RANDOM
HOUSE
LARGE
PRINT

A CHAIN
OF
THUNDER

A CHAIN

OF

THUNDER

A NOVEL OF
THE SIEGE OF VICKSBURG

JEFF SHAARA

RANDOM HOUSE
LARGE PRINT

Copyright © 2013 by Jeffrey M. Shaara

All rights reserved.
Published in the United States of America by
Random House Large Print in association with
Ballantine Books, New York.
Distributed by Random House, Inc., New York.

Cover design: Dreu Pennington-McNeil
Cover illustration: © Robert Hunt

The Library of Congress has established a
Cataloging-in-Publication record for this title.

ISBN: 978-0-307-99088-4

www.randomhouse.com/largeprint

FIRST LARGE PRINT EDITION

Printed in the United States of America

10   9   8   7   6   5   4   3   2   1

This Large Print edition published in accord with
the standards of the N.A.V.H.

Verily, war is a species of passionate insanity.
—MARY ANN LOUGHBOROUGH,
CIVILIAN, VICKSBURG, MISSISSIPPI

TO THE READER

This story focuses on the campaign that results in the siege and conquest of the crucial Mississippi River city of Vicksburg. It is the second volume of a series that explores the often-overlooked story of the Civil War in the "west." Quotation marks are necessary because to our eye today, "west" would certainly take us far beyond the shores of the Mississippi River. Yet, throughout much of the Civil War, events that occurred just west of the Appalachian Mountains were often overshadowed by the great battles to the east, which took place close to what we would refer to now as the great "media centers" of their day. Those events, from Kentucky to the Gulf Coast, from Texas and Arkansas, to Missouri and even New Mexico, were as bloody and as significant to our history as what took place in and around Virginia.

Throughout the war, both sides understand the critical importance of railroads and rivers, the two primary means of moving goods (and people) across vast distances. In the first volume of this series, **A Blaze of Glory,** the issue, primarily, is railroads, specifically the Union's effort to capture a critical rail junction at Corinth, Mississippi, which results in the Battle of Shiloh. Now, roughly one year later, the Federal armies, under the command of Ulysses S. Grant, seek to further divide and thus weaken the Confederacy by seizing the last major Southern obstacle to Northern control of the Mississippi River, the city of Vicksburg.

This story follows several pivotal characters through the spring and summer of 1863, as Grant and his generals push through the state of Mississippi, facing off against Confederate forces under the command of General John Pemberton. Some of the voices in this story will be familiar to any student of the war: Generals William T. Sherman and Joseph Johnston, as well as Grant and Pemberton. Brought forward from the first volume is Private Fritz "Dutchie" Bauer of Wisconsin, whose baptism of fire at Shiloh shapes the kind of soldier he will become. The fourth primary voice is something of a departure for me. The story of Vicksburg is not just a story of battles and generals, and so my research sought out the voices of the civilians, the citizens of Vicksburg, who suffer mightily and whose tenacity is a part of this story that cannot be overlooked. So often in war, civilians are tragically involved simply by being in the way. In Vicksburg, their ordeal affects the way many civilians throughout the divided country will come to view the horrors of this war. They come to represent what the conflict has become, evolving from what some saw as a gentlemen's spat between men of honor, into a brutal war that will deeply impact towns and cities, and their inhabitants. There is a poignant comparison to be made between Vicksburg and what has taken place a few months earlier at Fredericksburg, Virginia. In December 1862, the citizens of Fredericksburg embark on a mass exodus away from their town, fearing the horrific battle that does indeed occur. In the spring of 1863, the residents of Vicksburg are offered the same opportunity for escape, and yet an overwhelming percentage of them decide to remain in their homes. And thus, one of those voices is essential to telling this story, nineteen-year-old Lucy Spence.

I am not an academic historian. If you know of my work, you know that, from the Revolutionary War through World War II, my focus has been on the **people,** whose accomplishments and failures have become a visceral part of our history. This is a novel by definition because there is dialogue, and even if a character is well known historically, the point of view has to be described as fictitious. My research has always focused on a study of the original source materials: diaries, memoirs, collections of letters, the accounts of the people who were **there**. Often, when it fits the flow of the story, I quote their words verbatim. But in every case, their experiences and the events from the historical record are as accurate as I can portray them. If I don't believe in the authenticity of the voices here, neither will you.

I am frequently asked if there are veiled references in any of my stories to more modern events, a nudge-nudge wink-wink that what I'm really offering is a parable to more modern times. Absolutely not. There is no judgment here, no history-in-hindsight, no veiled references to any more recent event or person.

One enormous irony of the campaign for Vicksburg is that it ends exactly **one day** after the conclusion of the Battle of Gettysburg. Obviously, since Gettysburg is much closer to both Washington and Richmond, that battle has always received enormous attention. But it is a point of debate even today whether Vicksburg or Gettysburg had the greater impact on the outcome of the war. That debate I leave to others. This is a story told through the eyes of the characters, and to most of them, the events they experienced were the most important of their lives. To me, that's what makes a good story. I hope you agree.

JEFF SHAARA

APRIL 2013

CONTENTS

LIST OF MAPS

SOURCES AND ACKNOWLEDGMENTS

In response to numerous questions from readers, asking for some specifics on the original sources I draw upon, the following is a partial list of those figures contemporary to the events in this book whose accounts were particularly useful:

FROM THE NORTH

Lucius W. Barber, 15th Illinois
Cyrus F. Boyd, 15th Iowa
Sylvanus Cadwallader
Ransom J. Chase, 18th Wisconsin
Wilbur F. Crummer, 45th Illinois
Charles Dana

Thomas J. Davis, 18th Wisconsin
John J. Geer, USA
Philip H. Goode, 15th Iowa
Ulysses S. Grant, USA
Orville Herrick, 16th Wisconsin
Virgil H. Moats, 48th Ohio
Osborn Oldroyd, 20th Ohio
Hosea Rood, 12th Wisconsin
William T. Sherman, USA
Leander Stillwell, 61st Illinois
The Men of the 55th Illinois

FROM THE SOUTH

Emma Balfour (Vicksburg)
Sid Champion, 28th Mississippi Cavalry
William Cliburn, 6th Mississippi
Thomas Dobyns, 1st Missouri
Rev. William Lovelace Foster (Vicksburg)
Joseph E. Johnston, CSA
Rev. W. W. Lord (Vicksburg)
Mary Ann Loughborough (Vicksburg)
Lucy McRae (Vicksburg)
Dora Miller (Vicksburg)
John C. Pemberton, CSA
Samuel J. Ridley, 1st Mississippi
Charles Swett, Warren (Mississippi) Light
   Artillery
James M. Swords (Vicksburg)

Mollie Tompkins (Vicksburg)
William H. Tunnard, 3rd Louisiana

With every book I've done, I must rely on a variety of research sources, including the generous contributions of material from historians and readers. The following is a partial list of those to whom I offer my sincere thanks.

Tim Cavanaugh, Chief Historian, Vicksburg
   National Military Park
Dr. J. William Cliburn, Hattiesburg, MS
John H. Ellis, Matthews, NC
Patrick Falci, Rosedale, NY
Christopher Gooch, Cane Ridge, TN
Colonel Curtis J. Herrick, Jr., USA (Ret.),
   Annandale, VA
Evalyn E. Kearns, Atlanta, GA
Bruce Ladd, Chapel Hill, NC
Stephanie Lower, Gettysburg, PA
Keith Shaver, Murfreesboro, TN
Bob Springer, Jacksonville, FL
Paul Thevenet, Nazareth, PA
Edward Vollertsen, Monticello, FL
Nancy Warfle, Warren Centre, PA
Terrence Winschel, Chief Historian (ret.),
   Vicksburg National Military Park

Overview of Mississippi Theater of War

INTRODUCTION

From the earliest months of the Civil War, many of the strategists and political leaders of both sides consider control of the Mississippi River the key to victory. The original "Anaconda Plan," as designed by Union general in chief Winfield Scott, includes control of that river as an essential part of any strategy that will ensure victory (along with a total blockade of Southern seaports). In the South, Jefferson Davis is equally determined to maintain control of the river, understanding that free access for Federal troops and supplies along the waterway will split the Confederacy in two and eliminate the valuable trans-Mississippi states of Texas, Arkansas, and much of Louisiana as a source of troops, supplies, and food.

Throughout the first two years of the war, the superior numbers and strength of the Union navy successfully subdue various Confederate strongholds along the river, many of which, including Memphis, are not suitable for a strong military defense.

Once Federal forces become ensconced in Memphis, efforts are made to seal off the southern leg of the river. In April 1862, a stunning blow is delivered to Confederate hopes when Admiral David Farragut captures the crucial port city of New Orleans. In the process, Farragut destroys the fledgling Confederate naval fleet stationed there. Confident that his gunboats and oceangoing warships can subdue Vicksburg on their own, Farragut sails northward. Confronting the garrison at Vicksburg, Farragut's officers make loud, blusterous demands that the city avoid certain destruction and simply surrender. But the Confederate commander there, General Martin Luther Smith, understands the strength of his position. Though Farragut shells the town, Smith does not yield. In late May 1862, a frustrated Farragut concedes that his forces cannot complete the task alone, and he returns to New Orleans. But the mouth of the river is now firmly in Federal hands, and so Vicksburg becomes the last significant Confederate stronghold between Memphis and New Orleans, what most Federal strategists realize will be the toughest nut to crack along the entire length of the river.

At roughly the same time as Farragut's gunboats are making their efforts at opening the river, far to the north, Union general Ulysses Grant embarks on what becomes a bloody yet successful campaign to wrest control of the western half of Tennessee from Confederate forces. That campaign, which concludes with the Battle of Shiloh, opens the door for Federal armies to drive hard into Mississippi and Alabama, with the goal of capturing valuable railroad hubs and slicing the Confederacy into pieces. But Grant's superior, Henry Halleck, is not a man who recognizes opportunity. After his victory at Shiloh, Halleck vacillates, and thus he misses the opportunity to destroy a sizable army under Pierre Beauregard that is entrenched around the rail center of Corinth, Mississippi. When the Confederates escape Corinth, the entire face of the war in the West changes. Disgusted with Beauregard's failure to prevail at Shiloh, Jefferson Davis removes Beauregard from command and replaces him with Braxton Bragg. But Bragg's various campaigns are ineffective, and Davis knows he has to fill that command with someone more capable of inspiring his troops and defeating the enemy.

From the opening weeks of the war, Confederate general Joseph Johnston has openly feuded with Jefferson Davis. They have clashes of ego as well as policy, Johnston never accepting that Davis's presidency gives him legitimate control over how the war will actually be fought. Johnston has proven himself a capable battlefield commander at the First Battle of Manassas (Bull Run), and in subsequent actions on the Virginia peninsula. By his lofty rank as full general, Johnston is entitled to a sizable command, and so, despite their hostility, Davis acquiesces. Johnston is named to fill the vacancy created by the death of Albert Sidney Johnston, who is killed in battle at Shiloh. His authority now spreads over the entire department west of the Appalachians, all the way to the Mississippi River. As Bragg's superior, Johnston keeps his focus primarily on Tennessee, as Bragg struggles against Federal forces in a series of battles from Perryville, Kentucky, down through Stones River, near Chattanooga. By the spring of 1863, aided by the exceptional abilities of cavalrymen John Hunt Morgan and Nathan Bedford Forrest, Johnston's command in Tennessee settles into something of a stalemate with a Federal army commanded by William Rosecrans. But Johnston must deal with a new crisis more to his west. Realizing that Federal efforts are being directed more and more toward securing the Mississippi River, Johnston shifts his attention to the state of Mississippi. There his subordinate is another man Johnston finds utterly disagreeable: General John Pemberton. Pemberton commands the Confederate Department of Mississippi and thus is in control of the fortification efforts at Vicksburg. Pemberton, who is a close friend of Jefferson Davis, receives orders directly from Davis that

Vicksburg must be held at all costs. It is a strategy completely at odds with Johnston's own focus on Tennessee, and it puts Pemberton squarely in the middle of the Johnston-Davis feud. Backed by the authority of the orders he receives from his president, Pemberton continues to fortify and arm the earthworks and river batteries at Vicksburg. Pemberton becomes increasingly confident his defenses will prevail in the event that the Federal army and navy attempt any direct assault against the city.

In July 1862, Federal general Henry Halleck is called to Washington to assume the position of general in chief of the Federal forces. The choice is a wise one, but not for reasons Halleck might appreciate. In the various campaigns in the West, Halleck has proven to be an able administrator, but no one believes him to be the kind of battlefield commander the Union must have. Though the Federal armies in the West have been mostly victorious, capturing the important hub of Nashville as well as Memphis, and preventing new Confederate incursions into Kentucky, the war seems no closer to being decided. In October 1862, Lincoln promotes Ulysses Grant to overall command of the Federal armies along the Mississippi. Though intensely disliked by Halleck, Grant has considerably exceeded the expectations of his critics in Washington, and in his own command. While under Halleck, Grant notches significant victories in Tennessee, including the bloody horror at Shiloh. Grant understands the value of the Mississippi River, and with cooperation from the Federal navy, he believes the war's end can be hastened considerably by slicing the Confederacy in two. Appreciating that a direct assault against Vicksburg could be far more costly than Lincoln will accept, Grant maps out strategies to secure the city with as little loss of life as possible. Upriver, north of Vicksburg, the Federal naval forces are under the command of Commodore (later Admiral) David Dixon Porter, who agrees with Grant's new strategy that any attempt to capture Vicksburg must come from the north. As had happened in Grant's successful capture of Forts Henry and Donelson in early 1862, Grant understands the value of cooperating with the navy.

In the fall of 1862, shortly after taking command, Grant pursues a plan, championed by Federal engineers, to bypass Vicksburg altogether by rerouting the flow of the river. A canal is designed that will slice through one of the looping meanders of the river. If successful, the canal will allow Federal shipping to sail harmlessly past Vicksburg, out of range of Confederate guns. But engineering cannot compete with Mother Nature, and the plan soon becomes a boondoggle. The muddy swamps of Louisiana, directly across the river from Vicksburg, prove to be a far greater challenge than Grant's engineers predicted. After numerous failures, which include a significant loss of life from sickness, the canal idea is abandoned.

Grant then changes tactics. In December 1862, he leads a sizable force of infantry out of his bases at Memphis, driving down into northern Mississippi. His troops are the eastern half of a two-prong pincer movement, designed to engulf the city with overwhelming strength. But Grant underestimates the power and audacity of Confederate cavalry. Grant's confidence begins to wane as he learns of relentless harassment of Federal outposts by Nathan Bedford Forrest. But the greatest blow comes on December 20, 1862. Thirty-five hundred horsemen, commanded by Confederate general Earl Van Dorn, sweep into Grant's primary supply depot at Holly Springs, Mississippi. Grant's meager defenses there are caught completely by surprise, and the Federal army loses more than $1.5 million in matériel, which drains the energy from Grant's campaign. Grant is forced to retreat toward Memphis, though he does not order the withdrawal of the second prong of his pincer movement. Those troops, led by General William T. Sherman, continue their march southward by keeping much closer to the Mississippi River. In the swamps and boggy bayous near the Yazoo River, Sherman finds the going far more difficult than expected. Though he reaches a point only a few miles north of Vicksburg, Sherman is not aware that Grant has withdrawn, and thus is not aware that the Confederates are now mobilizing all their energy in his direction. On December 29, 1862, Sherman's forces are soundly and unexpectedly defeated at Chickasaw Bayou, and like Grant, a humiliated Sherman is forced to withdraw northward.

Still under orders from President Abraham Lincoln to secure Vicksburg by any means necessary, Grant uses that discretion to launch a new strategy. Once again, the Federal forces will make their move on the western side of the river, across from Vicksburg. But Grant has learned from past mistakes. There will be no canal, and no attempt at a push by infantry straight toward Vicksburg. The plans call for a maneuver by Grant's entire army southward, seeking a crossing of the Mississippi River well below the city. When the assault against Vicksburg finally comes, Grant is convinced the confrontation will be on his own terms.

Sherman and Grant are both aware that another failure will not only extend the war, but also likely will strip Grant of his command. As he continues to fortify the heights along the river, Pemberton pours his energy toward the construction of earthworks inland from Vicksburg as well, in the event there is another overland campaign. Joseph Johnston reluctantly accepts that he must focus on events in Mississippi, never believing that Pemberton's efforts will bear fruit. Whether or not he chooses to actively support John Pemberton remains to be seen.

PART ONE

In my opinion, the opening of the Mississippi River will be to us of more advantage than the capture of forty Richmonds.

—UNION GENERAL IN CHIEF
HENRY HALLECK

To secure the safety of the navigation of the Mississippi River I would slay millions. On that point I am not only insane, but mad.

—MAJOR GENERAL WILLIAM T. SHERMAN

CHAPTER ONE

SPENCE

VICKSBURG, MISSISSIPPI
APRIL 16, 1863

The ball was a glorious affair, the Confederate officers in their finest gray, adorned with plumed hats and sashes at their waists. There was dancing and a feast of every kind of local fare, even the wine flowing with no one's disapproval. By ten o'clock, most of the older citizens had retired, the senior officers gone as well, offering the reasonable excuse that there were duties to perform, an early morning that would come too soon. Those who remained were the young and the unmarried, no one among them objecting to that. The music continued, more lively now, the quartet of violinists respecting the youth in the room, waltzes that brought the officers closer to the young women, hands extended, those girls who had caught the eye, whose furtive glances spoke of flirtation, the daring willingness to accept the invitation of a young man who had the courage or the skills to lead a dance.

As the night wore on, and the matrons drifted away, Lucy had allowed herself a single dance, had caught a beaming smile from a young lieutenant, one of the Louisiana regiments. She knew nothing of a soldier's life, what authority he carried, but the face was handsome, a firm jaw and bright blue eyes, clean-shaven, the young man's hand extended toward her with smiling optimism, hinting of hope. She knew he had been watching her for most of the evening, and she had smiled at him once, was immediately embarrassed by that, quick glances to be certain that none of the others noticed. But now, as the energy of the ball rose with the youthfulness of those who remained, so too did her courage. And, apparently, his.

The waltz they danced to had been familiar, the violins doing admirable service with a pleasing rhythm that seemed to intoxicate her, the young officer admirably graceful. The couple was one of a half dozen who moved with elegance across the floor, but it ended too soon. With visible regret, the lieutenant had done what was required, had properly escorted her back to one side of the room, where the ladies sat, the officers returning to their own station, closer to where the wine flowed.

She sat, maneuvering the wide hoops of her finest gown, still glancing at the other girls, the rivalry they all observed. Such occasions were rare now. The welcome invitation had come from Major Watt, the officer spreading word that a gala was well deserved. But many stayed away, a gloomy acceptance that perhaps this kind of frivolity was not yet appropriate, not with the Yankees so close. For months now, the citizens had endured shellfire, Federal gunboats with the audacity to throw their projectiles into the city itself. Most of those boats were anchored far upriver, and the officers in the town boasted of that, that Federal sailors knew they could not match the enormous power of the guns dug into the hillsides across the riverfront. But still the shells came, and many of the civilians had heeded the advice of the army's senior commanders, had begun to move out of their homes, digging themselves into caves and caverns, most dug by the labor of Negroes.

The first serious violence had come close to Christmas, and the customary Christmas ball had been rudely preempted by one of the first great assaults, what so many of the townspeople described as the barbarity of the Yankees, their utter disregard for simple courtesy, for the sacred observance of Christmas ritual. Major Watt seemed to recognize that as well, and with the warmer weather came the army's gift to the town, driven by the kindness of this one major, who seemed to understand that the civilians would be buoyed by a party, a show of defiance toward the ever-present gunboats. Though the attendance was not as large as the major had hoped, the air of protest was there still, and like the others who attended the ball, the young Miss Spence thought it entirely appropriate that the townspeople make some effort to improve their own morale. Since Christmas, most of the people had gone about their business as though nothing were really happening upriver, as if the Yankees were there just for show, a protest of their own. Businesses continued to operate, the markets mostly able to stock their shelves, citizens freely traveling to the countryside. Even the occasional bombardments were part of the routine, and for the most part the damage had been minimal, the shelling more random than targeted. Like Lucy, most of her neighbors had sought the protection of Providence, that if a shell was to find them, it would be the hand of God and not the unfortunate aim of some devilish Yankee gunner. After all, the people of Vicksburg had done nothing to deserve such violence.

She watched her young lieutenant across the room, was disappointed to see a glance at a pocket watch. The music began to slow, and the atmosphere in the grand room was growing heavy with shared sleepiness. It was, after all, near ten o'clock, far beyond the bedtime of even the young.

Lucy felt the same weariness, suppressed a yawn, heard the talk around her, much as it had been all evening. The young women spoke of those things

Lucy had kept mostly to herself: who among the men in their gray finery were the best dancers, the most handsome, who had embarrassed himself by enjoying a bit too much wine. She held quietly to the warm glow that came from the single dance with her lieutenant, that it was her young man who outshone them all. She wondered about Louisiana, not the swamps that spread out for miles across the river, but down south, New Orleans, Baton Rouge, sophisticated places she could only imagine. Surely he was from the cities, she thought, a cultured man, familiar with music and libraries, perhaps from a military academy. Her imagination was fed by the sleepiness, and she blinked hard, fought to keep anyone from noticing that, saw him glance at his watch again, a scowl on his face. Then he glanced toward her, and she looked away, then back, wanted to smile, held it, scolded herself. He was speaking to another officer now, a captain, both men showing regret that this one beacon of color and gaiety had to come to an end. He began to move toward her, and her heart jumped, a blend of hope and alarm that he might ask to escort her home. She felt a slight shiver, and he seemed to hesitate, gathering courage of his own.

And now came a large thump of thunder, a jolt in the floor beneath her feet, the chandelier quivering, the entire room suddenly motionless. Another rumble came, but it was not close. She saw the lieutenant looking past her and realized he was staring toward the river, where the army had anchored its largest guns. Now the firing thundered closer, the officers speaking up, calming voices, that it was their own guns, not the enemy. To one side a door burst open, an older officer moving in quickly, searching, finding Major Watt, a quick word between them. Watt turned to them all and gained their attention.

"I regret," he said, "this ball has concluded. The Yankee boats are coming downriver, and you must retire to your shelters. Do not hesitate. Officers, report immediately to your posts."

There was authority in his words, and the men were quick to move, filing toward the wide entranceway, already disappearing into the darkness. She caught sight of the lieutenant, but he did not look back, and she pushed that from her mind, rose up with the other women, some of the officers lingering, standing to one side, allowing them to pass. There were questions, but no panic, so many of the civilians having experienced all of this before. Major Watt stood by the door, still their host, and offered a smile, pleasantries to the women, with the slight edge of firmness.

"Go on home, now. We shall deal with the Yankees. This has been a most pleasant evening. It shall be still, if our artillerymen have their way."

She passed the major, was outside now, a cool night, no moon, a hint of lantern light from the homes that lined the street. But quickly those grew dark, the usual caution, no needless targets offered to any Yankee gunner who might be telescoping this very place. She stepped onto the hard dirt, being careful to avoid the ruts from wagon wheels, and heard the talk around her in hushed excitement. She felt it as well, that there was something different about this assault. She looked in every direction, still no shells coming into the town, the sounds all toward the river. The soldiers were mostly gone, with only a few, the usual guards drifting past, offering assistance if any was required. Lucy saw a cluster of women moving uphill, not toward their homes, but toward the magnificent vantage point, what they all called Sky Parlor Hill. It was the highest point in the city, a knob of land the width of two city blocks, and during the daytime it was the most popular place for couples to gather, for picnics and courtship. For others, for the lonely, widows perhaps, the women struck hard by the pain of war, it was a place of solace, the perfect place to find comfort from gazing out toward the river, or across, to the flatlands of the Louisiana swamps. Lucy had climbed the heights often, enjoyed the silence, or the warm breezes that rose with the arrival of spring. More recently, her focus had been mostly northward, to where the Yankees had their camps, this high ground offering a perfect glimpse of a distant sea of white tents, and riverboats of all shapes and configurations. She had studied that with intense curiosity, had heard from the soldiers that the Yankees seemed only to be going about their business, more for a show of strength than for any real threat to the town. It was from upriver that the shelling came, though the Yankees had also positioned their guns straight across the wide river, as though taunting the town with their daring. The Confederates had offered daring of their own, the occasional raid, troops slipping across on small boats and rafts, harassing raids that drew pride from the civilians but seemed to accomplish little else.

She moved in line behind several others, most of them women, fumbling with the awkwardness of the ball gowns, helped along by a few old men, too old to be soldiers. The winding path led them higher still, and she was surprised to see a glow of orange light, beyond the hill, as though the sun were rising through a foggy haze, coming up from the wrong direction. She reached the top, breathing heavily, tugging at the hoops, adjusting her dress in the darkness, realized it wasn't truly dark at all. All around her were curious faces reflected in the glow of what she saw now were a dozen great fires, great fat torchlights on both sides of the river. She knew something of that, the soldiers openly talking for weeks about their preparations if the Yankees dared to bring their boats within range of the big guns. The fires came from enormous mounds of oil-soaked cotton, barrels of tar, wiping away the darkness that would hide any craft that tried to pass on the river. And now she could see them, silhouetted, a parade of vessels spaced far apart, coming downstream in single file. The guns began again, startling bursts of fire down below her, some out to the north, upriver. Out in the river, the fire was returned, small bursts of flame from the gunboats, the impact of those shells against the steep bluffs. But more shelling came from the Yankees, streaks of red and white arcing up and over, coming down far out to one side of the great knob. There was a response from the crowd, angry protest that the Yankees were doing what they had done before, blind destruction thrown into the town. She heard the impact, saw a brief burst of flames on a street close to where the ball had been. She looked again to the river, the firelight reflecting on the water, rippling eddies from the movement of the Yankee boats. Fog was spreading along the water, rising like a wall of reflected fire, the silhouettes of the boats blanketed, hidden. Voices around her rose, protesting the blindness, and she looked toward the town, no fog there, not unusual so high above the water. But the smell came, thick and pungent, brought by a sharp breeze. It was smoke.

Close beside her, a small man stopped, gestured with his cane, and shouted out, "They's hidin' from us! Bah! Go ahead with your tricks. We'll find ya!"

She wanted to ask, **Hiding?** But the man kept up the chatter.

"They's throwin' out smoke so's we won't see 'em. Mighty dang stupid. The gunners know the range. Too many of us. Give it to 'em, boys!"

She stared at the river, saw breaks in the smoke, glimpses of the boats again, still the single line, some coming closer, one turning sideways, as though out of control. She saw flames now, on the boat, and the old man said, "Got one! Sink that devil! Hee! Send her to the bottom!"

The cannon fire was increasing, a steady rhythm, the guns downriver opening up as well, shot and shell now launched in both directions. The sounds came in a chorus of thumps and distant thunder, more impacts in the town. She felt a twisting nervousness, stared hard at specks of fire from the boats, obscured then visible, the surface of the river glowing with the fires. There were cheers around her, and she saw a burst on the boat, another hit, the old man coming to life again.

"Good shootin', boys! Keep it up! Nowhere for those devils to hide!"

She moved closer to the man, but he ignored her, cheered again, spoke out loud, as though everyone would hear him.

"You see that? Took off her smokestack! I'll bet they hit the boiler next! Whoeee, you might see one of them dang things go up in one big show of hellfire!"

There was another burst of fire mid-river, and the old man's joy was infectious, more cheering for the raw destruction, the good work of the men who worked the guns. She had a sudden urge to go down there, to be closer to them, to watch the deadly work, different now, the targets genuine, the **enemy,** the guns doing what so many had hoped for. **Killing Yankees**.

Her name was Lucy Spence, and she had spent all of her nineteen years in Vicksburg. Her father had been a preacher, made his living mostly traveling the countryside, offering sermons to anyone willing to put a coin in a collection plate. For as long as Lucy could remember, her mother had been sickly, never traveling with her husband, and finally, keeping to the house, then her own room. With her father off for a week or more at a time, it was Lucy who had become the caretaker, the nurse. She had no formal training for that, or for anything else, and so the chores of a household had been learned by necessity. There had never been the luxury of slaves, not even a maid to care for Lucy as a baby. She had clung most strongly to the reunions, when her father would return home, joy and hugs and laughter. But as Lucy grew, and her mother lost strength, the joy faded. With Lucy more able to care for her mother, her father's journeys lasted even longer. When the war began, he seemed to welcome the necessity of traveling, often for many weeks, and though he spoke of hardship, the people growing poor, she knew from the look in his eye that he looked forward to those days when the journeys

began, when he no longer had to watch the skeletal
frailness of what had become of his wife. And so
it was no surprise that two days after Lucy turned
eighteen, her mother died, with no one but her
daughter to hear the last struggling breath.

Her father came home a few weeks after, had visited the grave briefly, tears and several days of sad
silence. But then he was gone again. Now, more
than a year later, there had been no word at all,
and Lucy had steeled herself against all of that, did
not press the army or the officials in Jackson, did
not really want to know where he had gone. If
he had ever been a husband, he had rarely been a
father. And most certainly, he was not one now.

With the war growing closer to this part of Mississippi, the army came in greater numbers, outposts and defensive works spreading around the
town. Lucy had been wary of soldiers, had heard
too much talk of barbarism, that the army brought
unruly men fueled by liquor and lust. She kept
away from the camps, from the defensive works,
avoided the men who paraded through the town in
small groups. But soon the fear faded, none of the
gossip coming to pass, no violation of some young
innocent. Even the liquor seemed to affect the civilians more than it did the soldiers, and soon it
was clear that the officers, those primly uniformed
men on horseback, actually controlled these men.
It was not a rabble. It was an army.

Comfortable now with the presence of the soldiers, Lucy kept mostly to herself, minding the family's home, sometimes helped by friendly neighbors. They were older women mostly, curious about this single girl who seemed to manage quite well. Their respect increased, though the help still came, lessons on cooking, on preserving meats, even a vegetable garden she tended herself. With her father absent for more than a year, talk of her disadvantages as an "orphan" simply drifted away. Not even the gossips taunted her, those who thrived mostly on vicious speculation. She was now an adult, in her own home, with every confidence that she could handle a household. To the neighbors, her greatest requirement was, of course, a husband. It was Lucy herself who realized with perfect logic that the opportunity had come to her along with this army. If it could be an officer, well, more the better.

Until now, the artillery duels had been mostly brief affairs, mere target practice. Throughout the chilly winter and into spring, the townspeople had often drifted down among the gun emplacements to watch the drills, the preparation. The artillery officers had encouraged that, their men showing off their accuracy, seeking targets on the far side of the river. Some had been offered by Yankees, men or wagons rising high up on some levee, inviting a response from the Confederate cannoneers. She had heard the talk, that it was something of sport, to both sides surely, and rarely did any harm result. But along with that playfulness, the talk had grown that the Yankees across the river were many, and now they were in motion, great columns marching south. Few of the officers would speak openly of that, and if the commanders had any real information about what the enemy was doing, they kept that to themselves, and so the soldiers spread rumors of their own. The boasting had been endless, the Yankees marching away altogether, those men across the river making their escape all the way to New Orleans. The civilians had come to believe what the soldiers insisted was true, that Vicksburg was a fortress, impregnable, that the bluffs that rose so high above the river could never be conquered. The presence of the massive cannon had only increased that confidence, and Lucy had toured through the artillery camps, awed by the sheer immensity of the great black barrels. The artillerymen were awed right back, pausing to watch any young woman strolling through their camps.

She kept her gaze on the river, could see more of the Yankee boats coming downstream from the far bend, outlined still by the great fires. The cheers were constant, louder when the impact on the boats could be seen, the destruction seeming to impact every boat that passed. Beside her, the old man spoke again, his cane pointing high in the air.

"Damn fools! Sendin' them boats down one at a time! Dang shootin' gallery! Oh . . . well lookee there. They's comin' closer! And listen to them hound dogs! They know what's happenin'. Even they hate the Yankees! They're cheering us on, sure as can be!"

The howling came all through the town, the dogs reacting to the sounds with as much enthusiasm as the people on Sky Parlor Hill. It was a strange sound, a chorus of howls, low-pitched and high, and Lucy sensed more than some echo of their masters' devotion to the Cause. They're afraid, she thought. They hear the screams of the shells and don't know what it is. Maybe it hurts their ears. Glad I don't have one. If he was that afraid, I wouldn't know what to do. Like having a frightened child. I don't envy the mothers.

She tried to see the Federal gunboats that were easing closer to the near bank, but the lay of the land and the rows of buildings below the hill hid them from view. She caught a glimpse of one slipping into the firelight, the reflection revealing the immense ironclad.

She moved closer to the old man and shouted above the din, "Are they coming? Will they land?"

"Missy, I served in the navy for thirty-odd years, learned somethin' about artillery. Hard to shoot pointing down. Some damn Yankee captain figured that out, too. Got hisself all shot to pieces, and so figured out that movin' closer to this side might protect him. Not gonna work, though. They ain't figuring on landing, no sir. There's a pot full of sharpshooters down low on the river, and if'n they don't kill every dang one of 'em, they'll be haulin' up prisoners!"

She coughed, fought through the smell of the smoke, looked at the old man, tried to see his face in the glow of firelight, familiar, a man some said was addled. But his words held authority, and she kept close to him, with an instinct that he really did know what was happening. He pointed the cane, kept up his monologue, didn't seem to care now if anyone heard him at all.

"Yankee navy's done for. Only thing that gave 'em hope. This is desperation, pure and simple! They's making a run for it, headin' to Orleens. I heerd word that a bunch of them Yankees upriver are already marchin' back to Memphis. Them scoundrels can do whatever they want back east, Virginee and all, but out here . . . they got no hope. No hope a'tall."

His speech was becoming redundant, a hint of boastfulness that began to sound more like exaggeration than fact. **Addled**. She focused more now on the sights, the stink of smoke, more explosions on the river, the parade of boats still ongoing, endless. The big guns farther downriver began firing, one more part of the great Confederate gauntlet, and she understood now what the army had done, that no matter how many boats came past, the army's guns were certainly too many, that Vicksburg was protected, invulnerable, just as the officers had claimed.

She felt stiffness in her legs, her eyes fogging, the sleepiness coming now, a long night made longer by the steady roar. There was nowhere to sit, the dress too clumsy, but the sleepiness was growing, the sights and sounds from the river blending together in a dreamy haze. She turned, moved past the glow on a hundred faces, and back toward the winding pathway that led below. She thought of her young lieutenant, wondered where he was, if he was a part of this spectacle, the marvelous destruction of those who dared to disrespect the town, the army, the Cause. I'll see him again, she thought. I'll ask him all about guns and boats. She eased carefully down the path, smiled in the darkness, Yes, you will be proud of that, will try to impress me with all that you know, will show off in front of your men. And I will blush and hide my smile, and enjoy every moment.

Behind her, up on the hill, people cheered again, the battle ongoing, the civilians knowing that no matter what the Yankees might believe about power, no matter the planning of their generals, the bravery of their sailors, tonight the vast fleet that dared trespass on this mighty river would be utterly destroyed.

CHAPTER TWO

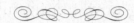

SHERMAN

DOWNRIVER FROM VICKSBURG
APRIL 16, 1863, MIDNIGHT

He had watched the spectacle with furious impatience, nothing for him to do but sit perched on the small yawl boat, staring into the sea of flames that lined both sides of the river. The advantage the fires had given the rebel gunners gave him a vantage point as well, and he knew that the first of the big boats he saw would be the **Benton,** Admiral Porter's flagship, leading the way. Sherman understood the plan, what the passage of the town and its batteries meant to the entire campaign. An army this size demanded an enormous mountain of supplies, far more than could easily be transported along the river by wagon train. The possibility of raids from rebel forces west of the river was very real, not to mention the sheer logistics of hauling those supplies across the river itself. The plan for hauling so much of what the army needed had come from Porter himself, the navy extending a helping hand to the army's strategy. Since Farragut was reluctant to make another foray upriver, and with most Federal supplies now coming through Memphis, the navy's efforts would have to come from the north, from Porter's fleet. On this night, Porter was doing exactly that. The fleet he was leading past Vicksburg consisted of seven of Porter's ironclad gunboats, providing escort to three transport boats and ten barges, all hauling mountains of supplies that were essential to Grant's plans to assault Vicksburg itself. Whether they would make the passing without enormous loss was a calculated risk Porter had worked out mostly on his own.

Not even Grant had authority over Porter, the army and navy commands separate, answering only to their superiors, who were far away. David Dixon Porter had the lineage of a man whose destiny seemed unalterably linked to the sea. His father had been a navy commodore during the War of 1812, and Porter himself had served with considerable distinction in the Mexican War. At fifty, Porter was several years senior to both Grant and Sherman, but he carried none of the arrogance of seniority, as though any man of the sea would presume to know how to manage an army on land.

Porter had been as cooperative to the generals as any one of them could have hoped, and Sherman knew that Grant and Porter had developed a close relationship, strategically and personally. It was no surprise to Sherman. He felt the same way toward both of them.

The mutual respect between army and navy made for an effective partnership, and already Sherman had worked closely with Porter, months before, the first attempts to drive toward Vicksburg through the swamps and small rivers north of the town. Those campaigns had collapsed under the weight of geographical handicaps and a stubborn rebel army. After Sherman's failed attempts to crush the rebels at Chickasaw Bayou, he had worked alongside Porter on a different plan, a plan that relied on what seemed to be the best use for the dismal waterways that snaked eastward from the Mississippi, again north of Vicksburg. Porter's gunboats had attempted to drive upstream as a hard spear of firepower the rebels could not stop, eliminating the greatest threat to Sherman's supporting infantry. But the plan had unraveled, ripped apart by rebel ambushes and the waterways themselves, too narrow for any good maneuvering for Porter's gunboats. Like so much of the lowlands close to the big river, the creeks were narrow, thick with overhanging limbs and fallen logs that nearly trapped Porter completely. Worse, the rebels had made good use of the resources nature offered them, their engineers overseeing the cutting of trees to obstruct the passages behind as well as in front of Porter's small fleet. With inevitable disaster facing the boats, Sherman had come to the rescue, leading infantry through the swamps and rugged patches of high ground that spread out from the creeks. Instead of a large-scale engagement across ridiculously difficult ground, the rebels had chosen to back away, their commanders too uncertain just how much strength Sherman was pushing their way. The maneuver gave Porter's sailors and Sherman's men the time they needed to clear the debris from the creeks, allowing the gunboats to slide back toward the Yazoo, and eventually, the big river. If there was humiliation in yet another failure to reach Vicksburg, Porter made no show of that, a graciousness Sherman appreciated. Sherman already knew of failure, from Bull Run to Shiloh, that stain that seemed to offer so much fuel to his enemies, mostly the newspapers. Whether his own men paid any attention to that, Sherman could not help the old torment, the fiery doubt that any time now, word would come that his enemies had used their influence to have Sherman swept out of command. It was an ongoing fear he had never been able to put away, not completely, not even with the successes the army had enjoyed.

Since late in 1862, the strategies Grant had devised for grabbing Vicksburg had been a shambles, some of it caused by poor planning and miserable execution, some by the tenacity and bold maneuver of the rebels they confronted. Sherman knew that the reasons, legitimate or not, would make no difference to those in Washington, and he was surprised and enormously grateful that Grant was absorbing these failures with a calm inevitability. With each failure came understanding; with each disaster, something useful was learned. No matter Grant's enemies, Washington had given him the precious gift of time. Sherman could not avoid his self-doubt, still suffered from bouts of anxiety that drove him awake through torturous nights. Sherman had wondered if Grant suffered as he did, if the quiet man with the soft temperament had masked his anxieties, if Grant feared the petty wrath of newspapers and desk-bound generals as much as Sherman. One clue to that came with the arrival of General John McClernand.

At Shiloh, as a division commander, McClernand had done the job, had even helped rescue pieces of Sherman's own division as they absorbed a brutal punch from the rebel assault. But McClernand was a political animal, said to be extremely close to Lincoln, and through McClernand's strenuous efforts around Washington, he had managed to be assigned to the western theater with the inflated self-importance of a man who carries the full support of his superiors, and more, the power to run the show his own way. But Grant also had his supporters, and his rank, and was highly regarded by Lincoln as well.

Sherman never had much respect for McClernand, and he wasn't surprised that McClernand would arrive with noisy expectations that overall command would be his for the taking. But the command officially belonged to Grant. Now a disappointed McClernand was merely one of Grant's three corps commanders, equal in authority, if not rank, to Sherman and James McPherson. It remained to be seen if McClernand would accept subservience to the man he had thought he was replacing.

As much as Sherman despised McClernand, his feelings for James McPherson were a complete contrast. McPherson was an engineer first, a West Pointer who had already earned respect for his skills and leadership. At Shiloh, McPherson had done as much as any capable man could to prepare the army for the blow they intended to strike against Corinth. Bad weather and bad orders from General Halleck had been the greatest obstacles to McPherson's success, but Sherman knew better than to fault a good man for any of that. Those plagues had affected the entire campaign. With Grant's reorganization of his army, good men were needed at the top, and McPherson had both the background and the ex-

perience to fill the position. Though Sherman had
to swallow hard serving alongside McClernand, he
welcomed McPherson's promotion.

Sherman's troops were camped far to the
north, where Porter's boats had begun their
journey. Sherman himself had ridden downriver on the western shore, moving through the
camps of the men who watched as he did, stunned
by the amazing show of fire and smoke and thunderous artillery. Sherman had not come merely to
sightsee. He had ordered four yawls, small, single-
sailed vessels that could be transported by hand or
mule team across the swampy ground west of the
river. Their purpose was rescue. Sherman knew
they were too small to be targets and could maneuver effectively around and past the larger boats and
barges, offering aid to anyone from Porter's fleet
who might be in trouble. The yawls were unarmed,
of course, manned by no more than three or four
crew, men Sherman had chosen for their skills with
the sail. At least if sailors went into the water, or any
of the boats were badly crippled, Sherman could
offer assistance once more.

The larger ironclad drifted closer, a hulk-
ing shadow, no lights but for a flicker of
fire high on one of her stacks. Sherman

motioned to the helmsman behind him, pointed, the yawl easing closer, and Sherman shouted, "Ho there! Benton!"

A voice came back toward him, very young, from the larger boat.

"Who calls?"

"General Sherman. I presume Porter is un-damaged?"

Another voice came now, older, grim and formal.

"Sherman. Why in God's name are you on this river? Are you mad?"

Sherman hesitated, had been asked that question too many times already.

"Perhaps. But I'm here to offer aid. Do you have casualties?"

"One man injured, not badly. Much of the fleet is still taking punishment. Something of a heart-pounder, I have to say. Come aboard!"

There was a stiffness to Porter's words, and Sher-man realized Porter had far more concerns than the condition of his own crew, and little time to be hospitable. He felt suddenly out of place, the small boat rocking unsteadily as the **Benton** drew closer, his small crew struggling to lower the sail, oars pushing her through black, choppy water. Dam-mit, what were you thinking? This man knows his job. I'm just in the way.

The two boats came together, ropes tossed, and Sherman saw a figure bending low, one arm ex-tended. For me, I presume. He grabbed the hand

and was pulled harshly up, landing clumsily on the deck of the ironclad. Men were moving away from him, their own jobs to do, and Sherman felt more uneasy now, as though blundering into the urgency of someone else's private matter. The voice came again, less formal now, a shadowy shape calling to him.

"Get down here, Sherman. They've got sharp-shooters all along that bank. Wouldn't do for me to tell Grant you were lost at sea."

Sherman followed into an opening, one hand touching the steel planking on the ship's bulkhead. Behind him, the single staff officer remained on the yawl, Sherman's instructions to stay out of the way. Sherman stepped down into a wave of heat, caught the sharp stink of men and smoke and powder. To one side, the row of big guns erupted, a blast of fire through their portholes that punched Sherman against a bulkhead. He fought to right himself, pain in his shoulder, his eyes trying to wipe away the blindness. On the far side of the deck, he could hear the gunners heaving and wrestling with their pieces, reloading with manic efficiency, and farther away, a steady chorus of artillery, the glow from the fires.

Porter shouted out, "Hold fire, Lieutenant! We're far past the worst of it, and I don't want them tossing a lucky one this way! Nothing much we can do now but wait here! We get a bit farther down, we'll anchor, wait for daylight!"

"Aye, sir! We'll drop anchor on your command."

Sherman could see the officer now, the man moving away, one part of this immense machine of boilers and pulleys and smoke. God, he thought, there's a reason I'm not in the navy. Too much damned work. And these boys stink a lot worse than anybody I've got.

There was the glow of a lantern now, deep in the bowels of the boat, and Sherman blinked through the smoke, fought the smells, saw Porter waiting for him, a sharp wave, bringing Sherman down into a small office.

Porter looked back, past Sherman, barked out again, "Prepare to fire the boilers!"

"Sir! We've lost our stacks!"

"So, we'll breathe smoke for a while. Better than drifting in the current. Once the transports are clear of the town, we'll put them on the west shore. There's a gap in the rebel guns up ahead." He looked at Sherman. "I assume we can count on your sharpshooters and artillery to keep any pesky rebs on their side of things. We still have the batteries at Grand Gulf to deal with, and I want everyone gathered up and ready for another fight!" He turned to the officer again. "Make sure the general's yawl is secured alongside. He's sure as hell not going to want to bunk with you wharf rats."

Sherman could see Porter's face clearly in the lamplight, intense weariness, the tension, a face blackened with soot and sweat. "Not sure why you're here, Cump. When I heard what you were planning, I thought Grant might grab you by the collar and keep you upriver."

Sherman put one hand against the bulkhead and steadied himself.

"He agreed this might be a good idea. Couldn't just sit up there and watch all of this like some damn Fourth of July fireworks show. Just thought we might be of assistance. Any of your people end up on the east side, not much I can do to help. But if they come over here, I can pick them out of the water." He felt suddenly foolish, thought, Can't sailors swim? Well, maybe not if they're wounded.

Porter surprised him, nodded, a smile cracking the grime on the man's face.

"Good. We'll probably need the help. Not too bad so far. We took a storm of shot, but it was mostly high up. Lost our stacks, caught a few right against the bulkheads. Thank God for iron. I think the rebel guns might be set at a high angle; almost everything went overhead. When it got really hot, we eased closer to them, hugged the east shore as close as I dared. No way they could get their bigger guns pointed that low. Helped. They had infantry out there, sharpshooters, but they didn't hit anything, even with some of the crew exposed on deck."

Sherman could see the tension returning to Porter's face, felt the impatience, knew the man was thinking more about what was still happening on the river. But Sherman couldn't help the curiosity, had so little experience on any gunship, certainly not under fire.

"I'm surprised . . . well, impressed. You made it through. That's a good sign. Grant's up there chewing his fingers off waiting for a report."

"We drifted mostly, kept 'em quiet. The barges might still be a problem, but I haven't heard about any disasters yet. Look, Cump, I need to get topside. . . ."

Sherman backed away, and Porter moved past, and once more the orders came. Sherman felt a rumble beneath his feet, engines coming to life, but the boat was still drifting, swinging slowly to one side. Sherman moved through the darkness, tried to avoid the crew, climbed up to the open deck, the vast glow of fire still to the north. He could see the other boats clearly, some as far down as the **Benton,** others still running the hottest part of the gauntlet, abreast of the town. But they came on, steady, some drifting sideways, no control but their rudders and the current. Sherman felt a bolt of alarm at that, boats out of control, saw two of the barges close together, a collision, one gunboat sideways as well. But the firing from the boats still answered the shore batteries, a chaos of splashes and blasts that seemed to swarm around every boat, streaks of fire launched up toward the town. Behind him there was a metallic splat, and he realized suddenly it was a musket ball, impacting the steel plate. The word burst in his brain. **Sharpshooters**. All right, Sherman, being out on this river might be the first stupid thing you did today, so don't get yourself shot. He eased past a quickly moving deckhand, slipped around away from the firelight. A hand touched his shoulder, startling him. Porter.

"Hell of a show, Cump. But by damned, it's working. Most of the gunboats are past the worst of it, and the barges, too. Can't wait to gather up those damn cowards we left behind. A few nooses might tighten up their damn morale." Sherman didn't know what he meant, and Porter seemed to read him, slapped him on the back. "Most of the crews of the damn transport boats wouldn't make the trip down. Too damn scared. Said they didn't sign up to be shot at. Wouldn't do to put them to work at gunpoint, so I called for volunteers from the troops you had camped nearby. Bunch of Illinois fellows, mostly. Not sure who they belong to, but their officers were obliging. I guess some of 'em know a good deal about riverboats. They manned the transports and several of the barges. I owe you for that. Or maybe General McPherson. Not sure. Let's just say, the army did its part. But those damn civilian sailors . . . well, sometimes it's good to sort out the vermin."

Sherman knew nothing of this, thought, It has to be McPherson's men. Damn good job. Grant will hear of that, for certain.

"Oh God. Direct hit."

The words came from farther along the deck, and Porter responded, moved toward the bow, a clear field of vision toward the worst of the chaos. Sherman followed, saw a burst of flames on one of the larger boats. He wanted to ask, Transport? But Porter moved away, disappeared down inside, shouting orders. Sherman stared out to the flames, remembered his binoculars, focused, could see men leaping into the water, small splashes, flailing arms. He felt helpless, the job he came here for now so necessary . . . and you're watching like some damn schoolboy. The **Benton** swung about, slow and ponderous, and Sherman saw a smaller boat moving closer to the burning wreck, perfect silhouette, one of his yawls, thought, I'll be damned. We're not sightseers after all.

He watched for agonizing minutes, saw the burning hulk drifting closer, men scampering over a blazing deck, what he had to believe were the last on board, the captain, certainly, a desperate effort to steer the boat away from the rebel shore.

"Ho there! Is General Sherman there?"

The voice came off to one side, and Sherman saw another of the yawls.

"Here! What's wrong?"

"Sir! One of the gunboats took a hit! We've pulled some people out of the water! They're mostly unhurt."

"Good! Get 'em to shore!"

Sherman felt a wave of satisfaction. By damned,

we did the job. I knew this was the right thing to do. That idiot McClernand's probably sitting over in that swamp somewhere hoping I'm out here drowning. Not tonight.

Porter was there again, another slap on Sherman's back.

"Fine work! Fine work indeed! The **Henry Clay** got hit pretty badly. She's done for, most likely. Hope like hell we didn't lose too many people. Good crew."

Sherman was curious now, saw more of the larger boats drifting past, the fires upriver beginning to die down, the thunder from the artillery duels more piecemeal now.

"How'd they do? How many got through?"

"Best I can tell right now, the **Clay** is the only loss. We'll know more by daylight. I imagine you'll see Grant before I do. Or send him a courier. Not much I can do from down here. Tell him that Rear Admiral Porter reports the mission has been a success. At least **most** of those supplies will be waiting right where he wanted them. The next job is yours."

CHAPTER THREE

BAUER

NEAR LAKE PROVIDENCE, LOUISIANA
APRIL 16, 1863

He had seen the great glow of fire from the river, had stood with so many others as the strange orange haze filled the horizon. Almost immediately they could hear the rumble of the big guns, and all through the camps, the chattering began, excited speculation what it all meant. The distant glow had broken through the darkness like the faraway signs of a massive forest fire, but there were no answers, nothing to dull the growing talk, speculation that spread like a fire of its own. For the Wisconsin men, the camps were well back of the river, too distant to actually see the bluffs that protected Vicksburg, to see whose artillery was doing the work, and what their targets might be. Some were not convinced it was artillery at all, some believing it to be exactly what it seemed, a fire; those men had a reputation for nervous talk, jabbering that the fire might be sweeping through the swamps, an unstoppable hell coming toward them. But Bauer knew enough of artillery to know the difference, said it aloud, **artillery,** others agreeing with him. But still the curiosity was rampant, just who it was and whom they were shelling. And what would happen next.

With the cannonade ongoing toward midnight, rumors began to spread of a great battle, a surprise assault from a massed rebel army. The officers were quick to silence that, to avoid the burst of panic that too many recalled from Shiloh. The voices of authority, Colonel Allen, his adjutants, rode through the men with loud observations of their own, a confident air designed to defuse what they all knew could become a full-blown stampede. Bauer heard those voices, stern and reassuring, that the direction of the sounds was too obvious, coming from the river itself. Vicksburg and any great rebel army was **over there,** the other side, and anyone in authority knew that most of Grant's entire army was **here,** west of the river. If there was an attack at all, it was not troops. The roar of the artillery fire was different than what they had heard so many times before, so much of it the deep thumping of the heaviest guns, far larger than anything the army had in the field. Bauer reached the same conclusion as the officers who paraded past. If there was a battle, the field was water. It had to be the navy. Even more reassuring, the men began to realize that there were no orders coming their way, no sudden train of supply wagons bringing ammunition or rations, no preparation to break camp. Bauer had noticed that immediately, and like the other veterans, it gave him more relief than confidence. Every one of those men understood what happened after the usual artillery barrage. That's when the infantry took over. But throughout the regiment, there was always the stupidity of the raw recruits, the "fresh meat." As the battle exploded along the river, those men absorbed it all with raucous enthusiasm, anxious to rush out through the night and see it for themselves, to join into whatever fiery collision was happening far beyond the swamps and lakes that separated them from the river itself. Bauer could only wonder at their disappointment when that order never came.

After two long hours, Bauer had become bored, the rumble of sounds seeming not to change, no movement one way or the other, just a steady roar that rolled at them straight from what the officers insisted was Vicksburg. All through the vast sea of encampments, men still gathered, many of them staring blankly at what Bauer thought resembled a sunset. But soon, many returned to their campfires, to their card playing or the discreet passing of a bottle. Bauer was bored with that as well, rarely enjoyed either vice, knew that reveille would come far too quickly. Though the chatter would flow through the camps for another hour, he had left all of that behind, drifting back to the tent, sleepy acknowledgment toward the others who moved as he did, who shared the wisdom of experience, that if it was an artillery battle after all, it was someone else's affair. Until the orders came to do otherwise, they were going to bed.

In early fall word had come in a letter from a neighbor, that both of Bauer's parents had fallen gravely ill. Within days, another letter arrived with the awful news that his father had died. The news was jolting in its suddenness, but the letter gave no real details what had happened, the letters coming as a courtesy from someone Bauer knew well. He had sought answers, had spoken to the sergeant, hoping for some dispensation, perhaps a brief furlough to allow him to see to his mother, if only to find out just how serious her condition was. Instead Bauer had been given the astonishing option of a ninety-day furlough, enough time to return to Milwaukee not only to care for his mother, but, as her only child, to have time to handle his family's affairs. He knew the furlough was no haphazard luxury doled out to anyone who lost a family member. The hints came first from Sergeant Champlin, the man showing surprising compassion, and Bauer knew that Champlin would sympathize more than most. He too had lost most of his own family not long after Shiloh. But there had been no allowance then for anyone to journey home from the miserable siege of Corinth.

As Bauer suffered the agony of ignorance about just what had happened to his family, Champlin had made his way up the chain of command, and the 16th's commander, Colonel Ben Allen, had agreed with Bauer's company commander that Bauer had served too well under fire, and with the regiment encamped in relative boredom at Memphis, what seemed to be a fairly quiet autumn for the army, Allen rewarded Bauer with generous consideration. Bauer had been seriously impressed by that, wasn't sure even now if the colonel actually knew who he was. But Allen was very aware of the names and the service of his veterans, the men who had struggled through the horror of Shiloh, had survived the waves of disease that crushed the army during the siege of Corinth. And there was no doubt among any of the officers, or Sergeant Champlin, that Bauer was no shirker. Unlike those few who had used any furlough to escape their service, when his ninety days had passed, he'd be back.

The time in Milwaukee had been dismal, consuming most of the autumn, and so he had missed the two fights that erupted in Mississippi, Iuka and a second conflict at Corinth, more horror stories embraced by the newspapers, tales of inept generals and the exaggerated barbarism of the enemy. Bauer knew too much of combat now to believe much of what he read, and through the fog of sensationalism, it was clear that both fights had been Federal victories. That was at least good for the morale of the civilians. But then came the inevitable lists of dead, one more reminder that the war was not just some vaguely tragic event confined to some far-off place.

In October, when word came of the victory at Corinth, Mississippi, the news that so aroused the town had only confused him. He had already done his part at Corinth, had marched into the rail center with the rest of the regiment, only to find that Beauregard's rebels had slipped away, avoiding what should have been a crushing blow by overwhelming Federal numbers. But that was May, months before, and as he read the newspaper accounts, he had to wonder if somehow it had taken six months for an account of the siege of Corinth to reach Wisconsin. But the details and the names were very different, and Bauer finally understood that this had been **another** fight at Corinth, and very soon some of the louder mouths in the town were trumpeting as fact that Lincoln and Henry Halleck had ruined their best chance to win the war west of the mountains by scattering their mighty army to the four winds, while the rebels had grown healthy again. Whatever truth there was to any of that, the battles spoke for themselves, and Bauer had read the accounts with gnawing helplessness. His own regiment, the 16th Wisconsin, had taken part in yet another fight for the same ground at Corinth that the Federal troops had occupied once before, filling the same works and occupying the same fortifications they had drained of troops the summer before. And this time Bauer had missed it.

The lengthy stay in Milwaukee continued to be far worse than he had expected, and not just for his absence from battle. His arrival home came two weeks after his father's funeral, and his mother's condition kept him closer to her for a long terrible month of suffering before she too succumbed to what the doctors told him was consumption. He knew a great deal more now about medicine and sickness, had spent too many nights enduring the awful noises of men around him plagued with various ailments that always infected the army. But those ailments had risen from the swampy water and muddy terrain that spread throughout Mississippi and Tennessee, places he had learned to despise. His parents had been strong, hearty, no hint that disease would suddenly strike them down.

While in Milwaukee, he had learned of many other deaths, some of them soldiers, who had returned from the battlefields with festering wounds that only grew worse, or troops who brought home sickness that never improved, their joyous homecoming wiped away by some plague that always seemed to overwhelm the doctors. He was surprised to learn of a smallpox outbreak, causing weeks of panic in the town, the older citizens especially aware that smallpox could sweep away entire families. The newspapers had jumped on that with stern warnings, that those who had ignored the availability of the vaccine should be made to comply with the governor's call for the entire population to receive the medicine. Those vaccinations had been available for years now, and Bauer's family had long ago visited their doctor, accepting the needle pricks without protest. It had amazed Bauer that so many in the town, and in the army, had responded instead with outcries against the vaccinations that seemed born of nothing more than superstition. Though the outbreaks had become much less frequent, the disease still came, suddenly bursting through those families who had thought themselves protected solely by the Hand of Providence. As had happened in every city, with each outbreak, more of the people lined up at the doctor's office, forcing themselves to accept that it could be Providence after all that had given them the vaccine.

After three months in Milwaukee, Bauer had suffered through more gloom than he had ever experienced in the army. His family's affairs had finally been settled, and he was surprised to learn that his father's sausage business had in fact been moderately successful. He had paid off a variety of debts, and offered his family's house to tenants who Bauer knew to be reliable. Once the details were handled, Bauer had no more reason to remain a temporary civilian. With the expiration of his ninety-day leave, he boarded the train that would take him to Memphis, where much of Grant's command had encamped. Bauer had done his best to carry the optimism that this time, when the spring came, the campaigns would be brief, would end this war once and for all. Surely, with the South absorbing so many defeats west of the mountains, they would be drained of the will to continue this bloody rebellion. But along the way, the newspapers filtered through the railcars, loud talk and condemnation of Washington, of the War Department, and the incompetence of blue-coated generals. The papers reported of a place in Virginia called Fredericksburg, details of how the traitorous rebel Robert E. Lee had thoroughly embarrassed the Federal army, driving them from the field in one of the most costly fights of the war. Bauer ignored the big talk from people who had never stepped on a battlefield; he knew that the "embarrassment" suffered by generals and politicians meant that there had been enormous casualties, no doubt on both sides. On the jostling ride southward, he couldn't avoid dragging himself back to Shiloh, and the more talk he heard the more gruesome the memories became. When he finally reached Memphis, he had had enough of railcars filled with big-mouthed cigar-smoking civilians. He had one goal now, a single-minded pur-

pose: return to duty, return to the men who knew
what this fight truly meant. The army was the only
home he had left.

When he reported to the camp of the 16th, he
couldn't avoid seeking out the casualty lists, that if
the men had been a part of more tough fights, or
had suffered inevitable waves of illness, there would
most certainly be the empty spaces in the tent, the
absence of men whose names he knew too well.
The first jarring shock came when he sought out
his friend Sammie Willis. The summer before, not
long after Shiloh, Willis had been promoted to sergeant. No surprise there. Willis was the best soldier
Bauer had seen, and it was clear that observation
had been shared by the company commander. But
when he arrived at the encampment in Memphis,
Bauer learned that Willis had been promoted yet
again, someone farther up the chain of command
making the decision that this small, rugged fighter
should become an officer. To Bauer's astonish-
ment, Willis was now a second lieutenant. Every
soldier knew that the lieutenants took more than
their share of battle wounds, that the top brass constantly sought out men to fill the boots of so many
who were taken down. What Bauer did not know
was that those freshly promoted officers were sent
where they were most needed, **anywhere** they were
needed most. Lieutenant Samuel Willis had been
transferred to fill a spot in a different regiment, the
17th Wisconsin. Though most of the Wisconsin

troops fought within the same brigades, and certainly they would be assigned within the same corps
of the army's new organization, to Bauer, Willis's
absence was a tragedy all its own. No matter how
close their camps might be, or whether the 16th
would ever stand alongside any of the other regiments from Wisconsin, to Bauer the 17th Wisconsin might as well have been serving on the moon.

After long weeks in Memphis, more of the usual
training and drill, adding new recruits to rebuild
the ranks, the 16th Wisconsin had been ordered
to the transport boats and sent downriver. Bauer
heard the grumbling talk again, the army's most
common commodity, that they were to serve as
one small part of Grant's futile efforts to maneuver past Vicksburg by waging hand-to-hand combat with Mother Nature. Bauer had been regaled
immediately with the tales of engineers and their
grandiose plans for digging what was called Grant's
Canal. The tool most commonly given the men
was the shovel, and Bauer received no more enjoy-
ment from that work than the new recruits who
worked alongside him, or the Negroes who had
been gathered in work crews of their own, many of
them runaway slaves. Bauer suffered his own blis-
ters, hardened his own calluses, feared dysentery as
much as he learned to fear snakebite and alligators,
all the while suffering from armies of ticks and in-
finite swarms of mosquitoes.

And then, the order came. In was time to march.

NEAR HARD TIMES, LOUISIANA
APRIL 21, 1863

For weeks the soldiers had spent their days slogging through muddy fields and narrow bayous, every watery hole humming with every kind of bug, and worse, lurking danger in every muddy footstep, every bog hole seeming to hold some creature whose sole purpose was to torment men. The rebels had come as well, but not many, small raiding parties, easily scattered by the vigilance of the picket guards. Bauer had heard the speculation from the officers, that the rebels were using darkness to slip across the river, and so patrols were sent out along the banks, searching for hidden rafts or small boats. But the steep riverbanks were no friendlier than the dark swamps, the blue-coated troops easily visible to watchful lookouts on the other side, rebel gunners itching to find a target. It was more of a game than anything else, the Federal gunners keeping watch of their own, waiting for the telltale puff of smoke, then launching their own shells back the other way.

The roads they used were often laid on the driest ground, the tops of the levees, and so, for long stretches, the troops marched in perfect view of the rebels across the way. But farther south of Vicksburg, between the smaller settlements the rebels occupied downriver, the gunners were few and scattered, nothing like the massed batteries that guarded the town itself. When the shell came, it was almost always too high, the men dropping low from instinct, the shell tumbling harmlessly into some bog. To the men like Bauer, the shells went by mostly unnoticed, the men focused more on the tramping of their sore feet, the rhythm of the march wearing at their brogans. Though the labor in the swamps across from Vicksburg had been a miserable duty, at least the supplies had been plentiful, even the food reasonably edible. But the veterans knew that, now that they were on the march, any wagon trains would stay far behind them, and if a man wore a hole in his shoe, he might just have to live with it. Or swap out his own with the shoes of a corpse, something no one wanted to think about.

SOUTH OF NEW CARTHAGE, LOUISIANA
APRIL 22, 1863

They had marched for nearly a full day, cooled by a brief shower that kept the dust low on the road. But there had been more showers, days of rain that made for slow going, long stretches of muddy bog. Most of that had been repaired by a carpet of cut trees, what the engineers called "corduroying." For the foot soldiers, mud was merely an annoyance, but the poor roads put a grinding halt to the artil-

lery, which in turn would slow the march for anyone else. Bauer had no idea how many miles they
had covered, didn't really care. That was a problem for the officers, and for the senior commanders **back there** somewhere, who always seemed to
think the army should be able to move as quickly
as a line could be drawn on paper.

For much of the day they could see the river itself, and Bauer felt drawn to the scene, the quiet
serenity of moving water, thick and muddy. He
knew enough of geography to understand that this
same water started its journey far to the northwest
of Milwaukee, emerging from springs and drain-
ages in country that some said still held Indians.
Bauer had never been to northern Minnesota, had
all the wilderness he had needed closer to home.
As a boy, he had hiked and hunted with his father
through land that bore little resemblance to what
surrounded them now. In April the Wisconsin
mornings still held a sharp chill, but here the heat
came early, any effort at all drawing a soaking of
sweat through the wool uniform. In the swamps,
the men who strained with the shovels had been
allowed to go half dressed, and even in the winter
season, the cold had never been what the Northern men were used to. The decorum of the uniform had been an encumbrance, made filthy by the
work, and a welcome hiding place for an amazing
variety of vermin. There were weekly bonfires in
every camp, so many uniforms too dirty to salvage,

and infested with God-knew-what kind of creature. The army seemed to recognize that allowing a man to go shirtless was more acceptable than the cost of replacing uniforms on a daily basis. It was one of those rare pieces of wisdom that surprised even the officers.

But now the shovels were gone. On the march, the uniforms were regulation, muskets on shoulders, bedrolls wrapped across one shoulder. The canteens had been filled with what Bauer could only hope was water cleaner than what flowed past him in the river. It had been a miserable lesson learned in southern Tennessee, when the troops often had to drink water straight from the Tennessee River. The sickness had infected enormous numbers of troops, had certainly contributed to the army's weakness when the rebels came. Bauer had at least made the effort not to drink anything he couldn't actually see through, though lately there had been little choice.

He stepped in silence, the only sound the tramp of the footsteps around him. He glanced toward the sun, falling low, knew the march would end soon, blessed rest for his feet, the opportunity for rations, however meager. Beside him were three other men, the march a column of fours, and far to the front he could glimpse the horsemen, the flag hanging limp, thought of Colonel Allen, the man lucky to be alive. Bauer had escaped any serious wound at Shiloh, but so many had gone down hard, including Allen himself. Amazingly, Allen had survived wounds that those who saw had been convinced were mortal. Whether it was the skill of the doctors, or Allen's own willpower, he had recovered to lead the 16th once more. No one was more pleased with that than Bauer. With the colonel's generosity in allowing Bauer the long furlough, his respect and affection for the man was that much stronger.

"A gunboat! Whoeee! Look at them cannons!" Others around him were pointing to the obvious, an ironclad moving upstream, what Bauer assumed was protection to the army on the march. He had seen the black smoke long before the boat appeared, watched it now, barely moving, just enough power from the rumble of the engines to counter the flow of the current. There were four big guns protruding from the side he could see, three more pointing forward. Yep, you stay right out there. No rebel's gonna come floating across here with you looking at 'em. After a few minutes, there was a fresh belch of smoke, the boat moving on past, upriver, and men all along the column were waving their farewell, acknowledging the comforting show of strength. Bauer had wondered about life on the water, knew boys from home who had spent their time on Lake Michigan, while Bauer preferred the deep woods. Some of those boys are right out there, he thought. Somewhere, some other boat maybe. Maybe New Orleans, those big ocean ships. Not sure I could take that. The river's smooth. The gulf, or worse, the Atlantic . . . people drown out there by the hundreds. I ever have to get on another boat, I'll stick to the rivers.

The levee beneath them seemed to flatten out, the road turning away from the river, and he saw an enormous house, white columns and a wide veranda. The men were flowing out into a field to one side, flat high ground, a good place for a camp. That order drifted back toward them, the horsemen moving that way, the captain relaying the word.

"Column halt! Prepare for camp! There's no tents, so find a good spot and keep close together!"

There were groans about that, but Bauer understood the meaning. This camp was for only one night, just a place to eat and sleep. This march still had a ways to go.

The captain waved them off the road, and Bauer followed, the column breaking down, men flowing along with their color bearer, directed into place by one of Colonel Allen's staff. The officers were gathering, the usual routine, and closer to the men, the sergeants took command, cursing and taunts, the amazingly stupid ritual that seemed to give such joy to the men who wore the stripes. The exception was Champlin, and Bauer saw him now, a quick drink from his canteen, waving the men out toward a cluster of trees.

"Move! Grab that shade while you can! It rains tonight, you'll know why!"

Bauer obeyed, moved beneath a low-hanging limb, lifted his pack and bedroll over his head, dropped down heavily, was suddenly very tired. He looked skyward, the oak tree spread out like an enormous skeleton, barely flecked with new growth, specks of green on the smaller branches. Beyond, the clouds were small and sparse, white puffs darkening with the setting of the sun. Men were settling down all around him, many reaching for their rations, and Bauer did the same. He unwrapped a small cloth bundle, smelled the bacon, almost raw, typical, stuffed it partway into his mouth, tried to bite off one corner. He tugged, the soft meat shredding, the pungent sour taste adding to the growling in his stomach. He focused on the challenge, swallowed a lump of greasy meat, then attacked a piece of hardtack. The square biscuit broke in his hands, something of a relief, sparing his teeth. He tossed a small piece into his mouth, the cracker crumbling into dust, grabbed the canteen, tried to avoid inhaling the floury dust. He took a short swig, stopped, held it away, clenched his jaw, closed his eyes. The water was awful. He took a long breath, his tongue working furiously to wipe away the remnants of hardtack and any hint of what was supposed to be water. The rumbling in his gut continued, loud enough to hear, and he let out a breath, stared again at the wad of soft meat, knew he had to do it all again.

"Private Bauer!"

The voice drew his attention, and he sat up straight, saw Sergeant Champlin, and behind him the captain, walking toward him alongside . . . Colonel Allen. He stood, the instinct of training, snapped a salute toward the officers.

Allen took charge and said, "The army's a mysterious creature, Private. I try to understand its ways, but I learned a long time ago it's best to just let things come as they come." He paused. "It was made clear to me some time ago that the War Department frowned on anyone who requested a transfer to a different regiment. That's not hard to understand. We need to know each other, to know we can fight together as a unit." He reached into a coat pocket, produced a piece of paper. "Apparently, someone has enough influence to allow at least one exception. I have an order here . . . calling for your immediate transfer from the 16th Wisconsin Regiment of Volunteers . . . to the 17th Wisconsin Regiment of Volunteers." He looked at Bauer now, shrugged. "Not sure I understand this, Private, but the order's plain. Usually this kind of thing comes after a promotion, but I've heard nothing of that. I hate to lose you, Private. You're a credit to

Wisconsin, and a credit to this army. We need all the veterans we can get."

Bauer tried to absorb everything the colonel was saying, questions bursting up inside of him. He nodded, saluted again, fought through a jumble of words.

"Yes, sir! Thank you! Uh . . . when, sir?"

Allen looked at the paper, a point with his finger.

"Says right here . . . immediately. Like I said, Private, it's pretty plain."

Bauer noticed a man behind them, keeping back, seeming to wait for the colonel to complete the duty. Bauer didn't know the man, a very young private, a coating of grime on the man's face, the sign of the day's march. The man eased forward now, hesitant, and Allen folded the paper, handed it to Bauer.

"You'll need this to get past the provosts, or any picket guard." The colonel turned, then motioned the man forward. "This man was sent to guide you to the 17th. I suppose . . . no reason for any delay."

The private stood stiffly, prepared to do his duty, and Allen turned away, scanning the men around him, all the faces on Bauer.

Allen said, "You new recruits . . . give a hearty farewell to this man. He could have taught you something. Like some of you others, he was at Shiloh, saw the worst of it. Hate to lose him."

The colonel turned again toward Bauer, who snapped the salute up once more. Allen returned it and spun away, moved back out into the field, trailed closely by the captain. Bauer heard a low voice, Allen.

"Leave it to the army. Who in the hell . . . ?"

Champlin was there now, stood close in front of Bauer, shook his head.

"I guess they're gonna promote you. Only thing makes sense. You're no damn officer. Somebody up the damn chain of command's got too many bug bites to think straight. Well, Dutchie, you best get moving. This here escort of yours looks like he's about to jump out'n his pants."

Bauer felt a swirl of thoughts, confusion most of all.

"I didn't ask for this. . . . I don't want to leave these boys . . . or you, Sarge. The colonel . . ."

"The colonel just read you that order. Now, stuff it in your pocket and follow this squirrely chap to wherever he's supposed to take you. And, like the colonel said, you best do us proud. He won't whip your ass, but I will. Get going."

Bauer saw the private waiting for him, expectant, a gangly boy with red hair, a slight smile, nodding toward him.

"We best be headin' out, sir. Afore's it's dark. Rebs be out and about. Other critters, too."

There was a distinct Irish brogue to the man's speech, and Bauer said, "Not **sir**. I'm just a private. I don't understand any of this."

The man nodded, then glanced at Champlin.

"Well, we best be goin' anyhow. My orders are to escort you to our camp, up ahead a ways, a mile or so."

Bauer looked at Champlin, who reached out, slapped his shoulder.

"Keep your head down, Dutchie."

Bauer nodded, no words, looked again to the gangly private, who said, "You need to hang on to them orders. Like the colonel said, it'll get us through the guards. I got orders of me own, pretty plain, too. We get to camp, I'm to take you directly to Lieutenant Willis."

The name jolted him, and Bauer looked at Champlin again, who said, "Well, now. There you go. They make that tough little squirt an officer, and he's already takin' over the whole damn army."

Bauer said nothing, a wave of confusion still, but the private began to move, beckoning him, and Bauer followed, a quick glance to the sea of faces close by, men calling out, the ones who knew him well offering a confused cheer. Bauer picked up his musket, his bedroll, fought to load himself back to a march. Now he followed the young man into the open field, imagined the scowling face of Willis, smiled. **Sammie**. Well, I'll be damned.

CHAPTER FOUR

SHERMAN

MILLIKEN'S BEND, LOUISIANA, ON BOARD THE *VON PHUL* APRIL 23, 1863

"You could have chosen an ironclad. I'd feel a hell of a lot safer if **my** family was behind a sheet of iron. Ellen would give me hell if I stuck her out here where some lucky rebel gunner might disturb her teacups."

Grant sniffed, seemed lost for a moment, the cigar smoke rolling up around his face.

"Fred doesn't mind. He's been jumping around here like a grasshopper, keeps borrowing my binoculars so he can catch some glimpse of the guns downriver. I think he's hoping we get shelled so he can see what kind of adventure this is. I guess . . . if I was twelve, I'd feel the same way. I don't."

"And Julia?"

Grant shook his head.

"She's not going anywhere near the fight. Not her place, and she knows it. I've got more to think about than worrying about my wife . . . or her teacups. When we reach the river crossing down south, I've ordered that none of the senior command haul along their families or their fancy baggage. This isn't the time for that."

"I know. I got the order. I don't figure I'll be needing my fanciest dress uniforms while we're stuffing our guns down rebel throats."

Grant gave a hint of a smile.

"I'm not so worried about you. Not as confident in . . . well, some of the others."

Sherman knew that Grant was thinking of McClernand, that it was still possible McClernand would try to distance himself from Grant's authority, would make every effort to conduct his part of the campaign his own way. Sherman said nothing, knew it was not the time to chew any fat over McClernand. He set the cigar aside, caught the sudden fragrance of . . . a woman. She was at the cabin door now, in a hoopless skirt, far more appropriate for the awkward confines of a boat, whether the commanding general's wife agreed with that lack of decorum or not.

"Excuse me . . . oh, General Sherman. How nice of you to visit."

There was softness in her greeting, with just a hint of aloofness, Julia's way, something Sherman was accustomed to. Julia Grant seemed to relish her position as the most "high ranking" of the generals' wives, a very proper air about her that Grant seemed not to notice. Sherman made a short bow.

"The pleasure is mine, Mrs. Grant."

Grant studied a map more than he acknowledged his wife; he seemed to know why she was there. Julia swept into the room, bathing Sherman in a fog of feminine smells, a radical difference from the smells of the boat itself, and Grant in particular.

"Ulyss, I don't mean to interfere in your army business, but Fred has become most difficult. He claims you have given him permission to accompany you, despite my misgivings."

Grant let out a long breath, straightened his back, as though bracing for an argument. "He's correct. I told him he could come, as long as he kept far back of any fighting and was accompanied by one of my aides. I don't see the harm."

Julia glanced at Sherman and put her hands on her hips in obvious disapproval. Grant clearly had been through this before. He put down the cigar, looked at her, a brief silence between them. Julia said nothing; she seemed to understand that Grant would have the last word.

"My dear wife, Fred is nearly grown. There are drummers in this army younger than he is. He'll be safe, and this is something he truly wants to do. It will do him good. I do not wish to have him feel . . . coddled. I see no reason. . . ."

"Fine. You are after all the commanding general."

She nodded, half-smiling toward Sherman.

"General. Please visit anytime."

She turned, left the cabin without another word to Grant. Grant shook his head, his shoulders slumping again. Sherman tried to hide a smile, thought, Well, he had the last word. But the **final** words were hers.

Grant shook his head and said, "She protects him too much. Not good for the boy." He looked up at Sherman, who fumbled with a cigar, as though oblivious to anything that had just happened. "She has to get used to this, I'm afraid. My son wants to be a soldier. There will come a time when neither of us will have a say in that. It's better if he learns what soldiering means."

Sherman still studied the cigar, said, "You're the commanding general. You can do whatever the hell you want, I suppose."

"Don't believe that for one minute, Sherman. No general in this army has more power than the wife who waits for him to come home. You are most certainly aware of that."

"Most certainly. That's why Ellen has been 'posted' at Cincinnati. She had expected to visit me before now, but the gracious General Burnside has cautioned her not to make the journey. Told her there are a good many guerrillas in the countryside. I owe him a favor for that one."

Grant seemed to react to Burnside's name, but said nothing. No one had ignored Burnside's catastrophic failure at Fredericksburg the December before, that general now assigned to some vague post in Kentucky. Now it was Grant who seemed anxious to change the subject. He looked toward the map again, a map Sherman knew Grant had memorized in every detail.

"McClernand is taking his time. Need to repair that situation, but it will require some diplomatic skills. Not my favorite activity. I would rather focus on the issue at hand without wrestling with . . . ambitiousness."

Sherman could hear the strain in Grant's voice, felt it himself, a twisting urgency to get this thing started. No matter what kind of criticism had flowed over Grant, Sherman had seen too much of the man's performance firsthand, the tactics and strategy that no one in Washington seemed to understand. He saw it now, Grant's focus on one thing, the most important matter at hand, and exactly what would come next.

Sherman stuffed the cigar back into his mouth, said, "I saw Secretary Dana this morning. Friendly chap. Insists he will stay out of our way."

Grant sniffed. "He'll stay where I tell him to, and then write the War Department that I prevented him from doing his job." He paused. "No, I'll allow him to go where he wishes. We accomplish our mission, do our jobs, he'll have nothing else to put in his reports. I do trust him to be honest about what we accomplish here. In that I have no choice."

Charles Dana was the assistant secretary of war, and so was the immediate subordinate to William Stanton, who, alongside Henry Halleck, was truly in command of this war. Grant's distance from Washington was a blessing, which was not the case for so many of the generals east of the Appalachians, who had struggled to find Union victories far closer to the capital. The campaigns back east had resulted in failures much worse than anything in the West, either costly stalemates or outright defeats throughout Virginia and Maryland. From McClellan's aborted campaign up the Virginia peninsula, to a second major fight near Bull Run Creek, and then of course Fredericksburg, no Federal commander had shown he had the skills or the fortitude to defeat the outnumbered and outgunned Confederates. Even the vicious fight at Antietam Creek had accomplished little more than halting a rebel invasion of Maryland, at a horrifying cost in casualties to both armies. No matter George McClellan's noisy claim of a great "victory" over Robert E. Lee, McClellan had allowed Lee to escape back into Virginia. It was all the more infuriating to Sherman that Grant would be so vilified by his critics, while the greater harm to the Union was happening east of the mountains. For the most part, Grant had given **this** army victories. But still the newspapers sought to embellish failure over success, as though anxious for that one great collapse that would force Abraham Lincoln to re-move Grant altogether. So far, Lincoln had resisted any condemnation of Grant, seemed more satis-fied with the army's progress in the West than he was with the parade of ineptitude closer to home. There was no doubt that Charles Dana had made the journey west to cut through the rumors and in-nuendo, to observe firsthand just how competent a leader Grant was. Officially, Dana was to open an active pipeline of communications with Washing-ton. But if Dana witnessed any failure of leadership, it just might open the door for John McClernand to step through, which of course was McClernand's expectation.

Grant rolled up the maps and shoved them into a leather bag. Sherman saw Grant's faraway look again, knew this meeting had to end, that Grant was deeply concerned about the progress of the army's march downriver. Sherman took one step toward the exit and stopped. He couldn't leave without pressing, asking the one question that was digging inside of him.

"How long you plan on keeping me up here?"

Grant seemed to expect the question. It wasn't the first time Sherman had asked it.

"As long as I need you here."

Sherman knew he wasn't being held back as any

slight to his reputation. It was just a part of the strategy, the plan that Sherman still not did fully believe in. Even before the first of the year, Sherman had objected to the entire notion of coming at Vicksburg from the water, and the engineering failures at slicing through the swamplands west of the river had been infuriating confirmation that Sherman was right. The effort to alter the flow of the Mississippi River seemed utterly ridiculous to Sherman, an enormous waste of manpower and time. Now, with Grant focused more on shifting his army south of Vicksburg, and driving into Mississippi below the town, Sherman was forced to go along with a strategy he still didn't accept. He continued to believe that the most efficient plan was to withdraw and regroup at Memphis, then drive southward from the Tennessee line into central Mississippi. The result could devastate rebel supply lines eastward, and the Federal army could capture the towns in northern Mississippi to use as bases of supply. Depending on the rebel response, there could be alternatives for Grant to wage a strong campaign toward a variety of valuable targets, Vicksburg among them. Grant knew how Sherman felt, but his tolerance for dissent was limited, something Sherman understood. He might not agree with Grant's plan, but he had to obey his orders.

Now two-thirds of Grant's army, the two corps under McClernand and James McPherson, were on the march downriver. Once well below the strongest rebel shore batteries, they would assemble on the west bank of the river, then cross as rapidly and with as much massed strength as possible, striking hard at any resistance in their way. The rebels had several outposts south of Vicksburg, most of them on the river itself, or just inland, guarding key intersections. But Grant knew enough of the rebel troop strength to understand how thinly they were spread, and even with heavy artillery that made the navy's job continually dangerous, the rebels simply did not have the manpower to fortify every possible crossing point. Once a massed fist of Federal strength could be established on the east side of the river, Grant was confident every advantage would be his. Just what he would do next, how quickly he would drive up toward Vicksburg, would be determined by what kind of maneuvers the rebels made in response to the landing. Since the rebel commanders in Vicksburg were forced by geography to protect more than twenty miles of riverfront, Grant had to believe that their forces were spread too thin to hold away the Federals' strength. If everything went exactly as Grant hoped, there was the possibility that the rebels might simply abandon Vicksburg without a fight.

To Sherman, the northern approaches were still far more practical. Despite the surprise attack at Holly Springs, Sherman still believed that keeping the supply lines open to the north would keep the army strong and mobile. The rebel cavalry's success at Holly Springs had taught Grant a lesson, and any supply depot would be heavily protected. To Sherman's frustration, Grant's plan now seemed to contradict that, the army moving even farther from Memphis and any other key depot where supplies were being stockpiled. One of the largest of those depots was Milliken's Bend, just upriver and across from Vicksburg, and vulnerable from an attack from the west, from rebel forces in Arkansas or southern Louisiana.

Their arguments had been brief, as far as Sherman dared to go, though he knew Grant would listen to him with more patience than he would any other general in the army. With the rest of the army marching downriver, Sherman's corps, accompanied by several of Porter's gunboats, would remain closer to Milliken's Bend. But they were not there just to protect transport boats and supply trains. It was one vital piece of Grant's plan, and Sherman had to swallow it whole, no matter his indigestion. While Grant moved south, Sherman would once again threaten Vicksburg from the north. But that threat was designed to be a feint, a loud and boisterous demonstration to bring rebel infantry out in Sherman's direction. Sherman had to agree with Grant that the rebels would gleefully accept another opportunity to bloody the Federals, inspired by memories of their victory at Chickasaw Bayou. If the rebels responded by shifting strength northward as Grant hoped, it could greatly weaken their strength south of the town, or their ability to maneuver reinforcements quickly enough to block Grant's inland push. No matter the soundness of the plan, Sherman knew that the morale among his men would suffer mightily, that they were to stage a counterfeit attack, what would feel like a mocking repeat of their humiliation in December. If there was an opening, if somehow the rebels ignored Sherman, or backed away, the option was open to him to drive on to Vicksburg, and even to attack the town. But Sherman knew better. The rebels were supremely confident in their strongholds and fortifications spread all through the swamps and bayous. They weren't going anywhere.

Even Grant understood that Sherman's maneuvering would be misinterpreted by the newspapers as another failed assault. The reporters seemed to dislike Sherman as much as he despised them, and would certainly taunt him for anything that hinted of failure. The newspapers could not be told of the actual plan, of course, and so the planned "retreat" would be seen as yet another humiliation, no matter that it was exactly what Sherman was ordered to do. Sherman had tried his best to ignore the reporters, not to read anything in the papers at all. But his men would, good men who had done nothing to bring shame on themselves. He knew he had to go along with Grant's overall plans, but ordering his officers to begin the maneuver was like chewing a mouthful of sand.

Below Vicksburg, Admiral Porter had insisted that any rebels coming from the west could be kept at bay, and that their various batteries and forts along the eastern shore of the river could be passed at will with minimal loss, allowing the boats to keep a supply line open to Grant after the crossing. After the stunning success of the passing on April 16, Porter had emphasized that very point a few nights later, by doing it again. There were far fewer boats this time, a half-dozen supply vessels, and there had been losses, but the majority of the barges and transports had escaped major damage. One of Sherman's greatest arguments against Grant's plan was that as Grant moved farther into Mississippi, his supply lines would be increasingly vulnerable, threatened certainly by rebel cavalry. Considerable troop strength would be needed all along the supply lines, and since Sherman's corps, once they made their own march southward, would be the final link in the chain, it was obvious who the guardians of the supply routes would be. That would be one more blow to the morale of his men.

Sherman crossed his arms, fought the urge to spit all of this out into words he would regret. There was commotion outside, men on the march, and he glanced out toward the shore, gritting his teeth, unable to hide his anger at what was already in motion. The words came out slowly, an agonizing effort to control his frustration.

"This is a dangerous enterprise, Grant." He paused. "Once you give the order, we'll march south to link up with the rest of the army as quickly as possible. I would hope that this **feint** is a rapid affair."

"You still going to bellyache about this? I thought it was settled. It's a little late for arguments. Can't do that, Sherman."

Sherman had not intended any argument at all, but if he was to abandon his own best ideas, and march downriver with the rest of the army, being **last in line** was still a thorn he couldn't ignore.

"I've always been concerned about the lines of supply. That's all. The campaign . . . well, we tried it my way, and the rebels busted our noses. It's your plan, and you know they'll hang you with it if it doesn't work."

Grant looked at the cigar, turned it slowly, Sherman noticing the elongated ash that hung off its tip. Grant tapped it on the ashtray beside him and said, "You spent the Mexican War in California. You missed out on one of the greatest military campaigns ever fought."

Sherman didn't expect this, had heard too much annoying chatter about Mexico, the army now populated with generals who had earned their lieutenant's bars under Zachary Taylor or Winfield Scott.

Grant seemed to sense he had jabbed Sherman in a tender place.

"I'm talking about General Scott, that's all. Don't go reading anything more into it. Back then, I was nothing more than a green assistant quartermaster, hauling blankets and tents, counting spare bedrolls. After General Scott busted up the walls at Vera Cruz, he gathers up the whole blessed army and hauls us off on a long march across hundreds of miles of pure wilderness. The enemy was retreating back to Mexico City, so we chased after them. Scott cuts us off from every kind of contact we had with the Gulf Coast, with the navy, and especially with Washington. No way to supply us, or even communicate with us. There were generals then who thought it was the most foolhardy strategy ever conceived. Some thought our little ten-thousand-man army was marching to our doom, that Santa Anna would just gobble us up, and no one in Washington would hear another word out of any of us. Tried it, too, all along the way, and we whipped them in every fight. We followed them right to the walls of Mexico City, and gathered up what we could, and Scott shoved us right through. We won that damned war because of a plan that none of his commanders believed in. And you know why it worked? He counted on three things going our way. He believed we were a far better army than the Mexicans and would whip them in a fight, no matter if we were outnumbered. We did. He believed the enemy would be completely surprised by our making such a march with speed. He was. And he believed we could live off the land while we were doing it. We did. I believe . . . that will work now."

"I can't say anything else, Grant, so I won't. You're in command. You tell me to use the Yazoo, I'll do it. You tell me to haul my corps downriver, I'll do that. I'm pretty sure you'll be wanting me down there pretty quick. McPherson's good, but he's not really tested. McClernand . . . well, he's McClernand."

"We'll see. You know what you're doing up here, and why. Just . . . make it work."

Sherman nodded, couldn't help a feeling of dread.

"I just hope we have a chance . . . downriver . . . for my boys to redeem themselves."

Grant didn't respond, and Sherman knew he couldn't, that redemption couldn't be a focus of any strategy. Grant glanced around as though checking on anything he might have left behind.

"When you get my order to move south, well, I expect you to **move**. Anything else? Every minute that passes, my army is farther away. At least, it had better be."

It was unusual for Grant to show visible impatience, and Sherman understood completely. Sherman lit another cigar, saw a naval officer moving close to the entrance of the cabin. The man saluted Grant and said, "Sir, we're preparing for you to disembark. The horses and your staff are in readiness onshore. Your Colonel Rawlins has instructed me . . . has asked me to retrieve you at your earliest convenience, sir."

Grant curled his face, glanced at Sherman without smiling, then back to the naval officer.

"I'm quite certain Colonel Rawlins **instructed** you. It's just . . . what he does. Never mind. Tell the colonel I'll be there shortly." He looked at Sherman again, put out the stub of the used cigar. "Sherman, I'll do what I can to get those people moving downriver. You do what you can to convince the rebels we're staying right here and smacking them from the north. That's it. Time to go."

Grant moved out to the open deck of the merchant steamer, no smoke from the tall stacks, the engines quiet. The shore was a mass of activity, supply wagons and artillery rolling out onto a network of roads that all led south. Grant stepped toward the plank, the naval officer there, snapping another salute, a formal farewell. Along the deck there were other crewmen, but they were not navy. The boat was, after all, a civilian vessel, and Sherman saw the crewmen eyeing Grant as though appraising him, most with a bored scowl. Sherman scanned them, thought of Porter, the admiral's fury at the civilian crews who wouldn't man their posts when it came time to run past the rebel guns. Maybe some of you?

He followed Grant, moved toward the plank, and caught their stares, now directed at him. Sherman stopped, a hard glare toward the men closest to him. He pointed toward Grant, already onshore.

"Remember **him,** gentlemen. That's the man who will win this thing."

The **Von Phul** was a merchant steamer that had been converted to Grant's temporary headquarters. But there would be no effort yet to bring her downriver. Sherman's concerns for the lack of armor plating was only one reason. It was utter foolishness for the army's commander to risk the kind of dash Porter's supply flotilla had made past the batteries at Vicksburg. Grant would make the ride to his new headquarters along the same route his army was using west of the river. As Grant made his way downriver, he began to hear reports of delay, primarily a roadblock from the front of the line, McClernand's Thirteenth Corps. Though Grant knew that McClernand's ambitiousness could become a problem, he at least expected the man to follow orders. Grant had insisted with considerable vigor that McClernand and McPherson move their troops to the potential river crossings as rapidly as the men could march. What he did not expect to hear was that, along the way, McClernand felt the need to halt his men in their camps, while he regaled them with a lengthy speech.

As Grant made his way down to his new headquarters, a landing called New Carthage, he fumed over how best to handle McClernand. Appreciative that Sherman had no idea of the infuriating delays, Grant was completely certain that if Sherman were in command here, McClernand would likely get his nose broken.

A s the rebel forces along the river continued to observe Grant's army in motion, communications flowed from Vicksburg back eastward to the state's capital, Jackson. There the Confederate general who commanded this entire theater waited eagerly for the reports that would bolster what he already believed, that Grant was retreating and that any assault against Vicksburg would come once more from the north. Whatever reports rolled into Jackson from below Vicksburg only served the expectation that those Federal troops in motion west of the river were very likely moving away altogether, perhaps downriver toward the only remaining Confederate stronghold below Vicksburg, the town of Port Hudson, just north of Federal-held Baton Rouge. Already, Confederate scouts along the Yazoo were reporting gunboats and troop transports moving toward the scene of their humiliating defeat in December, a blow the rebels were prepared to deliver yet again.

On April 17, new reports reached the Mississippi capital. A wave of Federal cavalry had emerged from their camps near Memphis, several different expeditions, said to be spreading out in a variety of directions. The most immediate concern was a column reported to be driving straight down through the heart of northern Mississippi. The Confederate command had cavalry of their own, outposts and squadrons positioned at every significant intersection. In a few short days, the reports from those outposts degenerated into confusion and chaos, word reaching Jackson that a fast-moving wave of Federal horsemen had caught several rebel cavalry units completely by surprise, that the skirmishes and confrontations had gone nearly all the Federals' way. In Jackson, the fear began to grow that the most logical target for the blue column would be the critical railroad link that connected Jackson to the east, far from Vicksburg, or that possibly, the bluecoats were aiming to drive hard into Jackson itself. In response, the Confederate cavalry, including several strong units whose primary mission had been to observe Grant's army to the west, were called away from their posts, an urgent effort to track down and destroy this daring raid.

The Federal cavalry was commanded by Colonel Ben Grierson, his seventeen hundred men showing a kind of speed and audacity rarely exhibited by Federal horsemen. So far, the war's most effective horsemen wore gray, John Hunt Morgan and Nathan Bedford Forrest, Turner Ashby and "Jeb" Stuart. But in Mississippi, Grierson quickly proved the superior of any opponent he faced. By employing a small squad of his scouts in ragged rebel garb to move out in advance of his main force, these "Butternut Guerrillas" successfully relaxed the alertness of any outposts in his path, bringing down the guard of pickets and skirmishers who protected any railcars or supply depots. When the pursuit from behind grew dangerously close, Grierson responded by dividing his forces, sending them in a maze of directions. When actually confronted by rebel muskets, Grierson kept his few lightweight artillery pieces in constant motion, firing into various directions, giving the definite impression that he had far more artillery at hand. By making good use of the spiderweb of roads in the rural country, his pursuers never could lay the ambush, or block Grierson from his actual targets.

At Newton Station, east of Jackson, Grierson struck, destroying the rail lines and capturing both supplies and rebel troops. Grierson then defied the rebels' expectations once more. Instead of withdrawing northward, where Confederates were gathering to cut off his retreat, Grierson continued to the south and escaped the baffled rebels by pushing his men and their mounts in a breakneck ride all the way to Baton Rouge. Though the rail lines were easily repaired, and the delays to the communication lines only temporary, Grierson's raid had one enormous consequence. With rebel cavalrymen chasing their tails all throughout central Mis-

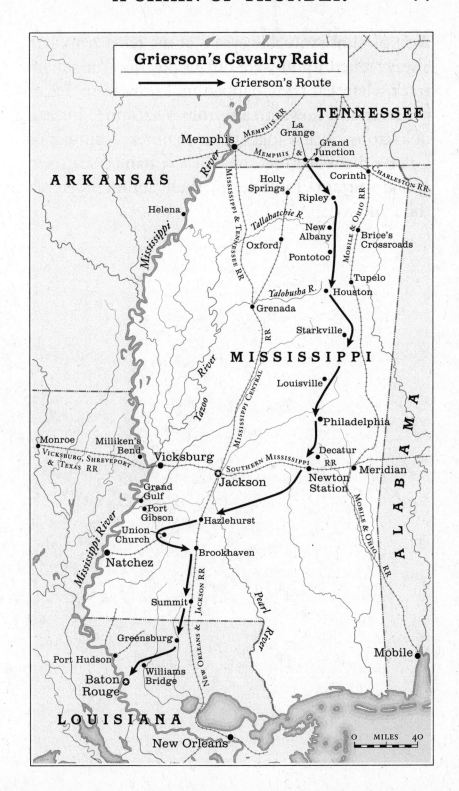

Grierson's Cavalry Raid

→ Grierson's Route

sissippi, those valuable eyes that the rebel army had always relied upon were out of position, unable to track what was truly happening to the west, across the river and downstream from Vicksburg. Instead of a strong cavalry juggernaut to observe and harass Grant's maneuvering, the rebels remained scattered and uncertain. In Jackson, their commander felt the same way.

CHAPTER FIVE

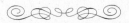

PEMBERTON

JACKSON, MISSISSIPPI
APRIL 27, 1863

"More reports, sir. A skirmish south of Newton Station. But the Yankees escaped."

Pemberton sat with his chin in his hands, stared at nothing, nodded.

"Escaped."

"Yes, sir. We have word that Captain Apcorn was captured, along with an undetermined number of our troopers. The Yankees had a significant number of artillery pieces, and were more than our equal."

"Artillery? I have not been informed that the enemy has brought along any sizable number of fieldpieces. How much artillery?"

The man shrugged, no response. Pemberton

looked to the teacup, the brew cold, sipped it absently. Artillery, he thought. One six-pounder? Or a dozen batteries? Is there infantry as well? No, I would at least know about that. But this bluecoat is a crafty one, and he moves too quickly to be hauling many guns.

Pemberton knew artillery better than any man on his staff, had served that branch of the army after his graduation from West Point. If there are siege guns, he thought . . . well, no, that would mean infantry, and so far, at least no one is flying in here chirping about infantry.

The sudden appearance of Federal cavalry through what seemed to be every crossroads in the state had worn on Pemberton, as it had worn on the rumor mills of Jackson. Already the citizens were in something of a panic, many loading up their belongings and fleeing the city. He could offer them no comfort, no encouraging words to stay in their homes. It was not his way, no elaborate gift for oratory. And worse, the troops stationed in Jackson were feeling the same edginess, skirmishes breaking out at night, more often between the guard posts and picket lines of his own men.

The staff officer waited, as though expecting something from Pemberton that would solve everything. Pemberton felt that weight too often, had felt it in South Carolina, had felt it every time he had been called to meet with Jefferson Davis.

Davis seemed to appreciate Pemberton's methods, the intense focus on details, planning, and paperwork. Pemberton had seen the same in Davis, the two men forming a friendship based on their shared view of how to command an army. But Davis's authority held far more gravity than this Pennsylvania-born field commander, and to Pemberton's dismay, his administration of the defenses for the city of Charleston had been met with stiff criticism from the very people he was assigned to protect. After considerable controversy directed at Pemberton from civilian officials, Jefferson Davis had no choice but to remove Pemberton from a department where his unpopularity had made him completely ineffective. The assignment to Mississippi had come next, and Pemberton had tackled that command with the same attention to detail. It was his experience with artillery that made him appreciate Vicksburg's enormous value and formidable strength, and Pemberton fortified the high bluffs with every large-bore gun he could secure. As was always the case in nearly every command throughout the Confederacy, Pemberton could never get the quantity of guns he requested, was competing for limited resources with every general who faced the enemy. But Vicksburg had much more strategic value than so many other defensive posts, and it took very little convincing to assure President Davis that the defense of Vicksburg had to be a high priority. Pemberton's cause was bolstered by the fact that Davis's own plantation was nearby.

But Pemberton's difficulties lay far beyond a sufficient number of artillery pieces. West of the Mississippi River lay enormous agricultural resources desperately required to feed the entire Confederacy. But the commanders there, notably Richard Taylor and Kirby Smith, seemed unwilling to offer their bounty to Pemberton at all. Pemberton was friends with neither man, felt the same strained relationship he endured with so many of the senior Confederates. He had always felt an iciness toward him from the men in gray, as well as the civilians they served. Pemberton was, after all, a Pennsylvanian, had come to the South only from a devout dedication to his Virginia-born wife. No matter his oath, his absolute dedication to the Southern Cause, or his friendship with Davis, the only way Pemberton would earn respect from his subordinates was to earn **victories**. But there was no great offensive campaign to be waged in Mississippi, no real opportunity to strike hard at the Federal forces who controlled so much of the great river. Davis understood, and Pemberton was fully aware that in his particular command, there was no more critical mission, nothing more essential to Southern hopes than keeping the Federals from absolute control of the river. North of Baton Rouge and south of Memphis, the most defensible bastion was Vicksburg. For now, though, Pemberton had to look the other way, east of Jackson, wondering why this wave of blue cavalry was sweeping down through central Mississippi.

Colonel Waddy leaned closer to him, as though examining Pemberton to see if he was awake.

"Sir? May I be of any further service?"

Pemberton leaned on one elbow, his chin cradled again by his hand.

"Find me some more cavalry, Colonel. If we had the strength, we would not be so . . . blind. I am quite certain General Grant knows of my resources. I wish I knew more of his."

Waddy seemed uncomfortable, shifted his weight, catching Pemberton's attention. Too much talk, he thought. Waddy is a good chief of staff, but he doesn't need to know my every thought.

"Perhaps, sir, if General Johnston knew of our predicament, he could order General Van Dorn—"

Pemberton's stare silenced the man.

"Perhaps you should be in this chair, Colonel. Then I could go riding off where I please and attend to the ladies of Jackson who find our officers so very charming."

The man stiffened.

"Sir, I assure you that I have no interest in courting any ladies here, or anywhere else. I am spoken for, and my dear Loretta awaits me right here, the guests of a fine family just a street removed from this headquarters."

Pemberton sagged, had experienced this before. John Waddy was just one more staff officer who felt no hesitation arguing with him, or displaying just a hint of disrespect. It wasn't Pemberton's way to handle his staff with an iron fist. The staff had learned that quickly, the men speaking out with far less formality than other commanders allowed. Pemberton waited for a pause in the man's outrage, then said, "You are excused, Colonel. Please request that the couriers be a bit more efficient with their reports. I must know more of this Grierson chap, and what he intends. Perhaps you're correct, that General Johnston can be persuaded to assist us."

Waddy backed away without a salute, was quickly gone. Pemberton looked again to the teacup, let it sit, pushed back in his chair. He rubbed his stomach, felt a hard knot, the nagging indigestion, the constant reminder that he was really not in control here. Johnston, he thought. Sits over there in Tennessee and lords over us like some sort of monarch. He despises the president and so he despises anyone who has Mr. Davis's favor. I offer my own correspondence to the president, no matter how trivial or personal, and I am treated as though I am a subversive to Johnston's great plan. It would be so very helpful if I knew what that plan might be. Tennessee. General Johnston must certainly be receiving great compliments from General Bragg, and so he keeps close to Bragg's affairs, while I am but a stepchild.

He stood, kneaded the pain in his stomach, heard commotion in the outer office, voices, that same annoying urgency that accompanied every incoming dispatch. He moved to the chair again, stayed behind it, supported himself against the back, blinked hard. There had been very little sleep, not since the Federal cavalry had begun their raids, and not when reports came from Vicksburg ten days before of the Federal flotilla driving past his guns. His patience dissolved, and he called out, "Who has arrived? What is it?"

He caught a glimpse of a dust cloud, saw it billowing from the ragged uniform of a sergeant, the man peering in toward him, more curious than respectful. One of his aides appeared now, neat, the perfect uniform, a distinct contrast to the sergeant. Pemberton didn't wait for the aide.

"What do you have for me, Sergeant?"

The man stepped in with too much volume in his boot heels, a show of the man's own authority. It seemed to work on Pemberton's staff officers, no one following.

"Sir! Sergeant Israel Duncan, at your service. General Bowen sends his respects, and wishes to advise the general that the enemy has assembled a large fleet of transport boats and gunships on the river below Grand Gulf. General Bowen apologizes for his speculation, sir, and offers that the enemy is preparing to cross the river somewhere to the south of that point, possibly at Bruinsburg."

Pemberton allowed the words to sink in, thought of Bowen. Good man, would not exaggerate.

"What of the batteries at Grand Gulf? How did we not prevent the enemy from passing there?" He felt his voice rising. "Is that not why we placed so much ordnance there? To prevent the enemy from passing?"

The sergeant's bravado seemed to wilt, and Pemberton slid around the back of the chair, sat heavily.

"Sir, General Bowen did not instruct me to report that. The general only wishes me to report that the enemy appears to be preparing a crossing of the river. There are great numbers of Yankees now camped at Hard Times, and at the plantations below. He requests in the most urgent terms, sir, that you authorize every available artillery and infantry unit to march in preparation to receive the enemy there. The general has withdrawn our outposts west of the river without loss."

Pemberton sat back and closed his eyes.

"That is good. If General Grant is in force, those outposts would certainly be lost." He paused, blinked, the dust of the man's coat drifting through the office. He tried to share the man's energy, the sense of authority, knew that if Bowen was correct, Grant might finally have revealed his intentions. But still . . . Grant might keep going, keep marching southward. What Bowen calls a fleet . . . could just be the boats to take Grant's army farther downriver.

After a long silent moment, he said, "You are excused. Return to General Bowen and offer my respects, and my appreciation for his vigilance. Have him confirm at his earliest convenience the accuracy of your report. If the enemy does intend to cross below Grand Gulf, we must certainly make an effort to oppose him."

"Sir, may I inform General Bowen that the army is responding as he requests? He was most insistent on that point, sir. The general has stated plainly that he does not have the strength to prevent the Yankees—"

"Yes, yes. If he is correct, there must be reinforcements sent to his position. I will look into that, Sergeant. We have other concerns right here, and there are still the reports of the enemy's movement **north** of Vicksburg. I must consider all the possibilities. Return to General Bowen."

The sergeant stood in silence for a long second, and Pemberton waited. There was something else the man wanted to say, but there was nothing but the sound of the man's breathing.

"Go now, Sergeant. I assure you, it will all work to our advantage. We have the interior lines, and the enemy is spread all over this part of Creation. It is our ground, and it will remain our ground."

"Yes, sir. **Our** ground."

It was a hint of sarcasm Pemberton had heard too many times before. But he had no energy for dressing this man down, forced himself to ignore the man's impudence. The sergeant withdrew, a trail of dust following him, the air in the office finally clearing of the odor of damp horses. He pulled in a deep breath, wiped his face, tried to clear away the dust, thought, **Our** ground. Is that what I must endure from them all? Is every order to be questioned, every observation held in suspicion? I did not put on this uniform and strap on this scabbard to be reminded every day that I am not a **Southerner**. The president did not grant me this rank believing that I would betray this cause. My wife . . .

Her image slowed the anger, and he thought of her soft skin, that marvelous perfume, her perfect attention to her dress, so beautiful. So . . . Southern. She knows why I am here. She does not doubt, she will not speak behind my back, she will not offer discreet insults to my face. I must prove to her only that I am a good husband, **her** husband. Of that she has no doubts. I fight for this nation because I fight for her. How dare any one of these soldiers insult that.

He fought to concentrate, withdrew a map from his desk, unrolled it, and called out, "Colonel Waddy? A moment, please?"

The officer appeared, hesitated, now stepped in, focusing on the map.

"Colonel, thus far, all we know of the Federal

cavalry is that they are keeping to the east of the city, correct?"

"Yes, sir. From the reports we have received."

"And now General Bowen reports that the enemy is in force opposite his position south of Vicksburg."

"Yes, sir. I heard Sergeant Duncan's report, sir."

"And we have also been informed that the enemy is in some force moving up the Yazoo River, correct?"

"Yes, sir."

Pemberton stared at the map, putting a finger on each of the three points.

"Well now. General Grant has provided us with a compass that seems to be pointing in three directions. I am to believe that the city of Jackson is under threat from the north and east, Vicksburg is under threat once more from the north, and now the Federal army is en masse across the river to our southwest. What am I to make of this, Colonel?"

Waddy stood back, and Pemberton could see he was nervous, hesitating.

"I cannot rightly say, sir."

"Well, I am not at all surprised that the enemy is advancing toward Vicksburg from the Yazoo. He knows the routes, knows the capabilities of our defenses. In December he erred in his calculations, and I do not believe General Grant will allow his commanders to make those same mistakes. When he comes, he will bring more strength, a better plan. It is what I would do. But we still have every advantage. Good high ground, the perfect vantage points for placement of artillery. The waterways will not allow safe maneuver for his riverboats. And I am quite certain that the enemy does not enjoy maneuvering in swampland. We can only assume that Grant will attempt to appease his many critics by setting **right** what went so **wrong** in December. Reputation carries enormous weight, Colonel. And Grant will protect his. We must see what we can do about that."

"But sir . . . General Bowen's observations at Grand Gulf . . ."

Pemberton stared at the map through watering eyes, still fighting the lack of sleep. He could not avoid a thorn of uncertainty. Bowen. He would not issue a false report. He would not panic.

"Yes, I am aware of the possibilities. Perhaps . . . General Grant is aware of what I would do in his place, of what we would anticipate in his movements. And so he sends cavalry to scare us, sends gunboats to shell our batteries. He has certainly succeeded in spreading panic among the civilians. And . . . this army is swirling around like a dervish, forced to look over our shoulders in every direction at once. But I have no doubt that their priority must be the same as ours. We must hold tight to Vicksburg, as they will expend much to take it. No matter the chaos General Grant causes our people, his intentions are clear, as they have always been clear."

"They are clear, sir? But you said—"

"Never mind, Colonel. I am merely pondering our alternatives, examining every option. It is, after all, my job, is it not?" He paused again, thought of Johnston, off in Tennessee, the man who would no doubt find fault with any plan Pemberton advised. There is no time for a parade of couriers, he thought. The enemy is coming, one way or another. I must respond.

"Colonel, we must move this headquarters to Vicksburg."

"Yes, sir. Begging your pardon, sir, but . . . when?"

"It will require a few days. Make ready as soon as we can organize the transportation. Assign more troops to the pursuit of that confounded Federal cavalry. I do not wish to leave the good citizens of Jackson in more of a panic than they are now suffering. We will advise the civilian officials here of our vigilance for their concerns. Vicksburg is Grant's objective . . . no doubt of that. But that is a military matter." He studied the map again. "It is possible Grant is intending to bypass Vicksburg and capture the capital. We must be certain, Colonel. Certain."

"Yes, sir. When . . . will we be certain, sir?"

Pemberton ignored the question, rolled the map, and slid it into his desk drawer. Waddy began to move away, stopped, then said, "Sir, I shall order the servants to prepare our baggage, at your command, sir. It will take some time for our wives to prepare, and I will see to that immediately. The senior field commanders will wish to know how to communicate with us as we travel, and I will send word to General Bowen and General Stevenson of our intentions, if that's acceptable, sir."

"Yes, yes, of course. Your wife will accompany you, then?"

Waddy seemed not to understand the question. "Well, yes, certainly, sir. Is that not appropriate?"

"Oh, no, by all means. The wives should remain close to their husbands." Pemberton thought of Pattie again, the strong will, the hard steel that had been so persuasive in bringing him south. You must be safe. You will be safe. I will have it no other way.

"Colonel, I will go to my quarters now. Mrs. Pemberton will require time to prepare, as you say."

"Very well, sir. I will see to your quarters once we reach Vicksburg, and make certain there is a feminine touch, sir."

"Vicksburg? Oh, no, Colonel. She won't be accompanying us to Vicksburg. I prefer to send her to a safer location." He thought a moment, saw a blank expression on Waddy's face. "Mobile. Yes, that's good. That's the place. She will go to Mobile. It will be far safer there."

CHAPTER SIX

BAUER

NEAR BRUINSBURG, LOUISIANA
APRIL 30, 1863

"You bring any coffee with ya?" Bauer shook his head, and the man spat, disgusted, turned away. "He's not a whit good to us then, is he?"

Bauer was still feeling overwhelmed, new faces and new accents, some of the brogue so thick he could barely understand what was being said. The men around him seemed to pick that up right away, were making a show now of speaking to one another with such speed, Bauer couldn't understand them at all.

He thought of coffee, more valuable than gold to some of the men. The small cloth pouch that held his had been empty for some time, just one more detail he had forgotten. Well, that would have helped, he thought. At least show them I'm trying to fit in.

"Line up by fours! We're marching to the boats. Keep your bayonets at your belts. None of that ass-stickin'. You wanna get tossed in the stockade, you jab the fella in front of ya. Not puttin' up with it, no more."

The voice was a hard roar, so typical of the sergeants. He had made it a point to stay close to Sergeant Finley, knew that in every outfit, the sergeants knew more than anyone else, even more than the officers. And if the sergeant hated you, your life would be a living hell. Bauer had been through that once before, a year ago in the 16th. Damn, he thought. Coffee woulda helped out there, too. At least show him you're here to fight.

Bauer wasn't sure just how to do that, had never been one for the loud boasts, or passing on advice to the new recruits. It was one of two options for dealing with any nasty sergeant. Either show him you're just as nasty, or else hide from him. Bauer hadn't been good at either one. He wasn't sure yet if Finley was as mean as he sounded, though he certainly had the **growl,** a thick, gruff Irishman, with arms like fat logs, his neck a deep red. He was shorter than Bauer, unusual, since Bauer was shorter than most everyone else. But Finley was obeyed without hesitation.

The 17th Wisconsin was a part of James McPher-

son's Seventeenth Corps, the Sixth Division, commanded by a Scotsman named McArthur. Though
every man Bauer had met had come out of Wisconsin, there wasn't another German in the bunch.
He had no reason to dislike Irishmen, though he
hadn't known any in Milwaukee. His father had
no particular prejudice toward anyone, a businessman's wisdom: Someone wants to buy your sausage, doesn't matter what his accent is. Bauer had
heard bits of their history, a horribly downtrodden
people, escaping the curse of British rule, much as
Bauer's parents had escaped the military turmoil of
1830s Germany. All he knew of these men was what
he saw: They were soldiers, wore the same uniform
as he did. And though this regiment hadn't fought
at Shiloh, they were bloodied. And from what he
had seen of their spirit, they would be again.

"Sergeant, make sure their canteens are filled. No
rain in three days, the creeks will be falling."

"Sir. Will handle it, sir."

Bauer couldn't help a smile, saw the newly pol-
ished lieutenant stepping quickly toward them, urgency in his steps. Willis looked at Bauer, no smile at
all, and said, "Well, Private, you making yourself at
home among all these micks? I see you still got your
teeth. Anybody kick your ass yet?"

Bauer still smiled, saluted, knew that no matter
how close they had been, Willis would demand it. It
went with the job, and so far, Bauer knew that Willis had taken every job very seriously. It went with

the uniform as well, and Bauer looked his friend over, a shine on brass buttons, a clean white shirt under a short jacket, the plain strap on each shoulder, the insignia of the second lieutenant. Willis pretended to ignore that, but Bauer could see the pride. Willis focused on the sergeant, Finley moving away, barking out instructions, men lined up at a pair of water wagons in a field. In the road, the column was already forming up, the lines of blue snaking far ahead, around a bend, and far behind, with the usual hum of grumbling from men who had slept in the open. Bauer felt a stirring in his chest, had pride of his own. He was a part of something powerful, an army that knew how to **win**. He looked at Willis again, the lieutenant staring out, appraising.

He caught Bauer's stare, stepped closer to Bauer, and said in a low voice, "Dammit, Dutchie, I'm hearin' talk that since we come from the same unit, you're my "special one." Not good for morale, and I'm not gonna bail you out of every thicket they put you in."

Bauer was confused.

"Special what?"

"My personal . . . pet. Word got out pretty quick that a good friend of mine was transferring in, and a whole bunch of these boys suddenly applied for transfers of their own, all kinds of bitching and carrying on about wanting to be in some other regiment with their brothers or cousins or God knows

who else. I had to listen to some pretty tough blessing out from Colonel McMahon. He approved
my request to bring you here because I told him
you were one tough rascal, and we needed veterans. These boys aren't new, but they haven't seen
enough fighting to be toughened up yet. I built you
up to be the meanest ruffian in Wisconsin, and the
best sharpshooter, too. And by damned, it worked.
The colonel took care of some kind of paperwork.
Didn't really expect that. Now the men are carryin'
on like I brought my sweetheart in here. Dammit,
Dutchie, you better not let me down."

Bauer was nervous now, saw faces looking at him
from the road.

"Geez, I'll do my best, Sammie."

Willis cringed.

"**Lieutenant,** you jackass. That's another thing.
I earned this rank and I aim to keep it." He raised
his voice, just loud enough to be heard by the men
close by. "You talk to me like an officer or I'll have
that bulldog sergeant put you in hell." The message
was received, some of the men laughing, Willis accomplishing just what he intended. He turned his
back to the forming column, his voice lower again.
"It's just gotta be this way." He paused, and Bauer
saw a hint of a smile. "Dammit, Dutchie, I'm sure
as hell happy to see you. We'll talk after the march.
I wanna hear what happened to your folks, if you're
inclined. And all about what's going on in Milwaukee. I haven't heard much from my wife . . . noth-

ing about my child." He paused, and Bauer saw the look he had seen too often before, Willis's strange reluctance to talk about his own family, about the birth of his son the year before. Willis said aloud, "We've got to move, and right now. The colonel wants us on the boats as quick as we can get there. All of you . . . fall into column."

Willis spun away, hands clamped behind his back, an angry scowl on his face. The others watched him as he moved past, seemed to accept just what Willis wanted them to think, that he had chewed Bauer out for some unnamed offense. Bauer saw their gaze, some of them laughing, a poke of an elbow, jokes at his expense. He put on a hangdog look, appropriate to being blessed out by any officer, shouldered his musket, joined the column. The sergeant was there, seeming to wait for him, pointed to a gap in the row of men.

"Right there, Dutchman. I want you on the outside, in case somebody tries to pick some of us off." Finley glanced up at Bauer's musket, seemed satisfied, and said, "I see they taught you right in the 16th. No marching with damned fixed bayonets. We got some idiots in this company who still think they need to have the damned potstickers in place every damn minute of the day. Already had three men sent to the damn doctor from gettin' stick wounds in their backside. Bayonets, mud, and marchin' don't go together." He spoke louder now. "You hear me?"

There were mumbles of acknowledgment, and Bauer stepped into place, glanced at the man beside him, a tall, lanky redhead, realized it was the young man who had retrieved him from the 16th. Bauer nodded, the man returning it, and Bauer thought of Willis's building him up into some kind of madman. Guess I should do something, he thought. A good growl of my own. Yeah, I'm tough as nails. I can whip any damn Irishman. Well, no, don't say that out loud. Being tough doesn't mean being stupid.

The bugle sounded now, cutting through his thoughts, the column beginning to move. No, let it go. You gotta prove something to these boys, do it when it counts. They gotta know I've done this before. The thought punched him, whatever pride he was feeling ripped by a wave of memories. Yeah, the enemy came and you ran away. No, dammit. That was back then. It ain't gonna happen again. Ever.

At Shiloh, Bauer had done what half the Federal army had done, had reacted to the surprise assault by fleeing the battlefield, a mass of blue rabbits. But that was the first morning, the first great shock to these newly arrived recruits who dared assume to be soldiers. The attack had slapped into the men like a bolt of lightning, the sudden shock that the rebels were in fact a big damn army, with guns and bayonets and artillery, determined to kill every bluebelly who stood in their way. But Bauer had recovered, had erased his own shame alongside the men who gathered alongside Colonel Allen, or any other officer who had found courage of his own. And the next day, he had marched "forward," part of the great drive that swept the rebels from the field. **Soldiers** again.

But still the voice was there, taunting him, his own conscience. So, what happens next time? He knew that Willis had confidence in him, friend or not. But Willis seemed to be immune from any kind of fear, had stood his ground at Shiloh when most of the men around him had simply melted away. He was nothing like some of the others, the big talkers, the men going through the training and the drills with hot words for what they would do to the rebels. Most of those men were simply gone now, broken bodies or shattered courage, gone from the army, back home regaling their audiences with magnificent tales of heroism, stories Bauer had heard in Milwaukee, stories that would only be told to civilians.

Bauer marched in step with the men around him, heard Finley doing what every sergeant did, shouting angry curses to keep the men in line. Bauer looked down at his worn black brogans, the roadway a half inch thick in dust, rising in clouds with every step. He looked ahead, tried to see Willis, knew the lieutenants walked with the men, some toward the head of the company, some behind. I guess Sammie learned all that stuff pretty quick.

Lieutenant Willis. I wonder if they know, the rest of this bunch, all these Irishmen, I wonder if they know how much Sammie **likes** this? Bauer thought again of Shiloh. Even after the fight had stopped, Willis seemed eager to do it all again, but that enthusiasm came with a perfect certainty from Willis that he would never survive the war, would never see his wife again, or his new baby, that any hope for a marvelous homecoming was a worthless exercise. Bauer had been shocked at that, and even if he had no sweetheart himself, he had thought often of that wonderful return home, warm hands, tears and relief. Bauer had to believe Willis's wife and baby were still there, back in Wisconsin, like so many others, a family waiting with hand-wringing anguish for their soldier to return. And you, Fritz . . . you've got no one at all. You should be the perfect warrior, fearless, no distractions from a pocket full of love letters, a curl of hair in some locket. He couldn't shake the memories of Shiloh, of a mad scamper through the thorny brush, tumbling into mud, one piece of a massive wave of panic. So, he thought, will that happen again? Will you run like a frightened rabbit? A worthless coward? Again? Sammie will be the same, no matter that new uniform. He won't run, ever, unless it's straight at those other boys. He'll fight this war by himself, if we let him. Can't let him. He glanced to the side, dusty faces and sweat, shouldered muskets, shuffling feet. We'll fight for him, follow him, no matter what. That's

what we're here for, isn't it? Me . . . and these Irishmen. Who'd a thought that?

The morning was cool, but very soon there was
sweat in his eyes, the heat of the march. He stared
ahead, saw the flags, the Stars and Stripes far to
the front, unmistakable, and the regimental colors, a green flag like nothing he had seen before,
the symbol that told everyone else who these men
were. And now, he thought, one German boy. Well,
Fritz, you know what Papa would say. Same thing
Sergeant Champlin said, same thing Sammie's
thinking right now. Don't let 'em down.

There was sharp thunder upriver, smoke rising beyond a sweeping bend, wide muddy
water that seemed never to change. On the
far side, he could see a mass of blue, men disembark-
ing from transport boats, but the thunder was not
here, no one doing anything to contest the crossing. He knew nothing of the orders, knew only to
follow the man in front, to obey the profanity of
the sergeant, to pass by the men on horseback, the
flags snapping in a sharp breeze. The column had
turned, moving close to the river, and the boats
were there, some against the near bank, others in
motion, moving across, packed with a mass of blue.
Some were returning, empty, belching smoke, but
not the smoke he saw upriver. The artillery seemed
continuous, and Bauer looked up at the officers,

their eyes on the sounds as well. They probably know what's happening, he thought, who those guns belong to. A duel? Maybe some of those navy gunboats and reb batteries on the shore? Like to see that, just once.

"Move!"

The words came from Willis, his jacket dusty now, his arm waving the men closer to the water, toward one of the flatboats that settled against the bank.

"Load up! Don't shove. There's room for half of you, so get real friendly. But nobody swims!"

Bauer was impressed. The orders flowed out from Willis as though Sammie had been an officer all his life. Made for it, he thought. Like Sergeant Champlin said, he's running the whole damn war. Bauer couldn't hide the smile.

The boat filled quickly, and Bauer stepped down, pushed from behind, was quickly jammed in tight to the others. There were curses, but not many, the men more interested in just what was happening. But there was nothing to see, nothing but heads and muskets. The artillery fire upriver seemed to stop, but the sounds around him were many and close, added to the stink of a dozen men breathing into each other's faces. Somewhere beyond the boat, a voice shouted out, "Heave ho!"

The boat lurched, the men leaning to one side, then upright again in a single mass. Bauer gripped the musket, held it tight against him, braced by the

men around him. The smoke rose high above him, black, more stink, the breeze sweeping the smoke from a half-dozen transports, all of them like this one, packed tight with men in blue.

The boat swung to one side, Bauer still blind, but the engines beneath his feet were slowing, and just as quickly, the boat bumped hard, knocking them all sideways. Bauer felt the weight crushing him, the men around him cursing in a long chorus, but they were finding their feet again, and Bauer realized the boat had stopped. The orders came again, the men starting to move, the massed crowd lightening, and Bauer followed the flow, waited as men in front of him stepped up onto a railing, then a plank, and then . . . land. The journey was barely a few minutes, and his feet welcomed the hard ground. The column was forming again, more orders, men on horses, the shore lined with boats belching out their blue cargo, more columns, horses, flags. He could see the countryside now, thickets of trees, a wide road, the ground inland rising up into hills. The bugles began, and they began to move, marching away from the water, where more boats still crossed, bringing the army out of the misery of the Louisiana swamps. Bauer kept his place in the column, the steady rhythm once more, the sergeant there, moving through his men, but this time there were no curses, no yelling at the men. A horseman rode past, moving toward the front, another holding the Stars and Stripes, several staff officers trail-

ing behind, the word always in Bauer's mind: **brass.**
Who? A general?

They climbed, the road leveling out between
stands of hardwoods. The ground here was far different than the flat, soggy swamplands of Louisiana,
the roads running along crests of narrow hills. On
either side of the road, the ground fell away into
thick ravines, brush and briars, the same kind of
terrain he had seen at Shiloh. There the rebels had
rolled up from the dense bottoms in a terrifying
chorus that swept the Federal troops away. Bauer
strained to hear, expected the sound of musket fire,
an army waiting for them, or perhaps just a picket
line, skirmishers whose job would be to slow the
bluecoats down. He couldn't help staring down
into the thickets, waiting for the zip and ping and
rattle, the sound of even a single musket. But the
sounds were only memories. From the land around
them, the Federal troops made their crossing and
moved inland with no enemy waiting for them at
all. No matter Bauer's expectations, or his fear, as
they marched farther from the river, there was only
silence.

T he next day, May 1, the lead corps of
Grant's advance, under John McClernand,
pushed their way toward the first objective,
the town of Port Gibson. Waiting for them was
Confederate general John Bowen. Bowen's cries for

reinforcements, for a strong enough force to hold Grant at the river, had not been answered. To his relief, there had been bombardments at the river itself, a duel at Grand Gulf between rebel artillery and Porter's gunboats. Porter's mission was to silence those guns, allowing Grant's army to cross at Grand Gulf as Grant had first hoped. But the rebel batteries were as well protected as they were along the river at Vicksburg. No matter the pressure from Porter's ironclads, Grand Gulf remained firmly in rebel hands. Despite what seemed like a setback to his plans, Grant's response had been to march farther downstream and make the crossing at Bruinsburg, where the rebels had no guns at all.

But the violent duel at the river had one effect that mattered greatly to John Bowen. It was clearly audible several miles to the north in Vicksburg, alerting the commander there, General Carter Stevenson, of the urgency of Bowen's situation. Stevenson responded by marching troops out of Vicksburg southward, hoping to add enough strength to Bowen's forces to form a stiff line that Grant might not cross. But Stevenson's men did not arrive in time. When the Federal troops collided with Bowen's feeble position, the Confederates were outnumbered better than five to one, Bowen's sixteen artillery pieces facing McClernand's batteries, which numbered close to sixty guns. Despite a stout effort, Bowen recognized the inevitable, and even with elements of Stevenson's troops reaching him later in the day, the tide of blue was far too strong. Shortly before sunset, with his small force in disarray, Bowen wired Pemberton.

"The men did nobly, holding out the whole day against overwhelming odds."

By nightfall it was over, Bowen receiving the order he had hoped for, to withdraw from the field. Very soon, Federal troops swarmed into Port Gibson, and the next day, Bowen had no choice but to pull his forces out of Grand Gulf, abandoning the artillery positions on the river that had frustrated Porter. With the rebels backing away, Grant had secured the first link in a chain. As more of the Federal army crossed into Mississippi, Grant moved with them, carrying a silent pride that this first part of his plan was a complete success. The beachhead was secure, the path open for his entire army to begin their drive deeper into Mississippi. Almost immediately, the order had been sent upriver that it was time for Sherman to march south.

As he rode with McClernand, Grant kept his thoughts mostly to himself, his usual habit when riding with men with whom he was not altogether comfortable. But McClernand would not keep anything to himself. With darkness rolling across the field, McClernand ordered his victorious troops to halt their advance, and once again, to Grant's furious dismay, McClernand made a speech.

CHAPTER SEVEN

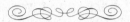

SHERMAN

GRAND GULF, MISSISSIPPI
MAY 7, 1863

"I could not have asked for a better result. The enemy has withdrawn beyond the Big Black River, and seems content to wait for us. I must credit your maneuver on the Yazoo for at least a portion of that. The enemy did not dare to deploy his troops in this direction with you poised to assault him from above. We planted the seeds of doubt, and those seeds bore fruit."

Sherman nodded, but didn't fully agree.

"I'm just happy to be here now. According to our scouts, we did draw some rebel forces to the north, but I'm not sure the feint was all that significant."

Grant said nothing, and Sherman knew it was an unnecessary argument. The two men rode at the head of a cluster of staff officers, trailed as well by Grant's son Fred and another group of civilians. Sherman could feel the grumbling inside his brain, could not help the doubts still, that he had been left behind as some sort of punishment for his failures in December. He had never received the first hint of that from Grant, but still . . . he was growing more angry with himself now, a debate that seemed to tear his mind in two, the fear and doubts confronted by a voice of reason, that out there, in the world beyond his own thoughts, no one doubted him nearly as much as he doubted himself.

Grant said nothing, the others behind them chattering in idle talk, the routine of the long ride. Grant's plans had not changed, with most of the army already on the march inland, farther still from the river. There had not been any other fights since McClernand's battle at Port Gibson, the rebels keeping away completely. That surprised Sherman, that not even rebel cavalry had harassed them. It has to be Grierson, he thought. Damn fine work. The rebel horsemen are still out there trying to find their own noses, and Grierson is safe at Baton Rouge.

He thought of Forrest now, the embarrassment Sherman had suffered at Fallen Timbers, the day after the monumental Federal victory at Shiloh. **Forrest**. Well, now we've tossed a little humiliation back **your** way. Good thing, though, that you're up there in Tennessee somewhere, tearing up . . . well, whatever you're tearing up. Stay there, for all I care. Probably a good thing for Grierson **you** weren't the one chasing him. This time we get to have the **hero**. That'll play up big in the newspapers back home. And we can sure as hell use some of that. I bet Baton Rouge is full of heavy-breathing reporters, all flocking around Grierson. Good. Keep them away from here.

Sherman glanced at Grant, could see Grant's face twitching, thoughts rolling through his mind, his lips moving just a bit. It's all right there, he thought. He's going through every detail. And that's why we're better than they are. Sherman glanced back, scanned the unusual variety of those who followed, noticed the boy, seeming to struggle on an enormous horse, the horse definitely in command of **that** battle. Sherman couldn't help a small laugh.

"Fred's horse . . . ought to be pulling an artillery piece or a supply wagon instead of hauling your boy."

Grant didn't look back, just said in a low voice, "He had to find whatever he could to ride. I'm not making him a special guest on this campaign. Not doing it for Mr. Dana, either. They wish to accompany us, they will make do. I had to borrow a mount of my own when I landed at Grand Gulf. My baggage was left on the far side of the river for near a week. By the good graces of Admiral Porter, I was finally able to bathe." He glanced at Sherman. "You might consider doing the same."

It was Grant's attempt at humor, at lightening whatever load Sherman was carrying. Sherman appreciated the gesture, could see that Grant was in a buoyant mood, unusual, and he scolded himself yet again for doubting Grant's support.

"There will be time for a bath later. Someplace more suitable than a barrel in the middle of a camp. We'll find some plantation house, maybe have a **mammy** or two scrub my back. Thought about wading into the river before we crossed it. But I did not wish to remain in Louisiana any longer than necessary." He paused. "Mississippi has not been kind to me. I am eager to amend that."

Grant said nothing, had heard too much of this already. Sherman pointed ahead, a gathering of troops at a line of wagons.

"Rations. I have ordered as much as possible to be brought from the river, ammunition as well. It concerns me that the enemy's cavalry could still injure us. Somebody out there is surely figuring out that Grierson is long gone."

Grant shook his head, rubbed a hand through his beard.

"We cannot carry all that is required. Two days perhaps. We will arrange to move up salt, hard bread, and coffee, and . . . the country can furnish the balance."

Sherman looked out to a wide field, a grand house set back from the road, a cluster of Negroes moving closer, joyously waving to the column of troops as they passed by. Grant followed Sherman's gaze.

"There is food aplenty around these estates. The owners have mostly disappeared, which saves us the necessity of haggling. The Negroes seem more than willing to offer up anything the plantations have in their larders. It will be most helpful." He leaned closer to Sherman, a hard stare Sherman could feel. "There is yet no danger here. No rebel force strong enough to cause us any . . . surprises. You should not dwell on that."

Sherman understood, knew that Grant could read him, that so often any threat of imminent crisis came solely from Sherman's imagination.

Behind them, Sherman could hear Colonel Rawlins, a brief sharp argument, heard the horse moving closer, knew, as Grant did, that Rawlins would make the inevitable report of any controversy. He moved up alongside Grant, and seemed to avoid Sherman when he could, a habit Sherman appreciated.

Rawlins leaned in to Grant and said, "Sir, there is some discussion about your decision not to join our forces with General Banks. Mr. Dana insists the order issued to you was clear, and that you have perhaps caused a problem for yourself in Washington. I deeply regret that he made this observation in full earshot of Mr. Cadwallader. I fear—"

Sherman interrupted, reacted to the name.

"You fear that damn reporter will write to his paper that we're out here defying orders. Again. Dammit, Grant, your colonel is right. Why do you allow these vermin to infiltrate your camp?"

It was already a controversy, fueled by Dana's obligatory telegram back to the War Department. The advantage for Grant now was that any message out of the Federal headquarters took a lengthy amount of time to reach its destination. Sherman had wondered if Grant included that in his planning, that there would be no line of telegraph poles thrown up behind them. Now any message had to be carried by hand, first across the river, then north, to the nearest telegraph at Milliken's Bend. From there the message would be transmitted through Memphis, before it could find its way east. Sherman saw another brief smile from Grant, thought, Yep, that's exactly what you had in mind.

To the south, Port Hudson was the other remaining thorn in the side of Federal control of the river, one last bastion controlled by rebel guns. It was not nearly as strong a position as Vicksburg, and the expectation in Washington was that capturing Port Hudson would be a far less painful task. The command of the Port Hudson expedition had first been given to Nathaniel Banks, whose experiences in the field were no match for Grant's. Banks had been one of the unfortunate victims of the rebel general now known as Stonewall, who had wiped clean the Shenandoah Valley of a Federal army that far outnumbered the Confederates under Jackson's command. Banks himself had absorbed two defeats from Jackson, and though many in Washington regarded Banks as the ultimate scapegoat for Jackson's success in the valley, some in the Federal command had reluctantly conceded that Stonewall Jackson's successful campaign had more to do with Jackson himself. But Banks's failures could not be ignored, and so he had been reassigned to command of the Department of the Gulf, presiding over the spoils of New Orleans and Baton Rouge, won primarily by the efforts of the navy. Grant had received instructions that, since Vicksburg had thus far been a tough nut to crack, far tougher than Washington expected, Port Hudson should now be the primary objective. Grant was to unite his army with Banks, creating an unstoppable force. Vicksburg could come later. It was a strategy Grant found completely unappealing. His army had already expended considerable energy around Vicksburg, and Vicksburg was, at least in Grant's mind, the highest priority. And besides, the more time that passed before Grant attacked Vicksburg, the more time the rebels had to bring in reinforcements there, possibly adding considerable strength to what was already a strong position. But Banks solved Grant's dilemma, sending word that he had embarked on an entirely new campaign up the Red River, which flowed into the Mississippi from the west. According to Banks, it would be at least another month before any attempt could be made to assault Port Hudson. That was all the justification Grant needed. Port Hudson and General Banks could wait.

Grant seemed to ponder Rawlins's concerns, then said, "Colonel, inform Mr. Cadwallader that I have been placed in overall command of this department, and will conduct this campaign in the most judicious way possible."

"But, sir, he will certainly report to his newspaper—"

"You heard me, Colonel. You might remind Mr. Cadwallader that Washington has vested in me the **last word** on the matter. If he has questions, certainly he may ask them."

Rawlins fell back, and Sherman gritted his teeth.

"Why the hell do you allow this?"

"Colonel Rawlins is most valuable to me. You know that."

"Cadwallader is the scoundrel that concerns me. He writes for that damnable **Chicago Times,** which is nothing more than a treasonous rag. There isn't a copperhead in that part of the country who doesn't call that paper his own bible. I've banned its distribution in my camps."

Grant turned toward him.

"You will countermand that order. No newspaper is to be banned in this army, no matter how disagreeable we may find it."

Sherman was caught off guard by Grant's sternness.

"Well . . . if you order it. I did not think it wise to allow the men to be drenched in the kind of talk that fuels sedition. I may not always agree with Mr. Lincoln, but we are fighting **his** war. There are too damn many loud voices in Illinois, and every state around it, calling for this war to end on Southern terms. It's outrageous. No, it's treason."

"I am not aware of any mutiny in the ranks. Have faith in your soldiers, Sherman. They are as outraged as you are by all of that talk. I've seen that myself. Any secessionist who comes through these camps preaching all of that nonsense is fortunate to escape without tar and feathers."

"I'd boil the tar myself. The reporters could use a little of that as well."

Grant said nothing, and Sherman felt his heart racing, the subject always digging hard at him, fueling an unstoppable anger. He had banished reporters from his own camps, but it wasn't an order he was comfortable spouting about. There was always the chance Grant would disagree and order Sherman to permit the men free access to Sherman's headquarters. Thus far, Grant had said nothing, seemed to understand that Sherman's dislike for newspapermen was his own business. But Grant seemed perfectly willing to allow any of the newspapermen free access to his own camp, a policy Sherman found utterly appalling.

"You're naïve, Grant. With all respects, **sir**."

Grant chuckled.

"Perhaps. Been accused of worse. But Sylvanus Cadwallader is no copperhead, and he performs his duties with admirable restraint. He clears all of his dispatches with Colonel Rawlins, and I have yet to read anything he has written that gives me a belly-ache. It is good to have civilians in the camps. They don't feel the obligation to salute me at every turn, and so they offer observations not tainted by obe-dience. And, I must admit, there are those times when it is good to speak my mind, to offer up frus-trations and opinions I cannot always share with my staff. Cadwallader is a good man. He listens well."

Sherman huffed.

"So does a spy."

NEAR AUBURN, MISSISSIPPI
MAY 11, 1863

Since crossing the river, Sherman's Fifteenth Corps had kept generally behind McClernand, their left flanks close to the Big Black River. Sherman had ordered a strong guard to be placed at each river crossing they passed, a wise precaution to prevent any sudden rebel attempt to cut behind the march. If the rebels made any attempt to slice through the Federal supply line, they would draw plenty of attention.

Out to the southeast, on a parallel route, James

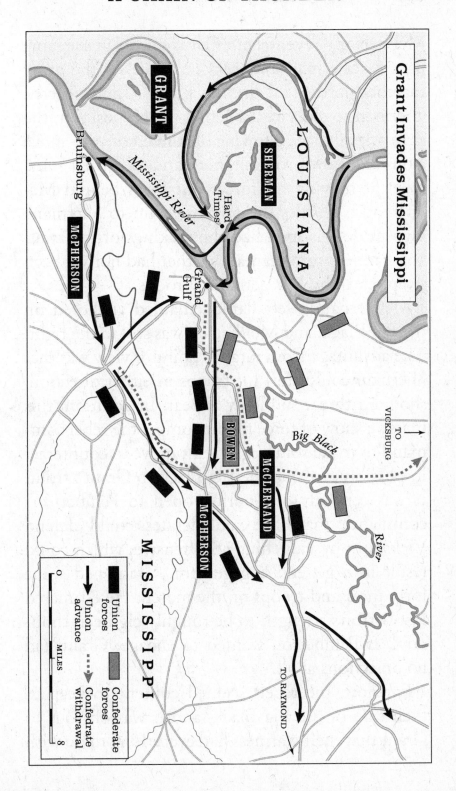

Grant Invades Mississippi

LOUISIANA

GRANT

SHERMAN

Bruinsburg

Mississippi River

Hard Times

MISSISSIPPI

Grand Gulf

McPHERSON

BOWEN

Big Black

TO VICKSBURG

McCLERNAND

McPHERSON

River

TO RAYMOND

Union forces
Confederate forces
Union advance
Confederate withdrawal

0   MILES   8

McPherson's Seventeenth Corps moved at the same pace as Sherman and McClernand. As the army marched farther up the Big Black, Grant ordered Sherman to shift to the center of the position, the network of roads allowing all three corps to move along their own routes. Sherman at least felt some relief at moving his forces out from behind Mc-Clernand. Besides the obvious balm to Sherman's own pride, his men had the pickings of the available rations from plantations that had not yet been swept clean by McClernand's troops.

McClernand's left flank remained anchored on the Big Black, and McPherson was still to the right. The advantage from Grant's point of view was that Sherman could shift his troops in either direction, should a threat suddenly appear. In addition, this massive show of force might compel the rebel command to make some significant move to counteract it, possibly crossing the Big Black to Grant's front. It was certainly one option open to Pemberton's command, that the Confederates could defend Vicksburg by launching an offensive, which could result in a general engagement. Grant had some forty thousand troops on the march. He estimated Pemberton's strength to be roughly eighteen thousand. If Pemberton wanted to engage, Grant had no objections at all.

For now, the rebels seemed content to keep to their side of the Big Black, and it was obvious to Grant that their wariness had everything to do with their complete uncertainty as to what Grant would do next. The Big Black flowed generally from the northeast, and Grant continued the march in that direction, offering the rebels no real hint of just when or where he would make a sharp turn toward Vicksburg, a move that certainly the rebels were expecting.

Sherman rode thinking of water. The canteens were mostly empty, a supply problem the wagons could do little to help. By now he understood that drinking water from any of the larger rivers could cause illness among the troops, a problem that had plagued the army since their drive up the Tennessee River the year before. There were creeks and springs inland, of course, and the men had become efficient at locating any good water source, often from the same plantations where they were finding their rations. But there had been no rain for nearly two weeks, and the creeks had been reduced to trickles, the few springs and dug wells inadequate for the needs of forty thousand men.

He turned, saw tired faces, his staff showing the effects of a very long day in the saddle.

"Colonel Dayton, send orders to the division commanders to halt the march. This day has lasted long enough. Captain McCoy, send a dispatch to General Grant, offer my respects, tell him that we are forced to halt the march for want of water, and offer my humble suggestion that the rest of the army halt as well."

The two men saluted him, moved back to the couriers, and Sherman did not have to watch them. I am blessed with good people, he thought. Always been that way. Major Sanger . . . will truly miss him. But he gave all he could, just didn't have the energy for what I required of him.

Dan Sanger had been with Sherman nearly from the beginning of Sherman's command, had been the sponge for so much of Sherman's fury, had likely kept Sherman in the saddle by allowing Sherman to spout off about every manner of aggravation, including every general who outranked him. But Sanger had mustered out in February, and Sherman could not object, had felt that instinctive weakness in the man, a sense that Sanger knew his health was failing. He had lost Captain John Henry Hammond, too, another of the good men who had done so much to salvage the command after the burst of disaster at Shiloh a year before. Another man whose health was failing him, he thought, who gave so much to me. What do you give them, Sherman? All right, stop that foolishness. You give them orders. That's your job, and theirs. Staff officers are an expendable lot, and have to be. No shortage of them, for certain. They're not all cowards, either, despite what I used to believe. Always thought that any man who sought out service close to the command was a man who fears hearing the musket balls. But . . . well, we've heard plenty of damn musket balls. Will again.

He dismounted, an aide quickly taking the reins from his hand. He had two horses now, his favorite a large bay he called Sam. He watched the animal lumber slowly away, thought, Yep, you're as tired as I am. You've heard the musket balls, too, had one nearly bust open your gut. No complaints from you about that one. I'd have hollered like hell. Well, hell, I don't hear much complaining from any of them, officers, aides, or the damn animals. Beasts of burden, all of them. I suppose, most of the time, I'm the burden.

The sun was setting quickly, the air cooling, the last hint of blue in the cloudless sky above him. He stretched his back, saw columns of his troops spreading out into the open ground, the camps coming together, fires started, coffeepots emerging from hidden places. There would be no card playing, not anymore, Grant's orders that once they began the great march inland, gambling was forbidden. Sherman didn't argue, had no patience for fistfights over a silver dollar. They'll get used to it, he thought. We'll try to give them something better to do.

A horseman galloped toward him, familiar, an officer from one of his division commanders, Frank Blair. Blair was new to Sherman's command, but Sherman had liked him immediately. Blair had been a politician before the war, a man of considerable public influence, had been extremely active in the Union cause, and now was a rabid supporter of the army's mission. Mr. Lincoln's war, Sherman thought. Blair would fight it all by himself. That kind of energy is good for his men. We'll make use of that.

Sherman recalled the officer's name now, Major Haskins, the man dismounting with clean precision, a good horseman.

Haskins saluted and said, "Sir, General Blair offers his respects and reports that a courier has come from the east, sent by General McPherson. The Seventeenth Corps's forward units are encountering some rebel skirmishers. General McPherson has thus ordered his divisions to encamp for the night and has ordered cavalry patrols and strong skirmish lines to avoid . . . uh . . . surprises, sir."

"Has General Blair observed the enemy to **his** front?"

"Not in any strength, sir. Scattered observers, cavalry squadrons, that sort of thing. We have cavalry patrols ahead of us as well, sir, up as far as Fourteen Mile Creek."

"Good. General Blair knows what to do. Tell him only that I offer my respects and advise him to remain on the alert. This is, after all, Mississippi. Damn rebels could be hiding out in every barn and every outhouse. General McPherson is doing the right thing. Avoiding surprises is always the best plan. Grab some coffee, if you care to, Major. Then return to General Blair."

Haskins saluted him, and Sherman followed his own suggestion, moved toward a growing fire, the coffeepot already hung above. The staff made way for him, and Sherman stopped, stared down into the fire. **No surprises**. Made that mistake before, won't do it again. If McPherson says there's an enemy out there, believe him. It's a whole lot better if the **surprises** come from **us**.

CHAPTER EIGHT

BAUER

SOUTHWEST OF RAYMOND,
MISSISSIPPI
MAY 11, 1863

Bauer munched the remnants of his hardtack, paid no attention to the flavor, something close to licking a pantry floor. What had been brought across the river had been issued immediately, chunks of meat held aloft on bayonets. It was a surprisingly bountiful gesture from a commissary that seemed to delight in feeding the men anything but actual food. But that bounty, what was supposed to carry them for ten days, had been consumed within two or three. No officer seemed willing or able to prevent their men from eating anything they were given, as quickly as they could. Bauer never gave it much thought, had done as so many had done, devoured the meat as quickly as possible. He still heard the talk, some men grimly fatalistic, that if they were marching to a fight, they would at least die with a full stomach. Now the commissary wagons carried only coffee and hardtack, the rock-hard crackers always in abundance.

Like most of the others, his canteen had run dry hours before, adding to the misery of the dry dust of the hardtack. Some men had come through with a water bucket, ladles pouring brown liquid into waiting cups. No matter his thirst, he would do everything he could to avoid anything that dirty. The fear of the hospitals had come to exceed any fear of the enemy, and though the cases of dysentery had been far fewer on this side of the river, the hospitals were always back there, somewhere.

It was nearly dark and Bauer spread out his bedroll, in his slow habit, laid it across anything soft he could find, tufts of grass, handfuls of the dreary gray moss that hung low from nearly every tree. Around him, men were doing the same, the entire regiment ordered to camp in what had once been a cornfield. There would be little talk tonight, no spouting off around roaring campfires, even the few coffeepots mostly ignored. The day's march had been as tedious as any he could remember, slow, stops and starts, no explanation why they could not just **move**. He had no idea how far they had come of course, never really knew that. But the slowness, the lack of a steady rhythm to the long stretches, meant they had not come very far, a few miles at best.

He patted the bedroll, satisfied that he had at least some padding, wadded his jacket together to form a pillow, and lay out flat, staring up. There were just a few stars, the darkness slipping in quickly. Around him the chorus had begun, great swarms of creatures that he guessed to be insects, frogs maybe, everything else in this infernal country that had a voice. Why night? he thought. They don't say a thing all day long. The sun goes down and they have some kind of contest to see who can croak and buzz the loudest. Just to keep us awake, I guess. Revenge for slapping at them all day, killing their cousins. There were the night sounds in Wisconsin, mostly crickets. But here the volume was much louder, especially if there was water nearby. On the other side of the river, the men often heard something completely different, a low bellow, what some said were ghosts, or some awful swamp creature cursing them for invading their homes. Then someone had figured out . . . it was alligators. Probably a mating call, he thought. Oh sweet lady gator over there. Come to your beau. Bauer drew no comfort in that. I'd rather it be ghosts, he thought. At least they don't eat you.

"Where's that damn Dutchman?"

Bauer sat up, knew Willis's voice.

"Here . . . uh . . . sir."

Dammit. He's still Sammie.

Willis was silhouetted now by a distant campfire, moved closer, leaned down.

"You?"

"It's me, Sammie. **Lieutenant**. Geez, can't get used to that."

Willis sat, said, "You will, by damned. I'll toss you in the stockade for insubordination."

Bauer couldn't tell if he was serious or not, but he knew Willis too well to test him. Willis seemed to scan the men around them, focused on a group of men out by one of the fires.

"Idiots are playing horseshoes. I figured we'd be arresting people for gambling. Colonel McMahon pretty clear on that one. Orders came from Grant himself. But it didn't take these boys long to find something else to do. How the hell do they see what they're aiming at?"

Bauer had no answer, had never played horseshoes, wasn't really sure how. Around them the voices were muted, most of the men too tired to do anything but sleep. After a long silence, Willis said softly, "Cavalry says the secesh are out there waiting for us. Talked to Captain McDermott about it, says it makes sense. They can't just let us march all over hell and back through their own backyards. We're headin' for some trouble, no doubt about that. But there's a whole potload of us, Dutchie. We're strong, mostly fit, too. Gettin' clear of those swamps helped. This is some pretty countryside, the fancy plantations and all. Guess I can see why the damn secesh are fightin' over it."

Bauer stared at the horseshoe players, heard a telltale clank, a raucous cheer. But the game was winding down with the darkness, the men starting to drift off their separate ways.

Bauer said, "I guess I'd fight if somebody marched into Milwaukee."

"Yeah? Who'd be doing that?"

"Uh . . . I don't know."

"Yeah, you don't know. Neither do these damn secesh. We're not shoving them out of their homes, rounding up civilians. We're not violating the women. Hell, I ain't seen anyone in this army taking shackles off one single darkie, settin' anybody free. But you can't tell these fool people any of that. We're foreigners. Trespassing. I thought this was one damn country. Never saw a KEEP OUT sign at the county line back home, or down there on the border with Illinois. But not here. They've decided we're so damn evil, they're gonna kill us over it. Fine. I'll kill you first, you stupid plowboy. Every damn one of you."

"I remember . . . one of the brass . . . talking to us about them stompin' on our flag."

"Colonel Peabody. They killed him at Shiloh."

"Yeah, Peabody."

"That's all fine and good. But now old 'Honest Abe' has done made a big stir about emancipating the darkies, and all he's done is rile up these plowboys to being even more mad at us. We'd have probably won this thing but for that. The secesh knew they were whipped, and Lincoln went and kicked the hornet's nest."

"I don't know, Sammie. Every farm or mansion we pass, there's Negroes standing out there waving at us, and no white man to be seen. They seem like they're pretty happy we're here. There's gotta be a reason for that. I suspect they won't be going back to work for any master, shackles or not. I hear that some of 'em's following behind the army, like it's a big damn parade. Sure sounds to me like they're being freed from **something**. Something that matters to them, anyhow. I just wonder about the . . . people. The white people. Seems they're just in the way, their homes and all. I saw some of the places burned up over there, across the river. We had no cause to do that. None I could see. Armies oughta fight armies, and leave the civilians alone."

"So, all these folks who've sent their sons off to shoot at us, you figure they're just the poor and innocent, caught in the way? They don't have a part in any of this? You wanna go up and tell General McPherson about this, maybe Grant himself? You got it all figured out, just how this war oughta be fought, who's the good and who's the bad. Like it's so damn simple. You trying to be smart, Dutchie? You takin' to figuring out stuff now? Damn miracle."

It was Willis's attempt at humor, always an edge of anger to it.

"Not me, sir. I'm just the son of a sausage maker. Dumb as a river rock."

There was a silent pause, and Bauer knew why. Willis said, "How you doin' with all of that? Really sorry."

"It's okay, Sammie. Papa went quick, a blessing. Mama . . . well, not as good. Watched her get weaker, thinner. Worst part of it, she didn't hardly know me at the end." He shoved hard against the memories, didn't want to see her at all, not right now. "It ain't good watchin' people die, Sammie. Not people . . . you love."

"And that's why you're down here waitin' for some damn secesh to rise up in front of you? You've seen plenty of men die. None of it's pretty. It's just . . . why we're here. You lose your belly for it, and somebody'll make you pay for that. Those damn secesh got plenty of belly for killing. I intend to fix that. Clean this country like a scrub brush if we have to."

Bauer had heard plenty of this kind of talk before. It was nothing like the boasting of the loudmouths in the training camps. Bauer had seen Willis in the middle of the fight, knew that his friend wouldn't hesitate to kill any rebel who stood in his way, whether by musket, bayonet, or his bare hands. Bauer had a twisting need to change the subject.

"These boys do pretty good at Corinth?"

"Not bad. Since they missed out on Shiloh, they're pretty ornery about anybody slappin' them in the face with that. Felt like they had to prove something. They know what the 16th did, they know that the 18th nearly got wiped out. I heard a fair number of Wisconsin boys got hauled off when General Prentiss was captured. They're sittin' somewhere in a rebel prison, most likely. If they survived at all." Willis paused. "Not me. Good luck to any damn secesh tries to take me captive. I'll rip his heart out before I let that happen."

"Hey, Lieutenant!"

The voice came from beneath a large tree a few yards away, and Bauer could see now, others sitting up, some of them close enough to hear their conversation.

"What is it? Who's that . . . Kelly? What the hell do you want?"

"Sir, I was just a-wonderin' sir, if we'uns could be getting some sleep any time this here evenin'. Hate to be interruptin' you tuckin' your boy into bed and all."

Bauer felt a hot glow of embarrassment on his face, but Willis responded with a spit.

"You slept all damn day on the march. I saw you. Tomorrow we tie you to the colonel's horse, so's you stand up straight."

There were laughs all around them, the taunting

aimed mostly at Kelly. Bauer lay back, stared up, saw Willis moving, then hesitation, the low voice again.

"Might see those scoundrels tomorrow, Dutchie. You keep close watch on your poor old **innocents,** too, all those plantation folks you feel sorry for. One of them's liable to put a musket ball in your head. You do your job, you hear me?"

"You can depend on me, Lieutenant."

Willis rose quickly, was gone in the darkness. Around Bauer, the talk faded away, none of the usual energy the others had for teasing him. The men were as tired as he was. He stared up into stars, heard the familiar whine of the mosquitoes, pulled one side of his blanket over his face, the only remedy, his eyes heavy, and he let out a breath, the sounds of the others fading away. But the one image stayed with him, always there, the frail sickness of his mother.

SOUTHEAST OF RAYMOND, MISSISSIPPI
MAY 12, 1863

The march started early, and from every path and side road, cavalry patrols had appeared, the horsemen moving with urgency. He watched an entire company moving past, a hundred or more, following their commander, other officers, a flag. Another

smaller squadron came past them now, from the
rear of the column, the officers shifting the infantry
to the side of the road to give the horsemen space.
Around Bauer, men cursed the clouds kicked up by
the hoofbeats, but Bauer felt something different,
not pride exactly; an appreciation for the power of
the horses. He coughed through the dust, wiped
at his eyes with rough hands, thought, I should
have done that, volunteered for cavalry. They'd
have taught me how to ride a horse, sure as rain.
No matter what happens, those boys see it all first,
get to hit the enemy in quick raids. That's gotta be
more fun than what we do, standing up there, staring into musket barrels. **Fun**. The word jolted him,
unexpected. But it was there, the expectation that
something was about to happen, that all the shovels
and mud and mosquitoes were behind them. He
felt the jitters in his hand, his stomach, his heart
starting to race. It had been so long since he had actually seen the enemy. And now it would be soon,
surely it would be soon. I'm ready, by damned. I
want this thing to get over with, and that's the only
way it'll happen. He tested himself for the fear, but it
was distant, not quite there. For now the memories
were replaced by something new. By **excitement**.

Up ahead, officers gathered, a large Stars and
Stripes, a quick meeting, one man animated, pointing to the front. The meeting was brief, the men
moving off quickly. Beside him, the skinny redhead
stood taller, trying to see beyond the vast column.

"What's happening? Do you know? Are there rebs up there?"

All around him, men tossed their taunts at the "foolish question," but Bauer could see them looking forward as well, the rhythm of the march quickening, more questions. Beside Bauer, Sergeant Finley barked out, "Stay in line! This is a march, damn you! You wanna sightsee, do it back home! They want you to know what's up ahead, they'll tell you."

Bauer knew the sergeant was right, that until the bugles sounded, there was nothing for these men to do but march. Bauer glanced at the young man beside him, knew only that his name was, of course, Red. The man was barely a man at all, no hint of a beard. He marched awkwardly, all legs and gangly arms that made him look like a freckled spider. Bauer could see fear on the man's face, nervous twitches, his head jerking back and forth, eyes distant, searching.

"Hey, Red, what's your name . . . your real name?"

The boy stared at Bauer like he had never seen him before, nodded, looked again to the front.

"Evan O'Daniel, sir."

Bauer couldn't help a smile, said softly, "Not **sir**. You'll catch hell for that."

"I know. All the time. I . . . was just raised to call folks . . . sir. Most everybody in this outfit's older than me. You, too, I suppose."

"How old are you?"

"Fif . . . Seventeen, sir."

Bauer had an uneasy twinge, looked hard at the boy, thought, Fifteen, for sure. Too damn young. They gotta know that. He ought not be here at all.

"Why'd you volunteer?"

The boy seemed to straighten, a show of pride.

"To fight the rebels, sir." He paused, and Bauer sensed there was more. "Had to get away from there, I suppose. Eight sisters. My papa was expecting me to be a man ever since I can recall. Soldiering . . . well, that's the best way I knew how."

Bauer tried to picture the image . . . eight sisters. Good Lord.

"They all look like you? All redheaded?"

"Some. All of 'em are younger. I need the army pay, to help out."

Bauer looked again to the front, heard voices behind them, the men who obviously knew much of this boy.

"Yep, Red, that thirteen dollars a month will have them living in luxury."

"The army might even **give** us that pay, one of these days."

"Don't hang your hat on that one, lad. Army's full of promises. They told me I'd be wearing a colonel's eagles by now. I ain't seen no sign of that. And the colonel hisself seems pretty pleased to leave it that way."

Bauer let the jabbering pass by, hadn't given much thought to his army pay. Anything he received he had always sent home, though the men hadn't seen any sign of a paymaster for months. There was grousing about that, mostly ignored by now, the men understanding that there wasn't much of anything around this part of the country to spend it on. He looked again at O'Daniel, who marched staring down. The boy embarrasses easy, he thought. Better get over that. All that red hair . . . and eight sisters? These boys must be making your life pure hell. Bauer looked again to the front, more cavalry emerging from a wood line to the left, moving toward the front.

"You been in any fights?"

O'Daniel looked at him, wide-eyed, and shook his head.

"No, sir. Just been here a pair of months. I kinda wondered about the pay and all." He turned, looked back to the man behind Bauer. "They are gonna pay us, though, right?"

The man laughed, slapped Bauer on the back.

"You tell him. You're supposed to be the old soldier among us dew-eared lads. How much pay you seen?"

Bauer thought about that, suddenly realized the others around him expected a response.

"A few times. They send the pay wagons in every few months or so. I don't give it much thought."

"You rich, then? That why the lieutenant pals up to ya? You loan out money, do ya?"

Bauer closed his eyes, shook his head.

"No. I'm not rich. The last time I saw pay . . . maybe last August, just sent it home. My parents did okay. But I'm the only child. My parents just died. Both of 'em."

The words seemed to strike them silent, and he regretted it immediately. Dammit, Fritz. Don't go putting these boys off any more than you already have.

"That's a pure awful thing, losin' your folks close together."

The words came from behind him, and Bauer didn't look to see the face.

"Thanks."

They marched in silence now, a gloom Bauer hated. The excitement of seeing the cavalry, the urgency of the march seemed drained from him, and he felt it from the others as well. Beside him, O'Daniel spoke, the redhead's words barely audible.

"I best be survivin' this war. They need my pay, for certain. Can't think of not havin' my folks back there a'tall. I couldn't stay in the army, for sure."

Bauer fought through his gloom, and the sergeant was there again, the usual growl.

"Keep in line there! This ain't some country picnic! Hey, Dutchman! You make it back home, maybe you should go courtin' one of Red's sisters! Ha!"

The sergeant's jab seemed to lighten them all, and the words came again, teasing, another slap on his back. He felt a sudden glimmer of affection, the men not as suspicious, the hostility from the

Irishmen seeming to fade. He stared ahead, didn't respond to the sergeant, could still hear the mumbling from O'Daniel, the words betraying the boy's fear.

Up ahead a bugle sounded, the order passed along to halt the march. He saw one of the colonel's aides riding back toward them, then past, a man doing his job, and Bauer thought, A dispatch most likely, for somebody behind us. The column was stopped now, the lieutenants shouting out the order to remain in the road, the sergeants responding by moving through the column, keeping the men together. Bauer paid no attention to the words. He focused to the front, heard it now, the peculiar hum, broken by thumps of artillery. The hum came again, like the buzzing of bees, and if the others around him, the redheaded boy, had no idea what it meant, Bauer knew too well. He had heard it before. It was musket fire.

With Grant's army still moving parallel to the Big Black River, the response from the Confederate command had changed from urgent curiosity to action. Flowing westward into the Big Black was a small tributary known as Fourteen Mile Creek. There the rebels finally chose to make a stand, a single brigade of mostly Tennesseans commanded by General John Gregg. Gregg was not there intending some grand assault, but rather to take advantage of a natural defensive position that might allow him to slow the march of Grant's troops, to possibly force Grant to show his hand. At the very least, Gregg might inflict a hefty toll of casualties on whatever Federal units stumbled into him. It was only by chance that the rebels had chosen the path taken by James McPherson's corps, and chance again that McPherson's lead division would belong to General John Logan, a man who knew how to control his men, to appraise what faced him and make the best moves.

Though Federal cavalry patrols had driven out well in front of their infantry, they had not fully located and appraised the force that stood in their way. As Logan's skirmish line approached the thickets along the creek, Gregg's first volley stung them hard, and the Federal troops recoiled under the sudden shock of a force whose numbers were masked by the rugged ground. But Gregg's initial success gave the Confederates a confidence that causes mistakes. Gregg knew as little about what he was facing as Logan did, and he responded to the initial chaos in Logan's front by seeking a rapid advantage. Gregg launched his three thousand men across the creek, believing he could flank the Federals and possibly crush whatever force was to his front. Despite the jolt to his frontline troops, Logan continued to push forward his remaining regiments, and Gregg soon discovered that he was facing an entire division, ten thousand men. By late afternoon, Gregg had held the Federals back for as long as he could. Realizing he might in fact be in serious trouble, Gregg ordered his rebel troops to withdraw, pulling them back through the town of Raymond and beyond, preserving most of his strength. Like Bowen at Grand Gulf, John Gregg understood the mathematics of what he confronted. The limited number of Confederates who had been sent out to follow Grant's progress could do little else but slip back across the Big Black and try to determine once more what Grant was planning to do.

"I ain't hearin' a blessed thing!"

Bauer ignored the big talk. With the day drawing to a close, the only signs of a fight came now from the ambulances, the houses along the road transformed into hospitals. It was nothing as awful as Bauer had seen before, the casualties not many. But to the men who had yet to see any man's body torn apart, the sight of blood stirred up an uncomfortable chatter. Beside him, O'Daniel still mumbled, and Bauer recognized a prayer. The redheaded boy had stared out with the rest of them at the first field where the wounded had come, where doctors in bloody aprons did their work. Bauer gave it only a glance, had feared that up ahead it might be far worse. But the fight seemed to have been only a strong skirmish, the two sides maneuvering and colliding with just enough force to produce the casualties, but not so much to bring the entire column into the mix.

Far to the front, the musket fire had stopped, but still there was the occasional thump, an artillery crew taking their last opportunity to find some target they couldn't see. Even the cavalry seemed to go somewhere else, and Bauer wondered about that, if some general had sent them farther forward, making sure there would be no rebels hidden away in some hole along the march. There were holes galore, the entire countryside cut up and rolling, as though the land had been shoved up against the river behind them like a great piece of carpet, nothing like the smooth ground far to the west. He glanced up, one more day ending, a few clouds in a darkening sky. The breeze had begun to blow, the entire column welcoming that, the wind chilling the sweat on their faces, the soaking sweat of their shirts. The officers hadn't told them anything, and Bauer suspected that would come later, in camp, some word on what the lead regiments had walked into. As the fight erupted against Logan's lead division, their own march had been halted for not much more than an hour, and the only chaos he had seen came from the officers who moved past in both directions, carrying information to those who needed to know. Foot soldiers don't need to be told anything, he thought.

The bugles began, the usual routine at the end of a day's march. Well, today, it wasn't us. He felt an odd blend of sadness and relief, saw one more ambulance move past, heard a sharp cry from inside, the voice of someone he would never know, the sound waking one more piece of memory.

He followed Sergeant Finley into a field, saw Willis now, speaking to the company commander, Captain McDermott, both men with hands on hips. Bauer looked more at the captain, knew he was a veteran, too, had been in most of the fighting many of the Wisconsin boys had come through. There was always comfort in that, so different from the clean-pressed freshness of the new officers, who knew only of training manuals and drill, who used their power of rank only to torment. We're probably past that, he thought. This has gone on for so long, most everybody's seen something of the enemy. He glanced at O'Daniel, the redhead looking at the sergeant, waiting to be told where he should go next. Well, maybe not everybody. They ought not let a youngster out here. Not even those drummer boys. This is no place for boys.

He followed the sergeant's directions, found a smooth piece of ground several yards wide, his camp for the night, would share it with a dozen men from the company. The bedrolls were laid out, men sitting, some already lying flat. Close by, a fire was building, a precious coffeepot, and jabbering from the men who always went first to the fires. He heard anger, protest, mindless bellyaching from men who had missed out on today's fight. The musket fire had done that to him as well, drawn out the lust, surprising even him. But that excitement had passed with the sight of those first casualties, and he could not erase those images now, bloody aprons, broken men.

He reached into his knapsack for the hardtack, ate the dismal cracker without thinking, tried to block out the big talk from the fire. To one side he saw the redhead, O'Daniel, sitting silently on his bedroll, staring off into some other place.

CHAPTER NINE

PEMBERTON

BOVINA, MISSISSIPPI
MAY 12, 1863

"Sir, General Gregg reports the enemy is in some force at Raymond. He was compelled to withdraw. There were casualties on both sides."

Pemberton stood beside his horse, stared down, kicked at the ground slowly with one boot.

"Of course there were. I informed General Gregg that he should not assault the enemy unless he was certain of victory. Did he not understand my order? Does no one understand my orders?"

Waddy looked down as well, shrugged, not the response Pemberton hoped for.

"I cannot answer that, sir. Your orders have been clear to me."

"Yes, and you are not in the field, Colonel. You do not know the location of the enemy."

"It appears, with all respects, sir, that none of us are completely aware what General Grant is intending to do."

Pemberton closed his eyes, annoyed at so much **obviousness** from his chief of staff. He moved away from the horse, aides scrambling ahead of him to make ready his new headquarters. No, he thought, none of us is aware of anything. And if they are, they do not see fit to inform me. I do not understand such a lack of cooperation. Or . . . obedience.

He turned, looked at Waddy again.

"Has General Loring indicated he is moving his troops to conform to my orders?"

Waddy seemed confused now, hesitated, then said, "Which orders would that be, sir? General Loring was ordered to support General Bowen, but you . . . we countermanded those orders."

Major Memminger stepped forward now, his attention caught by the conversation. "Sir, General Loring now insists that the enemy intends to destroy the railroad between the Big Black and the city of Jackson. He is hoping, sir, that you will order a general attack against the enemy's position."

"What **position** is that, Major? I am under orders from General Johnston to unite my entire army and pursue the enemy. I am under orders from the president to defend Vicksburg at all costs. I have the strength to do neither with any effectiveness. General Johnston has taken my cavalry from me and assigned those good men to aid General Bragg in Tennessee. I am left with scant resources to scout this countryside." He paused. "When did you speak to General Loring?"

Memminger glanced at Waddy.

"A short while ago, sir. He was on the road leading to the Big Black bridge. A courier directed me to him, saying he wished to speak to me directly. It was there that he offered his prediction."

"Did he not tell you to bring that . . . prediction to me?"

Memminger let out a breath.

"No, sir. He rather insisted . . . it was not important that you be informed."

Pemberton felt the heat rising, a brittleness in his temper he rarely showed.

"Major, you are my adjutant. After Colonel Waddy and Colonel Montgomery, you are the highest-ranking member of my staff. You will report to me any message . . . or **prediction** you might receive from any one of my commanders. Is that difficult for you to understand?"

"No, sir. Certainly not." Memminger shifted his feet, seemed to search for some way to make amends. He looked up at Pemberton now, a small light in his eyes. "Sir, I did happen upon Colonel Adams. He offers his respects and says that if you order it, he can bring the cavalry commands together. He advises that they are still somewhat . . . scattered."

"And how long did you intend to hold **this** information secret, Major?" Pemberton had no energy for this, knew that his staff was loyal to him, regardless of their failings. It was something Pemberton never took for granted, not with so many doubts about his own loyalty from so many of his subordinates. He thought of Wirt Adams, his cavalry commander, in charge now since Earl Van Dorn had obeyed Joe Johnston's orders and hauled most of the horsemen to Tennessee. But Van Dorn was dead, a shocking report less than a week old, the man shot down by a civilian for reasons that were still a mystery. And so, he thought, General Johnston will eventually claim Adams from me as well. It is inevitable. Pemberton pictured Adams in his mind, a small, handsome man, college educated, already accomplished as a superb leader of cavalry. Adams was from the neutral state of Kentucky, and Pemberton appreciated that Adams had snuffed out any indiscreet grumbling in his command about Pemberton's loyalty.

"You may respond to Colonel Adams that we cannot afford to bring in the cavalry outposts. As much as I require his eyes, uniting the cavalry will leave all of northern Mississippi unprotected. That confounded Grierson could yet make another raid, and the enemy might bring yet another column of troops down from Memphis." He looked down and shook his head. "I trust General Johnston is making effective use of my horsemen. But I surely could use them here. I cannot confront what I do not know."

"Sir, Colonel Adams does have cavalry patrols close to the enemy's position. Your orders were to maintain a vigilant eye on any Yankee movement. Colonel Adams is in obedience to that order."

"Yes? So half a hundred horsemen are scouting the entire Federal army? How is that possible, Major? I cannot fault Colonel Adams for doing what he can, but we do not know where the enemy has his greatest concentration. We do not know the direction of their movement. The enemy has cavalry as well, and they are perfectly capable of driving away any effort we make to observe them." His voice had risen, and he choked it off, saw faces across the open yard watching him. "I am ordered by General Johnston to make a massed assault against Grant's forces. General Loring offers his speculation as to where Grant is going, but he does not tell me anything of where he is **right now**. I have been attempting to divine the enemy's intent for some weeks now, and it is no clearer to me today than it was a month ago."

He stifled his frustration, moved on toward the house, an old mansion that still showed hints of the luxury that had once been so prevalent throughout this part of Mississippi. He stepped up onto a wide

veranda, saw a well-dressed civilian, the man offering a smile, a deep bow as he opened the front
door.

"General, you are most welcome in my home.
Please . . . what is mine is now yours. You are, after
all, our salvation."

There was an odd unpleasantness to the man's
well-wishing, the words forced, a show of politeness only because his land was now occupied by so
many men with guns.

"Thank you, sir. We shall not abuse you or your
possessions. I do not expect to remain here for long.
We must make every effort to destroy our enemies."

The man backed inside the house, seemed satisfied at Pemberton's intent, still the smile pasted on
his face.

"Please, sir, enter my home at your convenience."

"In a moment, thank you."

Pemberton turned and saw a column of soldiers
on the road, moving east, toward the Big Black
River bridge.

"Whose men are those?"

Waddy was on the steps, keeping close to him,
said, "Not certain, sir. Should I seek out their
commander?"

Pemberton said nothing, thought, What does
it matter? They are in motion, and those are my
orders, after all. They march to the river, where
we must be vigilant. I am still quite certain that
General Grant will come, and he will use the most

convenient route, possibly this very road. I truly believed he would move on us more quickly, from the south. And yet he hesitated, a slow march beyond the river that seemed without purpose, as though he too is uncertain. And perhaps he is. He is in enemy territory, after all, and perhaps his cavalry is not as skilled as I believe. Perhaps he searches for **our** greatest concentration, or perhaps he is avoiding a fight altogether. He is on trial, after all, loud voices in Washington calling for his dismissal. He must not disappoint and so he is surely cautious. It is possible that General Johnston is anticipating this very hesitation, and so, if I strike Grant unexpectedly, I could crush him. Or perhaps that is what Grant hopes. And so he spreads us out along the Big Black, looking for his own opportunity. He looked at Waddy, rubbed his fingers slowly through his beard.

"General Johnston believes that the enemy is a plum, ripe for the taking. Our orders are to take it. I had thought Grant's target might be Jackson. That kind of feather would do much for his reputation in Washington. But I cannot assume he will not strike us directly at Vicksburg, and he could still. Here we sit out east of the town, when even now, his fleet could be transporting troops downriver to strike us directly from the west. We must remain on the defensive. The president is correct. We must defend Vicksburg."

He looked past Waddy, saw Memminger, others, standing quietly, as though waiting for instructions.

"Major! Do you still have General Johnston's order on your person?"

Memminger moved quickly to his own horse and retrieved a paper from his saddlebag.

"Right here, sir. Do you wish to see it?"

Pemberton tried to hide his annoyance.

"That is why I asked, Major."

Memminger climbed the steps, presented the paper with a short bow.

"Sir."

Pemberton read the order again, Joe Johnston's insistence that the army be brought together, the various commands spread around Vicksburg to be pulled away from the river and united into a single crushing blow against Grant, a powerful force more than adequate to rid the state of Grant's absurd invasion. So, here I am, he thought. I have done what the general ordered, and removed myself from Vicksburg. Now I am to unite an army that is, presumably, scattered for twenty miles, while none of my generals has any certainty just where we should attack. We have engaged Grant twice on this side of the Mississippi River, with inadequate numbers, and so we have been brushed aside. Ah, but we were not prepared. So, I shall obey General Johnston. And if Vicksburg is even now being assaulted by Federal troops climbing up those bluffs, then I can explain to the president that I was, after all, following the orders of my superior. It would be convenient, however, if my superiors, or anyone else, could offer me some clarity on just what the enemy intends to do.

He handed the paper to Memminger, turned, moved into the house, the door left open, the civilian nowhere to be seen. He moved past the foyer, saw a sitting room to one side, and stepped that way, a small couch inviting him with bright purple pillows. He flexed a stiffness in his hip, thought, I could use something . . . soft. He sat, allowed the cushion beneath him to absorb the weight, a brief second of comfort. But it was gone now, replaced by a blossoming headache, rising up the back of his neck, a great steel hand gripping his skull.

Waddy stood in the entrance of the room and said, "Orders, sir?"

Pemberton stared up at a portrait hung above a small fireplace. It was a child, a girl, standing beside a large black dog, which stood taller than the child. He smiled at the portrait, tried to imagine the patience required to sketch such a scene, that no child would remain in such a pose for very long. You do not issue a stern command to a child, as you would a dog. He thought of Loring now, a division commander who seemed to regard Pemberton as much more of a nuisance than a superior. It was too common in this army, a plague of insubordination and disrespect that had followed him from South Carolina.

"I would very much like some tea, if the master of this house has any he is willing to share. Sugar as well, though that might be too much to ask. Such luxuries are growing scarce."

Waddy bowed, moved away, and Pemberton was alone in silence, unusual, none of the clamor of the army, of headquarters. That will come soon, he thought. They must know where I am, must know where to send their utterly unreliable information. He thought of Grant, had known him in Mexico, an audacious officer who took pride in launching himself into oddly dangerous situations. Pemberton had been there, standing back with the commanders, waiting dutifully for some instructions. He had observed, as the generals observed, a bloody affair against the stout walls and gateways of Mexico City, the last barriers that held Winfield Scott's army away from their final victory. Through a dozen field glasses, they had observed a young officer close to the Mexican position, the man hauling a single artillery piece to the belfry of a church, and when the cannon went into action, it seemed to dishearten the Mexican forces who absorbed the punishment. Very soon after, the city had fallen. The officer was virtually unknown, had led no infantry, had gone out on his own and done something that caught the attention of the generals. Pemberton had been sent to retrieve him, had learned the man's name, Lieutenant Ulysses Grant. I brought him back to General Worth, he thought, saw him lauded for his heroics, a hard slap on the back, laughter from men who did not often laugh. Grant will remember that day for the rest of his life. It is doubtful he will remember me. He did not come to West Point until after I had gone, surely would not know anything of me from there. He would know what they all know, that I left Pennsylvania to go south. And he will know that we shall certainly meet in the field. It would be so very convenient if I knew where he was.

He thought again of Winfield Scott, a Virginian who had never even considered holding on to his loyalty to that state, so different from so many of the others, Joe Johnston, certainly, and Robert E. Lee. Pemberton had spoken to Scott, a hard argument about Pemberton's resignation that Scott would not win. He made every effort to secure my loyalty, Pemberton thought, but it could not be done. My family in Pennsylvania still does not understand, and doubtless they never will. And had I remained in a blue uniform, what would I be now? A colonel, perhaps, keeping order in some heavy-artillery post in Washington, a comfortable office, something more suitable to my experience. Would they have sent me out into the field, offered me command of a regiment, a division? Perhaps it would have been **me** at Fort Sumter, brashly defying the order to surrender, standing defiantly against Beauregard and his artillery. Is it coincidence that General Lee assigned me to that very post, long after the heroics had passed? Now Sumter lies in our hands, a useless outpost against Federal gunships. The civilians did not trust me there, thought me capable of treachery, and so I am here, once more protecting a waterway. Not even my marvelous artillery can hold away a fleet of gunboats, and so the Federal navy has made mockery of our brilliant defenses. That Grierson fellow . . . their cavalry cuts our telegraph wires and wrecks our railroads. The Confederacy has done a truly wonderful job of creating an army, so many good men, so much passion for our cause, and yet I have no idea what must be done to eliminate this plague of blue mercenaries, cursed West Pointers who are no better officers than I am, whose rank comes from politics and friendships with Abraham Lincoln or that vile Henry Halleck. Grant is no more than a puppet on a string, dancing to preserve his reputation. That is our difference, surely. I am fighting for something far stronger, far more important than rank or political favor. It is the honor of the Confederacy, of an entire way of life. It is a way that I respect and love, and General Scott be damned, I will not betray my precious Pattie.

He wanted to stand, to pace the room, but the stiffness held him on the cushions, the headache beating him down. Right now, he thought, General Grant is adding to their mockery, mocking my own command. Perhaps he recalls me after all, perhaps he knows that in Mexico I was a staff officer, a messenger, while he was deploying artillery in the face of the enemy. Perhaps he suspects weakness, that I will not bring all I have to the fight. So I must find the means to change his mind. All those who doubt my loyalty, all those venomous snakes in the Richmond newspapers, they will understand my legacy when victory is achieved. Grant must be destroyed, and Vicksburg must remain a great citadel, unconquered, an impregnable dam across the Mississippi.

He forced himself up, moved to a window, sunlight bathing him, uncomfortably warm. In the wide yard, his staff was in motion, wagons and horses, and beyond, more troops moving past on the road. He fought against the headache, thought, I am certain of what must be done, of the fight I must wage, of the task I must accomplish. But, by God, it would be terribly useful if someone, General Johnston perhaps, would do more than issue proclamations telling me what I already know. It would be terribly useful if someone would tell me **how** I am to do it.

CHAPTER TEN

SHERMAN

SOUTHWEST OF RAYMOND, MISSISSIPPI
MAY 13, 1863

Grant had ridden forward, confirming the reports that came from McPherson, the cavalry monitoring the retreat of the rebel forces back toward the Big Black River. Sherman had heard the sounds of the fight at Raymond, was never really concerned that McPherson might be in trouble. James McPherson had spent a great deal of time with Sherman the year before, was one of the few senior officers in the army whom Sherman truly respected. During the campaign that resulted in the horrifying fight at Shiloh, McPherson had been the primary engineer who had scouted the various approaches toward the rebel positions. Then, the engineer's primary target had been the railroads, and the army had required an engineer's sense of maneuver, how best to approach an enemy well entrenched, how to cross the morass of swamplands and river bottoms with enough force to inflict effective damage. McPherson was the best engineer Sherman had ever known, and even now, with McPherson's promotion to corps commander, Sherman had every confidence McPherson could handle the job, would be a calming presence in places Sherman feared most. Early in the war, Sherman's demons had festered, rising up at the worst possible times, jeopardizing his men and his own career. The fear was there still, those brief moments when darkness hid the land around him, when a stray blast from an artillery piece would jar the night. Since Shiloh, those demons had kept mostly silent, but he knew they were there, knew they would wait for that special time, when his men needed his authority, his calm presence. He had done nothing to betray his fears, not to his men, not to Grant. But Grant's plan stirred the turmoil inside of him, one reason why he had argued against it, had hoped that somehow, the great citadel of Vicksburg would somehow just collapse, would fall into Union hands without the misery of another hard fight. By now the arguments were mostly gone, Sherman admitting to himself that Grant was doing the right thing. The invasion of Mississippi from across the river had seemed to catch the rebel troops and their generals mostly by surprise, as though the rebel command had been completely ignorant of Grant's bulldog determination, or the authority Washington had given him to carry out his plan. They certainly knew nothing of what Grant had intended to do, or what he was intending right now.

Sherman's confidence in Grant continued to grow. There had always been affection, some of that coming from what could only be called shared persecution, both men with so many enemies in Washington, a hostility neither man really understood. There had been failings, of course, the kinds of stumbles beloved by newspapers. But there had also been victories, and no matter the lack of "perfection" in executing all those great plans sketched out on paper, thus far no Confederate commander west of the mountains had proven himself Grant's superior. Sherman knew that nothing was certain, that a stray musket ball or an ill-timed artillery round could accomplish the same kind of disaster that had fallen upon the rebels at Shiloh. Then it had been Albert Sidney Johnston, a loss of such magnitude that the rebel forces there could not recover. It was one part of his own fear, that a single sharpshooter, one very lucky man, might offer up the musket ball that would strip this army of any one of its commanders. It was the recurring theme through so many sleepless hours: What would this army do without Grant? Would it fall upon Sherman? No, McClernand, most likely. And what of confidence then? He would obey, of course, but Sherman had learned from Grant's humility that an outspoken commander whose own hubris came before good tactics could lead this army to disaster. This was, after all, the enemy's ground, and the enemy could be everywhere, every hole and every patch of dark woods, waiting in ambush. Even Sherman's staff seemed to understand his anguish at the slow pace of the march, allowing the enemy time to maneuver, to make a good plan of their own. Sherman fought furiously against the single bolt of fear, that if the ambush came, it might be the commander who would respond with his own worst instincts, who would rout his own men with a terrified gallop away from the guns.

He had long ago accepted leadership as the most important responsibility of his life, was deeply appreciative that those above him, Halleck, and of course Grant, had shown more confidence in him than he believed he deserved. But Shiloh was a year past, and thus far the army, and Sherman, had yet to confront a similar disaster. The embarrassment at Chickasaw Bayou had been exactly that, an embarrassment, a humiliating failure, but that failure was about logistics and support, and a well-prepared enemy who held the good ground. The greatest lesson learned there had much more to do with tactics and positioning than the nagging doubts about his own abilities. No matter the hostile reaction of the cursed newspapers, or those fat

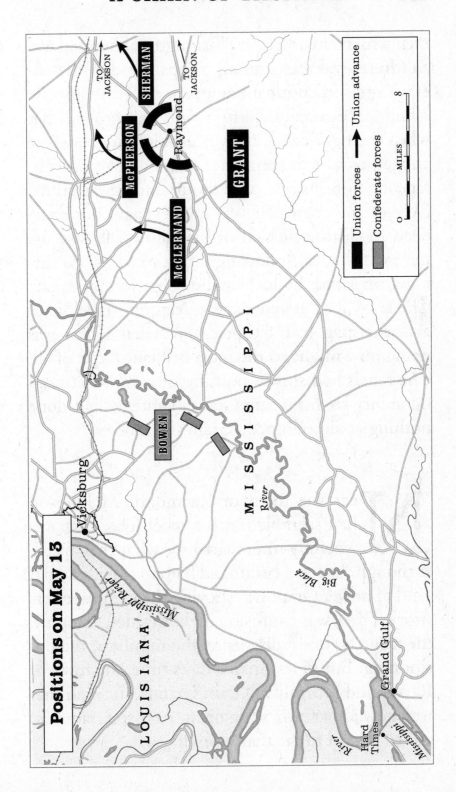

Positions on May 13

men who filled offices in Washington, Sherman was still **here,** was still leading troops through the enemy's ground. With no ambush, no great surprise assault, Sherman's determination had grown, that when the fight came, the voices might just be gone altogether, and in their place a different voice, courageous, furious, his own shouts into the terrified faces of the enemy. It was not revenge, not some need to cleanse himself of his failures. It was just the job at hand, following Grant's orders, executing a plan that he had finally come to appreciate. The army had driven a spear deep into rebel land, and Sherman had accepted that what Grant was doing now might be the most brilliant tactic of all. The rebels had shown nothing of comprehension, no ability to anticipate Grant's strategy, had done nothing at all to impede Grant's advance.

Near the town of Raymond, McPherson had stumbled into a rebel force that was woefully unprepared for what they faced, as though the rebel command had no real idea what kind of power Grant was shoving through their territory. There was confusion on both sides, certainly, the ragged ground disguising the numbers, the positioning. But in less than a day's time, the town of Raymond lay firmly in Grant's hands, the road that way now apparently wide open. And so Grant had gone forward to see that himself.

Instead of making a sweeping turn to hit Vicksburg from the east, Grant had ordered his three
corps to make the best advantage of what Pemberton was giving them. Between Vicksburg and the
capital city, the railroad and communication lines
were seemingly unprotected, Pemberton keeping his
forces west of the Big Black, and whatever strength
the rebels had in Jackson seemed content to remain
where they were. To anyone with a map, Grant's
army looked to be pinned between two halves of
a vise, such that a vigorous offensive from either
direction could catch Grant in a dangerous bind,
possibly cutting him off from a retreat back to the
Mississippi River, eliminating any hope of a supply line, any hope of reinforcements. But the rebels
had yet to do anything **vigorous** at all. It was the
kind of hesitation Grant had hoped for, and the orders that came to Sherman now were received with
complete enthusiasm. Vicksburg was still the ultimate target, but with no one yet standing in their
way, Grant ordered the army to shove northward,
slicing the connection between Vicksburg and Jackson, and then, with McClernand guarding against
any sudden attack from the west, McPherson and
Sherman would make a rapid march straight to
Jackson. If there was any strong force there waiting to surprise Grant at Jackson, a potential threat
to Grant's eventual assault on Vicksburg, that force
would first be eliminated. If the city of Jackson was
captured in the bargain, even better. Sherman knew

as well as his superior did that the capture of any
Confederate state capital produced headlines back
east. And should Jackson fall into Federal hands,
even Grant's harshest critics would be made tooth-
less. Sherman's opinion of newspapermen had not
changed, but even he had to admit that this time,
they might serve a useful purpose after all.

He had found a soft patch of deep grass near
a fence line, most of the rails long gone,
firewood for men who needed very little
to keep warm. But there were some fires, the hum
of low talk from tired men who had still not faced
the enemy. The talk was all about McPherson, the
brief fight near Raymond, the town now along
their own route of march. The rumors flew, unstoppable, that the rebel army was just beyond the
town, waiting, that McPherson had merely driven
back a tough skirmish line. Sherman did nothing
to stop that kind of talk, knew that nervous men
were alert men. If it cost them some sleep, they just
might take that out on the first rebels they saw.

Sherman's makeshift bed was close to the edge of
the road, the dense grass of the fence line too comfortable to ignore. He had actually slept, waking
once to the sound of hoofbeats, some courier moving quickly past. He had waited for the poke from
a staff officer, one more order from Grant, a report
from one of his own division commanders. But the

hoofbeats had passed with no other disturbance, and within minutes the sleep had come again.

He dreamed of California, the ocean, San Francisco, but there was something new, tearing the dream away, a hard, painful jolt in his back. He blinked, felt it again, a stiff kick, and now, a voice.

"Hey! Where'd you come by the liquor? You got any left? This old throat is a-mighty parched."

Sherman rolled over, still felt the pain where the man had booted him, tried to see the man's face, hidden by the darkness, the brim of a hat.

"What the hell . . ."

Sherman sat up, and the soldier let out a short gasp, backed away a step, turned, and with an eruption of motion, vanished down the road.

"Sir!"

Men were moving toward him, the familiar sounds of his staff, the voice of Colonel Dayton.

"Sir! Did something happen? Who was that man? An assassin perhaps? A spy? He ran off that way. We'll find him, sir."

Sherman probed the ache in his back, stood slowly.

"Don't bother, Colonel. Just one of our boys doing a little scavenging. Mistook me for a drunkard, sleeping off a good fog."

"Did he recognize you, sir?"

He couldn't help a chuckle, glanced at his shoulder straps, the two gold stars reflecting the firelight.

"Seems so. He'll run for a while yet. It'll give him

a story to tell his friends. You hear anything about that, ask a few questions. Otherwise, just let it go."

"My apologies, sir. The guards should not have let anyone slip into camp like that. There will be punishment, sir."

"I said, let it go. The boys have spirit. They're itchy for something to do. Have to admit, I share that. We march early, and we move quickly."

"Yes, sir. That order has been communicated to the senior commanders."

Sherman stretched his back, glanced at his pocket watch, tilted it toward the nearest fire. Midnight.

"Has Grant come back to us yet?"

"No, sir."

"Might not tonight. Might stay with McPherson." Sherman kept the words to himself now, thought, That engineer doesn't need Grant tucking him in tonight, but sure as hell he'll be nervous. The fight at Raymond loosened his men up a little. Good. Tomorrow, maybe we'll do some loosening of our own.

He sent the staff away, a half-dozen men who would still be cautious, who knew that whatever nameless soldier had been allowed to stumble upon Sherman might have had far more on his mind than a bottle of spirits. They worry about their own asses, he thought, as much as they worry about mine. Good. Keep them sharp. I doubt that thirsty fellow will go wandering through a strange camp again. Not this one, anyway.

He stepped out into the road, saw clouds moving past the moon, the night darker still. He realized suddenly he missed Grant, had a ripple of fear about where Grant could be. We need him, for damn sure. Don't you go riding into some fool ambush, or have some jumpy jackass guard mistake you for a rebel.

He pulled a cigar from his jacket, lit it, the smoke rising into his nostrils, warming him, fogging his eyes. He suddenly thought of Napoleon, a lesson from long ago, a text at West Point: Strike the enemy when he least expects it. And if he's divided, strike him harder. Well, from all we can tell, he's divided now. Grant's doing exactly what he should. Before we commence anything at Vicksburg, protect us from behind by busting hell out of anybody lurking out past our backside. Solves all kinds of problems, before they become problems. And, along the way, we might just grab a city full of civilians . . . and teach them just what a war really is.

CHAPTER ELEVEN

JOHNSTON

JACKSON, MISSISSIPPI
MAY 13, 1863

The rains had come, the streets of the city already soft, oozing mud stinking of the horses. He rode away from the train, stiff in the saddle, always observing, inspecting, the kind of attention to detail that kept his men alert. But the usual show was draining him, his strength barely keeping him in the saddle. The illness had come weeks before, some malady no one seemed able to treat, but there was no time now for the luxury of rest. He had come to Jackson, after all, because the president had ordered him to.

The feud between Johnston and Jefferson Davis had begun even before the bloodshed at First Manassas. In the United States Army, Joseph Johnston had held the rank of brigadier general, and so had outranked every other officer who had made the decision to go south. It was only logical to Johnston that his higher rank would grant him the same consideration in the new army of the Confederacy. But Jefferson Davis had a completely different view, and in what he could only describe as a slap from the president, Johnston had been named the fourth most senior commander, behind Davis's adjutant and inspector general, Samuel Cooper, as well as the now deceased Albert Sidney Johnston, and Robert E. Lee. Only Pierre Beauregard was subordinate to Johnston in the Confederate's highest ranks. Johnston certainly believed the credit was his for victory at Manassas, but Davis blamed him for the failure of the Southern forces to drive home their success by crushing the Federal army completely before it could escape back to the defenses at Washington. Johnston knew better, that both armies were ill-prepared for such a bloody confrontation, and that even in victory, the Confederate forces suffered from the inexperience of so many of the officers in the field. The fact that Beauregard had received loud praise from the newspapers for his own role in the fight had only added fuel to Johnston's fire.

In 1862, Johnston had commanded the Confederate forces that first confronted George McClellan on the Virginia peninsula, and it was there that Johnston suffered the greatest indignity of all.

Throughout his lengthy career, he had faced a variety of enemies, from the Seminole Wars in Florida to the war with Mexico, serving with enormous distinction alongside another of Winfield Scott's more prominent officers, Robert E. Lee. Johnston had been wounded a number of times in a number of engagements, his coat usually riddled with holes, the purest sign of a man in the thick of the fight. But the year before, in June, the confrontation with McClellan at the Battle of Seven Pines produced a pair of wounds too serious for mere pride. With Johnston unable to command from his saddle, Jefferson Davis had responded by replacing him with Robert E. Lee. Since their days together at West Point, Johnston and Lee had been close, as close as either man's temperament could allow. But now Lee was a rival, as he had been in Mexico, a thorn in their friendship that seemed far more significant to Johnston than to Lee. Since awarded command of the Army of Northern Virginia, Lee's star had risen, victories over a parade of inept Federal commanders, most notably the crushing success against Ambrose Burnside at Fredericksburg. Naturally, to President Davis, this was validation that Lee was the right man for that job. To Johnston, it was one more slap. But Davis could not just ignore Johnston's value to the army. The death of Albert Sidney Johnston at Shiloh had given command of the West to Pierre Beauregard, and although Beauregard was widely heralded in the newspapers as the

South's first real hero, the man who had ordered the firing on Fort Sumter, many in the army had a very different opinion of the Creole, many blaming him for the devastating loss at Shiloh, and various setbacks soon after. It was an opinion shared by the president, and by November 1862, with Joe Johnston healthy once again, Davis had appointed Johnston to the overall command in the West.

Since November, Johnston had kept his headquarters closer to Braxton Bragg's army in Tennessee, overseeing what seemed to be the greatest threat from Federal efforts to drive toward Chattanooga, and possibly Atlanta. It was a supreme annoyance to Johnston that he was assigned to command Pemberton's army as well, hundreds of miles from Bragg. To Johnston's efficient mind, his sphere of command was spread out over a geographical area no single commander could hope to manage. It was little more than Davis's attempts to put him in a position where success was impossible. Davis could then claim that his negative appraisal of Johnston was completely justified.

Though Johnston was far from Richmond, there were frequent reminders from the pen of Jefferson Davis that his command was most certainly not independent. The most recent order had come as a result of the crisis confronting John Pemberton in Mississippi, the obvious threat to Vicksburg. To Johnston's intense irritation, Pemberton had no hesitation bypassing his immediate superior in

Tennessee with a flow of urgent communications sent directly to the president. It was one more reason for Johnston to despair. He had very little respect for Pemberton. The man was, after all, a Pennsylvanian, and thus far Pemberton had done very little to inspire anyone that he was the right man to secure the defense of anyplace as valuable as Vicksburg. Now Pemberton was facing a very real threat. No matter the potential for disaster in Tennessee, Johnston had been bluntly ordered by Richmond to travel to the city of Jackson, to take charge of the growing threat from Federal forces now seemingly slicing through Mississippi at will. Johnston had learned only in piecemeal messages the details of what Pemberton was confronting; that told Johnston that Pemberton himself didn't fully grasp what was happening around him. Thus Davis's order for Johnston to travel to Mississippi actually made sense. Illness or no, Johnston was compelled to board the train to Jackson.

The train ride had taken three days, a naggingly methodical trip made necessary by the constant repairs to the tracks resulting from damage inflicted by cavalry of both armies. When Johnston finally arrived in Jackson, the rain seemed only to punctuate his lingering illness, his energy drained further by the parade on horseback to what had been arranged as his headquarters.

It was, after all, customary that the commanding general would keep to his mount, moving beneath the flag that signaled the gravity of his presence. Most of the time, he actually enjoyed that, made it a point always to show the men the finest uniform, the most prominent adornments, whether the bright sash at his waist, the silver spurs, or the feather in his hat. But there was little to celebrate now, the rain and his growling stomach making for a depressing arrival to a city he had no real interest in protecting. He would get an argument about that, of course, knew already that Mississippi's governor, John Pettus, had fled the area, reestablishing some kind of state capital at the town of Enterprise, near the Alabama border. It was no surprise to Johnston that Pettus, like every other civilian politician, was pleading that Johnston call forth a massive army to destroy Grant, an army that did not even exist in the imagination of Jefferson Davis. Johnston had no real concerns about Pettus or any worries about the state's civilian affairs. It was one more piece of the annoyance of trying to manage an army in the midst of anxious civilians. They would come, as they always came, would seek Johnston out in a display of obsequiousness, a false front from men who served this army only by offering an endless tide of complaints.

He peered out through a stream of water pouring from the brim of his hat, shivered, and followed the directions from a staff officer, the man just as miserable. They rounded a corner, and he saw the hotel, the Bowman House, an imposing structure highlighted by the prominent painting of a Confederate battle flag on the wall above the veranda. He halted the horse, impatient for the groom to take the reins, the man splashing up close to him, unspeaking, knowing what to do. Johnston swung his leg weakly over one side, dismounted into a thick splash of slop, hesitated, could not help thinking of the effort that had gone into the sheen of polish on his boots. He straightened his back, an instinctive habit inspired by his short stature, made every effort to move to the veranda with some kind of decorum. At the top of the steps, gray-coated officers spread out to meet him, some of them from his own staff, men who had hurried away from the train station to make ready his new office. But the others had a different look, worn men, the uniforms not nearly as dapper, rough beards and dirty hats. He didn't mind that. From their stare alone, it was quite clear that these men had met the enemy.

He stepped up to the veranda, protected now from the soggy breath of the shower behind him.

An officer stepped forward, with an air of importance. Johnston knew the look: someone's adjutant.

"Sir! Welcome to Jackson. Please come inside. This weather was unexpected. It has been miserably dry here for some time. I regret deeply that the skies have seen fit to insult your arrival."

"I've seen bad weather before, Major. I prefer to think of it as God's blessing on parched land. Or God's punishment on those who would despoil it. Who exactly are you?"

The man stepped back, another show of formality, and snapped a sharp salute.

"Major Ailes, sir. Adjutant to General Gregg. The general offers you his most respectful welcome, and wishes me to inform you that he shall arrive here in a short time. He is seeing to the placement of his brigade."

"Then I'll wait. Inside, if you don't mind."

Johnston stifled a cough, felt sweat in his coat, a chill that rippled down his chest, bringing another shiver. They made way for him, salutes all around, his own aides already inside, and he caught the scent of tea. He saw a young lieutenant and asked, "Which way to my room? I require a moment." The man knew his job, a short bow, pointed silently to a stairway, and Johnston ignored the salutes, moved quickly, climbed the stairs, felt betrayed by the weakness. He had no energy for show now, the last few steps a struggle, stopped at the landing, felt his breathing in hard gasps. Confounded afflictions, he thought. If not musket balls, then some infernal plague.

From behind him, at the bottom of the stairs: "Sir, General Gregg has arrived."

Johnston sagged, did not turn around, nodded

slowly, and said, "I told you . . . I require a moment. I assume there is a sitting room of some kind. Escort him there, and just . . . wait."

"Sir."

Johnston saw another aide in front of him, an open door, the smell of an oil lamp, yellow glow, warmth. He moved into the room, realized he was soaking the rug beneath his boots. The aide retreated, closed the door, and Johnston removed the hat, saw what was left of the grand plume, one more annoyance. He scanned the room, simple elegance, the bed, a pitcher of water at a basin, a hastily arranged spray of flowers on a mantel. He put a hand on his stomach, felt a rumble, but it was not hunger. The window rattled slightly from a gust of wind, the rain spraying on the panes, and he moved that way, stared out, saw muddy streets, wagons, horses in line along the front of the building, his own, Gregg's. He glanced at his pocket watch, nearly five, one more day passing by for a commander whose enthusiasm for command was draining away. It will never be my command anyway, he thought. If I had the authority, there would be so many differences, so many good people . . . **better** people doing the job. His mind blanked, no names coming to him, just who those people might be. He put one hand on the bedpost, closed his eyes, felt unsteady. The chill came again, a harder rumble in his gut, and he turned, searched, and said aloud, "Now, where in the devil is that chamber pot?"

John Gregg was much what Johnston had expected, a man in his thirties, hard face, sure of himself, the glint of steel in the eye that gives confidence to his men . . . and his superiors. He was no West Pointer, but then, Johnston knew that many of the younger commanders were not. Gregg was a Texan, had been among those so ingloriously surrendered to Grant's forces at Fort Donelson the year before. He had returned to duty through exchange, had been promoted to command of a brigade, but Johnston had too much experience with men like Gregg, had the instinctive sense that before much longer, this man would command a division, or more.

"We were made to retreat, sir. It was shameful, and I will make amends."

Johnston studied a map, his cold hand shaking, and he saw the glance from Gregg.

"I have been ill of late, General. It is passing. This rain has not been helpful. If not for this absurd condition, I should have taken command in Mississippi, this entire operation. The Federals are trespassing dangerously . . . for them, and from what I have been told, they are not yet aware just how foolish their strategy. General Grant has taken an enormous risk, has extended his supply lines and strung out his forces across many miles. He must guard every bridge, every roadway, and he is certainly limited by how many troops he can sustain in the field."

"Yes, sir. We did manage to hold back what we discovered to be an entire division, sir. My men carry shame for their retreat, but we did give them our measure."

"Enough, General. I have been informed of your encounter at Raymond. There is no shame in accepting the inevitable. You were severely outnumbered, and yes, you did perform well. There will yet be opportunity to repay the enemy for his arrogance."

"Thank you, sir. It is my honor to be of service to your command."

Johnston had heard this before, but there was gravity to Gregg's words, not the usual emptiness of those who sought favor.

"I was told by your adjutant that you were engaged in placing your brigade. What is your situation?"

Gregg leaned closer, and Johnston caught a thick odor of rain and horses. Gregg pointed at the map, a pair of roads leading west, out of the city.

"Sir, Colonel Adams's cavalry reports that General Sherman has marched northward and seems to be placing his troops in the direction of this road . . . here. Colonel Adams estimates his strength at four divisions. We are not completely certain of his intentions. This weather and General Sherman's pickets have prevented us from determining his precise location, or direction of march. But his columns are no more than twelve miles from the city. We have also determined that General McPherson's corps is on the march using the more southerly route, though we are not yet certain of their intentions. In the event the enemy does advance in this direction, sir, I have already begun the placement of those troops available to obstruct these two roads. But if they attempt to drive into the city, I fear we do not have the strength to prevent that. Unless you order otherwise, sir, I have instructed one brigade to position themselves astride each of the Federal routes of march. We shall give them our best efforts, sir."

"What is our combined strength in Jackson, General?"

"I have six thousand effectives, sir. My brigade and the reinforcements that arrived here several days ago. It is rumored . . . forgive me, sir . . . but I was told by several officers just arrived, that the president is calling forth a considerable number of troops to be marched here from the east. I was informed as well by General Pemberton that you would personally bring significant reinforcements here, to protect the city."

Johnston leaned heavily on the table, stared at the map through watery eyes.

"Yes, I know all about General Pemberton's expectations. His . . . dreams. The general has beseeched me to bring the entire Confederacy to his aid. It is the case with every general in every theater of this war. No place is more important than their own command." He paused, fought the weakness, did not need to tell Gregg anything about Pemberton. "I anticipate receiving those reinforcements within the next few days. No doubt this weather shall delay their arrival. But it will also delay any move the enemy is determined to make. You have done the right thing, General. It is likely that General Sherman has been ordered to cut our communication lines to Vicksburg. It is a wise tactic. But by putting his attentions to railroads and telegraph lines, it is possible that General Grant has given us an opportunity. Pemberton . . . General Pemberton has a considerable force at his disposal, a force that could inflict serious damage to the enemy from that quarter. Do we know General Pemberton's precise location?"

Gregg hesitated, and Johnston stood straight, looked at him, the man's beard still flecked with wetness, tired determination in his eyes. Gregg moved his hand slowly across the map, and Johnston could feel the man's uncertainty.

"My last communication from the general came from Bovina, sir. The general has marched a considerable force to the Big Black River. If the enemy should move this way, General Pemberton will be in his rear." Gregg seemed to animate, to understand what Johnston was already thinking.

"Very well. I shall prepare an order to be sent by the most effective means we have . . . that General Pemberton shall move to force an engagement with Grant's forces where he may find them. If he strikes the enemy with zeal, while we occupy them from this direction, we may accomplish what General Pemberton insists is our primary goal."

"Yes, sir. We may very well destroy the enemy."

Johnston looked at Gregg again.

"I'm not sure General Pemberton knows how to accomplish that. His **primary** goal is only to hold fast to Vicksburg. In that, he is in complete agreement with the president. It is their obsession." The words stopped, and he looked again at the map, had said more than Gregg needed to know. Yes, he thought, it is their obsession. It is not mine. Vicksburg is indefensible, no matter what "dreams" General Pemberton enjoys.

JACKSON, MISSISSIPPI
MAY 14, 1863

The rains had continued through the night, the misery of the weather equal to the misery Johnston could not avoid through a sleepless night. With the dawn had come a steady flow of reports from the two roads that led west, the cavalry doing all it could to determine just what the enemy intended.

He rose from the lush comfort of the bed, dressed

quickly, made every effort to offer the usual display for his staff, for anyone who came to his headquarters, that this man was clearly in command. The shirt was clean and white, the uniform one of several from his trunk, the staff making every effort to prepare every piece of the display. Even the plume had been replaced, the hat once more set upon his head before the dressing mirror, Johnston eyeing the sash, adjusting, the last detail in its place before he would meet with anyone beyond his own aides.

The breakfast was removed, the teacup drained, and Johnston moved out into the spray of mist that engulfed the veranda. The rains had grown harder, a dismal fog that seemed to crush the town, few citizens in the streets, the only movement coming from a team of artillery, splashing slowly toward the west. The defenses of Jackson were fair, but not strong, and Johnston considered that now, tried to think through the shivers that still plagued him. Gregg is a good man, he thought. If there is opportunity, he must act on it. The enemy cannot move quickly in these conditions, and if they move against us here, we will have the advantage of the defenses. It will allow us the time we require. And that might be the best gift of all.

He saw horsemen now, a limp flag, a half-dozen men moving close, recognized Gregg. Johnston glanced toward the doorway, moved inside, drier, warmer, knew Gregg would not have come himself if it were not essential. Johnston moved into the small office, looked at the map, studied what he already knew, rehearsed in his mind what he had already decided to do. The boots thundered across the wooden porch, aides welcoming Gregg, who was there now, dripping streams of water.

"Sir . . . my respects, sir."

"Tell me what is happening, General."

Gregg took a deep breath.

"The enemy is advancing on both avenues. I have deployed the brigades as you approved, sir. With the rain, his progress will be slow. They will not give us a strong fight with wet powder. But I anticipate pulling back to the city's defenses. It is our best opportunity to hold the enemy in place long enough for General Pemberton to strike him from behind."

Gregg was breathless, animated, and Johnston nodded, knew that Gregg actually believed what he was saying.

"Do we know the whereabouts of Grant's remaining corps, the troops under General McClernand?"

Gregg's movements suddenly stopped, the man pondering the question.

"I am not certain of that, sir. The cavalry—"

"Yes, the cavalry has not been able to find those people. Is it possible that General Grant has read the basic manual on military tactics, and placed General McClernand's troops to the west, with the purpose of holding back any threat to the rear of Sherman and McPherson?"

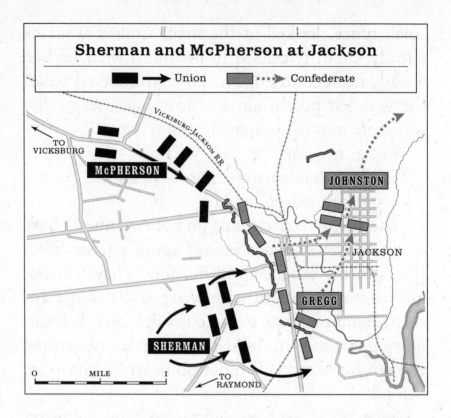

Sherman and McPherson at Jackson

Union   Confederate

TO VICKSBURG

VICKSBURG-JACKSON RR

McPHERSON

JOHNSTON

JACKSON

GREGG

SHERMAN

MILE

TO RAYMOND

"Yes, sir, that is possible. But you did order General Pemberton to advance with all vigor."

Johnston said nothing, thought of Gregg's words, **wet powder**. There will be no vigor on this day.

"You will continue to do what you can to delay the enemy's approach. That will allow us the time to move the stores, to pull as much as we can out of the city."

"Sir?"

"You will delay the enemy as long as practicable, General. Is that not sufficiently clear?"

Gregg seemed uncertain now, said, "Yes, sir. Most clear. But . . . remove the stores?"

"That is not your concern. Go. Offer the enemy your 'best measure.'"

Gregg stiffened, saluted.

"We shall do so, sir."

"Do not sacrifice your men needlessly, General. When you are pressed into the city's last line, you will order a withdrawal, as you wisely did at Raymond. You will serve as a rear guard to cover the movement of the rest of those forces we have here."

"Withdrawal? Forgive me, sir. Withdraw . . . where?"

"We shall make every effort to remove from the city anything of use to this army. That includes every capable man in this command." He looked down at the map. "We will march north, using the railroad if possible, and the roadway toward Canton."

"Sir . . ."

"You have your orders."

Gregg made a short bow, moved out of the room, more boots clattering across the wooden floor, shouts and orders taking Gregg and his staff outside. Johnston moved to a chair, sat slowly, ignored the map, the orders to Gregg drifting out of his mind. He stared toward the lone window, his mind filling with the hiss of driving rain. Time, he thought. He will give us time. It is, after all, the only plan.

He wanted to stand, to return to his room, the rumble in his stomach relentless. But the soothing rain held him in the chair. He tried to see the state capitol, the hotel facing that way, but the foggy wetness on the windowpanes distorted his view. It is this way everywhere, both armies, he thought. There will be little movement, little activity today. He thought of Pemberton, tried to picture him in his mind, barely recalled what he looked like. You would have us waste everything we have . . . holding on to that town. That would so please the president, would do so much to give rise to grand headlines. It is foolishness. Vicksburg cannot be held. It would be far more useful to remove every piece of defensive strength and deploy it elsewhere, closer perhaps to Tennessee. But that would cause outrage in Richmond. And, by all means, we must not agitate the president.

He struggled to stand, held himself up on the table, ignored the map still, saw his aides watching from outside, obedient, efficient, prepared for anything he would tell them to do. It is already done, he thought. We will withdraw as quickly as practicable, see to our own care. If the president wishes me to do more than that, he should come here himself, see what kind of foolishness he proposes, see the hopelessness of the task I have been assigned.

He thought of the wire, the last thing he had done the night before, the last task before he sought the comfort of the white sheets. The wire had gone to Richmond, sent soon after three couriers had ridden off into the rainy night, each carrying a copy of the order to Pemberton to bring forward his army, to engage Grant's army wherever he would be. But even then, he knew the order would serve no purpose, that Pemberton would obey only Jefferson Davis, both men holding tightly to the absurd fantasy of protecting Vicksburg. And so I will be ignored. There will be no attack, no crushing blow to Grant's forces, no means to prevent the enemy from shoving through General Gregg's defenses. And Vicksburg, he thought. It makes no difference how much value Pemberton or Davis or anyone else assigns to that place. There is no need for reinforcements and no need for a grand stand, no need to sacrifice this army. No matter those fantasies, I have given the president the most simple of truths.

"I am too late."

CHAPTER TWELVE

SHERMAN

JACKSON, MISSISSIPPI
MAY 14, 1863

The rains had finally halted near eleven in the morning, two full hours after the first wave of artillery fire had announced to all that Sherman's men had struck the rebel defenses. He had wondered if there would be a confrontation at all, the weather so utterly miserable that no infantry could make use of their muskets. For a while it was exactly that, a sluggish and careful advance against rebel troops who were hunkered down in well-designed earthworks, the only real fight coming from the trading of artillery shells. But with the rain blowing past, the infantry had gained momentum, musket fire adding to the power of the big guns. From the north, Sherman could hear more artillery, McPherson's men. But Sherman stayed close to his own men, knew that McPherson would do what had to be done. Grant knew that as well, and so Grant had stayed close to Sherman.

By early afternoon it was over, the rebels pulling away, a surprise. Sherman had anticipated something more, had ordered his lead division under James Tuttle to hold back if the forces they encountered were too strong, too well fortified. But Tuttle's men had pushed onward with only a brief burst of resistance, a scattering of rebel sharpshooters doing just enough damage to slow Tuttle's advance. Grant had been as surprised as his commanders, had fully expected the capital city to be stoutly defended, if for no other reason than pride. Though rebel artillery continued to thunder into Tuttle's advance, those guns soon quieted, rebel artillerymen leaving only a few pieces behind to retard the last surge of Tuttle's attack. Almost immediately, the reports came back to Sherman that the bridges were intact, and Sherman knew it was not some clumsy error by a rebel commander, but the rain. Wooden bridges could not be fired in such a downpour, and so Sherman's men had simply marched over swollen creeks they might otherwise have had to ford.

When the guns first engaged that morning, Sherman had sought a strategic advantage, had ordered one regiment to make a flanking maneuver to the right, to sweep in behind, probing for some opening that might open a way for more troops, an attempt to cut the enemy fortifications off from behind. Those men, the 95th Ohio, had felt their way cautiously, expecting at least a burst of fire from a waiting line of skirmishers. But there was no opposition at all, the rebel works they approached virtually empty. After capturing the few rebel troops and a handful of artillery pieces, the Ohioans called forward the rest of Tuttle's division with cheers of relief, the raucous ovations for a surprisingly easy victory over an enemy who had most certainly chosen to withdraw rather than make a stand. By midafternoon, Tuttle's men were parading unmolested into the heart of Jackson, Sherman and Grant close behind them.

Sherman pointed, but Grant had already seen the two horsemen riding toward them, one, the boy, holding clumsily to the reins, struggling to keep upright in the saddle. Sherman didn't smile, was not at all comfortable with Fred Grant's presence, a needless danger. But Grant seemed oblivious to that, still welcomed the boy's presence, that peculiar rite of passage from a father eager to see something of a **man** in his oldest son. With Fred was Cadwallader, the reporter, who held back on the reins, allowed the boy to move closer, to be the first to make his report. The words came in a flood of panting, nonsensical at first, and even Sherman couldn't help a smile.

"Father! We almost made it! We were so close! It was ours for the taking! A supreme trophy, something to bring home. Mother would be so proud. She'd have to be. We had it . . . so close!"

Grant held up a hand.

"Slow down, boy." He glanced at Cadwallader, Sherman watching the reporter as well, still not trusting him. Fred pointed back, and Sherman looked that way, saw the Stars and Stripes rising up the tallest flagpole in the city, high over the capitol building, heard cheers from gathering troops. Cadwallader kept silent, would allow the boy the adventure of telling the tale.

"Father, Mr. Cadwallader and I made haste to reach the rebel flag, flying right up there, right on the capitol! But when we entered the building, a soldier met us on the stairs. He had beaten us to it! It was the worst luck, Father. Only a minute sooner and it would have been ours!"

Grant stared at the flag now flying above the dome and said, "Whose flag is that? What regiment?"

Fred didn't respond, obviously uncertain, and Cadwallader said, "Fifty-ninth Indiana, sir. Fellows had a bit more hop in their steps than us poor civilians."

Sherman felt a sudden burn.

"That's Crockett's division. You're telling me that McPherson's boys beat my boys into the city?"

Cadwallader seemed to make note of Sherman's outburst, and immediately Sherman held back, cursed himself for revealing anything to a reporter.

Cadwallader nodded slowly. "Yes, General. It seems this particular race was won by the Seventeenth Corps."

Grant said, "Makes no difference. We're in the city. From all I can observe, we own the place. Didn't expect that. What in blazes happened to Joe Johnston?"

A pair of couriers was moving toward them now, easing through soldiers marching past, a column of Sherman's men adding to the forces already in the city. Sherman saw another horseman, a staff officer emerging from the main avenue that led to the capitol.

Sherman said, "Perhaps we're about to find out. That's Major Burgess, Buckland's man."

The couriers held back, recognized they were outranked by the third man, and Burgess rode up close to Grant, his eyes on Sherman.

"Sirs! Forgive my intrusion. General Buckland offers his compliments, and reports that, by all indications, the rebels have fled the city. There is a rear guard withdrawing to the north."

Grant motioned to the pair of couriers, permission to approach. Sherman saw the eagerness in their faces, men who carried "good news."

Grant said, "Report, gentlemen."

The senior man spoke up, older, a sergeant.

"Sir, General McPherson offers his respects and reports the same, sir. A sizable column of rebels is moving northward. The general inquires if you wish him to pursue their retreat."

Grant pondered the question, looked at Sherman, shook his head.

"No. General Johnston has no wish to engage us this day, for reasons I do not quite understand. He has something of a head start, and any pursuit could risk ambush. But clearly, the enemy did not believe his forces adequate to the task of holding us away from this city. We will accept the gift he has provided. There is clearly some tactical brilliance at work here that I do not comprehend."

Sherman looked at Grant, a low chuckle at Grant's rare show of sarcasm. "Perhaps it is as simple as that," he said. "The enemy didn't have the strength to defend the place. No need to fight if you know you can't win. I would imagine there are some unhappy civilians about. We should be watchful of that. One musket fired from a rooftop . . . could cause us a **problem**."

Grant turned to one of the couriers.

"Sergeant, return to General McPherson. Offer him my congratulations on a fine effort this morning. . . ." He glanced at Sherman. "And, for besting his **competition** in securing the enemy's flag. Be sure the general knows to guard that flag with some care. It could be . . . useful at some point."

The men saluted, turned, rode away quickly. It

did not escape Sherman that McPherson had sent two couriers, an engineer's calculations, two men with twice the chance of surviving, should the rebels still pose a threat. Grant looked toward Sherman, silent permission, and Sherman understood the courtesy. Grant would not issue an order to Sherman's own man.

Sherman said to the officer, "Major, return to General Buckland. I assume General Tuttle is in his presence. Offer my congratulations . . . and those of General Grant. Instruct General Tuttle to position his division with an eye toward encampment. But patrols should be deployed, houses and businesses searched. We shall have no surprises."

"Certainly, sir." The major hesitated, and Sherman could see there was more. "Sir . . . begging your pardon, but there is some commotion among the men, some protest, that we do more than . . . occupy this place. It is after all a prominent city to the rebel cause."

Sherman looked at Grant, who pulled out a cigar, rolling it in his fingers.

"My instructions from the War Department were explicit on this point," Grant said.

Sherman felt a letdown, knew his men would have their fire up, that trying to keep them in check would be nearly impossible. Sherman lowered his voice, a useless effort to keep his words between the two of them.

"It will be hard to hold these men back, Grant. Look where we are, for God's sake."

"I said nothing about holding them back. I believe the exact instructions I received from General Halleck were to 'handle the rebels without gloves.' Need I be more clear?"

Sherman pulled out his own cigar, the letdown replaced by a jolt of enthusiasm. The War Department, he thought. Someone there might actually understand what we're doing out here.

He saw a wide-eyed stare from McPherson's staff officer.

"You heard him, Major Burgess. I wish this town secured from any rebel miscreants, and we must see to it that nothing of military value remains."

Grant lit the cigar, said quietly, "Keep an eye on them, Sherman. Make good use of the provosts. Be sure the junior officers maintain control over their men. Nothing shall be done to harm civilians, is that understood?"

"Then perhaps it would be helpful if you remained with this command a while longer. We should make our presence known, you and me, be visible to the men, accompany some of the patrols. If there is to be discipline, we must be seen." He realized Cadwallader had moved up behind them, was most certainly hearing every word. Sherman hated the man for being there at all, knew that whatever he said to Grant would be etched hard in the reporter's brain. He aimed his words at Cadwallader now. "The instructions from Washington seem clear enough. Certainly, we must obey General Halleck."

Grant nodded silently, ignored Cadwallader, smoke from the cigar drifting away. He turned now, called out to the staffs trailing behind.

"We shall move through the city, ensure that the regimental commanders place their encampments with an eye toward defense, should the enemy return. We shall instruct them on the deployment of patrols, to check every home, every merchant for rebel stragglers. No quarter shall be given to anyone who attempts an assault on our troops." Grant seemed to notice Cadwallader now. "Perhaps you should escort Fred back to a place of safety. There could still be sharpshooters about, and Julia would never forgive me."

Cadwallader understood exactly what Grant was saying, the request not a request at all. The man made a short bow from his perch on the horse, nothing pleasant in his response.

"As you wish, sir."

They had gone with the troops through several businesses, some abandoned completely, some occupied by angry, defiant men. But so far there had been nothing dangerous, no potshots from poorly aimed flintlocks. The only threats were verbal, cursing citizens, who spewed out their anger and then wisely withdrew. What Sherman saw from most of the citizens was resignation, a matter-of-factness to the Federal capture of the city, many of the people already adjusting to what they must have believed would be a permanent occupation. Sherman knew better. Johnston had abandoned the city because he could not defend it, and if that decision had come only because the rebels were seriously outnumbered, Sherman knew that Johnston had the authority to call upon reinforcements and possibly turn the tables. A fight over a city this size would be destructive in the extreme, and with so many places for sharpshooters to hide, this kind of fight would be costly to both sides. If the Federals prevailed, and swept Johnston away, holding the city was still a useless option. The city was, after all, just a city. That it was Mississippi's capital gave it symbolic value. But Jackson had no more strategic value to Grant's army than did Nashville or Baton Rouge. To suffer casualties for a symbol might have appealed to those commanders who still believed in the chivalry of war, that any capitol building was as valuable as the men who defended it. Sherman and Grant had long ago escaped that. Once Grant had appraised the positioning of the two corps, McPherson had been ordered to prepare the next morning to retrace his steps westward. Sherman's men would remain in the city for a short time, with one very specific assignment.

Sherman understood that any foray through a rebel capital was a tricky affair, and not just from straggling snipers. He knew that everything they did within the city would be examined, criticized, praised, or condemned. He also knew that any condemnation would be aimed squarely at Grant. Though some of the troops would strike out with predictable violence, Sherman had to maintain some kind of control. Any suggestion that any massacre of civilians had taken place, whether justified or not, could cost both of them their commands.

G rant rode beside him, the streets glowing from fires that dotted each block. The orders had been explicit, that any kind of machine shop or factory be put to the torch, and for a while, those orders had been obeyed. But in any city with so many buildings of wood, fires spread, and already it was obvious that entire city blocks were going up in flames. Sherman had given orders to his regimental commanders to avoid mass destruction, orders that even the best-intentioned men would have difficulty obeying.

Daylight was fading rapidly, the glow of the fires brighter now, reflections on every window. They rode down a narrow street lined with small shops, many with second-story residences, curtained windows, a few half-hidden faces watching them pass. Sherman could not help the anxiety that Grant had no business wandering through this place. With the darkness, the streets had become ghostly, the flickering firelight dancing on every wall, the sky around them glowing orange. Out beyond the city, the roads to the south and east were busy with a one-way flow of traffic, refugees who chose flight, their wagons piled high, tugged along by horses too unfit for use by the rebel army. Of those who remained, many were soldiers, rebel wounded, cared for now by Sherman's medical people, alongside the occasional civilian doctor. They moved past an alleyway, and Sherman's head jerked that way, studying, seeking some threat in the fading light. The troops who moved with them had already searched the space, and he heard voices now, one man emerging, reporting something to a waiting lieutenant, the officer then jogging over to the parade of horsemen.

"Sirs, there are wounded men back there, the alleyway, a dozen or so. One rebel doctor, and we have him under guard. Do you wish me to arrest him?"

Grant deferred to Sherman, had done so all afternoon. These were, after all, Sherman's men.

"No. Use your brain, Lieutenant. If those were our boys, would you expect the enemy to haul

away our doctors? Bring up our own medical people, make sure any wounded we find are cared for."

The man saluted and ran back toward the alley,
giving the commands.

Sherman looked at Grant, who stared ahead, as
though not paying attention to anything Sherman
did. Sherman knew better.

"Sometimes I wonder who trains these damned
officers."

Grant smoked a cigar, nodded lazily.

"Let it go. You took care of it. They're learning.
We get better at this every day. All of us."

The street widened, a small square, and Sherman saw a cluster of rebel prisoners, sitting in a
tight mass, a half-dozen guards standing with fixed
bayonets. Some of the rebels carried wounds, ban-
daged arms, a bloody rag on one scalp. The officer
in charge of the guard snapped upright, acknowledging the two generals, and said, "General Sherman! General Grant! It is my honor to present these
prisoners, sirs! We caught these devils trying to slip
out of this building. They had given up the fight,
no doubt about that. No muskets at all. Cowards
dropped them somewhere. I guess they're not as almighty as they believe, right, sirs?"

Sherman had no energy for this kind of boasting, knew Grant despised it. Grant said nothing,
didn't look at the man at all, focused instead on his
cigar. Sherman spurred the horse toward the officer, leaned over slightly, closer to the man's face. It

was another lieutenant, the man's eyes wide, staring up into Sherman's anger.

"Get these men out on the road west. You plan on sitting with them all night? You seen the fires, Lieutenant? You thinking maybe you'll just camp right here and hope these damn buildings around you don't burn to the ground? Move out, or find a provost to take them. Now!"

The lieutenant's pride was washed away by the unexpected response, and he backed up a step, tossed up a salute.

"Yes, sir! We'll march these men right now! I had thought we should do just that, sir!"

Sherman's voice rose, a sudden flood of anger.

"You **thought**? This is a war, Lieutenant. You need to **think** about what we're doing here?"

"No, sir!"

The man turned, the guards hearing every word, the prisoners rising, and whether or not they knew who Sherman was, some of them responded by coming to attention. Sherman was surprised by that, had seen too much sullenness from rebel prisoners, a defiance that showed more hate than respect. But the lieutenant was right, these men seemingly happy to be prisoners. Sherman said nothing, eased the horse back beside Grant, who still worked the cigar. Sherman glanced toward Grant self-consciously, couldn't help wondering if Grant was measuring every move Sherman made, every order he gave.

Sherman pulled out his own cigar, lit it, said quietly, "Probably shouldn't have sliced that boy up in front of his men. But by damned, Grant, every time I see enemy prisoners . . . it just punches me. I can't look at any of 'em for very damned long without wondering what kind of stupidity is bred into these people."

Grant said nothing, and Sherman couldn't help feeling angry, his memories of Louisiana once so pleasant, now swept away by a war fought by some of the men he had considered friends. He pulled furiously at the cigar, a fog of smoke around him, and after a moment, Grant said, "Most of them are already marching west. Couple hundred at least. McPherson's got a good many. A pile of artillery, too. Dozen pieces, maybe more. Johnston just left it behind. Wish I knew what he has on his mind. Could be a whole damn rebel army gathering up north of here, waiting to put an end to this little foray of ours. We need to get moving to Vicksburg. I don't want your men cut off, so do your business here and move out west quick as you can. McClernand's probably dancing around like an angry squirrel out there, wondering how many rebel soldiers are set to bushwhack him. McPherson will get his people out that way pretty quick. I want no surprises, Sherman. We've got a job to do. You and everybody else in this command."

It was a scolding Sherman didn't need, and he realized now that Grant was already far ahead of

what had happened today, that capturing Jackson
had been a success that had nothing to do with the
city at all. Just why Johnston had withdrawn rather
than fight wasn't as important as the fact that he
was gone. Sherman wanted to say that to Grant,
the old lesson about Napoleon, hitting a divided
enemy one piece at a time. But Grant was off in
some other place, pondering some other mission,
what might happen tomorrow, or the day after that.
It was one reason Sherman had grown to love this
man, even though Grant was so very different from
him. Grant was in control of himself, kept any ti-
rades or outbursts hidden away. That's why he's in
command, he thought. Doesn't go blasting through
his officers like a keg of lit gunpowder. Sherman
thought of McPherson, suddenly realized that the
engineer had done the greatest portion of the fighting in the last few days, and, whether Sherman appreciated it or not, McPherson had driven his men
into Jackson first. Well, good for him. He's learning, too. Needs some success, gives him confidence
that he's up to the job. Sherman pulled out another
cigar and sniffed it slowly. Worry about yourself,
dammit. McPherson isn't some greenhorn fresh
from West Point. He's got confidence to spare. He
glanced at Grant, the smaller man's hat pulled low,
his half-hidden face silhouetted by the glow from
the fires. That's why he's **here**. If McPherson needed
a foot up his backside, Grant would be there. Hell,
I thought he was **here** because he liked me.

"Sirs! Up here!"

A horseman was waving at them, behind him, a handful of foot soldiers standing guard at a larger building. Rawlins was there now, moving out front, as though expecting some kind of crisis. Grant said nothing, moved the horse that way, and Sherman felt a tug in his gut, something about the soldier's urgency. He moved out closer to Rawlins, who ignored him, and Sherman returned the favor, saw one of the men holding a musket against his shoulder, aiming into the entrance of the building. Sherman touched the pistol at his belt, old instinct, and the officer said to Rawlins, "You gotta see this, sir! They're . . . it's like they're in another world. Couldn't care less about us."

Grant was up beside him now, dismounted, Sherman doing the same. Rawlins gave a hard whisper.

"Are they armed? Is it an ambush? The general cannot be put in danger!"

The officer laughed now, surprising Sherman, who stepped toward the open doorway. The man with the musket lowered it, started to laugh as well, and Sherman heard a strange chatter, the rattle of machinery. There was light coming through the doorway and Sherman still had his hand on the pistol, stepped closer, peered in.

The room was large, open, filled with rows of small tables, and at each one sat a woman. Each one worked with some piece of foot-cranked machinery, some of it for sewing, some winding great spools of thread into twists, stacks of cloth beside each of them. On the tables the cloth was taking shape, squares of thin canvas joining together, some being rolled onto wooden dowels. Grant moved past Sherman now, was fully in the lantern light, hands on his hips, the cigar clamped between his teeth. Sherman stepped up beside him, saw what Grant saw, the women working dutifully, completely occupied by their labor, not one of them paying any attention to the men in blue who stood before them. Grant glanced at Sherman, puzzled, and Sherman shrugged, kept his eyes on the women along the first row of tables. They still ignored the soldiers, and behind Sherman, more men filed in, muskets ready, something no doubt ordered by Rawlins.

Grant put his arms in the air and shouted out, "See here!"

Gradually the faces looked up, and now the machinery began to slow, the room growing more quiet, then suddenly silent. Sherman saw the faces eyeing them, no fear, no emotion at all. He noticed the canvas now, the larger pieces embossed with block letters, the initials **CSA**. Sherman understood now.

"They're making tents."

"Well of course we're making tents. It's our job." The woman's voice came from the back of the room, the woman standing, clearly annoyed at the interruption. "Last week we were to make blankets, but there was no wool. You expect us to do our jobs properly if you won't give us the right material?"

Sherman had no idea how to respond to the woman, waited for Grant to say something. After a moment Grant said, "Ladies, I regret that we are not the army for whom you labor. However, I also regret that this equipment is too valuable to be left in place." The women began to stand now, low sounds, most of them finally understanding just who these soldiers might be.

The woman in the back said, "All right, so if you all be Yankees, what would you do with us? Are we to be savaged, then? Butchered?"

The words brought small cries from some of the others, a sudden ripple of fear spreading through the room.

Grant said, "No, my God. No." He seemed to think a moment, another glance at Sherman. "You ladies may take with you all you can carry of the material here, the canvas. Take it away, use it for your families. I suggest you move swiftly. There are a considerable number of fires burning through the city. You must see to your families."

They stared, seemed to absorb what Grant was saying, some of them studying the blue uniform. Sherman could see confusion now, blending through the fear.

Grant looked at him, said, "Once they're gone, out of danger, put this place to the torch."

Grant backed away, the guards moving up closer behind Sherman.

"You heard him, ladies. Carry what you can, then skedaddle. With haste."

The confusion was replaced by understanding, and bolts of material rose up, slung onto shoulders, some of the women with their arms full, and quickly they began to file past him. He avoided their looks, had no interest in suffering the wrath of Confederate women.

Grant spent the night at the Bowman House, the proprietor not hiding the fact that Grant was using the same bedroom occupied by Joe Johnston the night before. With the morning, McPherson's troops were on the move, retracing their steps away from Jackson, the drive that would link those troops up alongside McClernand. Sherman would follow, but there would be a day's delay. Grant had left him in command of the captured city, with one very explicit order: Any piece of equipment, any machinery or warehouse or store of goods that could be of use to the enemy was to be destroyed. The next morning, Grant rode away from the city, moving out to supervise his other two corps, to put them into position for the next confrontation. With most of the civilians out of the way, Sherman began the morning by giving the same order to his officers that Grant had given to him. No matter the instructions to focus only on military assets, the men who carried the torches were not so selective. By day's end, most of Jackson lay in ashes.

He led the column back across the same bridges his men had swarmed over days before, passing by makeshift hospitals, Federal doctors working alongside their Confederate counterparts, still treating the wounded from both sides. Most of the walking wounded were already gone, marching out to the southwest, under guard, the Federal army's newest prisoners. As Sherman led his men along muddy roads, he couldn't avoid the wreckage that lay scattered along the way, muskets, backpacks, bedrolls, and broken artillery pieces. He thought again of the prisoners, men now marching to the landings at the great river. Eventually they would board steamers, transports, would be taken to Federal prisons far upriver. Along the way, they would march along the same roads that Grant's army had used inland. He studied the countryside, as he had done from the beginning, this beautiful, terrible place, some of it like Louisiana, so familiar to him, but much of it very different. Mississippi was more rolling, some places green and lush, clean and beautiful, more farms than swamplands. But there were similarities to Louisiana as well, the plantations, thick white columns across the verandas of glorious mansions, and behind, long lines of slave quarters. By now, nearly all of the grand homes and smaller structures were either empty or destroyed altogether. Sherman could not avoid thinking of the prisoners from this very place, Mississippi men marching through their own land, land swarmed over now by blue-clad troops. Do you need to be told, he thought, that this is your own damned fault? Why else are we here? It's an **army,** for God's sake, and we're fighting a **war.** And so your glorious plantations have been looted and burned, your slaves freed, the towns we march through half empty, people who scurry away like mice, terrified of us. Now all of those prisoners we've grabbed will sit in some fenced-in hole until this war is over. And a great many more will join them before this is through. How many will it require? How many men must we haul northward, until their leaders understand that we can't be driven away? How many will we kill before they are made to understand? There is nothing of decency and chivalry in this; it is not a **spat** between gentlemen. I have one job to do, and by God, I am no gentleman.

CHAPTER THIRTEEN

PEMBERTON

NEAR EDWARD'S STATION,
MISSISSIPPI
MAY 14, 1863

In directing this move, I do not think you fully comprehend the position that Vicksburg will be left in, but I will comply at once with your order.

The message had gone out to Johnston with a flurry of frustration, the response to Johnston's call for Pemberton to strike the rear of what was presumed to be Sherman's corps, also presumed to be stationary at the crossroads town of Clinton. But the cavalry had their reports as well, Wirt Adams providing intelligence that the

Federals were in fact engaged at Jackson, a force that included at least part of Sherman's corps. If Sherman was no longer at Clinton, then Johnston's order made no sense. But Clinton, like so many of the crossroads towns between Vicksburg and the capital city, could be invaluable to the maneuver of either army. And Johnston's order seemed to Pemberton to be explicit enough.

He left his camp at the Big Black River with a hard knot in his stomach, a column of troops to his front, men quickly exhausted by the rain and the slogging march on muddy roads. The order from Johnston to attack Grant's army had amazed him, but Pemberton was a subordinate after all, and Johnston's order would be obeyed. But those orders were in direct contradiction to the long-standing command he had received from Jefferson Davis, that Vicksburg should be protected at all costs. The farther Pemberton rode from Vicksburg, the harder the knot in his gut. At the very least, Pemberton had made some effort to obey both men, leaving two divisions at Vicksburg itself, preparation to hold off any surprise move should Grant decide to order an attack from the river. Pemberton had no idea how many Federal troops might still remain on the west side of the Mississippi. All intelligence from that quarter had been cut off by the efficiency of the Federal gunboats, and the complete unwillingness of the Confederate command west of the river to offer Pemberton any assistance at all. It was an agonizing reality that those troops were far more concerned with the possibility of a threat that might arise in their own backyards than in anything happening across the wide, muddy river. The need for Pemberton to satisfy both of his superiors only added to his fears, that with his army now divided, neither part had the power required to accomplish what he had been ordered to do.

Pemberton had not slept at all since leaving the Big Black River. With so much training in engineering, he had always believed that an army's greatest power lay in the overwhelming defense of a good position. The Big Black carved a deep gulch through the countryside and so seemed to him to be the perfect barrier to prevent Grant or anyone else from advancing unmolested toward Vicksburg. But now that marvelous security was behind him, and he continued the slow march toward the place Johnston had ordered him to go. He had received nothing else in the way of intelligence that Sherman might still be waiting at Clinton, all faces turned to the east, that Sherman's backside would be unprotected, ripe for a surprise assault. The reports from those few cavalry patrols that probed for Grant's army remained infuriatingly vague. Even Colonel Adams seemed convinced that the most reliable reports had come from the fighting close to Jackson, that most of Grant's army had moved that way, the sound of heavy guns echoing across the rolling land west of the city, alert patrols reporting back to Adams, then to Pemberton exactly what he had hoped to hear. If Grant's army had chosen to launch its assault against the capital city, Vicksburg might actually be spared altogether. At the very least, a serious bloodletting at Jackson might so weaken Grant that the Federal forces might salvage what they could by marching northward, vacating Mississippi completely. It made little sense to Pemberton that Johnston expected him to attack an army that was not where Johnston claimed it to be, especially since the cavalry gave every confirmation that many of the troops engaging Johnston at the capital belonged to Sherman. But Pemberton had received nothing else from Johnston that amended the order to advance on Clinton. As he rode through the rain, staring into misty fog and the backs of his tired men, he tried to imagine what Johnston was hoping to accomplish. It was possible that a stalemate in front of Jackson could give Pemberton an opportunity after all, striking into the rear of the Federal position there while Johnston engaged them from the front. It was the only faint glimmer of optimism Pemberton could muster. If his own subordinates could move with efficiency, make the difficult march before Grant's troops knew he was coming, this entire campaign might result in a rousing Southern victory.

He didn't believe that for a single minute.

The rain peppered his coat, a stream of water sliding down his back. The horse plodded as slowly as the men in front of him; behind him his staff was mostly silent, following Pemberton with the same lack of enthusiasm Pemberton had felt even as he encamped at the Big Black. We are blind, he thought, stumbling in pitch darkness toward a rendezvous with a general who cares nothing for Vicksburg. Regardless of what Johnston achieves at the capital, he would have me strip Vicksburg clean of any defenses, march my entire force out here on a dangerous escapade that would serve the purposes that exist only in Joe Johnston's mind. And what purposes are those? Glory? Victory? Some slap at the authority of President Davis? And why? Can he not understand the value of Vicksburg?

He wiped the wetness from his face, a useless gesture, stared again at the backs of the men who marched in front of him, the road still deep with mud. That is one blessing, I suppose. There is no dust. But what shall I tell these men? We search for the enemy, we obey our command to engage him . . . if we can find him. On ground of our choosing or his? I suppose that is not to be my concern. And how many is he? We are . . . sixteen thousand, perhaps, those of us east of the Big Black. Scattered along several roads, facing every direction, expecting . . . what? Should we fear an attack? From an enemy as blind as we are? Shall we stumble into each other like crutchless cripples, and keep our hopes high that the other is more cripple than we are? And all the while, Vicksburg sits as a magnificent prize, waiting to be plucked. And my president will not want to hear why I disobeyed him, why I chose instead to push good men out across open roads pursuing an enemy who seems to know more of this country than I do.

His depression had become overwhelming. He glanced upward, no hint yet of darkness, did not look at the pocket watch. Mid-afternoon, he thought. Hours before darkness, but I will not destroy the spirit of these men by marching them into utter exhaustion. Up ahead, he could see the small homes and shops of the rail depot at Edward's Station, a logical place for him to camp for the night. There was a telegraph station there, as at all the rail crossings, and he knew it was important to keep Johnston aware of his disposition, whether Johnston could receive those messages or not. No, I cannot rely on that wire to be intact, he thought. The direct line is certainly severed, or at least in Federal hands. Any message must be transmitted by some indirect route. Which route would that be? I must rely on those who deal with such things. Perhaps we should rely on couriers, and hope that they can ride with enough skill to avoid the enemy. But then, by the time any message is received, it is obsolete.

The staff trailed behind him, and he halted the horse, jerked it to one side, faced his aides.

"Stop here. Order the columns to halt, and prepare to camp. I will not march these men to death in this mud. Are there rations available? Did we consider that, for God's sake?"

Memminger rode closer, wore the same weary expression as the men around him.

"The wagons are far behind, sir. Should I send a courier to bring them up?"

"How far behind?"

Memminger looked down, painfully hesitant.

"I don't know exactly, sir. It is possible they have not yet been ordered out of Vicksburg."

Pemberton closed his eyes, drooped in the saddle.

"That would have been prudent, yes? To include a supply train with the march of an army?"

"Yes, sir. I awaited your order, and when you didn't . . . I assumed, sir, that you had issued the order elsewhere. Colonel Waddy assumed the same."

Pemberton didn't respond, rolled the man's words through his brain, one more detail of command, someone's failure . . . **his** failure . . . to authorize the obvious.

"Next time, Major, do not hesitate to inquire if such orders have been issued. I cannot be expected to wrap my hands around every detail."

Pemberton turned the horse, moved slowly toward the closest house, then abruptly stopped. This is madness, he thought. There is risk here in every move we make, and we have no control over our fate. He pulled the horse around, saw Waddy moving up close beside Memminger.

"I will take refuge in that house. Offer our respects to the owner, if he is to be found, and request use of his rooms. Then send word to my senior commanders, division and brigade, and have them meet me here. I must know their thoughts about our . . . expedition, about the orders I am to follow."

"Sir? **All** the senior commanders?"

"Is there some confusion about my order, Colonel?"

Waddy took his time responding.

"If I understand, sir, the commanding general wishes to assemble—"

Pemberton's voice rose, silencing the man.

"Bring me the generals. All of them! Anyone who can be located. I'm not going to place this army in further jeopardy without a council."

He turned away again, spurred the horse toward the house, heard the bugles, the first calls for the columns to halt.

"The leading and greater duty of this army is the protection of Vicksburg. Does anyone doubt that? Is that not why we have an army assembled in this part of Mississippi?" He paused. "You have all seen the order communicated to me by General Johnston? I have obeyed with some reluctance, a reluctance that continues to grow. If we engage the enemy now, a defeat could be of grave consequences. We must have the ability to make a rapid retreat to Vicksburg, should the need arise." There were some nods, all from the less senior commanders, the men who still showed him a hint of respect. He looked toward the far side of the room toward the cavalry commander. "Colonel Adams, do we know any more of the disposition of those enemy troops who are supposed to be awaiting us at Clinton? Or rather, those forces we are supposed to assault, with complete surprise?"

Adams sat with his back against a wall, seemed to appraise the others, a dozen men, some sitting on the floor, the more senior division commanders in chairs. Adams stared at his open palms, said, "As I reported earlier, sir, General Sherman appears to be engaged at Jackson. General McPherson's corps is there as well. McClernand's corps appears to be to our southeast, and there is one division, we believe, more to the south, near Dillon's Plantation. It is likely that McClernand has been charged with protecting the enemy's lines of supply, or is positioned as a general reserve. He is certainly providing the enemy with a screen, which could very well prevent us from doing what General Johnston has ordered us to do."

Loring stood now, and Pemberton dreaded this, knew that Loring would choose the opposite position from anything Pemberton believed.

William Loring had much the same background

as Pemberton, experience in the Seminole Wars, had lost an arm in Mexico, and had begun his service to the Confederacy in the East. But Loring had an indiscreet temper and seemed to relish controversy, so much so that the year before, a sharp disagreement between Loring and Stonewall Jackson had cost Loring his command in Virginia. To placate Stonewall, Loring had been sent to Mississippi. If Loring was disagreeable by nature, he was Pemberton's problem now.

"All I know is that the commanding general of this department has ordered this army to attack the enemy's rear. I believe we should do precisely that. Or does **our** commanding general wish to record his views that disobedience is the better course?"

Loring kept his feet, stared hard at Pemberton, the tiresome defiance that Pemberton did not need. Pemberton looked at the others, saw faces turning to Loring, a mix of reactions in their expressions. Pemberton struggled with the energy to combat Loring's typical hostility.

"Is General Loring aware that if we continue eastward toward Clinton, we are increasing the distance between ourselves and Vicksburg? And if there is a full Federal division to the south at Dillon's Plantation, any farther advance to the east would put those troops on our flank, or even to our rear. By our offensive actions, we could be providing an opportunity for the enemy to cause us some embarrassment."

Loring seemed to sneer, and gazed at the others, as though measuring his support.

"I can read a map, General. I have no doubt that Colonel Adams's scouts have performed their duty, and so we know that the main body of the enemy is to the east, moving on the capital. I, for one, choose to obey a direct order from General Johnston. Assaulting the enemy from behind could aid our cause immeasurably. What else must we discuss?"

Pemberton felt his heat rising.

"I have every confidence in Colonel Adams. As you just heard, the enemy, General Sherman in particular, does not seem to be resting carelessly in Clinton with four divisions, contrary to what General Johnston asks us to believe. We know there is an engagement at Jackson, and yet our orders remain as they have been: Attack the enemy's rear at Clinton. We do not know if **anyone** is in Clinton. What we do know is that the longer we remain distant from Vicksburg, the greater the risk that we lose the one strategic location I have been ordered to defend."

Loring seemed to ignore the force of Pemberton's concerns, still looked at the others. Adams stood now and said, "I assure everyone here that the reports from my cavalry are accurate. I only suffer the disadvantage of numbers, as you all know. But we have made our best effort to keep a watchful eye on the enemy's movements. It is possible that we have an opportunity at Dillon's Plantation. If a single Federal division is isolated there, they cannot believe they are under any threat. That could provide the opportunity to carry out General Johnston's order in the most practicable way. Destroying a Federal division would certainly have a negative effect on General Grant's zeal for campaigning. We do know he is being closely watched by his superiors in Washington."

Loring seemed to have far more respect for Adams than he did Pemberton, and Pemberton saw a slight nod. Pemberton said, "My preference is to withdraw back to the safety of the Big Black and await developments to our front. I understand that would place me in direct disobedience to General Johnston. Do any of you not see the wisdom of adhering to our primary mission of protecting Vicksburg?"

Loring pointed toward him with his single arm.

"**Your** mission? Mine is to defeat the enemy, wherever he may be."

"**Yours** is to obey your commander."

"My commander is General Johnston. Who is yours?"

Pemberton clenched his fists, knew this was a battle he could not win. The eyes of the men around him gave the message clearly, that a majority favored advancing eastward. General Stevenson rose now, seemed to be a calming influence on Loring, aimed a hard stare that silenced him, then Stevenson said, "Sir, it is quite likely that, through no fault of his own, General Johnston's orders are too far removed from current conditions. The enemy is most likely not in Clinton, as you say. All reports indicate a sharp engagement is taking place at Jackson. Thus, with our forces already out here, east of the Big Black, and with the enemy now making their assault on the capital, perhaps we should use the opportunity presented us to march southward, and drive a strong wedge through the Federal supply lines. If General Grant cannot supply his army, he will have no choice but to reconsider his entire campaign. General Johnston can find no fault with that, surely. Inflicting damage upon the enemy is our primary goal, sir. As deeply as you hold to the notion of defending Vicksburg, I would offer that defeating Grant accomplishes that goal in the best way possible."

Pemberton glanced back at Waddy, who stood near the closed doorway.

"The map, please, Colonel."

Waddy stepped forward and unrolled a thick piece of paper. Pemberton studied for a long moment, the others in the room continuing their own discussion, a low-pitched debate. His eye traced the flow of the Big Black, the network of roads that led up from Grand Gulf, any one of them a potential avenue for Grant's wagon trains. And all of them taking his army that much farther from Vicksburg.

"Am I correct that the majority of you desire to march this army eastward?"

There were murmurs, most of the men agreeing

to follow Johnston's orders, whether they had been made obsolete or not. He felt a sharp wave of uncertainty, a raging argument digging into him from the variety of opinions in the room. I cannot abandon Vicksburg, he thought. And yet, we must seek opportunity to destroy the enemy.

"This is still my command. I will not submit blindly to instructions from General Johnston that do not take into account our uncertainties. The risks are far too great. General Stevenson, though I appreciate your counsel, marching more to the south adds risk as well. We do not know the exact disposition of General McClernand's forces. We could open ourselves to a flank assault from that quarter that could devastate us piecemeal."

Loring assumed the defiance again.

"Then you would have us turn tail and scamper back to Vicksburg? At the very least, I would submit to General Stevenson's suggestion. Maneuver with an eye toward damaging the enemy must be our goal. Should we do as you propose, and abandon this position, we would be leaving General Johnston to his fate."

Loring stopped abruptly, and Pemberton heard a mumble from some of the others, knew what they were thinking. **Leaving Johnston to his fate**. Yes, the act of a man who would prefer to see his army defeated. The act of a traitor.

———

After lengthy discussion, debate and argument, the council of war concluded just before dark. The disagreements continued, a variety of opinions, some favoring Stevenson's plan to jab southward, possibly severing Grant's supply line to the Mississippi River. Others continued to insist that an attack as Johnston had ordered might be essential to the protection of the capital city, and that Johnston's very survival could depend on that kind of assistance. In the end, Pemberton had to choose, to issue the order that would decide just what these men did. The only decision he could muster was something of a compromise that satisfied no one. Thus far, in every engagement since Grant's crossing of the Mississippi, the Confederates had been outnumbered. Now a vigorous assault on the single Federal division at Dillon's Plantation could push the pendulum the other way. Whether Johnston would approve such a move was anyone's guess.

Just prior to dark, Pemberton sent his wire, giving Johnston details of just what the army was intending to do. Whether that wire could get through to the capital, no one really knew. When Johnston did learn of Pemberton's decision, it mattered little. The fight for Jackson had ended hours before Pemberton's council of war, Johnston's troops abandoning the city completely. Though Johnston issued Pemberton another order, that the two men join their forces at the town of Clinton, west of Jackson, it

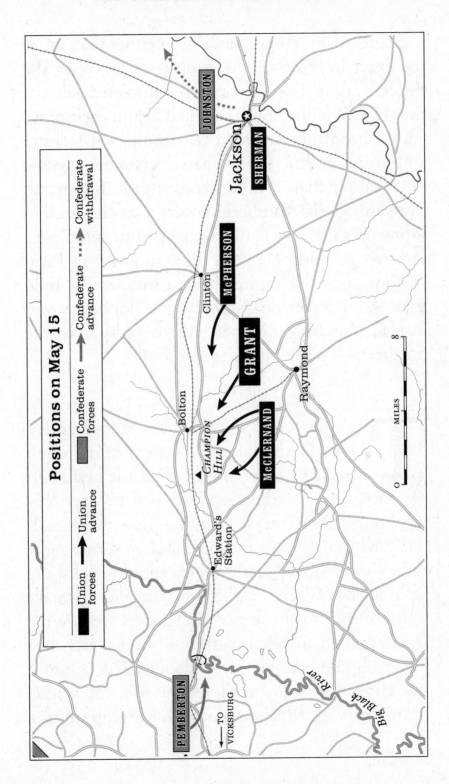

Positions on May 15

Union forces
Union advance
Confederate forces
Confederate advance
Confederate withdrawal

JOHNSTON

Jackson

SHERMAN

McPHERSON

Clinton

GRANT

Raymond

Bolton

McCLERNAND

CHAMPION HILL

Edward's Station

PEMBERTON

TO VICKSBURG

Big Black River

0   MILES   8

was hardly a practical plan, since neither man knew the exact location of the Federal army. With the Federal occupation of Jackson completed, an entire corps, McPherson's men, had begun their move back out on the very road that connected Jackson and Clinton. But Johnston's orders were specific once more, that Pemberton continue his march eastward, giving Pemberton every expectation that Johnston somehow had a route open to complete a rendezvous, adding several thousand men to Pemberton's forces. Despite those assurances, a mild tonic to Pemberton's uncertainty, Johnston was instead marching his men out of Jackson to the northeast—in the opposite direction.

The arguments continued the following day, May 15, and despite a variety of opinions, no one was certain just what the best strategy should be. Pemberton continued to wage that war in his own mind, mindful that every mile marched out beyond the Big Black was one more mile they would have to retrace should Vicksburg be attacked. While Pemberton struggled to make a firm decision, the army struggled as well. What was supposed to be an early morning march had instead become a half day's idleness. The columns were forced to wait, until at long last, the wagon trains carrying precious rations and ammunition reached them after a long march of their own, all the way from Vicksburg.

When they did move, the march was slow and pointless. What some had insisted should be a hard drive to crush the lone Federal division at Dillon's had instead become a confused stumble by Pemberton's three divisions across flooded roadways and swollen creeks. The divisions under Loring, Stevenson, and Bowen had taken the same roadway, Loring in the lead, the single narrow route guaranteeing another plodding march. Worse, Pemberton had not ordered Wirt Adams to deploy cavalry scouts to survey the routes immediately to their front, so that when the lead elements of any column arrived at the various crossings, many of those waterways were far too dangerous for troops to ford. In some cases, the head of the main column was forced to halt the march altogether, while behind them, decisions had to be made whether to wait for the flow of water to slacken or to march off in another direction, the attempt to find yet another route that might take them closer to the enemy.

With his troops positioned well south of the rail line that connected Vicksburg to Jackson, Pemberton understood that the most direct route to reach the capital now lay on the road that passed through Raymond. But that route was blocked by the flooded Baker's Creek. After long hours of shifting their routes, the army finally zigzagged and shoved northeasterly, still intending to reach the goal laid out for them by Joe Johnston, the rail crossing at Clinton. As night fell on the fifteenth, some of Pemberton's exhausted troops made camp in muddy fields, suffering through the meager rations brought them from Vicksburg. Others, Stevenson's troops in particular, were forced to march well into the night. With Loring's division still in the lead, the men were spread out in a confused line, still uncertain where the enemy might be. As Loring's men built their small fires, skirmishers had been sent to the east, protecting the men from whatever enemy might be probing toward them, patrols or cavalry scouts. As happened so often, those skirmishers found a line of skirmishers from the other side, pushing forward as well. The musket fire was light, scattered, but enough to let everyone on the field know that the two armies might be close to a major confrontation. What Pemberton did not know was that on the roads leading eastward, McClernand's entire Federal corps had been ordered by Ulysses Grant to push hard toward the rail crossing at Edward's Station. With nothing to hold them back, McClernand had made the short march in relatively easy fashion, his men well rested, going into camp, brewing coffee, eating their rations. To the north, along the railroad, the road to Clinton was thick with blue as well, the corps of James McPherson passing unmolested through the town.

The sight of a vast Federal column caused outrage and dismay from the citizens there, who had cheered the thunderous echoes from the fight at Jackson and had convinced themselves that Grant's invading horde would be crushed by Joe Johnston's guns. Instead, that "horde," more than thirty thousand troops, had received the order most of them knew was coming. Along three parallel routes that drove westward, Grant's army was on the march toward Vicksburg.

On the night of May 15, the skirmishers continued to probe and take their potshots, while patrols of cavalry engaged in brief clumsy duels with their counterparts, neither side truly knowing how close they were to the bulk of the enemy's forces. The encampments were barely four miles apart.

Between them lay a farm, to the east of Baker's Creek. It was one of so many farms that spread across the rolling countryside, and its boundaries included an imposing piece of high ground, a mostly bald hill, crowning a series of ridgelines that offered a panoramic view of the surrounding woodlands and cultivated fields. In the farmhouse close to the hill, a woman hurried about, securing valuables, storing heirlooms in hidden places. She knew something of armies, felt comforted that her husband was close by, a cavalry officer who served Colonel Adams with a cautious eye toward the protection of his own family. Their name was Champion.

CHAPTER FOURTEEN

PEMBERTON

NEAR BAKER'S CREEK,
SOUTH OF CHAMPION HILL
MAY 16, 1863

He stood outside, staring east, the sun already throwing a bright glow that swept the darkness out of a cloudless sky. His staff had gathered, Waddy close beside him, all of them staring, as he was, toward the first sound they heard. It was artillery.

"Do we know who that is?"

No one responded, and Pemberton searched for his horse, the groom not yet there. He felt his heart racing, stared again where the sounds were coming close, just down the road from his camp, the same camp where Loring had made his temporary head-quarters. The cannon fire increased now, a series of hard thumps beyond the woods to his front, and Pemberton couldn't wait for the horse. He said to Waddy, "Order General Loring to deploy his division in a line of battle!"

"Sir, he has done so. They made their camps in a line along the road. General Loring anticipated—"

"I don't care what he anticipated. I am more concerned with what is happening right now."

"Yes, sir. General Tilghman's brigade has been placed in line near the farmhouse, past that bend in the road."

Pemberton moved anxiously, shifting his weight, saw the groom, finally bringing the horse close. He jumped up quickly, the animal reacting to the shelling with nervous jumps, the same nervousness rolling through Pemberton.

"Sir! Colonel Adams!"

He saw the cavalryman riding hard, coming up the road from where Loring's men seemed to know what was happening. Adams will know, too, he thought. He must know.

Adams reined up, a small staff just behind, and jumped down from a horse whose flanks were thickly lathered. Adams saluted and said, "General! The enemy is advancing in force against our picket line! Their artillery is having good effect. General Loring is making preparations to receive them, and requests instructions."

Pemberton stared down the road, could see smoke rising, a low-hanging fog through the treetops. Loring isn't requesting anything, he thought. But thank you, Colonel, for at least offering me a show of respect.

The artillery fire seemed to intensify yet again, rippling thunder, more smoke. Pemberton thought of the map, the confusing array of roadways, plantation trails, too many to recall. But the ridgelines were plain, each one a strongpoint, where men could hold to high ground and force the enemy to come at them from rugged terrain below. He looked toward Waddy, saw the aides gathered, expectant, fear in their eyes. The thought flickered through him, that some of these men had never seen the enemy.

"Colonel Waddy! We must learn more of what we are facing! It would be good to speak with General Loring. Colonel Adams, with all respects to you, your service is most valuable when you are out in the field. Please return to your patrols and provide me with reports of the enemy's movements."

Adams acknowledged with a silent salute and was quickly gone, his small staff following. Good man, Pemberton thought. Valuable in times like these. I should be more forceful in my requests to General Johnston that we be given more horsemen. They were, after all, taken from me. One more outrage. And Colonel Adams deserves a larger command.

Pemberton brought himself back to the moment, stared down the road, more smoke billowing up, closer, more artillery. Yes, the scouts must move in haste, determine what troops those are, whose skirmishers . . . I suppose there is more than skirmishing . . . artillery, of course. But we should know who those people are.

He was surprised to see Loring now, trailed by a color bearer and his usual staff. Loring halted the horse, stared at Pemberton with no emotion, said in a calm voice, "It appears, sir, that the enemy is not intending to await our arrival at a place of our own choosing. My men were unprepared to receive an attack. I have ordered them to form a battle line with all haste, and to deploy the artillery batteries in the most advantageous position. With your permission, of course."

There was an eerie calm to Loring's words, and Pemberton saw an odd smile on one of Loring's officers.

"Yes, of course. Prepare your men to receive an attack. Do we know who that is?"

"It is . . . the **enemy,** sir. I have already put General Tilghman's brigade into motion. They have a commanding position along that ridgeline past those trees."

"No . . . they are too close . . . you must order General Tilghman's men to pull back, the next ridge to the west. The enemy's artillery could inflict grave damage." Loring glanced back, seemed to study the ground in the distance, drifting smoke opening up to reveal the ridge where Pemberton pointed. "There . . . back there," Pemberton said. "They will be in a better arrangement."

"That ridgeline is too exposed, General."

"But . . . your men are too close to the enemy's guns."

"I will arrange my men in the best position available. **Sir**."

Loring pulled the horse around, no salute, led his staff back into the smoke. Pemberton felt punched by the man's clear lack of respect. What must I do, he thought. We must make decisions on what we know . . . and I trust him to know his men. But I am in command. . . .

"Sir! A courier."

The man was escorted by one of Adams's horsemen. He slid slowly off his horse and approached Pemberton with a casual stride. Pemberton didn't know him, and the man seemed to search the others, appraising, then stepped closer to him, slapping dust from a filthy uniform. He offered a sloppy salute, betraying his obvious exhaustion.

"General, Captain Herron. General Johnston offers his respects, and advises you that he has been compelled to abandon the city of Jackson. The general repeats his order for you to rendezvous with his forces at Clinton. I am to ask, sir, if you are in preparation for such a move?"

Pemberton stared at the man, saw a slight stagger, the man too tired to hold his shoulders up. Pemberton had a sudden flash of doubt, that this man might not be from Johnston at all, a spy perhaps. He caught the smell of sulfur, the smoke from the growing battle rolling closer.

"Captain . . . Herron? Are you certain of this order? We are to continue to Clinton in the face of . . . this?"

"General Johnston was most insistent, sir. I have his order here. He is marching six thousand men to Clinton and anticipates your combined forces to be adequate to cause serious damage to the enemy."

The man produced a paper now, as though it had just occurred to him Pemberton should see the order in Johnston's own handwriting. Pemberton reached down, took the folded paper, broke the seal, and read the same order the captain had related. He sagged in the saddle, looked again toward the rumbling artillery, where he could hear a peppering of musket fire.

"Very well, Captain. You may wait with my staff and recover from your ride. They will provide you with breakfast, such as we have. I shall put my reply in writing, and when you are fit, you will return to General Johnston." He paused. "I will inform the general of our route of march, and inform him that we are facing . . . some vigorous skirmishing. But we shall obey."

Memminger was on horseback now. He moved close and said, "Sir! A courier . . . from General Stevenson. That's Lieutenant Gilroy."

Pemberton stared up that way, had heard no sounds of a fight from that direction. The lieutenant had ridden hard, reined up, frantic motion in his salute, a high-pitched chattering voice.

"Sir! General Stevenson offers his respects and reports that there are enemy troops to the east of his position. He wishes you to know that cavalry scouts have reported that, from all indications, the enemy could be moving in the direction of Edward's Station. The general wishes to know if he should move back up toward Edward's."

Pemberton felt the decisions rolling through him, thought of Edward's Station, a critical link on the rail line, the very place he had been strong just two days before. Yes, we should have kept behind the Big Black. We cannot stop them from cutting the railroad. Certainly they have done so now. We would be strong with that river to our front. But out here . . . He thought again of Loring. What will he do? Will he hold here? How strong is the enemy here? He stared up past the lieutenant for a long moment. The enemy is there as well? Then we are in some danger . . . all along our position. I suppose . . . we no longer have doubts where Grant has placed his army.

The troops advancing into Loring's position were the lead units of John McClernand's corps, the men who had been lurking to

Pemberton's east all the while that Grant was occupying Jackson. Pemberton knew the maps well
enough to understand that there were three primary roads that Grant could use, and from the reports of Stevenson's man, the Federal advance was
moving toward them on the two more southerly
routes. There had been no word at all of Federal
activity along the northerly road, the one that ran
directly along the railroad. It was the one piece of
optimism for Pemberton as he reread the order from
Joe Johnston. Clinton could still be reached, by
marching the army in column to the north, above
the railroad, then curling back to the east. Whether
the Federal forces already controlled that route or
whether they occupied Clinton itself had not been
addressed in Johnston's order. Pemberton began to
understand that his own subordinates had placed
their faith not in him, but in a man who was miles
away, this department's highest authority. It was a
safe decision for any officer. But the uncertainty
remained, Pemberton feeling a boiling agony that
his own generals might simply march off in any
direction they chose, following what Johnston ordered them do, whether Pemberton agreed or not.
Pemberton had already suffered through days of
nervous agony, pondering the threats to his troops,
the threats to Vicksburg, and now, the threats to
his own authority. If Johnston insisted they march
to Clinton, Pemberton had finally accepted that it
was an order he could not ignore.

With the enemy shoving close to Loring's front, Loring would be slow to move, if he could pull away at all. Pemberton understood as well as Loring that disengaging from an enemy assault was risky at best. The first moves would come above Loring's position, the divisions of Bowen and Stevenson. When they left Edward's Station, Stevenson had been the rear of the march, but now the column would be reversed, the men moving back to the north, retracing some of their steps from the day before. The army sat now in a snaking single file, and on its northern tail were the nearly four hundred wagons of the supply train. Before Stevenson could go anywhere, the wagons had to be moved out of the way, making way for the foot soldiers. Then the wagon train would have to be sent along some parallel route farther west, a time-consuming effort at keeping the crucial supply train out of harm's way.

As the sun rose higher, Stevenson's third brigade, under Stephen Dill Lee, anchored the army's left flank at a crucial crossroads less than a half mile below the prominent landmark of Champion Hill. But Lee did not sit still. Scouting the hill itself, and the rail line above, Lee could clearly see another advancing column of blue marching close to the railroad. Grant had used not just two, but all three of the roads that would take his army toward Vicksburg. Whether or not Pemberton held tightly to his decision to rendezvous with Johnston, Lee had a far more urgent mission. The Federal troops advancing above his position belonged to both McPherson and McClernand, one part of the seven divisions that Grant was sending Pemberton's way. Unless Lee reacted, and shifted his troops up onto Champion Hill, the Federals would march right past his flank, and could endanger the entire army. As they drew closer to Lee's position, the Federal troops reacted as well. Not long after 10 A.M., the division under General Alvin Hovey spread into battle formation near the roadway and faced the rugged ground slicing along the base of the higher ground. But Hovey would not yet advance. Instead he sent out scouting patrols, cavalry, one brigade commander to slip up toward the high ground and determine just what he was facing. With that information, Hovey understood that he had placed himself squarely above the entire rebel position. All he required now from his corps commander was the order to attack.

CHAPTER FIFTEEN

GRANT

The courier had found Grant while he was still in Jackson. The man rode disguised as a local farmer, no sign of a uniform at all. It was a wise precaution as he passed through so much of the countryside, and the picket lines and guard posts of the Federal troops who had occupied the city. Though the guards he first met were skeptical, his story and the letter he carried were convincing, and so he was led to the most senior commander in the camps close by, James McPherson. The man's appearance might have been a surprise to McPherson, but his identity was not, and quickly the courier was taken to General Grant. There was a single piece of paper, a handwritten order, which Grant did not keep. The courier, after all, still had a mission to perform, still had to keep up the appearances of a man riding hard to bring a written order from one Confederate general to the other. The handwriting belonged to Joe Johnston, the order sent to Pemberton that the Confederate forces were to rendezvous with Johnston at the town of Clinton. Johnston had no doubt assumed the telegraph wires to be useless. And so, three couriers had been sent toward Pemberton, taking different routes, each dedicated to a fast and discreet ride, the expectation that at least one would make it through and complete his mission. The man who had stood before Grant had done exactly that. What Johnston did not know was that one of his trusted couriers was a Federal spy. And so, with the courier sent back out on his way, Grant knew exactly what Johnston and Pemberton were planning. Whether or not Pemberton could ever reach Clinton, whether or not there would be an actual rendezvous, didn't matter. Grant knew now that Pemberton had been ordered to try.

NEAR CLINTON, MISSISSIPPI
MAY 16, 1863

It was barely daylight when the train appeared. There had been the usual column of thick black smoke, and the deep grunting of the engine. The surprised troops who marched alongside the tracks had been ordered to halt, their officers scrambling to pass the word to their commanders just what was happening. Orders were issued, a single artillery piece rolled up, unlimbered beside the track, its crew waiting, preparing to load the piece should the train not respond to the threat of a hundred soldiers with muskets that would be aimed straight at the train's engineer. As the train came closer, rounding a final bend, the stunned resignation on the face of the railroad men cleared away any anxiety the soldiers had about a violent confrontation. With the train slowing, the officers climbed up into the engine, their pistols pointed into the faces of the men, who quickly obeyed, bringing the train to a lurching stop in a shower of steam. Behind the engine were three passenger cars, and quickly troops scrambled aboard, terrifying the few passengers, who offered no resistance to the muskets and their sudden captivity at the hands of the men in blue.

Grant had been close by, riding to catch up with McPherson, and he responded to news of the train with surprise of his own, baffled that any train would be using this line at all. He moved the horse up alongside the now-silent engine and waited as the train's crew was escorted out of their perch, three men who faced their captors without defiance. Grant stared at them for a long moment, the guards poised with bayonets, an unnecessary display of force. One of the men was much older, a thin white beard, the blackened overalls of a railroad man, all three showing the dress of civilians. Grant aimed his question at the older man.

"You have come from Vicksburg?"

"Reckon so. I told them folks there was gonna be bluebellies out thisaway. Dang soldiers been straggin' into town for days now, all sorts of big talk about Yankees and whatnot. But the officer at the depot sent us on our way, said he had been given the go-ahead from General Pemberton hisself, that we could make our scheduled run. I just done what I was told. Damn fool. Me, that is, not the general. Well, maybe."

Another of the train's crew spoke up, far more afraid.

"What you aimin' to do with us? We ain't done nothin'. We got no muskets."

The older man seemed far more assured, no hint of panic.

"We got a dozen passengers back there. Brave folk, for certain. Some said they had family in Jackson, had to go make sure they was unhurt, what with the bluebellies tearin' things up. Can't fault 'em for that."

Grant saw nervousness in the two younger men, eyes focusing on the bayonets, the weapons still pointed their way. Grant couldn't help but like the old man, just one more civilian with a job to do, his life thoroughly scrambled by a war he probably cared nothing about. Grant held a cigar in his hand, pointed it back toward the three passenger cars, their occupants spilling out with some protest. He could see a pair of women among a throng of well-dressed men. The women wore fine colorful dresses, feathered hats, as though on some kind of formal outing. Of course, he thought. To anyone in Vicksburg, Jackson is the "big city," and so one must dress accordingly. He smiled at that, shook his head, called out to the officer herding the passengers into some kind of formation beside the train.

"Captain, no harm to these people."

"Certainly not, sir. What should I do with them?"

Grant thought a moment, an idea turning over in his brain. He kept up in the saddle, a higher perch, the symbol that might add gravity to his authority.

"Just keep them right there for now." He looked down at the old man, said, "No harm will come to these people, if you answer a few questions. Truthfully, of course. You never know just how **crafty** one of us bluebellies can be. Hate to resort to torture, that sort of thing."

The older man nodded slowly, no show of fear. He knows better, Grant thought. But he knows the position he's in, and what he's got to do.

"You'll be wantin' to know what we seen coming out thisaway. All like that."

"That's the first question."

"Well now, since you boys are a-headin' that way anyhow, don't see what harm it'll do to tell you what's out thataways. I seen some of your cavalry along the way, so I expect you done figured out what's happening."

"Perhaps."

The man scratched at his beard, and Grant saw the other two looking down, saw a hint of anger on one of the men. Grant said to the nearest sergeant, "Why don't you take these other two back to the passengers. The old gent and I need to have a private conversation."

The sergeant understood, the other two crewmen escorted away, one man shouting back over his shoulder, "You ought not tell them nothin', Zeke! They's gonna shoot us anyhow!"

The old man looked up at Grant.

"You ain't a-gonna do that, are you now?"

Grant pulled at the cigar, a show of thoughtfulness, as though he might actually be considering just that. But the old man didn't bite, still no fear. Grant shook his head.

"Truth. All I'm after. Of course, you can't have your train back. Not a good idea to let you roll on to Jackson. You wouldn't like what you found there anyway. Nope, you'll be walking along with us for a spell. We'll find an ambulance wagon for the ladies."

The man nodded. "Sounds fair. We done seen too much of you bluebellies out here. Might have to tell somebody about that. Not smart for you to allow that. Sounds like we's got us a bargain. I tell you what I seen already this morning, and you'll be nice to us, right?" He didn't wait for Grant to answer. "It weren't even daylight when we passed right by a whole passel of General Pemberton's men. Rough-looking bunch. Not all spiffed up like you folks. Don't much matter about that, I suppose. Man's gotta fight with his heart, not his trousers."

"How many of those men?"

The man looked down, then smiled.

"Yep. I'm gettin' to that. Didn't count 'em myself, you understand. Didn't have to. Back in Vicksburg, the word was passed around pretty open and all. Eighty regiments done moved out here, near twenty-five thousand muskets. Could be more, could be less. They left maybe twenty regiments in the town, dug in to all them earthworks and such. They's still diggin', too. They know you're comin'. So I can't rightly figure why they let this train make this run. Generals are supposed to be smarter than that."

"Supposed to be."

Grant was absorbing what the man had said, had already suspected that his estimate of Pemberton's available force was too low. That had come from the spy, the order Grant had intercepted. The old man was likely exaggerating about the numbers. Most civilians did. But the regiment count could be accurate. Flags were easier to count than men. The question rose up inside Grant now. Why in blazes would Johnston order Pemberton to march out here in the wide open, away from the protection of the Big Black? Even if they had joined up in Clinton, Johnston didn't have near the strength to add much to a fight, not from what we saw in Jackson. They have to know we're going to hit Vicksburg, and that's where they ought to be sitting, digging in. Unless Johnston's got more of an army out here that we don't know about. Better send the cavalry out north and east of Jackson, or make sure Sherman does that before he moves this way. But this old buzzard's probably right. Pemberton is following orders, pushing out this way . . . for what? Does Johnston think they can hit us hard while we're unprepared? Sorry old fellow, but I'm as prepared as I need to be.

"So, that what you wanted? I need to ease off into the brush, if'n you know what I mean. Comes with bein' old."

"In a moment. Anything else you can tell me? Any details."

"Nope. Don't really pay much attention to soldierin', all that business about who's doin' what. Just told you what I heard. And saw."

Grant was beginning to like this old man even more, wondered what other stories he could tell. But the army was up and ready, the columns in formation, and with a clear blue sky opening up above him, Grant knew they would move quickly.

"All right then. The guard will lead you to those bushes over that way. Thank you . . . Zeke?"

"Ezekiel Horne. Since you're a Yankee and all, seems fittin' we keep it more proper."

"Very well, Mr. Horne. You go do your business, then join the others. Nobody needs to go running off anywhere. You understand that?"

"We'll mind. My two boys there are a might jumpy, but I'll hang a leash on 'em. You just go on about your own business. But . . . if you can see your way clear . . . try not to hurt too many of our boys. Most of those soldiers out there ain't soldiers at all. Just local fellows, trying to guard what's theirs."

"They don't shoot at me, I won't shoot at them."

The old man rubbed his chin, nodded.

"I reckon that ain't gonna happen. What with Old Stonewall in the ground and all, things is only gettin' worse."

"Stonewall? Jackson?"

Grant stopped himself, didn't need to reveal any ignorance. The old man looked up at him with a squint in his eye.

"You didn't know about that. Yep. Word came to Vicksburg few days ago. They killed him somewheres in Virginia. The whole place is mournin'. You'd a thought every household in Vicksburg lost a brother. I imagine it's a good bit worse back east. Didn't know the fella myself, but heard plenty. He was takin' it to you bluebellies pretty hard, if you can believe what the newspaper said. Guess it had to end up like that. Ain't been a soldier myself, but knowed plenty of 'em, and some of 'em didn't come home. That Stonewall fella . . . probably had a wife and young'uns. Feel worse for them than anybody else." He paused, shook his head, then looked again at Grant. "Mighty fine-smellin' cigar you got there."

Grant didn't hesitate, just reached into his pocket, retrieved a fresh cigar, and handed it to the man, who sniffed it with closed eyes. He lowered his voice.

"I'll save this for later. Don't need jealous eyes stabbin' a hole in me." The man slipped the cigar into some hidden place, put his hands on his hips, looked again at Grant. "You seem like a decent sort, for a bluebelly. Hope you make it through this. Hope all of us do. God willin'."

Grant watched the man turn away, heading toward a discreet place in the nearby brush. The guard followed, keeping a respectful distance. Grant watched the old man still, saw stiff knees and a bent back. *Sorry, you old coot, but there will be plenty of shooting before this is done. You'll survive, I hope. Me too, maybe. God willing.*

NEAR THE CHAMPION HOUSE
MAY 16, 1863

He had stayed close to McPherson, knew that to the south, on the next good road that led to Ed-

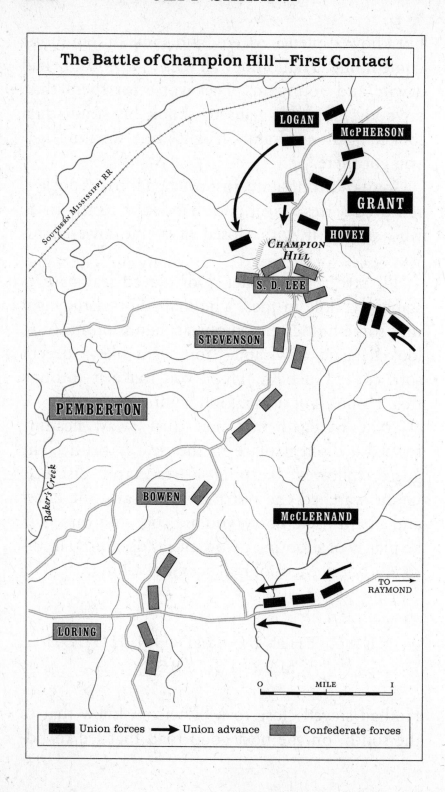

The Battle of Champion Hill—First Contact

LOGAN

McPHERSON

GRANT

HOVEY

CHAMPION HILL

S. D. LEE

STEVENSON

PEMBERTON

Baker's Creek

BOWEN

McCLERNAND

TO → RAYMOND

LORING

O   MILE   I

Union forces   → Union advance   Confederate forces

SOUTHERN MISSISSIPPI RR

ward's Station, McClernand's troops were positioned well, a stout blue line that would check any
possible advance the rebels might be attempting,
any possibility of a flanking move, or some kind of
surprise assault that John Pemberton might dream
up. Grant had very little fear of anything Pemberton might try, knew too much of the man to respect
his ability in the field. But there were good generals
under him, and Grant had already experienced the
tenacity of John Bowen from the first days since
crossing the river. Bowen was close, surely, and if
Grant wasn't altogether certain of the skills of the
other commanders Pemberton had brought out
east, to ignore caution could be dangerous.

All along the way, he had watched McPherson,
appraising, knew McPherson would be aware of
that. But the engineer had accomplished something Grant greatly appreciated. In an army where
promotion came often by friendships and political clout, McPherson had made himself genuinely
valuable. For more than a year, the man Henry
Halleck considered the Federal army's finest engineer had found a way to escape the staleness of
Halleck's headquarters and put himself out into
the field, whether leading a reconnaissance patrol
or supervising the construction of a bridge, and finally secured the command of the army's entire engineering brigade. Since Fort Donelson and Shiloh,
Grant had sifted through the competency of the
division commanders who answered to him, some

of those no longer with the army, some, like Sherman, elevated even higher up the chain of command. Throughout 1862, through the campaigns in Tennessee and northern Mississippi, Grant had seen something in McPherson that went far beyond numbers and charts or skills at geometry. It was the same kind of trait he sought out in every man chosen to lead, that certain intangible glint in the eye, steel in the spine, and even better, the ability to pass that on to the men in their own commands. With Halleck off to his new post in Washington, Grant had been greatly relieved that McPherson had remained. With Halleck's support, McPherson continued his rise through the ranks, and in October the autumn before, McPherson's climb up the chain had become official. Washington had elevated him away from the engineering brigade, to command of a full combat division. Since then, with Grant given far more discretion in reorganizing his army, he had implemented the corps system, what he believed to be a far more effective way of organizing a large-scale overland campaign. In each of his three corps, three or four division commanders were now subordinate to a single corps commander, who in turn was subordinate to Grant. While McClernand had not been Grant's choice at all, the other two, Sherman and McPherson, were the best he could have hoped for. Sherman's deep connection to Grant had extended back more than a year, and Grant had not wavered in his belief that despite

Sherman's various failings, he was likely the best fighter Grant had. McPherson might be more of a thinker, but so far, in various engagements over the past few months, he had only gotten better at his job, and he was now in control of a third of Grant's army. As they finally shifted the army's attention toward Vicksburg itself, Grant had chosen to make the advance by riding closer to McPherson, as he had done with Sherman since the crossing of the river. Sherman had become a friend, McPherson not yet in that place. But with Sherman busy back at Jackson, Grant had decided he wanted to watch McPherson work. If McPherson was nervous about that, more the better. Grant just wanted to be sure there were no significant mistakes. And riding with McPherson would be far more pleasant than moving out alongside McClernand. Grant was under no illusions that John McClernand would ever be his friend.

They had begun the day by riding west out of Clinton, the rail tracks there completely destroyed, the same kind of work Sherman was completing in the capital city. Edward's Station was the next goal, and from the reports of the cavalry, there was very little rebel presence along the railroad, no significant attempt by Pemberton to block his way. That had been something of a surprise to Grant, that Pemberton did not make every effort to defend the most logical route, and the straightest line to Vicksburg. Instead the Federal cavalry had reported that the mass of rebels the railroad man had seen were marching away from Edward's more to the south. Grant's first intuition was that Pemberton was trying to flank him, but Grant knew he had the numbers, and the position. If Pemberton drove down to try to sweep around McClernand's left, to possibly turn the army from below, it would not be difficult to shift McPherson around that way as a counter. With Sherman's work in Jackson nearly complete, Sherman had already been ordered to march westward with all speed. If the rebels drove up from the south against McClernand, Sherman could alter his line of march and possibly crush straight into the rebel flank. Though Grant didn't especially fear Pemberton as an opponent, it seemed as though the rebels were engaging in an odd game of chess, maneuvering to try to gain some kind of tactical advantage Grant didn't really understand. As long as his flanks were secure, Grant didn't really care. His goal was Vicksburg, and if Pemberton had several divisions out here east of the Big Black River, it only meant there were fewer defenders in the town.

With the artillery fire erupting south of Champion Hill, Grant had ridden ahead, leaving McPherson to oversee the rapid advance of his Seventeenth Corps. Grant reached the Champion house near ten in the morning, and his staff had secured the farmhouse as their headquarters. The house was by now unoccupied, word coming from amused aides that the lady of the house, Matilda Champion, had filled a wagon with her four children and a mountain of possessions and had scrambled away toward the west. Grant was relieved by her escape. It meant one less rebel to worry about.

He stayed up on the horse, focused on the broad hill, less than a half mile south of the house. For some time now he had heard the artillery fire down toward McClernand's position, heard it now, steady thunder beyond the hill itself. But the hill was not empty, and he saw the rebels in a solid line, mostly along the crest of the hill and the ridges that spread away. And now, more artillery, close to his front, the first streaks of fire, thumps and blasts coming toward him from high along the ridges. The staff had emerged from the house, even Rawlins curious to watch the spectacle, the shelling more of a nuisance from this range than a real danger.

From the right of the hill, Grant saw officers riding up at a fast gallop, a small staff behind, the color bearer bringing up the rear. Grant motioned to Rawlins and said, "Bring them inside. Those boys have something on their minds, and there's no need to have a conversation out in front of every pair of ears."

Grant watched the men dismount, saw the calm intensity of veteran commanders. Grant knew them, moved on ahead into the new headquarters, ignored the smell of lavender, family, cooking, interrupted now by the business of his army. In a few seconds, Rawlins escorted the two men inside, and Grant remained standing, extending a hand to the senior officer.

"General Hovey. Fine morning. Who might those people be up on that hill?"

Alvin Hovey commanded one of McClernand's divisions, was another of the Mexican War veterans, had served as a justice of the Indiana Supreme Court, and was now considered one of the rising stars in McClernand's corps. He had been detached from McClernand's front to pursue a separate route that eventually merged at Edward's Station. Now he was separated from McClernand not only by Champion Hill, but by what seemed to be a serious amount of fighting south of the hill. The second man was George McGinnis, one of Hovey's two brigade commanders, and another man with long experience in command.

Behind Grant, aides scrambled to clear a space in a sitting room, chairs pulled back. Rawlins rushed them out of the way, and Grant moved in, sat, then motioned to the others. Hovey sat as well, would be the first to speak.

"Sir, we were advised by General McClernand that you were en route this way. It is a relief to find you, sir."

"Easy, General. I'm here. I'm sure that General McClernand keeps a close eye on my whereabouts."

He paused, had no need to reveal anything about that to one of McClernand's own commanders. "Have you been in communication with General McClernand? Do we know just what he is facing down there?"

"Not directly, sir. As you suggested, sir, I have been more concerned with what we are facing right here. General McGinnis, please report."

McGinnis took the cue, spoke in a slow measured voice.

"General Grant, I have personally observed a battery of enemy artillery, a squadron of cavalry, and a line of infantry filing up into a position of readiness on that high ground. This primary road makes a bend away from the railroad and traverses the large hill. Clearly the enemy expects us to continue on that route, and they are using that vantage point to observe our approach. He is in battle formation, expecting to receive us. My cavalry reports that west of the road, the ground is open, less difficult than the high ground to our front. But, with your permission, sir, I do not feel comfortable moving out to the right without protection for my left flank. Colonel Slack's brigade is there now, but he would have to shift westward as well, as his flank would then be exposed. One division might not be enough strength."

Hovey interrupted, more nervousness in his voice, the excitement building now in both men.

"Sir, I have complete confidence in my brigade

commanders, but I agree that my single division could be vulnerable on either flank. If we are to take the offensive, we should move right. The enemy does not appear to be in strength anywhere west of the road, and so this high ground is his flank. If we can drive the enemy back off the heights, we can open the main road for a rapid advance."

"How much enemy?"

Hovey glanced at McGinnis, who said, "Not entirely sure, sir. They do hold the prominent vantage point. Alabamans, for sure. A brigade, perhaps more. My concern, sir, is that we do not yet know if he has a much larger force coming up in support. I did not feel it advisable that I remain in proximity to their deployment."

"That is understandable, General. No, we must make that **vantage point** our own."

Grant motioned to an aide and said, "Go now, back down the road to the east. General McPherson is advancing in this direction. Find him, and urge him to advance with all dispatch. I do not wish General Hovey's division to bear this burden alone."

The man saluted and was quickly gone, the energy Grant appreciated. Rawlins was there now, his usual place, waiting for Grant to put the rest of the staff into motion. Grant sat back, retrieved a cigar, said simply, "Map."

Rawlins seemed to anticipate that, an aide stepping forward immediately, a map produced, unrolled on a small table. Grant hid a smile. He had wondered if Rawlins could actually read his thoughts. He studied the map, then said, "On the north side of the high ground . . . there are just your two brigades?"

"Yes, sir. We are fit for battle, sir, I assure you."

"I am not doubting you, General. You have done exactly as you should. There is a time for audacity and a time for caution. Thus far in this campaign, every advantage has been ours, and I intend to keep it that way. By following protocol, you will no doubt draw praise from General McClernand. And right now, I prefer that you hold off any aggressive move until General McPherson arrives. His people are moving this way and are not far. I would rather go into this fight with two fists instead of one."

"By all means, sir."

Hovey seemed relieved, McGinnis tapping him on the leg, a sign of approval. Yes, Grant thought, we shall go by the book whenever possible. Mc-Clernand would have it no other way.

"Do you know what General McClernand is doing to the south? I have not received any word from him. I issued him orders that he move on Edward's Station first thing this morning. I have to assume that the enemy is attempting to prevent that."

Hovey nodded.

"I have reported to him by courier my situation here, but I have not yet received a response. The ground, I would imagine, is somewhat . . . difficult. We have heard the artillery down that way for two hours or more. From the sounds, it would seem a substantial body of the enemy is extended to the south, likely facing east. Which means . . . facing General McClernand."

Grant looked up at Rawlins, who waited for the order with the usual pulsing eagerness.

"Colonel, I want to know what General McClernand is doing down there. Send a courier . . . send two. Different routes. The enemy cannot be in overwhelming strength both here and down there. I wish to know if General McClernand intends to inform me of his actions. Make that very plain, Colonel. I want information."

"Right away, sir."

Rawlins was out quickly. Grant sat back in the chair, said, "By the way, on the march this morning, we came across your wagon train. Your commissary officers had parked in the middle of the roadway. It was not especially to General McPherson's advantage. There were some . . . oaths muttered, particularly by General Logan, whose division leads the way. I solved the crisis by issuing an order your teamsters would not obey from anyone else."

Hovey stared wide-eyed.

"I deeply regret this, sir. I will discipline Major Jernigan."

"Handle it your own way. Since it is very apparent you do not intend to fight this war by yourself, you should assume that additional infantry is advancing up to support you. In the future, park your wagon train to one side of the road."

"Most definitely, sir. Very sorry. I shall apologize to General Logan myself."

Grant tossed the spent cigar into a spittoon, conveniently placed beside his chair, no doubt by Rawlins.

"Better idea. When Logan's division arrives, which I expect to be very soon, show him the way to the fight. That should be satisfactory . . . for both of you."

By 11 A.M., Logan's division of McPherson's corps had reached the field and was placed out to the right of Hovey's division. With shells from rebel artillery pounding through their ranks, the men in blue began to shove down through the thickets and dense underbrush. As they gained height on the hillside, the ground changed, opening up to clear fields of fire as the troops drove their way toward the waiting rebels.

McPherson sat on horseback close to Grant, and Grant left him alone while keeping a sharp eye on the flow of orders, staff officers, and couriers in motion. Even as the first lines of troops moved up onto the hill, McPherson was shifting more of his people farther right, and Grant understood that the strength in numbers the Federals were bring-

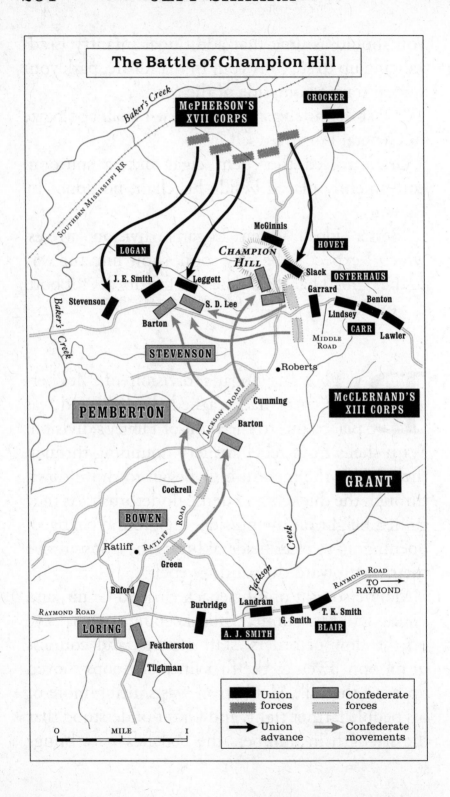

The Battle of Champion Hill

Baker's Creek

CROCKER

McPHERSON'S XVII CORPS

SOUTHERN MISSISSIPPI RR

McGinnis

HOVEY

LOGAN

CHAMPION HILL

J. E. Smith

Leggett

Slack

OSTERHAUS

Garrard

Benton

Stevenson

S. D. Lee

Lindsey

Baker's Creek

Barton

CARR

Lawler

MIDDLE ROAD

STEVENSON

Roberts

JACKSON ROAD

Cumming

McCLERNAND'S XIII CORPS

PEMBERTON

Barton

GRANT

Cockrell

BOWEN

ROAD

Ratliff

RATLIFF

Creek

Green

Jackson

RAYMOND ROAD

TO RAYMOND

Buford

Landram

RAYMOND ROAD

Burbridge

A. J. SMITH

G. Smith

T. K. Smith

BLAIR

LORING

Featherston

Tilghman

	Union forces		Confederate forces
→	Union advance	→	Confederate movements

O MILE I

ing to the field seemed to far outstrip the rebel defenses that had positioned themselves on the high
ground. Grant eyed each courier anxiously, wondered in nervous silence if the word would come
that Pemberton's entire army had shifted northward, that the hill might be masking a vast surge
of rebel troops who would turn the tables. With
the fight beginning in earnest, the fire from the
highest ground became more sporadic, small bursts
and volleys that betrayed the thin lines the rebels
had placed there. Grant stared up through distant
smoke, wanted so badly to ride up there, to find
Hovey or Logan or anyone else who knew exactly
what lay to his front. But for now, Grant's role was
here, near the Champion House, the focal point of
McPherson's command.

There had been other couriers, sent by Grant, a
nagging annoyance growing to a full boiling fury
that he had as yet heard nothing from John Mc-
Clernand. That fight, south of the high ground,
was still ongoing, and Grant's orders had been for
McClernand to advance with some caution. Even
now, no one was certain where Pemberton's greatest strength might be. But from all he could hear,
caution had become something else altogether, and
Grant could not avoid the feeling that McClernand was just sitting still. There were two roads
to McClernand's front, either one of which could
offer an opportunity for a hard thrust that might
slice through whatever force Pemberton had placed

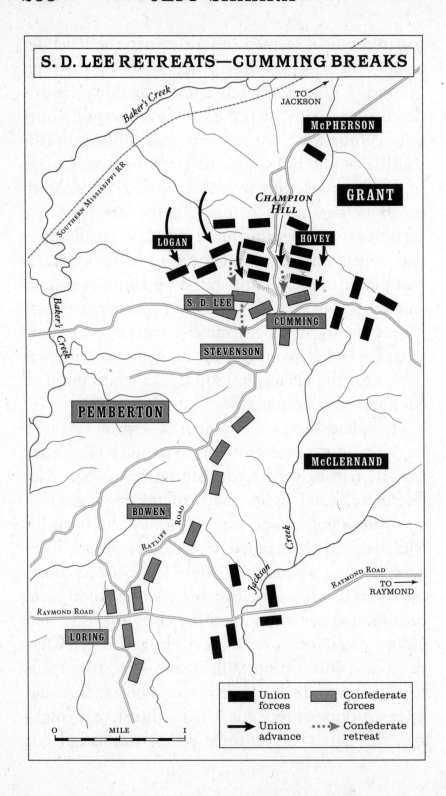

S. D. LEE RETREATS—CUMMING BREAKS

Baker's Creek

SOUTHERN MISSISSIPPI RR

TO JACKSON

McPHERSON

GRANT

CHAMPION HILL

LOGAN

HOVEY

S. D. LEE

CUMMING

STEVENSON

Baker's Creek

PEMBERTON

McCLERNAND

BOWEN

RATLIFF ROAD

Jackson Creek

RAYMOND ROAD

TO RAYMOND

RAYMOND ROAD

LORING

	Union forces		Confederate forces
	Union advance		Confederate retreat

0   MILE   1

there. But McClernand was showing no indication of a thrust at all.

Within an hour of McPherson's order to attack, the rebels were driven back off the high ridges and the bald crest of Champion Hill. Success had come from Hovey's tenacious offense and the sheer weight of numbers under his command. The first major break came not on the far flank, where Logan was continuing to stretch out the rebel position, but more to the center. There a brigade of Georgians under Alfred Cumming did what they could with the meager artillery and troop strength at hand, but Hovey's forces held every advantage, and faced with annihilation, the Georgians quickly withdrew. The gap in the Confederate center left the remaining rebel troops in a serious situation. The brigade of Stephen Dill Lee, the first men to recognize the immense importance of that ground, found themselves nearly surrounded by overwhelming numbers of Federal troops on both flanks. Instead of a retreat, Lee tried a rally of his own, launching a counterattack, a slashing drive to push through Hovey's tired troops, with a goal toward silencing or capturing a clearly visible Federal artillery battery. But Lee's forces were simply too few, their bold attack swept back soon after it began. Lee had no choice but to pull his men back down the southern side of the ridges and concede Champion Hill to the Federals.

Hovey's two brigades, under McGinnis and Colonel James Slack, scampered up and over Champion Hill, pushing down the far side with raucous energy. Though the rebels were unable to hold them back, as so often happens in such a rapid, overwhelming assault, the victorious troops could not maintain their surge. Hovey's troops had driven more than a half mile up and then down the rolling terrain, and inevitably, exhaustion took hold. Order had broken down as well, officers losing their own commands in the tangles and ravines, the Federal advance stumbling about now in a morass of confusion. Worse for Hovey, Logan's division, on his right, had not enjoyed such a rousing success across so many acres of ground. The ridgelines that extended westward from Champion Hill were far more difficult than the open ground high on the hill, and Logan's men were faced by a stubborn resistance from Confederate troops who would not break. Logan did what the maps required him to do. Recognizing that he faced the far left of the rebel position, he extended his own lines in that direction, attempting to sweep around the rebel flank.

To the south, Confederate general Carter Stevenson was attempting to manage a fight that had now spread over two fronts, to his east and north. Sending a brigade of Georgians under Seth Barton to the flank west of Champion Hill, Stevenson made

every effort to stem the tide against him and prevent the collapse of what was in fact the flank of the
entire Confederate position. Like Lee, Barton made
a gallant effort, but numbers and the unyielding
terrain worked against him. Barton was soon nearly
surrounded, and forced back as well.

As the hot afternoon sun slid over the field, the
Confederate left was in danger of collapsing altogether, much of the fighting rolling down closer
to the middle road, where John Bowen's division
faced east, steadily dueling with John McClernand's
Federals, who seemed content to pick and probe
the rebel lines, within easy earshot of the vicious
fighting on Champion Hill. As Pemberton kept a
careful eye on McClernand's troops to the east, he
could not avoid the danger that was rolling down
upon the entire rebel army from the Federal success
across Champion Hill.

CHAPTER SIXTEEN

PEMBERTON

NEAR THE
ISAAC ROBERTS HOUSE
ONE MILE SOUTH OF
CHAMPION HILL

"Is the enemy advancing? It sounds as though he is holding back! We must drive him then!"

Pemberton's horse squirmed beneath him, and Pemberton realized he was digging his spurs hard into the horse's flank. He tried to release the tightness in his legs, the same tightness that rolled through him, drawing his insides into a hard knot. He kept his stare to the east, to the troops he now knew belonged to John McClernand. For more than two hours those troops had waged a tough but stagnant fight on two of the roads that would have taken them to Edward's Station. But Pemberton's own lines had held firm, blocking the way, and seemed to be more than McClernand's blue-coats could handle. He searched for an aide, anyone who could answer his question. He shouted out the question again, staring into the dense smoke.

"Is the enemy advancing? We must continue to hold!"

"Sir! The enemy is not advancing with any force. We have no other word from that quarter. General Loring reports that the enemy is keeping to their lines and does not appear to be pressing this way!"

The words came from Waddy, exactly the response Pemberton was hoping to hear.

"Excellent! By God, yes! We are holding them back!"

He could not help the churning nervousness, had been completely surprised by the advance of any part of Grant's army. With so little cavalry to scout the field, there had been no hint of problems with the route he would use to reach Clinton, but now any attempt to disengage from the enemy could be disastrous. No, he thought, General Johnston can wait. For now we must hold here, keep them away. Surely Johnston does not know what Grant is doing, where the enemy troops are moving. He can't possibly know.

He spurred hard, the animal bouncing up in protest, but the horse began to move, a hard gallop to the south, where Loring would be. Throughout the morning, Loring had held position against the

Federal troops along the two roads that intersected Pemberton's army, the route that would take the Federal troops to Edward's Station. Pemberton had begun to accept what was happening, that the sudden appearance of so many blue troops could only mean that Grant was intending to maneuver a great mass of his army at a place that offered a straight-line advance toward Vicksburg. The horse jostled him, and he jerked one rein, turning the horse to the right, was suddenly not certain which way he should go. His brain rolled the thoughts over in a vast jumble, one thought above all else. They will drive upon Edward's, and then . . . westward. They shall not have Vicksburg, not without the hardest fight I can offer them. He searched manically for officers, for someone besides his own staff to give him information. For two hours now, those reports had been the same as what came from Loring. The enemy seemed content to pick and probe, no major effort at engaging his lines. His mind pulled him away from that, and he thought of riding instead to the east. But Loring was in control there, as best as Pemberton could see. No, I must move . . . this way, find the greatest point of crisis. The thought caused him to halt the horse abruptly, his feet slipping from the stirrups, and he fell forward onto the horse's neck, then steadied himself with a hard grasp on the horse's mane. He was breathing heavily, realized he was alone, had left his staff behind. He searched the woods again, a small field, amid smoke, chatter, and thumps of nearby guns. I must return to the Roberts house. My staff should have accompanied me. They should know that, whether I order them or not.

He pushed the horse into the road, passing wounded men, and in a few minutes he was back near his headquarters. He could see the open ground around the Roberts house and was surprised to see troops, a scrambling herd, out of control. He reined up the horse, saw his staff moving among them, shouts and chaos.

Men were rushing past him now, and he called out, "Who are you? What troops are you? You must not run!"

A few men were slowing, exhausted, some dropping to their knees. He saw an officer among them, a lieutenant, shouted to the man, "What unit is this? Why are these men running away?"

The lieutenant looked up at him, no recognition. "Cumming's brigade, sir. These are good Georgia men. We were run off by a considerable force of the enemy."

Pemberton looked to the east, no signs of any heavier fighting, more of the steady skirmishing he had heard all morning.

"What enemy?"

"Don't rightly know, sir. But there was a wood-pile dollop of 'em."

"Stevenson's men?"

The lieutenant stood, some of his men doing the

same, the panic drained out of them. They stood staring at Pemberton, more men gathering, drawn to the patch of open ground. The lieutenant said, "Well, yes, sir, we been put in General Stevenson's division. But we belong to General Cumming. Georgians fight together, sir."

Pemberton felt a maddening frustration. He doesn't know anything, he thought. Cumming . . . Stevenson's division. They were not to the east. They were . . . to the north.

Though the first contact from the enemy had come directly eastward, Pemberton had received a steady flow of couriers from Carter Stevenson, who held the left flank, farther to the north. Each message brought the same urgency, that Stevenson was facing an enormous force of the enemy. Pemberton had mostly ignored that, held firmly to what he could see himself, that Loring's troops were facing what could only have been a heavy portion of Grant's army. Stevenson is fresh, he thought. His men don't have the experience, and I must consider that. These men are proof of that.

"Lieutenant, assemble these men into line. March them back to their position. We cannot have our troops scattered all over the field. Does General Stevenson know you're here?"

"I don't reckon he knows where we are, sir. I can't say I know where he is, either."

Gradually the men were put into some kind of line, more officers arriving, a pair on horseback, flags, Georgia men. Well, good, he thought. Take command, get these men back into position. The order was unnecessary, the officers doing the job, their troops reluctant but obedient. His staff was gathering closer to him now, Waddy speaking out.

"Sir, we have received another courier from General Stevenson. He still insists he must have reinforcements, sir. His flanks are in peril. He maintains he cannot keep any connection on his right flank with General Bowen's troops."

Pemberton was confused, had not wanted Bowen involved in any fighting. Bowen's men were the most experienced on the field, had given much of themselves all throughout this campaign. Pemberton had hoped they would simply get some rest. But Bowen's position, filling in the center of the army between Stevenson and Loring, meant that Bowen was the connecting point between the other two divisions.

"Where is General Bowen, Colonel?"

Waddy looked past him.

"Right there, sir."

Pemberton turned the horse, Bowen seeing him as well, moving his way. Pemberton felt a surge of relief. Finally, someone who will **know** what is happening. Bowen rode up close, his staff strung out at a safe distance. The heavy skirmishing continued in the woods to the east, the stink of smoke swirling around the officers.

Bowen did not salute, said, "General Loring is

holding the right flank, and my men are now facing a considerable force. But the enemy is not advancing with any aggressiveness. Should they move
against my lines, the ammunition trains must come
up! My men must fill their cartridge boxes."

"Is that McClernand? Are those people still the
ones from this morning?"

Bowen looked at him with a tilt of his head.

"From what we can tell, yes. Does that matter? I
am far more concerned with what is happening to
the north, my left flank."

"The north?"

Bowen pointed, as though Pemberton wouldn't
know the way.

"General Stevenson has sent word through my
command . . . the enemy has pushed him back
from those high ridges, that big hill. Have you not
received his reports?" Bowen paused. "Have you
not heard the **fighting**? I have stayed close to my
men, but I did hear artillery up that way. I thought
you would have ridden in that direction."

Pemberton stared at the distant mound of high
ground, saw smoke now, the first he had noticed
it. The sounds of the fight to the east, mostly in
front of Loring, had consumed his attention, and
throughout midday Pemberton had kept closer to
the house he had chosen as his field headquarters.
He focused on the Georgians, more of them scampering through the open ground, and he realized
there was musket fire coming from the base of

the big hill, much closer, a fight pushing directly toward him. There was more artillery fire as well, to the left, farther away, the sounds of a fight spreading out beyond his own left flank . . . moving **behind** him.

"We must find General Stevenson! What is his location?"

Bowen hesitated, then said, "I have no idea. I've been occupied with holding my lines right here. General Loring reports a considerable force of the enemy to our front, still to the east. But my skirmishers say the enemy is advancing from the left, from that high ground. These men . . . they're Georgians. That's Cumming's brigade. They've been driven back?"

"So I've been told. I've ordered them to move back into position."

"Which position, sir? I thought Cumming's brigade had moved north, to assist Lee's brigade. My understanding was that they were in position on that high ground. If Stevenson's brigades were pushed back . . . well, sir, clearly they were. General Stevenson was most adamant that his lines were in some trouble."

"Yes, I know that. I've been hearing that all day."

Bowen stared at him, and Pemberton caught the look.

"I assure you, John, I've been keeping a close eye on the situation. You recall, I had anticipated that General Loring would crush whatever enemy

forces came at us this morning, possibly with your
help. But since we have not accomplished that, we
must work to protect our vulnerabilities. If General Stevenson is giving way, we must assist him.
From all I can see, your division has not yet been
fully engaged. It would be advisable if you shifted
one brigade to the left and sought out contact with
his right flank. Clearly the enemy is attempting to
drive a wedge into our position."

Bowen kept the stare.

"Surely . . . he is. I shall put my men into motion
with all speed, sir. But I would insist that General
Loring do the same. My right must be protected.
General Loring must be ordered to shift his strongest lines where the danger is the greatest. From
all I can hear . . . from all we know, that danger
is not to the east, but to the north." He paused.
"You should ride there, find General Stevenson. He
would know what is needed in his own front."

The words from Bowen carried heat, impatience,
and Pemberton ignored that, saw another tide of
men flowing back through the yard, some dropping down, leaning against the sides of the house.
Men on horseback emerged into the fields now,
officers, a flag, more infantry, the officers gaining
some control. Closer to the house, Waddy was taking charge, gathering the refugees, their own officers assisting, getting them to their feet. Close to
Pemberton, other staff officers were staring toward
him, questions on every face. He glanced toward

Bowen again, watched as Bowen moved away, his staff trailing behind him. Pemberton sat straight in the saddle, tried to show an air of confidence, that finally he understood what was happening.

"Yes! We must ride up there! Do you men hear the fighting?"

Heads turned northward, and he saw Memminger now, coming from that way, a hard gallop toward him. Memminger spun the horse to a stop, saluted him, and said, "Sir! General Stevenson again requests in the most urgent terms that we send reinforcements his way! The enemy is pushing past his left flank and has broken his center. He has lost connection with General Bowen. He is in a dire situation, sir!"

Pemberton began to form a picture in his mind, a map in his brain, what Grant was doing. He knew of the road that ran parallel to the railroad, the very route he should have taken to Clinton, the first order he had received from Johnston. Now, he thought, Grant is there, has cut us off. There can be no rendezvous, no great plan to join our armies. The fight is . . . right here.

"Major, send a courier to General Loring. I had asked him to crush the enemy to his front, but if that enemy is of no danger, then request that he disengage as many of his units as he feels he can and march them northward. The greatest danger is up there, not to our front." It was a sudden moment of clarity, that if Bowen was right, if Stevenson's urgency was accurate, the Federal troops who had begun this day with a gentle slap at Loring's men were by now content to just . . . stay there. We are being held in place, he thought, one hand holding us down while the other reaches around us. No, it cannot happen.

A courier was getting the order from Memminger, and Pemberton rode toward them, wiped sweat from his eyes with the rough fingers of his gloves. Memminger said, "Captain Selph will convey your request to General Loring, sir. Is there anything else?"

Pemberton saw the impatience on Memminger's face, the same as the courier, men waiting to do the job.

"No. Captain Selph, go now. Request that General Loring assist us to the north, with all speed!"

Selph saluted him, pulled the horse, slapped its haunches hard with his hat, and was quickly away. Waddy was there now, holding his own horse alongside Memminger, the two senior staff officers watching him, waiting for . . . something. He stared to the north, saw a low haze of smoke, heard thumps from artillery. He was suddenly angry with himself, thought, You should have given heed to Stevenson's reports! You should have ridden to every part of this ground! But they should have kept you better informed. Who is to blame here? They would engage the enemy whether I was here or not! I must find what is happening. Perhaps I should remain here, where they may find me. But General Stevenson requires assistance. He says he must have it. Well, I have done all I can for now.

"Sir! General Bowen is returning!"

Pemberton saw Bowen riding up hard, his hat in his hand, dirty sweat on the man's face. Bowen said, "General, I am maneuvering a full brigade to my left, to counter the enemy's advances. There is a significant retreat of our people all along that part of the line. General Stevenson's right flank is no longer organized. Loring must come up with me! There is still a considerable body of the enemy to the east. So far, they seem content to keep to their lines, but that could change. Have you located General Stevenson?"

Pemberton absorbed Bowen's words, thought, Yes, good, move troops to the left. **Counter** the enemy's advance. Yes, very good.

Bowen spoke again, leaning closer to him.

"General Pemberton! Has General Stevenson reported his situation to you? Is General Loring aware that we must respond to the enemy's move against our left? Have you ordered—"

Pemberton snapped around, cutting off Bowen's words.

"Yes! I have ordered General Loring to move up this way! We must not lose this army's left flank, and your right must be protected. I have not heard anything from Stevenson!"

Memminger spoke, his voice low, just above the sounds of the fight.

"Sir, I reported to you a short time ago. General Stevenson requests in the most urgent terms . . ."

"Yes, yes! I recall. Go . . . find General Stevenson, or send someone . . . and tell him we are moving troops in his direction. If General Loring cannot confront the enemy to his front, then he could be of great service here." He looked at Bowen, who seemed to watch him with annoyed concern. "General Bowen, you must push your people to the left. We must halt the enemy's intrusion! If General Stevenson requires assistance, you must offer it."

"Then . . . you wish me to continue doing what I am doing, sir?"

Pemberton was already ignoring him, focused now on the courier riding hard from the south, Captain Selph, the man who had gone to Loring. Pemberton eased the horse that way, saw a strange look on the young man's face, Selph seeming to avoid him, moving past, close to Memminger. Pemberton jerked the horse that way, felt helpless, useless, as though no one even knew he was there. Selph spoke softly, gave his report to Memminger, but stopped short as Pemberton approached.

"What is this? Did you find General Loring?"

Selph looked down, and Memminger shouted hard at him.

"Make your report, Captain! The same as you told me!"

The young man looked at Pemberton from beneath the brim of his hat, still hesitant, and Pemberton looked at Memminger.

"What is it? What is wrong?"

Selph spoke up now.

"Sir, General Loring will not comply with your . . . **request,** sir. He says he is engaged with the enemy to his front. He says that there is Federal cavalry close at hand, and he must protect his right flank. He reminds the commanding general that his division anchors the right of the entire army, and thus he must be vigilant. General Tilghman was with him . . . and they were in agreement that your request not be followed. They were . . . not kind in their response, sir. I cannot in good conscience repeat what was said."

He thought of Loring, the man's infuriating lack of respect.

"He would refuse my direct order? I will ride there myself and deliver that order personally!"

Memminger spoke now, leaning closer to him.

"Sir, you did not order him . . . you did issue a **request** that he move his people. . . ."

"I know what an order is, Major!"

Memminger sat straight, accepted Pemberton's authority, the **final word,** and Pemberton tried to recall his instructions to Loring. I ordered him . . .

certainly. I shall discipline him for this. There can be no such disregard for my authority.

"We must ride to General Stevenson. We must determine what is needed in that quarter."

Bowen was still there. He burst through the gathered staff and said in a harsh shout, "General, I already know what is in that quarter! It is the enemy, and they are driving a deep hole through our position!"

"Yes, you have reported that! Very well, you will move a full brigade to the left. Is that acceptable?"

Bowen lowered his head for a brief moment, nodded. "Yes. It is."

Bowen moved away quickly, and Pemberton eased the horse out into the road, saw a large field beyond the house, out toward the sounds of the growing fight. He stared at the distant hill, bathed in a soft fog of smoke, looked high at the sun, drifting westerly, the day slipping past. So, he thought, Loring will not obey me, and Bowen thinks me the fool. What must Stevenson think of me? Perhaps he has other concerns.

He dismounted, stood close to the horse, smelled the hard stench of sweat from the animal's thick, frothy hair. From the house a group of women emerged, surprising him, all smiles, seemingly oblivious to the sounds of the fight.

"Ladies . . ."

They ignored him, focused instead on the gathering soldiers, stragglers from the fight on the hill, some mingling now with Bowen's men, who were already marching quickly along the road. The men began to hoot, the column ragged, slowing, their surprise equal to Pemberton's. The women were brightly dressed, halted close by the roadside, suddenly fell into song. The cheers grew louder, and Pemberton absorbed the scene with an unnerving mix of admiration and fear, that these women had no place in the kind of hell that was erupting closer to their home. But he felt the cold thrill in his chest, raised a hand himself, his own salute with the men around him. To the north, a new burst of firing began, Bowen's men moving into the fray, confronting the blue-coated troops who had pushed much closer to his headquarters than Pemberton expected. He tried to ignore that, just for a moment, to relish this marvelously feminine surprise. Like the men around him, he was drawn first to the voices, the song that he tried to find inspiring, that clearly inspired the troops around him. They were singing "Dixie."

Bowen moved Francis Cockrell's brigade into line, expecting to confront the Federal troops who might by now be on their last legs. Sensing the opportunity that might be presenting itself, Bowen ordered forth another brigade, under Martin Green, and their strength

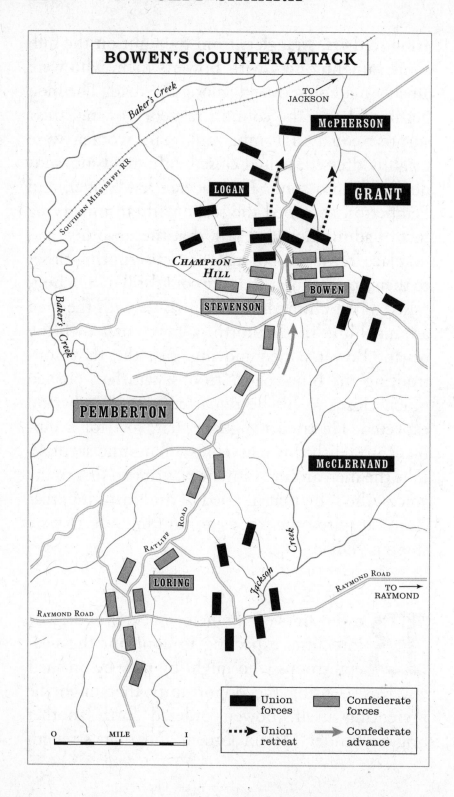

BOWEN'S COUNTERATTACK

TO JACKSON

McPHERSON

Baker's Creek

SOUTHERN MISSISSIPPI RR

LOGAN

GRANT

CHAMPION HILL

BOWEN

STEVENSON

Baker's Creek

PEMBERTON

McCLERNAND

RATLIFF ROAD

LORING

Jackson Creek

RAYMOND ROAD

TO RAYMOND

RAYMOND ROAD

	Union forces		Confederate forces
	Union retreat		Confederate advance

O   MILE   I

was increased further by the remnants of the original forces on Champion Hill who had struggled
mightily under Stephen Dill Lee. Forming into a
stout line of battle, Bowen's men drove northward
and almost immediately surprised Alvin Hovey's
exhausted Federals, the men who had fought up
and over Champion Hill. The Federal troops had
given nearly all their energy to the fight they had
every reason to believe they were winning. The
sudden appearance of Bowen's fresh lines drove the
Federal forces back across the same ground they
had won, past the scattered dead and wounded
from both sides. By mid-afternoon, Bowen's men
had retaken the hill itself and driven Hovey's men
back toward the Champion House, in full view of
Ulysses Grant. But Grant and James McPherson
had an asset that Pemberton did not: a full retinue
of reserves. Though Hovey's worn-out troops had
given way, in their place came a full Federal division,
under the command of Marcellus Crocker. Despite
John Bowen's audacity, Crocker's fresh troops were
too much for the Confederates to handle. Once
more the fight drifted back over Champion Hill,
and once more the Federal troops occupied the
high ground. As the afternoon sun drifted into far
treetops, the fight all across the ground around and
below Champion Hill was winding down for the
final time.

———

The collapse of Stevenson's position had brought the Federal troops down close to the middle road, had taken away what Pemberton had expected to be the best avenue of escape back to Edward's Station. After a confusion of countermanded orders, the brigade and regimental commanders took charge of as many of their own men as could be found, and the retreat began. But the order for a general withdrawal had not been made clear to Pemberton's commanders. Across every part of the field, scattered fighting continued, chaotic and desperate, while Confederate commanders tried to salvage what remained of their forces. On the primary north–south road where Pemberton's army had held their ground against McClernand's sluggish advances, great gaps had formed, some caused by the amazing stubbornness of William Loring. Ordered repeatedly by Pemberton to advance troops northward, Loring at long last had sent a single brigade, but only a brigade. Loring continued to insist that his right flank to the south was in some danger, no matter Pemberton's orders.

With daylight slipping away, the Confederate army had finally begun to move westward, crossing Baker's Creek, good officers doing what they could to protect the wagons and their own men. The urgency had increased dramatically when it became clear that the Federal troops to the east, the massive force under John McClernand, had finally begun

an advance of their own. Throughout the day, Mc-
Clernand had seemed content to keep his people
engaged in cautious, methodical probing, in small-
scale fights that erupted all along the Confederate
position. But with the fight to the north sweeping down well below Champion Hill, McClernand
had finally responded to Grant's continuing stream
of orders, had finally become an aggressor. The
sudden crushing blow by McClernand's forces had
only increased the peril faced by Pemberton's battered army.

Loring continued to battle the advancing Federals as best he could, which allowed many of Bowen's
troops to pull back across the first obstacle to the
west, Baker's Creek. There Confederate engineers
had bridged the waters, but the creek had calmed
considerably, and a great many of Pemberton's men
made the crossing by wading on their own.

Though Loring had finally shifted troops to
the north, he had maneuvered most of his much-
needed regiments along the wrong road, taking
his men in a more westerly direction, well behind
the roads and fields that had been fought over by
Bowen and Stevenson. As Pemberton's army withdrew across Baker's Creek, Loring's apparent mistake happened to place him in the best position
to protect the army's rear. But the Federals had exhausted themselves as well as their enemy. As night
fell, there could be no energetic pursuit.

Pemberton's army had suffered nearly four thou-

sand casualties, Grant's near twenty-five hundred.
As Pemberton pushed his demoralized army westward, he knew they would not stop at Edward's
Station. If there was to be any kind of effective
defense against Grant's advance, they would move
with as much speed as the men could muster, taking them to the one place Pemberton knew with
perfect certainty was the most secure defensive
position for his army to make their stand: the Big
Black River. Pemberton now understood that by
obeying Joe Johnston's orders, he had made a disastrous mistake, had weakened the forces he had to
rely upon to protect Vicksburg, a mistake he would
certainly not make again. But the Big Black could
not yet give his army the perfect protection they
would need. Pemberton could not be certain just
where Loring's division had gone, just how far back
they were, and whether or not Loring would has-
ten his men toward Vicksburg pursued by an aggressive Federal advance. So, as Pemberton's troops
dragged their way to the safety of the Big Black,
he was forced to keep a sizable number of muskets, the remnants of Bowen's division, on the east
side of the river, with the unburned bridges and the
deep gash of the river's banks to the rear of much
of Bowen's force, in the optimistic hope that they
could keep the Federals away from the bridgehead
until Loring's men could reach them.

What Pemberton could not know was that Loring had other ideas. In the full darkness of early

evening, Loring could not maneuver effectively without stumbling directly through the new camps of their victorious enemy. If he waited for the new dawn's sunrise, Loring knew that he would likely be directly in the midst of Grant's entire army. Locating a local guide, Loring instead maneuvered his men with impressive stealth along narrow pathways and dim farm roads, until they were clear of the Federal camps. But he did not march his men toward the Big Black. Instead, Loring preserved his own troops by escaping to the south and east, a long roundabout maneuver that took them not toward Pemberton, which would have added much-needed strength to the bloodied Confederates. Loring chose a different route altogether that would eventually take him east, toward Jackson. Loring had made his own command decision, that if his division was to take the field again, it would do so not under Pemberton, but under the command of Joe Johnston.

CHAPTER SEVENTEEN

PEMBERTON

BIG BLACK RIVER BRIDGE
MAY 17, 1863

"Is there no word?"

Waddy pulled his horse close beside him and said, "No, sir. Scouts report some activity to the southeast that could be General Loring's advance, but the Federals are fully in control of every major roadway. My apologies for such speculation, sir, but it could be that General Loring is entirely at the mercy of the Federals."

Pemberton stared through the field glasses, studying the ground east of the river, staring above the heads of Bowen's men, who had occupied entrenchments more than a half mile east of the river itself.

"We are all at the mercy of the Federals, Colonel.

We must make our stand here with the best energy we can muster."

He saw a cluster of officers, the colors trailing high, knew it was Bowen, the men reaching the bridge, moving quickly across. Waddy said, "Sir . . ."

"Yes, I see him. He will certainly see me. At least one officer in this army keeps me informed."

Waddy ignored the comment, and Pemberton waited for Bowen to approach, the staff keeping back, Bowen tossing up a salute.

"Sir, we are in place. When we filed into the entrenchments, there was a brigade of Tennesseans there already. Eastern men. I spoke to their commander . . ."

"Yes, General Vaughn. General Smith ordered them out here from Vicksburg when he received word of our . . . misfortune at Baker's Creek. I am not overly confident in them, General. They are fresh to this army, little experience with the enemy."

"Vaughn said as much. I placed them directly in my center, between my two brigades. That should keep them out of trouble. I doubt there will be much of a fight anyway. Once General Loring sees fit to join us, we can vacate that position and move back here west of the river. I'll send General Smith's brigade back to Vicksburg ahead of us. I rather like watching the backside of men who might be a tad disloyal. Never sure just who they're going to shoot at."

It was a comment Pemberton didn't need, a question of disloyalty always floating around any troops from the mountains of eastern Tennessee. The entire Confederacy knew that the people in that part of the country held a distinct loyalty to the Union, no matter that they were surrounded by fiercely rebel sentiments. But . . . they were here, they carried muskets, and Pemberton just couldn't think about anyone else's concerns of disloyalty. He had heard too many hints about his own.

"Vaughn is said to be a good brigadier. With your men flanking him, I have no concerns."

Bowen shrugged, had made his point, had done all he could to secure the position he had been assigned.

Waddy spoke up, as though Pemberton needed one more voice of agreement.

"Yes, sir, General Vaughn is a good man. Most loyal, sir."

Pemberton glanced at Waddy, Bowen ignoring both of them. Pemberton was beginning to hate the word, knew that "loyalty" was one of those standards that mattered around his own command the way "courage" mattered most to the infantry.

Throughout the night, as Pemberton made his own way through the retreating army, he passed soldiers, his soldiers, the men who knew more than anyone that they had failed to hold back the forces of General Grant. In the dark, the voices rolled past him, few paying attention to the horsemen who paraded by them with greater speed, officers of every unit flowing away from Champion Hill, feeling the same despair as their men. Pemberton had been just one more horseman, one more cluster of staff, one more flag. And so the voices had not been discreet, no one paying attention to rank or command, and those voices had been angry, low curses, talk of betrayal and defeat, all of it laid at the feet of the man who led them. Pemberton had tried not to hear that, but the voices were everywhere, on every pathway, grumblings from old sergeants or teenage boys, even the officers prodding their men with talk of how "someone else" would have to be their salvation, some speaking of Joe Johnston. It was the only optimism these men seemed to carry, that somewhere out there, Johnston was assembling a vast, fresh army to sweep through the flanks of the Federals, driving Grant away for all time. It was the only hopefulness he heard, and Pemberton could only move westward in silence, knowing that no matter what he had tried to accomplish against the forces Grant threw at him, it had not been enough. If there was any confidence in Pemberton at all, he heard it only from his own staff, small bits of encouragement that the move to the Big Black would regroup the scattered units, bring the key officers back together, that the army still had the spirit, the willingness to crush any force sent against them. Pemberton appreciated the optimism of his staff, whether it was counterfeit or not. The single day's fight along Baker's Creek, the struggle that swept both armies back and forth over the bare heights of Champion Hill, had been a worthless bloodletting. Pemberton knew that Grant, besides gaining a resounding victory, had also been allowed the gift of a day's time, to bring forth more of his army, Sherman certainly, though Pemberton had no idea where Sherman's troops might be. Word had come often of the conflagration at Jackson, exaggerated reports of wanton destruction throughout the capital, the murder of civilians, unspeakable violations of anyone who dared protest the viciousness of Sherman's tactics. Pemberton didn't believe that, not all of it. It was logical, after all, that any good commander would damage his enemy's ability to wage war, and so would target factories and storehouses. And it was just as logical that those who saw their property consumed by flames would react with a fiery response of their own, their only weapon a blossoming hatred for the men who used the torches.

He stared again through the field glasses, a cluster of trees to the left, the northern flank of Bowen's position. Scanning the field, he strained to see any kind of movement: flags, horses, some sign of Loring's advance guards. It was still early, but the open ground was already bathed in daylight, little cover for anyone who would approach, at least not directly to the front. No, Loring will most likely come in from down below, the right. The enemy . . .

well, they might not come at all today. They know
we are here in force, certainly. Grant took a hard
knock yesterday, and he will move fresher troops to
the front. And that would be Sherman. Sherman
will not linger in Jackson. There is no purpose to
that. Grant will want him out here, leading the way
toward Vicksburg. It is just . . . good command
decision, and I would do the same. The Yankees
have a duty to defeat us, as we have a duty to drive
them from this land. Yesterday we could not stand
up to their numbers. There was poor communication, poor work from the staffs of every general
on the field. I will seek the cause of that, in time.
There will be answers. Stevenson failed to hold his
flank. Loring . . . Loring betrayed me, no better explanation. He was disobedient to my commands. I
cannot tolerate that, not at all. Who would expect
me to? There will be a hearing, certainly, perhaps
a court-martial. He thought of the angry talk the
night before, men spouting out their frustration by
aiming their wrath at him. I must accept that, he
thought. It is my army, my command, and those
men have no understanding of the complexity of
it all. One word stuck in his mind now, a word he
heard often in the ranks, men bemoaning the lack
of a **Stonewall**.

He barely knew Thomas Jackson at all, was well
aware that Loring had been involved in a significant
controversy with Jackson early in the war, in western
Virginia. Loring had been placed under Jackson's

command, Stonewall already gaining a colorful reputation in Richmond as perhaps the South's most
effective field commander. Loring was the more
political general, and did not fully accept Jackson's
authority, or the strategies that Jackson imposed on
his subordinates. The feud was resolved when Loring was sent west. So, Pemberton thought, General
Loring has made himself a nuisance to anyone he
has served. What must he think of Stonewall now?
The great Jackson is dead, and this entire army . . .
this entire country mourns the loss. Would he be
alive had Loring been a more capable subordinate?
Already there are those who claim the Almighty has
punished the South for our cause. Certainly, the
newspapers in the North will embrace that absurdity. But is it not just as understandable that God
has provided us with a martyr, a source of inspiration? This army requires inspiration, certainly. He
looked toward Bowen again, the man moving in
the saddle, anxious to return to his men. You might
be the best I have, he thought. Perhaps you know
that as well. And so, perhaps that will keep you
loyal to me. You will understand the importance
of our duty here, that we must protect Vicksburg
above all else, no matter what **cause** drives General
Johnston. There is great value in Bowen's leadership, perhaps more than my own. His men follow
him with perfect obedience. His lines have not collapsed; his officers have not failed us, failed **me**. But
is Bowen a Stonewall? There is a danger to that, to

elevating men to mythical perches. In life, General Jackson led his troops to great victories. In death, he leads them nowhere. Perhaps that is the great lesson here. Some of us fight for the history books. Johnston. Perhaps. He does not fight for **this** command, for Vicksburg. So what else inspires him? Does he gain his satisfaction from infuriating Jefferson Davis? Is that enough for him? Who can be inspired by such motives? Pemberton sat back, sagging in the saddle, the field glasses by his side. All he has cost me is . . . casualties.

His mind was clouding, the intense weariness of the past twenty-four hours, mostly on horseback. He followed Bowen's stare again, brought the glasses up, aimed his gaze closer still, men on this side of the river, the best ground, the best protection the river could offer. The bridge remained intact, and in the river itself, a steamboat, the **Dot,** had been anchored, converted to a floating bridge of its own. Downstream, two others, the **Paul Jones** and the **Charm,** were perched as well, their equipment and obstructions removed, placed perpendicular to the flow of the river. The river itself formed a wide horseshoe, a vast U shape bisected by the railroad line, that would invite any approach directly toward the bridge. We are strongest there, even with Bowen's doubts about the Tennesseans. But if Loring will finally arrive it will not matter.

His gaze settled on an artillery emplacement, and he aimed the question at Bowen.

"How much artillery has been left in place east of the river, General?"

"I have three batteries, a dozen guns. Not sure how many guns Vaughn's boys have."

Behind Waddy, another man rode forward, and Pemberton was surprised to see him, grateful as well. It was his chief engineer, Samuel Lockett. Lockett said, "Begging your pardon, sirs, I have counted twenty pieces. Mostly six- and twelve-pounders. It is not a juggernaut, but it should slow the enemy down. The ground they must cross is flat and open. I do not envy the soldiers who make that advance."

Lockett had been with the army since well before Shiloh the year before, and when Pemberton assumed command of the department in Mississippi, he had been delighted to learn that Lockett would be his chief engineer. Lockett was a West Pointer, a young, energetic man who had served with distinction under Albert Sidney Johnston and Pierre Beauregard. Above all, Lockett's training had put him in a number of crucial situations, whether bridge building or the rapid repair of any roadway the army might need, including the escape routes over Baker's Creek the night before. Now he commanded the efforts Pemberton needed to straddle both sides of the Big Black.

Bowen seemed to appreciate the engineer's work.

"It was you who dug these works?"

"I supervised, yes, sir. I hope they are to your satisfaction."

Bowen nodded, returned to his field glasses.

"They're adequate. For now. We don't need to stay out there any longer than it takes. Those are tired troops, and right now, I'm guessing some of my boys are catching a quick nap. I want them pulled out of there as soon as our . . . job is done."

Lockett looked at Pemberton, who nodded approval.

Lockett said, "Sir, I am prepared at a moment's notice to fire the bridge, and if necessary, the three riverboats. We have bales of cotton along the riverbank, and many barrels of turpentine. The bridge in particular will be the greatest challenge, but once your men are across, the enemy will not have the time to take advantage."

Pemberton stared at the bridge.

"I admire your confidence, Major. Thank you for your efforts. Have you been in communication with your engineers in Vicksburg? How does that work progress?"

"Quite well, sir. There is much still to accomplish, a great many strongpoints to be fortified. But even now, the labor is ongoing."

Pemberton nodded absently.

"We shall require all your efforts, Major."

"Sir! Riders!"

Pemberton tried to focus the sleepiness out of his eyes, saw the movement, well to the right. He brought the glasses up, could see four men, dirty gray uniforms, a hard ride, slowed briefly by Bowen's men, then continuing straight toward the bridge. In a short minute they crossed, guided by officers who pointed them toward Pemberton. Pemberton felt a burst of excitement, was awake now, sat straight in the saddle, thought, There will be news, at last.

They reined up, tossed him their salutes, Bowen moving up beside Pemberton, clearly interested in what they had to report. Pemberton did not wait.

"Is General Loring close behind?"

The men were settling their horses, a sheen of wet foam on each animal, and one man spoke up, a captain, in the unmistakable uniform of cavalry.

"No, sir! We have not seen General Loring. We have seen no infantry at all. We have ridden from Baker's Creek, close to the enemy camps at the main crossroads. The enemy is on the move this way, began their march well before dawn, sir."

Pemberton rolled the word over in his mind. **Cavalry.**

"Have you seen Colonel Adams, then? Is he gathering his horsemen? I have not seen him since yesterday."

"Sir . . . Colonel Adams is gone, out to the east. The last word I received was that he had too many horsemen out beyond the enemy. He said he intended to gather as many of his squads as he could locate, and pull them eastward toward the capital. His last orders to me were to make every effort to find you, and report that he is preserving as many of his men as he can, and will rejoin you when the time is right."

Pemberton felt a cold stab.

"When the time is **right**? Does he know anything of General Loring? When is the time right? The enemy is on the march . . . in this direction, I presume?"

The man was suddenly sheepish, seemed to grasp the gravity of his message.

"I know nothing of General Loring, sir . . . except . . . we heard that General Tilghman was killed. The Yankees were speaking of it. We stayed close to their camps until near sunrise. I can't confirm any more than that."

Pemberton looked down, then glanced at Waddy.

"Do we know anything of this?"

"No, sir. I would have notified you."

"Yes, of course. If this is true . . . if Tilghman is dead, it is a disaster, one more disaster for this army. Such men cannot be replaced." He looked toward the horseman again, more questions rolling up inside of him, but there was a tired emptiness to the man, his report delivered, his single duty completed. Pemberton saw the last bit of energy draining from them all, thought, At least they have found us. General Loring . . . certainly has not.

Bowen said, "The enemy is on the march, you say. How many? How much force? Are we certain they are moving in this direction?"

The cavalryman focused on Bowen, seemed to recognize him, threw up a sudden unnecessary salute.

"Uh, sir . . . they're on the march, that's for certain."

"How many of them, Captain?"

"We didn't stay too close to 'em, sir. All we can say is . . . there's a passel of 'em."

Bowen looked at Pemberton, and Pemberton saw the hard frown, a pulsing anger.

"Well, General, I'm not sure how long we can hold our position on that side of the river. If General Loring intends to make his appearance, this would be a very good time."

The thump of thunder rolled over the field, faces turning that way. Pemberton saw the smoke, a single gray wisp, rising up from the cluster of trees to the north. Now there was more smoke, billowing out from the woods to the left flank, the thunder coming soon after. Closer, his own artillery responded, the shells streaking over the open ground, some over the heads of Bowen's men. Bowen said, "A new day, a new fight. With your permission, General, I will take my leave."

He didn't wait for Pemberton's response, spurred the horse, and was gone quickly, galloping across the bridge, moving out to be with his men. Pemberton felt the thunder of the shelling all through him, so familiar now, the pure sound of power, both sides, a duel expanding to batteries on this

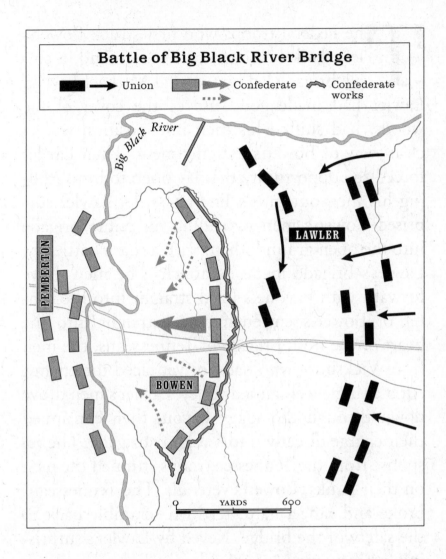

side of the river. He tried to lift the field glasses, no strength in his arms, and for now there was nothing to see, just an open field, the sky above streaked by the shells that bore one simple message. Grant's army had arrived.

The Federal troops who first struck Bowen's left flank belonged to McClernand, a single brigade led by General Michael Lawler. Lawler had made good use of the cover of the woods, had shifted his men into position with a clear view of Bowen's entrenchment. Then Lawler forced the opportunity that lay open to him. Rolling his men out into a line of battle, Lawler surprised Bowen's men by sliding his entire brigade into the open ground, then, with a sharp battle cry, Lawler's brigade made its attack. The men drove forward with bayonets fixed straight into the center of Bowen's entrenchments, straight into the heart of the fresh brigade of Tennesseans, the men from Vicksburg who had not yet faced the enemy. After a single well-aimed volley, Lawler's men drove down through the soggy bayou, then continued their charge directly into Vaughn's brigade. The response from the Tennessee troops stunned the men on their flanks, Bowen's veterans. The Tennesseans broke and ran, a hard, terrified scramble back to the safety of the bridge. Keyed by Lawler's surprising success, more of McClernand's troops drove quickly across the open ground, and Bowen's men, realizing their center had collapsed completely, could not stand up to the tide. In an hour's time, Bowen's entire force had made a rapid retreat of their own, a massive struggle to shove across the river bridge, others dropping down the steep embankments, swimming, or drowning, in their frantic escape. As more Federal troops pushed forward, the fight spread along the river itself, some of the Confederate troops shot down as they swam or made the climb up the far bank. The musket fire went in both directions, most of it ineffective, the river providing the safety it always had, the blue troops content to keep to the eastern side, rounding up prisoners and artillery pieces, the remnants of the army that once again could not hold them back.

P emberton had ridden back toward the railhead at Bovina, his staff preparing the railcar that would take him on to Vicksburg. But Pemberton could not just abandon the men at the Big Black; he knew deep in his conscience that there would be talk about that. It was his battle, after all.

He sat alongside the road, tall in the saddle, fighting the lack of sleep. They marched in something of a column toward him, men still flowing out of the woods from both sides of the bridge, finding their way to the route that would lead them away from one more disaster. The order had gone out to every officer who could be found, to organize their men as well as possible, putting them on the march westward. He had thought of making another fight, of putting his troops into line along the west side of the Big Black, where he knew they should always have been. Grant was there in force now, just beyond the deep cuts of the riverbank, and Pemberton could not help believing that no matter what he did, Grant would come, that Vicksburg was, after all, his primary goal.

The decision to withdraw had come with the successful firing of the bridge, and Pemberton stared at that now, a vast plume of black smoke, a billowing fire boiling up from Lockett's barrels of turpentine. He could not look away, the bridge a quarter mile to his front, the ground between flowing with his men, retreating once more. There was still musket fire, some from the north, a fight he knew nothing about, another crossing of the river above the rail line. Stevenson was there, doing all he could to hold back the Federal wave, making good use of the river's defenses. But Grant cannot be stopped, he thought, not for long. He has engineers of his own, and good cavalry, and it will not take them very long to find their own way across. He still stared at the dense smoke, could see flickers of tall flame as the bridge was fully engulfed in Lockett's fire.

For long minutes, the smoke boiled upward, the thick cover spreading out with the light breeze, covering what he knew was happening east of the river. Major Lockett had done exactly as ordered, had waited until the last possible moment to fire the bridge. Many of Bowen's men had made their way to safety, and Pemberton could only hope that those caught on the far side of the river were not many, the wounded perhaps, a few more. He would know the toll later, could not think of that now, would not think of Bowen, and what Pemberton had ordered him to do. Bowen was safe, that was certain, was putting his men on the march, westward, away from the river. There will be blame for this, too, he thought. Bowen will curse me for putting his men out there, vulnerable, the river at their **back**. But it was . . . the job at hand. How could we know the enemy would move so quickly? At least, Pemberton thought, we can pull ourselves away, make for the next best place of safety, the place we should have never left.

Pemberton turned the horse, no staff officers with him at all, no flag, nothing to let the men around him know just who was in command. He started to ride, moving along with them, his head low, heard his name, official, respectful. He stopped, knew the voice of Lockett, caught the smell of turpentine. Lockett was there now.

"Sir! The bridge is destroyed. The enemy must find other means to make their crossing. There is little time to lose."

"I know, Major. There is a train waiting at Bovina, to carry us to Vicksburg. The staff has gone ahead to make all the arrangements for my headquarters."

"Sir, my work here is complete. Might I ride with you? The commanding general should not be alone. Not now."

Pemberton wasn't sure what Lockett meant,

thought, Does he believe I am in danger? How much more danger can there be?

Around them, men began to call out, the recognition spreading, officers riding past with an offer of a salute. But many more did not, and the men in the ranks were much less discreet. He heard curses, attached to his own name, and no one seemed to care if he heard them or not. Some of the officers were doing what they could to bring control, to silence the fury, and Pemberton ignored that, carried enough anger for all of them, a silent fury toward the man who had done this, who had ordered him away from Vicksburg only to have this marvelous army crushed under Grant's boot heel. Beside him, Lockett kept his silence, seemed to know Pemberton was far away, with hard thoughts in other directions. They rode along at a slow pace, and after a long moment, Pemberton said, "I obey the orders I am given. And for that I will be condemned."

"Sir? I hardly think . . ."

"When the orders contradict each other, when my president tells me to carry out **his** instructions, when my commanding general orders me to do the opposite . . . which is the right decision?" He paused, Lockett not responding. "Good generals must understand that these men, the infantry, are the pawns in a deadly chess game. But I am no different. I am a pawn in a game of politics and pride. I must make amends for that. What do we know of General Johnston? Right now."

"I am not certain, sir. I have heard rumor that he is bringing together a strong force, possibly to attack the Federals from the east."

"Wonderful rumors, are they not? All will be saved. Victory will be ours. It could be true, as fantastic as that sounds. It could be true. I sent General Johnston a letter by courier early this morning, before the Federals attacked us. I informed him of our inglorious defeat at Baker's Creek, and how we would do all in our power to strike back at the enemy. I suppose I should send him a more accurate letter. Events seem to change in this department far more quickly than I can report them."

"Yes, sir. If you say so, sir."

The reins were loose in his hands, the horse following the march of the infantry more than his own control, and he stared at the backs of the men, battered, filthy, men who had faced the enemy once more and could not find a victory. We have one duty, he thought. The only duty. It was **always** the only duty. Major Lockett has done the job, will continue with the good work. The fortifications are strong, will be made stronger, and these men know now what they must do, the fight that must be made. It is in them still, surely, and if they do not fight for me, they will fight to hold to such a treasure, the place we never should have left. He stopped again, stung by a thought, turned, and looked back toward the burning bridge, still a fountain of thick black smoke. Lockett stopped as well, and waited.

"Are you certain of the destruction of the bridge? Perhaps you should remain there."

"Sir, I witnessed heavy timbers falling into the river. The bridge was full aflame. The enemy can make no use of it. There were sharpshooters lining the bank, keeping the Yankees at bay. We do have time, sir."

"Yes, of course. I do not mean to doubt you. I must rely on your talents a great deal now. I am no engineer myself. I trust your work on the entrenchments at Vicksburg are strong?"

"They will be. There is much to be done."

"There is always much to be done. I am never at rest, Major."

Beside him, more men were moving into the road, another regiment, following their colors, their officers, a soldier shouting something, more shouts, and again Pemberton heard his name. He forced himself beyond that, kept his stare at the bridge, one thought rising up above all others. We stopped out here . . . made a stand on the wrong side of the river. And so, we lost good men here . . . because Loring made us wait. Bowen may curse me for that. But if I ever see Loring again, I will shoot him in the heart.

No, you will not.

The smoke at the bridge was beginning to slow,

and he turned the horse's head, spurred the animal gently, Lockett following, close beside him.

Pemberton said, "Thirty years ago, Major, I began my military career by receiving an appointment to the U.S. Military Academy."

"Yes, sir. I did as well, sir. Graduating Class of 1859."

"Well, of course, yes. But there is one very great difference between us. Your future is bright; you are respected, skilled; you could be a prominent engineer in any army. Today, that career that glowed with so much brightness all those years ago . . . that career is ended in disaster and disgrace."

"Forgive me, sir, but I most heartily disagree. We have not yet had the enemy to our own advantage. That will change, and very soon. I will see to that, sir."

Pemberton saw the hint of fire in Lockett's eyes, and nodded slowly.

"The optimism of youth. You wear that well, Major."

They moved past the marching soldiers, and Pemberton stared out ahead, nothing to see but troops, the road, trees, and rolling ground. It was not so many miles to go, the place that was his to defend, the only duty left to him, the only duty that mattered. Before nightfall, they would be in Vicksburg.

PART TWO

You have heard that I was incompetent, and a traitor; and that it was my intention to sell Vicksburg. Follow me, and you will see the cost at which I will sell Vicksburg. When the last pound of beef, bacon, and flour, the last grain of corn, the last cow and hog and horse and dog shall have been consumed, and the last man shall have perished in the trenches, then, and only then will I sell Vicksburg.

—LIEUTENANT GENERAL
JOHN C. PEMBERTON

CHAPTER EIGHTEEN

SPENCE

VICKSBURG, MISSISSIPPI
MAY 17, 1863

She had been up on Sky Parlor Hill for most of an hour, alongside a group of women, those who came here often to watch the spectacle. The Federal gunboats had given them the usual show, thunderous, smoky blasts, streaks of red fire from their heavy mortars, the steel balls arcing up and over the hill, falling somewhere into the town below, mostly behind the hill. There were homes and businesses along the hillside itself, as far down as the rows of warehouses that lined the river, but the citizens had mostly abandoned those, and the Federal navy seemed to know that, paid far more attention to lofting the mortar shells high up over the bluffs. The Confederate batteries were all along the hillside facing the river, some hidden well near the structures, but for the most part, the gunners had selected their emplacements along empty ground, showing respect for those homes that might become targets, should the guns be placed too close.

The mortars had become routine to everyone but the dogs, who responded incessantly to the shrieks and tumbles of any kind of shell with what Lucy still believed were terrified howls. The dogs were on the hill as well, crouching alongside their masters, or standing tall, their loud barks and howling, protesting the chaos that poured over them. Whether or not the dogs could be convinced of anything, Lucy knew now that there was little to fear up on the tall hill, the Yankee gunners firing their charges well past, what seemed to be a concerted effort to damage the town itself. Despite the abundance of iron the Yankees threw at the town, so far any serious damage had been rare. One home had taken a shell straight through the roof, a crashing surprise into a woman's dining room. There was other damage as well, gardens churned up, streets pockmarked, craters opened up on sloping hillsides. But few people had been injured from the mortar rounds, though rumors spread, as they always did, that someone, somewhere had lost a leg, or a Negro had been killed out to the north of town, though no one was sure just who he belonged to. Lucy thought of that, so much ridiculous talk, was grateful that the hilltop was mostly empty of the old men, at least for now. When they made the climb, they seemed so eager to regale the women with tales as horrible as they were ludicrous, as though the old men knew all there was to know about war. Lucy had tried her best to avoid them, but they would find her, always found her, an attractive young woman without escort. Whether the old men had ever been genuine warriors, she was a perfect captive audience, too polite to move away, too solitary to distract herself in some chatter with the usual groups of women.

The women were there as well, even now, clusters of bright color along the crest of the wide hill, chattering in awe with each new volley from the boats. For most, terror of the Federal gunboats had faded, replaced more often by thoughts of their husbands. Most of the younger men were gone, somewhere east or south, standing tall against the Yankee invasion. No one in the town really knew much of what had happened since Grant had come across the river, where the Yankees had gone, or just what might happen next. But the men had responded as good patriots, adding to General Pemberton's forces, husbands and sons learning quickly what a soldier was supposed to do. The men weren't far away, confirmation of that coming from the frequent visits home by officers. The news they brought was mostly vague, hints of better things to come, of the inevitable victory, building up the expectations of some grand parade when the men came home. What came from the civilians who traveled was mostly rumor, those who made short journeys out to the plantations, visiting relatives, checking on their safety, whether the Yankees had indeed committed unspeakable acts. The old men picked up on that, and on Sky Parlor Hill, they filled the void with tales of Grant's viciousness, the certain brutality and savagery the Yankees would bring. By now, even the most sheepish women had learned to ignore that. All anyone really knew was that General Grant and a number of Yankee troops were marching out deeper into Mississippi, that there had been some kind of assault against the fortifications that protected the capital city, and that for all they knew the Yankees were long gone, perhaps all the way back to Tennessee.

So far, the only kind of enemy Lucy had seen were floating serenely on the river, mostly upstream, offering up their iron projectiles at regular intervals, so predictable they had become a part of the daily lives of the very citizens the boats were targeting. The gunboats operated with punctual efficiency, the entire town seeming to know just when the firing would begin, when there would be the midday pause, as though the Yankee sailors were taking time out for a noon meal. Then the firing would begin again, throughout the afternoon, until it was time for everyone, the Yankees included, to attend to their dinners.

For the few weeks since it began, the boats launching the mortar shells had been few, a small part of a much larger navy the civilians could see from the vantage point of the hill. Upriver, the Federals were clearly in force, and anyone with a spyglass could make out boats coming and going, from newly created wharves where wagons were loaded with whatever the Yankees were bringing down from farther north. Blue-coated soldiers could be seen moving through a great sea of white tents, going about their business, whatever that business might be. No one had explained to Lucy just why the Yankees were shelling the town in the first place, though the old men who claimed authority on such matters were quick to point out that the Yankees had to rely solely on their mortars, since the trajectory of fire from the heavy cannons could not reach the heights of the town.

For the most part, the Confederate gunners who manned the artillery emplacements along the river's edge kept silent. There were questions about that, those same old men wondering why General Pemberton did not respond, that any good aim from a Confederate gunner could send the closer gunboats skedaddlin' back upriver.

When the sights and sounds from Sky Parlor Hill couldn't hold her interest, Lucy would embark on another of her new routines, making a careful descent to the gun pits. She enjoyed speaking to the men who huddled with the cannons, though likely not as much as they appreciated visiting with her. When she planned those visits in advance, she would bypass the hill altogether, and bring the artillerymen a basket of cookies or some kind of cake. Usually her eye was caught by a young officer, the man making great show over her generosity as though she had brought the gift of angels to the soldiers of the Confederacy. But Lucy kept her own responses discreet. She still thought of the one lieutenant she had met at the formal dance, the young Louisianan. But it was foolish to imagine they would somehow find the opportunity for such luxury as a pleasant gala, another dance. It embarrassed her that she would harbor such playful images of peaceful walks in a garden, of allowing herself to touch the hand of this handsome officer. She fought against the romantic images of poetry and awkward conversation, all those things young suitors had to suffer through. Most of the girls would be carefully supervised by the watchful eye of a stern mother, and it pained her even now to realize it would never be like that for her. If there was any chaperone at all, it would be her own conscience. She knew what the women were gossiping about, knew all the speculation about the kind of girl who chose to live on her own. There might be an officer in her future, but she had to accept she might not ever see the young man again. All she knew of him was his regiment, the 3rd Louisiana, one of hundreds of men who had made their encampment out along the burgeoning entrenchments and earthworks inland from the town. She didn't even know his name.

In the days following the gala, so rudely interrupted by the Yankees, she had learned what many of the men in the town already knew. When Pemberton had marched his men out to confront Grant, the 3rd Louisiana, part of Forney's division, had remained behind, the officers quick to assure the civilians that the army was not about to abandon the town, that General Pemberton had ordered a sizable force to occupy their own earthworks. Those defensive works now spread for miles in a giant arc that bulged inland, curving back to anchor above and below the town right against the river. The men Pemberton had left behind had spent much of their time in construction, widening and deepening the earthworks, adding tall redoubts, steep defensive positions that gave confidence to the civilians, who welcomed the officers' assurances that the defenses would hold back any attempt by this devil Grant, should he be foolish enough to assault them. On Sky Parlor Hill, the mouthy old men disagreed, protesting that the army should be focusing more attention on the gunboats. Instead of so much good artillery aimed out at empty fields to the east, the guns should be brought along the riverbanks, adding to the firepower of the cannons that the old men groused about, the men angry that some weak-willed Confederate commander was not spending his time shattering every Federal boat that dared fire its mortar. Lucy had sought out some explanation why so many of the Confederate gun batteries along the river had kept silent. Her flirtatious artillery officer had obliged, with a high-handed demonstration of his expertise. If the big guns on the Federal boats couldn't reach the city, they could definitely play havoc with their counter-parts positioned farther down the hill. No matter what the old "experts" might say from the safety of Sky Parlor Hill, one successful sinking of a Yankee craft might provide a thrill to the civilian throng, but the Yankees would certainly respond by steam-ing a dozen more ironclads down the river to elimi-nate that sort of irritation. It was a simple lesson in mathematics: too many ironclads versus too few Confederate batteries. Upriver, the ironclads were being resupplied at will. At Vicksburg, the gunners had to make do with the ammunition they had at hand.

Though the town still seemed occupied by more soldiers than she could count, their camps and earthworks were at least a couple of miles inland. Any soldier seen wandering through the town was usually someplace other than where he was as-signed. The townspeople did venture out to the camps, on social calls, brief visits with kin, many of the women producing the fruits of their ovens, the same kinds of treats Lucy had offered herself. But the labor along the earthworks was intensive,

even the most genteel of officers insisting that the
civilians should stay out of the way. Those orders
were issued in the name of the chief engineer, a
Major Lockett, someone Lucy didn't know. She
knew nothing at all of engineering, knew only that
this major had put shovels to good use far more
than muskets. The parade ground drills that had
long entertained the town were gone, replaced by
the labor of sweating, filthy men who spent nearly
all of their duty time digging in the soft ground.
For Lucy, any hope of visiting her lieutenant was
dampened by advice she had received from her
neighbors, those few she felt comfortable confid-
ing in. They cautioned her against hoping for any
social encounter at all. Junior officers had very little
discretion when it came to such things, especially
with so much labor ongoing.

"Well, Miss Lucy, a fine beautiful day. Are
the Yankees providing suitable entertainment? Or are you planning a so-
journ down to the gun pits again?"

The voice was older, with a squeak she knew too
well.

"Well, good day, Mrs. Carrington. No, I have
seen enough for one afternoon. I have housekeep-
ing to attend to. Unlike some, I do not have the
luxury of a Negro."

"Well, that's fine, then. Consorting with an artillery crew is no place for a young lady of fine standing. Soiling one's dress, not to mention one's reputation . . ."

"Excuse me, Mrs. Carrington. I have no need to do either one. As you can see, my dress is . . . clean."

She stood, did a slow dancing twirl, knew that kind of frivolity could cause tongues to wag. There was no change in the sour expression of the older woman, and Lucy saw others now, standing back, low talk between them, laughter, Lucy unsure if it was aimed at her impropriety, or the grumbling surliness of the irritating Mrs. Carrington.

The Carringtons were just one more family terribly inconvenienced by the war. The husband owned a general store, and sold a variety of goods, cloth and trinkets said to come all the way from Europe. But those shelves had emptied rapidly, the first real hint of disruption to the normal routine of Vicksburg's citizens. The mortar shells had become just another part of that, the price to pay for Yankee audacity. But the shopkeepers, the men who ran the small cafés and dress shops, were beginning to show more than annoyance at the daily harassment that rained down on the town.

The cotton traders seemed unaffected, which was a source of grumbling by other merchants. Some said that the Yankees were helping to make those men rich, that the Federal army was buying the cotton for their own use, or allowing the bales of valuable fiber to reach port cities in the East.

Lucy had no idea why any of that mattered. Any man growing a healthy crop of cotton had a right to sell it, and if the Yankees were good customers, so much the better. She already knew enough of the disregard for Confederate currency, had actually hoarded a small stockpile of gold coins. She knew others were doing the same. Even the most patriotic Confederates seemed eager to accept and hoard their own supply of hard currency, be it gold or Federal scrip.

"Excuse me, Mrs. Carrington. I will take my leave. You may use the bench I had used. I tested the supports. It is most certainly strong enough for any two of me."

She swept past, knew the old woman was digesting the insult, probably trying to respond with one of her own. It was a simple sport Lucy had come to enjoy. She moved to the steps that led downward toward the main streets, offered a smile, a friendly nod toward one of the old men coming up toward her, making the slow climb on old bent legs.

"Mr. Keene, how nice of you to venture out. You will have a fine audience for your stories today. Mrs. Carrington in particular asked about you."

The old man smiled, dark teeth and a ragged brow, and tipped his small hat.

"Well, you best take care, Miss Spence. I hear talk of a fight out east. Old Pem is given the Yankees what for. It don't do to have a young lass like yourself wandering about, with no man to look after you. You ought to visit your soldier friends more often."

Her face froze with the smile, and she moved past him quickly, shook her head. **Gossip**. This town thrives on poking noses into places best left private. She imagined the young lieutenant's smile, had to assume that he would be nothing but appropriate, never anything too forward, no wink or any more of a touch than a brief clasp of her hand when he made his parting bow. He seemed every bit a gentleman, that's certain. Would you have thought you might marry a soldier?

She felt a joyful giddiness, but the steps could be awkward, and she pulled back from the pleasant fantasy, picked her way down carefully. Well, yes, she thought, I suppose that old bird is right. It would be nice to have even a moment's opportunity to see him again. Once this is over, he might certainly vanish completely, could march off to some other battle, or maybe just go home to Louisiana. Surely he thinks of me. He must. If it is meant to be, it will be. I do hope he remains here a good deal longer. It wouldn't do for him to suddenly march away. That wouldn't do at all.

She glanced ahead to the last flight of steps, then adjusted the hem of her dress, careful to avoid an embarrassing trip. Down below, along the main street she heard a wagon, shouts rising up above a clattering of wheels. The wagon appeared now, rounding a curve with a spray of dust. The driver was a soldier, and he halted the wagon, was already drawing a crowd, stood up, steadied himself from the jostling from the horse. He was pointing back down the hill, speaking in furious tones, words she couldn't hear. The crowd continued to gather, and Lucy hurried down the last few steps, moved closer, could hear the man now, the voice high and piercing.

"And they's coming! Sure as hellfire! They's coming! Old Pem done give us up!"

People were answering, some with jeers, the usual response to news that just didn't fit what everyone preferred to believe. Regardless of whatever horror stories the old men had used to frighten young women, it was unimaginable that the Yankees could do anything at all to threaten Vicksburg without General Pemberton's army stopping them.

She stepped closer, saw sweat and fury on the man's face, and heard a woman shout, "You ought not be comin' in here and scaring us folks! General Pem's done given old Grant a good licking! We heard about it yesterday! It's in the newspaper this morning!"

Lucy had seen that, the report of a fight out near the Champion farm, close to the railroad. It was the first news she had heard about Grant's army at all since the gunboats had rolled past the town a month ago. Unlike the old men, the soldiers who came back to the town, stragglers mostly, spoke only of success, that Grant had been driven far away, or would be very soon. But the provosts were efficient, and those idle soldiers either disappeared or were hauled off to someplace the civilians wouldn't see.

The soldier on the wagon jumped down, and Lucy saw him clearly, thick dust on a rag of a uniform, and she realized he was an officer.

"I'm telling you folks to get prepared. The Yankees is coming this way! They done whipped us at Baker's Creek, and this morning they whipped us at the Big Black!"

The response continued to be dismissive, even hostile, and Lucy saw frustration, resignation in the man's face.

"You folks gotta listen! There's gonna be trouble right here! Hey! Lookee there!"

He stepped up on the wagon again, pointed, and shouted out, "Now, what's all that then?"

She moved through the crowd, looked down the hill, past the wagon. Another wagon appeared, then two more, one an ambulance. Men on horseback followed, a quick gallop, no order, no formation. One officer moved up through them, raised his sword, tried to halt them, but the horsemen moved past him, determined, oblivious. From down several of the streets, men were gathering, most with muskets, hoarse cries, shouting, curses from officers. She felt a sickening swirl inside her stomach, kept by the side of the street, saw more men on foot, some dropping down, too tired to run, some wandering in breathless fatigue. More horsemen appeared now, moving past her quickly, the stink and grime of a hard ride. One man caught her eye. He pointed back to the east.

"We's whipped! Old Pem done sold us to the Yankees!"

He was quickly past, and she stood frozen, stared down the hill, a gathering crowd of civilians falling in beside her. The few men were becoming many more, some on foot, no kind of march, still no order at all. Wagons moved through them, froth-soaked mules and horses staggering up the hill, some of the wagons filled with men. She began to feel their fear, could see it in the faces, infectious, saw another wagon, different, filled with civilians, a family, knew them, her neighbors, their wagon in line with a dozen horsemen.

She stepped out and shouted, "Mrs. Cordray! Mr. Cordray!"

The driver saw her, gave a look of acknowledgment, then pulled the wagon to one side, and she saw the same fear, on dusty, wide-eyed faces. The husband stood, seemed protective of his family, focused more on keeping the flood of soldiers away. Lucy saw their two small children huddled low on either side of their mother, and the man shouted down to her, "The army is in full retreat! They're coming back here! Right now, there are men by the hundreds, by the thousands, moving into those earthworks out east! There's a lot of talk. Not sure what's true. But you see it now! Something terrible happened, and the army's coming back here. We were defeated, some saying badly, a disaster. Many dead. They're saying Grant is close, that he's going to attack us, right here! You must go home, Lucy! Now! See to your belongings. Come, you can ride with us!"

He picked up the reins again, anxious, impatient, and she obeyed, helped into the wagon by his wife. She settled in close to the youngest child, heard crying, both children terrified by something they could not understand, absorbing only what they heard from their parents. The wagon lurched ahead, and Lucy gripped the wooden rail, looked at the mother, her friend Isabel, a woman not much older than she was. Lucy saw red eyes, filled with tears and terror.

"What does it mean, Isabel? What has happened? No one has said anything about the Yankees. It's all just . . . **talk**."

She just shook her head, seemed too terrified to speak, pulled her children in tightly. They jostled with the movement of the wagon, the husband whipping the mule, shouting at men who clogged the street in front of them. The soldiers were mostly stopping now, milling about, men lost, no direction, no energy. Officers rode past, swords in the air, screaming oaths, trying to create order, and she looked at one man, more filth on a gray uniform, an older man, authority in his voice, the man halting his horse in front of a crowd of foot soldiers.

"Line up here! Form a line. We must move out to the works!"

Cordray eased the wagon past the soldiers, a slight gap in the throng of men, and he whipped the mule again, shouted the way clear, panic in his voice, adding to the terror in the young children. Beside her, Isabel grabbed Lucy's arm and said, "We came from the Big Black! We thought we could get to my sister in Jackson, make sure she was all right. But there was fighting! Lucy, it was awful. Men dying everywhere, explosions. The bridge was on fire! We are only back here by the hand of the Almighty. But so many of our boys are out there. So much talk about Yankees, about how we're beaten! We must get home, protect ourselves. What must happen now? What can we do?"

Lucy looked back at the older officer, the man's authority taking effect, the soldiers lining up. More men appeared from every street, their panic pursuing them. More officers were coming up, shouted orders turning the men around, guiding them back to the east, back out toward the earthworks, the great strong defensive position the engineers had labored over. Lucy focused on the faces of the officers, some not showing fear at all, just doing the job, pulling their army together, doing whatever had to be done.

Beside her, the mother rocked one child in her arms.

"Lucy, my dear Lucy. What of the children? What of our homes? What can we do?"

Lucy felt a strange calm, put her hand on her friend's, a soft squeeze. She put her other hand on the head of the smaller child, calming him, pulling his face into her skirt, quieting the terror.

"We will do what we can. Our soldiers know what they must do. If there is to be a fight here . . . then we will help them."

CHAPTER NINETEEN

BAUER

NEAR BOVINA, MISSISSIPPI
MAY 17, 1863

They crossed the Big Black on a make-shift bridge made from the felling of huge trees, the bark skinned away to prevent the men from slipping away into the narrow river. It was the engineer's genius for improvisation, since McPherson's corps were completely without pontoon bridges. Upstream, the army's only pontoons were in use by Sherman's men, another surge forward from the remaining third of Grant's army, all of them now pushing toward Vicksburg. The fight along the Big Black had produced enormous spoils for the men who had so completely shoved Pemberton's forces away, and Bauer couldn't help watching the commotion, vast lines of rebel prisoners, a makeshift camp already set up to hold them. The officers had passed along the good cheer from above, the enthusiastic congratulations to an army that, once again, had bested the enemy. In "B" company, Captain McDermott had made certain that every man in the ranks knew of the success of the others who had done the job, Willis and the other lieutenants passing along the numbers that the captain had passed to them. They had captured nearly seventeen hundred rebel soldiers and more than a dozen artillery pieces, most grabbed on the east side of the narrow river. There were casualties, too, bodies already set into rows, the blue shirts turning black, mangled corpses spread alongside the desperately unfortunate, those who had died from a single piercing wound. But the rebel dead were many more. They were being shoved into mass graves, and Bauer had seen that before, knew that watching the sickening process was usually a bad idea. At Shiloh, he had volunteered for the burial duty, for reasons he couldn't fathom now. Then the number of rebel dead had been astonishing, beyond anyone's worst nightmare, and the troops had mostly volunteered for the duty drawn by a promise of generous supplies of whiskey. Bauer had joined in, at least for a while, had gone about the gruesome business of digging the wide, shallow trenches, shoveling the rebel corpses in one at a time, until each pit was filled. The covering of dirt was always too thin, and Bauer had seen it himself, that when the first rains came, the men on top were exposed, curled and bony hands, smears of rotting flesh, unrecognizable faces. Around him, men were reacting to that sight now, and Bauer knew immediately that the numbers they were seeing at the Big Black weren't significant, that whatever had happened here was no great bloodletting. It wasn't quite so the day before. The regiment had marched along the northern fringes of what had clearly been a brutally contested battlefield, a place labeled by the officers for the nearby waterway, Baker's Creek. But the most prominent feature Bauer could see was the mass of high ground, a great bulge of mostly bare land that had absorbed the shock of artillery shells and fire, and even then was still pockmarked by the dead on both sides. The hilly ground belonged to a family called Champion, and the farmhouse was occupied now by blue-coated brass. Bauer felt certain he had seen Grant himself, a short, stocky man on horseback, smoking a cigar, in white shirt and rumpled hat, watching as the last division of McPherson's corps moved past. But any vision of the commanding general was brief, the march steady, strong, an army once more on the move. What caught Bauer's eye was the ground itself, the smells of a fight, smoke and sulfur and the awful stink of the newly created hospitals. The bodies were there, too, a great many more than what he saw at the Big Black, and when the officers spoke of the fight that rolled over that high ground, their voices were subdued, no boasting, no great hurrahs for their victory, no hearty cheer. But a victory it was, and Bauer had seen hordes of prisoners then, too, a mass of captured wagons and horses, and the most impressive sight always, dozens of big guns. But the business of the army was already sweeping through all of that, the captured rebels marching off somewhere, the artillery pieces now a part of Grant's own, adding to the power of this army that already seemed powerful enough.

That talk had spread through the entire regiment, and the officers had no good answer. Since coming across the Mississippi River, the 17th Wisconsin had been placed mostly toward the rear of the larger column, trailing behind the rest of McPherson's corps. To the Wisconsin men, all of those encounters, brief or not, had been nothing more than rumbles, a chorus of thunder from somewhere **up there**. There was hot talk growing about that, angry growling that for some reason, idiots in high places were keeping these men out of the fight. Bauer tried not to share that, kept the silence of the veterans, the men who knew what all of that rumbling could mean. But the talk came from the new recruits, men who had spent the early spring with shovels in Louisiana mud, building up the lust for carrying the musket, fixing bayonets, the big talk of those who still thought of all this as something glorious. For a week now, that "glory" seemed to be going elsewhere, a gift for some other regiment, some other part of McPherson's corps. The anger of the new men had surprised Bauer. Around him, the grousing was consistent and ugly, uglier by the hour. With so many fights in such a few short days, Bauer had pondered that, wondered if these Irishmen were being singled out just to be ignored, as though someone at the top believed they wouldn't do the job. That's a lot of bull, he thought. These micks are no different from anybody else. If someone up ahead thinks they're bad soldiers, they got a right to gripe about it. Nothing in any of them seems any different from the 16th . . . maybe the accents. Course, the best way they can prove they can fight is to . . . fight. Just . . . give us the chance. The word stuck with him for a long second. **Us.** Yep, guess so.

He marched again alongside the skinny red-headed boy, O'Daniel, who kept mostly to himself. Sergeant Finley kept to the boy's side of the four-wide column, and on Bauer's other arm, the terminally cranky Irishman he knew only as Kelly. The sergeant had stayed mostly quiet, no need for discipline, at least not for stragglers, not today. Bauer could feel the hot energy for a fight, itchy tempers in the men around him. It had kept him more subdued than usual, **the man who didn't belong there**. With no enemy to confront, Bauer had the uneasy feeling inside of him that the first man to inspire anyone's wrath might suddenly give birth to a massive brawl.

They were past any signs of the fight along the Big Black, moving through the same kind of lands they had seen throughout most of Mississippi. The ground was rolling slightly, with sharp drop-offs to one side or the other, low ground clogged thick with briars and vines. Beyond each ravine were stands of timber or open fields, some of those cultivated. He had learned to tell the difference between corn and cotton, or anything else these farmers had planted. It didn't much matter now, very little chance that anyone had stayed around to work the land in late spring, not with this mass of blue marching through. Damn shame, he thought. Waste. Good crops nobody'll eat or pick. Houses falling into ruin. Hell, we ain't gonna hurt none of 'em if they just let us pass. Sammie doesn't believe that, but no damn civilian's taken a shot at me. Not yet anyway.

Above them, the sky was darkening, rain clouds, and Bauer gazed up lazily, was drifting into that special silence, a dreamy kind of rhythm to the march where a man could actually go to sleep. The veterans had long ago learned that, sleeping on the march, steady automatic steps, the soft shuffling of their brogans on dusty roads. Even if there was no real cause for exhaustion, no scrambling mid-night marches, the sleepiness came anyway, driven mostly now by boredom. The time seemed to pass more quickly as well, long hours slipping past, until that blessed moment when the bugle would sound, calling them into the next place where there might be food. Bauer had become used to it, too many miles on too many roads, most all of the walking on Southern soil. It was a fine way to pass the time . . . unless the man in front of you suddenly halted.

He stumbled into the man, knocking both of them to the ground, a clatter of muskets and canteens, one cartridge box spilling out, a bayonet scabbard poking into Bauer's side. The shouts came quickly, more men tumbling down, jarred into alertness, the sergeant now, a hard yank on the redhead's shoulder, then pulling Bauer up by the collar, choking him.

"Get up, you damn fools! What ails you, anyway?" Finley moved through others, more men pulling themselves back up, the attention all paid forward. Finley called to another of the sergeants, a short stick of a man, named Heath. "What goes up there?"

Bauer heard it now, a high panicky **whoop,** saw men in motion, a manic scattering, launching off the road, a scramble to avoid . . . something. He pushed ahead, others as curious as he was, and Willis was there now, his pistol in his hand, one hand holding the men away, the careful aim, then a single shot straight into the ground. The sharp crack from the pistol backed them up, but more men were gathering from both directions, another lieutenant, pistol drawn, but there was no need. Willis called out, "Get back in line! Just a damn rattlesnake. You boys not seen these things? Hell, you probably step over a dozen every time you go wandering out through these woods. Probably squatted right on top of one more'n once."

The word passed back through the men, **rattlesnake,** hushed reverence. Bauer couldn't help a shiver, hated snakes of any kind, had too many memories of the swamps in Tennessee and worse, the swamps across the Mississippi River, where every log seemed to hide one.

The orders went out, and the men began to form up again, reluctance as they eased past the casualty, Willis still standing over it. Bauer was there now, and Willis was smiling at him.

"Hold up, Private," he said. "Give me your musket."

Bauer stepped out beside the slowly moving column, unshouldered the musket, and handed it to Willis, who dipped it down, slipped the muzzle under the snake, and hoisted it airborne. It took effort, a grunting strain from Willis, and Bauer grimaced, shivering again, was amazed to see the size, the snake as thick as his leg, near six feet long. Willis carried it a few feet off the road, lowered the musket, let the carcass slide down into deep grass. Willis tossed the musket upright to Bauer, who caught it, glancing at the barrel, where the snake had actually touched the steel. Willis called out, still had an audience.

"You boys pay attention to that. You kill one of those damn things, you don't go picking it up by the tail. Dead or not, those damn critters will turn around and bite you, sure as hell. Instinct, reflex. They still got fangs and they'll kill you dead." He paused, held a wide smile, and Bauer knew how unusual that was. Sure, he thought. He enjoys this. Scaring hell out of us.

Bauer fell back into line, beside the redheaded boy, heard low nervous talk all around him. Bauer looked to the side, Kelly there again, and Bauer said, "They got snakes in Ireland?"

"How the hell do I know? Ain't never been there. My folks came over 'fore I was born. You got snakes in Dutchland, or wherever the hell you're from?"

Bauer laughed.

"Sorry. Figured from the accents and all . . . most of you was born there."

"Some. Not me." Kelly paused, the march now rolling forward, the usual rhythm. "Wonder about that, though. What the army must think. They know we're mostly Irish . . . well, not you . . . but you know. . . ."

"Yeah. I know."

"Well, how come we're kept in the rear and all? I'm thinkin' it ain't no accident we ain't been in a fight."

Bauer had hoped that would fade away, the distraction of the rattlesnake taking their thoughts another way. But the jolting nervousness of the snake just seemed to ignite more of the fire toward an enemy many of these men had yet to see.

A voice came from behind Kelly.

"You're right about that. I been hearin' that they's gonna ship us back home. Some says we're not fit for fightin'."

Finley spoke up now, the hard growl.

"Who's sayin' that? You point him out to me."

There was no response, and Bauer knew when to keep quiet, saw Willis slide up close. Bauer was suddenly happy Willis was an officer, knew he didn't have Bauer's hesitation about joining into any kind of heat.

"Shut the hell up. Not having that kind of talk in this army, not in my platoon. You boys think they're holding you out of a fight? Well, that's only gonna get you stuck right up front next time. The boys who were marching up front have been carrying the load, and they've lost a heap of good men doing it. You in all kinds of hurry to join 'em? Fine. I'm telling you right now, the brass knows you've been in the rear, and so you're all fresh and rested up. You know what that means? That means when we run into the damn rebels again, they're gonna stick us right where the fire is."

"Suits me fine, Lieutenant."

The voice came from Kelly, others joining in, a chorus of agreement. Willis caught Bauer's eye, the smile long gone, replaced with a grim scowl.

"I said, shut up. They're not marching us for some kind of parade. I heard the captain, the colonel. They know we're fresh. That's all I know, and all you need to hear. You're so damned eager to jump into it with the secesh . . . well, you're gonna get your chance. Nobody's told me those Mississippi boys have surrendered. But when you see those sons of bitches standin' out there pointing their muskets at you, and that bugle tells you to charge . . . you damn well better be followin' close behind me. All this damn Irish blood, all this damn talk I'm hearing. When the time comes . . . it better be more than talk."

They halted the march in front of a grand plantation house, the usual cluster of Negroes welcoming them with joyous words most of the soldiers couldn't understand, many of the slaves accepting the soldiers' presence as reason enough to join Mr. Lincoln's war, no matter that they were only adding to the size of the column. But with the Negroes came the fruits of whatever the plantations could offer. The Irishmen who groused so loudly about being left out of the fight had one more reason to grouse now. Bauer held little enthusiasm for the scene Willis had painted, marching out into an open field to rush headlong into a stout formation of enemy bayonets, and he knew it was the one advantage of being positioned in the rear of the great march, at least so far. But there was one great disadvantage, and the men saw it now in every plantation and farmhouse they passed. Whatever prizes might have been there, whatever stores of meat and cider and any other spoils of war, they had already been sorted through by the soldiers who came first. The soldiers had been encouraged to scavenge for food, Grant's order that they live off the land, and Bauer was relieved to see that most of the larger houses were intact. And many still had slaves, a mostly raucous audience, but as more troops passed, more of the Negroes took advantage, their enthusiasm for the blue-coated presence reason enough for them to find the inspiration, or the courage, to leave behind what might be the only homes they had ever known. If the men marching now behind the column had any idea where they were going, it didn't seem to matter. This army was offering them an opportunity none of them had ever experienced, to go somewhere **else**.

The bugle had sounded, the usual rest, ten minutes or more after an hour's steady march. The troops settled down into the grass along the roadside, the broken-down entrance to another grand plantation house. The house was set back off the road a hundred yards, and guards were moving out that way, the usual caution against a potential rebel sniper. It was routine now, and the men ignored that, hadn't seen a rebel since the prisoners at the Big Black.

The men already resting were doing what they

always did, nursing sore feet, some searching through backpacks for something to eat. Bauer followed Sergeant Finley off the road, shuffled slowly through deep grass, saw an uprooted fence post, stepped carefully, searched every spot before putting down his foot. He scanned the ground around him, couldn't shake the image of the rattlesnake. There were snakes in Wisconsin, certainly, and Bauer had seen his share as a child. But no one had prepared him for the sheer quantity of the creatures that seemed everywhere throughout the South, and especially not the size. That thing was taller than me, he thought, weighed as much. Taller than the kid, Red. Probably swallow that skinny kid whole. He shuddered. Okay, stop that. You'll be seeing that damned thing in your dreams from now on. He leaned down, picked up one end of the fence post, hesitated, took a breath, prepared for the worst, tossed it up in a single violent motion, trying to catch a glimpse of what might be underneath. There was a sudden clutching grab under his backside, and his brain reacted with a piercing stab of panic, feeling the bite of all snakes everywhere. He leapt, a hard, shrieking scream, and a roar of laughter engulfed him from behind. He turned, the panic still there, saw Kelly close behind him, more laughter from the others, louder, increasing, men dropping down, rolling on the ground, teary-eyed glee. A dozen more joined in, and Bauer tried to stop the shaking, saw Kelly's hands pounding on his own knees, a single word pushed through the laughter, hands rising up in the air.

"**Snake!**"

Kelly collapsed into complete hysteria, and Bauer realized the joke was most definitely on him. He glanced back to the dead, bare ground beneath the fence post, nothing but a few grubs, and he let out a breath, lowered himself down, sat on the post, began to laugh with the men around him. Kelly was down to his knees now, tears on his face, uncontrollable, and Bauer saw Finley, the sergeant holding his stomach, bending over. The laughter spread, word passing, men describing Bauer's reaction with exaggerated gestures, nonsensical words. Willis was there now, curious, scanning the odd spreading hysteria, and looked at Bauer, who couldn't hold back his own tears, so much laughter too contagious to avoid. Willis moved up close to him, and Bauer tried to stand, felt Willis's hand on his shoulder, keeping him down.

"What the hell did you do?"

The words wouldn't come, Bauer trying to gain control, and Willis waited, couldn't help a soft chuckle of his own. After another moment, Bauer pointed at the dead place on the ground, where the old fence post had lain.

"Thought there might be a snake."

Kelly had his composure now, and said, "Sorry, sir. He wanted a snake. I gave him one. He jumped about four feet in the air."

Kelly was laughing again, but the joke was passing, the men quieting, sleeves wiping faces, red eyes, and Bauer felt a hard slap on his back, Finley, who said to Willis, "Wasn't nothing to it, sir. Boys just let out a little steam. Your Dutch friend's good for something after all. We'll be up and ready when the bugle blows."

Willis stared at Bauer for a long moment, then shook his head.

"Yes, Sergeant, he does his share every now and again. But we're sitting here for a bit. We're sending some scouting parties out looking for rations. They want us to join in. Several farmhouses down that far road there." Willis looked back toward the rear of the column, pointed. "Wagon coming up. Take three of the boys. I'll go with you. We'll move with the wagon, try to find something worth carrying to camp. The colonel will let us know when the column's up and moving. For now, the rest of the men can hold here. Not sure what's going on, but the colonel thinks we may need some extra rations tomorrow. Whenever I hear that, Sergeant, I pay attention. Let's see if we can fill that wagon." Willis looked down at Bauer. "Pick him. We could use a source of amusement."

Finley chuckled.

"Yes, sir. Just let us know if you sees any more of those dang snakes."

———

The wagon came at them on the narrow road, a quartet of soldiers perched high on a mound of cloth sacks. Behind trailed a dozen Negroes, mostly quiet, as though they belonged there. The driver of Willis's wagon eased to the side, making room, the other wagon obviously too weighed down for much maneuvering.

From the other wagon, a sergeant called out, "Well, hello there, boys! Fine day for stealin' us a secesh feast. Uh, Lieutenant. Sorry. No disrespect, sir."

"None taken. That's what we're out here for. What did you find?"

"Meal, sir. Corn, most likely, and some molasses. We'll be making some slapjacks tonight, for certain. But there's a whole heap more back there. We only made it to the second house. The first one been burned to ashes already. I guess somebody up front didn't like what they saw. But there's a couple more farther down the road. These darkies told us about a big one. Some local bigwig."

Willis waved the wagon's driver on past, a sergeant offering a hatless bow, then a casual salute. Willis waited for the wagon to get clear, the Negroes filing past, smiles now, yellow, toothy grins. Willis tapped his own driver on the shoulder.

"Let's go. A mile, they say. I want to get this done before dark. Don't need to be out here in secesh country after dark with nobody looking after my ass but these four fools."

Bauer felt the insult, knew better, that if there was any trouble at all, Willis was likely the best shot in the company. Bauer also knew: He wasn't too bad himself.

The wagon lurched forward, the mule nodding its head with each step as it drew the wagon through softer sand. They were moving uphill now, harder ground, and Bauer saw what must have been the first of the farmhouses, a blackened mound punctuated by skeletal remains of timber. Smoke still rose from the wreckage, the breeze carrying the stink of burnt wood and anything else the house contained.

Beside him, Finley said, "Bet some stupid secesh farmer took a shot at one of our boys. Won't do it again."

Willis seemed edgy now and said, "Could be. Don't get lazy. If there's one, could be more. Anybody who's not one of us, you can bet he hates us worse than the devil. Remember that."

They rolled past the second house now, a modest home, nearly untouched. There were no slave quarters, at least not that Bauer could see, and he thought on that, said, "Wonder where the darkies came from? The folks in these homes don't seem to have much. Not rich, anyway. Just . . . farms."

The driver said nothing, pointed ahead, and Willis said, "There's your answer. If any place had darkies, that would be it."

To one side of the road, the wooded ground

spread open to a vast yard of lush grass, the borders lined with waist-high bushes, neatly manicured. The house was set back at least two hundred yards from the road, tall columns across a wide veranda. From where the wagon halted, a pathway turned off, the entryway, a well-groomed cart path passing beneath an arch of iron lattice. The driver waited for Willis to give the order.

"Go on," Willis said. "Turn in. Muskets loaded?"

Bauer had seen the others loading back at the main road, had done the same. He glanced at the percussion cap, old habit, the last part of the lesson, the final part of the process. The men in the wagon beside him responded with clipped answers, all eyes on the grand house. Bauer saw Willis draw his pistol, and he tapped the driver again.

"Slowly. If anybody's in there, they'll know we're not being neighborly. If they're gone, they probably buried everything of value somewhere around back. But we're not here for grandmama's silver, you got that? If you can't eat it, leave it be."

Bauer studied the grounds, saw a row of small cabins stretching far behind the house, complete contrast to the clean white of the mansion, the cabins a rustic heap of dark wood. He could smell smoke, different than the destruction of the farmhouse. It smelled like roasting meat, and Kelly said, "Somebody's back there, sir. Smokehouse maybe."

"Slave quarters. Seen plenty of this before. Stop here."

The driver obeyed, and Willis jumped down, then motioned silently for the others to follow. Bauer slipped off the rear of the wagon, checked the musket one more time, felt the bayonet scabbard at his waist. Willis moved toward the front door of the house and motioned for the others to spread out to each side of him.

Bauer saw movement from beyond one side of the house, jerked the musket up, aimed, and saw now an old black man.

Kelly had done the same. "Well now, sir," he said. "**Somebody's** home."

They all stopped, muskets coming down, and Bauer saw deep creases in a haggard face, the man bowing, smiling as he moved through the yard.

"Ah . . . heah . . . **Missuh Lincom's boys**." The old man was smiling through a minimum of teeth, clasped his hands in front of him, nodded profusely. "See alls of ya."

Bauer couldn't help a smile, the man's pure joy contagious, and Bauer returned the smile, tried to sift through the man's thick accent, not really sure what he meant.

Willis said, "Howdy, old man. Anyone else around? You got a . . . master or something? Anybody with a musket?"

The man kept nodding, still the smile, said again, "Missuh Lincom's boys. Prizin for you." He pointed back toward the corner of the house. "Heah, sum good enjiyin'. Prizin for Missuh Lincom."

Kelly said, "Not sure he understands you, sir. Don't know what he's saying."

The old man pointed with more energy, started to move that way, motioning for them to follow.

"He wants us to see something," Bauer said. "I bet he knows where everything is. Sure smells good."

The old man nodded, a hint of comprehension, and pointed back behind him again.

"Yassuh. Yassuh. Wids me. Yassuh. Gots enjiyin'. Yassuh. Big prizins."

The old man started to move away, waving the men with him, and Finley said, "Think we oughta go with him, sir. He's got a burr in his pants about something."

Willis still held the pistol. "Slowly," he said. "Keep your eyes open."

The old man waved harder, faster, impatience growing.

"Heah! Heah! You be enjiyin Ole Missy."

Willis stepped forward.

"All right, old man. We'll see what's doing." He turned, looked at Bauer and the others. "Spread out. Sergeant, take these two and go through the house. I'm guessing it's empty, but make sure. Check inside any big piece of furniture. Could be somebody hiding out. There'll be a cellar. Don't go wandering down into the dark until we all get in there. If there's rations to be had, that's where it'll be. We'll see what this old coot wants, then join you in there. You see anybody in there, holler like hell. I don't like surprises."

Willis pointed the pistol at the old man, just a brief threat, a piece of caution. For the first time Bauer saw uncertainty on the old man's wrinkled face, a hint of fear. Willis lowered the pistol again, the message delivered.

"It's all right. I'm just being careful." Willis glanced back at Bauer and Kelly. "I'd bet a month's pay this old boy's not playing any games with us. I've heard they can't hide what they're thinking. He's all grins. Just . . . stay alert."

The three men kept their distance, and the old man seemed utterly delighted at the small parade that followed him, made quick steps on rickety legs. Bauer eased up closer to Willis and said in a low voice, "Kinda odd, Sammie. There gotta be a thousand soldiers by this place already today. What's he got they ain't taken from him yet?"

Willis growled, his voice a hard whisper.

"We don't know if anybody's been here at all. We're pretty far off the road. Maybe some cavalry, but they had better things to do. And, dammit, call me **sir**. You thick?"

Bauer fell back a step, knew an apology wasn't called for, not now. Old habits, he thought. But by God he's still my friend. Friend, **sir**.

They moved out around the right side of the grand home, and Bauer saw a single broken window, the curtain intact, a single piece of evidence

that someone had made their inspection of anything worth having. He kept in step behind Willis, an eye toward the window, could hear boot
steps in the house, Finley, the others. Nice place,
he thought. Wonder who lives here? Gone now, for
sure. Too many of us. Somebody'll put a torch to
this one, I bet. Hope it's not us. Just hate that. Burn
a nice damn house, just . . . because. He knew Willis didn't share that kind of compassion for anyone
in this part of the country, but Bauer had seen too
much of what seemed to be useless destruction,
raucous parties of soldiers, sometimes drunk, at-
tacking the homes of people who might have nothing at all to do with the war. He still kept that to
himself, knew that many of these men felt that if
any of these civilians didn't want this war, maybe
it would stop. But . . . children? Willis was still
moving, keeping pace with the old man, and Bauer
quickened his step, saw Kelly doing the same. They
were close to the slave quarters now, a long row of
cabins set back into tall trees, many more than he
could see from the road. He said aloud, "Bunch of
'em. Guess that's the ones we saw. Or maybe there's
a pile of 'em still here."

Willis didn't look back. "You're as dumb as a boat
anchor. You think they wouldn't be pouring out
here to cheer us like damn heroes? This old boy's
got the place to himself."

Bauer felt some relief in that. "Maybe we don't
have to burn the place, then, huh?"

Willis turned to him.

"We have orders, Private. Find rations. So we're gonna find rations, then get back to the main road. Who said anything about burning the place? What the hell's the matter with you?"

Bauer knew the orders, passed down months before about the destruction of civilian property. But somehow, orders or not, fires seemed to start by themselves. Bauer thought of Louisiana, the march downriver, the amazing stupidity of a landowner stomping out to confront an entire column of blue-coated soldiers, with curses and threats. The results were predictable, and once the man's larders had been emptied, the torches came out. But throughout the march into Mississippi, the property owners were mostly gone, had certainly hidden away those things the army might prize. But if the Negroes were still on the land, the soldiers knew there would be food, something even the most loyal of slaves eventually gave up. It was one more reason why the Negroes joined the march. The troops left them very little to eat.

The old man kept moving, past the first of the slave shacks, then stopped with a giddy laugh. Willis held them up, Bauer halting, the musket ready, watched the old man kneel low, rubbing his hand through a thick bed of straw. Bauer saw the rope now, a thick, short strand, and the old man stood, holding the rope, made a bow toward them, and pulled.

The leaves slid away from a wooden hatch, which swung open, showing a wide, dark hole. Willis held up his hand and gave a quick shout.

"Watch out! Who's in there! You in there, come out! Not playing out here!"

The old man dropped the hatch to full open, then stood back with smug satisfaction.

Willis stepped closer, his pistol pointed down into the hole, stopped, and said, "Holy Mother of God. You! Get up here!"

Bauer moved closer, his curiosity in full boil. From down in the hole he heard what sounded like a whimper, saw a hand in the air, dirty white skin, a grip on the steps of a ladder. Now a tangle of hair came up, then the face, smudged and thin, with red, hostile eyes. The ladder was narrow, unsteady, and Bauer stepped closer.

"Let me help her."

"Back up, Private. She got down there, she can get up."

The woman stepped up on the ground now, surprising, a fine dress, a smear of dirt she tried to cover with wrinkled hands. She stared at them with a hard glare, sharp eyes through wrinkled skin, her eyes darting to each of the soldiers.

"She's probably scared to hell, Sammie. What's going on here?"

The old man spoke up now, still the beaming smile.

"Yassuh! Heah Missy be! You be enjiyin'!"

"She don't look so scared to me."

Willis softened his tone. "What's your name, madam? What you doing down in this hole?"

She studied Willis, a silent test, and Bauer saw no fear at all.

"Lorena Baggett. This is my family's home. My husband's gone. Took the grandchildren."

"Where? He a soldier?"

"No. My son was . . . he was killed at Corinth. Hero, he was. Took a good number of you blue-bellied devils with him, they say. My husband took the children. I'm sick. Fever. Told him I'd stay close, keep guard on the place."

Kelly moved closer, stared into her face.

"I don't see no sickness. She's lying. Your husband's a secesh soldier. Officer I bet."

Her hand gripped the cloth buttoned to her throat, her arms tight across her chest, a gesture of protection.

"I got no reason to lie to the likes of you. I can't stop you from doin' anything you're gonna do, so if you have need to torment an old woman for your entertainment, go to it."

Willis still held the pistol, and ignored the challenge.

"So, you hid out in the ground? Sick with a fever?"

She hesitated, stared hard at Willis, appraising him, what Bauer knew could be a mistake.

"The root cellar, yes." She pointed at the old man. "Ollie's the only one who stayed. He's too lame to escape, and I told him to keep quiet. Guess he's back to his old ways." She pointed to the east. "We heard the fight at the river. That's when my husband took the children. . . . They're gone to Vicksburg. I suppose . . . that's where you're headed, too. You'll spill buckets of blood, if General Pemberton can help it. You'll all be in hell."

Bauer saw the woman trying to hold herself straight, the pride, a hint of defiance, but the weakness betrayed her, and she seemed to stagger. Behind her, the old man pointed to her, held out his hand, seemed more impatient now.

"You be enjiyin Ole Missy! Heah! Missuh Lincom heah, jez?"

She winced at the words, didn't look at the old man, and Bauer began to understand. The man's hand was extended, dull yellow palm upward, and Bauer saw a strange leer in the old man's smile.

"Good God, he's wanting to sell her to us."

The woman looked back at the old man and said, "I thought you were one of the smart ones, Ollie. You would betray me?"

The pitch of her voice was higher, a growing fury, no effort at hiding it.

Willis put the pistol in its holster.

"He's just getting back at you, you stupid old woman. Justice. He wants us to pay for what you're worth. What did you pay for **him**?"

She didn't react to the insult, as though expecting

little else from Yankees. She turned to Willis again, the defiance increasing, a harder tone in her voice.

"I don't rightly know. My husband bought him in Jackson . . . years ago. There's papers in the house, unless you took them."

"No, we're gonna do better than that. We're gonna take **him**."

She seemed to absorb the thought, her fury complete, a hard shout.

"You can't do that! Ollie's part of this family. He's . . . **mine**."

Bauer felt a sickening turn in his stomach, the perfect hate in her eyes, staring at **him** now. He couldn't hold back the words.

"Seems to me, madam, it's the other way around."

Willis held up his hand, quieting him, but Bauer was pulsing with anger, had soaked up too much of her high-handed tone. Willis said, "He's coming with us. You can, too. We got a doctor who'll look you over. You rather stay here, that's fine, too."

From the rear entrance of the house, the other men appeared, hurried steps now, curious. Finley jogged close and said, "Nothing in the house but furniture, sir. What we got here?"

Willis kept his stare at the woman.

"What we got here, Sergeant, is the lady who's gonna tell us how we can fill that wagon. Isn't that right, madam?"

"Steal what you wish. I'll not help you."

Willis chuckled, and Bauer saw the grin on the old man's face.

"Don't think she'll have to, Lieutenant," Bauer said. "We got a new friend."

The old man still had his hand out, and Bauer thought, he has no idea what's happening. Willis moved over to him, his hand resting on the butt of the pistol, stared at him for a moment, then took one of the old man's arms, and Bauer saw the scars, a deep gash across the man's wrist.

"They had you in chains before?"

The old man nodded slowly.

"Ollie be **punshed**. Not in a while now."

"Well, not today, Ollie. And unless you actually **like** this old woman, you can come along with us. Your friends are already trailing after the army, and somebody'll be looking after 'em. And you. All you gotta do first is tell us where the . . . uh . . . victuals are kept. Anything down in that root cellar?"

The old man shook his head, pointed to a small shack, back behind the slave cabins, what appeared to be an outhouse. He put his hands on his hips, another smile.

"Missuh Lincom's boys. You be eatin' fine this day. Hams . . . bacon. Sacks a corn flour. Massuh done hid t'all in a hoe back dey. Den you be wardin' Ollie for Missy heah?"

Bauer smiled and said, "I think he's hoping we'll pay him something. Reward."

"Yaz . . . Missy heah."

Willis said, "Sorry, you old buzzard, but we're just soldiers. Not a dollar between us. Not sure what you'd do with any silver anyhow. Now, you help us with those rations, and I promise you, 'Missuh Lincom' will appreciate it, even if your master's wife here doesn't."

Willis turned, motioned to Bauer, and there was a sharp crack, the old man suddenly bent over, dropping slowly to his knees, falling facedown in the leaves. Willis lunged toward the woman, grabbed her arms, spun her around with a hard grip around her waist, and Bauer saw the small pistol, tumbling out of her hand. She didn't fight, and Willis released her, stepped back, his own pistol aimed at her head, a long second of silence, cold stillness. Bauer felt his heart racing, stared at the body of the old man, a twitch in the man's leg. He didn't know what to do, waited for something from Willis, and the woman said, "Take him now, if you want. He never did mind me well."

Willis bent down, picked up her pistol, stuck it in his belt, and moved up close to her face, a hard growl.

"No, madam. You'll bury him."

He turned to the others, motioned them toward the place the old man had pointed, and said, "Load the wagon. As much as we can haul. I'll stay with her."

Bauer stared at the old man, the twitch gone, the man's face buried in the leaves. Bauer felt tears, fought the sight of the man's smile, his joy at the sight of the blue soldiers, erased by the hatred of one old woman. He felt something turn inside of him, realized Willis was watching him.

"So, Private, you still think these people are just . . . caught in the way?"

Bauer looked at the woman, saw a deadness in her eyes, staring at nothing, slowly looking toward him again. He gripped the musket hard, wanted to do something . . . anything, felt the familiar anger, the heat building, the fights, the rebel soldiers, saw it in her eyes, the hostility, the clear-eyed hate. She was no different from anyone with a bayonet, anyone across those smoky fields. She was the enemy.

The others were moving toward the small shack, no one speaking, and Bauer looked at the house, then back at Willis, saw a nod, a cold anger Bauer had seen before. It was an order, but there were no words. Bauer knew exactly what he wanted to do. He called out to Finley now.

"Sergeant, there plenty of rags in the house? Furniture?"

"Yep. Bed linens. Ladies' garments and such."

He looked back at Willis now, no change in the lieutenant's expression. Bauer said, "Then, with your permission, sir, I'll burn this damn place to the ground."

CHAPTER TWENTY

SHERMAN

CHICKASAW BLUFFS,
NORTHEAST OF VICKSBURG
MAY 18, 1863

The prisoners came in single file, two dozen surly, rugged men, a few looking up at him as they passed. He said nothing, didn't have to, some of them staring at the rank on his shoulder, the color bearer behind him, and whether they recognized the face, or whether any of their guards had told them already, they seemed to know exactly what he knew: He had seen these people before.

Sherman kept the thoughts to himself, glanced back toward his aides lingering close by, the men who knew just how much distance to keep. He couldn't tell them anything of this, wouldn't gloat, wouldn't strut about like some peacock, waving his arms as though all the land he could see had now become his private domain. But he felt it, pulsed in the saddle, didn't hide the smile. If the prisoners had seen him before, aimed their weapons at him before, he had done the same to them. It had been five months now, nearly half a year since Sherman's great failure, the humiliation these men had handed him from these same heights. Then he had come at them up the Yazoo River, the various creeks, the muddy swamps that were as much an asset for the rebels as their artillery. But they had won that day, had smacked him with an inglorious defeat. Now he had returned the favor. It wasn't from the river, no more trudging through swamps. This time he had come at them from behind, the 4th Iowa Cavalry, sweeping up and through the earthworks at Haines's Bluff to grab those same cannon that had done such good work against him in December. It wasn't much of a fight, many of the guns disabled, the crews mostly gone, a disappointment for the Iowans, certainly. But the message had been clear, to both sides. The rebels no longer held their strong perch overlooking the waterways that flowed inland north of Vicksburg. Sherman didn't know if the rebels had good intelligence, had known the Federal cavalry was close. Right now, he didn't really care. What he saw now, staring northward from the great high bluffs, was flat dismal swamp and meandering waterways that had been swept clear of rebel guns. For Sherman it was exoneration, though he knew that no one else would make much of a bother about that. Grant maybe. Grant would understand, he thought. He has his own failures, his own reputation to polish. Well, Grant, here's mine. We wanted these damn creeks open for the navy, and right now, the navy can steam right up to the closest landings they can find. If there's anybody in Washington or anywhere else who thinks Grant's a fool for cutting himself off from his base of supply . . . well, to hell with you. He's got that base right here. And by damned, I gave it to him. Nobody'll put that in a newspaper, nobody will even mention my name at the War Department. But Grant will know, and right now, he's the only one who matters.

He didn't want to leave, could see a plume of black smoke, the first of Admiral Porter's boats already steaming closer, word passing from signalmen to riders, to grateful sailors who could bring their supplies that much closer to the army, with no danger from any rebel marksman. He wanted to wait, to watch the boat until he saw the waving hands of the sailors, maybe Porter himself, shake his hand: Job well done, Sherman. He glanced skyward, the afternoon slipping past. No, it's time to go to work. One job done today. More to do tomorrow. And sure as hell, Grant will want to talk about it.

He turned the horse and moved back down the short hill, keeping to one side of the road until the last of the prisoners went by. The camps were com-

ing together quickly, tents spread across an open
field, one more message he hoped the prisoners absorbed. We didn't just chase you away from your
guns. We took this whole damn place. It is **ours**.
He moved the horse into deep grass, saw more
flags, larger tents that would house the regimental commander, the staffs, and his own, some of
the men whose jobs were only beginning. He saw
them now, jabbed the horse with the spurs, a short
gallop toward a cluster of officers. He wiped away
his smile, but the energy was still there, and he always enjoyed that moment, making a hard ride
straight into a conversation, or even an argument
that they might not want him to hear. The talk was
animated, but there was no hostility, the men too
familiar with the new duty that had suddenly fallen
into their laps. Sherman halted the horse, nearly
collided with his own color bearer, who was scrambling to keep up. Sherman caught the eyes of Con-
dit Smith, his quartermaster.

"Colonel . . . everything going smoothly?"

"My men are awaiting the boats, sir. There will
be much to do, and we shall accomplish that as
quickly as possible. I am well aware that the army
requires our services more now than at any time
in a while. We shall get the job done, sir. Colonel
Macfeely and I are just going over the logistical arrangements, setting up the storage depots. We have
already received a message from the supply boats

that by tonight, we might begin transfer of goods from boat to land."

Smith's businesslike efficiency was betrayed for a brief second by a short, satisfied nod, and Sherman realized that his quartermaster was very pleased with himself. About damn time, he thought. After a month of shouting at wagon masters, you might actually have something to do.

"Fine, Colonel. Put your men to good use. The army could use some new supplies." He looked at his commissary officer. "Colonel Macfeely, I want the men fed as rapidly as possible. I want commissary wagons on the road tonight, and rations distributed with all haste."

Macfeely seemed to share Smith's good spirits, a clipped salute, unnecessary, but Sherman returned it as Macfeely said, "It will happen as you order it, sir. This army will once more have the victuals intended for them."

Sherman absorbed that.

"Well, Colonel, I'm not sure that will help morale. But at least we don't have to rely on jayhawking these plantations anymore. Living off the land is one thing. Eating that land is something else."

He turned the horse, knew Macfeely wouldn't get the joke. Yes, we'll have rations, finally. But these men have spent a month feeding at the breast of Southern plantations. I'll give the damn rebels one thing: They know how to grow food, though maybe not what we need to keep an army in the field. Never seen so damn much molasses and salt ham in my life.

Macfeely called after him.

"We made the coffee a priority, sir. There should be a considerable supply reaching us by midnight." Macfeely paused as Sherman halted the horse. "Thought you would want to know that, sir."

Sherman didn't look back, kept the smile tight inside. Yep, he got the joke after all. Rebels might fatten us up with sugar and cornmeal, but they don't know a damn thing about coffee.

He rode back into the road, the prisoners long gone now, other horsemen moving in both directions, the cavalry, some of them the Iowans who had done the good work with the rebel cannon. He saw their commander, Swan, who shifted directions, approached him, a formal salute.

"General, we are moving the last of the rebels back to the temporary stockade. Your provosts have them now. I'm not sure yet what to do about the hospital. Best we leave it . . . unless you prefer otherwise."

"What hospital?"

"Oh, sir, I thought you knew. The rebs mostly retreated without giving us much of a scrap, but they left behind a whole load of wounded men. Some of 'em had been there a while. It's a pretty nasty place, sir. I've got my own doctor there, and if it's possible, I would appreciate some assistance there. There are rebel doctors there, and they're still willing to help out, certainly."

Sherman hadn't really expected that.

"I suppose they intended to hold to these bluffs for a while," he said. "I would have moved all those people into Vicksburg." He paused, a new thought. "Any of **our** people there?"

"Not that I saw, sir. I did look. It has been a while since our last encounter up this way. Any prisoners they had would probably be . . . gone."

"Well, Colonel, if any of my boys made it out of that place alive, they'll most likely be in Vicksburg. Something to look forward to."

"Yes, sir. Absolutely, sir."

He could see Swan moving in the saddle, the impatience of a good officer.

"You did fine work today, Colonel. See to your men."

"Thank you, sir."

Swan saluted once more, was quickly gone, a squad of his cavalry waiting for him farther down the road. He knows, Sherman thought. He knows exactly what his men did here, and why this place is so damn important. And how much I appreciate it.

FOUR MILES
NORTHEAST OF VICKSBURG
MAY 18, 1863

Early that morning, Grant had ridden with him,
the two of them crossing the Big Black together,
but throughout most of the morning, Grant had
spent more time putting the orders together, pushing each of his corps commanders where he wanted
them to be. The rebels were on the run, a hard retreat toward Vicksburg, and if there wasn't to be
another fight this day, at least the rebels had to
be pursued.

Sherman knew the orders, had kept his forward
regiments on the march pushing against any kind
of resistance the rebels might throw in his way. But
Grant had found him again, something of a surprise, since Sherman's men were far to the right of
the primary rebel fortifications. They sat now on
horseback, a fork in the road, the left the better
road, a continuation of the primary road that led
back toward Jackson, the best route for moving
troops toward Vicksburg as quickly as possible.

Sherman's columns were there already, and he
didn't need Grant's order, had already sent one regiment to the left, and for more than an hour there
had been a scattering of musket fire, the certain
signs of a rebel rear guard. The musket balls flew
past, but the fight was distant, little danger.

Grant studied the map, then handed it back to an

aide and said to Sherman, "Keep your men moving that way. The rebel works are strong there. Mine would be. They'll expect us in force, and we need to get there before they have too much time to prepare for us. Who are those people leading the march?"

"Eighth Missouri. Colonel Coleman. He knows to push like hell. Everything we've heard tells me it's only skirmishers, hoping to slow us down. Coleman won't sit still."

"Good, yes."

Grant seemed tired, lines of grime on his face from a full day in the saddle. Sherman had waited for this moment, itched to give Grant the report of the capture of Haines's Bluff, had rehearsed just how much embellishment, how much flair he should use. But Grant showed the effects of the long day, and Sherman said nothing, would keep it for another time.

Grant pointed toward the right-hand fork, Sherman's men spreading out that way as well. "Graveyard Road, the map says. Moves to the town closer to the river. Keep the pressure up there. We need to shove straight to the river, keep anybody from slipping by us. Who's out there?"

"Regulars. Thirteenth United States. Captain Washington. He knows to get to the river, drive back anybody they find. It's all right, Grant. Nothing to worry about up this way. Not yet."

Grant seemed to understand the message, Sherman's polite way of saying that Grant ought to be looking over someone else's shoulder. A musket ball whizzed by, and Grant eyed a patch of timber, said, "Let's move out of the way. I could use something to sit on besides this saddle."

Sherman followed him without speaking, the staff moving out that way as well, keeping their distance, no one dismounting but Grant and Sherman. Sherman spied a fat log, pointed.

"There. Not sure it's any better than a saddle."

Grant sat down in the grass beside the log and leaned back with a groan. Sherman did the same, realizing the soft ground felt better than he expected. Yep, he thought. It's been a long day.

Grant lit a cigar, and Sherman waited for Grant to speak first.

"Sherman. Fine work. Your men made a good march. It helped to have the pontoon bridges, eh?"

Sherman hadn't given that much thought, hadn't thought at all how the other two corps had made it past the Big Black River. Grant smoked hard at the cigar, leaned his arms across his knees, stretching his back. After a long second, Grant said, "McPherson's coming up behind you. Took him a little while. Had to clean up the enemy. Left us quite a haul back there. McClernand took another road, down to the left. Guess you knew that."

"Yes, sir. I do actually read your orders. The rest of my people are moving up pretty quick."

There was another scattering of musket fire, mostly toward the left-hand road.

"Skirmishers," Sherman said. "That's all. The rebs won't stay out here for long."

"Maybe so. But I wouldn't put your headquarters here until you're certain just how close those rebs have stuck their picket line."

There was no humor in Grant's words, and Sherman looked back toward his staff, saw Rawlins talking to his own officers, lively conversation, and Sherman thought, Telling tall tales to men who've done the deed. Nothing new there.

"You going to stay up this way? I would have thought McPherson—"

"McPherson knows what to do, where to set his people. Not your problem." It was a gentle scolding, and Sherman knew not to take offense. Grant closed his eyes for a brief moment, stabbed the butt of the spent cigar into the ground beside him. "I've already set up my headquarters back a ways, a farmhouse." Grant paused. "Found one of our own people there, wounded, or sick. Bad shape, for certain. He's a riverboat captain, Illinois man, got captured somehow, and the rebs made him pilot one of their boats for 'em. He's a bit happier today than yesterday. His family's plenty happy having Federals in their parlor than what's been staying there." Grant took a long breath, looked out toward the column moving past. "We get everybody up . . .

well then, tomorrow's the day. I want to hit those people before they can get set." Sherman knew the tone, Grant's determination, thought again of the failures. "Make sure we occupy Haines's Bluff, block off any route of escape to the north. I want strength there, nothing to hold up any of our supply boats."

"Working on that right now. The rebs mostly cleared out."

Grant pulled out another cigar, Sherman taking the cue with one of his own. Grant leaned forward on his knees again.

"It will help a great deal having the supply lines up here, this close. Communication lines, too."

There was no enthusiasm in that observation, and Sherman said, "So, you plan on writing letters to Washington any time soon? I rather thought you preferred silence."

Grant didn't smile.

"Cadwallader, Dana. That's for them. They can write any damn thing they want. But now they'll stop griping to me about how long it takes to get word out. You hear about Cadwallader?"

"Somebody shoot him?"

Grant glanced at him, still no humor.

"Captured a handful of reb prisoners all by himself. Riding out in some fool place he wasn't supposed to be, and stumbled right into a passel of 'em, just sitting there, waiting for somebody to come along and grab 'em up. That's a good sign. Their morale's got to be falling apart. All they've done is fight and get whipped and pull back and do it all again. Not good for the spirit."

"We'll drive them out of Vicksburg tomorrow. They've no fight left, I'm thinking."

Grant straightened his back, another stretch, shook his head, and pointed the cigar toward Vicksburg.

"I knew John Pemberton in Mexico. Not the smartest man, but he's bullheaded. He never should have retreated back to Vicksburg. Joe Johnston's out east somewhere with a pretty decent-sized army, and they haven't been **whipped** by anybody. That's where Pemberton should have gone. Instead, he's decided to hole up in that town, digging big damn ditches, sitting there waiting for us."

"We'll make him pay for that. Besides, he had to protect Vicksburg. You said that yourself."

Grant looked at the cigar, rolled it in his fingers.

"It won't work. We've got the numbers, and your men, **all** the men know what **winning** feels like. His people are running scared and are being told to dig holes. Bullheaded."

Grant stood slowly, motioned to Rawlins, the staff preparing to ride. Grant moved toward his horse, took the reins from an aide, stopped, then looked toward Sherman.

"You get Haines's Bluff cleared out, and it'll do

you some good to walk out all over that place. Take some time and do that. One reason I wanted you up here on the right flank."

Sherman felt a sudden burst of affection for Grant, couldn't hide the smile.

"Already been up there. Caught a glimpse of one of Porter's boats coming up the Yazoo. My quartermaster is all over himself with excitement."

Grant nodded.

"Feels pretty damn good, eh?"

"Pretty damn good."

Grant climbed up on the horse, but Sherman wasn't ready to see him leave, not yet.

"Hey, Grant." Grant turned to him, and Sherman could see from the tired squint in Grant's eyes, he had to be thinking of a feather mattress. "You know I didn't think much of this plan. Not at all, not from the beginning. But . . . I just had to tell you . . . not sure what's gonna happen tomorrow. But everything that's happened . . . this has been one of the greatest campaigns in history."

Grant nodded, said in a low voice, "I'll remember you said that. But keep that kind of talk to yourself. This isn't over yet."

CHAPTER TWENTY-ONE

PEMBERTON

VICKSBURG
MAY 18, 1863

He watched the destruction of the houses with a disgusted gloom, the Confederate engineers doing what had to be done, leveling and burning any structures that could give some shelter to an advancing foe, and more important, opening up fields of fire for the Confederate guns set far back behind the entrenchments. But Pemberton couldn't avoid thinking of the families, the civilians caught in the way, whose homes simply had to go. He had hoped they would leave anyway, had pressed the town's elders that it would be best for the civilians to abandon the place, especially while the routes eastward were still open. Now those routes had been closed shut by Grant's army, and to the west, the river was no better alternative. But the people had surprised him, had protested vigorously that no one, not the Yankees, and not John Pemberton, could force them from their homes. It was a stubbornness caused mostly by the pure inconvenience of hauling anyone's worldly possessions out along some dusty road, most people content to just sit, to ride out whatever storm the Yankees could bring. Already they had absorbed the artillery barrages, and no matter Pemberton's warnings, too many of the civilians just didn't comprehend that a fight for the town could produce far more deadly violence than the occasional mortar shell. As had happened in so many towns before, the civilians had no grasp of just what the war might do to them, to everything around them. And so they had remained. But their stubbornness came at a price, and whether the Federal artillerymen knew or even cared if civilians stayed put, the shelling of the town had increased dramatically. With artillery now launching shells from both up and across the river, and now, with Federal artillery batteries digging in much closer to the east, the barrages came at all hours. Many of the families had responded to this new terror by abandoning their homes, had sought instead the protection of caves all across the sloping terrain that spread beyond the town and across the open ground that led to the army's earthworks. Some of those shelters were natural, caverns and shallow crevasses, but many more now were man-made, the labor provided mostly by Negroes. Pemberton had been surprised by the organization of that, neat arrangements where the people paid money to the men with strong backs, the Negroes responding with what seemed to be enthusiasm. Nearly all of those men were slaves, of course, but in the town, many were not field hands at all, and yet they took to the labor with a smiling attitude that surprised the soldiers, performing the work as though it was simply the right thing to do. The fact that their owners might pay them for the extra labor, or that others, neighbors perhaps, would offer them currency for a day's work with a shovel, certainly contributed to their willingness to attack the soft ground, opening up caverns, widening the fissures, strengthening the caves with wooden beams. Pemberton wondered if there was much more to the eager cooperation of the Negroes, something the black men could never say to their owners. Everyone in the town knew of Lincoln's emancipation order, and the town's citizens had reacted with the same disgust and derision that Lincoln's order had received all through the South. But in Vicksburg, the Negroes had kept mostly silent, few of them daring to risk brute punishment from their masters by loudly supporting Lincoln's call that these men be freed. But now, with the crushing pessimism spreading through the town that Pemberton could not hold the Yankees away, he sensed that the cheerful willingness of the Negroes to provide underground shelter for their masters came more from hope of some greater reward from the men in blue.

This was not a conversation he could have with anyone in the town. There was already too much sentiment against him, brash talk of Pemberton's betrayal of the Cause, that his failures to defeat Grant were just one part of his treasonous calculation to barter away Vicksburg as penance for his own betrayal of Pennsylvania. The talk sickened him, and he continued to struggle privately, to do all he could to steel himself against the open hostility of the very people he was trying to protect. It had been that way from the beginning, of course, certainly in South Carolina. But suspicions could be erased by proving himself loyal the only way that mattered: on the battlefield. So far, Ulysses Grant had prevented that. He tried to picture Grant in his mind, wasn't exactly sure what the man looked like now. But the name itself had become so much more than that of a respected foe, a capable adversary to be met on some field of honor. There was no honor now, only survival. With every day that passed, every dose of tragedy given his army, Pemberton's hatred of Grant grew. There would never be an opportunity to cleanse himself of that, except by killing the man himself, the nightmarish fantasy of aiming the pistol into the man's face, putting the bayonet through his heart. But he forced himself to accept what he already knew, that there could be no honor in that. The only honor he would find would come on the battlefield.

THE COWAN HOME, VICKSBURG, MISSISSIPPI MAY 18, 1863

Pemberton stood among them, all faces on him, every man sharing his gloom. But Pemberton had one more surprise for his commanders, the very reason for calling another council of war. He waited for them to sit, could not help noticing their number, fewer now than before, Loring gone, Wirt Adams as well. Tilghman . . .

"Gentlemen, as you know, following our necessity of retreat to Vicksburg, I sent a message to General Johnston, detailing our disaster at the Big Black, and advising him of our intent to occupy our defensive works around Vicksburg. This includes withdrawing our forces away from the northern outposts close to the Yazoo River. Those men, and whatever artillery we could salvage, have been added to our position here. As you know, the option was available to me to continue in obedience to General Johnston's order, and make every attempt to maneuver this army to a rendezvous with him. This I did not choose to do. I am deeply distressed that General Johnston does not accept my belief that Vicksburg is of value. That is a direct

contradiction to the orders I have received from
President Davis. Well, you know that. If any of you
doubt the stubbornness to which General Johnston holds in this view, allow me to read . . . this."
He held up a paper. "This was received today, by
what means I am not exactly certain. I am grateful
for the tenacity of our couriers, and their uncanny
ability to escape capture. They serve us well. This
is of course sealed by the hand of General Johnston." Pemberton paused, looked at the faces, his
four division commanders, their chief adjutants,
no one appearing eager to hear whatever he was
about to tell them. He was not surprised. He took a
long breath, read from the paper. **" 'Your dispatch
of today by Captain Henderson was received.
If Haines's Bluff is untenable, Vicksburg is of
no value and cannot be held. If therefore you
are invested in Vicksburg, you must ultimately
surrender. Under such circumstances, instead of
losing both troops and place, we must if possible save the troops. If it is not too late, evacuate
Vicksburg and its dependencies and move to the
northeast.' "** He stopped, glanced at the faces, saw
no change of expression. "This was sent to me . . .
yesterday."

He turned, a pair of his staff officers standing at
the doorway.

"Captain Selph, please store this in a secure location. It is a document of some value to me . . .
to this army." He turned to the others, fewer than

a dozen men, still no one speaking. "We will be
called upon one day . . . to answer for what we
will do here. According to what I have heard, the
morale of the army is strong. We shall do all in our
power to drive away the threat to this town, and to
this army." He looked toward the engineer. "Major
Lockett assures me that his efforts have been fruitful. Though there is much to be done, the earthworks have been improved and repaired, and that
work continues."

Lockett nodded, then spoke. "The defensive
works had deteriorated somewhat during the army's absence, due mostly to inclement weather.
And there is some shortage of spades. We have perhaps five hundred in total. I had hoped for a good
many more."

Pemberton tried not to react to that, knew Lockett had pressed him months ago for more earth-
moving tools, pickaxes and shovels. From Lockett's
tone, it was clear the engineer recalled that as well.

"Thank you, Major. Please maintain a strong
hand over the sappers and the men doing the work.
The defensive lines must be strong and durable."

Lockett said nothing, and Pemberton knew the
man already understood the task assigned him.

"We have made every effort to put the strongest forces along the front lines. Those troops who
have not yet engaged the enemy should be our best
weapon, and thus they are placed accordingly. General Stevenson, your men have given a great deal to

this fight thus far, and therefore I have placed you to the right, an area I believe will be untested for the near term. You are our right flank."

Stevenson fidgeted, then said, "Yes. We're in place. The men are doing what they can to make amends."

It was an unnecessary apology, but Pemberton understood that Stevenson's division had been most responsible for the failure at Baker's Creek, and so Pemberton had to respond to that, had assigned his men the one part of the line farthest from the Federal advances.

"General Forney . . ."

"We are in place in the center. I have made certain our right rests on the railroad line, and that we are in contact there with General Stevenson's left. It is a good position."

Pemberton didn't have to wait, Martin Smith eager as always.

"We're ready for them, sir. Our right adjoins General Forney at the graveyard road, and we have secured our left to the river. We were not able to salvage all of the wagons and supplies from the bluffs, but the men are eager for a fight. The scouts report that the enemy's boats are in motion along the various approaches, including the Yazoo River itself. Though we no longer hold those heights, he will not have an easy time of it. We shall make them pay dearly for their daring."

Martin's enthusiasm seemed forced, counterfeit,

a direct contrast to the posture of John Bowen. Bowen was staring down, seemed preoccupied, one finger rubbing dull black leather on one boot. Pemberton wanted to say something, offer some encouragement to the one man whose troops had borne the lion's share of the fighting, but Pemberton couldn't muster the kind of energy Martin had shown. Bowen looked up now, glanced at the others, seemed to avoid Stevenson, one more piece of the tedious personality conflicts Pemberton had tried to ignore.

"We are in reserve," Bowen said, "as you ordered. My men require time. There are a great many men not fit. I want everyone in this room to know in absolute terms the duty performed by my division. I will not boast of great accomplishments . . . only of sacrifice. A great many good men . . . my men . . . have made that sacrifice. They will do so again if called upon. But there are morale problems. . . ."

Bowen stopped abruptly, looked down again, and Pemberton said, "Thank you, General. We are all aware of the valuable service performed by your command. God willing, your men shall have time to regain their fighting spirit. . . ."

"They do not lack for spirit! They lack for . . . leadership. The talk is ugly and indiscreet, and for that, I am to blame."

The outburst silenced Pemberton, the fire in Bowen's eyes as much anger toward him as the enemy. Pemberton fought to find words, thought,

He does not believe that. His men would not find any blame with **him**.

The others stirred slightly, uncomfortable with Bowen's anger, and Pemberton knew that every one of them recognized where the blame would lie. After an awkward silence, Pemberton said, "Had General Loring—"

Bowen seemed to erupt.

"This is not General Loring's fault! I should have liked him in this room, yes. He **should** be in this room. I should have liked him to obey your orders and attend to his duties as a part of this army. But we cannot change what is. Perhaps General Loring will ride to our rescue after all. Is that not what we are hoping . . . all of us? We are outgunned here. The enemy has every advantage except the ditches we dig. This is not Fort Donelson. There is no convenient avenue of escape the enemy has left open for us. In a very short time, we shall be surrounded by gunboats and bluecoat infantry, and they will have the advantage of resupply and reinforcement. Our best hope lies in the willingness of General Johnston to come to our aid with a vigorous advance. Is that not perfectly clear to you all?"

Pemberton closed his eyes for a brief moment, blinked them open, felt himself sagging at the shoulders.

"General Johnston does not seem compelled to assist this effort." He paused. "General Bowen, at this moment, we have only our duty to concern us.

That duty is to defend this town against the enemy. I am supremely hopeful that if General Johnston should see his way to join us, he could very well strike a blow that will force General Grant to re-think his strategies." He paused again. "I would welcome any suggestions how we may persuade General Johnston to do that."

Bowen looked up at him, a searing glare, the man's face showing a hint of gray, a flicker of ill-ness. Bowen said, "Have you . . . **asked** him?"

The room shook, a hard rumble beneath his feet, and Forney said, "The enemy has begun this after-noon's parade. It has become annoyingly predict-able, and rather consistent in the timing. Perhaps we can make use of that to set our watches."

Pemberton did not smile, waited for more, the incoming artillery dropping down, whistling past with the usual variety of sounds, one high scream passing directly over the house. The officers began to move, and Pemberton knew they would all be eager to return to their commands.

"Gentlemen, please. There is a purpose to this council . . . beyond the reading of General John-ston's unfortunate dismissal of my strategy. I must know if you are in agreement . . . that this course is the proper one. Yes, I will beseech General John-ston to bring his army to us. But I would hope that I might inform the general that we are here in agreement, that this place must be held. This army is prepared to fight the enemy . . . of that I am certain. Are all of you? There is no mistaking that General Johnston is ordering us to abandon this place. That . . . I cannot do."

Bowen stood slowly, weakness in his legs. He glanced at the others, heads nodding, and Bowen said, "We are here, are we not? If we did not choose to follow your command, then we should have followed after General Loring."

The opinion was unanimously expressed by the council of war that it is impossible to withdraw the Army from this position with such morale and matériel to be of further service to the Confederacy. I have decided to hold Vicksburg as long as possible, with the firm hope that the government may yet be able to assist me in keeping this obstruction to the free navigation of the Mississippi River. I still conceive it to be the most important point of the Confederacy.

He reread the letter, Waddy standing tall above him.

"This is adequate. I shall also prepare a communication for the president. He must be informed what has happened . . . why it has happened."

"What do you mean, sir?"

Pemberton sat back, pushed through an aching stiffness in his shoulders.

"I **mean** that my influence with General Johnston lacks any gravity at all. General Bowen is correct that we must hope for General Johnston to come to our assistance. But I cannot expect such a thing just by requesting it. Perhaps the president can persuade the general on what course he should follow."

"Certainly, sir."

Pemberton looked up at Waddy, who reacted by standing stiffly.

"Such formality is not necessary, Colonel. I regard you as something of a friend."

Waddy remained stiff, stared ahead, as though Pemberton were grading him.

"Thank you, sir."

Pemberton dropped his gaze and stared at the desk.

"So, are you of the opinion of so many others . . . that I have sold this town to General Grant?"

Waddy reacted now, the formality swept away.

"Oh my, no, sir. Not at all."

"There is talk, you know. A great deal of talk. Bowen's division . . . the citizens."

"Yes, sir, I have heard such things. I have ordered the staff to do away with any such slanderous chatter, to silence it with great vigor."

"Kind of you, Colonel. But I cannot change anyone's opinion of my actions, unless I first give them a change of results."

"Yes, sir."

Pemberton stared at the papers in front of him, an accounting of goods, rations and ammunition, most of it prepared by Waddy himself, some from the commissary and ordnance officers.

"It seems that we are greatly in need of percussion caps, Colonel."

"Yes, sir. That is a primary task. I have ordered . . . operations in that area to be undertaken with extreme effort, sir."

Pemberton swallowed the word. **Operations,** an army euphemism for smuggling.

"Dangerous work. The enemy will give those men no quarter. Anyone caught bringing any matériel into this place will likely be regarded as a spy. Any rations will be confiscated, certainly, but not even the enemy would punish the hungry. Ammunition, powder, caps . . . very different affair. Men will be shot for that."

"Then they should not be captured, sir."

Simple logic, he thought. The certainty of the young.

"Very well, Colonel. Have my letter sent to General Johnston by whatever means is required. At least three copies."

"Right away, sir."

Waddy took the paper, folded it carefully, and moved out of the room. Pemberton sipped the tea, weak, the water bitter. He heard noises, looked to the door, the house's owner, Cowan, a thin, frail man, his hat clasped in both hands at his stomach.

Behind the man, Lockett appeared, the civilian giving way with a bow, Lockett pausing, always proper protocol.

"Come in, Major."

Lockett stepped closer, boots on the wooden floor, and now the civilian was there as well, stood close beside Lockett, the engineer puzzled, looking down at the small man with the obvious question in his mind. The civilian spoke first, pointing to the teacup.

"I regret, General, that I can do no better. The supply boats have stopped completely. Well, you know that, of course. I shall endeavor to locate more luxury items for your headquarters, honored as I am you would choose my humble residence."

The man scurried away, was gone quickly without any response from Pemberton. Pemberton looked at Lockett and shook his head.

"I wish that man would stop issuing me apologies. This home is most adequate for our needs. I must remember that these people are not army. They do not respect our ways of doing things. This is never easy, forcing ourselves into anyone's home. But luxuries . . . I cannot just order anyone here to provide for me."

Lockett held a thick sheaf of papers, was studying a diagram of some kind of structure, his attention more on the drawings. He looked toward Pemberton, as though just realizing Pemberton was addressing him.

"Oh . . . well, yes, sir. Actually, you can order them to do anything you wish. Most likely they will obey. The army is all that stands between them and the enemy, and they most certainly know that. And the army is . . . you."

Pemberton stared at Lockett, saw calm logic on the man's face, the mind of an engineer exercising perfect clarity.

"It is not that simple, Major. Every town is the same. These people never seem to grasp what we are doing here, how crucial this operation is. I have heard a great deal of complaining as to how their lives have been inconvenienced by this war, by our arrival in their midst. I suspect, should General Grant have taken up residence here, they would treat him with as little regard as they do me."

Lockett looked at him now, no humor in the man, and Pemberton knew that Lockett had heard the same grousing, the angry suggestions that just by his birthright, Pemberton was surely a traitor. Pemberton shook his head.

"Yes, yes," Pemberton said. "I did not bring them victories. I should be condemned for that, I suppose. That is, after all, what civilians expect of us."

"Yes, sir. I suppose." Lockett looked to the drawings in his hand again, then seemed to snap to attention.

"Oh, sir, the reason for my visit . . . I wish to report that the river batteries are in fine condition, fully stocked with ammunition. There are reports . . . and I did observe myself, that the number of enemy gunboats has increased at their bases upriver, and that there is definitely movement into the Yazoo River. The enemy no doubt is targeting Yazoo City as a means of protecting his flanks. It is of course a wise precaution. Unfortunately, there is little we can do to alter that course. According to your Major Memminger, all supplies that could be brought into the town from the bluffs are now . . . here."

"I am more concerned with your opinion as to the strength of our defensive lines."

"As strong as they can be, sir, given the time and manpower we had available. Most of the main works are fronted by exterior ditches six to ten feet deep. There are ramparts and parapets for the infantry, and at last count, I recorded one hundred and two artillery pieces ready for service. We are even now cutting timber to create abatis in the exterior trenches. I have also suggested the use of surplus telegraph wire as further entanglement."

Pemberton couldn't help feeling impressed, at this man who did his job without complaints. He leaned forward, arms on the desk, tapped his fingers, nervous energy.

"So, there it is, Major."

"Sir?"

"The enemy is moving up, will no doubt put his people in direct opposition to our entrenchments. Do we know their disposition?"

"I know that Sherman is to the north, closest to the river. But my attentions have been focused mostly on the labor. Much remains to be done. Should the enemy target the entrenchments with their artillery, I have ordered that the men seek protection whenever necessary."

Pemberton nodded slowly, stared at the teacup.

"Sherman shall make it necessary, Major. The others. Very soon. Grant will see it so."

CHAPTER TWENTY-TWO

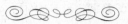

BAUER

THREE MILES EAST OF VICKSBURG
MAY 19, 1863

The march had ended at dusk the evening before, the men filing into yet another open field. But this time there was tension in the officers, orders firm and quiet, the men pushed out into lines that kept them facing westward. To either side of them, other units were doing the same, and immediately the wagons had come forward, but not with rations. It was shovels, axes, and other tools, everything an army would need to prepare defensive positions. There was grumbling about that, too many memories of the Louisiana swamps, mud and snakes. But the shovels were mostly for artillery, big guns rolled into positions not too far behind the camps of the infantry. Across the narrow road, all down through thickets and cuts, dense brush and patches of open ground, the infantry prepared for whatever rest they could find by keeping to lines that resembled a human wall, guarding against some surprise the rebels might suddenly throw at them. The regimental commanders were vigilant, staff officers moving quickly through the darkness, assured that each unit had bonded its flank to other units who did the same on down the line. The flank of McPherson's corps was anchored on the right, to the north, by Sherman, on the south by McClernand.

All through the night more of them came forward, filing into place, led by staff officers who knew the geography, and most important of all, who knew just where the enemy had gone, and where he should be right now. More artillery came, too, teams of horses pulling forward the caissons and limbers, their crews ordered to dig the guns into the earth, as much cover as the shovels could offer. The work went on all night, the steady thumps of axes bringing down trees, widening roads, opening up fields of fire. When the dawn came, there were a few campfires, mostly deep in the gullies, the smoke drifting out in a gray haze, not precise enough to offer any rebel artillery battery a target. But the camp wagons with the precious food stayed back, and so breakfast came from the backpacks, those men who still had hardtack sharing it with those who had eaten all they had on the march the day before. There was water now, small creeks where commissary officers filled buckets, but it was no better than most of what they had had to drink for the past month. Still, the canteens were filled, and for the first time in weeks there was an unspoken sense that the march had ended. The dark, rolling ground around Bauer was becoming much more than the usual roadside camp. Wherever they were supposed to be, they had arrived.

"Whoeee, lookee there! They're burning down the whole place!"

It was the loudest voice Bauer had heard in a while, and he peered from under his cap, sat up, could see men climbing the steep sandy hillside for a better view, pulled himself up and followed them to the crest of the ridge. The sun had set hours before, a glorious orange reflection that had outlined a scattering of farmhouses back behind the rebel earthworks. But now the glow had returned, reflected across the faces of the men who rose up to stare, mostly silent, curious, baffled. The fires offered a silhouette of mounds of distant earthworks, some of that natural, some man-made, but they were too far away to see any real details. Out front of the ridgelines, trees were being cut by the sappers, the men with axes, instructed by the engineers, and Bauer had seen that before. The

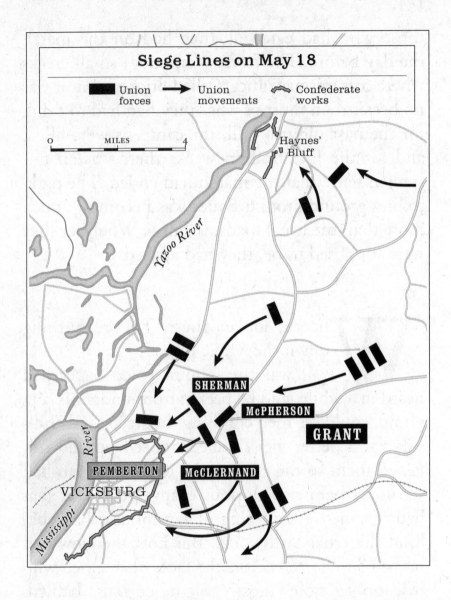

Siege Lines on May 18

Union forces — Union movements — Confederate works

O MILES 4

Yazoo River

Haynes' Bluff

SHERMAN

McPHERSON

GRANT

River

PEMBERTON

VICKSBURG

McCLERNAND

Mississippi

ground was being **prepared**. But the fires they saw now were more distant, closer to the town, possibly in the town itself.

Bauer stared, fixed, and said in a low voice, "They burning down their own town?"

Kelly was beside him, standing tall, waving his hat.

"You betcha! They heard what old Sherman done to Jackson, and they's gonna save us the trouble!"

Finley was there, behind Kelly.

"What do you know about Jackson?" he asked.

Kelly ignored the tone of the sergeant's question, said, "Old Sherman burnt it to the ground! Hell, Sergeant, we all heard about that. You could see the smoke from miles away! Didn't take no cavalry scout to spread that word. Now, lookee here! It's happening again, and we ain't even had a chance to do nothing! Phooey! I was hopin' we were finally gonna get our chance!"

Finley stood up taller, stared out with the others, his haranguing of Kelly silenced by the spectacle.

"Be damned. Maybe that's what they's doing. Well, for the love of Mike! We're not gonna get a chance to do nothing! Not a damn thing! Stinkin' low-life secesh done taken all the fun out of this here war!"

More men were climbing up, and Bauer glanced to the side, a sea of faces, some across the road, men from other units. Behind him, a hand on his shoulder, the man pulling himself up, a harsh hiss of a familiar voice: Willis.

"Get your damn heads down! Back down here! This ain't some damn parade! You'd think you were gawking at dancing girls! The rebs are burning down houses, clearing their own field of fire. That's all! According to the colonel, they been doing it for a couple days now. You think that's so damn exciting? It means they'll have a better shot at you when we move that way."

Bauer thought of that, a slight shudder, didn't want to imagine anyone out there with a better field of fire. He tried to make out details, but the fires were too spread out, parts of the field nothing but a glow of orange. Above him came the sharp sound of a bee, but it wasn't a bee, and he flinched, stared out still at the fires, more buzzing, a crack close past his ear. High above, a streak of fire, the blast coming down behind, in the low ground, another out to one side, more artillery shells coming down farther away, and Willis shouted now, "Get down! They're shooting at you! You're targets, you stupid micks!"

Bauer squatted down, slid off the embankment, blinded from the firelight, let gravity pull him back down to the flatter ground. The others were doing the same, reacting to the sound of the musket balls. The artillery shells were few and scattered, but they added punctuation to Willis's warning, and a new fear took hold in some of the men, some falling past Bauer, tripping over one another, a sharp cry of panic from one man who screamed as he tumbled and ran past. Most of the men just stopped in the low ground, but some were yelling out with the terror of what they couldn't see, one artillery shell bursting in the darkness a few yards behind them, dirt and brush tossed through the men, adding to the fear. Finley was down now, calling out with more volume than Willis, "Hang here! It ain't bloomin' banshees! They's not coming after ye! Just sit tight! It's just rebel pickets!"

Others were taking up that call, all along the hillside, and Bauer sat frozen, his heart thumping hard, his knees pulled up tight. He blinked, forced himself to stare into the dark. The artillery fire slowed, then stopped, and Willis called out what was already in Bauer's mind.

"They're just testing you! Finding the range. You all stood up there like you were watching a parade ground drill, and their skirmishers saw you. They got field glasses, too, you know! That oughta tell you how close we are to what we came for. Anybody feel like griping about being left behind? You think the army's done forgot about you still? This is the front lines, boys!"

The men were calming, and Bauer felt a stab of concern, had yet to be in any kind of fight alongside these men, did not expect they would react with such a burst of chaos. He wanted to stand, to help Willis calm them, bring them back into line, but Willis was moving slowly past, his words doing the job. Behind them, farther down into low ground, across the thickets, other officers were taking charge, more voices of authority, picket lines of their own slipping forward to keep any prying rebel eyes just far enough away. Willis was staring up the hill, his face caught by the glow from the house fires.

"Just sit tight. We got nowhere else to be until they tell us."

Finley stood close to Willis, and even in the shadows Bauer could see the sergeant's massive thickness, a squat tree trunk of a man.

"They'll be all right, Lieutenant. They's just not used to seeing such things. Damnedest thing, though, people burning down their own houses just to get a better look at us. Might be saving us some work."

"That ought to tell you something, Sergeant. They know we're here, and that we're not planning on just waiting around. You boys . . . all that talk about being left out of the fight. Looks to me like the brass has put us out here where we can lead the way. I told you boys before . . . we're rested up. That's what the army knows how to do. Use up some fellows until they're too worn-out, then give them a rest. Well, right now, those boys who did the deed at that Champion place are filling in behind us, getting rested up. And **we're** up **here**. Anybody confused about that?"

There were a few responses, no one arguing the point with Willis. Bauer could see through the darkness now, the trees and open ground more visible, the first hint of dawn, saw men in groups, some spread out along the base of the hill, many more back in the open. There was a different kind of quiet to them, no one sleeping, a few in motion, crawling toward him, many more sitting with their backs against the hillside.

Bauer closed his eyes, wasn't ready for the dawn yet, felt a chill from cool air, but the shiver came from somewhere else, some other place planted deep inside him. There was never a good time for this, for all of that preparation, none of the veterans ever feeling oh so comfortable that the inevitable fight would be **better** this time because trees had been cut down. He kept his eyes closed, a churning in his brain that would do anything to keep this day from beginning. When the march first halted, he had slept, but that was barely a memory, hours before, some other place on ground that seemed to burst with thorns. He gripped his legs harder, eyes still closed, thought of bees, the deadly pieces of lead, so many, so often. He kept his eyes closed, his head down hard against his knees, his mind opening up into a childlike fantasy. If I can't see you, then you can't see me. . . .

Army corps commanders will push forward carefully, and gain as close position as possible to the enemy's works until 2:00 P.M. At that hour they will fire three volleys of artillery from all the pieces in position. This

**will be the signal for a general charge
of all the corps along the whole line.—
Major General Ulysses S. Grant—Special
Order 134**

The order had been passed down to the most junior officers, those men surrounded now by their
small commands, Willis standing among two dozen
seated men who sat in silence as the order was read.
Willis recited from memory, no time to put all
of this to paper, stared out toward his platoon, a
nodding glance toward Captain McDermott, who
stood out to the front of his entire company. To one
side, a cluster of horsemen stood tall, their voices
hushed, hands pointing, a variety of flags scattered
out in the field around them. Men rode away now,
others coming close, and Bauer watched the scene
play out, could see agitation, anger in the brass.

Now Willis was close beside him, said in a low
voice, "We've got a hell's gambit in front of us,
Dutchie. It's after one-thirty. The captain said he
just got this order. Strange. This sorta thing ought
to be passed along a whole hell of a lot sooner than
the time we start the advance. Has to be somebody's
mistake. Don't like mistakes, not from the brass.
Dammit anyway."

Bauer looked at him, saw tension in black eyes,
knew that look too well. Whatever demons drove
Willis to stand up to the enemy were at work now,
the man's words clipped, each one a small punch.

Bauer whispered, "We'll do all right, Sammie. These boys are eager, no doubt about that."

Willis seemed not to hear him.

"Wouldn't be Grant doing that. Had to be some jackass staff officer, taking his sweet time putting on his fancy sash and polishing his damn sword before he decided to get out here and put that order in our hands. Not McPherson, either. Good man, I think. For a West Pointer."

That answered a question for Bauer, his own uncertainty about their corps commander, a man few of the foot soldiers would ever see. From the beginning of training there was a prejudice against the men from West Point, generals who had learned of war from books. But no one faulted General Grant, not after Shiloh, and even the crankiest veterans had begun to concede that book learning might not be such a bad thing for those men who made the decisions.

Bauer said, still in a whisper, "You think General McPherson's a good one? Didn't know about that."

Willis looked at him, no change in his hard expression.

"You think it matters? He gonna make you a better fighter, or make sure you're safe? Shut up, Dutchie. I gotta get out front, meet with the captain, the other lieutenants." He paused. "We better be ready, that's all I can say. The rebels might run, but the river's at their back. They'll fight before they try to swim. There's gonna be some lead tossed at us, for sure." He looked at Bauer again, no sign of softness, but the words betrayed that. "Keep your head down, Dutchie. We shove our way into Vicksburg, I want to see you there. You run off . . . well, you ain't gonna run off."

Willis moved away quickly, in short, precise steps, and climbed up the sandy embankment, the place where Captain McDermott was assembling his lieutenants. Bauer watched them gathering, the company commander obviously angry, sharing something with his officers, and Bauer thought about Willis's words, **tossing lead**. He looked around at the others, saw faces down, some men praying, almost no one sharing conversation. His eye caught the shock of red hair, the boy O'Daniel, his hat off, sitting with a fixed stare, one hand rubbing the stock of his musket. Bauer moved a step that way, but saw the boy's face now, tears. Bauer stopped, knew what the boy was feeling, knew the fear, that when the muskets began, the fear could lead to uncontrollable terror, that the boy might run.

Finley moved up beside him, seemed to follow his gaze, moved to O'Daniel, jerked him up to his feet, the boy's face a plaster of wet grime.

"You wanna go home to your mama, Red? Well, you do your job today, and we might all do just that."

Bauer took a step forward, felt a sudden hatred

for the big sergeant, had no patience now for the stupidity of mindless cruelty.

"He's got no mama. Let him be."

The words came out with more volume than he expected, and Finley turned, his shoulders bowing up, a massive fist rising up, the man's eyes fixed on Bauer's face.

"You telling me how to talk to my own men, Dutchman? You'll eat those teeth. . . ."

"Sergeant!" Willis moved quickly, stood between them, and Finley hesitated, lowered the fist. "Put these men on their feet. We've got a half mile to march before we begin the attack. No time for this. You hear me?"

"I hear you, sir."

Finley turned but the others were already rising up, muskets in hand, and Willis said aloud, "Some of you . . . if you got family possessions . . . think of leaving them here."

Bauer had heard these words before. He didn't want to see that, didn't want to know who around him was that frightened, or that certain they weren't going to survive what they were about to do. The men took the lieutenant's advice, some pulling out letters, small Bibles, a pile forming beside a small tree. It was a strange show of faith, that the items would be untouched, no thievery from the men who came up behind them. The fear was rolling up through him now, unavoidable, infuriating, and he

fought to hold back tears, his hands shaking, steadied them on the stock of his musket. He closed his
eyes, could hear the men all across the wide field,
gathering themselves, some with no idea what was
coming, green men eager for the fight. The pile by
the tree was growing, more Bibles, papers, charms
on leather straps, but many of the men were falling
into line, the order already given, battle formation,
the bugler off to one side blowing out the awful
cadence. His hand pressed against his shirt pocket,
nothing there, and he focused on that, felt a dull
throb of aching sadness that there was nothing in
his pockets worth saving, no one back home who
would even know what might happen to him.

T he volleys from the artillery had streaked
overhead, more bugle calls, and all across
the wide fields the march began. They
stepped to the sound of drums, their part of the battle line pushing through a cornfield, the low green
stalks trampled quickly. Bauer kept his eyes on the
higher ground to the front, and already he could
see movement, rebels behind their earthworks, reacting to the wave of blue pouring their way. The
musket fire had begun even before the artillery fire,
sharpshooters sent out well in front of the advance,
an aggressive picket line, men in blue scampering forward into any kind of protected place. The
rebels were firing back, seemed to pay more atten-

tion to the men closest to them, the greatest threat right in front of them, were not yet offering any great volleys toward the snaking lines of blue. The smoke had begun to rise, small wisps from hidden places, some drifting above the vast mounds where the rebels waited, and with every pop of a musket, Bauer felt a flinch inside him, a blink of his eyes, a shaking in the hand that supported the butt of his loaded musket.

He glanced to the side, saw the familiar faces, the names he had come to know, **Irishmen**, wouldn't think on that, on whether that meant anything at all. His brain was chattering in rhythm to the scattered musket fire, nonsensical thoughts, manic words, answering the sickening churn in his stomach. He felt the sweat in his clothes, the hard breathing in short gasps, looked down to his feet, his brogans digging deep into soft soil, each step a desperate effort to stomp away the fear that he might run. **Tossing lead**.

"Tighten up the line! No gaps!"

The words growled through him, Sergeant Finley doing his job, the only voice he heard, the drumbeats behind them distant, many more men in formation there, strengthening the lines, adding to the power. Drive them back, he thought. No need for a fight at all. They'll run maybe, just . . . go. He looked again toward the rebel works, saw an eruption of fire, an artillery piece firing toward them, the shell passing far overhead. The thunder of that reached him now, followed by another, but up front, the sharpshooters were taking advantage, rebel gunners too exposed, and so the cannon fire was weak, scattered. The lack of artillery made for an eerie kind of silence, but it was not silence at all, the drums and the muskets making their own kind of soft rhythm. He strained to see ahead, his steps slowing, hesitant, the fear in his brain trying to hold him back. The dirt beneath his feet was soft, tilled soil, his brogans snagging on the green cornstalks, and he stumbled.

Finley was there, always there, and said, "On your feet! Keep together! Close up that line!"

The chattering of fire in front seemed to increase now, and they passed a man, hunched down, loading his musket, giving a sharp single cheer, "Go get 'em, boys! They can't shoot without showing themselves! Hee! We're giving 'em hell!"

Bauer ignored the man, stared still at the rebel works, close now, fat mounds and tall walls of raw earth, and beyond them flags, heads peering up, then gone, the whistling zip of musket balls still from the sharpshooters. He tried to guess the distance, two hundred yards, close enough, too close, the screaming voice in his head, Get down! But his feet would not obey the panic, the steps automatic, in time with the men beside him, behind him, the earthen walls closer still.

From beyond the fat mounds of earth, more artillery came, cascades of thunder, most of it overhead, but then the solid shot found them, tumbling through the men themselves, rolling and bouncing into the lines, crushing everything they touched. The canister was there as well, thick clouds of hot iron, a hot rush of air, ripping the ground in front of him, tearing gaps in the men with sickening efficiency. He knew of all that, had seen it before, knew the sounds, the crack of bone, the curdling tear of flesh, screams and cries, even the smallest wound too painful to bear. And now the tops of the earthworks seemed to come alive, muskets rising up, pointed forward, voices calling out, a chorus of cheers, some hint of a rebel yell, but those men weren't coming; there would be no great terrifying charge. The first volley blew out in a hard blast of smoke, the singing of a hundred bees zipping past him, the dull smack of cracking bone, one man falling out of line, tumbling down in a heap, another close to him crying out in a hard shriek. He lowered himself, a reflex, pulled his shoulders down, making himself smaller, a useless gesture, and now the second volley came, quickly, too quickly, the sounds ripping past his ear, a man behind crying out.

Behind him he heard Finley's voice: "Tighten up! Keep moving!"

Bauer did not stop, fought the voice in his brain, terror and hate. But still he moved forward, feeling the man beside him, the entire line pushing closer, Willis now, out in front of the line.

"No firing! Wait for the order!"

Another volley burst out from the earthworks, the smoke thick and billowing, and Bauer flinched again, caught the stink of the smoke, a fog drifting toward them, the rebels hidden from view, and now the bugle sounded again, the horrible sound, so familiar, so much training, the order to charge. He saw Willis raise his pistol in the air, turn to them, his hand in a circle, and now Willis turned again toward the rebels, lowered his head, and surged forward.

Bauer did as the men around him, a jogging run, the rebels firing again, the sounds of the fight growing all along the line, far out beyond the Wisconsin men. There was cannon fire now, thumps in every direction, but not many, most of the fight coming from the muskets. Bauer kept his eyes on the fat earthen walls, fought through aching legs, searing heat in his lungs, heard the order, someone, a voice.

"Fire!"

He stopped, raised the musket, no target, smoke and dirt, hesitated, searched for something, anything to shoot at. He pointed high, to the top of the wall, saw a flicker of movement, yanked on the trigger, the musket punching his shoulder, more smoke, the butt of the musket released, dropping to the ground, his fingers fumbling in the cartridge box, a frantic shivering as he tried to reload. Around him, men were doing the same, and he saw them out to both sides, vast lines of blue, more moving up behind. In every direction, men were falling, others firing their muskets. Out front, some of the men were rushing up close to the earthen walls, dropping down into low ditches, struggling through piles of brush, cut tree limbs, more obstacles. The rebels kept up their fire, not massed volleys, just steady and regular, a hum that sliced the air all around him. He stumbled, low ground, saw men lying flat, facedown, the dirt around them punched by musket balls, and Bauer did the same, flattened out, a ball striking close to his head, dirt on his face, the musket shoved up in front of him, a useless gesture of protection.

"Up! Let's go! Keep in line!"

He saw Finley, the big man waving, grabbing men, pulling them up from the cover, and Bauer felt weakness in his legs, his brain screaming him down flat, another ball striking beside him, Finley cursing, men around him moving forward. Bauer pulled himself to his feet, a brief panic. Did you reload? He glanced at the percussion cap, **yes,** relief, followed a cluster of men, all moving with Finley, many men to one side, shouts and screams and smoke. The rebel fire came through them in sheets, men falling in line, a half dozen going down at once, Finley standing, waving them on, looking at Bauer, pointing, words he couldn't hear. Bauer slogged through soft sand, fought thorny brush, his legs tangled in wire and tree branches, bodies, one man writhing, blood on his face, and Bauer knew not to look, not to stop. He pushed ahead, saw Finley still watching him, the face different, and Bauer stopped, Finley's eyes holding him, the man's anger gone, hands motioning to him, a casual wave, the sergeant's mouth moving slowly, blood now on his lips, flowing down his chin. The eyes stared out past him now, and Finley staggered, fell, straight toward him, and Bauer was there, over the man's body, felt panic rising up inside him, sickness, saw a small pool of blood on the sergeant's back. He put an arm down, froze, wouldn't touch him, his brain yelling at him, It doesn't matter, and he felt a hard grip on his shoulder, was jerked to one side, his knees giving way, saw Willis, hot fire in his eyes, no glance at Finley.

"Let's go! Get to that wall! Climb! The rebels can't fire down! You with me?"

Bauer began to move, Willis still watching him, others moving past, and Bauer stared for a long second across the wide ground, the bare approach to the rebel works, saw men down, some crawling, some not moving at all. But there was order still, lines of men moving up behind, officers leading them, sergeants keeping them together, volleys fired, then answered, the sounds a roaring chorus in Bauer's ears, and now one more sound, the bugle. He searched for it, frantic, needing to see that, the terror holding him frozen, his brain searching for the sound, the musket balls still thick in the air, and he heard it again, felt the hand again, jerking him. Willis.

"Retreat! The order to retreat! Dammit! This isn't gonna work! Let's go!"

Willis moved away, motioning to the others, some men rising up from whatever protection they had found, but many more were moving out across the open ground, holding to some kind of line, pulling away in good order. The rebels still fired, and Bauer heard the first cheer, close above him, backed away, the musket ready, aimed at nothing, fired, the fear still there, his feet avoiding the bodies of men, and he moved back with the others, saw wounded men helping others, some bloodied men walking on their own, cries and screams and musket fire still coming from the rebel earthworks.

They withdrew back across the open ground, through the trampled cornfield. Bauer struggled to keep upright, soft dirt and cornstalks beneath his feet, looked back toward the rebels, saw hands in the air above the earthworks, muskets raised high, a single flag waving in a broad arc, taunting the men in blue as they withdrew from a fight that on this day they would not win.

The assault had taken place along the primary roadways, those places that made for the easiest assault, and the places the rebels had fortified with more strength than any other. Since many of Grant's troops had not yet reached their assigned positions, the strongest push had come mostly from Sherman's part of the field, the right flank of Grant's lines. Though the other two corps were engaged, those attacks were often piecemeal, a weaker and more uncoordinated attempt against a position that the Federal generals could now see was far more stout than they had expected. For an hour or more, charges were launched and repulsed, Federal sharpshooters and scattered artillery fire helping to keep the rebels pinned in their works. But behind the earthen walls, no one ran, no great gaps were forced open, and for now, the rebels held the best ground. Grant's prediction that Pemberton would stay put was proven true.

CHAPTER TWENTY-THREE

SHERMAN

NEAR THE GRAVEYARD ROAD
MAY 19, 1863

The sun was setting, shadows drifting across the open ground, a welcome shroud hiding the bodies of too many of his men. He had watched the assaults from a low hill, staring straight into a massive fortification bristling with the muskets of the enemy. There the assault had been made by the men he respected most, the 13th Regulars, men who knew of combat and training and went about their deadly work without complaint. On this day, that work had proven disastrous, and Sherman had forced himself to see it, to know firsthand what he had asked them to do, what kind of sacrifice they had made. He had begun the day with ripe optimism, that this incredible campaign was

drawing to a close, that very soon the rebels would
be whipped completely, the reward for a plan that
Sherman had finally accepted as brilliant. He had
imagined the newspaper headlines already, all those
noisy fat men back east, dangerous and stupid.
The thought had inspired him even as the assault
began, the pride any good commander feels for
his men, capable veterans, men who deserve to be
lauded, who deserve to have their names read aloud.
As the three artillery volleys echoed across the field,
he had ridden just a bit closer to it all, watching the
troops move forward, could not avoid thinking of
newspapers, of reporters who would have no choice
but to put aside their pettiness, their mindless nip-
ping at his heels, like so many mongrel dogs. With
the regulars in motion, a stout battle line that no
one could turn away, he issued a silent command to
the reporters, suddenly wished they had been there,
could see this. They will have no alternative, he
had thought. Write about this. Write about Grant's
marvelous strategy, and perhaps even make some
casual remark about just who watched it all, who
sat on his horse on this hill, while the veterans of
the 13th Regulars poured up and over those rebel
walls.

When the artillery began sweeping through them,
the fantasy dissolved. Still he had watched, no field
glasses necessary, the smoke swallowing up those
good men, the volleys decimating the formations.
It was over in an hour. The sunset now was a bless-

ing, darkness over a place where his own foolishness had let him believe it would be easy.

It was too soon for any specific casualty reports, and he didn't want to see that anyway. It would come, the regulars making their own counts, as the other units did. The report would be delivered by the hand of a junior officer, and not the man Sherman had seen so many times before. There had always been the cheerful salute, the eagerness of the young captain to return to his men, the calm efficiency of a leader. But that man was still out there, shot down doing exactly what he was supposed to do, leading his men into the terrible fight. Sherman stared at the ground, saw the man's face, Edward Washington, one of the most capable officers in the army, a man Sherman had long predicted would rise through the ranks to command a division. Washington had taken his men right up to the rebel works, but the volleys were thick and furious, and Sherman was certain he had witnessed the single worst moment of the day, the moment when young Captain Washington went down.

Sherman stood close beside the horse, one hand holding the saddle, had waved off the aide, kept still for a silent moment, his stare downward, thought, He cannot be dead, surely. But I saw him drop, so many others with him. The colors were right there, two dozen yards from the base of those blasted walls. But those are strong positions, stronger than I had believed, too strong to be overrun by those men unequaled by any other soldiers in this army. We lost too damned many good men because we hoped the rebels would just . . . what? Run away? Captain Washington knew better than that, would surely have known from the first wave of canister, the first volley of musket fire. He would know what kind of a fight he was in. He pulled them as close as they could go, and it wasn't close enough.

Sherman glanced out that way, almost too dark to see now, a scattering of musket fire all down across the rebel works. He knew it was the sharpshooters, still seeking a careless target, or skirmishers, sent forward to prevent the rebels from making a reckless foray into the open ground. There was fire from the rebels as well, what he assumed to be that particular kind of viciousness aimed at anyone who dared to slip into the open to retrieve a wounded friend. And so the boys we had to leave out on that open ground will stay out there, and if they can move at all, they'll use the darkness, and find their way back.

He knew there were some men up close to the rebel works who had survived, who were hunkered down into the cover the rebels had provided them. The safest place on the field was closest to the base of the rebel strongholds, no way for anyone above to aim straight down without exposing himself to a certain cascade of lead. But it's dark enough now, he thought. They'll slip away. Maybe they can bring the young captain back with them. He glanced up.

No moon, not yet. One blessing. Maybe Washington is all right, just a tough wound. He shook his head. You know better. If it wasn't musket fire, it was canister, and those were the worst wounds of all. No one survives that, not at close range. Dammit, anyway! Arrogance! We thought they'd scamper out of here like frightened mice! Grant did that, convinced us just how superior we are. Sherman put a quick grip on that anger, forced that thought away. No, there is no blaming Grant. I believed it, too. We've licked these devils at every turn. Why should that change? Is that it? We cannot be defeated . . . we are invincible? You know better than to believe that nonsense. They're backed up, the last refuge. Grant was right. Pemberton may be a jerk, a desk officer, but he's got to hold on to this place. It's all he can do, the only important responsibility he'll ever have. Just be thankful it's not Bragg or Leonidas Polk behind all that dirt. They'd have counterattacked, might be running right over this hill while you stand here scratching your ass. They licked us, that's all. But Pemberton likes his dirt, and if he's not some armor-coated warrior, he at least knows he has the best ground. Today they made use of it, and punched us in the face.

He felt the urge to climb up on the horse again, to ride out closer, to command any efforts in seeking the wounded, anyone who might still be out there. But that was foolishness, the rebels certainly primed to target any hint of sound. He saw the aide now, the man charged with caring for the horse, waiting patiently to do his job. Sherman patted the horse on the neck, let the thoughts drift away. The day is over, and this big boy needs some rations. I suppose . . . me, too.

He turned from the horse, stopped, punched one fist into an open palm. Dammit to hell. Those were regulars, the best men in my corps, in this whole damned army. We fed them to a slaughter mill today. Can't have that. If they're going to die for me, I need to give them a better way to do it, a chance they might actually win this thing. Today . . . there was no winning. But by God it was glorious to see them try. He had a thought, tried to see the face of Captain Washington again, looked around in the darkness, knew the staff was lurking nearby.

"Colonel Dayton. Respond."

The man came close quickly, knew Sherman too well.

"Yes, sir."

"Where is Captain Kossak?"

"Right over there, sir. With Captain McCoy."

"Good. Take me to him. We need to make every use of this dark. I want that engineer working all damn night putting my men into the ground. The enemy's figured out how to do that, and so have I. We pushed our people pretty damn close, and I'm not giving up all that ground."

Kossak appeared now, the man always stiff-backed, formal, a crisp salute.

"General, I am at your service, sir."

"Fine. You're supposed to be. I want shovels put to use right now. Anyone who went through that hellfire today will be the first ones to dig a hole. Put 'em to work. Everyone else in the frontline area. Dig like gophers until the sun comes up. The rebels know we're not pulling out of here, but I don't want them thinking they took the best we've got to give. Get to it, Captain."

The engineer moved quickly, and Sherman heard the orders going out, knew that a handful of supply wagons were close, that the engineer could find all the implements he required close at hand. But those wagons weren't for the men, no comforts of a healthy camp. He knew that the meager wagon train had followed his march all the way from Jackson. The most valuable commodity they hauled was ammunition. And now . . . shovels.

Sherman tried to see Dayton's face, a thin man, taller than he was.

"Colonel, have we heard anything from the bluffs? I thought we had that new supply route open. We have a fresh wagon train anywhere close?"

"Um . . . not quite, sir. That work is continuing. Colonel Macfeely is up that way now, as far as I know."

"Well, what I know is that these men are eating rations fit for sewer rats. I promised Grant we'd get a supply line into use immediately. This isn't . . . immediately. My boys took a licking today, and they need something besides moldy crackers. You got me, Colonel?"

"I'll send word. . . . No, sir, I'll go out myself and locate Colonel Macfeely. I'll bring you his report as quickly as possible."

"Now, Colonel."

Sherman saw the other aides moving closer, a cluster of shadows. There would be no firelight, his position within artillery range of too many rebel gunners.

"Where's Grant right now?"

McCoy stepped forward now, a young, sickly man who seemed to jump every time Sherman spoke to him.

"I believe the general is at his headquarters . . . back that way, sir."

"Well, I believe I need to talk to him. He might be surprised by what I'm about to do, and he doesn't care for surprises."

He waited for the question, McCoy responding.

"Begging your pardon, sir, but what are you going to do? Should I accompany you?"

"You'll do more than that, Captain. You'll issue the order. Send couriers to every artillery command in this part of the front. The rebels are over there slapping each other on the back, big talk about how they **whupped** us today. I never want to see anyone in that so-called army smiling, you understand that? Don't even want to imagine that. Order the artillery to open up a barrage all across the position."

"But, sir . . . it's dark."

Sherman stared at the young man, regretted McCoy couldn't see the heat in his glare.

"This is a modern army, Captain. We have cannons that can fire in the dark. Your job is to see that they do. But make sure they aim a little high. We still have boys out there who need to get in off that open ground. I want the damned enemy to know that we didn't appreciate what happened today, and if they think they'll spend this night celebrating about it . . . well, we'll change their minds."

GRANT'S HEADQUARTERS
EARLY MORNING, MAY 20, 1863

Grant paced, unusual, crushing the cigar in his hand. He looked at McPherson.

"They've got good ground then?"

"Very strong ground, sir." McPherson glanced to one side, where McClernand sat, leaning back in his chair. "My own scouts have conferred with General McClernand's engineers that the enemy's entrenchments have been extended in an arc that anchors toward the river to the south. To my own front, we could plainly hear them laboring to improve those works all through the night. I imagine they'll continue that every night. Nothing is ever perfect, sir. I recommend we continue with nightly artillery assaults."

Sherman nodded, then said in a low voice, "You may depend on that."

Grant continued to pace, and Sherman looked toward McClernand, the back of his chair against the wall, his lips pursed, as though pondering just when to offer his own special brand of wisdom. Sherman caught McClernand's eye, the man turning away quickly, a response that satisfied Sherman's feelings for the man. Sherman pulled his own cigar out of his pocket and said to McPherson, "Care for one?"

"Oh, thank you. No. I haven't eaten much this morning. Doesn't sit well inside."

Sherman ignored McClernand, hoped the man noticed the slight. He had no intention of giving up a valuable cigar to a man he couldn't abide.

Grant stopped his pacing, didn't look at any of them.

"We were disorganized. The assaults were made without good order, before we were fully in position. We attacked them straight across the most open ground, the roads and pathways, the very place they would expect us to come. It was a mistake."

Sherman lit his cigar, mimicked McClernand now, leaned back lazily in the chair, kept his stare on the man, who still avoided looking back.

Grant didn't seem to need a response, but Sherman said, "It was arrogance. I threw the best unit I have out there and was perfectly certain they would drive the rebels right into the river. Deadly stupid."

Grant looked at him, and seemed surprised.

"The regulars?"

"The regulars lost half their strength. I'm not letting that go."

McClernand spoke now, let the chair drop noisily forward.

"This is hardly the time for a formal inquiry, General. The blame for such losses rests in this room, if I may suggest. Our time would be better spent preparing our next objectives."

Sherman held the cigar in his hand, rolled it over, fought the urge to launch it like a dart into McClernand's face.

"I never said anything about an inquiry. I intend to see that the 13th Regulars be remembered for their gallantry. With your permission, Grant, I'll order that their colors carry an inscription that means something to **them**. Not just the place. I'm thinking . . . **First at Vicksburg**."

He waited for the inevitable protest from McClernand, and Grant anticipated that, held up his hand, silencing the others.

"Agreed. See it done." Grant shook his head, flicked an ash from the cigar. "Half their strength? I did not expect such a thing. Not at all."

McPherson said, "None of us did, sir. My men took casualties, to be sure. But none of my regiments suffered such losses. General Sherman, please offer those men my deepest respects."

Sherman didn't expect that, saw soft sincerity in

McPherson's gesture. McPherson had served Sherman well the year before, had done good work at Shiloh as the army's chief engineer. No matter their equality of command now, it was obvious that McPherson fully accepted Sherman's superior rank.

"I will do exactly that, General. Thank you. Captain Ewing and Captain Smith will appreciate the recognition. Every man in that battalion feels the loss of Captain Washington."

Grant seemed suddenly impatient.

"Offer your condolences to whomever you please, gentlemen. We took far more casualties than I anticipated, in every unit that made the assault. We underestimated the enemy's backbone for a fight. I am not content to have this army stand out here now and throw artillery shells at earthworks. The enemy believes he's guarding a citadel, that his fortifications are impregnable. We did nothing yesterday to dissuade him of that notion. That will change. Two days hence, we shall make another assault." He glanced at McClernand. "This time we shall go into the fight with both fists, all across the front. We shall launch our attack precisely, in one coordinated blow. I do not believe the rebels can stand up to that kind of power. They have shown no inclination to hold any ground that we choose to take from them. Vicksburg will be no different. They have suffered a month of defeats at our hands, and there is nothing, piles of dirt or otherwise, that will change that. Yesterday, we were . . .

the word is **sloppy**. With respect to your regulars, Sherman, we gave the rebels a gift. Not just casualties. We bolstered their spirits. No doubt we did much to improve their morale, morale that heretofore was shattered to pieces. That must not happen again." He looked toward the closed door. "Colonel Rawlins?"

Rawlins appeared as he always did, as though perched just outside with the doorknob in his hand.

"Sir?"

"Have orders prepared for each of these men, and have those orders issued to all independent commands. Have Cadwallader and Secretary Dana informed as well." Grant looked back toward Sherman, the other two. "There is to be no confusion about this, any of you. You will all meet with me here well before reveille on the twenty-second, to align our timepieces. No one shall have the excuse of a delay, or a lack of preparation. Or the excuse that his watch stopped. You may return to your commands and begin preparations."

Sherman smiled, knew it was rare for Grant to show this kind of fire. He stood, the others as well, and Rawlins was already out the door, orders issued to the staff, men going into motion all through Grant's modest headquarters. Sherman hesitated, but there was nothing more to say, even McClernand grasping that this meeting was not for any kind of discussion.

Sherman stepped outside, a cloudy, cool morning, the sun just over the trees to the east. He moved to his horse, two of his staff officers already mounted, an aide offering him the reins. Sherman climbed up, slapped the horse with energetic affection, and said in a low voice, "Two days. In two days we shall settle this thing."

CHAPTER TWENTY-FOUR

SPENCE

VICKSBURG
MAY 20, 1863

She had insisted on staying in her home, but her neighbors, the Cordrays, would have none of that. Already, that family's terrifying ride in from the Big Black River had given them all the incentive they needed to move quickly down away from the streets, to a sloping hillside where many other families were already finding shelter. The first to seek safety in the various low places, the caves and deep ravines, had endured ridicule, but no one scoffed at them now. As she rode in the Cordrays' carriage down the narrow trail, Lucy couldn't help noticing the old men moving that way as well, those same big talkers who held court on Sky Parlor Hill, as eager as their women to seek the safety of a hole in the ground. Lucy had no means to provide a shelter for herself alone, and so the Cordrays had made every accommodation for her, the girl grateful for their care, even if they seemed to think she couldn't survive on her own at all. She swallowed that with the same effort it took to walk away from her home, leaving behind all of her family's treasures. If there was to be looting, so many homes now unoccupied, it would have to come from the people of the town, or perhaps some miscreant soldier, and Lucy had to believe that there was decency in these people. Even the soldiers, the men willing to fight for the safety of the town, surely those men would guard not only the civilians, but also their precious homes.

The street where her house stood was not yet completely abandoned, some of the families determined to make a kind of defiant show. But Cordray had been convincing, had persuaded her that dying under a heap of rubble would do nothing at all to aid the efforts of the army. When they came for her, their wagon was heaped with all manner of things, glassware and portraits, and Lucy had marveled at the value placed on such things, as though a hole in the ground could somehow be made to feel like home. She took few things of her own, had never expected to be away for more than a few days. The Yankees launched their artillery barrages with far more frequency now, but there was little accuracy, and those who remained steadfastly in their houses seemed to surrender themselves to the Hand of Providence. If an enemy shell was to find them, it was simply meant to be. Lucy had a difficult time with that, would not just sit in her parlor praying that the Yankees obliterate someone else's home instead of her own.

The most precious cargo in any of the wagons was of course the children, and already, word had spread that some of those had been victims, horrifying injuries from exploding shells, or the occasional impact that crushed down through a roof. Lucy hadn't seen any seriously injured children, but for Mrs. Cordray, and any of the mothers who herded their young into the makeshift shelters, the rumors were serious indeed. As they reached the entrance to what appeared to be a brushy archway, Lucy had dismounted the carriage with more curiosity than fear. Not so Mrs. Cordray. There had been tears, a great many tears, and Mr. Cordray had been sternly persuasive with his wife that if the children were to survive this holocaust, they had to be sheltered inside the earth. Lucy had tried to comfort her friend, could see more than just a fear of cannon fire in the woman. The children had scampered into the cave with the innocence of adventure, no fear at all. But Lucy could feel shaking in Mrs. Cordray's hands, a sweating terror of the cave itself, more fear there than from the bursting shells. It was her husband who had finally convinced her to go inside, by clawing back the brush that guarded the open-

ing, clusters of bushes that served more as shade
than protection from artillery. It seemed to work,
Lucy as relieved as Cordray when the woman finally slipped inside, Lucy following closely behind.
Almost immediately, Lucy understood her friend's
reluctance.

The cave itself had been hollowed out of a soft
hillside, timbers placed overhead, supported by logs
wedged vertically from the floor. Whether those
supports would be effective, Lucy had no idea. But
someone had gone to great effort to burrow out
this musty place, what was now a gaping hole hollowed back into a hillside. Cordray had seemed satisfied, and there was some comfort in that, though
Lucy didn't really know if that show was meant
more for his wife than for any knowledge he might
have about the science of what lay over them. On
all sides, the dirt walls were damp, and the muddi-
ness of the floor had been planked over with pieces
of flatboard, the kind of siding that sheathed the
walls of many of the smaller homes in the town,
those houses usually occupied by the town's poorer
citizens. She had wondered about that, if those
homes had been dismantled to provide for these
shelters, but very soon she realized that the caves
were not just for those more affluent. All across the
hillside were these same kinds of openings, some
far more elaborate than others, some mere dugouts,
offering space for a single man to crawl in out of
harm's way.

Her exploration of the Cordrays' cave had been brief, all that was required. There was one separate room, dug farther into the hillside, a rag of a curtain partitioning it from the larger room. That would of course be the Cordrays' sleeping area, an embarrassing reality to Lucy that she tried not to think about at all. Her own bed was a thin mattress, brought from her own home, covered with a thin sheet, a blanket rolled at one end. There was room for one trunk, holding a few articles of clothing, though Lucy had tossed together a variety of garments with no real idea what she would need. No one offered any idea how long they would remain in the caves, or how anyone would pass their time.

The children would sleep close to her, and she could not complain of that, knew she was a guest. The smells of the cave, the lack of privacy, the absurd notion that this was somehow a home at all seemed almost comical to her. But Cordray took it very seriously, sought ways to improve the cave without trespassing too deeply into the earthen space that might suddenly poke through into a neighbor's shelter. The neighbors gathered frequently, assessing the quality of their sanctuaries, offering advice, and occasionally a helping hand. Lucy had volunteered for that as well, but Cordray refused. He seemed quite at ease treating her as merely another of his children.

With most of the artillery fire coming from the

river, it had been something of a surprise when a new fight suddenly erupted out to the east. Lucy had wandered out to find some kind of vantage point, but the army's entrenchments were nearly two miles inland, and her only view was of a distant, smoky haze. The men seemed to hang on every kind of sound, always explaining, picking out the specific kinds of shell fire, muskets and howitzers and long-range guns, arguments breaking out over what kind of fire they were hearing. Lucy tried to keep away from that kind of silliness, had heard too many "experts" up on Sky Parlor Hill. Even with the distant smoke, she wasn't certain it was a battle at all, the rumbles and bursts sounding as much like some distant thunderstorm than anything of blood and death. But then the wounded came, hauled back toward the town in ambulance wagons, and many of the homes were quickly commandeered as hospitals. The ambulances had been a shock, but more, had dug something deep inside of her, a nagging urgency for her to do something more than sit in some damp, dirty hole.

The entrance to the cave faced southeast, away from the worst of the shelling from the river, but the ragged maw was aimed straight toward the army's nearest defensive positions, soldiers and wagons moving in both directions with purpose, unsmiling men who rode their horses along the farm trails that wound past the caves, few of them paying any attention to the curious and nervous civilians.

The artillery fire had grown quiet, a pause that she knew might be very short. With the sunrise, she had stepped outside, twisting and straightening the tightness in her back, the inevitable discomfort of the makeshift bed. There had been something of breakfast, the magnificent smell of cooking meat in the cave next door, their neighbor, a man Cordray knew well, offering to share his bounty with Cordray's family. Lucy had accepted willingly, had enjoyed a thick slice of dark bread soaked in some kind of grease, a meal completely alien to her, but after a night in the wet cave, she had gulped down the doughy feast without any embarrassment for the drool down her chin. Now the bread had seemed to gather itself into a solid lump inside her, and no chamber pot could mask the embarrassment of that.

She sat on a small wooden chair, one of the treasures brought out from the Cordray home, the only piece of real furniture they had. Behind her she could hear the children in the cave, playful, chirping laughter, and now they rushed past her, into the first sunlight, pursued by their mother, and close behind them all, the old hound dog that belonged to the Cordrays' lone servant, James.

"Ezekiel, you come here! Now! Hilda, bring your brother back here right now!"

Mrs. Cordray stood beside Lucy with her hands on her hips, the children only reluctantly obeying.

"This won't do, Lucy. I cannot impart to them the seriousness of this. Their father doesn't even make the effort. He and the rest of the men in this infernal place seem to believe they can solve every problem the soldiers have if they just smoke their tobacco and argue all hours of the day. If we had spirits down here, I'm quite certain they would happily imbibe. It would only add to their wisdom."

Lucy stood, the children responding more to her than to their mother, a torrent of giggles as the girl tried to pick the younger boy up, a playful game, the hound scampering around them, barking all the while. Lucy moved out to them, the dog breaking away, sliding up toward Lucy on its stomach, the usual request for attention.

She reached down, rubbed the animal's ears, and said to the children, "You two . . . listen to your mama. It's best you go inside now."

Behind her, Isabel Cordray repeated her own command.

"Now! Inside!"

The children moved past, wearing the inevitable pouts. The dog kept close to Lucy, content now to sit beside the chair. Lucy stretched her back again and said, "It will take some time, Isabel. This is just playtime for them. Sleeping in the outdoors. I heard one of the men down the way telling a gathering of children some story about bears."

"Oh, yes, that's just fine. Those children won't sleep a minute." She paused, and Lucy could see the sadness, the woman glancing down. "Lucy, I don't know what this is about. I don't know why the Yankees hate us so. I had never even seen a cannon before this war. . . . The shell fire sounds like all the world is coming to an end. Where is the Almighty in this? The men . . . my husband seems to believe this is all so . . . necessary. Is that what God believes? We must kill those men before they do the same to us? This is madness, Lucy. Utter madness. I am living in a hole of dirt, while my home endures the violation of a war I do not want."

She was crying now, silent tears on her cheeks, and Lucy felt helpless.

"I don't understand it, Isabel. Not at all. But there are a great many in this country who believe in what we're doing. Intelligent people, worldly people. Some of our soldiers . . . the generals . . . they are educated men. They fight to protect us from a great evil. That's what I know. That's what I've heard."

"Look at us, Lucy. Look where we are, what we are doing. There is evil right here, an abomination. God did not intend His children to abide in holes of dirt. When I'm in there, I feel the very earth squeezing into me, swallowing me. I am terrified, Lucy. This awful place . . . it is no more than a tomb. The men tell us with great assurance that we are now safe. Yet we make our homes now in what could be our very graves."

Lucy felt the weight of Isabel's gloom, had no response, couldn't offer the bland confidence of the men who seemed to know so much. Isabel turned, wiping at her face with a handkerchief, then stared at it for a long moment.

"Are we unable even to cleanse our clothing? My handkerchief is already soiled, and I have no other with me. My husband has forbidden me to return to our home. He tells me we must make do. He tells me this will allow us to feel sympathy for our soldiers, that by our sacrifice, we support their quest for victory. Tell me, Lucy, how is my filthy handkerchief helping this war?"

She moved to the entrance of the cave, halted, and drew a long breath.

"Please keep that dog outside. It is unpleasant enough without . . . that."

Lucy put one hand down on the dog, who seemed perfectly content to remain by her side. She stared out across the hillside, saw more children, a chase in progress down the hill, joyous screams, one more angry mother calling out. More soldiers came past now, moving quickly along a ridgeline, the wider trail that led out east. She watched them, saw an officer, couldn't avoid thinking of her young lieutenant, wondered if he could soothe Isabel's despair, if he had answers to so many of the doubts, the fears.

Or, she thought, perhaps he is just a good soldier, doing what he is told, what his duty calls for him to do. Perhaps that is what they all do. But then . . . where does that begin? Who decides to make this happen, and who will decide to make it end? And how long must we live in . . . dirt?

She returned to the small chair, leaned it back against a stout timber that framed the entranceway. Beside her, the hound rolled over on its back, silently begging for attention. She obliged, one hand rubbing the animal's stomach, still stared out to the east, the sun high over the trees now. She wanted to climb up again, to walk along the ridgeline, and see if there was anything new to see. More officers rode past, high up on the next ridge, one of them slowing his horse, looking her way, and she caught his gaze, turned away abruptly. Don't shame yourself by appearing flirtatious. My goodness, look at you anyway! She held up her dress at the knees, smears of dirt along the hem, thought of Mrs. Cordray. No, there shall be no laundry day down here. There is a creek deep in the ravine. We must make do, if it comes to that. She laughed. So, you would wash your undergarments in full view of anyone who passes? Have you no shame? She rocked the chair forward, couldn't fight the angry feeling of pure boredom. This is how we fight a war. Well, then, victory is certain.

The sun had set a half hour before, and she had returned once more to the small chair, slapped at mosquitoes that whined around her face. For most of the day, the mortars had come as they seemed always to come, thunderous blasts in every part of the town: beyond, upriver, and down. The dark brought its own entertainment from the shelling, not merely the high screams and massive blasts that shook the ground. She understood now that Cordray had chosen his cave well, facing away from the river, far less likely to be struck by the haphazard impact of the iron ball. She had heard much of that kind of talk, that the earth was the best protection of all, that no mortar shell could penetrate several feet of solid ground above them. Yet with each blast, Lucy felt the trembling, as though the entire hillside absorbed the punch with a ripple that spread like pond water, expanding outward, until the sounds and the shaking drifted away. Inside the cave, the shells that landed close by brought dirt down from the ceiling, and so, despite the linens and the blankets and the covering on the earthen floor, the shower of dirt was a reminder even to the children that this was a brutal necessity, not some family outing.

She stared up, the stars clear and bright, and waited for the next mortar round to cut across the sky. She didn't have to wait long. It rose up from well beyond Sky Parlor Hill, the slight scream audible now, the red streak falling far to the right, the impact muted by the lay of the land. More came, ribbons of red, hanging high above even as the shell fell away, the fiery streak fading slowly, then disappearing, only to be replaced by another, then many more. The dogs responded now, always, the howls adding to the chorus from the sky. She had learned to ignore that, focused on the shells, made a game of it, tried to guess where the next one would come, if it bore in straight across the river, or came from the north. But the game was frustrating, the numbers increasing, no guesswork to it at all.

She saw it now, one of the shells bursting high above, exploding into a spray of fiery stars. She jumped, delighted, the stars falling away like golden rain, fading quickly. She waited for another, felt childlike, saw another burst far downriver, waited for the telltale thump, thought of the grand fireworks show, July Fourth, years before, a child's marveling at the science of explosives. She felt that way now, a joyful glee with every new starburst, framed by more streaks of red. There was coolness in the air, and she heard an owl in the distance, the night sounds not quite wiped away by the artillery. There was the high-pitched scream of a new shell, much closer, and she stared up, the shell bursting nearly straight overhead, glorious and perfect, the child's voice in her uncontained.

"Oh my goodness. How beautiful."

She didn't expect a response, but the Cordrays' servant was there, standing off to one side, gazing out, as she was.

"Ah reckon 'tis, Miss Lucy. Don't do for nobody to be's out thataways, that's for certain. Cuts a man in pieces."

She watched as the last of the starburst faded, saw more red streaks out to one side.

"I suppose you're right, James. I just didn't expect any of this to be so . . . grand. War, I mean. The ambulances . . . I expected that, I suppose. I've decided, I'm going to help with that, if they'll allow me."

"Oh, no, missy, don't you gawn out'n heah. Mr. Cordray done been plain on that. We's safe right heah, and James is gonna stay where I's needed. That's heah, for certain. I sure don't want Ole Rufus to go off to no soldierin'."

She saw the hound, a fierce wag of its tail, a loyalty to James that Lucy couldn't ignore. James has his master . . . and so does the dog. I wonder if James ever thinks of that. I suppose . . . God has His ways.

She had always liked James, enjoyed what seemed to be his genuine kindness. He stood with a slight crook in his back, what Cordray said was too many days in the fields. And so James worked around the Cordray home, various jobs at repair, at pitching hay for the mule, or any errand either of the Cordrays might need.

Lucy enjoyed talking to the man, guessed him to be close to sixty, James himself having no idea of his age. She had wondered about his home, his earliest memories, but if he remembered any of that, he kept silent, wouldn't reveal anything about his days before coming to Vicksburg. Lucy had prodded him to recall anything about his youth, a mistake, the only time she had seen James angry. He had barked at her about minding her business, an indiscretion that could have resulted in some harsh punishment, had Cordray heard the man's protests. But Lucy kept that encounter to herself, apologized to James even as he apologized to her. She felt only embarrassment, had trespassed into some place James held to himself. But the apology from James held genuine fear, both of them aware that speaking out rudely to a white woman could be a deadly offense. For weeks after, she had made every effort to pretend the incident had never happened, but James had reacted to her by keeping some distance. Only now, with the family moving to the cave, did he seem more comfortable speaking with her. Lucy had wondered if it was because there was some sort of equalizing in their new predicament, the white people of the town now reduced to living in much the same way as many of the field hands. It was not a question she could ask Cordray, certainly. And she knew better than to ask James much of anything.

James sat now, staring up, as she did, the dog resting its head on the man's leg.

"He loves you, doesn't he?"

"Ole Rufus? Reckon so. He's a lot like me. Too old for much else but sitting around in the sun. 'Bout the only good friend I ever had. He ain't gonna run away, that's for sure."

He laughed, a soft cackle, and Lucy tried not to read any meaning into that.

"If I decide to help the soldiers . . . I would appreciate it if you didn't tell Mr. Cordray. I don't think he believes me capable of anything."

"I won't say nothing, lest he asks me. I cain't do no lyin' to the man. You ought not be thinking such things anyway. Mrs. Cordray needs help with the babies, that's for certain. You oughta stay right here."

"We'll see. Maybe this will all just . . . stop. The Yankees will go on off, out of here, go somewhere else. I heard Mr. Hepperman saying that General Pemberton has better than twenty thousand men out there. That's hard to imagine, wouldn't you think? How many men would it take to fight off the Yankees? How many of **them** are out there? It's all just too . . . strange."

Behind her, a man's voice, stern and unfriendly, Cordray.

"Here! Miss Spence! You ought not stay out that far. James, you know to bring her in close. This dirt over our heads serves a purpose, Miss Spence. I implore you to make use of that. One unfortunate mortar shell . . . well, let's not talk of that. James,

Mr. Hillyard has requested your assistance tomorrow. He's preparing a number of dwellings around that next hill to the south. He'll pay you well. Go see him at first light."

Lucy turned, Cordray only a shadow, a hint of light from the night sky outlining his form.

"Why would Mr. Hillyard be constructing so many dwellings? He has no family, but for his wife."

"He's selling them. Wish I had thought of that. Smart businessman. He'll pay James, and a couple more boys, and turn a hefty profit. He can't sell anything out of his store on the main street, so he'll sell what he can here."

She felt a glimmer of anger.

"Why wouldn't he just help out, like some of the others? He would sell the caves? That's outrageous."

"Don't mind that, Miss Spence. People have to do what they can to get by in this war. It's like those cotton merchants . . . smart men. Selling cotton to brokers who have safe passage right through the Yankee lines. Simple business sense, Miss Spence. You offer a product to satisfy a demand. There's profits to be made. Some people can't provide these dwellings for themselves. Someone has to step forward."

"For a fee."

"Well, certainly. Like I said . . . I wish I had the means, the servants in numbers to do the same."

She felt a bitter disgust, turned away, caught the

fading streak of red light, a fiery thump coming down off to the left.

"Well, I certainly appreciate you allowing me to be here . . . or would you have me pay rent?"

"Nonsense, dear child. Your father was a good man, despite what some . . . ah . . . well, I always enjoyed his company. Least I can do is repay that by allowing you to share this temporary home. Really, child . . . rent?"

Cordray laughed, moved away deeper into the cave, mumbling something she couldn't hear. But the meaning was clear. You're just a girl, Lucy Spence. Unless you intend to work in a dance hall in Jackson, you can't possibly understand what money is for. Well, she thought, I'm not going to become one of those camp followers, just so I can participate in a man's idea of "commerce." She realized James was still there, his dark skin disguising him, the man easing back inside the cave, seeming to wait for her to follow. She knew he wouldn't stay in the cave, not with the family, and she said, "James. Where do you and Rufus sleep?"

"Don't you be worryin' none about us'n. We gots a safe place, down in the brushes."

She thought of Cordray's instructions to James, that he'd be paid for his labor. And what would he do with money? Knowing Mr. Cordray, he'll just take it away . . . for "safekeeping."

The streak of fire was quick and sudden, no sounds until the shell erupted a few yards in front of the cave. She was shoved backward, fell hard, dirt spraying over her, a hard ringing in her ears. She blinked through the dirt, wiped her eyes with the hem of her dress, fought to see, heard screams, shouts, men coming closer, a hand on her, gripping under her arms.

"Child! Dear God! Child, are you all right?"

Lucy spit out dirt from her mouth, grit in her teeth, tried to sit up, the hands helping her, Cordray.

She shook her head, tested, moved her legs and arms, one hand pushing into her ribs.

"I'm unhurt. I think. It just came down right out front. I didn't see it."

Outside the cave, men were gathering near the blast site, and she caught the biting stink of smoke and sulfur. To one side, another blast shattered a tree, fire igniting the leaves, the treetop tumbling down, the men flattening out, some crawling quickly to any cover they could find. More came now, and she felt herself pulled backward, Cordray dragging her inside, deeper into the cave. She heard crying, the children, the voice of Mrs. Cordray, terrified, a poor effort at calming them. The little girl ran to Lucy now, hugged her, words coming between sobs, in a high, tinkling voice.

"Lucy, Lucy. You hurt? They hurt you?"

"No, Hilda, I'm all right. Just . . . dirty."

Cordray released her, went to his wife, the little girl staying closer to Lucy, still sobbing.

"Loud, Lucy. Hurt my ears."

"I know. Me, too."

"Why?"

The blasts continued, calculated, the impacts coming down in a wide sweeping formation, gunners doing their job.

"It's the war, Hilda."

Lucy felt even more useless, unable to comfort even a child, the little girl falling onto her, more heavy sobs. She wrapped her arms around the girl, tried soothing words, stroked her hair, could feel dirt on her hands, dirt she was putting on the child. The voices outside had grown quiet, the men moving away, satisfied that no one had been seriously hurt. She caught the smell of tobacco, James slipping into the cave, the dog close beside him. James leaned low, fear in his words.

"I done tole you, Miss Lucy. I done tole you."

"Yes, James. You told me. I'm safe now, all right?"

She was suddenly angry, her patience drained away by the incessant sobbing of the child, and she pushed the girl off her, Mrs. Cordray there quickly, taking her away. Lucy crawled forward, firelight at the cave's entrance, the one fat tree still burning, the great open pit a few yards in front of the cave, the crater where the shell had impacted. She thought of the little girl's question, the single word . . . **Why?** Just . . . because. That's all I know. All I'm supposed to know. Only the men seem to know. She felt the fury building, stood, wiped at her dress, a futile gesture, spit again, unembarrassed, dirt grinding in her teeth. The family was wrapped up in themselves, Cordray giving soft words to them all, and for a long moment she felt utterly alone. She moved again to the entrance of the cave, the fire in the tree dying down. There was loud talk, one more discussion between some of the men up the hill, loud opinions, worthless anger. She heard the name Lincoln, thought of that, knew so little of politics and government, and Yankees and their generals. She had seen Pemberton, everyone calling him Pem . . . thought of her lieutenant. **Out there**. She tried to see his face, wouldn't ever forget that, no matter what else might happen. God preserve him, guard over him. Please. I ask thee. The prayer dissolved in her mind, and she looked back into the cave, a single candle coming to light, Cordray wiping his daughter's tears, his wife holding their son, the boy not yet six. Lucy brushed again at her dirty dress. I live in a cave, she thought. For how long? Until Mr. Hillyard grows rich enough from selling his caves to helpless people? Does God smile down on **that**?

She moved outside, into the cool air, and took a breath, pushing the smoke and stink from her lungs. The shells continued to fall, but it was not the strange gracefulness of the arcing mortars. These shells came from the east, sharp streaks that sliced close over the ridgelines, impacting with fiery collisions. There was no beauty now, just the horror, the shelling very different, far more angry, a viciousness that terrified her. There were more fires, trees engulfed in flames, a pair of blazes on the next ridgeline, the silhouette of men moving past. I cannot do this, she thought, just sit in a hole in the ground like some helpless animal, while my lieutenant risks his very life . . . while they **all** risk their lives.

She turned, moved back inside the cave, toward the candle. Mrs. Cordray was watching her, then said in frightened words, "Oh, dear Lucy. You mustn't go outside. You could have been hurt . . . or worse. Please, for God's sake, be more careful."

Lucy nodded, couldn't say anything to this woman, knew that a mother's whole world was engulfed in the desperate need to care for her children, and no matter his stern talk and useless advice, Cordray was doing everything in his power to keep them safe. That's what families should do, she thought. They will be safe. But . . . the soldiers. None of them are safe. And if this is to go on, if these cannons and muskets are to do such damage, those men will need help. I know something of nursing, of what can be done to care for the afflicted. I must tell them that. I must let them know I will not suffer this war by trembling uselessly in a cave.

CHAPTER TWENTY-FIVE

BAUER

NORTHEAST OF THE
3RD LOUISIANA REDAN
MAY 22, 1863, DAWN

It was one more morning in a place he had grown to hate. But if there was one glimmer of hope through the gloom they all felt, it came from the rumblings of the supply wagons, filled with fresh rations. So far, talk of a new avenue for the supply trains had been only talk, the usual rumors, fueling the griping throughout the camps where the men had to make do with hardtack. Some had gone scavenging, avoiding the provosts and ignoring the orders from their own officers, slipping out through the countryside at night in hopes of discovery of that rare farmhouse still intact, some larder overlooked by the hundred men who had come before. But on May 21, all of that stopped. The rumors became fact, the appearance of dozens of wagons offering a boost to the morale of the men who had begun to doubt they would ever know morale again. The wagons came from the north, the newly opened routes that led down from the high bluffs up toward the Yazoo River. Though campfires were forbidden, the meat was welcome, soft bacon and smoked hams, and then, the greatest luxury the soldiers had thought they might never see again: coffee.

Bauer sat in a gathered pile of soft leaves, tall hardwoods above him, hiding the stars. The daylight had not yet come, but the men needed little prodding to rise up from whatever kind of bed they had fashioned. The bugler had done his duty, reveille coming at 4:30 A.M., but by then most of the men were already on their feet at the coffee wagon. Some of the meat they were given was raw, as it always seemed to be, and though the men were not allowed their fires, the cooks were, the commissary officers cautiously building the small pits deep in the ravines for the sole purpose of brewing coffee. In the dark, there would be no telltale smoke, no target for the rebel gunners, some of those barely three hundred yards away.

The coffee burned his lips, but the steam rose up in a marvelous fog, and he held the cup close to his face, would enjoy every part of the experience. The coffee was awful, of course, nothing like his mother could make, what any of them could make in their own kitchens. Here it had boiled for half the night in water that none of them wanted to drink, but the men caressed their tin cups in a silent reverie, and no matter how bad this coffee might be . . . it was coffee.

He had eaten his fill of ham, a thick slab he gripped with his fingers, an amazing saltiness he tasted even now, licking those fingers of any hint of the greasy film. The others around him were mostly silent, some still eating, full mouths and casual belches, others just sitting, as he was now, staring toward the east, waiting for the dim gray light to brighten, the red glow that would take all of this momentary bliss away.

As the army drew closer to Vicksburg, even the veterans had expected an easy time of it. Three days before, when the orders came for the surge against the rebel earthworks, they had marched out expecting the rebels to just melt away. Bauer could still hear the raucous cheer of the sharpshooters, the men who took careful aim at any rebel who happened to show himself. The sharpshooters had called out their own wishes to advance with the infantry, even those men believing they were going to miss out on that glorious sight of the enemy running away. Bauer had seen some of that at Shiloh, whipped rebels who had given up the day, who had lost their nerve or their spirit. Despite so much casual optimism, when the advance began, Bauer suffered again through the fear, braced himself for the sound of the musket balls. He knew that some of the men around him who made the charge on May 19 had never been in any kind of fight before, and those men had absorbed the shock of their unexpected defeat with a depressed silence. To the veterans, there was outrage, as much at the enemy as for the men **back there** who had sent them forward. The rebels hadn't run away after all, had instead built a strong defensive line, and every man who saw it knew that the generals had made a mistake. Bauer held his feelings deep inside, had no anger toward the officers, felt no shame for their defeat. What mattered most was survival, and if you won the day, or were chased from the field, getting through it all without a serious wound was a victory all its own. The other kind of victory mattered mostly to the generals, and Bauer had watched those fights go in all directions, glorious triumphs following panicked flight, cowards turned to heroes, then back to cowards again. And always came the terror. He knew that would never change, no matter how many times they ordered him into the field. But this time he didn't run, had kept in line with the others, had absorbed the punishment the rebels had dished out all along the places the ragged attack had struck.

He had seen men die, of course, a great many men, especially at Shiloh. Even the men in blue were mostly nameless strangers, and you learned to step over them, didn't see faces as much as you listened for voices, the wounded who might still need help. The dead were . . . dead, nothing anyone could do for them, and so Bauer had learned to move past the corpses with the callousness of an undertaker. Even the smells had become routine, made more tolerable once you knew just what the smells were, what happened to a man who lay in the soil for more than a couple days. His work on the burial details had taught him what the chaplain still preached to them, that when the soul had departed, the body was only that, a body. The dead man was most certainly in some better place, nestled into the hand of God. There was some comfort in that, more so for the true believers. Bauer wasn't certain where he fell among those ranks. His family had been Lutheran, and in this army, few outside of the German regiments seemed to know what that meant. Since the death of his parents, Bauer had tried to show more dedication to attending the chaplain's Sunday services, the Irish priest doing what he could. From all Bauer had heard, the chaplain was a good man, would offer comfort to anyone who asked, Catholic or not, and on Sundays he seemed to speak directly to Bauer, as though he knew what kind of pain a man would feel when both his parents were suddenly taken away. The Sunday mornings had helped him a great deal with the thoughts of his family, the reassurance that his parents were in that special place, a place where he might be able to see them again, though he was in no hurry for that. It was all the more ridiculous for the bellyaching Bauer had heard, all those men insulted that the army had left them behind. Three days before, when they had lined up and marched into the green cornfield, those men had their first real shock, their first corpse, the first hair-raising cry for help. Those men would be changed now, some of them for the worse. When those men were ordered to do it again, they might be the ones to run away, to find any kind of escape. If enough of them ran, it could become contagious, a panicked stampede. There was no sermon from the chaplain about that, no remedy except to fight through your own terror. On the nineteenth, Bauer had done exactly that. And then the new shock had come, unexpected, all of that comfort from the chaplain suddenly jerked out of him, wrapped in a black shroud and stuffed into some distant hole. It was not just the fight, not the musket fire or the artillery, or even the nameless men who tumbled out of line. The wounded had called for their mamas, nothing new there, the dead men had stayed dead, collapsing like sacks of meat into the soft green cornstalks. Even now, most of that was already gone, one more fading memory, one more piece of experience. But then . . . he saw the face of Sergeant Finley.

He barely knew the man, the gruff beast of an Irishman, the man surely born to be a sergeant, as though God could find no other place to put him. Before every assault, there were the men you felt uneasy about, the men who seemed to know when their time was due. There had been a few of those on the nineteenth, the Wisconsin men who had stripped themselves of precious belongings, expecting never to return. But Finley wasn't like that, seemed to be tougher than any musket ball, tougher than the war. To Bauer, that was a different kind of comfort, something that inspired him to follow the man, to obey his grouchy commands, and, yes, to fear what he might do to you if he became truly angry. Bauer couldn't find a way to accept Finley's death. He tried to pray, more of a complaint, a protest to God: You made a mistake. You took the wrong man. He wasn't meant to die. He didn't leave his Bible or his letters back by that tree; there was no fatalism in the man at all. Getting shot should have made Finley madder still, his Irish wrath certain to drive him up over that wall of earth to take his nasty revenge on the rebel who pulled the trigger. But . . . no. He was still out there, lying in a crumpled heap at the base of the rebel works, a terrible, terrible mistake.

Bauer had retrieved a second cup of coffee, the strong brew curling his nose. He sat with a dozen men, most of Willis's platoon, men who knew that with the rising of the sun, something important would happen. Other men were shaking off the damp chill, arms slapping sides, the various itches from whatever insect had burrowed into a temporary human nest. Bauer stared back to the east, the sky showing just a hint of the first glow, and he sipped from the cup again, heard low voices, heavy Irish brogue, familiar now. He could finally understand them, the slang, the odd curses. He had wondered about Willis, how a new lieutenant would adapt to that, but it was never that way. They would adapt to him. It was Willis, after all. You paid attention to him because it was the smart thing to do, and any soldier worth his salt learned just which officers he could trust. And the sergeants. The face came, the snarling growl planted inside Bauer's mind. Finley. Dammit anyway.

Men were gathering closer, silent blue shadows moving up to create the formation. Bauer could feel the strength building, the entire regiment pulling in closer, the officers putting them along the base of one more rise. They were closer to the rebel works now than they had been on the nineteenth, no cornfield to wade through. From all Bauer could see, the ground in every direction seemed to be nothing but slices in the earth, narrow ravines, small rolling hills, with only a few open fields where the enemy gunners could find a target. Bauer watched more of the men coming up, an entire company, and the cup began shaking in his hand, reflex, that first stab of fear. He had enough coffee, tossed the dregs to one side, thought, Well, I suppose they told Sammie the truth. We're going to do it again.

Word had come down the day before. The failure on the nineteenth had indeed been a mistake, a clumsy, disorganized effort. The message came down through the division commander, General McArthur, to every regimental commander, Colonel McMahon passing it down to the company commanders, who gave the word to their lieutenants. The night before, Willis had come to his platoon, gave them the briefest of instructions, Willis's way. Once the shooting started, if the men didn't know whom to follow, or what to do, they wouldn't much matter anyhow.

Bauer saw him now, and Willis moved slowly, picked his way, and Bauer knew he was searching.

"Morning, Lieutenant."

Willis eased that way, casual, as though seeing Bauer purely by chance. But Bauer knew from the man's motions there was no accident to this at all. Willis sat down beside him, pulled his legs up close, hat low on his head, his arms crossed on his knees.

"Nasty business, Dutchie."

The voice came in a whisper, but no one around them seemed to care now, too used to this friendship that had long passed being a source of ridicule.

"What business?"

"Today. Artillery will start up any time now. Ought to be a hell of a barrage. Three hours' worth. They been hauling caissons up all night, pulling the guns up close. There are batteries in those trees back there, gathered up in force closer to the rebs than I've ever seen. They figure on blowing holes in the reb works, I guess. Might take the backs of our heads off, too."

"So . . . for sure, we're going out again?"

"I already told you that. Jesus, Dutchie, you heard the orders."

"I know. But things change. You know generals."

Willis looked at him, and Bauer felt the glare. Willis didn't have to say anything. Bauer knew that what either of them understood about generals wouldn't fill a tin coffee cup.

"We'll line up in platoon column. Small formations. I guess that makes us smaller targets. But Captain McDermott says it's orders. Should make it easier for us to snake our way through the reb obstacles, all that cut timber and such. Somebody was paying attention to our little disaster three days ago. Not all generals have wood skulls."

Bauer saw an officer moving through the low brush, seemed to be searching, and Willis stood quickly.

"Sir? You need me?"

"Just checking on us, Lieutenant. There's three more companies to our right, three more backing us up. You seen that fort out there?"

Bauer knew the voice of the captain, was suddenly curious. McDermott never seemed to make idle chat.

"The earthworks down to the left? Yes, sir. The flags say it's Louisiana boys."

"Yep. We'll be going in alongside some Illinois fellows down that way. General McPherson just came back from Grant's headquarters all in a lather. Breathed a little hellfire to General McArthur. Probably the same thing Grant did to him. There'll be no mistakes this time. We go out at ten o'clock. The whole bunch of us, all across the lines." Bauer could hear nervousness in the captain's words, only adding to the stirring cauldron inside him. McDermott continued: "No need for a pocket watch. The assault will begin as soon as the artillery quits."

"Yes, sir."

"Oh, one more thing, Sammie. I'll get you a new sergeant as soon as we can get organized. No point in bringing in anybody fresh or giving out a promotion until we get clear of this place. You all right with that?"

"Of course, sir. I can handle these boys. They probably aren't as scared of me as they were Finley, but I think I can change that."

McDermott slapped Willis on the shoulder, and Willis snapped a salute. McDermott moved away, and Willis eased back toward Bauer, then sat down. Bauer could see his face now, a hint of daylight. Bauer smiled.

"Sammie? He called you **Sammie**?"

Willis let out a breath, Bauer's words catching the attention of the men close by.

"Well, it's my damn name, Private. Officers can do that, you know."

Bauer couldn't hold back the laughter, a fountain inside of him opening up, so much of Willis's scolding, all that **propriety**. The question burst out of him.

"What do you call him? What's his nickname?"

Willis didn't need a heavy dose of Bauer's teasing.

"I call him Captain McDermott, you jackass."

Bauer lay back in the leaves, still laughing, the shaking in his chest coming from some odd place, rising up, unstoppable. Around him, men were beginning to laugh as well, caught by the contagiousness of it, whether they knew the joke or not. The questions came now, even through their chuckles.

"What's funny?"

"What's eatin' him?"

"Tell me the bleedin' joke!"

The laughter spread, and Bauer couldn't stop himself, his eyes watering, a tight aching in his stomach, tried to hold it back, but the laughter took him over completely, no thoughts of anything but . . . Sammie . . . the captain . . . the laughs unstoppable, spilling up out of him in a loud rolling wave. The tears came harder now, and he curled over, his face in the leaves, felt a slap on his back, the others sharing the moment. The aching grew worse, the tears flowing heavily, his arms gripping hard to his body, still facedown, ignoring the others, the laughter slipping into something else, raw, painful, more tears . . . Finley . . .

And then the artillery began.

MAY 22, 1863, 10:00 A.M.

It had begun promptly at seven, and for three hours, the artillery poured over them with deafening roars, the shells seeming to rip the air no more than a few feet above the ground. Bauer had kept flat, the men around him doing the same, hands over ears, faces down, always the fear that a shell would burst, a misfire, scalding iron blowing straight down into men who had no place to go. After the first half hour, Bauer had begun to relax, the hands still planted against his ears, but the rumbles and screams rolled into one long lullaby, and for the first time in three days, he had slept. There were no dreams, the big guns shaking the ground just enough to keep him stirring, but the sleep did come, the shelling rolling up and over him like waves, the ground beneath him like a softly pulsing ocean. When the sleep left him, the guns were still in full fire, and he pulled his hands away, a mistake, his ears punched, ringing hard, the hands clamped up once more. Around him men were doing the same, most flat on the ground, a vast blanket of blue, most of them motionless, eerie, a sight that startled him, a memory. But there was no blood here, no wounded, just an army, waiting for the good work of the big guns. He wanted to climb the slight rise to the front of them but knew he would see that soon enough. For now the cannon fire was glorious, and he focused on that, the sheer brute power of what must be happening **over there**.

He jumped, a hand grabbing his calf, saw Willis on his hands and knees, the look in his eyes that had a dangerous meaning. Willis tapped him hard, no words, nothing to hear, and then Willis crawled away, moved up the rise, seemed to know something. In seconds, the cannon fire began to fade, scattered shelling, a distant battery, and then no sound at all. Bauer sat up, his hands off his ears, still the ringing. Men around him were doing the same, muskets coming up, cartridge boxes checked, the ammunition handed out the night before. Bauer saw the captain moving along the sloping hill, saw a man on a horse, Colonel McMahon, shouting orders, Willis responding, motioning to his platoon, words Bauer couldn't hear. The muskets were upright now, settling onto shoulders, the order unmistakable, and Bauer stood, raised the muzzle up close to him, reached into the cartridge box, retrieved the paper cartridge, the routine so familiar. He tore the paper with his teeth, spit out the bitter taste, poured the powder into the barrel, stuffed the lead in after it, the ramrod out quickly, finishing the job. He fingered the percussion cap, felt his hands shaking now, fumbled with it, turning it over, but the training was there, perfect rhythm, and he cocked the hammer, pushed the cap onto the nipple. He closed the hammer again, gently, saw Willis watching him, steel glare in his eyes, and

Bauer's ears were clearing, the words reaching him, one more order.

"Bayonets!"

Bauer obeyed, and all through the brushy field the men were doing the same, the glint of steel in the sunlight, the men pulling themselves into narrow columns. Bauer saw the colonel again, the horse moving along the ridgeline, a sword in the man's hand, pointing straight up, then a slow, sweeping curve, toward the enemy.

The bugle sounded now, back behind them, the line of men reacting, climbing the rise, and Bauer tried to ignore the thunder in his chest, dug his feet into the soft soil, men on either side of him, behind him, the colonel out front, moving now to one side, other officers leading the way, controlling their men, smaller groups, the plan. Willis motioned to his small platoon to keep together, Bauer fourth in line behind Kelly, and just behind him, the red-headed boy. The ground was flat for a dozen yards, then made a shallow dip, then flat again, and beyond, no more than two hundred yards, great thick walls of dirt. Bauer stared, eyes fixed at the top, saw a long cut tree lying on the crest, saw now heads, muskets, lining every foot of the log. There were deep V's cut into the earthworks, the black maw of cannon protruding, one pointing at **him**, more cannon all down the line, some back behind the fortifications, barrels elevated, their crews scrambling furiously. He glanced to the side, the mass of blue moving out across open ground in perfect parade drill, the reflection off the bayonets, the men moving in slow, precise steps. Bauer jerked his eyes back to the rebel cannon, the great mounds of dirt, thought now of their own artillery, three hours . . . and the rebel works were just as they had been, the muskets in line along the top of the log, and to the left, a great fat fort, flags, the words of the captain, **boys from Louisiana**. He shivered, kept shivering, his feet moving by jerks and starts, pulled along by the men on both sides, his eyes seeing movement, men, heads, faces. . . .

The sharpshooters were already at work, pops and pings launched all around him, some from behind, small sprays in the mounds of dirt. The rebels began to answer, but then Bauer heard the shout, an officer, somewhere out there, and the entire fortification erupted into smoke, flashes of fire, the musket balls whipping past him, men staggering to one side, another platoon, half the men cut down. The artillery fire came now, sheets of canister, and Bauer knew not to see any of that, no staring off to see what might be happening to any of the others. He hunched his shoulders, pulled himself shorter, helpless gesture, more musket balls zipping past, a crack of bone in front of him, the first man behind Willis dropping, rolling to one side, a scream, hands on a bloody face. Willis turned briefly, shouted a curse to them, waved them forward, more quickly, a slight jog, the men on both sides doing the same. The canister came again, high, sweeping the air over Bauer's head, a blast of hot breath and he ducked, reflex. They were running now, several of the platoons reaching the first obstacles, cut tree limbs, sharpened to a point, brush and wire, and Willis scrambled up and over and through, Kelly doing the same, and Bauer followed. The smoke was rolling through them, blessed camouflage, but the voices were plain, high above them, more volleys coming, shouts on all sides, yells from the rebels. Bauer felt a stabbing in his leg, jumped, no! But it was a branch, a tear in his blue pants, and he worked himself free, dropped the musket, bent low, grabbed it, looked up at the earthworks, saw musket barrels protruding over the top of the log, splinters from musket fire, the sharpshooters doing all they could to keep the rebels down. To one side, the ground was low, and the muzzle of a cannon erupted in a hard, crushing blast, Bauer deafened, Willis falling against the earthen wall, close beside the maw of the gun. But the sharpshooters saw that, too, and Bauer heard a handful of zips, cracks, and pings, lead striking the cannon barrel, men behind the dirt calling out, orders, clear, drilling into him.

"Pull back!"

Willis slid along the side of the dirt wall, waved furiously, his men moving up close, Bauer still back, looking toward the cannon, but the barrel

was gone, one man lying flat in the V, blood flowing onto the dirt. Sharpshooters. He embraced the
word, looked up, and heard Willis.

"Get up here! Flatten out!"

Bauer stumbled forward, held the musket across
his chest, and lay back against the dirt. He glanced
at the percussion cap, hadn't fired, looked straight
up, the hill steep, a slight slope back to the rebels. He tried to breathe, the smoke choking him,
and stared back across the open ground they had
crossed. He was stunned by the sight of a dozen
more platoons coming right into the same place,
climbing down across a wide, shallow ditch, struggling to crawl over the tree limbs, caught in the
tangle of wire. Men were shot down now, some very
close, many more farther out in the field, the fallen
now scattered all across the ground, far out on both
sides. But the men still came, officers leading the
way, pistols in hand, some men kneeling to shoot,
cut down, others running hard, tumbling into the
ditches. Above them the muskets continued, the
smoke thick, stifling, Bauer's eyes watering, lungs
burning. Willis was shouting now.

"Follow me, dammit!"

Bauer saw Willis digging his feet into the soft soil,
trying to climb, shoving his pistol back into the holster, climbing with both hands now. But the hillside
was too steep, and Willis slid back down, one fist
punching the dirt, red fury on his face. He turned
to his men, others trying to climb, no better at it,

Bauer feeling the desperate helplessness, raised the musket, no targets but musket barrels a dozen feet above him, one man suddenly leaning out, pointing down, and Bauer fired, no aim, the man disappearing into the smoke. More rebels began to lean out and over their wall, but the sharpshooters were waiting, a rebel soldier suddenly tumbling forward, falling in a heap beside Bauer, Willis firing his pistol into the man's chest. Bauer stared, thought of the bayonet, but he knew death, watched the man rolling over slowly into the brushy thicket. Bauer scrambled to reload his musket, saw Willis trying again to climb the embankment, again the wall too steep. Willis turned, then leaned against the dirt. Bauer saw the raw anger as Willis shouted out.

"Where the hell are the ladders?"

The men who couldn't get to the dirt walls were driven back to whatever cover they could find, the open ground littered with bodies. Along the earthworks, men huddled, all they could do, but those men were the most fortunate, since there was very little the rebels could do to them. The sharpshooters were the most effective weapon the men in blue could offer, keeping the rebel soldiers down behind their cover, picking apart the artillery teams, blunting any attempt the rebels made to reach out to the men close below them.

In the first thirty minutes, the Federal attack was crushed to a halt, and those men who could obey the order to retreat did so willingly. But the fury in the soldiers had spread to the generals, and by early afternoon, the orders had come, attack again, another massed assault against the earthworks that no one seemed to know how to breach. The soft soil had absorbed much of the Federal artillery fire, and in many places the ground was simply too steep for the men in blue to climb. In those places where the rebel works were more accessible, the firepower behind was strongest, and so any attempt by Federal troops to drive through the more forgiving fortifications was met by a storm of fire that no one on the Federal side could absorb for very long. As the afternoon passed, the Federal troops had no choice but to withdraw, some accomplishing the only victory they could, planting their colors against the sides of the rebel works.

Even before nightfall, the Federal troops who huddled against the base of the earthen walls were called away, a mad scramble back through the same difficult barriers they had crossed, back across the narrow patches of open ground to the safety of the closest ravine.

He sat again, near the same place he had left his backpack, the coffee cup still stained with the remnants from that morning.

Around him, men did the same, some nursing wounds, a doctor slipping through them, checking bandages, searching for anyone who required aid. Bauer stared into nothing, the stink of the smoke still in him, the sight of that carpet of blue, sickeningly familiar, dozens of men down, some of the wounded making their way into any kind of cover, some crawling back to the ravine. The musket fire was confined mainly to sharpshooters on both sides, a duel that had become a game, carefully hidden men on both sides seeking any glimpse at all of the careless. The musket fire from across the way had one purpose Bauer tried to ignore, but the cries of the wounded were everywhere, one man no more than fifty yards above Bauer now. The man screamed mightily, asking for water, for any help at all, and Bauer tried not to hear, but the man's voice was too vivid, reaching into him, into the others around him. There was low cursing, and Bauer saw Kelly stand, a hard shout now.

"Stop it! We can't get to you! Wait for dark! Bloody hell!"

Willis was there and grabbed Kelly by the shirt collar.

"That could be you! Sit down! We're waiting for orders."

Bauer felt a punch from that, let out a shout of his own.

"They gonna make us do that again?"

Willis turned to him, no friendship in the glare,

just hot words: "What if they do? You gonna run?"

Bauer wanted to stand, energized by a growing fury of his own, Willis bowing up to meet him, fists coming up, but a horseman was there, then another.

"Attention! Knock that off!"

Willis dropped his hands, and Bauer saw him straighten, trying to regain some kind of decorum. Bauer saw Colonel McMahon, a staff officer close behind him, and coming toward them, the captain, more of the lieutenants.

Willis ignored Bauer now and said with a strong exhale, "Orders, sir?"

"Hell no. This day is done. They can hang me if they want. I'm not sending my boys into that fire again." McMahon seemed to catch himself, the officers continuing to gather, waiting for more. After a long moment, he said, "General Grant wants to take that ground; let him lead the way."

Around Bauer, some men looked up, but others ignored the officers, few seeming to care what any colonel had to say, not even their own. The talk went on, and in every part of the field the officers were doing their jobs, messengers going out in all directions, reports and regrouping, organization and every other detail of command. Bauer ignored it all, stared down between his knees, had nothing left, a flicker of sadness for the men still out there, for his sudden anger at Willis. There would be mending for that, but not now. He rolled back onto the leaves, the shadows lengthening through the brushy ravine, and now the wounded man called out one more time, a hard, shrieking yell. Bauer pushed it away, fought the only fight he had left, pulling himself away from one more horror across a bloody piece of ground, and made a desperate search for that dark, quiet place.

CHAPTER TWENTY-SIX

SHERMAN

ONE QUARTER MILE NORTH OF STOCKADE REDAN
MAY 23, 1863

The day began with a soft cool rain, which seemed to silence both armies. But it was more than wetness that kept them quiet. The Federal forces had absorbed far more losses than Sherman ever expected to see, and no doubt the rebels were licking their wounds as well. With the rain came a pause, a chance for both armies to see to those who needed care, to reorganize and refit. As much as it galled Sherman to give the enemy any time at all, he understood the crushing reality that it was the men in blue who had been bloodied far worse than anything they had done to their foe.

He had watched the assault from behind a cluster of trees no more than two hundred yards from the massive fortress the rebels called the Stockade Redan. With so much artillery fire beginning the attack, Sherman had believed that the way would be cleared, that no enemy defenses could stand up to so much shelling. But the soft earth that made up so much of the enemy's defenses had absorbed most of that with comparative ease, and though Sherman could see some damage, it was mostly back behind, a few pieces of shattered rebel artillery, wagons destroyed, craters blown out of thick dirt walls. But none of the damage had been what he expected, nothing blown through the rebel defenses that anyone could describe as an opening. From his perch close to the rebels' fortification, he had watched with utter helplessness as those first men charged across the open ground with ladders and axes, the critical seconds those men would need to drive across the wide ditches, to lay planks across the tangled thickets, to throw ladders up against the tall earthen walls. They were called the Forlorn Hope, a dismal name passed down through history, given to any group who would lead the way, who would make the first effort, not to fight, but to carve out the pathway, to do whatever was required so the bulk of the army behind them could do the job. Sherman's Hope totaled one hundred fifty men, volunteers from several regiments, their bravado inspired first by the promise of a sixty-day leave.

Sherman had wondered about that, if the army was such a miserable place that so many men would welcome a chance for a simple vacation, knowing that in return, the risk was enormous. It had to be more, he thought. It had to be a kind of badge of honor, something they hadn't found in any of the fight so far. Some of them were misfits, perhaps, or men who had been shamed among their units for some indiscretion, the one singled out by the abusive sergeant, the one who spent too much time in the stockade. And so there could be redemption, the chance to prove worthiness, achieve instant heroics. All you had to do was survive. Or maybe not. There are dead heroes, too. A pile of them . . . right out there.

Sherman stared at the rebel mounds, the wide ditch just in front littered with broken ladders and lumps of blue and black, what had been so much of his Forlorn Hope. All that artillery . . . all those shells. Has that ever worked? Even I believed they could make it. The enemy's defenses should have been broken to pieces, and if we couldn't knock down their walls, then sure as hell we would have sucked away their will to fight. They haven't had much of that in a while. Until they got behind those fat piles of dirt.

With the halt in the artillery barrage, he had stared hard through his field glasses, expectant, a **hope** of his own. But all I saw were busted-up artillery pieces, he thought. Someone's good aim. That helped, no doubt. But the rebels . . . they knew it would stop, sooner or later. And so they huddled down in their dirt, and did what my men did: They just waited.

Sherman had seen the first volley, the Forlorn Hope drawing wonderfully close to the enemy's obstacles, the ladders on shoulders, excited, breathless men who were so close . . . and then the muskets had come up, a thousand rebels emerging from hidden places, far more than he had thought would be there, as though they knew just where the first wave would come.

He stared through the misty rain at the rolling ground, blanketed with the bodies of his men, some of them from the Forlorn Hope, many more the men who followed. This was a bloody awful mess, he thought. And how much of it was my fault? Grant must know that, must know that we didn't go in as one big fist. The damn colonels . . . what? We gave them coffee for breakfast and so they forgot there was supposed to be some kind of organization to this thing? How clear did I have to be?

He tried to find the usual anger, but he felt drained, depressed, knew that if Grant was to find fault at all, it would start first with Sherman. The others, too. Maybe. He expected us to swing a hundred hammers at the same instant, and we told him we could. We set our damn watches, for God's sake, every one of us with their minute hand in the same place. And so, when the cannons stop, my men stagger into this thing in bunches, scattered, ragged organization, regiments with no flank support, some of them not moving at all. He wanted to be angry at . . . someone. But it wasn't one failure, a single idiot he could pluck from the camps, a tirade he could launch at one brigade commander, one regimental commander. It was all of us, he thought. And that means . . . it was me.

"Sir! General Grant is approaching."

The staff had kept their distance, some knowing him well, not wanting to be within range of his wrath, others very aware that he was within musket range of rebel sharpshooters who could be watching this very spot. Sherman had thought of that, had kept close behind a fat oak tree, the same place he had watched the disaster unfold. But the rain offered just enough haze to disguise who he might be, this officer standing too close to be someone important. Right now, he didn't feel important at all.

Grant dismounted a dozen yards back behind a rise, then seemed to hesitate, Sherman watching him. Grant was frowning at him, hands on his hips, a cigar stuffed in his mouth.

"Get back here, Sherman!"

He moved without answering, a quick scamper up and over the sandy knoll, removed his hat, then slapped his thigh with it, dislodging a soaking of rainwater. He knew a salute was called for, Grant seeming to wait for that. The names were one thing, the stark informality that shocked most of the other generals. But this was still the army, and Sherman tossed up the salute. They stood silently, a strange awkwardness, Sherman feeling anxious, trying to read Grant's mood, looked to one side, a cut tree stump.

"Mind if we sit?"

Grant shrugged, and Sherman moved that way, sat, regretted it immediately, the wetness driving up to his bottom. He still held the hat, ran the brim through his fingers, Grant keeping silent. After a moment, Sherman's impatience got the best of him.

"We're supposed to learn from our mistakes, Grant. Nice fresh ones, too. These were only three days old. I can't speak for the others . . . but this corps didn't learn a damn thing. I look at those damn ladders out there, busted all to hell, a couple of 'em still up against those dirt walls. The rebels haven't even bothered knocking them away." He stopped, knew he was chattering, mindless nervousness. He looked up at Grant, who still held the same posture, no smoke from the wet cigar, barely a stub now.

"At least you had ladders."

Sherman wasn't sure what Grant meant, but there was no humor in the words, the spent cigar tossed away now. Sherman felt the burn of curiosity, fought against his need to keep his mouth shut.

"Nobody else had ladders?"

"I wouldn't say **nobody**. There were some. A few

made it to the enemy. Most didn't . . . or somebody couldn't find them to begin with. Too late to worry about that now."

Sherman felt the aching need for his own cigar, fought that, waited for more from Grant. He expected Grant to give him a serious blasting, but that wasn't Grant's way, at least not often. Grant stared out past him, seemed lost in thought, and Sherman heard the pop of a single musket, then a response, the sharpshooters playing their game. The silence was maddening, and Sherman stood again, paced, felt a surge of questions rising up. There were failures . . . everywhere? Everybody? Who? Was it as bad to the south?

Grant looked at him, seemed to read him, and said, "This won't work."

Sherman succumbed, pulled out a cigar, tried to light it, but the wetness had soaked through everything. He gave up, chewed it furiously, was increasingly nervous, his gut rolling over, the cigar chewed to mush in his mouth.

"If it makes you feel any better, you weren't the only one who didn't get the job done."

Sherman pulled the mess of tobacco from his mouth, tossed it away, tried to be as casual as he could.

"Who else?"

"Everyone."

Sherman was puzzled now.

"But you were right here with me when McClernand sent word. . . . He said he grabbed a big slice of the rebel works, broke clean through. Was he pushed back?"

Grant put his hands on his hips again, glanced back toward the gathered staff officers, stepped closer to Sherman, and lowered his voice.

"I rode down there as quick as I could. Well, you know that. Had to see it for myself. That's why we ordered the second charge. Well, you know that, too. He told me he opened a breach. Isn't that what you're supposed to do when someone opens a breach? Shove through it? Take every advantage? I'm pretty sure there's a textbook at West Point that says something about that. But all I saw down that way was a couple of regimental colors stuck in the dirt. His men made some good progress near the railroad cut, but they couldn't hold it long, and they left a good many of their number behind when the enemy drove them back. Whatever Mc-Clernand 'captured' was in his mind. There were brigade commanders down there wondering why we were going in a second time. I heard plenty of that. Too much of it. We had colonels and captains who knew more about what we should have been doing than all the generals in this army!"

Grant's voice had risen, the disgust obvious, a show of rage Grant tried to clamp down, another self-conscious glance back toward the staffs. Sherman had thought McClernand's breakthrough might have been the one genuine success on the field, had actually convinced a skeptical Grant that it might be true. As Grant had ridden away, Sherman had to digest what was immediately a huge bitter pill, that McClernand might have exaggerated his success, something to make him even more insufferable than he was now. But . . . there was no breakthrough at all?

After a long moment, Grant said, "McPherson did no better. He's pretty hot. The man knows something about engineering, after all, and even he couldn't find his ladders. Not sure who to blame for that. I'll leave that to him. But he took a pile of casualties. Well, we all did." Grant paused. "As I said, this won't work." He glanced back again to his staff, and Sherman saw Charles Dana, the one civilian among a cluster of officers. Grant lowered his voice again. "Washington will get the reports of this. I'm not waiting for a reply. Not even waiting for the secretary to compose his letter. There was always the option of going into a siege. I didn't want to go that way. . . . I didn't think we'd have to. But I was wrong. And if I don't admit that, Secretary Dana will do it for me."

Sherman knew that Grant hated the idea of a siege, that even behind their heavy defensive works, the rebels weren't likely to make a stand, might not fight at all.

He thought of the map, which he knew at least as well as Grant did.

"If you order us to pen him up," Sherman said, "it has to work. There's nowhere for Pemberton to go. Not up this way, for certain. I'm anchored on the riverbank out here. And Porter's not letting anybody cross that river." He stopped, knew the other flank couldn't be his concern. At least not out loud.

Grant nodded; once again he knew what Sherman was thinking.

"McClernand's in the process of extending his lines down to the river, and we've got reinforcements headed this way who can complete that job. You're right. Maybe the first time in a week. Once he's penned up, Pemberton's got nowhere else to go."

Sherman absorbed the insult silently, grateful that was as far as Grant wanted to go. But it only meant Grant was holding a good deal more inside, just Grant's way. Sherman glanced up, the rain a steady drizzle.

"What about the casualties? We pulled some of the wounded back last night. But in this country, the heat will be back pretty quick. We need to pull in as many of the bodies as we can."

"When I say so."

Sherman was surprised by Grant's response.

"The smell's gonna get pretty strong."

"Yep. When I say so."

Sherman didn't know what else to say, but unless

Grant ordered it, he wasn't going to risk any more of his men to any sharp-eyed rebels. Grant looked back toward his staff.

"I'm going back to my headquarters," he said. "Secretary Dana seems a bit uncomfortable. So am I. And not from this weather." He paused. "I truly believed we'd be in Vicksburg by now. Instead we've handed the enemy a major boost in their morale. Well, Sherman, we broke 'em once, we'll break 'em again. Call your senior commanders together. I'll send word to McPherson and McClernand to do the same. I want it made clear. Tonight, we bring up every wagon load of digging tools we've got. The enemy knows he's given us a hard punch in the face, but Pemberton has to know we're not going anywhere. That will be very clear to that **Pennsylvanian** by tomorrow morning. Who's your chief engineer?"

"Captain Comstock."

"Right. Put him to work."

A musket fired close by, adding to the distant fire scattered all down through the lines. Grant seemed to hear that for the first time.

"I'm not going to have us sitting out here picking at each other. Every damn one of the West Pointers in this army knows something about engineering, including you. If this is going to be a siege, it's going be an active one. I want artillery to raise Cain every day, and I'll make sure Porter's gunboats do the same. If Mr. Dana wants to write letters, he can send one upriver to Memphis that I'm ordering every available regiment west of the mountains to roll in here and beef up our strength. In the meantime, we'll start digging ditches of our own, and shove them closer to the enemy as quick as we can."

Sherman absorbed that, thought, Shove a ditch? Grant was animated now, angry, his hands in motion, something Sherman had rarely seen.

"Engineering, Sherman! Figure it out." Grant paused, seemed to take control, calming himself. "We tried my way. Now we'll take what Pemberton's giving us. He likes dirt piles . . . we'll give him dirt piles." Grant stared out to the east now. "One more thing. Pull some of your people away from the heights up north. There's no threat to us there, and Porter's got plenty of naval guns near Yazoo City. Send some of your people out to the Big Black. We built three nice strong bridges over that stream, and I'm guessing Joe Johnston might find them useful. Until we know where he is, and what he's doing, let's not get caught pointing all our guns the wrong way."

CHAPTER TWENTY-SEVEN

SPENCE

ONE MILE EAST OF VICKSBURG
MAY 23, 1863

The quiet from the Yankee guns had been a surprise, and Lucy had emerged from the cave as though testing whether the silence was real or just some odd illusion caused by the damp earth around them. Since before dawn, the rain had been steady and light, and for the first time, it had occurred to Lucy that a downpour might be as dangerous as Yankee artillery. The greatest threat so far was the direct overhead impact from one of the massive mortar shells, a couple hundred pounds of solid steel that would most likely crush through most of the caves. But the rain could do its damage slowly, oozing mud that could cause a sudden collapse, burying anyone inside just as effectively as a Yankee shell. If Lucy was philosophical about that, careful to observe any signs of loosening mud, the thought had burst upon Isabel Cordray like a bolt of lightning. Lucy had done as much as she could to calm the woman, Cordray straining his patience with his wife's manic fears, none of which helped the mood of the children. With the Yankees seeming to hold off on their shelling, Mrs. Cordray had taken full advantage, had done what many of the others around them had done, using the peace, no matter how brief it might be, to hurry back to their homes. Cordray had accompanied his wife in their carriage, the children going as well. But Lucy would remain, her own choice, protecting whatever belongings the Cordrays had brought to their dirt shelter, presumably protecting the shelter itself from an unwanted occupant. That task had been given her by Cordray himself, though he didn't specify just what she should do if some vagabond decided to move in.

Cordray had assured Lucy that their return would be hasty, that his intention was to load the carriage with practical necessities left behind the first time around. That first day, the threat of artillery shells had inspired far more panic than reason, and already those who had little faith in any kind of lasting peace were making the journey back to the caves laden with all manner of household goods. Lucy watched them with curiosity, women hauling carpetbags, presumably stuffed with every type of

feminine necessity, from brushes to dressing mir-
rors to fresh garments of all kinds. The men seemed
to have a far greater grasp on the useful, and so they
made the pilgrimage back to their caves carrying
sacks of flour and cornmeal, kitchen utensils and
hand tools.

The rain seemed relentless, though not the kind
of violent storm that came so often in the summer.
She kept to the small chair, just inside the cave's
entrance, sheltered from the steady drizzle, wondered about the servant, James, had seen little of
him or his dog, Rufus, since the opportunity had
come for paid labor. The cluster of caves on this
particular hillside was one of many, and Lucy had
been surprised by the sheer number of people who
had escaped their fears by moving down into the
ravines and thickets, could see legions of black men
providing most of the labor, while in every open
field children were scampering about, most of them
oblivious to the reasons for this strange adventure.

Lucy had made a journey out toward the camps,
inspired by the meager fantasy that she might find
her young lieutenant. Already she had been given
a route to follow, a friendly officer on horseback
pointing out the direction of the 3rd Louisiana.
But others had ridden past, and their cautions
came, a trio of officers suggesting she might actually be a spy, Lucy not certain if they were serious
or not. There was no menace in the men beyond a
stern coaxing for her to return to where she came

from. There was a hint of condescension as well, a suspicion that she might not be quite sane. If her lieutenant was indeed real, and if he was where he was supposed to be, there would be time enough for her to see him. **Later**. Lucy took their concerns seriously, but a new day brought new determination, her fantasy strengthening that somehow by going to the camps, she could offer some aid, perform some kind of womanly work that would help. If her lieutenant happened to learn of that, more the better. Despite the foolishness of it all, she still embraced the image, imagined the crisp uniform, the lieutenant standing tall as he ordered his men to perform their duties. The sounds of the first significant fight on the nineteenth had inspired her to see more, to learn just what was happening in a place where so many thousands of soldiers were supposed to stand facing one another. The other women who hovered near their caves regarded her hopes of visiting the soldiers as one more reason to doubt her chastity. Since she had assumed command of her family's home in Vicksburg, she had endured enough sniping from the town's biddies, and she ignored it now. But her questions remained, and Lucy knew that despite so much talk by those who claimed to **know,** she would have no idea what an army camp actually looked like, or what duties her lieutenant might actually be performing. It was impossible to imagine the sight of thousands of soldiers in one place, all those cannons, and out across the way, the enemy, men in blue. It was like some game, an absurd thing for men to do, like so many children, even Cordray's little boy playing war, the other children as well, right now, on those hillsides not so far from where their own fathers might be making the fight.

Cordray had returned to the cave without his family, the carriage parked alongside so many of the others on the road above them. Like the others, he carried all he could manage, a heavy sack of flour, and in his free hand, a pickax. Lucy had thought of helping, wondered how much more might still be in the carriage, but he moved past her quickly, unloading his burden deep in the cave. He emerged again, glanced up at the rain, and wiped his face with a dirty handkerchief.

"She's being stubborn. I can't let her stay there. I just can't. There was an officer on our street, a colonel, aide to General Pemberton, and he told me the fight yesterday was the worst he'd ever seen. But today the Yankees are sitting tight. But he warned us all that once the rain stops, they might attack our boys again. This calm . . . it won't last. The Yankees took it awful bad, hundreds killed, he said. Our boys, too, not as many, but . . . well, look there."

He pointed up toward the road, two ambulances moving past a long row of parked civilian carriages. Cordray held the pickax up, as though he had some job in mind, and said, "I'll retrieve the rest of the goods I brought. . . . No reason for you to soil your hands. Some of the sacks are heavy. Is James about?"

Lucy looked at the crusted mud on her hands, dirty fingernails, small cuts from hauling brush for Cordray, the kind of work servants were doing for some of the others. It was an attempt to shield the cave's opening, as though by building up a wall of sticks, they would be safe from the shelling.

She shook her head.

"No. I haven't seen him. I assumed he was over the next hill. There is a great deal of labor there, new caves."

She tried to keep the edge out of her voice, knew she had to be grateful for Cordray's hospitality. But her patience was gone, dragged away by the weather and the mud.

"Well, all right. I'll have to unhitch the mule myself. We've got to do a better job of this cave, Miss Spence. The Yankees are giving us some peace, and we must take advantage. It would be most helpful if you return to our home and convince Isabel to return. The officer was certain the Yankees would commence their fire at any time. She ought not have taken the children. I believe Hilda's ailing. She's feverish, it appears. Perhaps you can reason with my wife. I certainly cannot."

"Is it not safe, truly? I would rather be in my own home."

Cordray looked at her with a condescending

shake of his head, the same look she had seen from the soldiers.

"Child, there's a shell crater directly beside your front door. Four feet deep, twice as wide. Mortar shell, no doubt. You've got one broken window, at least. I stuffed a tablecloth in the gap, and it'll do for now. But you've got no business up there on your own. From what I can see, the houses on our street are empty, all of them. Except for mine. Confounded wife!" He turned quickly, moved back into the cave. "You can go to the carriage and wait for me. I'll be along to fetch the rest of the things . . . food mostly. Some china and silver, anything to convince my wife that this infernal hole might yet resemble a home. You can drive a carriage, yes?"

"Yes."

"Well then, please go to my residence and see if you can persuade her to abandon this foolishness. I'd sling her over my shoulder, if I could."

He moved back inside, and she heard grunting, Cordray doing something with the pickax, and Lucy wiped the wetness from her face, her dress soaking, thought, Men and their talk. You **sling** Isabel anywhere, she's liable to use that pickax on you.

She watched more of their neighbors coming down the hill, more carriages halting along the roadway, men hauling all manner of goods, including furniture. Servants were there as well, one man leading a sway-backed cow on a loose rope. Well, she thought, at least there's milk. Perhaps Mr. Cordray can trade his skill with the pickax for a cup for his ailing child. She thought of Hilda, the girl always sickly. Living in caves . . . who would not be sickly out here? And for how long? Is all of Vicksburg to move out here, become some underground village? It won't be long before shopkeepers bring their wares out here.

She was soaked from the rain, felt a chill, moved into the cave, retrieved a damp towel, wiped her face, did what she could to clean her hands. Cordray was far in the back, slinging the pickax, a pile of loose dirt building beside him. He glanced at her.

"I'm constructing another room, space for a kitchen. If she can tend to her cooking, perhaps she'll feel more at home here. No smoke, though. Can't really have a fire in here. A few of us are going to build a fire pit the lot of us on this hill can use. If there's still meat, we might actually be able to cook it. Though where we'll get dry firewood on a day like this is a mystery. Damnable war!" He looked toward her again, then bowed his head. "My apologies, child. I'm afraid we are all being tested. Go on up to the carriage. . . . I'll be right behind."

She moved back outside, trudged her way up the muddy hillside, climbing toward the crest of the hill, was wearying of being regarded as some sort of helpless damsel. She reached the narrow road, moved up close to the Cordrays' carriage, the mule standing motionless in the rain. She patted the mule's head, a friendly reflex, and immediately regretted it. Her hand was smeared with a stinking wetness, animal hair and sweat, nothing for her to do but . . . wipe it on her dress, one of two she had brought to the caves, the other already soaked through and smeared with dirt.

The road skirted the crest of the hill eastward, and she saw a pair of wagons moving toward her, ambulances, splashing their way through the muddy potholes, the mules that drew them as muddy as the wagon wheels behind them. She kept behind the carriage, and the first ambulance halted, the driver waving to her with a flirtatious smile. She tried to ignore him, was suddenly aware of the sounds that poured out from inside. One man was talking, a manic jabbering, and the driver called out, "Crazy one, he is. Tetched by whatever struck him down. The others . . . well, they's be just the usual."

The thought burst through her, that the opportunity might finally have come.

"May I see?"

The driver laughed, ignored her request, the ambulance moving again. The second one was there now, more sounds, a muffled crying, and the driver was nothing like the first, this one a brute of a man, thick black beard, hatless, and she fought through her first instinct to stay away from him. But her curiosity pushed her courage forward, and she called out, "Halt, please! May I look at the men? Might I assist?"

The driver halted the wagon, appraised her, no smile, shrugged.

"Look all yer want, missy. These ones not be lastin' the night, I'm guessin'."

She moved out into the ruts, her foot plunging nearly knee-deep in a mud hole, one more piece of misery. She heard a chuckle from the driver, ignored that, went to the rear of the ambulance, pulled aside a filthy piece of canvas. Inside were four men, wedged in close together, one of them near naked, blood in a thick smear across his torso. The smell engulfed her, and she stepped back, gripped the canvas, steadying herself, her eyes fixed on the grotesque sight. One man was awake, saw her, his eyes wide, a dirty cloth around his neck, his mouth moving, small choking sounds. One hand rose up, reaching to her, curled fingers, pleading through whatever wound he had taken in his throat. Now another seemed to waken, his head tilting up, staring at her as she did to him, his head dropping back down, no strength in him, and she heard the man's voice, soft tearful words.

"Mama. Come get me, Mama."

The wagon suddenly lurched forward, the driver saying nothing, moving away, his own job to do. The canvas was snatched from her hand, and she stared with an open mouth, the smells still inside her, the sight of the blood, the man's bare skin, the awful words. Behind her came another wagon, the ambulance moving toward her with the same slow gait of the mule. She stepped out of the road, her stockings soaked with the cold ooze from the mud, some force inside of her rising up, sickness, sadness, and a sudden burst of fury.

"You! Where are you taking these men?"

The man didn't look at her, called out, "Hospital, miss. Up there a ways."

"Take me there, if you please."

The man halted the wagon, looked at her, no change of expression.

"You got a husband up there?"

"No, I just . . . want to help."

He stared at her for a long, silent moment, and she saw age, the eyes cold, as though the man had done this terrible job his entire life.

"What you wanna do that for?"

"I have done some nursing. These men need help. That's all. I just want to do what I can."

"Who you belong to, anyways? Don't want no trouble."

"I don't **belong** to anyone. I'm Lucy Spence. I live in the town."

"Well then, Lucy Spence, if'n you don't mind ridin' up next to a feller like me, you climb on up here. You don't want to be ridin' back there, I promise ya."

She moved to the wooden step, raised her dress

clear of the mud, the man watching with more interest than she cared to see. He reached out a hand,
and she suddenly wished mightily for her gloves.
But those were down in the cave, as soiled as anything she wore now. She grabbed his hand, stepped
up, sat on the wooden plank, the man courteous
enough to slide to one side.

"All set, then?"

"May we please go?"

He slapped the mule with the leather straps, and
she felt his leg bump hers, the touch curling her
up inside. She felt paralyzed for a long moment,
suddenly heard a voice, back by the carriage. It was
Cordray.

"Miss Spence!"

She leaned out around the side of the covered
ambulance, saw him waving both arms.

"Where you off to? What are you doing?"

"I'm sorry . . . I can't tend to Isabel just now. I'll
be at the hospital. They need my help."

It was a grand mansion, perched on the crown
of a hill, and across the sloping ground she
could see most of Vicksburg. In the open yard
a dozen tents were pitched, dull white canvas in
two rows, and beside each, wounded men lying on
litters, some on the wet ground.

The driver halted the ambulance and said, "Here
we go, miss. You sure you wanna . . ."

"Yes, thank you."

She dropped down, saw now red liquid dripping down from beneath the floorboards, blending into the muddy ground. She felt the shock of that, a brief stab of nausea, but the driver seemed not to notice her reaction, climbed down himself, waited for the approach of three men who emerged from the nearest tent.

They moved at a methodical pace, stepping to the rear of the ambulance, no one in any kind of hurry. She joined them, saw stares, surprise.

"Well, hello there, miss. You'd be a nurse?"

She held the word for a long second, put on as much casualness as she could muster, had no more patience for condescension.

"Yes. You a doctor?"

The man pointed back toward the tents, and she saw a black hat perched up on a thick beard, the man coated in a bloody white smock. His head was down, and he plodded out to the ambulance.

"Hold on there. Let's make sure there's any point to bringing them inside."

He seemed not to notice her, waited while the men slid the first wounded man out on a litter. She stepped back out of their way, saw that the wounded man had a black tourniquet tied around his thigh, his leg shattered below the knee, a shred of a bloody rag all that remained of his trousers. She looked away, the smell punching her, and she closed her eyes, forced herself to look again. The second man was out now, a gaping tear in his gut, the wound stuffed thick with bloody cloth, what had been the man's shirt. She saw his face, very young, heard a whimper, tears on a blood-crusted face, and now, tears on her own. The doctor looked at her now, with cold, silent eyes, and said, "This one yours?"

The question shocked her, but she studied the face, was suddenly terrified of the answer.

"No . . . no. I'm here to help. I've done some nursing."

"Well, if you're a nurse . . . you best be doin' some nursin'. But not this one. He's not gonna make it another hour."

A third man was pulled out, and the doctor leaned in close, then slapped the man's face, seemed to wait for a reaction, and put a hand on the man's neck.

"He's gone. Put him over there."

The men holding the litter said nothing, carried the man over to a row of bodies lined up under a fat tree. They slid the body off onto the grass, the litter too useful for men who might still be alive. Lucy watched it all in frozen stiffness, the thought of helping any of these men now something horribly ridiculous. But the ambulance was empty now, no flow of red from underneath. The driver climbed back up, jerking the mule back out toward the road, looked at her, and she tried to hide the tears, the rising sickness, angry at herself for not being stronger.

"Hey, miss. You change your mind . . . nobody's gonna say nothin'."

She had no words, nodded, the only thank-you she could manage. The ambulance was out in the road now, joining the others as they moved back eastward, empty, toward the army.

CHAPTER TWENTY-EIGHT

PEMBERTON

THE COWAN HOUSE—VICKSBURG
MAY 24, 1863

"It's a sight to behold, sir! Half the town, maybe more! Glorious, indeed. I so admire their spirit." Waddy was staring out the window, and turned to Pemberton now, a beaming smile. "Reverend Lord delivers a mighty fine sermon, so I've been told, sir."

Pemberton didn't look at him, held a letter in his hand, his own writing, scanned it for the fourth time.

"That might be all that drew those people, Colonel. I wouldn't excite yourself so."

Waddy seemed disappointed, and Memminger appeared now, drawn from the outer room by the obvious enthusiasm in the colonel's voice.

"Is there something happening here, sir? Do you require my attendance?"

Waddy responded, pointed to the window.

"Robert, have you seen the people? The street is alive with them! They came up here for the Sabbath service, but you can see it in their faces. They are happy, laughing! Certainly, word has spread of our successes. Wonderful sight! The morale of this place is as high as it ever was. The people know of victories, and we have given them one."

Memminger went to the window, but Waddy kept his stare on Pemberton.

"Sir, surely you must feel it."

Pemberton tossed the letter to one side and sat back in his chair.

"Morale? Just what is that, Colonel? We have won this war? Our nation is now free of Federal tyranny? The Yankee army has abandoned its quest to crush us under Lincoln's boot heel? For any of that, I assure you, my morale would be brightened. Those would be **successes,** Colonel."

He could see a flash of disappointment on Waddy's face, felt suddenly guilty, had no reason to drain away anyone's good spirits.

"Sir, I only mention what I see in the people . . . out there. I've spoken to a good many this very morning, as they came into the town. Their mood was considerably buoyant, sir. It was a delight. They share the army's good cheer."

Pemberton kept his attention on the paperwork

on his desk, saw another letter, slid it closer, blinked through tired eyes. He read a few lines and stopped.

"The army held the enemy back," he said. "We inflicted casualties aplenty. Do you believe it is sufficient, Colonel? Do you, Major? Do either of you believe this campaign has suddenly come to an end?"

Both men were looking at him now, their mood driven downward by Pemberton's gloom. He picked up the letter and held it out.

"You understand what this means?"

Waddy leaned closer, trying to see which of the correspondence he held, but Pemberton ignored that, pulled it back, stared at the bold handwriting.

"I am frustrated beyond all measure. They refuse to understand the urgency. Is there such complication to the proper handling of corn, gentlemen? How can this cause such controversy?"

It was Waddy who had brought him the letter, and the colonel seemed to understand Pemberton's mood now.

"Sir, they have their ways. It has always been like that with farm people. They're accustomed to doing things—"

"The army has its ways as well, Colonel. I am weary beyond exhaustion trying to explain to so many civilians that the army must have rations to sustain itself. There is corn in every part of this country, beans and bacon and God knows what else. We could always rely on those farms around the Yazoo for sustenance, but the enemy has severed us from those. So, we go elsewhere and every day the urgency increases. And do the people respond? Well, this is how they respond. It is . . . outrageous."

He tossed the letter onto the desk, the paper sliding off to the floor. Memminger was there quickly, retrieved it, read the letter.

"It says . . . they will not comply with the army's request to shell the corn."

Pemberton folded his arms across his chest and sniffed. "That's what the words say. The message is far more irritating. They are simply too lazy to do what must be done. The army has always received its corn in sacks, shelled and ready for grinding. Even that is far beyond what we normally do. The farmers used to grind it for us, provide us with sacks of meal. It has always been so, at least in my command. We do not have the manpower to handle unshelled ears. We cannot be expected to shell our own peas, or smoke our own bacon. We're fighting a war, for God's sake!"

The word seemed to punch Memminger, and Pemberton held up a hand.

"My apologies, Major. I should not use such language on the Sabbath. One acquires bad habits after so many years in the army."

Memminger didn't respond, and Waddy said, "Perhaps, sir, we should make allowances to the farmers. Many of them have suffered depredations at the hands of the Yankees. Yet still they make available—"

"Corn on cobs. Absurd. I thought this had been dealt with months ago, long before Grant and his hordes infested this place."

"Yes, sir. Certainly, sir."

There was resignation in Waddy's response, and Pemberton tried to push that away, could hear people in the street, conversations, children at play.

"They should return to their sanctuaries. The Yankee artillery has been more scattered this morning than I expected. But that will change at any time. The Yankees do not respect the Sabbath."

Neither man responded, and Pemberton suddenly realized they might be thinking of **him**, that he rarely attended church services. He looked again at the first letter, a copy made for his own records.

"This one makes five. Since Wednesday, I have sent five letters to General Johnston beseeching him to advance to our aid. Colonel, you said you had a report on his troop strength?"

"Yes, sir. It is estimated he could have as many as twenty thousand on hand. More are said to be joining him. His headquarters has been reestablished in Jackson."

Pemberton looked up at Waddy, then Memminger.

"How did you come by that information?"

"Oh, sir, the mail system has been most impressive. We have created an underground link northward, and nearly all our correspondence has made it through without detection. Your own letters to General Johnston were secured in that way, and I have every expectation he will receive them."

"I should like to know more about that. Underground? Spies and couriers and whatnot?"

Waddy seemed to welcome the change of mood.

"Yes, sir. It's the same way we anticipate a flow of supplies. They've been using the river, the swamps, passing right under the Yankee noses. There's a . . . well, let us call him a **messenger,** who floats downriver at night on something of a crude raft, drifts right by the gunboats. Says he can hear the Yankee sailors eating their dinners."

Pemberton was impressed, had become too used to the immediacy of the telegraph line, nonexistent now.

Memminger said, "There's messages coming straight across the river, too, sir. I heard some of the Missouri officers talking about mail coming from home."

"We have men receiving letters from home . . . and we have shortages of every kind?" Pemberton looked to his letter again, a desperate plea for the one piece of war matériel he knew was in desperately short supply.

"Do you believe we can bring in percussion caps this way? I made mention of our need to General Johnston. It is a serious problem."

Waddy nodded, his good spirits returning.

"No question, sir. Even if General Johnston cannot help us, others from the west can, certainly. One man riding alone can carry a significant number of caps."

It was the one irritating supply issue Pemberton had focused on most seriously. The supply depots in Vicksburg held an enormous number of musket cartridges. But without the caps to fire them, the muskets were useless.

"Very good, yes. Send word anywhere you feel it could produce results. I have notified General Johnston, and surely he will help."

"Sir, would not General Johnston do more than that? I beg your pardon, sir, but knowing the size of the command he is assembling in Jackson, I feel certain he will use that strength to strike at the enemy's position. It could be precisely the stroke of fortune we require, sir."

Pemberton rolled Waddy's words in his mind, thought, There is no "fortune" to anything Johnston does. He will come because it is the right thing to do, and if that does not sway him, he will come because the president will surely order it.

Memminger returned to the window.

"Most of the carriages have cleared the street, sir. Only a few still there. I see Reverend Lord. I admire his courage, calling the people to services on the Sabbath. Surely the Almighty has placed a hand of protection over such piety."

The shriek of the shell whistled past the house,

and Memminger backed away from the window in a surprised lurch.

Pemberton kept to the chair, looked again at the letters, the correspondence from irate farmers, other letters from townspeople with complaints about their safety, some offering Pemberton their wordy advice about how to deal with General Grant.

Waddy knew the look, that Pemberton would absorb himself in the papers, nothing else for the staff to do at the moment. Another shell blew past the house, a thunderous blast somewhere below the street.

Waddy said, "The enemy is back at his work, sir. We should return to our own."

"Yes, of course."

They slipped quickly out of the office, and Pemberton looked toward a small narrow bed against one wall, had a sudden need for sleep. He leaned forward on the desk, pushed himself upward, stood, still leaning against the desk. He heard a fresh chorus of shelling, some far in the distance, most of it coming from across the river. Their infantry will not attack our good defenses again, he thought. Even Grant is not a complete fool. He paid a terrible price for his arrogance, believing we would not fight, that our fortifications were inadequate to the task. No, he will have learned that lesson, and so he will keep his people back in their protection, as I keep my men in ours. He will give us the gift of time because he has no other alternative except the slaughter of his army. But such a stalemate, a siege of this town, will be of no benefit to us at all. If we are to defeat him, drive him away, we must have help from outside. Johnston . . . twenty thousand troops? Surely he will come. Now . . . **that** will be good for morale.

NEAR STOCKADE REDAN, NORTHEAST OF VICKSBURG MAY 25, 1863

The civilians seemed to rise up out of the ground, drawn by the small parade of horsemen, the color bearer showing them all just who this was. They gathered in small groups, some calling to him, waves and salutes that Pemberton acknowledged with a brief wave of his own. As he rode farther into the hilly countryside, he was impressed by their ingenuity, some of the dwellings seeming far more elaborate than mere holes in the ground. Some had carefully framed entrances, thick brush drawn into hedges, whether someone's notion of landscaping or a bit of protection against spent shrapnel. Between clusters of caves were dug-out fire pits and cooking areas, certainly created for communal use, neighbors providing for neighbors. Some of the caves were revealed only by the stub of pipe that poked up through the hillside, makeshift chimneys, some of those made plain by the wisps of smoke that flowed out, whether for cooking or warmth. But the people did not linger long in the open, and as he moved by them, he watched as they disappeared again, back down into whatever protection they had. There was no mystery to that. All along the ride from his headquarters, the sounds had been there, a slow, steady scattering of artillery fire, mortars and long guns, solid shot thumping into the hillsides, the occasional fiery blasts from fused shells. There seemed to be no aim, no careful design to any of that, the randomness digging into his artilleryman's sense of order. The color bearer kept just behind him, good decorum, the rest of the staff strung out far behind, good spacing between them. It was routine that they not cluster together, that any one of the enemy's projectiles could do serious harm to the army's command structure. For that reason as well, he had left Waddy behind, the young man capably handling the army's business in the town. There was shelling there as well, most of that coming from the Federal navy, or the guns set west of the river. Like the artillery to the east, there was no sense to it, no design beyond random terror, as though the Yankees were only tossing up their shot and shell for the purpose of scaring people.

Out front, his aide pointed, and he saw the small flag in a deep ravine, a cut in the earth well back of the massive fortification. The aide kept to one side, allowed Pemberton to ride in first, and quickly the reception was forming, staff officers and couriers in

motion, a show of respectful formality he appreciated. General Smith emerged now, the man standing tall, the familiar sternness Pemberton had come
to expect.

Martin Luther Smith was another of those few
Northerners who had placed their allegiance with
the Confederacy. Smith was also a West Pointer,
a veteran of Mexico, and throughout his service
had earned an excellent reputation as an engineer.
When the war broke out, Smith, a New Yorker by
birth, had surprised many by proclaiming his support for the Confederate cause. Unlike Pemberton,
Smith was much more a field commander than
an administrator, and in an army hungry for experienced leadership, he had risen quickly to the
rank of major general. The December before, it
was Smith who had bloodied Sherman at Chickasaw Bayou. In April and early May, when Pemberton led much of the army through his unfortunate
confrontations with Grant, he had assigned Smith's
division to remain in Vicksburg, confident that
Smith, along with John Forney, would maintain a
vigilant defense. Now Smith held the crucial left
flank of the army's fortifications, and his own skills
at engineering were a fine supplement to Major
Lockett's designs. Whether or not Smith might be
as effective in the field as John Bowen, Pemberton
had been drawn to the man for one obvious simi-
larity in their backgrounds. Pemberton had to assume that Smith had suffered the same indignity

Pemberton had, all that anonymous talk about the Northerner's potential for subversive disloyalty.

Smith was clean-shaven, seemed always to wear a hard frown, a seriousness that commanded obedience. He bore a slight resemblance to Jefferson Davis, a trait that Pemberton assumed only increased Smith's acceptance from his troops. But unlike the president, Smith didn't demonstrate any kind of warmth toward Pemberton at all, went about his job with a cold dedication, which Pemberton found disappointing. Though Pemberton was never quick to make friends, he had hoped their shared backgrounds might make Smith a trusted comrade. But friend or not, Pemberton had no complaints about Smith's performance. In the two Federal assaults on May 19 and May 22, it was Smith's men who had inflicted the greatest damage on Sherman's troops, an irony that even Sherman would understand.

Pemberton began to dismount, was suddenly struck by the smell. It drilled through him, bringing up a thick wave of nausea, but Smith seemed oblivious, offered a salute.

"General, welcome to my headquarters." Pemberton returned the salute with a twist on his face, and he heard groans from the aides behind him. "Ah, yes, very sorry about the odor, sir. I have offered the Yankees some assistance with their dead and have thus far been rebuked. It could be that General Sherman doesn't trust me."

Pemberton felt his skin crawling, heard one man behind him retching, wouldn't see that. He dismounted, one hand over his mouth.

"My God, what is this? Have they not sought their dead at all?"

Smith kept his same dour expression.

"No, sir. Very strange, if you ask me. Never knew the Yankees to be so disrespectful of their own casualties. But . . . well, there you have it. If you wish, we can ride forward to the redan. You can see it for yourself. Every night, we labor to repair any damage their artillery does our earthworks, and I fully expected them to use the darkness to send litter bearers into the field. I can't say the sharpshooters wouldn't have taken a few of those fellows down, but I did expect them to take the chance."

Pemberton saw the Stockade Redan a quarter mile away, could see movement, the scattering of musket fire.

"They're just . . . right where they fell?"

"It's a nasty affair, sir. My men are pretty upset, to say the least. They've tossed some pretty profane epithets out that way, but no bluecoats have responded."

Pemberton was surprised to see Lockett now, the engineer riding hard toward him. Lockett dismounted, gave a brief show of attention to both generals, and said, "Sir! I didn't know you would be coming out this way. My apologies for not being informed. I was supervising the deepening of the artillery pits. It's aggravating in the extreme, sir. None of the guns can fire without drawing a half-dozen replies, and the enemy has been effective at destroying many of our forward pieces. The artillerymen have shown reluctance to engage, and frankly, sir, I can't really blame them."

Smith said, "There's another reason for that. We don't have sufficient ammunition to duel the Federal guns. They're bringing their artillery up much closer than I would have thought wise. Should make for prime targets, but we try to take advantage . . . well, I learned pretty quick that when you're outnumbered six to one, not much point in picking a fight."

Pemberton absorbed that. "Surely that is an exaggeration, General."

"Not by much. They're bringing in more guns every night. We can hear them working. And there's more. It's not just guns. They've begun to dig earthworks of their own, trenches and whatnot."

"Well, I would have expected that. Despite what some in the town believe, we have not driven the enemy away. Grant is putting his people into siege operations. I suppose I would do the same in his place."

"Not sure about that. They're not just digging ditches to sit in. They're coming closer, digging out into the open ground, taking advantage of the terrain."

"How much closer?"

"Well, sir, it might be best if you take a look yourself. You'll see it pretty plainly. There's one trench extending our way in the shape of a snake, so we can't toss out any enfilade fire. They're digging trenches in parallel as well, with narrow cuts adjoining them. Somebody over there knows something about engineering."

Lockett said, "Or good common sense. Doesn't take education to dig a ditch. Sir."

Pemberton saw the defiant pride on Lockett's face, Lockett showing none of the effects of the amazing stink. Smith was watching him, and Pemberton made every effort to ignore the smells, but the thought of riding out closer had no appeal at all. Smith called for his horse, and Pemberton held up a hand.

"Not necessary, General. I do not need to see what you're facing. I'm sure it is equally as grotesque all down the lines. But I will not allow this to go unanswered."

He turned, then motioned to Memminger, who seemed grateful for any distraction.

"Major, prepare a dispatch. General Smith will choose an appropriate officer to cross the field under a white flag. We shall urge General Grant to retrieve his dead, in the strongest yet most respectful terms. It is possible they expect deception on our part, so make it plain that this request comes only from myself."

"Yes, sir. Right away, sir."

"I do not pretend to understand Grant's thinking. It is possible he is doing this purposely, to inflict misery on our troops. I shall request that he agree to a cessation of fire . . . in the name of humanity. Surely he cannot disagree to that." He paused, his hand coming back up to his face, nowhere to escape. "It is no wonder these men believe the Yankees are barbarians."

CHAPTER TWENTY-NINE

BAUER

NORTHEAST OF THE 3RD LOUISIANA REDAN
MAY 25, 1863

The flags went up all along the Confeder-ate works, flickers of white as far as Bauer could see. For much of the morning he had been on sharpshooter duty, a reward of sorts, since the alternative was to file down into the newly dug trench works with a shovel. But with the flags of truce came a gradual silence, big guns all across the field growing silent, the sharpshooters called back by their lieutenants, some, like Bauer, left where they were.

The artillery fire had been so constant that Bauer had stopped hearing it, and like the men around him, he no longer flinched when the larger guns close behind them did their work. The rebel defenses were battered regularly, the only respite from the gunners coming at night, and then primarily to give the Federal infantry some sleep. During the darkness, the Federal pickets could plainly hear the rebels at work, and each dawn, they saw the results. Much of the damage caused by the artillery had been repaired, whether it was cut limbs or piled dirt. There were other changes as well, the rebels seeming to modify their defenses with various tweaks and changes, someone's "new idea" how to increase the effectiveness of the rebels' fields of fire. From the first assaults against the rebel positions, the usual routine had been for the rebel riflemen to stand on parapets, just high enough to take their aim over a shooting log, or compacted earth. So far that simple tactic had been brutally effective against masses of advancing blue troops. But with the change in Grant's strategy, the Federal sharpshooters had made tweaks of their own, and very soon those men had moved into their camouflaged hiding places, and sighted various weaknesses in the rebel positions. Bauer learned quickly, and already he had keyed in on those places where the dirt walls showed a careless gap, some glimmer of an opening that would reveal a man's movements. And still, there were those with the foolish bravado that inspired them to stick their heads up above their cover. Those were the easiest targets for the Federal marksmen, and Bauer soon discovered that there were a half-dozen men just like him, buried in various hiding places, who would send a peppering of musket fire at nearly the same instant. It was no better for the rebel artillerymen. Several of their guns had been wrecked completely by the Federal artillery, the blue gunners having the advantage of maneuver and sighting into targets that were placed mostly in fixed positions. What guns they did not destroy, the sharpshooters made nearly unworkable by the carefully aimed musket fire that picked off the gun crews. Bauer had realized, even before Willis had mentioned it himself, that if their own artillery had been more precise with their massive bombardment on May 22, or if the sharpshooters had been given more time, the assault that day might have been considerably more effective. As it was, no one was expecting any such order to come down from the commanders again. In the full-on frontal assaults, Grant's army had absorbed nearly three thousand casualties. Whatever kind of new plans were being put to paper in the headquarters behind their positions, the Federal troops had to believe that no one would expect them to launch another suicidal attack against those infernal earthworks.

Bauer was buried deep in his hiding place when the word came forward to cease all activity, no firing at all. In the predawn darkness, he had slid into a place someone else had been using for days now, a dug-out bowl in the soft dirt. To his delight, and considerable relief, the daylight revealed that he was squarely behind a fat tree trunk, surrounded by the ragged remains of a rotten tree scattered about in large sections, offering a variety of perfect shooting positions. So far he had fired more than a dozen rounds, each reload now more difficult from the fouling of the barrel. But with no one out there responding to him, it was one more reason he was beginning to enjoy the duty. Despite the amount of care he took seeking out the individual targets, he really had no idea if he had actually inflicted any damage of his own. But he understood what harassment meant. That was exactly what he was supposed to do. If he actually hit someone, more the better.

The order to cease fire had been shouted to him by Willis, was repeated all down the line, and Bauer obeyed, knew better than to dwell on it. He had no idea when the truce had been negotiated. But the **why** had become gruesomely obvious. In his hidden perch, he was no more than a few yards from the first of the blue-clad corpses. The man's uniform was near bursting, the bizarre transformation that happened to all the dead after a few days, a mystery he assumed the doctors understood.

When the burial crews moved out past him into the fields, he sat quietly, hoped no one would order him to join in. He had done that job once before, at Shiloh, had his fill of it then. Men with shovels spread out all across the ground, and he stared up at the rebels, concerned, but there was no fire at all. With the truce clearly in place, a swarm of rebels suddenly emerged from over and behind their earthworks, some offering to assist, most just staying back, sitting high on their shooting log, or gathering along the ditches at the base of their earthen forts.

The burials were quick, efficient, a few officers scattered throughout the burial parties, brief orders, and he saw Captain McDermott standing by as the men closest to Bauer dragged a half-dozen bodies together. He wasn't sure about McDermott, how much of this the captain had seen, whether a company commander had the stomach for it or not. There had been only a single day of rain since the nineteenth, and so some of these corpses had been in the field for six days, most in the wide open, soaking up the Mississippi sun that turned skin to black leather. Bauer could never erase the memory of the eyes, muddy sockets, empty holes, or the teeth that suddenly protruded in what seemed to be a grotesque smile. Not all the bodies were as bad as that, and out in this broad field, Bauer knew one reason why. Some of the men had been dead only a short time, had been too badly wounded to make their way back to the protection of the lines. The aftermath of the assaults drove the horror of that into every man, no one able to hide from the men who called out, screaming, crying, pleading. But he knew that routine as well, and if the wounds were too serious for the man to move himself, they were most likely too serious for him to survive. Some of those were close enough to where Bauer sat that he saw their skin, puffed up and white, and other changes that affected so many of the bodies, arms extended upright, the peculiar curling of the fingers, what Bauer had to wonder was something conscious, a dying man's last act, reaching out for salvation, for help, for . . . mother. He shoved those thoughts aside, stared down now, his brain focusing on the sounds, the men with the shovels starting to do their work. Behind him, he heard steps, turned, saw Willis, fully upright, walking out toward him.

"Might as well get up. Just 'cause they haven't shot you yet, doesn't mean they don't know you're here. You do this job right, you don't give them the chance. That's the whole point."

Willis walked up close, sat on the dead log, no pistol at his belt. The officers would take any truce seriously, no one daring to suggest any trickery. Willis noticed Bauer looking at his empty holster.

"Any of you idiot riflemen just can't control himself, and thinks those targets over there are too tempting . . . well, the punishment for that will be pretty severe."

"Not me."

"No, I know you're not that stupid. But think about this. We've got half a hundred men out there from this regiment alone, and down the way, both directions, there's maybe a thousand more, just handling the bodies. On both sides, everybody just stares at each other, respecting that little white flag. Everybody's got their musket right close by, or there's a pile of gunners back there next to their twelve-pounders, knowing that lanyard is hanging right beside him. But so far anyway, nobody's messed this up, nobody's **violated** the white flag. That's one of those things left over from the old days, I guess, when wars were fought by the **rules**. Gentlemen and all. You see any gentlemen in this regiment? Any of these Irishmen'll bust out your teeth, you call him that."

"Yeah, I know. Hey, look. The whole outfit is coming out. Gunners, too."

"Yep. We were waiting for the colonel to give the word. That came down with orders for the truce, that the whole lot of us could take it easy. I heard some of the Missouri boys have family over there, cousins and whatnot. The generals figured we ought to have a chat about all of this, maybe. Make new friends. Before we go back and blow them to hell."

"How is any Missouri boy, or anybody else, supposed to find some kin or something in miles of this stuff?"

Willis shrugged.

"No idea. Not me. I got nobody over there. Expect neither do you. Be kinda fun, though. I heard some of the boys talking about doing some horse trading. Those rebs are supposed to have pockets full of good tobacco, for one thing. We got coffee, and I know damn well that's worth something to trade for." Willis stood, looked at Bauer. "Let's go. See us some rebels up close."

Bauer felt a tug of hesitation, had seen too many rebels up close as it was, mostly men aiming bayonets into his gut. He was surprised by Willis's cheerful calm, but Willis was already moving out into the open, the others, too, even the colonel, down off his horse, walking among the men, a quick word to the burial parties. Bauer watched that work again, saw men dragged into shallow ditches, covered by a few shovelfuls of dirt. That won't last long, he thought. This place'll have bones sticking up all over the damn place, long after we're gone. At least it'll take care of the smell, or most of it anyway.

He noticed now that the ditches were dug wide apart, all of them straight lines perpendicular to the rebel defenses. He climbed up from his hole, worked through stiff legs, caught up with Willis, and said in a whisper, "Why they burying the bodies like that? Why not just dig 'em in where they're sitting? It's nasty enough without pulling some poor boy's arm off, or leaving his guts behind." Bauer shivered, had tried too hard to forget those kinds of details.

"Orders. And that's why you're not an officer. They're burying them so's we'll know where they are. Nice straight lines, pointing out away from us. Word I got from the colonel is that before too much longer, we're gonna have our own trench lines pushed out this way, right across this field. Every day, we're gonna be a few yards closer to the enemy. It wouldn't do for a man with a shovel to be digging like a madman and suddenly chop his way into one of these poor souls."

Bauer absorbed all of that, saw one man hammering a cross into the ground at the near end of the elongated ditch. Respectful, he thought. And even better: a marker to tell us where they're buried.

He leaned closer to Willis, a low voice.

"You're right. I wouldn't have thought of that. The rebs probably hadn't figured that out, either."

"Doubt it. They will in a few days. The colonel says that General Grant doesn't have the patience for us to sit out here and jawbone with the rebs for very long. We can't charge 'em across this open ground so we'll burrow at 'em underneath."

They joined with a cluster of men in blue, all of them moving forward, slow steps, some still hesitating to walk calmly across the same ground where so many others had gone down. But Colonel McMahon called out now, a melodic brogue that Bauer had come to enjoy.

"Fraternize if you wish. But the terms call for us to keep back a ways. No one goes up into the reb positions. They don't want us a-peekin' around. Can't blame 'em. We'll be a-findin' out what's over there soon enough."

Men were laughing with the colonel's words, more of them at ease, moving past more of the burial parties. The ground was rolling, one deep ravine off to the left, and beyond that, the massive fortification that had drawn Bauer's attention every day. It was an anchor point along the rebel defenses, faced by some of the men from Illinois, a huge triangular fort manned, they said, by men from Louisiana. He wanted to go down that way, but the colonel's words took away that urge. Wouldn't be able to see much of it, he thought.

"Wonder what kind of fighting man comes from Louisiana?"

Willis didn't look at him, just said, "I'm sure they'd be happy to tell you. They're just secesh to me. Once they're dead, they don't smell any different than these boys out here."

Bauer looked to the west, beyond the rebel works, the sun sinking low toward the river, what he had heard was three miles or more that way.

"How long we gonna be out here? After dark, that might be a little . . . dangerous."

"The truce started at six; the colonel says we bring everybody back before nine."

"Be full dark by then."

Willis looked at him, a rare smile.

"I don't know, Dutchie. They might make you an officer yet."

Men were calling out now, and Bauer saw hands waving, amazing smiles on the dirty faces of the men he had been trying to kill. A cluster of men came forward, climbing out through their own defensive obstacles, one man tangled in the same telegraph wire that Bauer had stepped through. Bauer kept walking, heard friendly greetings, playful taunts, some of the men in blue extending hands, hearty shakes shared all along the lines. Willis slowed, Bauer as well, and Bauer knew that no matter how much calm Willis was showing, he would never be "buddies" with any of these men.

"Hey, Yank! I gots me a handful of cigars. You got any bacon, maybe? Yankee newspapers?"

The man stepped close, a gap-toothed smile, and behind Bauer, some of the men from Willis's platoon were there, Kelly pulling a paper from his coat.

"I got this here one from back home, Reb. I heerd you boys like to read all about stuff from them places you'll never see."

The two men drew close, Bauer watching the scene play out, two men who might have been haggling in a general store.

Kelly said, "Where you from, Reb?"

"Looseeana. Some of those boys down yonder ways from right here. M'ssippi. There's Tennessee boys up thataways. You boys'd be from Wisconsin, then? That's what they tells us. I cain't say as I ever need to see nothin' up Wisconsin way, but . . . well, we whip you boys, maybe we'll be visitin' anyways. I always said I wanted to see **foreign lands**. Hee. You from Ireland, then? I hear it in your talk."

Kelly seemed to warm to the man quickly, took a cigar from the man's hand, smelled it slowly.

"My family's Irish."

"All I know 'bout Ireland is snakes. You got lots of 'em. Read something about that."

Kelly laughed, then looked around at Bauer.

"Well, Reb, if you be wantin' to know about snakes and such, we got us an expert right here. Dreams about 'em every night, ain't that right, Dutchman?"

Bauer couldn't help a smile, felt an odd attachment to both men, some piece of joy in their conversation.

"Yep, I guess so. Don't care for 'em. Spent too much time in your blessed swamps. Shiloh."

The Louisiana man eyed Bauer, still the smile, a hint of an edge that made Bauer uneasy.

"Well, then. We had you boys all set to skedaddle right into that blamed Tennessee River. Ought'na stopped this thing right there. I wore out a good musket that day. Busted a bayonet. . . ."

The man stopped, seemed to realize he had gone too far. Bauer thought, "Busted a bayonet" where? A man's chest?

Another man came close and slapped the Louisiana man on the back.

"Hey, you boys done got acquainted with my cousin Zep. Hey, I seen you boys totin' that newspaper. Mighty fine of ya to bring it out here and such. Zep make you a trade?"

Kelly held up the cigars.

"I figured you'd wanna see it. It's three weeks old, but around here, that's like . . . this morning."

The second man looked at Bauer.

"You don't look none too friendly to me, Yank. This fightin' and all . . . it offend you?"

Bauer shook his head, still uneasy, felt a hand on his shoulder, Willis.

"He's happy as can be, boys. I recall we got a good look at your backsides at Shiloh. Of course, you got a good look at ours. His, in particular."

Bauer was stunned by the comment, but Willis got the response he was after, both rebels laughing out loud, Kelly joining in. Bauer tried to feel it, couldn't escape the thought of the man's bayonet. The man called Zep moved around behind Bauer, still laughing.

"Yep, I recall that one. All I did was yell 'snake,' and off he went. Hee."

Willis slapped Bauer again, harder now, a message.

Bauer lowered his head, played the part.

"Yep. You got rattlesnakes in Tennessee big as cannon barrels."

"That we do, friend. Tie 'em together, they make dandy lassos. Made one my pet when I was a boy . . . after he ate my dog and all."

Both men broke into gales of laughter, Kelly as well, even Willis joining in. More men had gathered, small trades passing back and forth, trinkets and parcels, but Bauer had nothing in his pockets, didn't see anything being passed around that appealed to him at all. The laughter and friendly jibes flowed out, much of it at his expense, and he forced himself to smile through it all, one of the rebels calling out, "Hey, Lieutenant! They got an officer over here!" He looked at Bauer with a wink. "You know these officers. Don't matter what army they's in, they gotta flock together. Like crappies in the wintertime." He looked at Willis now, a mock stiffness. "Don't mean no disrespect, sir."

Willis still seemed to flow along with the good humor.

"Sure you do, Reb. That's why you keep shooting at me."

"Hee. Well, yes, sir. You can say that."

The rebel officer moved closer, his uniform ripped at the side, smeared with dirt. He extended a hand toward Willis.

"A lieutenant, then? As well, sir. James Gramling. Baton Rouge. My apologies for my appearance. One of your solid shot came right through my perfect little observation post back there. Dang soil in this part of Mississippi a little too soft for my taste."

Willis took the man's hand.

"I suppose that's why you've piled up so much of it. We'll just have to make our solid shot heavier."

"Ah, yes, very good. That's the truth. I heard tell you're Irishmen. You, sir, don't sound like it."

"Most of the regiment . . . this ugly-looking fellow here is German. My family's English."

"Well, there you go. Mine, too. See? That's just one part of the foolishness of all this. We're the same folks, you and me. How much longer you think this fight'll last? After all, what are we really fighting about that can't be solved by a good old-fashioned handshake."

"And maybe a duel or two."

The lieutenant laughed, pointed at Willis, then said to his men, "See? I told you. They're not so different. It ain't ever the soldier, is it, friend? Just the generals. Politics and all. It can't last much longer, all this killing and such. Don't you agree? I don't imagine you'll be wanting to stay out here in these sandy holes much longer. And when it's done, we'll be doing a whole lot more of this . . . right here. Swapping tobacco and talking about families. How long you figure on carrying this thing on, then?"

Bauer caught something strange in the man's question, a small voice in Bauer's head. *He's asked us how long this is going to last . . . three times.*

Willis slapped Bauer on the back again, a brief, hard grip on Bauer's shirt. *Another message.* Willis said, "Well, Lieutenant, I think this fight will go on as long as it has to. My commander tells me there's rumors all over the army, yours and mine, that old Joe Johnston is riding hard to come right up our backside. Maybe that's all it'll take."

The lieutenant's smile faded slightly, a clear glimmer of understanding.

"Well, now, you know, you might be right about

that. If old Joe does show up, well, you boys will be in a pretty sorry state, wouldn't you say?"

"Pretty sorry. Course, he doesn't show up, we'll be swapping tobacco and telling all our stories right back there. . . . What's that place called? Vicksburg?"

The lieutenant nodded, smiling broadly.

"And so we shall. In all honesty, Lieutenant, you seem to be a man who has a grasp on things. And if two lieutenants can be having such wonderful repartee, just imagine what the generals could do."

Willis shook his head.

"I have no idea what generals do. I have a job, and I do it. Try to get my boys to do the same."

"Well, sir, in that we are in agreement." The man glanced up, the sky darkening quickly. "I suppose, very soon, we shall once again engage in that . . . um . . . job."

"Very soon. Perhaps I will see you in Vicksburg after all."

The man stopped smiling now, seemed to exhaust his artificial goodwill.

"Sir, no insult intended to a fellow officer. But if it is my choice, I shall only meet you again in the presence of the Almighty."

"As you wish. I suppose we must still determine whose **choice** will govern matters."

The man did not respond, made a short bow, turned, moved out through his men. Bauer realized he was soaked in sweat. He stared at Willis and said in a whisper, "He was trying to learn things, find out information."

"That he was. Guess he figured General Grant's gonna confide in **me** what our next move will be. Or maybe he just wanted to know how long it's gonna take us to drive his rebel ass into the Mississippi River. Imbecile."

Voices were calling out, and Bauer saw hands waving, the colonel and Captain McDermott, gathering the men. Bauer heard rumbles now, and all across the field, the talking stopped. Heads were turning toward the sounds, to the west, toward the last glow of the setting sun. The thunder came from the town itself, and Willis said in a hiss, "Move away, Dutchie. Pass the word as you go. Nobody does anything unfriendly. Let's just say our happy good nights."

Bauer was surprised to see Colonel McMahon now, a hint of urgency in his movements.

"Lieutenant, pull your men back. Those are mortars. I guess the navy didn't get the word. No trouble . . . just get these boys back home."

The colonel moved away quickly, more orders to the other officers, and Bauer saw the flow of blue-clad men backing away, the rebels doing the same, moving up into their defenses. He watched the astonishing spectacle, had to see it for one more minute, far into the distance, as far as the darkening sky would let him see. For nearly three hours, the two armies had come out of their holes and shared something of themselves, whether the swapping of precious goods, or just the teasing and taunting of opponents playing some kind of amazing game. He focused on the men from Louisiana, saw faces still looking out toward him, the one man, Zep, looking back at him with that maddening smile. Bauer was surprised, uncomfortable, had seen enough smiling. The man stood straight now, offered Bauer a salute, and Bauer managed a feeble wave, turned, wouldn't see the man again, wouldn't see the respect and the frivolity and the hints of casual friendship. He moved back through the dim light and saw Willis waiting for him.

"Good thing, Dutchie. If you'd have saluted him, I'd have kicked you in the ass."

Bauer kept walking, his head down, Willis moving with him, calling to the others to keep in step. They passed by the rows of fresh earth, the smell of dirt and corpses blending together, the work of the burial parties complete. The men in blue flowed down into the shallow draw, then back up, no one speaking, the men filing quickly back to where they had been when the truce began. Bauer moved toward the fat stump that marked his hiding place, and Willis said, "Get your musket. Somebody else will take that position tomorrow. There's got to be one Irishman in this lot who can shoot straight. Get something to eat."

Bauer stopped, stared down into the dug-out hole, his musket lying upright to one side.

"No. I want to do this again. Let me come out here tomorrow, Sammie."

"You sure about that? You sure you didn't make 'lifelong friends' out there?"

The sarcasm was heavy in Willis's words, and Bauer ignored that, bent low, pulled his musket up, let it hang in one hand.

"I'm sure."

They moved back toward the snaking entrenchments, down into the hollows and cut ground, a gathering mass of blue, the darkness covering them all. From back behind them, the first big gun erupted, then another, flashes of fire that burst out from the artillery pits, the hard scream of shells ripping the air close overhead, a long second for the impact against the great masses of earth and timber across the way, flashes of fire that swept away any thoughts of white flags.

CHAPTER THIRTY

SHERMAN

NORTH OF STOCKADE REDAN
MAY 26, 1863

The reporters came through with that look he knew too well, wide-eyed wonder, their ridiculous tactic for seeming only to seek some piece of dazzling information, tempting any soldier to reveal his own exploits, as though any of the reporters would write the man's life story. Through it all Sherman saw the plot for what it was: men seeking the exclusive tidbit of information for their own newspaper. Naturally, any such prominence would be a direct dig into the pride of the other reporters who shared their camp, the ongoing competition that Sherman knew would produce stories in print that were far more fantastic than anything that occurred on the battlefield.

They approached him warily, though the small, stocky man seemed without any fear at all. Around them, the artillery fire was bursting in a casual rhythm, big guns down to one side working now, then quieting, another battery out to the west doing its work. Civilians rarely seemed comfortable this close to artillery, something Sherman didn't mind a bit. But the first man seemed oblivious, had his focus squarely on Sherman, rode closer, called out.

"Ho, there, General! A word, then?"

Sherman caught the Irish brogue in the man's words and waited for more. There was always more. The four men rode closer, following in a cluster behind the Irishman, and Sherman felt suddenly surrounded, nowhere to hide. He looked out past them, toward Grant's headquarters, Grant establishing himself in close proximity to the link between Sherman's Fifteenth Corps and McPherson's Seventeenth Corps to the south. Sherman couldn't fault that, knew that Grant would rather be anywhere on the field than closer to McClernand. And Sherman appreciated that Grant was available to him not only for tactical meetings, but for conversation as well, that might have nothing at all to do with the army. Grant's headquarters tents were perched high on a hill, set just back out of sight of rebel gunners. So far it had been something of a surprise that Pemberton's artillery had made no effort to pepper any of the farthest positions of the army, even those lines that were clearly in view. There were two possibilities, and Sherman's own artillerymen had pointed out that there was no evidence thus far that the Confederates had any long-range guns in their arsenal, the Whitworths in particular. And the rebel cannon could only be manned at great risk to their crews. Sherman knew there was one other possibility as well. This was, after all, a siege. Pemberton's supply lines were severed completely, at least when it came to anything substantial. It was quite likely that Pemberton was conserving his limited supply of ammunition.

Sherman looked out toward the main road and saw Rawlins, leading a pair of couriers. Sherman started to wave, recognized the indignity of that, thought, He'll rescue me from this horde, if I can just get him over here. He knows better than to let these scoundrels run loose like this.

But Rawlins didn't stop, and Sherman watched with growing dismay as Grant's chief of staff rode past, pushing his horse too hard. Sherman hated that, had too much respect for the animal beneath him to see anyone abusing a mount. But it was Rawlins, the usual habit of making every ride the most important of the day, perhaps the entire war. Once Rawlins was well out of sight of the rest of Grant's staff, he'd slow down and go about his business with the kind of efficiency Grant required. He was, certainly to Grant, an invaluable part of the army. Sherman had to respect that, even if Rawlins seemed to hover over Grant like some nervous grandmother.

There were more horsemen on the road, moving the other way, toward Grant's headquarters. It was a squad of cavalry, the familiar flag of the 4th Illinois. Sherman saw their captain, Embury Osband, leading the way, moving with purpose. Osband had been a part of Grant's security detail for many months now, and where Grant went, Osband took charge. Sherman watched the cloud of dust rising up behind the horses, thought, He's got something to tell Grant, no doubt about that. Damn it all. I could use a little security of my own right now.

The reporters had made their way up close to him, the Irishman moving up too closely, as though seeking some private word.

"Ah, there, General, how ye bein' this fine day?"

Sherman looked at the others, saw the appropriate hesitation, all of them perfectly aware that pushing into Sherman's privacy was a risky thing to do.

"Who are you?"

"Ah, but you know, General. Richard Colburn, the New York **World**. Made a name for meself in this here army already. Freed meself from the bloomin' rebels with nothing more than a gill of horse manure."

Sherman knew the story, could tell by the frowns from the others that they had heard it too many times already.

During the various maneuvers by the navy, pushing supply barges and other craft past Vicksburg, three newspaper reporters had been captured, including Colburn. Colburn insisted that he had loudly claimed British citizenship, and had browbeat the rebels so completely, they had released him with deepest apologies. Sherman suspected the rebels tossed Colburn out of their camp because they were tired of hearing the reedy whine of his voice.

"What can I do for you, this **fine day**?"

"Ah, yes, then, General. Can you tell us when operations might be commencing against the enemy's position, then? I mean, you've tried the thing twice. Surely, General Grant's to give it a go one more time? Reinforcements are arriving daily, so I've been told. Coming downriver from Memphis, General Hurlbut, a few others. Seeing that it takes a good week to send our reports back east, it would be helpful to know somewhat in advance, if things are about to go heatin' up, see?"

Sherman didn't know anything about Hurlbut's arrival, beyond Grant's orders calling for every available unit in the theater to push toward Vicksburg. Sherman knew the trick, Colburn testing whether the report had any truth to it at all.

"Surely, Mr. Colburn, you do not expect me to reveal our tactical plans."

They were all leaning forward, hanging on for more, and Sherman turned the horse abruptly, then moved off. He heard them mumbling, thought, Stay there, damn you. Don't follow me. He looked to his staff, most of them inside his headquarters tents, and he ran orders through his head, something he could shout out to bring someone out there, some reason to excuse himself. He saw his engineer, Kossak, the man emerging from a tent with a roll of paper in his hand. Sherman pumped his fist in a short punch. Good! That engineer's got no more affection for newspapermen than I do.

"Captain!"

Kossak made a short acknowledging wave and trotted quickly toward Sherman.

"At your service, sir."

Kossak noticed the four civilians now, seemed to stop in his tracks, and Sherman said nothing, just stared at him, Kossak seeming to grasp exactly what Sherman was doing.

"General, I have these drawings for you. We must examine them in haste. They are . . . mightily sensitive, sir."

Sherman grimaced, knew that word would excite the reporters even more, pouring honey on the ground for a swarm of flies. Kossak stood at attention now, the roll of papers shoved formally under his arm. Sherman turned to the civilians and said, "There now. You boys run along. Serious work to do here, and this man is my engineer. Figures and whatnot, all of that geometry business. Nothing you can write about."

Colburn kept coming, the horse slipping up close to Sherman's again, a low voice.

"Now, General. Anything you'd be planning . . .

well, General Grant ha'nt said a word about it. So, you'd be doing some workin' out here without his knowledge, eh? Might we know what's happenin' then?"

Sherman felt the usual growling temper, reached his boot out, a slight kick in the rump of Colburn's horse, creating distance between them.

"This is an army, gentlemen. We have army work to do. When you can be notified of the details, General Grant will notify you. With all due respect . . ." The word stuck in his throat, and he saw the friendly gleam from Colburn now changing to determined annoyance. "Please depart this area," Sherman said. "I'm certain I saw Colonel Rawlins gathering up some of you fellows on the road. Probably issuing some notice, something you can all use. I wouldn't miss that."

They seemed to take the bait reluctantly, glances out toward the road, Colburn hanging back, still looking at Sherman.

"Ya know, General Sherman, if you was a wee bit more sociable to us fellas, we'd be a bit more . . . uh . . . sociable to you. Just doing our jobs, as it were."

"Right now, my job is figuring out the best way to grab that town out there. There's time for being sociable and there's time for killing rebels. You want **sociable,** go see Colonel Rawlins."

Colburn nodded, a hint of a smile.

"As you wish, General. Be seeing you later, then?"

He didn't wait for Sherman's response, rode off, caught up with the others. Sherman let out a long breath and looked at Kossak, all business, the roll of paper sliding out from his arm.

"Thank you for the help, Captain. What's that?"

Kossak glanced again toward the reporters, seemed to gauge the distance as safe enough for conversation.

"I've been keeping careful track of the entrenchments, sir. Might need to know precisely where our people are digging, should our artillery be called forward. That, and . . . well, begging your pardon, sir, but I'm rather pleased with the layout of the work so far. This will be a maneuver worthy of study for the future."

"For future engineers."

"Well, yes, sir."

"Fine, Captain, you want to write a text for West Point, you do that in your leisure time. Right now, there is no leisure time."

"Oh, no, sir. I understand. But you should see this. It's . . . well, it's beautiful, sir."

Kossak held out the papers, began to unroll them, and Sherman looked past him, down a wide hill, ravines and cut ground, thickets of trees, some of those being cut down. Far in the distance was the formidable fortress the rebels had named Stockade Redan, the place where so many of Sherman's men had fallen. He could see now what the engineer was talking about, what was drawn in detail on his papers. From the deepest ravines to Sherman's front, up onto the flatter fields, men were working half buried in the ground. The trench lines were laid out in a zigzag pattern, others, farther to one side, in parallel lines, connected by shortcuts. The artillery fire continued, the blasts striking the rebel works regularly, tossing sand and broken timbers skyward. Sherman raised his field glasses, scanned the works, no sign of rebels, no hint that anyone was there at all. Through the artillery, he could hear the pops of musket fire, knew it was all his own, the sharpshooters taking aim at anything that might be a target. He shared the engineer's pride, that this plan was working, that the rebels seem to have no answer for Grant's army digging their way closer, the distance shrinking every day.

"How close are we now, Captain?"

"Within ninety yards in places, sir. By tomorrow, closer still."

Sherman focused on the ground closer to him, saw spades tossing dirt up and out of the trenches.

"Risky. The rebels will do something about this before long. I would. Can't just let us waltz right up under their noses. We losing many people? There's rebels who can shoot, too."

"Not many at all, sir. If you notice the cotton bales, the straw."

Sherman saw the fat lumps, scattered about the field, but there was nothing random about that. At the leading edge of every trench, where the shovels were doing their work, the men in the ground were protected by a fat barrier, certain to stop any musket fire.

"Nice work, Captain. I assume this is going on all down the lines?"

"Indeed, sir. General McPherson is doing precisely what we are. I can't speak for General McClernand . . . haven't ventured down that far, but I know from Captain Comstock that General Grant has issued the same working orders to everyone. It's only a matter of time, sir."

Sherman lowered the glasses, heard the hard shriek of an artillery shell, could see the red trail to his left, the shell impacting flat against the redan's wall. The answer came now, a burst of smoke from behind the works, the ball impacting somewhere in the ravine below. Sherman waited, knew what was coming. The blasts impacted the rebel cannon before its smoke had even cleared, a half-dozen fiery explosions he could hear now. It has to be that way in every position, he thought. They try to hit us back, and we swarm on them like wasps. Or reporters.

"Very good, Captain. Keep me advised of your progress. There might be a textbook in this after all." He turned, looked back toward the road, no sign of the civilians, more cavalry riding past, the business of the headquarters. "And before much longer, we'll have something those reporters will want to crow about." He looked at Kossak, the man impatient to be gone, to return to the work. "Tell you what, Captain. When it's time to give these reporters what they're after . . . I'll let **you** do it."

CHAPTER THIRTY-ONE

SPENCE

CONFEDERATE HOSPITAL—
THE GREEN HOUSE
MAY 29, 1863

She held the boy down, couldn't avoid his blood on her hands. Already her apron was soaked through to her dress, the sticky dampness oozing through everything she was wearing.

"Here! Harder!"

The doctor grabbed her hand, pressed it on the boy's chest, a thick pool of soft goo that spread up through her fingers.

"Hold it there . . . tight. Stand up . . . lean over him. More pressure."

She obeyed, stood upright, bent out over the boy, her weight pushing down, the doctor now moving to the boy's head, removing a thick bloody bandage.

"Oh Lord."

The doctor stood straight across the table from her and shook his head.

"No, missy. Let it be. The wound's taken too much of his brain . . . behind the neck. He's done."

She felt a rush of panic, could feel the boy's heart beating through the mush in his chest.

"No! He's alive!"

The doctor wiped his hands on a rag, was already moving toward the next man, another table close by. She was furious now and shouted, "No! Come back! You can save him!"

He turned to her, and she saw the calm, the exhaustion, his strength overpowering her will, draining away the fury. He held out the rag and said, "Missy, we tried to stop the bleeding. It might have saved him. But the head wound is too severe. I can't explain this to you again."

"He's too young."

Her words were soft, a plaintive cry, but the doctor was working on the next man, a mess of an arm wound, more blood, the man reacting to the doctor's touch.

"Leave me be! I'm all right, you see?"

There was terror in the man's voice, and Lucy saw his face, frightened eyes, panicking madness.

"I'll take a look at it, son. Might be able to fix you up in no time. Missy, over here, please."

Lucy pulled her hands free of the soggy slop of

the boy's chest, stared at the face, silent, pale. She couldn't move away, not yet.

"Missy. Here, now!"

She wiped at her hands, the rag wet with the blood of a half-dozen men. She said the words again, silently, a plea for the boy. He's not more than fourteen. Can't be. We could still . . .

The boy suddenly bowed up, his chest foaming, gasping for one great burst of air. But it was one breath, one final sound, and she heard a hard gurgling, and then a soft rattle that seemed to come from the boy's throat. She knew the meaning, had seen it already, all morning long, the shock of witnessing a man's last breath. The boy's eyes were still open, and she turned away, wouldn't look at that, wouldn't touch him to shut them. It was the worst thing she had done, touching any of the men who died in front of her, feeling the body suddenly soulless. There should have been comfort in that, and she scolded herself for her uneasiness, knew the boy was with the Almighty now, the pain gone, the wounds healed in ways only God could do. She felt like crying, again, but the tears wouldn't come, were no longer there.

"Missy . . ."

"Coming, sir."

She slipped around the table, stopped, made way for two men who moved quickly by her, lifting the dead boy. She knew there was need for more space, the corpse just taking up room. The two men didn't speak to her, a relief. There had been too much of that already, teasing this wisp of a girl, sickening jokes about the blood on her clothing, blood in her hair, the apron doing her no good at all. But the men were as exhausted as she was. She glanced once at the boy as they lifted him up, the body carried quickly from the tent, and now, more men came in, carrying a litter, a man bawling like an infant, a high-pitched sobbing that sliced through her. She fought that, stepped to the surgery table across from the doctor, focused now on the new patient, older, a sergeant. It had stopped mattering, that first curiosity if the man was an officer, the terrible burst of panic that it might be **her** officer. But now the faces were losing meaning, just men, soldiers engulfed in their own nightmares, each one different, but all so much the same.

The sergeant looked up at her, a small ray of hopefulness.

"Ma'am? You be takin' care of me?"

"That she will, soldier. Finest nurse in this hospital."

Lucy tried to manage a smile, the doctor looking at her now, measuring, and she put a hand on the man's forehead.

"Yes. I'll take care of you."

The doctor called out toward one of the ambulance men nearby.

"Here! I need your hands." He looked at Lucy, the command she had heard all day. "Chloroform."

Lucy went to the table close by, wrapped her fingers around the small brown bottle, tried not to see the crust of dried blood on her hands.

"Here, Doctor."

"Apply it to the cloth. You know how."

She pulled the cork from the bottle, picked up a small dirty bandage from the table, put it over the bottle, and tilted it up for a long second.

"Now, to the soldier, missy."

She moved with automatic motions, bent over, the man's terror returning.

"What you gonna do? You suffocatin' me?"

She tried to show reassurance, keep the tremor out of her voice, and said, "Not at all, Sergeant. This will make you feel better. The pain will stop."

"The pain ain't all that bad. I'm all right! What you gonna do then?"

The fear in his voice was increasing, and the doctor said, "**Now,** missy. Don't delay."

She pressed the cloth over the man's face, and he jumped, terrified, but the doctor clamped down on his undamaged arm, the other man putting weight on the man's legs. In a few seconds the sergeant stopped struggling, and Lucy stood back, waited while the doctor tested the man, sticking him with a small needle, making sure he was as near unconscious as they could make him.

"I'll need both of you for this. Missy, hand me the scalpel. Butch, have that tourniquet ready. I'll need it quick, once I get the skin cut."

Lucy saw what seemed to be the remnants of a tourniquet high on the man's arm, and said, "He's got one already."

The doctor grabbed the strip of cloth, yanked, the tourniquet coming free, and tossed it on the ground beside him.

"Wasn't doing any more good. The scalpel, missy."

She picked up the small razor-sharp knife from the table and handed it to the doctor, careful to keep the blade pointing back toward her.

"Tear open the sleeve, Butch."

"Yes, sir."

The man complied, the wound exposed, shattered bone, torn flesh. She was becoming used to this now, a man's arm reduced to the simplest of terms. Meat. The doctor made fast work with the scalpel, cutting through the bloody skin, the ripped muscle, exposing what was left of the bone.

"Tourniquet, Butch. Tie it tight . . . right there."

The man moved quickly, experienced, and Lucy was grateful for so little fresh blood.

"All right, missy, use that curved instrument there, the silver one. Hold the muscle out of the way. I have to get up a ways, past the worst of it."

She moved closer, knew this part as well, slid the flat metal into the cut flesh, pulled the muscle up the man's arm, holding it back while the doctor slid his fingers along what she could see of the bone.

"That's it. Right there. Butch, here, take the scalpel. Now, hand me the saw."

The man retrieved the small rectangular saw from the table, a quick exchange of instruments with the doctor, the doctor not hesitating. He pulled the saw back and forth across the exposed bone, and Lucy shut her eyes tight, her jaw clamped, but she couldn't escape the sound, the teeth of the saw slicing quickly through the man's arm.

"That's it. Missy, check on him when you can. When he wakes up, he's not gonna like what he finds. This wasn't too bad, though. He'll probably survive this."

She took a hard breath, was engulfed by a new wave of nausea, infuriating, steadied herself against the table. The doctor had moved away, and she saw the worst part of it now, the doctor tossing the arm onto a pile of limbs. The arm landed with a soft thump, rolled partway off the pile, just one of a dozen arms, piled together with legs and fingers.

She looked at the sergeant's face, the man breathing softly, just a peaceful nap. The doubt came now, a foolish curiosity she could never ask the doctor. Is he asleep or not? Does the chloroform just freeze him, keeping him still? Might he know everything that had happened? She touched the man's forehead again, cold silence, and she said softly, "I'll return very soon, soldier."

"He can't hear you, miss. Dead to the world, at least for now." The words came from Butch, a smirk she had grown to despise, one more ambulance driver who had become so utterly callous about his job. And about her. "Doctor, I best be headin' back out to the lines. There'll be more, pretty certain."

"Go on, Butch. We're not going anywhere. Missy, over here please. This one's a leg. Oh my Lord, both of 'em. Real mess. Shrapnel."

She moved that way, wiped her hands against her apron, too tired to search for the rag, felt a small soft lump between her fingers. She looked at it, knew already what it was, a piece of flesh from the man who had just lost his arm. Meat.

She saw the face of a nurse, an older woman who never smiled.

"Get up, Miss Spence. Doctor, she's awake."

Lucy felt the floor of the tent beneath her, tried to sit up, her head spinning. The doctor was at one of the tables and glanced her way.

"Get her out of here. Missy, go outside, sit for a while. You feel like coming back in here, I sure could use you."

She stood slowly, helped by the other nurse, heard laughter, a pair of ambulance drivers carrying a litter, dropping it down on the hard table.

"Well, there, Miss Nursie, things getting a little rough in here? Maybe you best go make some tea for your husband."

"Leave her be, Henry. She ain't been doin' this long."

Lucy felt something familiar about the friendlier man, realized now it was the teamster who had brought her to the hospital. He tipped his hat, a brief gesture of kindness, and she nodded his way.

"Thank you. I'll be all right."

The nurse still held her under one arm.

"Doubt that," the nurse said. "Go on outside. Or go on home. Can't have fainting spells in here. You could kill somebody. Look at the back of your dress. This floor's no place for such foolishness."

There was nothing kind in the woman's words, and Lucy slid free of her grip, had already absorbed too much of the woman's surliness.

"I'll be fine. Thank you."

She moved quickly past the pair of tables, the familiar sounds, cries and soft whimpers, one man saying some kind of prayer, the words jumbled nonsense, the man falling silent.

She was outside now, the air hot, steaming, the smell of the wounds and the wounded, the smell of her own dress, the brown crust coating her hands, jammed under her fingernails. She walked out past the tents, three rows now, the need increasing every day, more injured men, too few doctors to treat them. She thought of the doctor, a hint of kindness in a man who went about his work with bored matter-of-factness. She was one of a dozen nurses, the standard being one nurse for every eight men. She hadn't understood that at first, part of the quick training she had been given by the older nurse, as though Lucy should already know the routine. The doctor knew otherwise, had seen through her show of courage, her need to be helpful, had tolerated her inexperience, at least for the first day. But there was no time for tolerance of any kind now, the flow of wounded from the east steady, the ambulance drivers pressed into service restraining the most violent of the wounded, the doctor quick to administer chloroform to silence anyone who disrupted the flow of work.

She walked out across the wide yard of the house, beyond the tents, avoided the big oak tree, the place where the rows of corpses lay. There were burials ongoing, men with shovels down the hill, graves just deep enough to hide a body from anyone's sight. She watched them working, laughter, one man handing a bottle to another as they stabbed their spades into the soft soil. She stared, indignant at their lack of respect for the awful duty, the men drinking liquor to steel themselves from a job that was no worse than anything she had been told to do, anything she had already seen. But she kept silent, knew better than to speak out to drunk men, the queasiness in her stomach keeping her from the sight of what they were doing.

"Hello, miss. You be wanting a ride, then?"

She turned to the voice, the ambulance driver, his hat in his hand.

"What do you mean? Where?"

"Well, forgive me for sayin', miss. But I been

watchin' you for a while now. This ain't the sorta thing you was cut out for. Maybe I take you back to your papa, or wherever you came from."

She wanted to be angry at the man, but she had absorbed all she could, rubbed her fingers together, wondered if her hands would ever be clean. She said nothing, moved toward him, and he led the way, back to his ambulance, climbed up in front of her, held out a hand, pulled her up beside him. Without a word, he grabbed the leather straps and slapped the mule, the wagon lurching ahead, back toward the caves, and beyond, toward the men who couldn't escape the punishment from the Federal guns.

She knelt by the small creek, let the cool water flow over her hands, dug at her fingernails for the last specks of dried blood. The creek was used by the cave dwellers on both sides of the hill, a gravelly stream that ran through the base of the ravine. The water was drinkable, and the women had finally succumbed to the necessities of life underground, the only place close by where they could try to wash what needed washing. They came out of their shelters when the artillery seemed to fall elsewhere, but those moments were brief, and anyone who dared stand in the open was risking a horrible fate. Those stories had flowed over the hillsides, a child killed by shrapnel, a cave-in that crushed one of the Negroes, a dozen accounts of injuries from the horrible effects of the shredded iron from the mortars. For days now the shelling hadn't stopped for more than a few minutes at a time, and as always, there was no order to it, no aim, no purpose anyone could explain. The mortars were still the worst of all, coming again from the river, and now coming in from the east as well. The men had gathered with their predictable chatter, but Lucy had stopped listening, her brain wrapping around the only piece of this war that mattered to her now. She had run her hands through the most graphic filth she could ever have known, parts of men's bodies she had never seen before, wounds that bathed her in blood and fluids that smelled worse than death itself. The amputations had been the worst, and no matter that doctor's casual routine or encouraging words, the nurses had told her that half those men would not survive anyway. The greatest surprise had been the comfort she had drawn from the quick deaths, what she now realized was a blessing. She had felt guilt at the odd sensation of welcoming a man's death. But when the wounds were the worst, unending, unstoppable pain, harsh screams, men begging for mercy, for any relief at all, the suddenness of death had been a relief, as though the unspeakable suffering had been swept away by the Divine Hand.

She studied her fingers, as clean as she could

make them, heard footsteps through the low brush, a voice, Isabel Cordray.

"Well, here you are. My husband told me what you were doing. Oh my, Lucy! You look a horror!"

Lucy glanced down, was still wearing the apron, every part of her clothing bloodstained.

"Yes, I suppose I do. This dress will never recover, I'm afraid. I don't have another in the cave."

"Well, I do, most certainly! Come back to the cave." Isabel put a hand over her face. "Oh, my word! The smell. Forgive me, dear, but you cannot come into the cave in this condition. I cannot abide that odor. And you will terrify the children."

"They aren't terrified now?"

Lucy had grown exhausted by Isabel's complaints, the perfectly miserable **inconvenience** of life in the cave. She heard it all over the hillside, the men gathering to complain about Pemberton, the helplessness of the army, the women seeming to complain about everything else.

Isabel stared at her, seemed to weigh the options, and Lucy thought, she isn't going to make me disrobe out here, no matter how disgusting I appear.

"Oh, well, come on then. I'll send my husband out to visit his friends while you change your garments. He prefers their company to mine anyway. And of course, those men are all so terribly eager to solve all our woes. Such opinionizing, I've never heard. What kind of lesson is that for the children?"

Lucy kept her silence, fought the temptation to

mention anything about the hospital, what that might do to their lofty opinions. She followed Isabel back up the hill, saw women coming down the path, hands rising up, a short scream, one woman staggering back at the sight of her. She was too tired for conversation, made a small wave, and the women seemed to melt together, protection against whatever kind of demon she appeared to be.

"Oh my, Miss Spence! Are you wounded?"

"No, but thank you for your concerns."

Isabel spoke up now, as though suddenly proud.

"She's been nursing at the hospital. Treating the wounded soldiers."

"Oh, my. Truly a ghastly thing, Miss Spence. I understand there are two hospitals. One for illnesses, and one for the wounded. Could you not have ministered to the sick instead? Surely it would be a simpler ordeal."

"The sick will either die or get better. The wounded men . . . well, there is no medicine for that. Only hands."

She moved past them, Isabel following, heard the low comments, the judgments, more opinions. The climb was steeper than she recalled, her legs weak, and she stopped, tried to catch her breath. Isabel stopped with her, kept her distance, and Lucy said, "The nurses told me I couldn't do the job. Today I didn't help matters any. I fainted."

"A fainting spell? Oh Lucy, how humiliating."

She swallowed the word, stared at her friend for a

long moment, Isabel starting the climb again, and
Lucy said, "I'll be along."

She sat down in the grass, the sky darkening with
the setting of the sun. The rumble of the artillery
shells shook the ground beneath her, a mortar shell
crashing down on the far side of the creek. She
thought of the climb, the safety of the cave, stared
up at the last bit of daylight, still too tired to move.
The mosquitoes were finding her now, and she
watched one land on her wrist. She slapped it away,
thought of the astonishing variety of bugs and vermin that infested the earth. Like us, she thought.
And so we will remain vermin until this misery has
passed, and we shall never stop complaining about
how terrible it all is.

She thought again of the hospital, the amazing
calm of the doctor, the pure terror in some of the
soldiers, men who would wake from a forced slumber to find a piece of themselves gone. She couldn't
escape those images, one man missing his lower
jaw, another with his eyes shot away. The shrapnel was by far the worst, bodies ripped open, bones
exposed, guts, lungs. And brains. The faces were
there, but there were too many, too much of it,
terrified hands grabbing for her, cries and shouts.
And what did you do, brave girl? You helped them
by having a fainting spell. She thought of Isabel's
word: **humiliating**. Yes, it was. That old crab of a
nurse . . . she knew it would happen. So, what do I

do now? Spend my days in the cave, or down here, doing the washing with a flock of cackling hens? Or shall I linger near the men, while they curse General Pemberton and wring their hands about politics and show off their knowledge of artillery?

She pictured the hospital, the tents for the surgery, alongside the grand house where the men would recover. Those who did recover. You cannot just pretend they aren't there, she thought. What good can you do out here? I don't care about the war or General Pemberton or what kind of savages the Yankees might be. Like everyone else in this town, I was rooted out of my home so I would not die by the hand of some blue-coated gunner I'll never see. Complain about that? Certainly. I did not bring this war. It found me. It found all of us. She thought of the shopkeepers, a chorus of cursing about the lack of goods for their shelves, the Yankees keeping the supply boats from bringing all those trinkets, new clothing, shoes, hairpins, and perfume. Such an **inconvenience**. How inconvenient is it for those men . . . the boy who died today, the man who lost his arm?

She knew she wouldn't stay away, that a fainting spell was no excuse for curling up in the safety of a cave. Tomorrow, she thought. I will go back there. Mr. Cordray can transport me, in case no ambulance happens by. Or I can walk. She dropped her head, stared at the grass, bugs there, too, something certain to inflict its bite. No, there will certainly be ambulances. There will always be ambulances, until all of this ends.

She leaned back on her arms, the grass soft beneath her, more rumbles from beyond the hillside, a red streak overhead now, coming down a hundred yards away. People were scurrying up away from the creek, the cluster of women pouring uphill in a frantic scamper to safety. More shells fell closer, a trio of impacts to one side, another shell, smoke and dirt tossed skyward. She watched the women in a mad dash up the hill, felt none of that, the terror drained away. She looked to the east, where the men from Louisiana would be, had stopped thinking of her lieutenant. He was just one of many, the same as the broken men who cried out to her, whose wounds soiled her dress, dying as their blood poured into her hands. I will go back tomorrow, she thought. I must.

She lay back in the grass, watched the red streaks sailing above, the slow, deadly arcs of the mortar shells, the stunning bursts of fire above the ridgeline, the thunder of the solid shot, her thoughts taking her to that special time, the Fourth of July, a child dazzled by the rockets bursting above the river. She tried to sit upright, but the weariness was complete. She laid her head back in the soft grass, and went to sleep.

CHAPTER THIRTY-TWO

PEMBERTON

THE COWAN HOUSE—VICKSBURG
MAY 30, 1863

"Your name, then?"

The man stood at attention, and Pemberton could see he was very young, beardless, most of his uniform a ragged mess.

"Seaman Thomas Smith, sir."

"Seaman Smith. Welcome to Vicksburg. Though I suspect you've seen quite enough of this place. No matter. I'm beginning to feel the same way."

The sailor kept his defiant stance, and Pemberton looked at the note prepared by his staff, the information he already knew.

"So, Seaman Smith, you were a crewman on board the **Cincinnati,** yes?"

"I was, sir. I am now."

Pemberton had no energy for a chess match.

"Seaman Smith, your mighty craft now rests in the mud on the bottom of the river, or were you not aware of that? Surely, some among my guards have regaled you with the marvelous triumph of our batteries over your once-proud vessel?"

"She'll return to action, sir. The **Cincinnati** shall have its honor restored."

"Not likely, boy. She's in twenty feet of water. All you can see is what's left of her stacks."

The young man seemed to wilt, fought to keep his back straight.

"So, you escaped. Some did, I heard. Some didn't. Your captain lost a good portion of his crew. Friends of yours, no doubt."

"I . . . don't know about that, sir."

Pemberton knew the boy was likely telling the truth.

"Says here we pulled you out of the river, after you floated downstream on a hay bale. Fortunate young man. We pulled a few less fortunate from the water as well. I can show them to you if you wish." The sailor seemed to flinch, a break in his armor. Pemberton tried to feel some sense of accomplishment in that, but it was hardly a challenge. "No, I won't do that. But you're my prisoner now, Seaman Smith. I'd toss you in with the lot of them . . . but maybe it's best you stay by yourself. When this is all over, there'll be more seamen joining you. Your navy is no match for the batteries we have here. I suppose your captain knows that better than anyone."

Pemberton motioned to the sergeant of the guard, **Enough,** the two men standing behind the sailor nudging him toward the door. As he reached the door, the sailor looked at him, a brief, hostile glance. Pemberton waited for the guards to exit and said to Waddy, "Close it. You can stay."

Waddy obeyed, stood before the desk now, a broad smile.

"Proud cuss, isn't he, sir?"

"Ought to be. Those ironclads have given this place a larger dose of misery than anyone here deserves."

"All the more reason to celebrate the **Cincinnati**'s destruction, sir. The Yankees are certain to understand the meaning. They are unlikely to be so brazen in the future."

Pemberton leaned back in the chair.

"We've sunk . . . how many of their gunboats, Colonel?"

The smile disappeared, and Waddy said, "This is the first . . . in a while, sir. But not the only one, certainly."

"We were fortunate. You fire enough iron at something with portholes in it, and sooner or later, you'll hit one."

"Oh, sir, there was a great deal more to it than that! The Yankees attempted to duel with our strongest columbiads. They could not endure such a storm of fire!"

Pemberton wiped his hands on his face, stroked his beard slowly, heard a soft knock at the door, the telltale sign it was Memminger.

"Let him in, Colonel."

Memminger entered with caution, another habit, making certain Pemberton wasn't deep into some highly sensitive issue.

"What is it, Major?"

"Oh, sir, very sorry to intrude. Mrs. Balfour offers her courtesies, and apologizes for interrupting your duties, sir. She only wishes to extend to you her gratitude for your attendance at her home yesterday. She says you honored her family by your presence, and they will cherish the memory of such a celebration of the success of the shore batteries."

Memminger seemed to run out of breath, and Pemberton couldn't help a smile, knew the major had practiced memorizing that entire message.

"Fine, yes, you may prepare a note, something gracious. I haven't had a peaceful meal like that in a while."

He wasn't in the mood to be polite, had only accepted the invitation from the neighbors next door to his headquarters out of a sense of protocol.

"Yes, sir. Right away. I shall bring you a draft of what I prepare."

"Oh for God's sake, Major. Just offer them a polite thank-you. I don't have to examine every piece of handwriting you employ here."

"Yes, sir. Of course, sir."

Memminger was gone now, and Pemberton felt the punch of guilt, had no reason to criticize either of his top aides.

"Colonel, you are dismissed. I should like a moment alone. I should wish to prepare my own personal correspondence."

"Of course, sir. It will be dark soon, sir. I would not advise even a candle."

"I know. I have learned to write my wife even in the dark. Whether or not a letter from me will ever reach her hand . . . well, I shall make the attempt."

"Certainly, sir. I have every confidence in our couriers."

Pemberton retrieved a blank piece of paper from the desk, the stack nearly gone.

"Colonel, is there more writing paper about?"

Waddy seemed hesitant.

"No, sir. We made sure you had the last of it."

"So. Make note of that, Colonel. The least of our luxuries has already been depleted. How much longer will we endure the enemy's presence before we exhaust everything else?"

He could tell that Waddy was chewing on his words, had something to say.

"Out with it, Colonel."

"Sir, I didn't want to bother you with a trivial detail. The servant who brought Mrs. Balfour's note . . . he said that the meal you enjoyed last evening was the last of its kind they expected to have. Mrs. Balfour went to a great deal of trouble to provide a bountiful table. I had urged her not to go to such extremes, but she insisted."

"And you're just telling me this now? After I gorged myself on ham and biscuits?"

"Well, sir, she insisted I make no mention. It was a celebration, after all."

"So, what are they stuffing themselves with today? The scrapings from their cellar floor? This is not good, Colonel. Not at all. I have my critics here, certainly. But so many of these people have treated me with great hospitality. I'm not certain they know the price of that."

"Sir?"

"Colonel, we are under siege. General Grant is even now in the process of sealing up our final escape route to the south. We do not have the means to prevent that. We do not even have the cavalry strength to maintain a vigilant watch on his movements. Whatever rations this army has in its possession . . . is what we have to eat. The same goes for the civilians. I have been avoiding this. . . . Somehow I hoped it would not become this dire. But it will only get worse. General Stevenson has been serving as chief commissary officer. Prepare an order that he put the troops on one-half rations, beginning tomorrow. I cannot order the citizens around here to do anything, but caution should be extended that they conserve as much as possible. See to it, Colonel."

Waddy seemed to soak up the message Pemberton was giving him, hesitated. "Sir. Are you certain this is necessary?"

"I do not wish a council of war on this matter, Colonel. You have my instructions."

"Yes, sir. I will prepare the order."

Waddy was out quickly, the door closing behind him. Pemberton pulled himself out of the chair and moved to the window. He could barely see the Balfour house, the darkness hiding every detail of the town. There would be no lantern lights, no fires, not with so much Federal artillery so close by. We sink one gunboat, he thought, and this place erupts in celebration. The Balfours insist on braving a journey out from their cave just to provide me a celebratory dinner, dodging artillery rounds so they can boast of our great victory. And yes, we captured a sailor. One sailor. I should have told him that . . . the only seaman in our stockade. If it stays that way, he'll have something to tell his grandchildren. Unless his own artillery tosses a shell into the holding area.

The fight that destroyed the Federal ironclad *Cincinnati* had taken place three days earlier, a cannonade that brought civilians out of their cover. The fight began in the morning and lasted long enough to allow an enormous throng to swarm up onto Sky Parlor Hill. To the civilians, the sight was magnificent, Confederate batteries blasting a storm of shells that ultimately was too much for the gunboat to endure. Her captain managed to withdraw upriver, just past Federal lines along the shore, but the devastation was nearly total. Losing a fifth of her crew, the ironclad had settled into the muddy river bottom not far from the river's edge.

Pemberton received the reports of the **Cincinnati**'s demise from his own staff, who seemed to treat the success as the greatest victory of the war. As it was now, the ironclad might still be salvageable by Federal naval engineers. At the very least, the boat's heavy artillery pieces were submerged more or less intact, a prize for either side to recover. But Pemberton knew the Federals would guard those guns carefully, and so he had ordered demolition crews to slip upriver after dark and destroy the boat where it lay.

And for what, he thought. They have twenty more upriver, as many downstream. The word came to him, planted into his brain, what seemed to matter so much to everyone but him. **Morale**. Yes, fine. A symbol of our might.

He looked to his desk again, saw the note received the day before, written four days before that. It had come from Johnston, a response to the litany of letters Pemberton had been sending east. Despite his staff's assurances, Pemberton had faint hope that any

of his correspondence would actually reach Johnston's new headquarters in the ruins of the burned
capital, but to his surprise, at least one had. It was
one of the several urgent requests for Johnston to
do something with the troops in his command to
relieve the pressure from Grant.

Pemberton had read the note without disguising
his outrage, one more effort by Johnston to distance himself from anything Pemberton was trying
to accomplish.

**I am too weak to save Vicksburg; can do
no more than attempt to save you and
your garrison. It will be impossible to extricate you, unless you cooperate and we
make mutually supporting movements.
Communicate your plans and suggestions if possible.**

Pemberton read it again, focused on the word
suggestions. Perhaps, General, you can pay some
heed to my prior suggestions, and attack Grant's
army. Of course, that assumes the **impossible,** that
we can be successful here at all. I suppose it is a
good thing that I am made aware how little regard
my commanding officer has for our necessity of
maintaining this position. It is very clear that he
has little respect for the fighting spirit of my men,
or the skill we have used in designing our defenses,
the capability of our generals. . . .

He sat heavily. **Morale**. Yes, a fine word. Perhaps we should remove the **e,** pay more heed to **moral**. What is **moral** about a commander who chooses to ignore such a situation as we have here? Against the orders of the president? Is there confusion as to what we require?

The letter had been brought in by a courier who also carried twenty thousand percussion caps, another of those morale builders. Fewer than one cap per man, he thought. But . . . it is something. Perhaps a million more would be helpful. He looked toward the window, fully dark now, knew that Waddy's advice was sound. There would be no lantern, no candlelight in his office. He thought of his staff, hardworking men, doing all they could to manage the business of the army. They do believe in such things as victory, that somehow we shall be rescued, whatever that might mean.

From both soldiers and civilians, the word had spread, filtering back to his headquarters, that Johnston was indeed coming, that relief from Grant's stranglehold was inevitable, the Federal army still ripe for defeat. It was one more surprise in a campaign full of surprises, that so many people, his own officers, would grab so heartily at rumor. He stood again, nervous energy, his anger frustrating him, nothing he could really do. I cannot speak of this, not to anyone. General Johnston claims he is too weak to help us. If I reveal that to anyone outside this headquarters, they will lose hope. And that, I suppose, is what drives them all. And tomorrow they are put on half rations. They did not expect that. I did not expect that. They may embrace this morale, this hope. But if we remain here much longer, they will have to embrace . . . hunger.

A QUARTER MILE WEST OF THE GREAT REDOUBT JUNE 2, 1863

He was responding to the urgency in a message from Major Lockett, imploring him to ride forward, to observe something the engineer seemed reluctant to put to paper. He saw the man now, sitting with three others, familiar, staff officers of General Forney, who commanded the center of the line. Lockett seemed content to wait for him, and Pemberton was annoyed with that, thought, You summon me to ride out here with such haste? I do not see any crisis.

His color bearer had slipped up close beside him, and Pemberton was annoyed at him as well, motioned with his hand, **Back up**. Is even my staff to show such a lack of decorum?

Forney's staff saluted him, one man speaking out, a major whose name Pemberton couldn't recall.

"Sir, with your permission, we shall inform General Forney of your presence."

"I do not intend a lengthy visit. It is not necessary for General Forney to make himself available." He looked at Lockett now. "I hear artillery to the north, Major. Musket fire in every part of the line. Is there something new to this? I have problems aplenty in town. The supply of corn flour is nearly exhausted. There is apparently no meat at all. Were you aware of that?"

Lockett glanced at the departing staff officers, offered his own salute now, and waited patiently for Pemberton to return it. Pemberton waved his hand across his brow, the most patience he could display, and Lockett said, "Yes, sir. I have heard a great deal of distressing talk from the men along the front lines. Their rations are diminishing in the extreme, and they are enduring considerable aggravation from the enemy. We suffer casualties every day from sharpshooters, from that artillery."

"These men are on the **front lines,** Major. They should expect casualties. I do not wish to hear of distress. I have citizens pushing their way into my headquarters daily, demanding that I win this thing. Just like that. Win it. Their caves do not have fully stocked pantries, and so I am quizzed as to why the general store has empty shelves. What do I tell them, Major? My army is suffering as well? Such talk helps no one."

Lockett was silent for a moment, then said, "Well, sir, what I wish to show you will not improve your demeanor."

"My demeanor is not your concern. Keeping the

enemy out of Vicksburg . . . that is the only duty that should occupy your attention."

"Sir, I suppose I could have sent this information in a message. The fewer among us who know of the enemy's actions, the better. I am concerned that the morale of the men will suffer."

Pemberton cringed. That word again.

"Morale is not your concern, either, Major. What is so important—"

"Sir, the enemy is entrenching forward. He is advancing under strong cover and is moving his entire position closer to our defenses. All the division commanders have requested that I devise some means of stopping their progress. I admit, sir, I am somewhat stymied."

Pemberton was puzzled, looked out toward the great fat earthworks, saw a burst of dirt from an artillery shell, another down the line. It was the same as it had been for days now, the Federal gunners targeting anything they could see, any movement. As far as he could see, there was nothing anyone was doing they had not been doing for a week.

He heard hoofbeats, saw Forney, leading his staff, the same men whom Pemberton had just seen. He sagged, thought, Does no one follow my wishes? I have no need to see Forney.

"General, welcome! I assume Major Lockett has given you the latest information. The enemy has taken to the ground, like so many moles. I had thought perhaps a council was in order, to plan some strategy to counter their actions. Is it true, sir, that General Johnston is en route, to strike the enemy's rear flank?"

The words rolled across Pemberton like a blanket of thorns.

"You will not speak of General Johnston's intentions. If I find out what those intentions are, I will tell you. Right now, it is best if the army continues to believe there is some salvation awaiting them."

Forney seemed surprised by Pemberton's attitude, made a quick glance at Lockett, and said, "We must all believe that, General. If we lose faith in our actions here, there is no reason to fight on. But the situation is changing, and we must find the way to change along with it. The enemy is pushing his people to close range, too close for our artillery to be of use. He must certainly believe he can launch an assault from close range at some point along our lines. We must strike back at him, prevent that before it begins."

Pemberton stared past him, could hear the thump of artillery far to the right, a great many thumps suddenly coming toward him from the town, the incessant shelling from the river. He saw an ambulance now, riding away from the redoubt, the mule pulling it toward him with a slow stumbling gait. The driver seemed to perk up at the sight of him, moved past now, a wave rather than a salute.

"How do, sir! Them Yanks is picking at us like skeeters. Wouldn't do for ya to poke your head up to take a look-see. That's what these boys here was doin'. Not good a'tall."

The ambulance moved past, and Pemberton absorbed the man's advice.

"Major, it is certain that if I make any attempt to observe the enemy's activities, I will become something of a target, wouldn't you say?"

Lockett nodded, his head down.

"Yes, sir. I thought you should know what the enemy is up to."

Forney's voice rose now, a show of frustration.

"General, we require some instruction out here as to how you wish us to counter the enemy's movements! My men are being shot down if they so much as sit upright. I'm hearing so many complaints about the lack of rations—"

"Enough, General. You know your duty. You hold the rank of major general because you have been taught how to deal with the enemy. So . . . deal with him! Major Lockett, carry the word to each division commander that I will expect them to counter the enemy with aggression and wisdom. You have provided the earthworks. I am relying on my commanders to provide the fight!"

Forney stared at him, no expression, and after a pause, Forney said, "As you order it, sir. However, since these men are being told to make a strong fight, it would be most helpful if someone **back there** could find a way to provide rations."

CHAPTER THIRTY-THREE

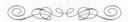

BAUER

NORTHEAST OF THE 3RD LOUISIANA REDAN JUNE 6, 1863

It was common sense, no one surprised that the rebels would try to find a better way to avoid the brutal punishment they were taking from the sharpshooters. All along the massive dirt walls, holes began to appear, and it didn't require a naval officer to understand that what the rebels had done was create what could only be called port-holes. The officers had studied the new configuration with their field glasses, and word had passed that the holes were in fact jabbed through the thick dirt using any kind of pipe, including stovepipe, wrecked cannon barrels, or anything else that was simply hollow. The Federal officers had sent that down to the sharpshooters, who had countered that tactic with some common sense of their own.

Bauer had shifted position, a new hiding place dug out of yet another rotten tree stump, a mound of dirt shoveled up in front of him, covered with a small piece of leather, a perfect rest for the musket. On both sides of the mound, brush had been jabbed into the ground as camouflage, so that even with the telltale wisp of smoke from the musket, any rebel gunner would have a difficult time finding a precise aim. The iron sights on his musket were set exactly in the direction that a stovepipe was pointing at him. Firing a few preparatory rounds, Bauer had drawn a bead straight down the pipe. All he needed was a glimpse of movement, a hint that a rebel marksman was taking aim through what was supposed to be his new safe place.

Bauer kept his head low, eyed the small round hole, no more than eighty yards away, could see a speck of daylight on the far side. He paid no attention to anything to either side of his intended target, couldn't have made any other shot without adjusting his position completely, possibly disturbing the brush that framed his hiding place. He had anchored his musket solidly on the leather pad, and he eased his shoulder forward, just enough to feel the butt of the musket. One hand rested on top of the breech, clamping the musket in place as he pushed his shoulder more tightly against the butt. He had already bruised himself severely by holding the butt too loosely, the recoil of the musket punching him backward, a lesson quickly learned. The musket was hard against him now, poking at the painful bruise, and he ignored that, removed his hand from the breech, the iron sights still centered on the hole. He could feel his heart beating, the cold anticipation, stared at the speck of daylight, the far side of the rebel works, tried to control his breathing. It was only a few seconds, and he saw the flickering motion now, the daylight suddenly gone. He tried to keep himself calm, deliberate motion, no time to waste, squeezed the trigger, the hammer striking down on the percussion cap, the musket erupting in a smoky blast. He looked up over the musket, stared angrily at the blinding smoke, said aloud, "Clear away. Now!"

The breeze obliged him, the gray fog drifting off, and he sighted along the barrel, into the stovepipe, could see the speck of daylight again.

Behind him, a surprise. The voice of Willis.

"Well, you didn't miss. No sand flew. I've got your relief here. I guess it's his time. Need to find out if he can shoot straight."

Bauer watched as Willis crawled forward, another man behind him, the redheaded boy, Private O'Daniel. Bauer was annoyed, wasn't ready to be replaced yet. He looked back out toward the rebels and said, "Not sure what I hit. Can't tell at all."

"Does it matter? Looked to me like you sent a ball right down that pipe. Pretty sure about that.

If there was some poor joker on the other side, he's on his back with a hole in his head, and a handful of his friends gathered round. They'll think it was a lucky shot, and one of 'em will step up there to get his revenge." Willis turned to O'Daniel. "Get into position quick. You might have a shot right away."

O'Daniel slid forward and said in a low nervous voice, "Good shooting, Dutchman. My turn now. Some don't think I can do this. Just show me a reb, and I'll show you what I'll do to him."

Bauer eased back slowly from the firing position, thought, Words don't do it, son. But he knew what the boy was trying to prove, that the whole company would want to know how he did out here. Bauer handed him the musket and said, "I didn't reload."

"No need. Mine's all set. You can take yours on back with ya."

Bauer realized O'Daniel had brought two muskets, one in his hand, one slung across his back. Smart, he thought. Shoulda thought of that.

The boy moved up to the sandy mound, was in position now, said something to himself, more nervous jabbering, and Willis said, "Take it easy, Private. Slow, careful aim. You take too long to get set, and one of those butternut farm boys might get off a shot."

O'Daniel acknowledged with a wave of his hand that made Bauer flinch. The boy had always been reluctant to stand out, to do anything to draw attention to his obvious youth. But youth was very apparent now, the boy shifting positions, in the open, still nervous, words now, a brief prayer.

Willis was close beside Bauer now, said, "The men insist on betting. Never heard so much worthless talk, but every man coming out here's got a dime wager on how many rebs he's gonna kill. There's a dozen betting against this one. He hits somebody, he'll be the richest man in the platoon. It's stupidity."

"None of that for me. Still have no idea if I hit anything. How would any of 'em know?"

"Can't. Like I said. Stupidity. But if it slows 'em down out here, makes 'em more careful, then fine. I'm not gonna tell 'em they can't do it. But sooner or later, somebody's fists are gonna fly because the rest of 'em insist he missed."

Bauer hadn't succumbed to any of that. No one could win a bet if you couldn't see if they had hit anything. Or anybody. The best they could hope for was no obvious evidence they had missed, provided by the sand around the pipe. The company had several good marksmen, O'Daniel not yet among them, and Bauer had wondered how many of the others had claimed to make a perfect shot when their fire was so inaccurate that no telltale punch in the sand just meant the ball had passed completely above the enemy's works.

O'Daniel was still agitating, slid his musket forward onto the leather pad, the second weapon leaned up on the sand, and he sat up again, seemed to gather himself, peering out, adjusting the second musket, leaning it up a few inches closer to him.

"Careful, Red," Bauer said. "You're in the open. Too much movement . . ."

He heard the crack, O'Daniel's head flopping forward, falling onto his musket, the barrel pointing straight up now. Willis cursed, crawled forward quickly, pulled hard on O'Daniel's collar, yanking him back. Bauer saw the hole in the boy's forehead, a small fountain of blood flowing over his face, the eyes closed, no movement at all. Willis shoved Bauer's shoulder, said, "He was too eager. . . . I knew better than to bring him out here. Dammit! Get up there and stick one in that rebel's eyeball!"

Bauer crawled to the musket, cold in his chest, angry at himself, thought, I should have told him, warned him. Taught him.

Willis jarred him to the job.

"Shoot the bastard!"

Bauer saw Willis dragging O'Daniel behind a thick clump of brush, and Bauer leaned against the sandy bank, tried to steady himself, his hands gripping O'Daniel's second musket, his breathing in hard gasps. Willis had the boy laid out flat, cursed, looked again at Bauer, pointed out, the black glare in his eyes.

"Shoot! Only one of 'em knows exactly where you are, and he'll be watching this spot!"

Bauer tried to soak up the idiocy of making himself a target to a rebel who knew exactly where he might be. But there was no arguing with Willis, ever, and Bauer forced himself to roll over, sliding the musket into place, trying to push himself into position, one part of his brain screaming at him to stay low. Musket fire began now, close by, one of the parallel trenches a few yards from Bauer's firing pit. He looked back, saw Willis dragging the boy that way, a quick scamper, others jumping up, grabbing O'Daniel's body, sliding him down into cover. The muskets fired again, an effort by the others to keep any rebel's head down. Bauer watched the scene, the muskets pulled back, reloaded, and he clenched his fists, kept low, too low, heard Willis hissing at him, "You're the only one who can do it. Shoot the bastard!"

The words added to the jumble of noise in Bauer's brain, and he closed his eyes, thundering heartbeats, tried to take himself out there, to see beyond the stovepipe, knowing what Willis knew, that the rebel had made a good shot, would be looking to do it again. Right now, he thought, that man's staring out here, waiting, watching.

The ball spit hard into the sand in front of him, Bauer flinching, hunching downward, and Willis's words came again.

"Now! He's got to reload!"

Bauer poked his head up, lined his eyes on the musket's sights, thought of the second weapon the boy had brought. Oh God, the rebel . . . he could have one, too. Might not have to reload . . .

The zip of the ball passed close to his left ear, a small breath of stinging air, and Bauer grabbed his ear, no damage, fought the screaming need to duck out of the way. He steadied his hand, found the hole of daylight, tried to calm his breathing, slid the musket out and in, anchoring it, flexed his fingers, stared down the sights. The daylight in the hole was obscured now, clear movement, a musket barrel sliding forward, a man's face, magnified in his brain, the target. Bauer aimed carefully, squeezed the trigger, the musket firing in a hard lurch against his shoulder, more blinding smoke. But there was another sound now, distinct, his ears focused on the direction, a hard, sharp scream from beyond the hole. Men were shouting out now, anger, cursing him, and Bauer released the musket, his hands shaking, slid low, hard breathing, turned, leaned back against the bank of sand. He looked over to the trench, saw faces watching him, the men protected by the cotton bales. One man was cheering now, a fist in the air, and Willis pointed to the rebel works.

"They'll be looking for you. Don't wait."

Bauer reloaded, rolled back over, slid the musket into position, kept it motionless, his eyes just above the musket, the sights aligned, aimed at the stovepipe, a circle of daylight, clear, no movement.

He stared until his eyes watered, and he blinked through sand in his eyes, heard the muskets firing again close by, knew it was useless, just noise, an answer to the cursing from the rebels. Someone's friend, he thought. Maybe their sergeant. And maybe I shot him in the eye. Like he was trying to do to me.

The rebel works showed no other movement, the muskets from the Wisconsin men nearby keeping the enemy's heads down. Bauer held his stare on the pipe, words chattering through his brain. Nobody's sticking their heads up over there, he thought. They're gonna keep using this pipe, 'cause they think they're so damn smart. Some officer's wonderful idea, a pipe through the sand, a perfectly safe place to put your weapon, your face. He saw another flicker in the speck of daylight, startling, and he calmed himself, took a breath, let it out slowly, squeezed the trigger one more time.

He slid low again, reloading, went through the automatic motions, tore the cartridge with his teeth, poured the powder into the barrel, caught sight of Willis again, still watching him, and Willis showed him a fist, pumped it slightly, and gave him a smile.

"What in blazes are they doing down there?"

Bauer stopped digging, straightened

his back, the work stopping for a brief moment. The cotton bales were close in front of them all, other protection as well, hay bales, logs, anything that could be dragged forward during the night to stop a musket ball.

Far down to the left, Bauer saw what the men were pointing to, a stack of what seemed to be rail ties, piled in a neat square, stacked much taller than a man.

Beside him, Kelly said, "It looks like some kind of tower."

The officer in charge came forward, another of the lieutenants.

"What's the rest for? I didn't order you to stop."

Kelly held his shovel in his hands and said, "Sir, look down there. That the Illinois fellas?"

The lieutenant glanced that way, and Bauer saw a shrug.

"Indiana. They built a damn tower. Their colonel was bragging about it to Colonel McMahon. They got some sharpshooter, thinks he's Daniel Boone. Coonskin cap, the whole outfit. An officer, no less. Their colonel said that thing's high enough, they can shoot right over the top of the earthworks, pop any of those Louisiana boys right off their parapet. All right, rest time's over. The captain's got a wager going with the fellows on either side of us about which company will be the first to draw up to spitting distance of the rebel works. I'm counting on you boys to win."

The lieutenant moved away, back through the trench, and Bauer saw a sergeant motioning to them with a wave of his hand.

"You heard him, gents. Now we know why the officers spend so much time hiding back there behind them trees. They's playin' card games with our immortal souls. Best ya keep diggin'."

T he commissary wagons had slipped up closer to the front lines, and when the labor parties completed their shifts, the rewards waited nearby. Bauer had stuffed himself with ham and cold pickled cabbage, the noontime meal following a pile of slapjacks that morning, more ham to go with that.

He licked his fingers, the last remnants of honey, a surprising luxury handed out in small dabs throughout the company. The hero's name was Hough, the man stumbling into a beehive, enduring the torture of a mass of stingers to secure the amazing treasure. Hough was one of the sergeants who Bauer had guessed would take over the vacancy left by Finley's death, and Bauer knew the sergeant's generous gift had now planted Hough firmly among the unit's most beloved men.

Bauer sipped from the tin cup, the water actually drinkable, a spring back behind their position that was serving the entire regiment well. He looked down into the cup, could actually see the bottom, a luxury he had come to appreciate as much as the amazing amount of food. He had enjoyed all he could hold, started to toss the last remnants from the cup, thought better of that, drank the last gulp. For a long moment, he sat in silence, ignored the frivolity that was breaking out around him. For days now, the men had welcomed the rations and their relative safety along the front lines with outbursts of athletics, wrestling matches, knife tossing, what seemed to substitute for the aggression they all felt for the enemy. The labor was just that, shovels instead of muskets, but this was nothing like the swamps of Louisiana. The ground here was mostly dry, a mix of sand and soft clay.

O'Daniel's death had thrown a pall over the entire company, putting even the hard cases into a kind of mourning that had surprised Bauer. Bauer wanted to believe he was growing immune to that, but the pain was always there, even for men he had nearly forgotten about. Every death he witnessed now seemed to dredge through him like an iron plow, bringing it all back, all those memories from Shiloh, every face coming back to him, the look in their eyes. It felt like a strange revelation to him that when those men died, they went away, and stayed away, and no matter how angry or sad he was, nothing brought them back. He wouldn't speak of it, not even to Willis. The others spoke of death in that religious way, the souls going to Heaven, Divine justice, always some kind of reason. But the boy's death just made him angry, every time he thought about it. If he's in that better place, there's a whole family in Wisconsin whose "place" is so much worse. There will be gallons of tears from all those sisters, every life changed by his loss. He thought of the chaplain. This is a question for you, Father. Is this Divine justice? Or did God just make another mistake?

He stared at the tin plate, the last piece of salty ham, tried to see the boy's face, the ridiculous shock of red hair, felt nothing at all. Something's wrong with you, he thought. Or maybe we always knew that boy was done for, like he brought it with him. Even he seemed to know it. All that talk about how much he was needed back home. Look at me. Nobody **needs** me worth a lick, and I ain't got so much as a damn scratch. He thought of Willis, the man's perfect calm in the face of the most terrifying fights. Like he just doesn't care. Maybe that's how it's done. That's what makes a man good at this. You're not scared to death if you don't care about dying. That boy . . . cared too much.

He shook his head. Stop thinking. The best thing you can do right now is find a place to take a nap. He let out a long, low belch and put a hand on his stomach.

"You'll give away our position, Private. We're not running out of rations, you know. Don't be such a damn hog." Willis walked up close, stood over him, didn't sit. "Boiling up some beef for tonight, they tell me. Lots of cabbage, too, pickled and otherwise. And sweet potatoes. There's a damn mountain of those things back there. I guess they're afraid if they don't feed us for a change, we'll up and quit. Let's go."

Bauer kept his hand on his stomach and said, "Go where? I'm pretty comfortable right here."

The humor faded from Willis's voice.

"Get on your damn feet, Private. We have a mission."

Bauer rose slowly, stretched lazily, and Willis pointed to his musket.

"Take that along. You're gonna make us all proud. I got permission from the colonel to make a visit to that tower."

"The rail tie thing? Why?"

"You're not curious about it? The provost guards are chasing after people all over the place who're trying to get close enough to peek inside. We can go down there and march right in. I got us orders. Damn, Dutchie, show a little appreciation."

Bauer retrieved the musket, and Willis was already moving away.

"Forward, march, Private. We don't have all afternoon. You've still got another shift up front with the shovel."

NEAR BATTERY HICKENLOOPER, OPPOSITE THE 3RD LOUISIANA REDAN

The tower was massively thick, and Bauer stood in admiration, not so much for the structure as for the man who had come up with the idea. He looked at the man now, ignored the lieutenant's straps on the coat, focused instead on the man's head, the fat coonskin cap. Willis slapped Bauer on the back and said, "Lieutenant Foster, this is Private Bauer, 17th Wisconsin, Company B. Finest marksman in the outfit. We would be privileged if the 23rd Indiana would provide us the opportunity to have Private Bauer take a stab at one of those Louisiana fellows over there."

Foster stood with his hands on his hips and appraised Bauer, spit a stream of brown goo past Bauer's foot.

"This ain't no carnival show, you know. We're keeping the enemy's heads down over there, so's we can get these earthworks pushed up close. That's the job, Lieutenant . . . what's your name again?"

"Willis."

"Willis. I'm Henry Foster. Call me Coonskin. Guess you figured out why. Wisconsin boys, eh? Never known any crack shots from up your way. Tell you what, Private. You follow me on up there. I'll show you how this duty's performed." He paused, tilted his head, looked at Willis. "You got the fee?"

Willis was prepared, held out the twenty-five-cent piece, Foster taking it without comment. Bauer wanted to ask Willis what had just happened, thought better of it, couldn't avoid staring at the absurd hat.

Bauer waited for the next move. Foster stepped back and said, "All right, Private. Your lieutenant's paid the toll. You're entitled to a real treat."

"Thank you, sir."

"Coonskin. You call me sir again and I'll toss you off this thing."

Foster moved into the tower, climbed up on the natural steps made by the uneven rails. Willis leaned close to Bauer and said, "Make us proud, Dutchie."

Bauer felt the odd sensation that a game was afoot, moved into the tower, watched Foster scurrying up like some demented bug. Bauer followed, felt his way a step at a time, saw Foster above him, a hand down.

"Gimme your musket."

Bauer obeyed, climbed up the last few feet, the top of the tower a small platform, enough height for a man to squat without being seen.

Foster said, "Now, you listen here. There's rules to this. You don't just stand up there and start shooting to beat hell. Rebs too smart for that. You got to catch 'em when they're angry, when they ain't thinkin' straight. Load that thing."

Bauer nodded silently, fought the instinct to say **sir**. Foster peered up, spit another stream of tobacco out the side of the tower, then sat, leaned against the thick brown wood, his back to the rebel position. Bauer completed the loading, the question burning inside of him.

"Mr. Coonskin . . . how is it this thing hasn't been blown to bits? We're awful close."

"Oh, they've tried, Private. It cost 'em a couple of six-pounders for their trouble. Captain Hickenlooper, he's General McPherson's chief engineer. Well, he's put a battery right over there, within a hundred fifty yards of those rebs. You can be sure they're not too pleased about that. But anytime one of their guns tries to hit this thing, or anything else for that matter, Hickenlooper's pieces blow it to hell. Day or night. It's a sight to behold. But the rebels learn quick. I been squattin' up here for a couple days now, pickin' those boys off right regularly. A few of my boys done the same. Not right for a platoon commander to get all the fun. So, naturally, the rebs over there hate me plenty. They keep bringing their best squirrel shooters up there on their parapet to pick me off. Only problem for those boys is . . . this squirrel shoots back." Foster removed the coonskin hat, put his hand inside, three fingers poking through. "You see this? They catch sight of this fur, and it gets their blood boiling. Like I said, Private. Fun."

Foster picked up a small stick and inserted it into the hat.

"Now, get yourself up and ready, on your knees.

I'll draw fire. You pop up and aim quick, and I promise you, you'll have a target."

Bauer felt nervous now, knew Willis was watching everything down below, heard voices, others as well, taunts and teasing. He double-checked the percussion cap, and Foster raised the coonskin cap slowly, the fur rising just above the wooden rail. He slid it to one side now, then moved it back the other way, and now the crack came, the musket ball smacking the wood outside the tower, close behind Foster's back. Bauer saw a beaming smile, and Foster motioned him upward, then shouted out, "Aaaagh!"

Bauer rose up, leveled the musket on the rail, and scanned the rebel works in a frantic search. Across the way, the redan had dug-out rifle ports above a platform, and he saw the motion, a handful of men in a cluster on the parapet, field glasses, one man with a musket, reloading, another musket coming up. Beside him, Foster kept the hat in motion toward the corner and called out again.

"Aaaagh. You got me. Dang, it hurts!"

Bauer tried to concentrate, aimed at the man with the field glasses, the two round eyes staring toward him, and Bauer let out a breath, slowly, the sights lined up perfectly, and fired the musket.

Foster was up quickly, field glasses of his own, and shouted again, this time down toward the ground.

"Whoeee! Got him! Hey, boys, get ready to take

some turns up here. Rebs are gonna pitch a fit. Wisconsin here just took down one of their officers!" Foster planted the coonskin on his head and looked at Bauer. "Nice shooting, Private."

Bauer felt a strange stirring in his stomach.

"Should I reload?"

"Nah. You're done. Twenty-five cents gets you one round. I need my boys to get back up here and go to work. We're still digging all around us every minute of the day and night. We're working the shovels in shifts. Doing shifts up here, too."

The voice came from below.

"Coonskin! Hang on up there. There's an officer here who's coming up!"

Foster scowled.

"Sightseers. Every hour or two some colonel's gotta have a peek. Somebody's gonna get their head blown off."

Bauer heard the man climbing, small grunts, boots on the wooden timbers, caught the smell of cigars. He saw the hat now, wide-brimmed, and the man reached up to the platform, Foster taking his hand, the last bit of effort. The man looked at both of them, nodded politely, no smile, and said, "Don't mean to be in the way. Marvelous thing you've done here. Captain Hickenlooper says you're helping his efforts considerably."

"Thank you, sir."

The man glanced at Bauer, a slight nod, then stood slowly, leaning his arms up on the rail, staring out. Bauer had a jolt of fear, wanted to say something, caution the man, and the musket fire came now, the officer offering too much of a target. But the ball whistled past, another smacking the wood, and the officer reacted, squatted down, and said, "I seem to have attracted a bit of attention."

Foster smiled.

"That's what we're up here for, sir."

"Well, you boys go on about your business. Just had to see this. Well done. Well done indeed."

The man dropped down quickly, and Foster motioned to Bauer, pointing down. Bauer started the descent, waited for the officer to clear the way, dropped the last few feet, saw Willis, silent, wide-eyed. The senior officer stared up for a long moment, lit a cigar, nodded approvingly toward the tower.

"Yep. Well done."

He moved away now, a pair of aides waiting for him, the man slipping down into a ravine, then back, quickly out of sight. Willis made a sound, and Bauer saw him staring out that way, and Bauer said, "What's wrong, Sammie?"

"You know who that was?"

"Some senior commander. Coonskin said something about a colonel."

"You didn't see his straps?"

"Didn't look. Sorry. Did I mess up?"

Willis laughed now, a rare outburst, and Foster emerged from the tower now.

"What's ailing you?" he asked. "You got some joke I need to hear?"

Willis kept the smile, looked toward the ground.

"I'd say so. You get him visiting you often?"

Foster adjusted the fur hat, said, "Always some dang parade coming through here. Looks like he didn't even have a horse. Who was he? Division?"

Willis looked at Bauer now, still the smile.

"No. Little bigger chest than that, Coonskin. That was General Grant."

They walked through the guard posts, Willis leading the way, crossed a wide hardpan road. Bauer worked to keep up with Willis's pace, hadn't seen him this energized in a long time.

"Sammie, you in a hurry? There's time for me to do my shovel shift. Don't worry."

Willis led him down into a deep cut, men nodding to them, silent acknowledgment, no conversation. Bauer struggled to catch up, both men climbing a steep hillside, and Willis halted just before the crest, catching his breath. Bauer was there now.

"How in blazes you know that was General Grant, anyway? I didn't see any fancy uniform."

"That's why you're a private. You think that if they make you a general, you're gonna parade all across the front lines like some prize-winning rooster? He had his stars on his shoulder, but that's it. No dress uniform, no horse, no big staff trailing out behind him. Smart. That's why he's Grant and you're not."

"Wowee. I was right next to him. Sammie, they shot at him! I'd have been there if he'd a been killed!" Bauer flopped down, sat on the sloping hillside. "Maybe I shoulda told him I shot down a reb officer. Guess he'd have been pleased with that. Or maybe not. Mighta gotten him really ticked at me. That wouldn't have been good at all."

Bauer was suddenly consumed with worry, and Willis sat beside him.

"What's eating you? Old Coonskin confirmed you got an officer. Good shot."

"Well, you sure about that? I hear officers don't care for us taking down their own kind."

"You're talking to an officer right now, you jackass. Take it from me, you kill any rebel you see. If he's got brass buttons, you kill him twice. Besides, that good shooting you did won me a bet. We had a wager with those Indiana boys. I guessed right, that you'd do the job. Picked up a silver dollar for it."

"You won a bet? What if I'd have missed?"

Willis pulled himself up to his feet and motioned for Bauer to do the same.

"Then you'd owe me a dollar."

CHAPTER THIRTY-FOUR

SPENCE

ONE MILE EAST OF VICKSBURG
JUNE 11, 1863

It had been another brutal day in the hospital, but the numbers of wounded had seemed to slacken just a little. Lucy had barely noticed that, but the doctor had, with another observation as well. A great many of the men they treated now had head wounds, musket balls piercing faces and scalps. It had not occurred to her at all that if this was the new routine, it meant that up at the front lines, there would be far more men who had no reason to visit the hospital at all. A head wound was more often fatal, and the ambulances wouldn't bother to bring those men far off the lines. For Lucy, the greatest relief had come from the fewer number of gruesome shrapnel wounds, something the doctor appreciated as well. Instead of the decision to remove a limb, or try to rescue a man from the crushing trauma to his organs, the decisions and procedures were much simpler. Lucy knew better than to ask why the kinds of wounds had changed. She was just happy to be accepted as one of the nurses, no matter the hours or the job she had to perform. Even the woman most critical of her seemed finally to welcome her willingness to help.

The men had gathered at the fire pit, the usual banter, loud voices with complete knowledge of the situation on the front lines. Lucy moved toward them, carrying a large oval platter, too tired to eat, too hungry not to. She moved up close behind Mr. Cordray, waited for a pause in the jabber, tried not to pay attention to what was being said. She was there now to fulfill one simple chore. The men were cooking slabs of meat over the fire, and Lucy had been sent by Cordray's wife to bring back whatever allotment of the meat was theirs. She stayed back from the men, the platter growing heavier, and she focused with bleary eyes on the pattern in the china. She knew it had come to the cave along with other luxuries from their home, a valiant effort to make the cave seem more comfortable.

The men seemed to notice her now, and Cordray turned to her, eyes on her dress.

"Oh, greetings, Miss Spence. That's my wife's garment, is it not?"

"Yes, sir, it is. I had little choice. I hope to have time to visit my own wardrobe tomorrow, and I can provide for myself. I have apologized to Mrs. Cordray for soiling her dresses. Every effort is made at the hospital to prevent any nurse from suffering even the smallest bloodstain."

She ignored their scan of her clothing, didn't care if they picked up the sarcasm in her words. Cordray seemed oblivious to all of that and said, "Well, you should apologize to me. Those dresses are purchased by my funds, not hers. I work hard for my meager earnings, and right now, none of us are able to work at all."

"Leave her be, Cordray. I've seen the hospital. The nurses are doing work no woman should ever experience. There is indecency there that would put my own wife to hysterics."

The voice came from another of the cave-side neighbors, whose house in Vicksburg lay close behind Cordray. Lucy nodded politely, appreciated the courtesy.

"Thank you, Mr. Atkins. I am just doing my part. These soldiers are paying a horrible price to protect us. But, Mr. Cordray, I shall not trouble you any further by causing ruin to Isabel's dresses. I shall bring down my own. Any of the ambulance drivers would be pleased to assist me."

Cordray sniffed.

"That's another thing, Miss Spence. You seem to be keeping company with men of considerable disrepute. Some of those teamsters are a dreadful sort. You should be more concerned with decorum, your place in this community. A young girl cannot afford to toss aside her dignity with such carelessness."

Lucy felt a boiling heat in her brain, saw the arrogant sneer on Cordray's face, but her rescuer spoke up.

"Now, John, you can stop that sort of speculation. I have spoken to a number of the teamsters, and there is nothing in their gossip to suggest that Miss Spence has been a part of anything sordid. In fact, quite the contrary. Miss Spence, forgive me for saying, but you have earned a considerable reputation among those men, and among the doctors as well. It is no secret that you are not formally trained for nursing. I admit to admiring your courage in assisting there. Few would do such a thing. Certainly not you, John."

"My place is with my family. I do not wish to insult you, Miss Spence, but I had assumed you would do more to help out with the children, or assist my wife with the hardships we are suffering. I did not expect you to be gone all hours, tending to those soldiers."

Cordray turned to the fire pit, stabbing a slab of meat with a long fork, and Lucy suddenly realized he was spouting off as a show for the others.

"If you wish, sir, I shall return to my home in the

town. I do not wish to be a burden, and it is actually a bit closer to the hospital."

She waited for a response, wondered if he was all bluff. The others watched him, expectant, and she could see smiles, the men fully understanding that Cordray had dug himself into a hole more embarrassing than his own cave. He toyed with the meat, didn't look at her, just said, "Nonsense. You are our guest. It is far too dangerous at your home, as it is at ours. Bring the platter closer. The meat seems adequately cooked."

He stabbed what seemed to be a large steak, and she held out the platter, the meat slapping down, juice spilling over the sides.

"Please have Mrs. Cordray divide that among the children, and of course, yourself. I shall be along shortly."

Lucy looked at the meat, charred black on the edges, a puddle of red juice, the wonderful smell now filling her, adding to her growling hunger.

"Thank you, sir. I will try to be more considerate of your family's needs."

She wasn't even sure what that meant, knew it would play well with the others, would likely prevent Cordray from speaking ill of her behind her back. But a voice spoke up, another of the men whose cave sat down the hill from Cordray.

"Hold on there. So, tell me, John, just how do you know it's prepared correctly? Ever cooked that before?"

"You know very well I have not. Does this have to be more difficult than it already is?"

Lucy looked at the meat, was ravenous now, itched to escape the banter, and said, "It appears to be the perfect steak, sir. We are grateful for such bounty. Whose cow was butchered?"

The milk cow had vanished days before, supplying the needs of a handful of families, the beef more valuable now than the milk. Lucy saw men looking down, a strange reluctance to answer the question. Cordray said, "You should not question these things, Miss Spence. You have been helpful to the wounded soldiers, to be sure. But we have learned of other forms of assistance, of other needs the army has. Like the soldiers, our supplies of flour have been consumed. The hams are gone; there is no molasses or salt. Our coffee comes from straw and the skin of sweet potatoes. If this war is about sacrifice, then so be it. But I will not have my children go hungry. None of us wishes to be out here, none of us wishes to starve. I fear, as we all do, Miss Spence, that if our army does not break the chain the Yankees have wrapped around us, starvation is a possibility."

Lucy studied his face, saw genuine sadness, the others agreeing with silent nods, one man uttering a soft word.

"Amen."

Lucy looked at the steak again, one part of her too hungry to care what they were talking about.

But their collective mood and the looks on their faces carried meaning. Her curiosity was suddenly overpowering.

"I do not understand. Yes, I agree we must make sacrifices. I see those sacrifices every day in the wounds of the soldiers."

The other man spoke up, Atkins, her defender.

"Miss Spence, I would suggest you take that dinner back to John's children, and enjoy your meal. The less spoken of this the better."

"The less spoken of what?"

Cordray stabbed another steak, the plates coming toward him in the hands of the other men.

"Here, Charles. I wish I had more to share." He repeated the move, the men gradually filing away, and Lucy held her ground, knew he would speak to her only when he was ready. The last of the meat was gone now, the neighbors adding a small polite farewell to her, a gesture of kindness, as though soothing any hurt put on her by Cordray.

He turned to her now and said, "I don't know if that will be any more acceptable if it gets too cold. Come, child, let's go to the cave. My wife will just have to make do. I do not wish an argument with her, and the children must be fed."

She studied the meat, felt a turn in her stomach, and said, "What is this?"

He moved past her, then stopped, resigned to a response.

"Miss Spence, the army has now issued orders

that their commissary people limit the rations to the troops to one-fourth what they normally receive. And yet even that has become impossible to fulfill. We had a staff officer come through here today who passed this information to us, as a form of counsel. We are being advised in the strongest terms that we do as the soldiers are now doing, and seek any means necessary to ensure our survival." He paused. "I am told by the colonel that the meat is actually quite palatable. The soldiers are said to find it agreeable, considerably more so than an empty stomach."

"What is it, Mr. Cordray?"

"I regret, Miss Spence, that I have had to put the ax to my mule. This, I'm afraid, is mule meat."

She had hesitated only slightly, her hunger too severe. But then came the surprise. The meat was not only palatable, she actually enjoyed it. The children had eaten as much as she had, their hunger suddenly obvious, though even the sickly girl seemed more thin than Lucy had noticed. But the meat had satisfied them all, at least for this night. All, of course, except Mrs. Cordray. Lucy had ignored the argument, the perfect stubbornness of the woman who could not stomach the thought of eating a mule. Cordray had made every effort to soothe whatever anxiety she had, to no avail, something Lucy was accustomed to seeing now. After a half hour's fruitless effort, he had sat down with Lucy and the children and satisfied his own hunger. Lucy had no idea what Isabel had eaten, if anything at all. But with a full stomach, and at least one night's comfortable sleep rolling over her, Lucy didn't really care. As she drifted into slumber on her thin pad of a mattress, her only thoughts were about numbers. If the soldiers were eating their mules, and the civilians did the same, how long would it be before that resource too would be exhausted?

THE GREEN HOUSE HOSPITAL
JUNE 14, 1863

She huddled low beside the table, a spray of dirt tumbling hard on the tent above her.

"Get down here!"

The doctor was beneath the table, and Lucy saw terror in the man's eyes. He reached for her, missed her hand, and said again, "Get under here! Are you mad, girl?"

"But the soldier . . ."

"Nothing I can do for him until the shells stop."

She was angry now, furious at the shells that tore through the hospital, furious now at the doctor.

"This man is bleeding! You're a coward!"

Another shell impacted down the row of tents, screams and cries, the smoke rolling through the tent, choking her. She saw the doctor with his hands curled hard over his head, ignoring her completely, and she struggled to stand, heard more impacts out away from the tents, more shells shrieking in close, a sharp blast now above them, shrapnel tearing a gap in one side of the tent. She ducked low, saw through the opening, white smoke, fire, another explosion throwing a plume of dirt skyward, shards of iron whirring overhead. She knelt, her hands still up on the table, gripping the edge, her fingers soaked in the soldier's blood. Beneath the next table, she saw another nurse curled up, huddling, desperate fear. She loosened her grip on the table, the ground thundering beneath her again, the tent walls shivering from the impacts, another long rip. She waited for the next explosion, anticipating, flinching, but there was nothing, long seconds of no sound but the ringing in her ears. Around her, the tent was swirling with thick smoke, and she spit a hard cough through the burning in her throat. She struggled to pull herself up just enough to see the wounded man, unconscious, oblivious.

"Missy, get down!"

She ignored the doctor, saw the other nurse looking at her, tears and terror through the grime on the woman's face. The silence continued through the hard hiss in her ears, and now there were voices, the ever-present barking of a dog. She gripped the edge of the table again, her eyes on the wounded man, no expression on his face, the scalp to one side ripped away, just one more man with a head wound. She looked out toward the tent's entrance, saw men running, and beyond, an ambulance in a shattered heap, one man splayed out on the ground.

"Outside, Doctor!"

She moved out quickly, expected more of the blasts, but quiet had settled over the hospital, a lull in the shelling. She ran to the wreck of the ambulance, saw three men in the midst of the splintered lumber, broken and bloodied, a gaping hole in one man's chest, an arm ripped away. She tried to reach down, something holding her back, knowing that all these men were dead, that whatever wounds had brought them to the hospital no longer mattered. She looked to the teamster now, more horror, the man's head nearly severed, blood in a pool around him, the face staring up with a look of shock, familiar, Henry, her friend, the man who had provided her transportation on his ambulance.

She fought the shock, but it came in a hard wave, knocked her to her knees, and she felt the tears, unstoppable, began to sob. She tried to control herself, pulled her apron up onto her face, holding the tears, the stink of the blood on her hands overpowering. But the sobbing wouldn't stop, the grief flowing out of her, thoughts of the man's kindness, his caution, his protection. She slid to one side, sat, felt the bare dirt, the ground around the ambulance still smoking, the blast ripping away the grass. There was a hand on her shoulder now, and she wanted to scream it away, but the voice came, the doctor.

"Missy, there's nothing we can do for these boys. Must have been a direct hit. This crater . . . had to be a mortar maybe."

"Does it matter, **Doctor,** what kind of shell it was?"

"No, guess not."

She gathered herself, wiping the tears away with the apron, the sleeve of her bloody dress. She felt stronger, and stood up, helped by his hand, the crying draining away. The doctor released her and said, "They ought not be shelling hospitals. How much bigger does that flag have to be? Surely they can see it!" She glanced up, hadn't paid much attention to the yellow banner that flew above the house, knew only that it was meant to signify a hospital. The doctor was shouting now, aiming his words toward the river. "What's wrong with you? Are you savages after all?"

She couldn't avoid the image of him beneath the table, her own words.

"Doctor, I regret if I insulted you."

He turned to her, a look of anger that suddenly frightened her.

"I am supposed to be helping wounded men! I am not supposed to be suffering artillery fire! If I fear being blown into pieces, so be it! Is that what a hospital is to be? A target? Do **we** throw cannon fire at their wounded men? Do **we** take aim at the helpless?"

"I don't know, sir. Perhaps we do."

She stood in what had been her sitting room, unrecognizable now, the sunlight pouring in from a wide gash in her ceiling. The floor was a shamble of debris, plaster and wood and what remained of her furniture.

"I told you, Miss Spence. There is little here to save."

Cordray backed away, and she stayed put, frozen, absorbing the sight of what had once been her parents' home. She wanted to go through the rest, the way blocked by the destruction. The doorway to the kitchen was obliterated, a skeleton of a wall forming a barricade.

"Perhaps there are utensils . . ."

Her words drifted away, Cordray not there to hear them, the man moving back out to the street, others gathering, low talk behind her back. She tried to find the strength to move through the rubble, another man moving up behind her, a soothing voice.

"Miss Spence, this place is not safe. The roof could collapse. I am deeply sorry, but you should not remain."

Cordray was there again.

"Miss Spence," he said, "we should return to the caves. It will be dark very soon, and it is not safe to be out here. Mr. Atkins has been generous to allow us the use of his mule and carriage. I do not wish to put him in any more danger than we are in now."

Lucy focused on the single word. **Mule**. She turned, saw the faces watching her, the street surprisingly crowded, two dozen or more. It was as she had heard, that there were a great many residents who had kept to their homes, no matter the outrageous danger. She studied them, saw a woman praying, thought, yes, there but for the grace of God . . . this would be your home. But today, whatever "grace" there is has clearly ignored me. And perhaps before this is over, there will be no grace left in the world. She looked at Atkins, always the kindness, but there was no kindness in her now, her bitterness seeping through.

"How much longer before **your** mule provides the greater need than a ride into town?"

Atkins seemed hurt by the question, and she felt a burst of guilt.

"Forgive me. I am sorry, sir."

"No, Miss Spence. You are correct. We have exhausted the other beasts. My Blossom will be next, I'm afraid. My wife cannot bear to think of it. But, like Mr. Cordray, we must provide for the children."

The name stuck in her mind, and she fought the sudden need to laugh. Blossom? You named your mule . . . Blossom? And now, she thought, we shall consume Blossom.

She turned back to the wreckage of her home,

felt a shaking hysteria, cold in her hands, her chest, saw now a small portrait in the rubble. She took a step that way, knelt, pulled it gently from the debris, the glass plate cracked in half. It was an image of her as a young girl, a sharp, frowning glare, the memory of that coming back to her in every detail. She spoke in a low voice, didn't care if anyone heard her.

"I remember suffering for this, just so my mother could have it on the mantel. The man who did this made me sit still for an eternity." She tossed it onto a pile of crushed wallboard, the glass plate falling into pieces. "I suppose . . . we shall do the same now. We shall endure this for eternity."

Cordray responded, "Nonsense, child. This will end very soon. There shall yet be salvation. Have you not heard? General Johnston is advancing rapidly. The Yankees are certain to be destroyed."

She saw the hopefulness on Cordray's face, that he believed the words. She glanced back at the rubble of her home, then stepped down into the wide street, the people backing away, a sea of pity keeping their distance from her monumental stroke of misfortune.

Atkins said, "We shall help you rebuild. After all, we are neighbors."

"And if General Johnston does not come?"

Cordray seemed annoyed now, a glance at Atkins.

"You are but a girl, Miss Spence. You cannot know the workings of our army. This shall all be concluded in our favor, I assure you. Today you suffered mightily, a most unfortunate blow. The Yankees have no shame, no decency, that they would do this. But we must suffer privations for the good of our cause. In the end, the Almighty shall reward us for our nobility."

She moved out past the two men, stood at the carriage, looked now at the mule.

"Well, Blossom, shall we ride back to our holes in the ground? Then we shall show **you** our nobility."

CHAPTER THIRTY-FIVE

SHERMAN

SHERMAN'S HEADQUARTERS
JUNE 16, 1863

He wiped the butter from his chin, savored the sweetness, the biscuit warm in his mouth. He had already eaten three, a pool of butter on his plate.

"These are outstanding, Captain. Truly. My compliments to the cook."

"I will tell him, sir. And Colonel Macfeely will be most pleased at your approval."

Sherman glanced toward the others, every man with a buttery plate.

"Who would have thought the enemy would have provided for us so? One thing I know about this place, gentlemen. My stay in Louisiana taught me that Southern people do know how to fill their

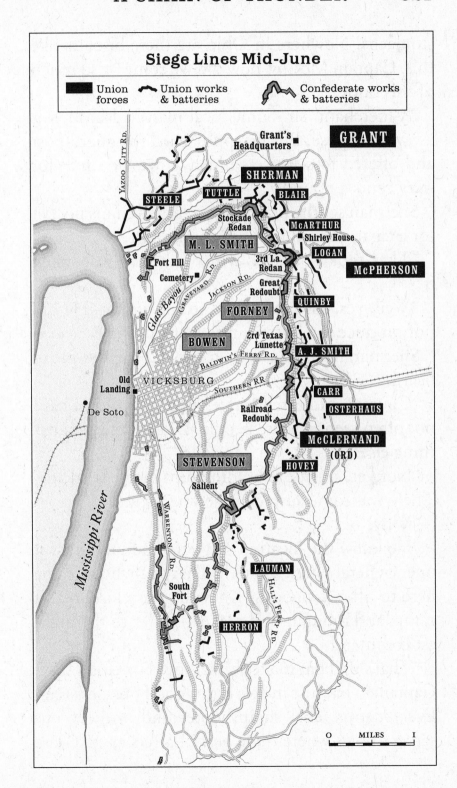

Siege Lines Mid-June

Union forces — Union works & batteries — Confederate works & batteries

GRANT

Grant's Headquarters

SHERMAN

STEELE — TUTTLE — BLAIR

Stockade Redan

McARTHUR

Shirley House

M. L. SMITH

3rd La. Redan

LOGAN

McPHERSON

Fort Hill

Cemetery

Great Redoubt

QUINBY

FORNEY

2rd Texas Lunette

BOWEN

A. J. SMITH

BALDWIN'S FERRY RD.

Old Landing

VICKSBURG

SOUTHERN RR

CARR

OSTERHAUS

De Soto

Railroad Redoubt

McCLERNAND
(ORD)

STEVENSON

HOVEY

Salient

Mississippi River

WARRENTON RD.

LAUMAN

South Fort

HALL'S FERRY RD.

HERRON

O   MILES   I

Yazoo City Rd.

Jackson Rd.

Graveyard Rd.

Glass Bayou

stomachs. Nowhere in Ohio are there biscuits like this. Captain McCoy, how did we come by so much of this butter?"

"A merchant, sir. Some local man had hidden it away, I suppose. But he approached the guard post and offered to sell us as much as we required, for sixty cents a pound."

Sherman set the plate aside, reached in his pocket for a cigar, cocked his head to one side.

"That took courage. We could have just taken it."

"Well, yes, sir. He seemed to know that. He did not produce the butter until we paid him."

Sherman lit the cigar, then stroked the stubble of beard.

"Courage **and** intelligence. A combination I have not often seen in these people. Did he offer us anything else?"

"Not yet, sir. We're holding him in the stockade. There was some suspicion he was a spy."

"Why?"

"He knew the location of your headquarters, for one. General Grant's as well. That was why he came here to offer his goods. Knew he was close to this camp, and thought he'd make his offer to the highest command."

"That's it? That makes him a spy? For God's sake, Captain. That just makes him a good businessman. Every damn rebel sharpshooter and artillery observer knows where these headquarters are. Release that man with my apologies, and request that he go home and search through whatever hiding places he has left. There's no telling what he might yet offer us." He glanced at the cigar, felt a burning bite on the tip of his tongue. "Better tobacco, perhaps. I'd pay him whatever he asked."

"Yes, sir. I'll see to it."

McCoy rose, set his plate close to Sherman's, the orderly knowing the sign, the man coming in quickly, stacking up the empty plates. Sherman saw a half biscuit on one plate, the owner, Dayton, rubbing a full stomach.

"You not going to eat that, Colonel?"

Dayton seemed to snap out of a pleasant stupor, and shook his head.

"No, sir. I had quite enough."

"Good."

Sherman picked up the piece of biscuit, made a quick wipe across the tin plate, tossed it into his mouth. He stood now, felt an overwhelming need for a nap. But the breakfast was just the first duty in what he knew would be a long day.

With so many reinforcements marching into Grant's position, Grant's lines had finally sealed off every approach to Vicksburg, anchoring hard against the river above, on Sherman's right flank, and now below, on McClernand's left. The new men had mostly come down from Memphis, one division under Francis Herron, two from Burnside's Ninth Corps, commanded by John Parke.

With the addition of Hurlbut's division, Grant's army had swollen to more than seventy thousand troops. Sherman wasn't completely certain how many rebels Pemberton had inside the enclosed ring, but no one in the Federal command doubted that what Grant had in place now would be plenty of strength to complete the job.

He moved outside the tent, his orderlies coming awake, the horse saddled, ready for whatever he required. He hesitated, thought again of the marvelous notion of a nap. No, not now. You ate too damned much. Live with that.

"Ah, General. A most pleasant good morning to you, sir!"

Sherman winced at the voice, saw Cadwallader riding toward him, the newspaperman climbing down from the horse with admirable skill. The need for a nap vanished, Sherman building the energy required for any conversation with the man who followed Grant like a foxhound.

"Mr. Cadwallader. Have you had breakfast?"

"Oh, quite so. The men over that hill had a pot of the most delectable chicken, and their cook had prepared loaves of the best bread I've had in a while."

"Those would be Illinois men."

"Correct, sir. Most hospitable chaps."

Sherman felt a tug of warning.

"They do a lot of talking, then?"

Cadwallader knew very well how Sherman felt

about him, something Sherman had never tried to hide.

"Please, General, do not concern yourself with any improper communication by your men. In fact, I came by here to confirm what is quickly becoming common knowledge. I prefer having my facts verified before I send my dispatches back east. Surely you would agree with that philosophy?"

"What facts?"

Cadwallader glanced around, seeming to search for eavesdroppers. He pointed to a log, a place Sherman spent a considerable amount of time.

"May we sit?"

"I prefer it. Ate too much."

Cadwallader laughed, moved to the log, and sat on the ground, the log to his back, making plenty of room for Sherman. Sherman lowered himself down, fought to keep his brain focused on the man who might just as likely be writing something about **him**.

"General, now that the lines are completely sealing in the rebel position, I must speculate that their capitulation will occur very soon."

"I thought you were going to talk facts. Not speculation."

"Well put, sir. I have learned not to inquire of those things General Grant does not first make known to me. I do know of our troop strength here, and I also know that General Grant has placed you in command of near half the force. Further, I know that you have ordered General Blair to march out between the Yazoo and Big Black, to guard against the sudden appearance of General Johnston's forces. There are estimates that Johnston has gathered as many as forty thousand men in his command. A sudden attack by that many rebel troops could prove most embarrassing."

"It could. It won't. So far, your information is mostly accurate. We don't know how many men Johnston has, but forty thousand is probably an exaggeration. We have plenty of eyes out there in the countryside, in case he tries to surprise us."

"A point of curiosity, if I may? Your troops are not guarding the Big Black. Is that not risky?"

Sherman didn't answer, knew his instructions to General Blair had inspired questions from Grant as well. Frank Blair had been ordered to position a sizable force well back of the Big Black, a stretch of high ground that gave the Federal troops control over vast swaths of lowlands. Sherman knew that if Johnston made it across the Big Black, Blair's deployment would severely limit the rebels' ability to maneuver. But none of this would concern a newspaperman. Not yet anyway.

"I have eliminated as much risk as possible. As I said, we have a great many eyes patrolling the countryside, including a number of cavalry units. If he comes at all, Johnston will certainly not sneak up on us."

"Will he come?"

"Ask **him**."

Cadwallader laughed again.

"Oh, very good. Yes, I should like that. Would make quite a story, that one. Perhaps after this messy affair concludes."

Sherman was running out of patience, had expected to ride up toward Blair's command, confirming that Blair's troops were placed as Sherman had instructed. He had no real reason to doubt Blair's abilities, the man being one of those division commanders who had served him well throughout the past year. Blair had been an attorney before the war, was another of the Mexican War veterans, had already led troops in the field with distinction. Sherman was perfectly comfortable that if he gave Blair an order, it would be carried out. Still, it never hurt Sherman to see that for himself.

Cadwallader was silent now, pensive, staring ahead with a look that sent a twinge of alarm through Sherman.

"I really have duties to perform. Is there anything else you require?"

Cadwallader looked down, and seemed to assemble the words.

"General, I have made an observation I find disturbing. Should I write the details into my dispatches, it could cause your commander profound difficulties."

Sherman sat up away from the log, his back straight, and felt a stab of anger.

"What kind of difficulties?"

"I hesitate to mention anything. . . ."

"Dammit, you will mention it, and right now."

"General, I am not here to inflame, no matter what you may think. Allow me to be blunt. Last week, I accompanied General Grant up to Haines's Bluff, to make the river journey to your outposts around Satartia. As you know, the general felt it necessary to visit his various outposts there, to confirm the security of his lines."

"I know all about that. Those outposts are under my command."

"Yes, well, you must also have observed that General Grant seemed to come down with some affliction. On board the steamer, the general's condition seemed to worsen, and when he retired to his quarters, I did not observe him until the next morning. But I have every reason to believe that the general was deeply intoxicated."

Sherman stood, a bolt of lightning through his brain.

"What **reasons**?"

"Oh, General, I do not wish to cause any damage to General Grant's reputation. Please understand. This is why I am speaking to you. In this army, there is no one closer to him than you are."

"I asked you . . . what reasons?"

"Well, sir, I did observe his doctor offering the

general a glass of wine, the doctor suggesting the beverage could be a useful tonic. The general did imbibe."

"How many glasses?"

"Oh, only the one, that I saw. But his absence for the rest of the evening could only have been explained by further consumption. I also suspected the general had been drinking considerably prior to that evening. He was certainly in poor condition."

"Because he was ill?"

"Well, possibly. But it is not like General Grant to take to his bed in the middle of such a journey of inspection, with enemy troops potentially in the area. There were several moments on board the boat when the naval officers did offer him a salute of sorts. The liquor certainly seemed readily available."

Sherman curled his toes in his boots, felt the sudden urge to kick Cadwallader in the teeth.

"You will not print anything of this. None of it. I will look into the matter myself." He leaned down, close to Cadwallader's face. "None of it. Do you understand me?"

"Do not try to intimidate me, General. I came to you for this very purpose, to enlighten you on what could be very damaging to the general's command. I will write none of this in my dispatches, for now."

The conclusion was left hanging, the man's smugness infuriating.

"So, you will write it no matter what I find? What the facts might be?"

"Did I say that? You are a reasonable man, General. What would you have me do?"

Sherman stood straight again, threw the spent cigar to the side, spit out scraps of tobacco.

"Do not assume I am reasonable. What would I have you do? Should you do anything to damage General Grant, I would have you walk straight into the Mississippi River until the only remaining article of your being was your hat. Should you try to surface, I would have a dozen sharpshooters ensure that you not succeed."

Cadwallader looked down at his hands, flexed his fingers, seemed to ponder that image.

"I do not completely believe you, sir. However, I wish you the best of success in your investigation."

NEAR GRANT'S HEADQUARTERS
JUNE 16, 1863

Charles Dana walked beside him, neither man speaking, Sherman making certain they were out of earshot of Grant's staff. Sherman wasn't yet sure he could trust Dana, but by now, with so much constructive activity ongoing around Vicksburg, any report Dana sent to Washington would most likely be positive. Sherman had grown sick of intrigue and political wrangling, had never had a stomach for men who spoke out of both sides of their mouths. But Dana had been with Grant on the journey to Satartia. Whether he would be honest with Sherman was a mystery, and certainly Dana had no reason to give Sherman any gifts. If Sherman was to gain any real information, he had to swallow the fact that he first had to be honest with Dana.

"I know why you're here."

Dana stopped, was holding a coffee cup, drank slowly, tossed the remnants to the side.

"Was it ever a secret?"

"Some think so. Some believe you were sent here by the War Department, by Secretary Stanton himself, to find reasons, or excuses, to have Grant removed from command. Some believe General McClernand is your ally, that he has been sending missives to the president, encouraging that same action. Some would see your presence here as a blatant attempt to smear Grant's name and reputation. Some would suggest that Grant's campaign against the enemy has been more successful than Stanton or General Halleck had expected. Or hoped. Some would—"

"Enough, General. You have a bayonet stuck in your gizzard. Pull it out. What do you want of me?"

Sherman was pulsing with anger, fought to keep it inside.

"So, you make no denials?"

"Of what? I was sent here to observe, and to report those observations to Washington. That is my job. I have no ambition for higher position in the government, no need to hang anyone from the gallows. I do not find it useful to make enemies for no good reason. Is that denial enough?"

"What happened on the journey to Satartia?"

Dana stared at him for a long moment, seemed to chew the question.

"It was a risky affair. The rebels had made a move toward capturing some of our outposts in that area, as you know. We did not complete the journey, on my responsibility."

"Your responsibility?"

"Yes. I assume you knew that after we left Haines's Bluff, General Grant had become terribly ill and had taken to his bed. When the boat neared Satartia, two of our gunboats met us with warnings to withdraw, that it was not yet safe for the general to visit there. I woke him to determine what he wished us to do. But the general was thoroughly incapacitated by his illness, and he requested that I make the decision whether to continue the journey or not. General Sherman, I am not a soldier. The decision I made was to turn back to Haines's Bluff until the area had been secured. Admittedly, I was hesitant to endanger the general's life, and my own."

Sherman knew that even before the inspection trip, Grant had been falling ill, but he hadn't been told just how sick Grant had become. He weighed Dana's story, looked hard at the man, then said, "During that time, did Grant imbibe strong spirits?"

Dana seemed surprised.

"You mean . . . was he drunk? Oh my, no. I observed him throughout the journey, and I witnessed what I can only describe as severe difficulties with his stomach. I believe he had a fever as well. I knew of no great stock of liquor on board the boat, though, of course, I am not so naïve to believe those sailors did not have spirits somewhere. Colonel Rawlins and I—"

"Rawlins was there?"

"Well, yes. Certainly."

"What of Cadwallader?"

"Yes, for a while. I try not to intersect Mr. Cadwallader. I believe, if I may suggest, sir, that you and I have one trait in common. I do not completely trust newspapermen."

"But—"

"Yes, I know, I am one. If not for something of a feud with Horace Greeley, I would still be at the **New-York Daily Tribune**. I place all blame in his direction, of course. But I assure you, General, I am acquainted with far more newspapermen than you will ever encounter. I trust only a few of them. And I dislike nearly all. I will speak nothing more of Mr. Cadwallader." He paused. "I am very much aware of General Grant's past history. I know that there are some in this army who would enjoy seeing Grant fall into a state of inebriation, and thus provide opportunity for, well, someone else to fill his position."

"Then, in your mind, Grant was not . . . drunk?"

"Not to my eye. I don't know why this is a point of discussion, and perhaps I should not ask. But should you wish another point of view, perhaps you should inquire of Colonel Rawlins."

Sherman shook his head slowly, tried to imagine that encounter.

"I'd rather not bother the colonel. His duties keep him in motion constantly. I hate to interrupt any activity that engages him."

Dana laughed, stood facing Sherman, his hands on his hips.

"I understand completely. Let me tell you something, General. If I had wanted Grant relieved of his command, I could have concocted all manner of tales that no one back east could verify for months. The general has enemies, to be sure. But they are not all in Washington. Some are much closer. Surely you know that."

Sherman felt an enormous relief, pulled a cigar from his mouth, unlit, had chewed it to a soggy nub.

"Thank you, sir. You have been of service to this army."

"Not that much. General Grant suggested I accompany one of your cavalry detachments to scout General Johnston's possible location. Along the way, my most notable accomplishment was falling off my horse. They spent more time caring for me than they did the enemy."

Sherman didn't laugh, his mind already moving on. He felt the need for an exit, still had a ride to make to the river.

"Regardless. Thank you for your time, sir."

Sherman saw his groom far behind him, holding his horse. He motioned to the man to come forward, and Dana said, "General, your loyalty toward General Grant is well placed. I assure you of that."

Sherman looked at the man, saw serious eyes, no smile.

"I know."

NEAR THE CAMP OF THE 55TH ILLINOIS
JUNE 16, 1863

The prisoner wore little more than rags, no shoes, seemed as frail as a corpse. The guards held him up, the captain standing before him, a hard shout in the man's face.

"Where did you come from? Are you seeking information? We shoot spies, you know."

The man seemed to sag, held up only by the guards, and Sherman stopped the horse, dismounted, the surprised captain falling silent. He turned toward Sherman, saluted, and Sherman said, "What is this?"

"A prisoner, sir. We captured him a short while ago. I was questioning him, sir."

Sherman looked at the man, who blinked toward him, seemed too weak to stand.

"You get his unit?"

"No, sir. He won't say much. We'll get what we want, though. Just give me some time."

Sherman heard the unnecessary bravado in the captain's voice, said to the prisoner, "You hungry?"

The man seemed unable to focus on him, nodded slowly.

"Feed him. Then he'll tell you anything you want."

The prisoner seemed to perk up, soft words.

"Thank you, Yankee."

Sherman was suddenly curious.

"Where'd you find him, Captain?"

"Down in that draw, sir. He was drinking water from the creek. We snuck up on him."

"Was he armed?" The captain hesitated, and Sherman saw through the man's bravery. "No, I don't suppose he was. Is it possible, Captain, this man is a deserter?" He motioned the guards away. "Let the man sit down. He's not going anywhere."

The captain repeated the order, and the rebel collapsed downward, his head slumped onto his chest. He raised it slowly, as though using up the last bit of his energy.

"Mighty kind of ya, Yankee. 'Fraid I was gonna be shot afore I could make it in."

"Where you from, soldier? You **are** a soldier, I assume?"

"I was, I suppose. Never kilt me no Yankees, though. Promise you that. Never."

Sherman didn't believe him, knew it didn't really matter anyway.

"Where's home?"

"Right out here a piece. Joined up to keep you bluebellies away. Guess it ain't workin'. You said something about food?"

Sherman saw a guard returning, a small plate of beans and bread. The rebel saw it as well, the man's hands reaching out, undisguised eagerness. The man devoured the rations in seconds, wiping his mouth with the back of his hand, licking at the remnants on his skin, then licking the plate.

"Guess you were hungry."

"Yes, sir. Truly. Ain't had nothing but cush-cush for days now."

"What?"

The captain spoke up now, as though imparting crucial information.

"Sir, we've been hearing that a good bit. There have been others come in, near starving, like this one. They all talk about eating pea-meal, some kind of mush."

The rebel said, "Ground-up peas. They try to make it into bread, think they're foolin' us. Nasty stuff, beggin' your pardon. Can't hardly eat the stuff a'tall. Like rock on the outside, raw slop in the middle. If you can even swallow the stuff, it rolls your guts over real bad. I'd rather have hardtack. But they say there's no flour even for that."

Sherman stood over the man, waved the guard closer, and said to the captain, "I assume you have a stockade for the prisoners?"

"Yes, sir. Back behind those woods."

"Put him there. And make sure you feed all of those boys. It wouldn't hurt to let one of 'em escape now and then. Might spread the word that there are rations here aplenty, bring in a whole damn regiment."

"By all means, sir."

The prisoner was hauled up to his feet, seemed stronger now, the guards taking him away. Sherman watched the man, blackened bare feet, shredded cloth for pants.

"Captain, did you really think he was a spy?"

The officer lowered his voice, bringing Sherman into the conspiracy.

"Oh, no, sir. But he didn't know that. We put the fear of God into some of them, they tell us everything we want to know."

"How about you just feed them, Captain. Like I said, they'll not only tell you everything they know, they'll show you where they put it. How many like him have come through your lines?"

"Dozen or so, sir. Last few days. You think there'll be more?"

"If they look like him? A great many more. But it doesn't really matter."

"Sir?"

"Never mind. Just do your duty, Captain."

"Yes, sir."

Sherman left the man, climbed quickly to the horse, his aides waiting patiently. He knew they had watched the entire encounter.

He turned to McCoy and said, "You heard of Napoleon, Captain?"

"Certainly, sir."

"'An army marches on its stomach.' Napoleon said that, hell of a long time ago."

"Yes, sir. I've heard that."

"If the rest of Pemberton's men are eating the kind of rations that man described, this whole affair will end very soon."

"Yes, sir. I see that, sir."

Sherman spoke out to the aides.

"A change of plan. We're going back up to Grant's headquarters. If he doesn't already know about the deserters, he needs to. He might actually smile."

CHAPTER THIRTY-SIX

SHERMAN

GRANT'S HEADQUARTERS
JUNE 17, 1863

Sherman was beyond furious, had crushed the cigar in his hand, threw it sharply against one wall of the tent.

"This is more than an outrage. It is . . . vainglory and hypocrisy! Even his own men would see this for what it is. No one in his command would be humbugged by such stuff!"

Grant studied the newspaper, his composure unchanged.

"Again, where did you get this?"

"General Blair. There were papers delivered to them up by the river. That's the **Missouri Bulletin**. No doubt, McClernand's claptrap has been published in every newspaper where he believes he has any influence at all. How dare this man issue a congratulatory order to his troops, when there are tens of thousands of men on this field engaged in precisely the same activity!"

Grant still studied, and Sherman forced himself into silence, could see that Grant was reading every word. Grant nodded slowly, then said, "Most impressive. Anyone reading this would believe General McClernand has won this war by himself. Possibly several wars. **'Your victories have followed in such rapid succession that their echoes have not yet reached the country.'** Clearly, General McClernand has sought a remedy for that."

"Grant, anyone who reads this nonsense must certainly conclude that he is the greatest hero this country has produced! This is a perversion of the truth to the ends of flattery and self-glorification! And there is one monstrous falsehood! He accuses myself and General McPherson with disobeying your orders on May twenty-second, as though he alone faced the enemy's guns! I should like to offer that opinion to the men of the 13th Regulars! Their reaction would be more pronounced than my own."

Grant put the paper down and held up a hand.

"Easy, Sherman. Sit down. I am not certain this is authentic. Though, it is dated May thirtieth, and is titled 'McClernand's General Order Seventy-two.' That would seem to carry some authority."

The entrance of the tent was suddenly alive with

motion, and Sherman saw Rawlins, clutching a newspaper, the man in a run, nearly stumbling into the tent.

"Have you seen this, sir? The latest edition of the **Memphis Evening Bulletin**?"

Grant held up his copy of Sherman's paper, and Rawlins said to Sherman, "Are **you** aware of the credit claimed by General McClernand? Are you aware of the blame he has assigned to everyone else? A thousand deaths should be laid at his feet, and yet he claims his army alone has won victory in this campaign." Rawlins paused, out of breath, and Sherman waited for more, knew that Rawlins would fill the air for him. Behind Rawlins, another of Grant's senior staff officers moved in, a man Sherman knew well. Colonel James Wilson had served Grant for more than a year and had already endured a confrontation with McClernand that had been hard to keep secret. Sherman saw the look of curiosity on Wilson's face.

"Well, Colonel," Sherman said, "it seems your good friend McClernand is proving his disloyalty."

Wilson seemed reluctant to respond, and Grant said, "None of that, Sherman. There will be no judgment just yet."

Grant looked again to the paper, and Rawlins said, "Sir, during the assault on May twenty-second, it was General McClernand who insisted the battle was won, who insisted we continue the attack. He claimed victory when there was none. His exaggerated boastfulness cost the lives of men in every command on this field! And now, he would alter the pages of history. . . ."

"Enough, Colonel." Grant rolled the paper up tightly and tossed it to Sherman. "I must know if this did indeed come from General McClernand's hand. Sherman, you know more than anyone in this army that newspapers are not always reliable purveyors of truth. McClernand has good friends in many places, who would leap at any opportunity to elevate their favorite. I had thought this sort of thing had been silenced by our successes in this campaign, by the positive advantages we now hold. I must know who wrote this. Colonel, prepare a communication to General McClernand and verify if this 'Special Order' is indeed from his pen."

Rawlins was still angry, one hand crushing his own newspaper.

"Yes, sir. Immediately, sir."

He was out of the tent quickly, Wilson following, and Sherman said, "And what will you do? You know very well this is a violation of your own"— Sherman peeked downward, a small scrap of paper pulled from his pocket—"your own Special Order One Hundred Fifty-one."

Grant leaned back.

"So, you came prepared to remind me of my own orders? Well, go ahead. Recite it."

Sherman shoved the paper back into his pocket, thought a moment.

"I admit . . . I do not recall the precise language. But the point is very clear. It is forbidden for anyone in this command to issue to the public any official letter or report. This isn't actually a letter or report, but it is styled an **order,** though it isn't really an order at all. But there is no doubt this was manifestly designed for publication, for ulterior political motives. Is there any other conclusion? Your order demands that anyone who perpetrates such an act have their name set before the president, for immediate dismissal. You have that authority, Grant."

Grant rubbed his beard with one hand.

"Let us hear his response first. Before I toss anyone under the wheels of a train, I should like to know it is justified."

Sherman pondered that image, thought, That would be acceptable in any event. I should certainly assist.

"It's your decision, of course. I have my own feelings about the matter."

Grant seemed wearied by the comment.

"Of course you do. But for now, let's show some discretion, shall we? I would imagine you have better things to do right now than report violations of my orders. So, go do them."

Sherman nodded, could see the soft burn on Grant's face, thought, He's more angry about this than he will say. That's just fine.

He moved out into the sunlight, saw Wilson, who seemed to be waiting for him.

"Colonel, you have something you wish to talk about?"

Sherman walked past him, Wilson falling in beside him. Wilson seemed eager to speak, as though spilling out some burden he had carried for too long.

"Sir, General McClernand has, for some time, been a close friend of my father. I have observed the general's rise through the ranks of this army with some interest. But I do admit, I cannot understand his lack of decorum."

"Vainglory, Colonel."

"Sir, with all respects, it is more than that. I delivered an order to his headquarters some time back, and he responded with oaths toward General Grant that were . . . well, sir, I was shocked. He spoke most inappropriately. He actually said he was tired of being dictated to by the general, as though General Grant had no authority over him. He further gave insult to any of us who attended West Point, as though we were somehow inferior to his own judgment on the battlefield."

Sherman stopped walking and looked at him.

"Did you respond?"

"Most definitely, sir. It is one thing to question the authority of your commanding officer. It is quite another to cast insults toward the United

States Military Academy. I took that rather . . . personally, sir. I admit that I might have issued a few oaths of my own. I did threaten to pull him from his horse and beat him senseless."

Sherman stared, wide-eyed.

"Indeed? Very well done, Colonel. I should pay good money to witness such a show."

"Sir, I am not proud of my loss of temper. And, to General McClernand's credit, he did retract much of what he said. He explained that he was simply expressing intense vehemence on the subject."

"How utterly convenient. So, we are allowed to spit out every oath that comes to mind, question Grant's authority, and insult anyone we please, in the name of . . . vehemence?"

"It would seem so, sir. Please, I ask you . . . this is not an issue I hope to make public."

Sherman turned, walked away from Grant's headquarters, stared at the nearby wood line, the trees offering shade to Grant's tents. He glanced up, the sun bright, a clear blue sky, the day growing hotter. Wilson followed, and Sherman could feel the young man's concern.

"Do not worry, Colonel. None of us will enhance our careers by planting boots in McClernand's backside. As it seems now, General McClernand has placed his head precisely in the same place. And possibly, his command."

JUNE 17, 1863

Enclosed I send you what purports to be your congratulatory address to the Thirteenth Army Corps. I would respectfully ask if it is a true copy. If it is not a correct copy, furnish me one by bearer, as required both by regulations and existing orders of the Department.

Ulysses S. Grant,
Major General, Commanding

The newspaper slip is a correct copy of my Congratulatory Order, No. 72. I am prepared to maintain its statements.

John McClernand, Major General

The following day, June 18, Grant issued the order that removed John McClernand from command of the Thirteenth Corps, and replaced him with Major General Edward O. C. Ord. The man who was charged with delivering the order was Lieutenant Colonel James Wilson.

JUNE 19, 1863

Sherman sat alone in his tent, turned the paper over in his hand, looked at the ornate pattern on the back side, a series of flowers on a pale yellow background. He looked toward the flaps of the tent, and called out, "Captain McCoy, are you close?"

McCoy appeared, leaned into the tent.

"Yes, sir?"

"This is a newspaper? Are you certain?"

"Yes, sir. It was carried by a deserter. He claimed it is all they receive now."

Sherman waved the young man away, examined the paper, looked again at the print. He spoke out loud.

"Very damned interesting. They print their newspapers now on wallpaper?"

He scanned the article, what seemed to be a lead story, made a short laugh. Well, he thought, this is what the people are learning of this war. Yes, once again, the newspapers are the ultimate voice of absurdity. He couldn't resist sharing the humor.

"Captain!"

McCoy appeared again, and Sherman pointed to a camp chair.

"Sit. Are you aware we have suffered a defeat of massive proportions?"

McCoy slid down into the chair.

"If you mean that newspaper story, well, yes, sir,

I suppose I am aware of what the rebels seem to believe."

"What they believe is up for argument. What they are telling the citizens of Vicksburg is . . . right here. It seems a large force of rebels has crushed our outpost at Milliken's Bend, and thus has cut our supply line in that quarter. We are certain to starve." Sherman read further. "Well, the grand hero of the day is Dick Taylor. I supposed we could expect that. He's the son of Zachary Taylor. Did you know that?"

"Yes, sir. There had been some talk that we might expect an expedition against our positions west of the river, some fear that Taylor or someone else would hit us in a vulnerable place."

"Well, according to this, that's exactly what happened. And with magnificent results for the rebels. Strange how only yesterday, I received a letter that had just passed through there from my wife."

"Sir, we can certainly depend upon the rebel to make false claims. Should they give their soldiers the truth, there would be mass desertions, certainly."

"Don't be so confident of that, Captain. I have been surprised more than once by the tenacity of the rebel soldier, no matter if he has shoes or clothing or food. This report is nonsense, of course. I am aware of what took place at Milliken's Bend, and admittedly, I was surprised that our colored troops there performed admirably. They were considerably outnumbered by Taylor's forces, and yet, with some assistance from the navy's gunboats, they prevailed. I did not expect that kind of fighting spirit from the Negroes. We must remember that. There are a good many in this army who do not believe the Negro should carry a musket. I am among them . . . or was."

"If you say so, sir. I have not had any opportunity to witness Negro troops in combat."

"Few have, Captain. It is possible we shall in the future. I should like to witness that myself, to observe just how much zeal they show when fighting for our flag."

"Yes, sir."

He saw McCoy shifting in the small chair, a glance outside the tent.

"You're dismissed, Captain. You look like you have a dozen itches waiting to be scratched. Go scratch them."

"Thank you, sir."

The young man was gone quickly, and Sherman looked again at the odd version of the newspaper, examined the back side, the colorful decoration. This came right off the wall in someone's home, he thought. Or perhaps they have rolls of it in storage somewhere. And so this is the only thing passing for paper. That pea-meal mess is perhaps the only thing passing for rations. What is passing for ammunition?

He tossed the paper aside, felt itches of his own, a

frustration he had suffered for days now. Total war, he thought. That's the only way to accomplish our goals. This kind of thing, a siege . . . there is nothing satisfying about a victory gained this way.

Sherman stood, paced inside the tent, felt the sweat in his shirt, the day hotter still. Burn the place to the ground. Give them nothing to hold on to, nothing to attach their loyalty to. That's what this will become. It's the only way. Grant will come to see that, eventually. He has no more stomach for this kind of campaign than I do. He moved to the tent's opening, stepped out, stared off toward the rebel works, bare hills, long man-made mounds of dirt. Patience, Sherman. This isn't Jackson, and there are still a good many boys beyond those ditches who would put a bayonet in your heart. He thought of the deserter he had seen. That's the key, after all. How much of a fight can they make if they're starving? That's what Grant has to do, after all. There will be time still to burn that place, and maybe a whole lot of other places. That's how this war will end. It's how I'd like it to end. Hard to mistake who wins when you've got nothing left in your belly or your cartridge box and your home is gone.

He let out a breath, and stared toward the rebel works, the nagging thought drilling into him. Time. It has to take time. And I hate waiting.

CHAPTER THIRTY-SEVEN

PEMBERTON

THE COWAN HOUSE—
PEMBERTON'S HEADQUARTERS
JUNE 21, 1863

On Saturday, June 20, the shelling had come in a storm that was unlike anything the Confederates had yet seen. For nearly a full day, mortars and cannon unleashed shot and shell that seemed to carpet the town, the earthworks, and most of the open land in between. Throughout the daylong barrage, the commanders along the defensive works fully expected the artillery attack to be a preliminary to yet another massed assault by Yankee infantry. When the bombardment finally ceased, Confederate sharpshooters and artillerymen braced for what was sure to come. But for all the destruction unleashed by Federal artillery, their soldiers never appeared. Across from the Confederate lines, the Yankees seemed content to pursue their labor, burrowing ever closer to the Confederate defensive lines.

"It was for show, sir. That's it. Just a show of force."

Pemberton stared at the plate in front of him, Waddy's words drifting past him. He probed the piece of beef with his fork and said, "This steak is dismal, Colonel. Tough as my boots."

Waddy hesitated.

"Sir," he said, "it is the best we could summon. There was a lone milk cow nearby, and the owner was extremely gracious in offering it. I suspect that whatever food the citizens have left is being carefully hoarded. Perhaps hidden. There are reports of thievery, some of it from our own troops."

"Nonsense. Our soldiers would not do such a thing."

"If you say so, sir."

Pemberton looked up at him, saw Waddy staring down, had no energy for this. There had been too many pieces of bad news already.

"Colonel, what were you saying about the artillery? I admit it was somewhat frightening to me. The aides and I hid out in a cellar nearby, but I feared the entire structure would collapse upon us."

The picture stayed in his mind, huddling low in the darkness, the young couriers and orderlies suffering through the same fear that engulfed him. He had not expected that, had not ever been terrified. But the Federal shells had stirred up something deep inside of him, a fear let loose by his sheer exhaustion.

"I am an inspiration. They told me that. We sat on wet dirt, and breathed in dust from above. Hours of that. And they called me an inspiration. Thank God for loyalty, Colonel."

"Yes, sir. The men are behind you, sir. No matter what may happen. There is a fighting spirit in this army that no Yankee can match."

Pemberton pushed the steak away, no appetite at all.

"Pity that such spirit does not extend to our generals."

"I cannot speak on that, sir."

"You choose not to speak on it. I understand. Your loyalty is appreciated. This is most certainly a test for us all. I'm just not sure . . . to what point. If the opportunity one day presents itself, I should like to face General Johnston and ask him why he chose to sacrifice us. There is so much he could do, and yet . . ."

"Surely, sir, the general will come to our assistance. The latest report I heard is that he has more than seventy thousand troops assembled. Such a force would be unstoppable."

Pemberton saw the glimmer of hope in the young man's eyes, could not avoid the question.

"Do you actually believe that, Colonel? Those numbers? The **report** you heard? Just who issued that report? Did it come from the general? Some missive I was not shown?"

He saw the man's hopefulness slip away.

"Sir, I only convey what is being spoken of with certainty. I do not have any other word from General Johnston that you have not seen."

"You are forgiven your optimism, Colonel. I am not allowed such luxury." He pulled open a drawer and retrieved a single piece of paper. "This is what I must rely upon for my optimism. I have heard nothing from him in more than three weeks, and finally, he acknowledges receiving only two of my dispatches. I advised him we might have in our commissary twenty days of rations . . . and he responds to that by claiming with perfect clarity that Vicksburg and this garrison cannot be saved."

"But, sir, the general also offers a plan for our escape." Waddy leaned low, pointed to a line in Johnston's letter.

By fighting simultaneously at the same point of his line, you may be extricated.

Pemberton dropped the paper into the drawer.

"Yes. I am to choose the point at which he is to attack. Tell me, Colonel, how is such pinpoint communication possible? I can well advise him that I believe the Warrenton Road is our best hope of escape, and then, perhaps in a week or two, General Johnston will submit to the plan. Though of course, we will not know when that would take place. It is an absurdity, Colonel."

There was silence between them, a long moment of gloom, and Pemberton pulled the plate back toward him, sliced through one corner of the steak, held the meat up, studied it.

"A milk cow, then?"

"Yes, sir. There will likely be no more beef. The citizens are relying on scraps of anything they can find."

Pemberton put the meat in his mouth, chewed, the meat barely yielding. After a struggle, he swallowed and said, "I suppose I should offer my gratefulness for this feast."

"It has been done, sir. Major Memminger prepared his usual response."

"Of course he did. Colonel, you may take this away. Enjoy it yourself, and perhaps share it with anyone outside who wishes it."

Waddy took the plate but seemed hesitant.

"Sir, I would not enjoy such an offering, with so many of our troops hungry. General Stevenson has ordered daily rations cut to fourteen ounces per man, and even the general admits that a portion of that is nearly inedible."

"What portion?"

"The pea-meal bread, sir. We have a substantial supply of peas in the commissary, and efforts have been made to create something that will be palatable. But grinding peas into flour has not proven especially useful. General Stevenson has expressed his displeasure at the grievous error by the commissary officers. He insists the farms had food aplenty to supply our needs, and yet we failed to properly stock our warehouses. He suggests that any estimate we make as to our ability to feed this army . . . might prove overly optimistic."

"I am aware of that. The rations have been stretched as far as we dared. But I have done all I can, Colonel. It is a little late for General Stevenson or anyone else to offer complaints to this command."

"I have heard some grumbling, sir, but still, the men are performing their duty. As for rations, there is some improvising, to be sure. I am concerned about the more desperate preying on civilians. We should increase the provost guards. There has been some desertion as well."

"That cannot be helped, Colonel. Every army who has ever marched has suffered from those few who will not perform, who seek small favors in return for betraying their own comrades. Let them go. They are of no use to us anyway, and they consume rations." Pemberton paused. "We are holding Yankee prisoners, are we not?"

"Yes, sir."

"It is inhumane to starve them, even if our own men must be the priority. Perhaps we should release them from captivity, return them to their own lines."

Waddy seemed to ponder the thought, then said, "But, sir, prisoners can be of use, in exchange for our own men. It has always been that way."

"And, so, we would trade for men who we must care for? Where is the gain in that? Order the prisoners released and have them marched out to the Federal lines under flag of truce. That should make for a celebration in the enemy's camps. Perhaps . . . they will offer some generosity to us. Perhaps our pickets will receive a bit more kindness from their counterparts."

"I'm sorry, sir. I don't know what you mean."

"Yes, yes. It is forbidden for our pickets to fraternize and trade with the enemy. Those are my orders, after all. But I know what must be happening out there. We are not fighting a foreign enemy, after all. They do speak the same language. I am not so naïve to believe that our men are keeping their silence. Desperate men resort to desperate measures. The Yankees most surely are taking advantage of that."

"But your orders . . ."

"Would you prefer more of them simply desert? If our troops are not fed adequately, they will continue to weaken. With weakness of body comes weakness of spirit, no matter how much faith we have in their backbone for a fight."

"Yes, sir. It is truly regrettable we did not adequately prepare for these events."

Waddy stopped, and Pemberton saw uneasiness, as though Waddy had crossed some line of decorum.

"I will not find fault. If we can provide fourteen ounces per day, then that is what we shall provide." Pemberton looked at the remnant of the steak, a piece the size of his hand. "This piece of meat is surely larger than that."

"Yes, sir. Most likely, sir."

Waddy stared at him, and Pemberton saw a flash of frustration, thought, He has his own criticisms, no doubt.

"Speak up, Colonel. You have something to offer?"

Waddy seemed to clamp his jaw tightly, then shook his head.

"I agree with General Stevenson that errors were made," Waddy said. "There was time . . . before the enemy drew close . . . a more efficient effort should have been made to negotiate with the farmers. The warehouses could have been filled." He paused. "If there is blame . . . perhaps it should rest with your staff. I must accept that."

Pemberton was surprised, knew Waddy had very little authority to make any contracts with the farms.

"Nonsense, Colonel. Do not fault yourself. Sometimes these things are out of our control."

"You are the commanding general, sir. Is not everything . . . in your control?"

Waddy stepped back, as though trying to erase what he had said.

"I suppose, Colonel, every responsibility must eventually settle onto this desk. But I cannot make every decision, guide every hand. Perhaps you will have a command of your own one day. You will learn what I have learned, how often it feels as though a rope is tied to each limb, each one pulling in a different direction. It is more than any man can bear for long. I would rather not speak of this any longer. The subject is simply too . . . distressing."

"Sir, that is why we must have faith in General Johnston. We believe we have rations for two weeks, at least. If the general can make his assault before then . . ."

Pemberton felt something snap in his brain, Johnston's name driving through him like a dull sword.

"I am not interested in hearing of Johnston again! Do you understand me, Colonel? No matter what kind of rumors are drifting through this place, there will be no assault from General Johnston! I am sick of hearing such ridiculousness! Yesterday, we suffered the most vigorous artillery assault I have yet experienced, and we dare not respond, for lack of ammunition. Our sharpshooters sit idly, hiding their heads, unable to answer the enemy's muskets because we have no excess of percussion caps."

"Sir, with all respects, we did receive some two

hundred thousand caps only this morning. The courier did a remarkable job of slipping past the enemy's guards."

"Yes, yes, I know about that. Tell me, Colonel. Did that courier also lead into camp a herd of beef cattle? Wagonloads of corn flour? I suspect not."

"No, sir. My apologies, sir. It's just that . . . those rumors of General Johnston are of great value to this army. Any hope is better than none at all."

Pemberton eyed the steak, the knife still in his hand. He sliced another bite, stabbed it with the fork, didn't hesitate, fought again with the toughness of the meat.

"If it's **hope** you wish for, Colonel, if this army believes in the miraculous, then, fine, I shall do my part. Have Captain Cooper available. I will prepare another dispatch for General Johnston." He struggled to swallow the thick lump of meat, cut another piece, held it up, watched a single drop of brown liquid falling away. "Perhaps I can offer him a plan that he will accept. There is no paper left, correct?"

"No, sir. But the captain is most reliable, sir. Anything you relate to him shall be recalled precisely to General Johnston."

Pemberton could hear the rising enthusiasm in the young man's voice. He attacked the beef again, heard a faint rumbling growl, then looked at Waddy, who held one hand on his stomach.

If it is absolutely impossible, in your opinion, to raise the siege . . . I suggest that giving me full information in time to act, you move by the north of the railroad, drive in the enemy's pickets at night, and at daylight the next morning engage him heavily with skirmishers, occupying him during the entire day, and that on that night I move to the Warrenton Road, by Hankinson's Ferry, to which point you should previously send a brigade of cavalry and two field batteries, to build a bridge there, and hold that ferry . . . I suggest this as the best plan. I await your orders.

**John C. Pemberton,
Lieutenant General, Commanding**

The church bells had begun early, came again now. It was another gesture of hope, this one offered by Reverend Lord. Pemberton knew that few people were going to the church services now, the risk just too great. Throughout the town, nearly every home, every building had sustained damage, some of that obliterating the structures completely. There was damage in his own headquarters, a gaping hole in one wall, yet his staff continued their good work, wrestling with the desperate demands of officers in every department of his command.

He watched a small crowd of people as they moved into the shell-pocked street, those with the devotion to their faith so strong that they would not ignore the reverend's call to a sermon. Will that sustain them? Pemberton thought. It will not fill their bellies. It will not give this army what we have been denied. Despite the increasing rate of desertion, the staff seems eager to reinforce some belief in me that the army still has the spirit for a fight, empty stomachs or not. If that is true at all, he thought, how long can that last? Until Johnston saves us? He turned away from the window, couldn't avoid the familiar fury at the thought of the man who seemed not to care at all for the town, for the army who defended it, for the orders of the president. How does such a man reach a lofty command? Johnston chooses which fights he shall wage based on . . . what? The certainty of a victory? Well, that "certainty" has passed by us here. All we can do now is survive.

He moved to the desk, too angry to sit, thought of Waddy, the hope of the young. The courier, Cooper, had taken his dispatch already, a journey that Pemberton couldn't fathom at all, the man with the courage to shove through every kind of danger. Just so General Johnston can know we are not yet defeated, he thought. Just so he will know that I am still in command here, that there is a **plan** that might yet save this army. And perhaps Colonel Waddy's optimism will be justified. Perhaps the rumors will prove true, perhaps this army's spirit will be enough to sustain us. Perhaps Johnston will come after all.

He said aloud, "And perhaps the Almighty himself will appear on the great river, and part the waters so that we might walk away from our peril."

He moved back to the window, with hard, fast breathing, and clenched his fists. He felt like punching the glass, a loud, shattering blow that would be heard all the way to Richmond.

CHAPTER THIRTY-EIGHT

SPENCE

NEAR THE
3RD LOUISIANA REDAN
JUNE 24, 1863

The storm clouds had come late the night before, adding to the misery of the trek eastward. With so much of the livestock devoured by the soldiers, and of course, the civilians in their caves, the hospitals were becoming useless, too far from the front lines where so many of the wounds were inflicted. Few ambulances could make the journey back to the Green house, simply because there were too few animals to pull them.

Lucy had ridden in one of the last available wagons, the doctor and several others doing the same. Space was made for the surgical instruments, rolled up in cloth pouches. But there was little room for tables, for any kind of furniture at all. When they reached the spot the officers had chosen, they would make do with the army's tents and whatever means they could find for caring for the wounded troops.

With so much work to do establishing the new hospital, the nurses and orderlies labored well into the night, suffering the rain and the mosquitoes and a scattering of Federal artillery. When the tents were secure, it was too late for her to make the long walk back to the Cordrays' sheltering cave, and so she slept beneath the ambulance, a blanket that did little to keep the rain away. The tents offered shelter, of course, but wounded men lined the ground inside, the doctor going to work as soon as he arrived. With the first hint of daylight, she was already awake, was given a small handful of some kind of cracker, struggled to swallow what someone said was a biscuit, a bitter slab tasting of the dirt she sat on.

The sun had barely risen now, and soldiers were encamped all around the tent, some stretched out on blankets of their own, seeking some protection from the rain beneath bushes or a ledge of rocky hillside. With the daylight, the rain had stopped, and she could see what seemed to be caves, dug-outs in the sloping hillsides. But they were nothing like the civilian shelters. There were few carefully shaped walls, few timbers for supports, most simply a hole dug out of the muddy ground. In every direction were men, some sleeping, some sitting alone, others in small groups. The campfires were few, any smoke at all a target for Yankee artillery. But even with no targets, the Yankee gunners sent their fire, shells coming down on the hillsides as they had in the town, random and haphazard.

The wounds were few, but the brutality of the suffering was more graphic now than what she had seen in the hospital. Many of the men resembled skeletons, some barely clothed. It was the one blessing from the summer sun, that no one was freezing to death, even the nights sticky and humid, few blankets required. But as the morning passed, the blessing became torture, the men doing all they could to shield themselves from relentless sunlight that sapped a man's energy completely. The doctor dealt with that, too, men simply falling out with the heat, delirious with hunger, or suffering dysentery from filthy water. The springs and clean running creeks were few and scattered, and often, any man who tried to fill a bucket was subject to target practice from Yankee sharpshooters who had positioned themselves precisely. It was no secret where the water sources were, and the Yankee infantry had pushed so much closer to the primary fortifications that the sharpshooters had free rein in the night to find those hiding places where a musket could reach back behind the Confederate works.

Another tent had been brought, another doctor, much older, a foul-smelling man named Prine, who scanned Lucy up and down with a probing leer.

There were other nurses as well, a handful of women scattered out into several of these smaller makeshift hospitals, three of those with Lucy now. She knew them all, acquaintances in horror, and the duty was as it had been before, ministering chloroform to screaming men, caring for those who survived whatever the doctors had done to them. She had tried to become better at that, comforting words, what seemed a hopeless gesture to a man with a piece of his body shot away, or gasping for breath in what could be his last hour of life. It was still the worst part of the job, the doctor telling her whether death was imminent, or whether the man might survive his wounds for a night longer, perhaps another day. All the while, she did what she had been taught, encouraging words as she changed a dressing, helping hands with the most distasteful bodily functions, hearing the confessions, the fears, the begging, the prayers . . . until the man was finally silent. Then she said a prayer of her own, often interrupted by the orderlies who hauled the corpse out to someplace along the hillside where the burial parties would do their job.

The artillery shell came down within yards of the tent, the canvas shivering, the ground jumping beneath her feet. She steadied herself against the makeshift table, a front door that had been salvaged from one of the burned houses. Across from her, Dr. Prine eyed her.

"Pretty little lass," he said. "Hard work for such a young one. Any of these lads live through this, they'll remember you. Probably find you a beau that way. Angel of mercy, that's what they'll say. There's a price, though. For you, that is. You'll never forget this, any of it. It'll come to you in the middle of the night, maybe for years. Look at your hands. The blood's been there so long it's stained you. Like the devil's inkwell. Hee."

She tried to ignore him, knew she couldn't for long. He was after all, in charge, and the man lying between them was whimpering softly, a huge slice through the man's rib cage. The doctor caught her look and said, "Shrapnel wound. You seen many of these?"

"Yes. Many."

"Well, then you know there's not much we can do about this one. His liver's in the wide open, and half his intestines, what's left anyway. Keep a bandage wrapped around him best you can, but he's bleeding to beat Cain. Don't spend too much time. Four more over here, every one of them as bad. Musta been a direct hit on this bunch."

She worked with the cloth strips, saw a hint of embroidery, what had once been sheets, torn now into bandages. Up along the hillside were the remnants of the burnt-out homes, what she thought had been destroyed by the Yankees. But the soldiers had corrected that notion, several of them a part of the teams that burned them down. She thought of that now, her mind drifting away from the horror beneath her hands. We burn down the houses on purpose, to make way for our artillery fire. What did they do with the people? She thought of Cordray, the caves, so many dwellings on every hillside, every slice in the earth. There, I suppose. They must know, surely, that they have no home to go back to. She closed her eyes. Like me. The word settled into her now, a word she was sick of hearing. **Sacrifice**. I have nothing else to give, she thought. She looked down at the man beneath her hands, felt him squirming slightly, the chloroform wearing off. He moaned now, and she called out, "Dr. Prine! He requires chloroform."

"Not now, Nurse. I'm holding a man's brains in my hand. You'll have to manage."

The man screamed now, tried to sit, collapsed beneath the pressure from her hands, screamed again. She felt a wave of panic, her fatigue draining the strength in her arms, and she leaned close to the man's ear, a hard whisper.

"Mother is here! Be calm. It will be all right."

The man's eyes darted past her, a desperate attempt to see, the words still coming from him, softer now, her lie having its effect.

"Mother is here! Thank God. Thank the Lord. Mother . . ."

"Yes. Right here. Now, you lie still. I'll be right back. Just lie still, you hear?"

"Yes, Mama."

She lifted her hands, searched frantically for the brown bottle, saw it in the hands of an orderly, the man waiting for a command from the doctor. She moved that way, too tired to ask, grabbed the bottle from the man's hands. She ignored his curse, moved back to the table, the man lying calmly, still the soft words, "Mama . . . I'm coming. I'll be seein' you. . . ."

She removed the cork from the bottle, something holding her back, and she saw the man's face, the eyes open, staring through the smear of blood and dirt, no words now. Calm. The orderly was there now.

"The bottle, miss? The doctor . . ."

"Yes, here. I don't need it. I believe the doctor will confirm . . . he's dead."

"They'll all be dead soon enough. Not sure why we're doing this job. I'd rather be killing Yanks."

The man took the chloroform from her, moved away, and she thought of his boastfulness, so completely foolish, as though it were better to inflict this grotesque damage on someone else. But there was no energy for protest, for logic or caring about the war, or which side had the most of . . . this. She turned, motioned to a pair of orderlies, the men who would take this latest corpse to its place in the ground.

———

"Got an officer here! Make way!"

The words had no impact on the doctor, and Lucy didn't move at all, just watched as the litter bearers brought the man in, lifting him up on the table with care, as though he were a fragile package. The doctor, Prine, was there now, and Lucy had the chloroform already, the duty too familiar, held the small scrap of cloth, removed the cork, and the doctor held up his hand.

"Hold on there, Nurse. This one's not too bad."

The officer was holding one arm across his chest, his hand gripping a bloodstained shoulder, a pained grimace on his face.

"Remove his hat," Prine said. "Let's open his shirt. Lieutenant, you'll have to let go. We'll have a look, but I don't see much blood. Your men have it worse than you, so far."

Lucy pulled the hat away, the face clean, the only sign of damage the small spot of blood on his gray coat. The man spoke through gritted teeth.

"Shouldn't have been out there. Stepped into the open, tried to get across . . . they must have been waiting. Stupid mistake. Knew better."

Lucy stared, the thick hair, the face young, brutally handsome. She felt the shock of recognition. It was her lieutenant.

Prine pulled her hand down onto the officer's and said, "Here. Hold that arm down. This might hurt, and I need to see the wound. Be brave, Lieutenant. Just need to get a look."

The man seemed to brace himself for the worst, and the doctor pulled back the coat, dropped his hands to his side.

"Musket ball . . . didn't hit the bone. You're not bleeding enough to lose the arm. Lucky man. Nurse, wipe the hole clean, put a bandage on it. He'll be out of here in a few minutes."

The officer stared at the doctor, in breathless relief.

"I'm not going to lose the arm? I'll be all right? Doctor, thank you! I thought it was mortal."

Prine turned away to another patient and said, "They all do. Officers worst of all."

Lucy waited for him to look at her, saw the sharp blue in his eyes, still the fear.

"Hold your hand down, please, sir. I need to clean the wound. This might hurt a little."

She exposed the wound completely, the hole clean through soft tissue. She knew enough by now to understand the musket ball had missed any vital artery. She worked quickly, watched his eyes, waited for recognition of his own, that delicious surprise when he realized who she was. The wound was packed now, and she said, "Please sit up. I need to wrap the shoulder."

He obliged her, focused mostly on the men around him, as though seeing if they were his. The groans were there, another man screaming, noises that floated past her now, and he said, "No one here is from my command. Thank God for that. I lost one man this morning. Corporal Bourgeois. Musket ball to the head. Nothing we could do. Keep your heads down. That's all I've been saying for days now. But they can't stand it, they have to look, to see if they can find the sharpshooters, or watch the Yankees digging their ditches. And then one gets a ball through his skull, and for an hour or so, they'll listen to me."

She stood back, couldn't help a smile, and said, "That's it. You're fine now. It will be sore as the dickens for a few days. But you didn't lose the arm."

He looked at her now, studied the bandaging, probed gently with his free hand.

"Thank you, Nurse. Thank you. I was truly afraid."

"You have no reason to be. I . . . the nurses here know how to take care of their soldiers."

She felt light-headed, a glow of joy she hadn't felt in weeks. She waited for him to realize the obvious, studied his face, his eyes not meeting hers at all. The suspense was agonizing, and she moved to the side, more into his line of sight.

"Lieutenant, it is good to see you again. I thank God you are not seriously injured."

He looked at her, studied her face, then shook his head slowly.

"I'm sorry, miss. Are we acquainted?"

"The ball . . . April. The night the Yankees sailed past."

She saw nothing in his eyes, just another shake of his head.

"Sorry, miss. With all apologies, I do not recall meeting you."

She felt the joy sinking into a burning dread, red-faced embarrassment.

"We danced."

"Oh, very nice. I'm certain I enjoyed that."

"You don't recall? Truly?"

"Very sorry, miss. Can I leave now? The doctor said I could."

She stared at him, felt completely idiotic, a hole punched through her.

"Yes, Lieutenant. You may return to your duty. You are quite finished here."

He stood, steadied himself, and she wanted to help, but something held her in place, what strength she had left drained completely away.

"Thank you, miss. You were most kind."

"Yes, I was. Have been, for some time now."

An officer entered the tent, moving to the lieutenant, and said, "Oh, thank the Lord, Lieutenant. We weren't sure how badly you were hit. Can you return to the line?"

The young man saluted and said, "Yes, sir. Right now, sir."

He moved outside the tent, gone now, and she lowered her head, felt far more than foolish. A child, she thought. Fantasies of a child. The older officer lingered, then said to the doctor, "Sir, I request you and your people make every preparation to receive a serious number of casualties."

The doctor looked up from his table, and she saw another man coming into the tent, filthy white apron, her doctor from the Green house. She felt relieved to see him, so much kinder than this older man, Prine, who seemed to delight in studying her form. The officer acknowledged both doctors with a respectful nod.

"Gentlemen, I am Captain Trevaux, 3rd Louisiana, adjutant to Major Pierson. We have detected the enemy working beneath the ground. He is attempting to dig a mine that will place him directly beneath our position. So far, we have been unable to locate any tunnel, and there could be more than one. Our brigade commander, General Hebert, has issued orders across the entire redan that we be prepared for an explosion of their mine at any time. If that should occur, there could be a large number of casualties. You must be prepared."

Prine sniffed.

"Captain," he said, "we are not prepared for anything more than you see here. What would you have us do?"

The other doctor moved past Lucy, ignored

Prine's surliness, and said, "Tell Major Pierson and your general that we shall do all we can."

"Very well. It would be helpful if you would spread word to the other hospitals all across the rear of our position, and beyond. If we are fortunate, the enemy shall suffer far worse than we. Gentlemen."

He made a short bow and moved quickly away.

The two doctors came together, low talk, some semblance of a strategy.

Lucy waited for a break in the conversation.

"Doctors," she said, "there are no patients waiting at present. Might I be excused for a few minutes?"

The older man looked at her, that same piercing leer.

"Don't wander off too far. Critters about. The kind with two legs."

Lucy ignored the insinuation, moved outside, cleared her lungs of the stench of the tents. She walked up the hill, felt the oppressive heat, the ground muddy and steaming from the rainstorms. Far beyond the crest of the hill she could see the redan, but much closer, men were at work, shovels and dirt flying, a new earthwork. There was an officer there, unfamiliar, the man clearly in charge, speaking now to other officers, issuing instructions in a firm, clear voice. She tried to ignore the ache in her empty stomach, stepped that way through a fog of curiosity, but the meeting concluded, the officers spreading out to their own men. The man in charge stood tall, observing the work, and she sensed something different about him, something she hadn't seen in many of these soldiers in weeks. He seemed proud.

"Excuse me, sir. I am sorry to intrude."

He turned, obviously surprised by her presence, then, her appearance.

"You're a nurse?"

"Yes, sir. I needed some relief, just for a moment. We just arrived out here last night, during the storm."

"Pardon me for saying so, miss, but this is not the place for you. Dangerous games are afoot, and before too much longer, the enemy is most likely to make a violent attempt against this very position."

She weighed his words, watched the men working, some of them watching her. She felt no hesitation now, her decorum swept away by the disappointment that still engulfed her, the utter silliness of her fantasy for the young lieutenant, so easily wiped away.

"So, you would put your soldiers back here, for protection. Are you General Hebert?"

The man said, "Are you a spy?"

She liked the question.

"If I was, would that make me . . . memorable?"

"Odd question. Odd girl, you are. Then, you're not a nurse?"

"I'm a nurse. Just not a memorable one, according to your most charming of lieutenants. I came up with the doctors, since there is so little transportation back toward the town. They have set up a hospital back down this hill, in those tents. Should your **hopes** be realized and the enemy gives you a battle, I'll do what I can to help your wounded, General. I've grown quite accustomed to digging the blood from my fingernails."

"Well, miss, we shall try not to burden you with too many wounded. I would prefer no one be wounded at all, if that were possible. But that goal is unlikely to be attained. It is, after all, why we're here. And, please, I am not General Hebert. I'm an engineer. Major Lockett."

One of the men spoke up, a shovel propped up on his shoulder.

"That's right, little gal. He's the one telling us where to toss up all this here dirt. I'd call him an expert at it. Only thing is . . . we can't eat this stuff. Uh . . . begging your pardon, sir. Been a while since we seen a fine filly like this one up here. She's a might messy, though."

"More energy with the spade, less with the mouth, Private. I want these trench lines completed by tonight. All of you, pay more attention to how many men you might protect with those spades."

Lucy watched the work ongoing, dirt in neat piles out in front of a long, narrow ditch.

"So, Major Engineer, how come you're not riding a horse? You eat him?"

"Fine talk from a nurse. My horse is . . . no longer

available, yes. But it would be foolish for me to sit up here for all the world to see. Federal sharpshooters can probably sight us standing here right now. For all I know, they're not trying to kill me because they can see you."

She felt a bolt of alarm, looked out toward the larger fortifications, could see clusters of men barely visible, a few scattered, standing on a ledge, muskets by their side.

"If I was a spy, I'd want to know why you're digging back here. Awfully far from . . . up there."

"If you were a spy, I'd have you shot."

There was no humor in his words, and Lucy knew the game had ended. She watched the workers a minute more, Lockett ignoring her now, caught glimpses from the men, too curious not to offer a quick look.

"Major, I will leave you to your digging. I am very sorry to have bothered you."

"No bother. But I would keep yourself back below this hillcrest. With the enemy laboring as they are, I'm fairly certain I know their intentions. I just don't know . . . when. I'm just preparing for the worst."

The emptiness in her stomach was stirring up now, and she suddenly realized she had no idea what she might eat. She knew better than to ask the engineer for anything. You're not supposed to be up here at all. It is hardly appropriate for you to make yourself some kind of . . . mascot. She moved away, stepped down through the grass, avoided a crater, saw scraps of metal, a broken wheel. Off to one side, at the base of the hill, she saw a row of graves, long, wide ditches rounded over with fresh earth. She turned away from that, thought of Lockett's preparation, his description. For the **worst**. Her mind took her back to the hospital, all she had seen and touched and smelled. She looked at the red stains on her hands, the stinking crust beneath her nails. Before this passes, how much worse must it be?

CHAPTER THIRTY-NINE

BAUER

NORTHEAST OF THE
3RD LOUISIANA REDAN
JUNE 25, 1863

He crawled forward, the men up front moving back his way, the change of shifts this time coming well before dawn. The men who slipped past him seemed in good spirits, none of the grousing about too many hours in the inclement weather, or bellyaching about their hunger. With the rainstorms two days past, the muddy ground had mostly dried out, the nights now just cool enough to keep a man from sweating as he huddled low in the trenches closest to the enemy. The sharpshooting duties had grown more mundane as well, bleary-eyed boredom, the rebels seeming to grasp the obvious, that a duel with the men in blue was likely to be a one-sided affair. There were still casualties, careless men on both sides who allowed their bravado to interfere with common sense, revealing their hiding places by standing up tall, taunting the enemy with claims of imminent victory, idiotic mouthiness about the rebels' lack of food, or any other insult that came to mind. Bauer had seen some of that courage coming from a bottle, some illicit find, apple cider, other concoctions the men continued to scrounge from so many hidden cellars. The officers had done as much as they could to prevent that, but even the officers were guilty of raiding places they had no business searching. The unfortunate behavior went against explicit orders from above, but even the commanders could not prevent bored men from seeking some adventure in the middle of the night, whether the penalty was a stint in the stockade, or the most severe punishment, the musket ball from a well-hidden enemy.

Any real information about conditions behind the rebel earthworks had come from the steady flow of deserters, men who crept out of their holes in the darkness, soft whispers asking for safe passage, encounters the pickets were growing accustomed to. Bauer had seen a few of them, stinking and filthy, escorted past him by armed pickets, mostly during those nights when Bauer worked the shovel. He didn't speak to them, but there was no mistaking their intentions. Some of them had wept as they moved by, their pride crushed by the hope of an opportunity to sit unmolested by a campfire, to soak up a cup of real coffee while they slurped down a plateful of bacon or real beans. With each rebel who came through the lines, the men in blue could feel the sagging fortunes of the ones still out there, the men still dangerous, still eager to kill a Yankee, who huddled low behind the massive earthworks. Bauer was only one of thousands who pondered just how much longer this could last.

The digging had mostly ended, and when Bauer went forward now, it was with his musket. He had rarely liked picket duty, had had a hard fill of that the year before. Then it was the swampy snake-infested lowlands that had erupted into the hell of Shiloh. But out here, the trenches were deep, the ground dry, the men well fed before beginning the shift.

He settled into the flattened place, soft dirt pressed hard by the men before him. He stared at darkness, a spray of stars overhead, leaned against the dirt. In front of him, the loose soil had been stacked in a long roll, adding height to his protection, some of that his work. He didn't miss the shovels, but still, the work had been no more than a good bout of exercise, a definite improvement over some parade ground drill far to the rear. That nonsense was ongoing in other regiments, and Bauer knew better than to ask anyone about that, even Willis, lest it trigger some sudden inspiration for the Wisconsin men to join them. There had been some mention of the drills, the company commander, Captain Mc-Dermott, using the phrase that no doubt made his superiors happy: **efficient readiness**. Bauer gazed upward, his eyes lost in the stars, thought, We're ready enough. The rebels are two dozen yards in front of me, over that big fat hill, sitting in holes like this one, and it sure as hell isn't gonna take some bugler to put us into the right kind of formation. When it comes time, all we do is climb up and over, and shoot anybody who's still waiting for us. God help us, maybe there won't be anybody. It'll be like Corinth again, all kinds of commotion and bluster, and when the order finally comes, there'll be nobody home. That would be the right way to win this thing.

He worried about the inevitable fight to keep his eyes open. They all knew the penalty for falling asleep, talk spread by the officers that a man could be shot for sleeping on guard duty. If anyone in the company forgot that, Willis and the other lieutenants were quick to remind them. Not going to let you down, Sammie. Not sleepy at all right now. This might be fun, actually. Wonder who's out there this time? He glanced to the left, knew Kelly was there, a half-dozen yards away. But there would be no conversation between them. The job was too important, and if there was little danger of armed infiltrators, Bauer truly hoped it would be his turn to escort some rebel deserter back to the big tents in the rear.

"Hey, Yank!"

Bauer waited, looked toward Kelly, then the other way, another man to his right he didn't know.

"Hey, Yank! Wake up!"

He heard Kelly whisper toward him, "You gonna answer him?"

"Yeah, secesh. I'm right here, aimin' this musket at your head. What you want?"

"Now, Yank, no need to be so hot about it. No officers around, is there?"

Bauer felt foolish now, couldn't have found a target if it was right in front of him.

"I'm here. What you want, secesh?"

"Call me Zep."

The name sent a small jolt through his brain.

"Hey! I saw you . . . met you when we buried the bodies."

"Which one er you?"

He thought a minute, remembered Willis's tease.

"I'm the ugly German. Wisconsin."

"Yep. I recall. You is one ugly fella, too. Bunch of Irishmen in your unit, then."

Kelly spoke up now.

"You got that one, secesh. Zep. What kind of name is that?"

"The one my pappy gave me. What's your'n?"

"I'm Fritz Bauer. They call me Dutchie."

Kelly responded, "Patrick Kelly. You and your buddy traded me a cigar."

"Yep, I remember you boys. Well, Wisconsin, you're sitting across from Looseeana's finest. I'd say there's about four hundred of us on this part of the picket line."

Bauer was in the game now, smiled.

"That's all? We got eight companies out here, just in case you boys try something."

He heard a low laugh, realized the man wasn't more than a few yards away.

"Well, then, I reckon we'uns got the whole dang armies out here, just ready for a skirmish. Funny, for a couple thousand pickets in breathin' distance of these bare feet, you're mighty quiet."

Bauer knew this would exhaust itself quickly.

"Well, maybe I overstated it a little. There's me . . . and Kelly. Maybe that's it."

"Don't much believe that, neither. Don't worry, Yank, I ain't about to go leading some hell-for-leather charge nowheres. Unless you promise me I'll find the coffee wagon."

Kelly jumped in.

"Come on over, Zep, and I'll take you there meself. Mighty hot and mighty strong."

"Well, we got a pot of squirrel stew over here that I ain't about to leave behind. Feel free to haul a big ole cup of that coffee over thisaway, anyhow."

Kelly laughed and said, "Hey, Zep! I traded with

your cousin . . . don't recall his name. Nice fella. He out here, too?"

Bauer recalled that now, the swap, newspapers for cigars, Willis talking to a rebel lieutenant.

"And your lieutenant . . . Gramling, maybe?"

There was a silent moment, and Zep spoke now, a different tone to his voice.

"My cousin . . . that'd be Farley. Shot in the eye. Never made a whimper. I guess you could say he didn't even know what hit him."

"Sharpshooter?"

The word leaked out of Bauer, and he regretted it immediately, thought of the stovepipe, one more horrible day.

"Well, reckon so. The lieutenant's back there in the hospital somewheres, so they say. Took a ball in the top of his head. Saw his brains, sure 'nuff. If he's alive, it's a dang miracle." He paused, and Bauer said nothing, Kelly silent as well. "I reckon you boys have learned to shoot a bit since I last ran into ya."

Bauer couldn't erase the image of the stovepipe, the speck of daylight. Kelly answered first.

"War, I guess. Sorry. Especially for your cousin."

Zep didn't respond, and Bauer was beginning to hate this conversation, didn't want to know who it was he might have killed. He thought of the tower now, that crazy lieutenant with the coonskin hat. I shot an officer . . . maybe his. But that's down a ways, and there's plenty of damn lieutenants. Even Sammie would agree with that.

There was other talk now, farther down the line, low chatter, questions, boasts, empty threats and promises of every imaginable exaggeration. Bauer sat back, stared at the stars again, but Zep surprised him.

"You bluebellies'll probably come at us again, 'fore long. It ain't gonna be easy, not for none of us. You all seem like decent folks, but I guess . . . it don't really matter. You try to climb into that big ole fort right here and when I stick you with this here bayonet, I won't ask your name."

Bauer stared out, then glanced at the musket leaning up in front of him. He tried to remember the man's face, or the cousin's, thought, Maybe it wasn't me who killed him. Probably not. Or maybe it was.

"You're right, secesh. I'm guessing we'll be coming over that dirt pile again, and it won't much matter which one you are."

Willis had them seated in low ground, seemed to count them, as though recalling each man's name.

"Now, listen up. You finish breakfast, you stay ready to move. They haven't told me a hell of a lot, but the colonel got orders that something's going to happen today. I heard this for a while now, and maybe some of you heard rumors. What I know is we've been doing a hell of a lot of digging, down to the left, near that tower. We're so damn close to the reb position, somebody figured out we oughta just keep going and burrow a hole right underneath 'em. All I know is what the captain said, and all he knows is what the colonel felt like telling him. But there's a flock of engineers down that way, and some coal-mining boys have been brought in. Saw that myself. Rough-looking lot. They've been working for the past few days, and I guess they did what they came to do. The colonel said General Grant himself came by, checking on 'em, and . . . well, I take that kind of rumor pretty seriously. So should you. So . . . check your muskets, fill your cartridge boxes, your canteens. The colonel says some of the units along this part of the line are ordered to provide handpicked sharpshooters, including us. So, Dutchie . . . that's you."

There were groans, Kelly slapping him on the back.

"Well, hell-a-mighty. They don't think micks can shoot straight?"

Willis was all seriousness.

"Shut up. You'll all be in this before it's over with. When I see the colonel that grouchy, I know something's about to happen. But all of you, keep your damn mouths shut. No spewing off about this to anybody else, Wisconsin boys or not. I don't know what any other unit is being told, but right here, you're my little half acre of hell. You'll do what I say or your ass will end up in the stockade. Maybe missing a few teeth along the way. This is for real. You have questions, keep 'em to yourself. I don't have answers."

ACROSS FROM THE 3RD LOUISIANA REDAN JUNE 25, 1863, 3:00 P.M.

They were dug in within a hundred yards of the redan, muskets loaded, officers behind them staring out through field glasses. Bauer didn't know the men on either side of him, knew only they came from Illinois and Indiana, quick introductions, maybe a handshake, any names he heard already forgotten. There was nothing social about this duty, the men chosen to be on this line by officers who knew their marksmanship. Bauer slid the musket up into a soft groove in the sand, onto the leather pad that kept the sand out of the musket and helped steady the shot. There were others back behind them, their perches elevated, more muskets trained on the rebel position, their firing line above the heads of Bauer and the others to the front. To one side stood the tower, what had once seemed so completely ridiculous now a testament to the overwhelming superiority of the Federal position.

Bauer had to believe that across the way, rebel gunners peered up at that monstrosity every hour, each one itching to launch the solid shot through the wooden rails that would bring the tower down in a heap of broken lumber. When he arrived on the firing line, others were speaking of it as well, the same sense of wonder that this amazing tactic had actually worked. Lieutenant Coonskin was known by all, if only by reputation, and Bauer learned quickly that many of the others on this firing line had done just what Bauer had, taking aim at the unfortunate rebel who had once been safe standing on his own rampart. The men around him spoke of the rebel artillery with a hint of arrogance, that more than once, the bravest rebel gunner had made the effort, wheeling his cannon to a firing position, only to be obliterated by the volleys that poured out from Hickenlooper's battery. Any rebel artillery was now kept far out of sight, back into dugouts, perhaps, or off the line completely. Even far behind the rebel earthworks, any gunner who had range of the tower had to know by now that Hickenlooper's guns had range on him.

"Keep at ease, men. Nothing's happening yet."

The officer was off to one side, field glasses staring out, lowering them now, an Illinois man Bauer didn't know. Beside Bauer, a man spoke up, clearly from the same unit, respectful recognition.

"Captain Jewell, what're we looking for? Begging your pardon, sir, but the rebs are sure keeping low.

There hasn't been a single cap sticking up. It's like there's nobody there at all."

"You know better than that, Corporal. Your job is to find a target. There might not be anything happening right now, but be patient. General Grant's just down the line, with General McPherson. They wouldn't be out here if it wasn't important."

Bauer turned, stared that way as they all did, hoping to catch some glimpse of Grant, or even the corps commander. Beside him, an older man.

"Don't be a mud brain. You think those generals are gonna stand up here where we can all give 'em a salute? They didn't get to be generals by being blooming morons. Just do your job."

Bauer glanced at the man, a short gray beard, a man with the same frightening look he had seen from Willis, a man who knew something of killing.

"What unit . . ."

"Forty-fifth Illinois, boy. Done told you once. I wanted to be out there with the first wave, but Colonel Maltby told me himself he wanted my eyesight back here. You got a reputation, I suspect. That's why you're here. Me, too. They want my musket where it'll do some good. Any fool can run up a damn hill."

First wave? Bauer pondered that, clearly a man who knew a great deal more than Bauer did.

"I got picked for this because I can shoot pretty good, I guess," Bauer said. "Done some sharp-shooter duty. Seventeenth Wisconsin."

"Well, Wisconsin, if Colonel Maltby's gonna lead some kind of attack against those works, I'm damn sure gonna do what it takes to make it easier on him. That means picking off rebels. You clear on that?"

"Don't know Colonel Maltby. . . ."

"You will, soon enough. Finest regimental commander in the army. Nothing we wouldn't do for him. McPherson must feel the same way, chose him for this job."

"What job?"

The man looked at him, then spat out a stream of tobacco juice to one side.

"They didn't tell me precisely. All I know is something's gonna start up pretty quick, and Colonel Maltby's in charge."

Bauer stared out over the barrel of the musket, nothing moving along the rebel works, little sound close by but the low chatter of the sharpshooters.

"You know the Coonskin fellow?"

The man motioned toward the tower.

"Right up there, I suspect. Best shot in the whole dang place."

Bauer looked that way, again nothing to see, a row of men in blue, muskets up, ready.

"Guess that's good. He's kind of . . . interesting."

"He'll shoot the eye out of a blue jay, and he's already played hell with a passel of rebs. Happy he's up there. You should be, too."

"Guess I am."

The other way, a single musket fired, voices now, an officer calling out.

"Keep still! There's nothing moving over there!"

The man next to Bauer spit again, sighted down his musket, and said, "That'd be Graves. Most impatient man in the whole outfit. Shoots at shadows, rabbits, snakes, even says he hit a mosquito once. But sometimes he's just a damn fool."

"He that good a shot?"

"He says he hit a mosquito, I'd believe him. Seen him knock the hat off a reb at near four hundred yards. Right over there. Plugged the fellow from Coonskin's perch. Earned him a spot out here, for certain. What'd you do?"

Bauer wasn't sure how to respond.

"Sharpshooter duty. Knocked down a few." He felt the urge to boast of that, knew he had shot a half-dozen men through the stovepipe, until the rebels learned that their clever invention wasn't so clever after all.

"Not gonna talk about it, eh?"

"Not inclined to. They're just men. I've done what they told me to do."

"Some advice for you, boy. Stop thinking of them as men. They're rebs. Secesh. The enemy. You been on picket duty, talked to 'em?"

Bauer thought of Zep.

"Yeah. This morning."

"You wanna be a good sharpshooter, or maybe even train to be a long-distance sniper, you need to beg off that picket duty. I've watched too many boys sit out there and make friends with those rebs, like we're all just out here for fun. Some say it doesn't affect 'em, that they can go right out the next day and kill all those new 'friends' they made, stick a bayonet in the gut of a man they just traded coffee with. But I've seen the look. They hesitate. They start remembering the man's name, all that friendly talk about a wife and kids and 'back home.' All that'll do is get you killed."

"Guess so."

"You better guess so. You're sitting in this ditch next to me, and it weren't my choice. Just chance. But I want you killing people as quick as you can, before some lucky fool over there can take aim at my damn head. I'll do the same for you."

Bauer didn't respond, believed the man completely. Behind him, an officer moved close, huddled low behind the mounds of dirt.

"Eyes to the front!"

Bauer focused on the gun sights, stared out toward the massive redan. The ground there was constructed in a long V shape, the point aiming toward the Federal line. There was movement to one side, a dozen men slipping out into the trenches that curled closest to the rebel works, within twenty-five yards of the tallest mounds of earth.

Beside him, the older man said, "Watch the top. Any reb's gotta stand up tall to have a shot at those boys. Makes a perfect silhouette." More men appeared now, packing the main trenches in a line four across, like a column of march. Behind Bauer, the captain again, nervous jabbering.

"**Forlorn Hope**. That's what they call them. Those boys up front. Forlorn Hope. Captain Hickenlooper himself's leading them. God help him. General Logan's over that way, says Hickenlooper's boys did this, so it's his place to lead the way."

The words were meaningless to Bauer, and he stared out to the cluster of men in the farthest trench, saw them down low, no one moving, as though just . . . waiting. He felt his breathing quicken, didn't really know why, could feel the tension in the men around him, the captain's anxiousness annoying, the man thankfully moving away. Bauer stared at the top of the redan, nothing, no movement, no hint of anyone there. The line of sharpshooters was deathly quiet now, the instructions from the officers filled with a kind of finality that made each man focus on the job he was supposed to do. Handpicked, he thought. Sammie thought I needed to be here. Where? Nothing's happening. He glanced up, the sun pressing him down, no shadows in the trench, no cool place. In both directions, men were doing the same, staring out silently, muskets up, and he felt frozen, uncertain, sweat in his eyes now, rolling down his face. He caught a glimpse of movement, high above, a bird, huge, then more, in slow, drifting circles. The silence from the men was magnifying the sounds of the open land around them, chirping birds, crickets, and close to one side, a bird landed on the dirt, startling him. The bird fluttered away, and Bauer tried to concentrate on whatever was supposed to be out there, whatever the officers were expecting. He felt drained of energy, a chill of sweat in his shirt, glanced to either side, still no one talking.

"Eyes front!"

Bauer didn't respond, knew the order was directed at him. He put his cheek against the stock of the musket, kept his stare out to the top of the dirt wall, his mind drifting, and he glanced down to his pocket watch, instinct, but the watch was long broken. The words came out to no one, his brain trying to latch onto some thought, something to focus him.

"What time is it?"

The man beside him responded, soft words through hard breathing.

"Half past three."

Bauer nodded, wanted to thank the man, felt an odd rumble beneath him. He gripped the musket, braced himself, a quake coming up into his legs, felt a bolt of panic, looked out, the rumble growing, spreading out in every direction.

"What . . . ?"

Across the way, the rumble grew, louder now, the rebel works seeming to shake, rising slowly, like some great uncoiling beast. The blast came now, yards wide, the fat earthworks rising up in a cloud of black smoke, dirt and timbers, rising higher, the thunderous explosion blowing closer, dust in his eyes, and he blinked through that, stared with paralyzed shock, watching the earth itself bursting to life, tossing guns and pieces of wagons upward like so many toys, still rising, the plume of earth not merely disguising or shading the rebel works. It was the rebel works.

CHAPTER FORTY

BAUER

THE 3RD LOUISIANA REDAN
JUNE 25, 1863, 4:00 P.M.

The Federal artillery far in both directions responded to the eruption of the mine by throwing out a heavy barrage of shot and shell, a diversion designed to keep the rebels in place, to prevent any great wave of reinforcements from surging toward the rupture in the redan.

Bauer blinked through the smoke and dust, saw flickers of blue, the Forlorn Hope moving quickly into the gaping hole caused by the blast. Behind them, the first wave of assault troops rose up from the Federal trenches in a rapid blue wave, pouring up into the thick cloud of smoke. Hickenlooper's Forlorn Hope had been charged with clearing away as much of the debris as possible, to make way for the rapid push by a hundred or more men of the Illinois regiment, those men hoping to shove a breakthrough completely through the rebel position. In the trenches now, more men moved forward, the next wave, waiting for the order to climb out and charge into the opening. Bauer searched frantically for a target, even a hint of a rebel soldier who might try to stand up against the blue tide. But the smoke and the debris hung thick in the air, the mass of blue troops disappearing as quickly as they surged through the remains of the rebel works. The men around Bauer were as anxious as he was, many calling out, cursing the rebels they could not see. Bauer shared their helplessness, but so far, there was no great battle, no sudden volleys of musket fire greeting the Federal advance, no sign that the rebels had been up on their parapets at all.

His mind raced, straining to see, trying to understand what was happening. Behind the sharpshooters, the officers seemed as paralyzed as the men before them, no one issuing orders, no one really in charge. The noise came only from the charging soldiers, a rapid scramble up and through the shattered embankment, the clouds of smoke still thick, obscuring whatever enemy the Illinois men had found. For a long moment, Bauer stared at the blue advance, flinching at every sharp sound, waiting for the inevitable, the horrific clash of muskets. To one side, Hickenlooper's artillery battery opened up, a series of thunderous blows that Bauer had to

believe were aimed far past the Federal troops. But
there was nothing to see of that, either, no great
fiery blasts among any rebel mass, the shells from
the battery blending in now with much more shelling from Federal artillery farther down the lines.
Bauer had heard this before, the Federal gunners
supporting one another, every battery along the
lines opening up, as though Grant himself was giving the enemy a sign, we're coming, all of us, and
this time we won't stop until we drive you into the
river. Bauer tried to feel the energy of that, but the
waves of sulfur smoke began washing over him, watering his eyes, some of the men near him coughing, heads down, others straining as he did, trying
to see just what was happening.

And then, the musket fire came, well back of the
smoking crater, farther away than he expected. It
rolled toward them in a solid, rattling chant, the
pulses of sound close together, row upon row of
rebel soldiers standing, aiming, firing. From his
perch, Bauer caught a glimpse of a flash, up beyond
the blasted earth, more flashes, closer now, the Illinois men responding. Behind him, an officer, the
captain.

"Give it to 'em, boys! Give it to 'em!"

The words were meaningless, the officer seeming to know that, the great boisterous cheer losing
energy, even as others tried to take up the call. But
the musket fire was distant, too distant, strange, as
though the rebels had been pulled away, no one

up on their closest parapets at all. The volleys poured back and forth, and Bauer could see the first wounded now, men staggering back out of the smoke, stumbling, falling among the churned-up dirt, rocks, timbers. Close in front of him, more men went forward, into the trenches, an officer, sword in hand, pointing the way. Some of those men broke ranks, helping the wounded, pulling them into the safety of the trench lines, while others climbed through the wreckage of the redan and disappeared into the rising clouds of smoke. The artillery kept up its fire, close by, deadening Bauer's ears, the hard ringing penetrating his brain. Still he searched with the musket, expected to see rebels, to the side, perhaps, high up on the adjacent ground undamaged by the mine explosion. He felt the raw fear about that, that if the Illinois men had failed, had collapsed, the rebels would show themselves on the flanks, rising up from some hidden cover. Then the job would fall on the sharpshooters, on **him,** to push them back, to make the good shot, the very reason he was there. But there was no back-and-forth, no surge and retreat that anyone on the sharpshooter line could see at all.

From the first days the mining operation had begun, the Confederates had been frantic in their attempts to locate the exact positions of the tunnels, men sitting low in holes in the earth, the digging and chopping by the Federal miners clearly audible somewhere close by, closer every day. Despite their efforts, the Confederate engineers could do nothing to halt the digging that was very soon right beneath their feet. What Major Lockett could not accomplish by stopping the Federal miners, he could instead combat by letting them complete their task. With the sounds of the excavation straight beneath the redan itself, Lockett had guessed when the Federal effort would end, and Lockett planned accordingly. When the mine exploded, the obliterated ramparts and mounds of ruptured earth were almost completely devoid of men. As the soldiers of the 45th Illinois drove through the ragged gap blown through the face of the 3rd Louisiana Redan, the enemy they expected to see simply wasn't there. To the stunned surprise of Hickenlooper's Forlorn Hope, followed closely by Colonel Jasper Maltby's first assault wave, the Federal soldiers found no great expanse of shattered bodies, no throngs of tortured wounded, no sign that enormous numbers of Louisiana men had been tossed skyward. Instead, as they made their way through the crater, they discovered exactly what the rebels had done. Major Lockett had constructed another stout earthwork, well back of the leading edge of the redan, had withdrawn the Louisiana troops away from their parapets, lining them up in wait for the inevitable destruction of the forward-most walls. Pushing farther through the smoke and debris, the Illinois troops were suddenly confronted by an extended line of freshly shoveled earth, set back far enough from the blast that the rebels Lockett had positioned there were completely untouched by the explosion. The first wave of Federal troops shoved through the crater, climbing up the sloping hillsides far inside the redan. Emerging from the smoke, they saw several hundred rebel troops, a dense row of muskets raised and aimed, waiting for them.

As Colonel Maltby's first lines collapsed, reinforcements were called forward, the Federal commanders realizing quickly what the rebels had done. The blue surge drove out through the trench lines, then up into the crater itself. But the crater could only hold so many men, and quickly the Federal forces spread out along the base of the redan, some moving forward, to the far embankments of the crater itself.

The order to the sharpshooters was specific and urgent: Run hard to the front side of the redan, spreading up and out along the crest, taking aim at any rebel troops who might be driving toward the crater. Bauer ran with the others, down into the trench lines, back up, across open ground. The walls of the redan were soft dirt, and he stared toward the breach, the crater, the smoke still thick, the sounds of the fight ongoing. To one side, an officer waved his sword, driving the men up onto the embankment, a stretch of high ground that spread out away from the chaos in the crater. Bauer collapsed on the crest, a line of men on either side of him, most of them lying prone, again sighting with their muskets, seeking targets. He tried to steady the weapon, his breathing in hard bursts, dirt in his eyes, smoke choking him. The officers were still calling out their commands, but the sharpshooters were mostly silent, a few firing their muskets. Bauer stared into smoke, saw flashes in the distance, the thick lines of rebels far away, men in blue pushing that way, slow progress into a storm of fire. The crater itself was thick with men, too thick, many of them pulling away, back out into the open, climbing up the face of the redan, trying to do what the sharpshooters were already doing, to find some way to make a fight. On the far side of the crater, rebels began to appear, easing up to the crest, shooting down into the blue, most not aiming, the targets dense and easy. Bauer aimed the musket, a long shot, saw a cluster of rebels along the crest nearest to him, focused, still shaking, the musket firing, a jolt to his shoulder. Others fired as well, the targets visible, a surge of rebel troops coming up close to the edges of the crater. Bauer pulled the weapon back to him quickly, sat up, reloaded, rolled over again, searched. But the rebels had learned, were mostly down behind the embankments, few making the foolish attempt to stand tall and fire downward, completely exposed to a hundred blue marksmen. Bauer saw movement, rebels gathering within a hundred yards of him, shouted that way, but the others had seen as well, more muskets aimed that way.

The artillery began again, muzzle blasts behind the rebel works, answered by a storm of shells from Federal guns passing close over Bauer's head. He flattened out, instinct, closed his eyes, heard the shells splitting the air very close to him, cursed the artillerymen. But the shells were high enough, impacting far back along the rebel position, more shells launched down the line, more support from distant guns. The roar was deafening, screeches and rumbles from the different shells, his own reflex pressing his face into the sand. After a long minute, the shelling seemed to move away, toward new targets, and he looked up, wiped the roughness from his eyes, struggling to see anything at all. The rebels were in a solid line now, across the crater, the men in blue making a fight upward, many falling, shot down in the smoking crater itself. Officers still came forward, and Bauer marveled at that, a color bearer scampering forward, more officers, the men reaching the far side of the crater, right below the rebels, what seemed to be the safest place to be. Bauer sighted the musket, scanned the crest above those men, struggled to breathe, wiped at his eyes again. Beside him, a man fired, calling out to the rebels, the man reloading now, leaning close to him.

"Hey, boy! This is some kind of holiday, eh? Sometimes it's good to hug the bosom of Mother Earth."

Bauer saw the man's face, gap-toothed grin, the man rolling away, aiming, firing again. He called out to his intended targets again, and Bauer felt the strange confidence, no fear, the man going about his job with perfect efficiency, whether he was hitting anything or not. Bauer stared out to the far side of the crater and asked him, "You see anybody worth shooting at? They're so damn far away."

"Who cares? They want us shootin', well, I'm shootin'!"

The man laughed, manic, a chattering giggle, and Bauer tried to ignore him, stared out again, saw rebels slipping along the hillside away from the crater.

"There!" he said.

Bauer aimed, fired, too quick, made a loud grunt, angry at himself, slid back down the hill, reloaded, saw an officer climbing up toward him, the man struggling in soft sand, his sword in his hand.

"Prepare to advance! There's too many of us clogging up the breach. We're going over here! March toward the far side of the crater!"

Bauer saw the fear in the man's eyes, the officer trying to steady himself on the steep slope. A bugle sounded now, somewhere below, and Bauer saw a line of men coming up from the trenches, climbing toward him, more officers, colors, and the officer saw as well, waved the sword over his head, shouted out, "Up! Advance! Don't be frightened!"

The man was moving away now, along the hillside, more shouts to other men. Bauer soaked in the man's words, the absurdity, moronic foolishness. **Don't be frightened**. He shouted a response, curses, angry words that meant nothing, no one to hear, and screamed at himself now, "Get up! Go!"

He hesitated, hard shaking in his legs, squeezed the musket, forced himself to rise to his feet. Along the crest, others did the same, the new line of men climbing toward them closer, their officers calling out.

"Go! Advance!"

Bauer felt the push from behind, raw energy, moved with the men around him, dropping down off the crest, across a parapet, down farther, fought to keep his balance. He tried to see the rebels, any rebels, but the footing was treacherous, pain in his legs, his breathing hard through dust and smoke and burnt powder. He was off the slope now, flatter ground, open, the crater close to one side, and he saw men lying flat in every direction, lifeless, others aiming the musket, some men huddled low, seeking any cover they could find. Behind him, the fresh wave of men came down, pushed by screaming sergeants, the orders of the lieutenants, any other officer trying to do the job. He pressed forward slowly, didn't need to be shouted at to know where the fight was, where his musket was needed, where he was supposed to go. He followed men who stepped out into the crater, the ground beneath his feet ragged, stinking, split jagged timbers, wreckage blocking his way. Around him, men were tossing aside what they could, opening a path. But those men went down quickly, the rebels up on the far side of the crater responding to the advance, flashes of musket fire in waves, the stinging rip of the air around him slowing Bauer down, pushing him to the earth. He flattened out, gripped the soil, pulling himself into the ground, the man's words in his head, **the bosom of Mother Earth**. The air ripped past his ear, the ground punched close in front of him, and he froze, couldn't fight the terror, felt paralyzed, but the words burst through his brain, his own command, fury at himself, at the coward he had been, that he was trying to be now. Move! Get up!

He looked up, saw men in blue huddled low against the far embankment, and back the other way, more men trudging through the debris at the great breach, adding to the strength of the Federal push, adding bodies to those who had fallen. Officers were pulling men back now, the crater too crowded, nowhere for them to go, a color bearer running past him, back, out of the hole. Others came forward, a line of men coming down to one side, avoiding the breach, tangling with the chaos of the men already there. The debris offered cover, and Bauer rose up to a crouch, saw a small mound of smoking earth, stumbled that way, curled up, pulled his knees in tight, his musket hard against his shins. He fought with himself, what he should do now, where he could go, where he **had** to go, saw an officer standing close to him, waving the sword, the man suddenly collapsing. But another officer came up, shouting out, gathering his men. The ground to one side erupted in a spray of dirt and fire, a blow from rebel artillery, and Bauer heard the response, a new wave of Federal fire, deafening, streaking overhead, gunners pushing their charges achingly close to the heads of their own men. Bauer held the grip of the musket across his knees, pulling tighter still, trying to breathe, to see, the small bit of protection just high enough to block the rebel musket fire.

The officer was still there, still waving his men past, and he looked at Bauer, pointed the sword, and gave a hard shout over the din: "Up! Advance! Let's go!"

Bauer saw the strength in the man, searched for it in himself, begged, cursed the terror. But the officer wouldn't leave, only called out again, "Up! Get up, son! Show those men who you are!"

Bauer absorbed that, thought of Willis, images flashing through him, Finley, the gruff sergeant, no fear at all. The officer moved away, colors close behind him, men surging past, and Bauer straightened his legs, rolled over, took a long breath, wiped away the cold shivering in his knees, his hands, the

ice in his chest. He stood shakily, pulled the musket up tight to his chest, saw the rebels high up
across the crater, steady fire, some now down in the
crater itself. Men were struggling, bayonets, muskets as clubs, the rebels pushing forward, but not
many, the blue troops taking hold, driving them
back. Bauer started to move forward, glanced out
to the side, the crater narrow, a small ocean of bare
dirt, men in any cover they could find. The musket
fire went both ways, but the rebels had the ground,
the height, and Bauer saw a mass of blue along the
base of the crater, saw the officer, followed still by
the color bearer, moved that way. He tumbled forward into more soft sand, men tumbling onto him,
others shifting their position, making space. He lay
on his back, gasped for air, the musket against his
chest, could see the blue troops out across the crater, many of those pulling away, blending into a
fresh surge of men through the yawning gap. On
the far side of the crater, Federal troops lined the
crest, doing what he had done, trading fire with the
rebels right above him. He watched it all, a helpless spectator, heard an artillery shell coming down
hard, back behind the rebels. Some men were still
in the open, firing up from churned-up earth, using
the blasted ground for cover, some men shoving
wooden timbers up as protection. An artillery shell
burst now, the rebel gun to one side, blasting a pile
of timbers to splinters, ripping into the men behind
it, the men who thought they were safe. The mus-

kets aimed for the rebel cannon, Federal artillery responding as well, the rebel gun gone now, pulled away or destroyed. To one side of the crater, rebels appeared along the crest, Bauer now exposed, the men around him responding as he did, taking aim, a burst of musket fire punching the dirt along the crest. Across the way, the Federal troops along the redan took up the fire as well, keeping the rebels down, behind their great mound of earth.

The rebels seemed to have pulled away, the men around Bauer safe, for now, the muskets coming down, men gathering up, an officer, another, heated exchange. Beside him, Bauer saw the face of a boy, terrified animal eyes, tears, and Bauer said, "It's all right! Don't be frightened!"

The boy stared at him, and Bauer expected the boy to bolt away, had seen that look before, knew what the boy was feeling. But the boy nodded toward him and said, "What do we do?"

"We fight! You see a rebel, you shoot him!"

The words were meaningless, a hundred men spread out on the sloping dirt, little fight in them at all. Some were without muskets, and Bauer saw weapons out in the crater, some close to fallen men. Damn!

"We're done for! They're coming!"

The words came from a few feet away, one man on his knees, ready to run, a sergeant there, shouting at the man, "Get down! Nobody's coming down here! Get ready! Load your weapon!"

Bauer felt strength in the sergeant, had seen that before, and the man responded, flattened out, seemed to calm. The sergeant crawled along the men and said, "You stay put! The rebs'll stay back and we're in the best place in the field!"

One of the officers was there now, and Bauer felt the control returning, the discipline coming back.

"Keep low, men! You see the enemy, fire at will! Anybody see Colonel Maltby?"

"Sir, the colonel went down . . . out there."

The officer lowered his head and said quietly, "Damn. Well, until somebody back there tells us to move, we're staying right here."

With so many Federal troops outside the redan, the rebels were content to keep to their position along the back side of the crater, and beyond. The fight had settled into something of a stalemate, and with the fading daylight, the Federal troops shifted into whatever positions they could find within the crater and outside the edges of the redan. The musket fire was still there, but slower now, men choosing targets, most of that from the Federal side. Bauer huddled against the wall of the crater, engulfed in the stink of powder, the smell of the fight held in the crater like water in a bowl. The men closest to the rebels were still the safest, and the few rebel muskets that offered fire were aimed out far past Bauer and the men at the base of the rebel position. But here, so close to the newly dug parapets where the rebels made their perch, Bauer had no target at all, the men straight up above him, a glimpse of a musket barrel, a bayonet, smoke from the muzzles.

Bauer studied the men around him, some hatless, shirtless, a few with wounds, blood on arms. Others did as he did, gripped the musket, gazing upward, the faint hope that a rebel would make a mistake, would erupt into that mindless heroism, that when the enemy was so close, some men would leap into the fray, slashing with the bayonet, the knife, firing the pistol. The men in blue seemed to expect that, sergeants slipping among them, the officers with their unnecessary warnings about "being ready."

He hadn't fired the musket in a while now, still no targets, some of the men around him having none of that discipline. Men fired still, aiming straight up, worthless effort, the sergeants shouting them down. But Bauer lay flat against the dirt, the musket ready, angry hope that a target would appear. The officer seemed to know better, nervous jabbering that the rebels were in the good cover and would certainly stay there, while the men in blue were caught in a place they would have to spend the night. Back across the maw of the crater, others kept up the musket fire, pinning the rebels down in their protection. Above Bauer, the rebels kept their muskets quiet, almost no return fire. He could hear them, voices, orders, the same kinds of panic and discipline, that even with so many of the enemy so very close, there was very little anyone could do about it.

And then, he saw the dark ball, the odd, egg-shaped piece of steel. It rolled down the hillside next to him, kept rolling, below his feet. A man jumped quickly, snatched it up, threw it back up the hill, the blast coming right above Bauer's head.

"Ketcham!"

"Watch it! There'll be more!"

Bauer flinched from the blast, the question bursting out of him, others as well.

"What was **that?**"

The sergeant closest to him stared upward, expectant, and said, "Ketcham grenade! They take a few seconds to ignite. You see one, throw it back! If you're too late . . . well, it won't much matter."

Bauer had heard something of the grenades, had never seen one, never used anything like that in training.

"Who's Ketcham?"

"Who the hell knows, Private. You gonna ask around?"

The next one came now, rebels shouting out as it rolled down the hill, the iron ball tumbling off to one side, no one close, the blast tossing dirt up in a fiery burst. Bauer heard a man screaming, others moving quickly, the word Bauer had come to hate.

"Shrapnel! Get a doc!"

"There's no doc! He all right?"

"No, hell he's not all right! Got him in the chest!"

Bauer absorbed the chaos, heard cheering from above, one voice: "Hey bluebellies! We got a thousand of them things! Wait till dark, then we's gonna have a real party!"

One man stood, fired his musket, still no target, the man dropping down, reloading, cursing.

"You damn rebs! If we're out here after dark, we're coming up there and slit your damn throats!"

"Got a better **idee,** Billy Yank!"

Bauer saw the grenade coming down in an arc, felt his heart stop, the ball landing with a soft thump beside him. The shouts came, but he rose to his knees, grabbed it, hard and cold in his hand, a wisp of smoke, and he slung his arm in a high toss, the grenade going straight overhead, igniting now in a cloud of fire. He closed his eyes, flinched again, heard shreds of metal whistle past, the sand around him absorbing the shrapnel. He dropped down again, the heartbeats thundering in his chest, heard the officer, far to one side.

"Be ready! Be quick about it!"

Bauer stared upward, the daylight fading quickly, the familiar fear returning, the taunt from the rebel driving home. Dark. Can't see 'em. A thousand of 'em.

"Hey, Billy Yank! How's this?"

The iron ball rolled down in a furrow of soft sand, a smoking fuse, much larger, and the sergeant was there, grabbed it, shouted out, and with a loud grunt, slung it back overhead. The toss was perfect, the shell exploding on top of the hill, the shouts and screams now coming from the rebels.

"Good work! Be ready for more!" Bauer looked to the voice, calm authority, an officer moving up quickly from somewhere out in the crater. "I'm Major Stolbrand. Those artillery shells have a fuse. If it's still smoking, throw it back."

"Bauer, sir."

"Let's go to work, Bauer. All of you! Try to catch those grenades in the air. They're not that heavy. The bigger shells . . . well, if we can throw a few of those back over, the rebs'll get tired of that game pretty quick."

Bauer watched the major crouching low, his eyes alert, darting back and forth, and Bauer did the same, waited, breathless silence, the men all along the sloping ground knowing what to expect now.

With the darkness, the grenades still came, but the men were ready for them, the fuses just slow enough to provide flickering light, that even in the darkness the Federal troops could see them. The men responded with the same urgent energy as the sergeant, the shells hurled back up to the crest of the hill, returned to their owners. Bauer stayed close to Major Stolbrand, mimicked his actions, the man clearly understanding what kind of weapon the Ketcham grenades were, the horrific damage they could inflict, the breathless moment of time the men had to get rid of them.

As the darkness settled completely over the crater, the rebels began to tire of this deadly sport, Stolbrand and the men close to him becoming far more skilled at countering the grenades with alertness, speed, and a good arm. If Bauer knew nothing of this absurd game before, he discovered quickly that he was learning from an expert. The major had come forward through the crater to scout the ground for a Federal plan to position an artillery battery at point-blank range to the rebel works. Charles Stolbrand was General John Logan's chief of artillery. With full darkness, the effort began to bring Federal cannons forward, creating a protected battery that would certainly decimate the rebels who tried to hold their position on the far side. But the rebels were not idle. After a desperate scrounge along the rebel lines for additional percussion caps, the rebel muskets again came to life, the men from Louisiana now equipped to stop any further Federal advance, especially the vulnerable artillery crews.

With neither side able to dislodge the other, by the following afternoon, Grant was faced with yet another agonizing frustration. Though the mine explosion had accomplished what the engineers had hoped, the rebel engineers, particularly Samuel Lockett, had made the only countermove they could. It worked. Late the next day, Grant ordered the attack called off, and under a curtain of covering fire from the strong positions outside the redan, the Federal troops who endured a night so close to the enemy were able to escape the crater and return to their lines outside the 3rd Louisiana Redan.

For Bauer, the escape started one more weary journey back to his unit, to the Irishmen who had witnessed the mine explosion from a distance, who had spent the long night wondering about the fate of their Dutchman. Those men had done all they could to hold down or distract any rebels across their part of the line, meager assistance for the men who made the assault on the crater. For Sammie Willis, the lieutenant who had given his friend the honor of becoming a handpicked marksman, the wait was the worst of all.

CHAPTER FORTY-ONE

SHERMAN

NEAR COX'S FERRY—
THE BIG BLACK RIVER
JUNE 27, 1863

He walked out from the horse and scanned the open land east of the waterway.

"No movement, then?"

"No, sir. Nothing we've determined with any certainty. They're out there, we know that. The last report put the bulk of his troops close to Vernon. But even those forces are minimal in strength. They are spread out through the various villages east of the river, but so far, there is no sign they are forming for a general advance."

Sherman looked at the young man, and couldn't help being impressed.

"Captain Ballou, you have performed admirably."

The cavalryman seemed to know how rarely Sherman offered praise.

"I'm only doing my duty, sir. But, thank you."

"Any reports from up north? Anything moving out of Yazoo City?"

"Sir, Lieutenant Joel took a patrol up that way, encountered a few rebels. Wirt Adams's boys. Pretty sure about that. But they were just an outpost. No sign of any bodies of infantry making any move at all. I admit, sir, it is most curious."

"What's curious?"

"Well, sir, we have heard from a number of rebels in the vicinity, captured scouts mostly, all of them insisting that Johnston's army is coming this way. There are reports that he has as many as one hundred thousand effectives."

Sherman tilted his head, the brim of his hat shading his face from the blistering sun.

"Then we'd be in a bad way, wouldn't you say, Captain?"

"Well, yes, sir. That was my thinking."

"And yet, you scouted all over hell and New Jersey, and couldn't find them? Pretty hard to hide a hundred thousand men. And if you gave that a little more thought, Captain, you'd wonder why Joe Johnston would want them hidden at all. I would think he'd make as much noise as he could, do everything possible to scare us right out of our pants. That's the point, isn't it?"

"Sir?"

"Scare us out of our pants. Chase us the hell out of this country. Save Vicksburg from the evil blue plague. So. Where the hell is he?"

The captain seemed suddenly uncomfortable, as though Sherman was about to unleash some punishment on him. Sherman saw the uncertainty, a glimmer of fear on the young man's face, not what he wanted to see.

"Relax, Captain. You've sent patrols out along the railroad, out into every little burg the rebels could be hiding."

"Well, yes, sir."

"You find any sign that there's a hundred thousand men out there?"

"I regret . . . no, sir."

"For God's sake, Captain, I'm paying you a compliment. You didn't **miss** them. You didn't find them because they're not there. I'm guessing you didn't trip over Horace Greeley, Jefferson Davis, or Abigail Adams, either."

The captain seemed to relax, as though getting the point.

"No, sir. They're not out there, either."

"No, Captain, the rebs are investing all their hope in . . . **hope**. Johnston's out there scratching himself, wondering if we're going to let him sneak into Vicksburg and reinforce Pemberton. Are we?"

"Not if he comes this way, sir."

"No other way he can come. He has to cross the Big Black sooner or later, and we've got people at every shallow ford. If he has engineers who think they can build a bridge, I'm assuming your horsemen might notice that."

"Yes, sir. We are continuing the patrols along every part of the river."

Sherman raised the glasses again, scanned distant trees, patches of brush, open land that Grant's army had trampled weeks before.

"You care to hear my estimate of this situation, Captain?"

"Certainly, sir."

"Johnston isn't a complete fool. He knows how strong Grant is, and how much support we're getting from the navy, both on the Mississippi and the Yazoo. He knows we've stripped most of this country of supplies, which will make it a problem for him to feed his army on the march. He might have cavalry support, but you've not had any real . . . **problems** out there, have you?"

"No, sir."

"Grant has a nagging fear of Forrest and Morgan, but we know they're off in Tennessee. Van Dorn gave Grant a bloody nose at Holly Springs, but Van Dorn's dead. Damned helpful, that was. So, there's no great horde of rebel cavalry going to rout your men out of their saddles, right?"

"Not that we know of . . . um . . . no, sir, there are not."

"Correct response, Captain. There are not. So, Joe Johnston knows he has two options. Number one:

He can do nothing. Or two: He can try to push his way straight through this army, which will add several thousand prisoners to what we're going to capture when Vicksburg finally falls. Those sound like reasonable options, Captain?"

"The first one, sir."

Sherman smiled, moved to the horse, took the reins from the groom, and climbed up.

"You're learning. But it doesn't mean this is over, that there's not another bloody nose lurking out here somewhere. You understand that? You keep your men in motion, patrol this stinking little river. Have Lieutenant Joel, or Thielemann's battalion, keep an eye on the Yazoo."

Sherman wheeled the horse around, his staff waiting, gazed once more across the Big Black, thought, If he did come . . . might enjoy that, actually. Rather enjoy giving out my own bloody noses.

GRANT'S HEADQUARTERS
JUNE 28, 1863

"How soon, Lieutenant?"

The young man kept stiffly at attention.

"Sir," he said, "Captain Hickenlooper insists the next mine will be ready for demolition the day after tomorrow."

Grant sat back, looked up at the young man, then turned to Sherman.

"Hickenlooper might be the most valuable man McPherson's got down there. But he came near to getting killed when the first mine went up. Lieutenant, you tell Captain Hickenlooper that if he leads any more attacks on his own, I'll have him driving a hay wagon." Grant paused. "Well, no, don't do that. I'll send a note to McPherson, with my suggestion that he take a little better care of his engineers."

"Begging your pardon, sir, Captain Hickenlooper is an artilleryman."

Sherman chuckled. "Lieutenant, when they put you in charge of handing out jobs in this army, you can decide which position a man like Hickenlooper should hold. My understanding is he's both. Just deliver the note, like a good boy."

Grant didn't react to Sherman's jibe, said only, "Return to your station, Lieutenant. I've no time for this."

The man saluted, clearly intimidated by both generals, and made a quick exit. Rawlins was there now, made a quick glance toward Sherman, then said, "Sir, the prisoners have been sent back to a rest area. They're faring well, considering the hardship."

Sherman was confused. "Rest area? We fill up all the stockades?"

Grant snatched a paper from his desk drawer, and Sherman could feel a lack of patience, Grant's words coming in a clipped growl.

"Our people, Sherman. Pemberton sent them

over here under a flag of truce. Released them out-right. Didn't ask for anything in return."

Sherman's eyes grew wide.

"That's interesting as hell. No request for exchange?"

"Nope."

"General Sherman," Rawlins said, "the prison-ers . . . our men reported they were not being fed adequate rations. Their captors seemed in as dif-ficult a circumstance. I suggested to General Grant that the enemy released our men just so they didn't have to provide for them."

For once, Sherman agreed with Rawlins.

"Yep, interesting. My frontline units report the desertions are increasing. The 55th Illinois took in a dozen last night alone. It's working, Grant."

Grant stopped his work, stared ahead, seemed to gaze at nothing. Sherman could see the lack of sleep in the man's face, the tired eyes and drooping shoulders. Rawlins seemed to focus on that as well.

"Sir," he said, "I shall have some coffee brought this way. General Sherman, is that acceptable?"

"Compared to what?"

Sherman held the thought, saw the frown from Rawlins, understood exactly why. Rawlins had be-come Grant's most fierce protector, especially since Cadwallader had spoken out about his suspicions of Grant's drinking. Sherman regretted the entire affair and scolded himself for the idiotic stab at humor.

"Coffee would be fine, Colonel. But I'm not staying. Grant, I want to head up toward Haines's Bluff. I've been keeping a tight hold on the cavalry and every outpost where Johnston might surprise us. No mistakes this time. We've come too far, done too much."

Grant nodded slowly, a cigar in his hand now.

"We haven't done enough. I'm sick of losing men in every assault, with nothing to show for it. McPherson's got work going on seven mines, and if that lieutenant delivered his message accurately, we're close to blowing hell out of another enemy fortification. But that can't go on, unless we grab something significant. Tossing people a mile in the air sounds like a marvelous tactic, if there's enough of them. So far, we've punched holes, and had them punched right back. If the rebels are starving, they're not doing it fast enough to suit me. Go on, get out of here. Check on your outposts. I do not want to hear that Joe Johnston is suddenly ramming a bayonet up our backsides."

Sherman knew when to take Grant seriously.

"We've got Johnston where we need him," he said, "which is . . . somewhere else. There won't be any surprises in that quarter. They've freed our prisoners, Grant. And they've got nowhere else to go. It's a matter of time. Take confidence in that."

"It's not confidence I lack, Sherman. It's patience."

CHAPTER FORTY-TWO

SPENCE

TO THE REAR OF THE
3RD LOUISIANA REDAN
JUNE 29, 1863

The mine explosion had frightened her worse than any experience with the wounded men, a dark cloud of dirt and debris, with a deep rolling thunder that terrified the patients in her care even more. With the battle that followed, the flow of wounded began again. The wounds themselves were nothing more severe than what she had seen already, shrapnel as well as the shattered bones from musket balls. The sadness of that didn't escape her, that what had once given her nightmares had now become routine, no different than the shrugging calmness of the doctors. The other nurses seemed as battered by their experiences as she was, both the old and young going about their duties with soft-spoken matter-of-factness, calming the most agitated men, holding back the skin and muscle for the amputees, putting hands deep into bloody tissue when the doctor required it.

There was no food at all around the hospital, but still the troops came, emaciated men who begged for any kind of scrap. Not even the officers seemed able to keep the discipline in their men, and so, many of those men drifted away, not to the front lines, but the other way, some going as far as the town. Word had spread among the caves, warning of bands of desperate and dangerous men. The civilians assumed they had to be soldiers, but Lucy had no reason to think that the civilians she had seen weren't just as capable of the kind of lawlessness that was spreading deeper into the lives of every family. Livestock had long since disappeared, the rare milk cow vanishing during the night, chickens and goats and pigs gone completely. And the thefts weren't confined to livestock. Anyone known to have a larder at all might be a victim, confronted by a band of men with muskets, or a lone, frail creature who might only have a knife. Some had no weapons at all, but the threat that showed through their desperation was weapon enough.

———

She walked slowly back toward the caves, her work done for now, the day calmer than the one before. Dr. Prine had allowed her to leave in the early afternoon, the journey much simpler, and much less dangerous in daylight. For all his crudeness, the unmasked stares, Prine still showed concern for her safety. The talk of lawlessness had spread to rumors of a new kind of desperation, some of the thieves not content to slip unseen into someone's pantry. The talk had spread of robbery, anyone walking alone subject to attacks by bandits. Lucy hadn't seen any of that, knew better than to accept the rumors as fact.

She reached the crest overlooking the Cordrays' cave, and so many others', people mostly inside their shelters, protecting themselves as much from the brutal heat of the sun as they were from Yankee artillery. With the heat came an even greater need for water, and as the nearby creeks fouled, and sickness spread, efforts were made by men who journeyed to the big river. But the Yankees had responded to that as well, Cordray himself dodging musket fire from Yankee sharpshooters on the far shore of the Mississippi. The river's muddy water was just as likely as the dirty streams to pass on the dysentery, or any other ailment already affecting the weaker among those in the caves. It was no better in the town, for those few civilians who huddled in their cellars, in a feeble attempt to guard some valuables, treasured mementos too cumbersome to be hauled to the caves. Most of the homes showed damage, and word had come of injuries and deaths from the shelling, those too stubborn or too helpless to secure a hole in the ground far more likely to suffer from the Yankee artillery.

The ground sloped away toward the caves, and she stumbled, an aching weakness in her legs, a hollow pain in her stomach. She fought to right herself, took a deep breath, stepped downward through the trampled grass. She had eaten nothing at all since the evening before, and then, dinner had been only a mash of sweet potato. There was smoke rising up from the cooking pit, and she caught the smell, a hint of roasted meat, her steps quickening. She saw Cordray, two other men, an iron pot over a small fire, the smells drilling through her in a rapturous glow, the pain in her stomach billowing up. She was there now, the men noticing her, the pained look she had become used to, reacting to the blood on her dress. She wore mostly the same dress every day, wouldn't ask Isabel Cordray for any more favors. Cordray's wife had been among the weakest of the adults, had suffered from too many ailments for Lucy to push any harder for considerations from the family who still regarded her as a guest.

"Miss Spence. You look a fright again. I admire your tenacity. If not your stubbornness."

She ignored Cordray, looked at the pot, the aroma sweeping her away, the growling hunger pouring through her.

"What is that? Did you find . . ."

"Squirrel stew."

The words were matter-of-fact, Cordray stirring the pot with a tin spoon.

"My word . . . you shot squirrels? That's wonderful." She fought to hold herself back, thought now of the children, the young girl more sickly than her mother. "Is there a bowl? Should I retrieve some kind of vessel?"

"Here." Cordray handed her a small china bowl. "Careful. It's hot."

He ladled the stew into the bowl, the amazing steam rising up, her brain begging her to drink it down, burn or not.

"Should I take this to Mrs. Cordray?"

He stirred the pot again, the men producing bowls of their own, and said, "No. She's too ill. The children have eaten already."

She blew softly across the brown liquid, the agonizing wait, put the bowl to her lips, a small sip. The thin gravy flowed through her like heavenly molasses, and she blew the steam away again, another sip, caught a piece of meat, chewed, tender, far different than the mule meat. She began to gulp the stew now, made an indiscreet slurp.

"Easy, child. That's all we have right now. Beyond the skins of the sweet potatoes, it's all we have for the rest of the day."

The bowl was empty too quickly, her tongue swabbing anything remaining, and she felt the warmth of the liquid inside of her, the aching hunger softened.

"It was wonderful, sir. Squirrel? Who was it that shot a squirrel?"

The others looked at her, moved away without speaking, and Cordray said, "We didn't shoot anything. We have no weapons here. The trap was successful. I suppose we should be grateful for what the Almighty provides." He paused, and she could see the anger building on his face, expected him to lash out at her. He pounded the spoon against the iron grate of the fire pit, startling her. "Do you know what is happening here, child? You know of hospitals and nursing, I suppose, all of those things that concern soldiers. I have not objected, not yet. It is not a respectable duty for women. Not at all. Not with so much else . . . with this outrage against us, who have done nothing to call for this. And now, our own . . . these damnable merchants . . ."

"Merchants?"

"Child, we are barely surviving out here, any of us. I am not a wealthy man, and so I cannot afford to feed my family. But, in town, right now, there are men who hoard flour and corn and molasses. All I would need to do is pay their price. Flour is merely six hundred dollars a barrel! One generous soul is offering to sell biscuits for four dollars each! Molasses . . . twelve dollars per gallon. There is beef.

Beef, child! Some say the Yankees are supplying it for only three dollars per pound. All one has to do is pay them in gold!"

"That cannot be, sir. The people would not do such a thing."

"Oh, they will most certainly do it, child. And all the while, my wife stays ill, my children grow weaker. All this talk about General Johnston . . . how he will save us. I hope when the general arrives, he puts those merchants in the gallows. Our most respected commander, **Old Pem** . . . does nothing at all!"

He stopped, drained by his fury, and she saw him looking away, as though embarrassed by his sudden loss of decorum. "My apologies, child. I must remember that every day we survive the Yankees' artillery, we are more fortunate than some." He looked at the empty bowl in her hand. "I hope you found your meal acceptable."

"Yes, indeed. Thank you, sir. Your generosity is most appreciated."

She didn't know what else to say, watched silently as he turned back to the fire pit. He filled his own bowl, scraping the spoon through the empty pot, then held the stew in front of him and said a short prayer. She realized she had not blessed her own, and waited silently for him to finish. He repeated her routine, cooled the steaming stew with his breath, then slowly drank from the bowl. She saw him grimace, struggling to chew, then swallowing, gulping down the rest.

He turned to her, seemed to sag, and said, "It would be helpful if you would speak with my wife. I fear for her health. It is one thing to suffer from the plague of Yankees. But she will not eat. Not even hunger will move her. I admit to being frustrated, child. She is the most stubborn creature on God's earth."

He began to walk to the cave, Lucy close behind, and she said, "Yes, certainly. It is not wise for her to just . . . starve herself. The children have been fed, though. That at least is something."

"Yes. Something." He slipped into the cave, and she stopped, felt the heat of the sun, sweat through her clothes, caught a hint of the stink she carried, thought of the creek. At least, some kind of bathing. I should take a pan down there, do something to clean what I can. I cannot expect this family to endure . . . this.

She heard Cordray call out, and he emerged from the cave, holding out a crude box of wire in his hands.

"Success again! Thank God. At least there will be something for tonight. Go, child, tell Mr. Atkins the trap worked again. Perhaps his contraption will be as effective."

Lucy stared, took a step back, the small cage bursting with frantic movement. It was a rat.

———

She heard the man's voice, a plaintive call, looked up from the trickle of water at the creek. Through the low brush he came, the servant, James, at a jogging run down the hillside. He stopped, bent over, a painful chorus of sharp, raspy breathing, his age and ill health showing itself. Lucy felt a tug of alarm, stood where he could see her, and shook the water from her hands.

"James! Are you all right? Are you injured?"

She saw now he was crying, and he dropped to his knees, his hands hanging low, looking skyward.

"Oh, dear me. Dear me. He's gone, for certain. Gone, Miss Lucy."

She felt a hard, icy twist in her stomach, had never seen James emotional about anything.

"What has happened? Who's gone?"

He looked at her with a stream of tears on both cheeks, shook his head.

"I didn't b'lieve 'em. Thought dey was making fool of ole James. But I heerd more from the others. He's gone. Oh Lawd. I cain't hardly stand it, Miss Lucy. He's all I gots."

"Who, James?"

She knew the answer already, felt tears of her own, his pain seeping into her.

"Ole Rufus, Miss Lucy. Dey done took him. Mr.

Atkins tole me. I thought dey was lyin', but dey tole me where. . . . Oh Lawd, Miss Lucy. I seen him. What dey done. He's been skint. It's all what's left."

He sobbed now, his head dropping, and she felt her tears flowing, wanted to say something, anything, to stop this.

"It can't be anything, James. He'll be back. You know Old Rufus. He wanders off now and again."

"No, he don't. He's done got too old, just like ole James. I always reckoned we'd go to the same grave, him and me. The Lawd'd wanna see us both, when the time comes. I saw what dey done, Miss Lucy. I saw him."

He let out a breath, but the sobbing came again, and she stood over him, shared the awful helplessness. She tried to feel anger, fury at the men who would do this. But it wouldn't come. She felt the emotions coming from her own agony, the filth and blood, tending to broken men, the pure indecency of everything she had seen and eaten and smelled and felt with her own hands.

She knelt close to the old black man, hesitated, put a hand on his shoulder, felt the shaking in his body, the pure grief, the loss of his friend.

When the sun went down, the shelling began again, the civilians moving inside quickly, but she remained outside the cave, watched the red streaks, heard the thumps and distant thunder, and noticed now for the first time that something was missing. What had been done to James's best friend was an act of raw desperation repeated in the town, and all throughout the cave-spotted hills. Until now, every time the shells came, it had been the same, the whistle and shriek of the mortars and the cannon fire answered by a scattered chorus of howling dogs. But tonight there were no howls, no response at all to the steel and fire from the sky. There were no longer any dogs.

CHAPTER FORTY-THREE

PEMBERTON

PEMBERTON'S HEADQUARTERS
JUNE 29, 1863

The letter began with compliments, the formal respect paid to his authority, what he quickly saw as window dressing for what the writer intended to say.

> Men don't want to starve, and don't intend to, but they call upon you for justice, if the commissary department can give it; if it can't, you must adopt some means to relieve us very soon. The emergency of the case demands prompt and decided action on your part. If you can't feed us, you had better surrender us, horrible as the idea is, than suffer this noble army

**to disgrace themselves by desertion. I tell
you plainly, men are not going to lie here
and perish, if they do love their country
dearly. Self-preservation is the first law of
nature, and hunger will compel a man to
do almost anything. You had better heed
a warning voice, though it is the voice of
a private soldier. This army is now ripe
for mutiny, unless it can be fed.**

Many Soldiers

"It is an outrage, sir! The Yankees have been
spreading such pamphlets through our ranks for
days now. Some of them float in off the river carried by the most absurd contraption, balloons, no
less!"

Pemberton stared blindly at the paper, the words
flowing together, his eyes unable to focus.

"Exactly how did you come by this, Colonel?"

"It was delivered here last night, a coward's way,
darkness to hide his treachery!"

"So, how do you know this came from the
enemy?"

"It has to, sir! No soldier in this army would dare
to issue such a brazen threat!"

"Many soldiers." He tossed the paper onto the
desk and stood silently for a long moment. "I wish
I shared your outrage at the enemy's propaganda.
The missives I have seen have been directed to our
troops, encouraging them to desert. True?"

"Yes, sir."

"This one is directed to me. There is something of . . . spirit here."

"Sir, you cannot suggest this is written by the hand of a Confederate soldier."

Pemberton didn't respond, just turned and walked toward the door. He stopped and looked back to his office, Waddy raising the letter again, studying it, no attempt to hide his disdain. Pemberton looked at the others scattered throughout the living room of the house, men responding to his presence mostly by casual stares, as though he might actually order them to do something.

"Tell me, gentlemen, is there some of that mule meat available? I rather liked that . . . considering."

JULY 1, 1863

The second mine erupted just after 3 P.M., along a front manned by the Confederate 6th Missouri, men who had taken up station within musket range of the first crater. Once again, Southern troops had been able to detect the mining operations close beneath them, and once again, Lockett's engineers had failed to stop the Federal efforts. But this time there was a telltale sign that the explosion was coming. Across the way, the ongoing Federal artillery assaults had suddenly stopped, the sharpshooters falling silent, and the Missouri officers took that as a sign of the inevitable. They were correct. When the massive explosion came, the loss of life exceeded what had happened the first time, but not by a great deal. A detail of workers, mostly slaves, had been deep in the ground, engaged in Lockett's efforts to locate the mine. They were never seen again. In addition, a handful of guard posts along the redan were shredded, along with the men who occupied them. As had happened before, many of the Confederate troops had been pulled back, prepared to receive another massive shove from Federal infantry. But this time the Yankees did not rush forward, no real attempt at all to exploit the blasted opening in the redan. The blast was followed only by a thunderous shelling from Federal artillery, which blistered the defenders who rushed forward to seal the breach. As the daylight began to fade, the Federal forces seemed content to keep to their cover, while in the redan, the Missourians tended to their dead and wounded. As happened before, Samuel Lockett's men took charge of the essential repairs to the earthen walls and parapets, a rapid effort to seal the breach. When he learned of the second mine, and the utter lack of any offensive by Federal infantry, Pemberton could only assume that the eruption was as much for show as it was any attempt to crush his defenses. It was one more signal, a sign for Pemberton that Grant had every advantage, that as time went on, each day would bring more destruction from Federal troops, many of whom were within a few yards of Pemberton's defenses.

He rode with John Bowen, the staffs trailing far behind, always alert for the scattered artillery that came down with the usual randomness. The night was clear, stars overhead, sultry, Pemberton feeling the sweat in the saddle, heat rising off the horse. The redan was close now, the road dipping down along a familiar hillside, then back up, no campfires to light the way. Bowen had said almost nothing, and Pemberton had seen something in the man he hadn't noticed before, a sad sickliness, Bowen moving in slow, plodding motions. Pemberton didn't bother to ask, knew Bowen for what he was, a first-rate battlefield commander who would never admit to weakness. Though Bowen's men had taken the worst of the fights near the Champion farm and the Big Black, having his men kept in reserve was more an insult than anything practical. Pemberton had no patience for that now, knew Bowen probably had even less. So far, Forney and Smith had accomplished as much as Pemberton could have asked of them, the fresher divisions lining the miles of defensive works, and so far, tossing back every major advance Grant had made against them. The mines were more of the same, and Pemberton had taken some encouragement from what must have been reluctance on the part of the Federal commanders to throw away any more men in some fruitless charge against such effective defenses. It was the one bright light in the rapidly growing sea of despair that spread through the army. Regardless of Grant's amazing surge through the Mississippi countryside, since he had put his people around Vicksburg, the Yankees had been whipped in every fight.

Pemberton saw horsemen up ahead, though it was too dark to see who it was. But the voice came now: Lockett.

"Sir, welcome. Thank you for making the ride. I thought it important to show you how we've reconstructed the defenses where the enemy set off their mines."

Pemberton said nothing. Bowen responded.

"Major, how many more of these projects do the Yankees have?"

"I can't say for certain, sir. We know of at least three more, but so far, we have not been successful in locating the tunnels. That part of it is most frustrating. I must offer credit to their engineers. Certainly they have some experience in these kinds of efforts. Coal miners, no doubt."

Pemberton said, "If you say so, Major. Is that the only reason we're out here?"

Bowen took the response from Lockett and said, "We're out here because the men need to know their commanding general shares their interest in self-preservation." He paused. "I assume that is a satisfactory reason?"

The phrase stuck in Pemberton's mind: **self-preservation. The first law of nature**. He looked at Bowen through the darkness, the words from the anonymous letter still digging their way through him. Lockett was speaking again, moving away, guiding them to whatever work the engineer wished them to see. Pemberton followed behind Bowen, the horse moving in sluggish steps, and he ignored Lockett's narrative, fought through one question rising up in his mind. The letter . . . signed by **Many Soldiers**. Should I wonder . . . if there were **Many Officers**?

THE COWAN HOUSE— PEMBERTON'S HEADQUARTERS JULY 2, 1863

They gathered at the appointed time, responding to his call for a council of all his division and brigade commanders. They found seats, most on the floor, little regard for seniority, Bowen close to him on one side, Forney in the back, sitting against the wall. Stevenson and Smith sat on the left, against another wall. The brigadiers sat between the more senior men, and Pemberton stood at the far end of the room, watched them situate themselves, growing silent as they sat. He had rarely insisted on the kind of protocol where the major generals sat in a cluster, their subordinates spread out behind. But here the seating was almost by design, and Pemberton couldn't avoid a nagging suspicion that the four division commanders had spaced themselves out to avoid any hint of some conspiracy, as though they had already met, made decisions that would strip his authority. The letter was in his pocket still, read more than a dozen times. **The army . . . ripe for mutiny**.

He scolded himself silently, had no reason to suspect anyone of plotting against him, but those thoughts were there nearly every night, the exhaustion pulling him out of a sound night's sleep, forcing him awake, to stare at the plaster ceiling of his room, ghostly shapes emerging in the patterns of the spiderweb of cracks, created by the scattered blasts from Federal artillery. It had been that way for several days now, and he had wondered about the men in this room, the generals who stayed out front with their men, who heard the complaints and the anger, who saw the suffering of their men firsthand. Bowen's words came back from the night before, the casual insult, that Pemberton should show more awareness of what his army was enduring. And what benefit would that do for our cause? The difficulties come from the enemy . . . and from our alleged savior, General Johnston.

"Gentlemen, you have been told of the various

dispatches received here, sent to us by the courtesy of General Johnston?" He pointed to one corner of the room. "Colonel Waddy has placed copies of those dispatches on that table, should you wish to examine them for yourself. I would only say that, despite my most strenuous entreaties to the general, he has given me decidedly differing messages. Like you, I have believed his presence here would change the tide of events. Despite my faith that the general would make such a decision on our behalf, the latest correspondence I received from him two days ago indicates once again his unwillingness to commit such a . . . meager force. He claims to have but twenty-three thousand men assembled." He heard grunts, mumbles, knew the rumors of far greater numbers had spread all through his command. "I cannot say with any certainty how many men General Johnston could bring to this fight. And so, I must rely on what he tells me. If I am in error in that judgment, any one of you may correct me."

No one spoke, and he caught the eyes of his four division commanders, saw no protest, no sign that any of them expected anything more from Johnston than he did.

"I should like to hear from you if there is some strategy you believe to be sound, that will extricate us from this crisis."

Stevenson stood, then nodded to the others.

"General," he said, "my men have a cheerful

spirit, but for such short rations, are much enfee-
bled. Should we attempt a forced breakout, many
of my men would be unable to suffer the marches.
I would assume that any breakout would require us
to reach and cross the Big Black River, without the
enemy drawing us into a general engagement."

One of the younger men spoke up, Francis Shoup,
a brigade commander under Martin Smith.

"Sirs, can we not embrace some faith that General Johnston will yet relieve us?"

Pemberton yielded the response to Smith.

"Francis, your enthusiasm for continuing this
campaign is laudable. But the men can barely rise
up from their dugouts. I have seen able men stagger about like drunkards for lack of rations. Even
if General Johnston presents himself in a line of
battle against Grant's eastern flanks, it does nothing to increase our commissary. We do know that
Sherman has been charged with defending Grant
from any attack from the east. With the reinforcements that we have observed coming into Grant's
positions, I have every reason to believe that Sherman's stand out toward the Big Black would not be
easily defeated."

Forney spoke up.

"The reinforcements you refer to were marched
in plain view of our camps, both above the town
and across the Mississippi. That was no doubt a
message, Grant making very sure we know what
kind of strength he brings to this fight. With all

respects, General Pemberton, my men might have spirit in their souls, but they cannot hope to match a far larger force, which is far better equipped, and we must assume . . . well fed."

Bowen kept his seat, seemed clearly to struggle with his voice.

"Gentlemen, I have no faith that General Johnston will arrive here in time to do more than witness our ignominious surrender."

The word stung Pemberton, questions in his own mind slowly cleared away.

"I must ask you all. Do you believe surrender is our only option?"

Bowen did not hesitate.

"Yes."

Smith nodded, repeated the word, Stevenson seeming to struggle with saying it out loud.

"If it is the consensus . . . then I would agree."

Pemberton felt the heat in the room, sweat on his face, saw the discomfort in every man there. Gradually they looked at him, tired eyes, sharp glares, the optimism of the younger men, the dismal acceptance from the others.

"Thank you for your presence here. I would suggest you return to your commands."

Bowen spoke up, a loud burst of words.

"Would it not be better if you **ordered** us to return? Is that not, after all, your place here?"

Bowen's head dropped, a silent moment, the others holding their reactions to themselves. Pemberton had no urge to scold Bowen even with such a show of disrespect. He looked at the man, saw more of the weakness, thought of summoning the doctor. But Bowen was a proud man, and Pemberton thought, Just let it rest. Nothing can be accomplished by a clash over . . . words.

"Very well. You are all dismissed. Except General Bowen. Please remain."

They began to move, hands extended by the junior commanders, Smith and Forney and Stevenson helped to their feet by the men who served them. They moved quickly toward the door, Waddy there, and other aides, clearing the way. Almost no one spoke to Pemberton, the occasional nod, a flinch of a salute from the youngest men. He said nothing, allowed them to leave on their own terms, knew that every man in the room would swallow this in a different way. Many had suffered significant casualties, though losses from any fighting paled against what they were losing now to sickness or desertion.

Bowen stayed where he was, seemed too weak to stand, and Pemberton watched him for a moment, Bowen's head down.

"General Bowen, I shall return in a moment."

Pemberton followed the last of the brigadiers to the door of the house, saw the men mounting horses, aides scattered about, the color bearers coming into line. There were civilians as well, a ragged crowd, two dozen people, men mostly, gathering off to the side of the street, making way for their generals. He heard the voices now, angry, defiant, a blend of hostility and desperation, calls for food, for safe passage, for sanctuary. He had nothing to give them, no response that would satisfy anyone. He backed away and motioned to Waddy, who closed the door.

"**A**m I to apologize to you for my impudence?" Pemberton sat in the chair, a few feet from Bowen.

"I ask nothing of that. It was a council of war, and you spoke your mind. That is, after all, the point."

"I did not truly speak my mind. None of them did. Even in our darkest hour, we maintain some dignity. The enemy must respect that."

"Then you will make certain of that."

Bowen looked up now.

"How?"

"You were once a close acquaintance of General Grant, yes?"

"I had my residence near his. We spoke from time to time."

Pemberton weighed his words.

"You wish me to give you an order? I shall do so. Tomorrow morning, I shall have prepared a letter, which you will carry under a flag of truce, and present it to General Grant."

"Saying what?"

"You already know. I shall request that General

Grant agree to an armistice, and that he shall also consent to the appointment of a body of commissioners who will agree to precisely what terms General Grant will accept. . . ." Pemberton stopped, the words not coming, a sudden grip of emotion. Bowen was looking at him, and made a slow nod.

"For the surrender of this army."

CHAPTER FORTY-FOUR

GRANT

JULY 3, 1863

The white flags appeared at ten in the morning, the Federal gunners halting their fire, the infantry cautioned to remain alert, no one really knowing what the rebels were trying to do. Within minutes of the sudden silence, three horsemen rode out through the Confederate position, including the man charged with delivering Pemberton's letter to Grant, General John Bowen.

The aide had come in a fast gallop, relating the news that the rebels were on the way, word going first to the nearest command officer, General Andrew Smith. The aide had passed along

Smith's message that the men were being escorted under guard straight to Grant's headquarters.

Grant waited, chewed the unlit cigar, tried to hide the churning nervousness. He had rarely showed deep emotion to his staff, to anyone in his army, and he fought that now. But the white flags had been an unmistakable sign, and if no one knew exactly what was happening, the troops soon reacted with a jubilant cheer, the same emotion rolling through Grant, no matter how effectively he could hide it.

He saw the men approach, accompanied by Smith and his own guards. Smith seemed to be a good choice for this, had served under the mostly disagreeable thumb of John McClernand, was a subordinate now to McClernand's far more likable replacement, Edward Ord.

Two of the Confederates were officers, and Grant studied them, saw the perfectly grim expressions, men who seemed to carry their purpose like an anvil on their backs. The third man was clearly an aide, held a white flag of his own, glanced around nervously at the gathering of Grant's staff, the cavalry guard under Captain Osband drawn up in a neat formation. It was more show than Grant felt necessary, but he appreciated it now, saw that Osband had put his men in clean shirts.

The rebel officers dismounted, Federal grooms stepping forward crisply to take the reins of their horses. Grant stood with his hands on his hips, dropped them now, felt suddenly clumsy, thought, How does one do this, after all? I don't salute them. Wave? A hearty **haloo**? Sherman might punch them, just for good measure. A hearty kick in the shins. No, none of that. That might be the best reason imaginable that Sherman's not here.

The men seemed to hesitate, and Grant thought, They don't know what they're supposed to do, either. Maybe Smith knows. He served McClernand, after all, so he knows all about political properness.

Smith stepped closer, ahead of the two Confederates.

"General Grant," Smith said, "I have the pleasure to introduce you to emissaries from the enemy's camp. This is Major General John Bowen, and Colonel Louis Montgomery. They have brought you a letter from General Pemberton, sir."

Grant looked at Bowen.

"Yes, I know you well. Sorry not to have shown recognition. You have . . . um . . . changed somewhat in appearance."

Bowen seemed weak, and struggled to keep his posture.

"Yes, General. We were neighbors in Missouri, some years ago. I am flattered . . . rather, I am honored you would recall."

Bowen produced a piece of paper, seemed anxious not to linger, and Grant looked at the other man, younger, a hint of defiance on Montgomery's face.

"It is a pleasure to make your acquaintance, Colonel . . . Montgomery. This heat is a dismal thing for us all. Perhaps we should retire into my tent."

Montgomery didn't respond, and Bowen said, "If you don't object, sir, I wish to deliver this into your hands with all speed."

"Well, you two might not have a problem with this infernal sun, but I rather prefer the shade. Please follow me, gentlemen."

Grant moved into the tent, Bowen following, Montgomery close behind him. The tent wasn't much cooler, and Grant saw General Smith peering in, the unspoken request to be some part of this. Rawlins was there as well, seeming to appear from nowhere, and Grant nodded his approval to both, his teeth working the butt of the cigar into mush.

The tent was nearly as hot as the outdoors, and Grant wiped sweat from his brow.

"Not much better, I admit," he said. "All right, please allow me to read your message, General."

Bowen handed the folded paper to Grant, and Grant could see that the paper itself had none of the finery suitable for a commanding officer. The words crept through him. **Another shortage**.

Major General Ulysses S. Grant
I have the honor to propose an armistice for several hours, with the view to arranging terms for the capitulation of Vicksburg. To this end, if agreeable to

you, I will appoint three commissioners, to meet a like number to be named by yourself, at such place and hour today as you may find convenient. I make this proposition to save the further effusion of blood, which must otherwise be shed to a frightful extent, feeling myself fully able to maintain my position for a yet indefinite period. This communication will be handed you under a flag of truce by Major General John S. Bowen.
Lieutenant General John C. Pemberton

Grant read the letter again, felt an urgent need to mention something about eating mules, couldn't avoid a burning impatience at Pemberton's reference to an **indefinite period**. He chomped the cigar to bits, spit it out, forced himself to calm, and said, "General Bowen, your mission is completed. You may return to General Pemberton and convey my deepest regrets, but I refuse his request."

Bowen looked down, nodded, and Grant thought, He's not surprised one bit. This is a letter written by an administrator, whose pride is influencing his judgment. Bowen is a fighter. And right now, he knows his army has very little fight.

"General Grant, I too have regrets that this unfortunate affair cannot be concluded with General Pemberton's suggestions. Perhaps it would be better if you met with the general personally. You could make your views known to him with more . . . efficiency than I could hope to."

Grant saw the pain in the man's eyes, wondered now why Bowen had been chosen for the job. Requesting terms. He's a West Pointer. This must be the most distasteful assignment he has yet been given.

"Perhaps that is wise. Please return to General Pemberton and, if he desires it, I will meet with him at three o'clock this afternoon, at a place to be indicated by flags of truce, in front of General McPherson's corps." He paused, then looked again at the letter.

"Perhaps I should respond in writing. Colonel Rawlins, summon an aide, with pen and ink."

"Right away, sir."

Grant looked at Montgomery, the man's stern demeanor fading somewhat, from what had to be the nature of his mission, crushed further by the heat. He looked again to Bowen, saw stooped shoulders, a man who seemed to suffer more from an ailment than a blow to his pride.

"General Bowen, do you wish to sit?"

Bowen straightened and took a long breath.

"No, sir. Thank you for your courtesy. This has been a difficult experience for us all. Wouldn't you agree?"

"More difficult for some." Grant regretted the words, had no reason to taunt Bowen. "Your men fought well, particularly at the Champion farm."

"Thank you, sir. Not well enough."

Rawlins returned now, with the aide in tow. Grant pointed to the camp desk.

"Sergeant, be seated. Write down the following."

The man obeyed, studied the two gray-clad officers with wide, curious eyes. Grant looked again at Pemberton's request, then said:

> **General John C. Pemberton,**
> **Commanding**
> **Your note of this date is just received, proposing an armistice for several hours, for the purpose of arranging terms of capitulation through commissioners, to be appointed, etc.**

He paused, glanced up at Bowen, thought, Bowen knows better than to toss any matter this important to the hands of . . . commissioners.

> **The useless effusion of blood you propose stopping by this course can be ended at any time you may choose, by the unconditional surrender of the city and garrison. Men who have shown so much endurance and courage as those now in Vicksburg, will always challenge the respect of an adversary, and I can assure you will be treated with all the re-**

spect due to prisoners of war. I do not favor the proposition of appointing commissioners to arrange for the terms of capitulation, because I have no terms other than those indicated above.
Ulysses Grant, Major General, Commanding

The sergeant wrote furiously, and Grant waited, the paper handed quickly to Rawlins, who passed it to Grant. Grant read his own words and handed the letter to Bowen.

"Please read it, General. I wish no confusion, should something happen to you in transit."

Bowen read, gave a hint of a smile, and Grant waited for him to finish.

"Something there catch your eye, General? Should I rephrase any passage so that General Pemberton will be more clear on my meaning?"

The smile had vanished, and Bowen said, "No, sir. You have stated your wishes plainly. I merely noted your choice of words. It is well known in my army that, since your triumph at Fort Donelson, your initials have come to signify more than just your name. It is a subject your own soldiers speak of with pride, prisoners especially."

Grant had heard enough about that, the soldiers referring to him as Unconditional Surrender.

"It is unfortunate that we cannot always control

the gratuitous musings of our troops. I am quite certain that 'Stonewall' cared not one bit for that title. Rest his soul, of course."

"If you say so, sir. If there is nothing else, and with your permission, I shall return to General Pemberton and convey your response. Your respect for the flag of truce is most welcome."

"Yes, you are dismissed."

Bowen handed Grant's letter to Montgomery, made a brief bow, and Bowen caught Grant's eye for a quick second, a nod very different than hostility to an enemy. They moved away now, mounted their horses, the cavalry guard moving into position to lead the way back out toward the rebel lines.

T he word of the scheduled meeting had spread, and Grant had no problem allowing his most senior commanders to observe. They met beneath a squat oak tree, within easy musket range of the rebel position, the white flags fluttering now on both sides. He stood staring out toward the massive forts, could see men standing tall, staring back at him. Whether they knew who he was, or just why he was there, it really didn't matter. Pemberton's note had stuck with him, the audacious claim that the rebels could hold out indefinitely. There could be some, he thought. But all those deserters . . . they're not just spewing out all that talk about the conditions there just to impress us with a good yarn. He recalled one man, escorted by guards who had to hold the man beneath the arms so he could walk. The obvious question had come, asked by Rawlins, just who the man's commanding officer was. The response had angered Rawlins, as so much did. But Grant took the man at his word. **General Starvation**.

He saw the entourage, expected that. Pemberton was a man for protocol, always had been, and Grant couldn't blame the man for it, not now. Behind Grant was an entourage of his own, the corps commanders, McPherson and Ord, and a handful of subordinates, including John Logan and Andrew Smith.

He noticed Bowen trailing behind Pemberton, observing good order, and despite the grumblings from so many deserters, it seemed clear enough that Pemberton was still in command. He dismounted now, the others doing the same, a cluster of aides, the officer from that morning, Montgomery. Pemberton stood tall, seemed to gather himself, a self-conscious tug at his coat, what Grant could see was a new uniform. Pemberton stood motionless for a few seconds, and Grant stepped forward, closer to the visitors. He stopped a few yards from Pemberton, who returned the favor, walking toward him, then stopping as well. They faced each other for a long, silent moment, the tension thick all around them, and Grant couldn't avoid feeling as though they were about to fight a duel. Pemberton seemed uncertain, reluctant, as though waiting for Grant to begin whatever was to happen next. Grant chewed again on an unlit cigar, as much nervousness knotting him up as he had usually seen coming from Sherman. Wish he was here now, he thought. He'd just . . . start jabbering. No, he's out doing his job, checking on his outposts, worrying about some surprise attack from Joe Johnston. Well, we'll see about that right here.

Grant had no idea what the rules were for this kind of meeting, could see that Pemberton was still waiting. Now Montgomery stepped forward.

"Major General Grant," he said, "I am honored to introduce Lieutenant General Pemberton."

Pemberton barely moved, and Grant thought, So, of course, you should remind me I'm outranked. But I'm not the whipped dog here. Grant took a breath.

"General Pemberton," Grant said, "we served in Mexico together. I recall you well. You were a few years ahead of me at West Point, though. I would not assume you recall meeting me."

Pemberton's expression didn't change, a stern calmness, and he seemed to expect more from Grant, but the pleasantries were only in the way. Grant had never been good at chatty conversation, felt even worse about that right now. Pemberton shifted his stance.

"General Grant, I must request you to detail

those terms you would require of my army for the surrender of Vicksburg."

Grant thought, The letter . . . surely he can read.

"My terms are as I wrote them to you this morning."

Pemberton's attitude was hostile, abrupt.

"If that is all you would say . . . then this conference might as well end. I assure you, sir, there will be more bloodshed, and you shall bury more men than I."

Pemberton spun around as though to leave, and Grant was surprised, thought, Even now . . . this is about pride? He would dictate terms to me? He felt a low boil rising up inside him, watched Pemberton step deliberately toward his horse, slowly, as though a carefully designed performance. So, that's it. Grant fought the urge to shout out something, anything, let us compare **our artillery,** our **rations**. But he kept it inside, said loud enough for everyone to hear, "Very well. It shall be so."

Grant looked back toward his own commanders, saw shock, dismay, and now Bowen called out.

"Sirs . . . General Pemberton . . . allow General Grant to select one of his commanders to meet with me, here, now. We should not abandon this endeavor."

Grant saw the anxious look on Bowen's face, thought, Yes, if you were intending to continue this fight, you'd be back in your own headquarters. But you know better.

"I have no objection," Grant said. He turned, motioned to Smith to step forward. "As you are already acquainted with General Smith, I see no reason why the two of you should not . . . discuss this further. Be aware, of course, that nothing you two decide shall be binding upon me, without my approval."

Smith was beside him now.

"As you wish, sir."

Pemberton turned back toward Grant, motioned to Bowen to advance, and said to Montgomery, "You will join them."

Grant played the game now and said to McPherson, "You will join them as well. Just . . . get on with it, shall we?"

McPherson walked closer to him and said in a low whisper, "Sir, what if they will not capitulate?"

Grant turned away from the Confederates and said to McPherson, with Smith easing close as well, "Gentlemen, if they were truly capable of making this fight, of surviving this siege **indefinitely** . . . they would not be out here."

After some discussion, disagreement, and a valiant effort on Bowen's part to gain as much advantage as he could, the meeting ended with a proposal that Grant had to take seriously. The notion of unconditional surrender implied no concessions at all, but Grant had taken something away from Bowen's deportment that impressed him. The conclusion, the precise terms Grant would accept, had been left partly open, though both Smith and McPherson had echoed Grant's sentiments that very little would be offered. After discussing it further with his senior commanders, what amounted to the only real council of war Grant had yet employed, Grant communicated both to Sherman and to Admiral Porter that the discussions had been fruitful. Thus would the armistice stand, at least for now. At ten that night, the final terms were put into writing, and passed through the lines to Pemberton's headquarters.

General Pemberton,
In conformity with the agreement of this afternoon, I will submit the following proposition for the surrender of the City of Vicksburg, public stores, etc. On your accepting the terms proposed, I will march in one division as a guard, and take possession by eight a.m. tomorrow. As soon as rolls can be made out, and paroles be signed by officers and men, you will be allowed to march out of our lines, the officers taking with them their sidearms and clothing, and the field staff and cavalry officers one horse each. The rank and file will be allowed all their clothing, but no other property. If these

conditions are accepted, any amount of rations you may deem necessary can be taken from the stores you now have, and also the necessary cooking utensils for preparing them. Thirty wagons also, counting two two-horse or mule-teams as one, will be allowed to transport such articles as cannot be carried along. The same conditions will be allowed to all sick and wounded officers and soldiers as fast as they become able to travel. The paroles for these latter must be signed, however, whilst officers present are authorized to sign the roll of prisoners.

Ulysses S. Grant, Major General,
Commanding

The response came late that night:

General Ulysses Grant,
I have the honor to acknowledge the receipt of your communication of this date, proposing terms of capitulation for this garrison and post. In the main your terms are accepted; but, in justice both to the honor and spirit of my troops, manifested in the defense of Vicksburg, I have to submit the following amendments, which, if acceded to by you, will perfect the agreement between us. At ten o'clock

a.m. tomorrow, I propose to evacuate the works in and around Vicksburg and to surrender the city and garrison under my command, by marching out with my colors and arms, stacking them in front of my present lines. After which you will take possession. Officers to retain their sidearms and personal property, and the rights and property of citizens to be respected.

**John C. Pemberton,
Lieutenant General, Commanding**

Rawlins read the letter, then stifled a yawn.

"He is attempting some chicanery, sir. There is no specific mention of taking an accurate roll of prisoners. His army could be scattered to the four winds in a matter of days. In time, we would find ourselves fighting those same men."

Grant drank from the coffee cup and sat back in the chair.

"You are correct, Colonel. These amendments . . . it's that Confederate honor. When I heard he had signed on with the Confederacy, I believed Pemberton was a man who had made a catastrophic mistake, throwing his lot with the wrong side of this affair because he had been swayed by Southern friends of bad influence. Perhaps bad character as well. Compare him to Sherman. Sherman was as deeply rooted to the South as any of us here, and I believe he loves Louisiana to this day. Yet I know of no man more likely to defend the Union, and with fists and clubs if necessary. Pemberton is behaving as though his reputation depends on his having the final word on the subject. Notice, he demands the time for capitulation be set two hours later than I proposed. Ten A.M. It is ridiculous in the extreme."

"Sir, I wonder how General Sherman would respond to this sort of . . . haggling?"

"There is no mystery to that. For weeks now, the navy has fired incendiary shells into the town. Sherman would request with some vigor that we increase that effort." He paused. "Right now, it is best that Sherman is elsewhere. I could not suffer that kind of spirit at this late hour. There is a time for the brutality of total war, Colonel. But there is also a time for total acceptance of the obvious. The rebels cannot feed their own men. The civilians in the town are suffering mightily. Rebel deserters are increasing in number every day. John Pemberton has capable subordinates serving him who know very well that their army is in defeat. He must respect their judgment, and I have seen no indication that his generals are anxious to continue this fight. If there was agreement with Pemberton's show of pride, I'd have seen that in John Bowen. Pemberton would not have chosen that man to deliver his message or accompany him to a meeting, if Bowen was the sole voice of dissent. Bowen knows this is over. The rest of them must share that conviction.

The time for posturing has passed. Bring the sergeant in here. Then wake up Secretary Dana. He shall be a party to this. I want Washington to receive a copy of these correspondences at the earliest opportunity. Dana will get the job done. Try to leave my son be. He'll complain like a hornet, but I don't need a twelve-year-old's energy fluttering about at this hour." Grant looked at his watch, well after midnight. "Colonel, have you noted that it is now the Fourth of July? I would have thought Pemberton would have avoided such a momentous event on such a momentous day. There will be repercussions for that, from the Southern civilians especially. Be certain of that." He paused, snapped the watch closed, and stuffed it into his pocket. "Too many men . . . too much blood, Colonel. We had a singular mission to accomplish here, and it has proven more costly than I anticipated. But now we shall see it done. No more negotiations or arguments. This shall end now."

General Pemberton,
I have the honor to acknowledge the receipt of your communication of 3rd July. The amendment proposed by you cannot be acceded to in full. It will be necessary to furnish every officer and man with a parole signed by himself, which, with the completion of the roll of prisoners, will necessarily take some time. I

can make no stipulations with regard to the treatment of citizens and their private property. While I do not propose to cause them any undue annoyance or loss, I cannot consent to leave myself under any restraint by stipulations. The property which officers will be allowed to take with them will be as stated in my proposition of last evening; that is, officers will be allowed their private baggage and sidearms, and mounted officers one horse each. If you mean by your proposition for each brigade to march to the front of the lines now occupied by it, and stack arms at ten o'clock a.m., and then return to the inside and there remain as prisoners until properly paroled, I will make no objection to it. Should no notification be received of your acceptance of my terms by nine o'clock a.m. I shall regard them as having been rejected, and shall act accordingly. Should these terms be accepted, white flags should be displayed along your lines to prevent such of my troops as may not have been notified, from firing upon your men.

Ulysses Grant, Major General,
Commanding

JULY 4, 1863

Grant had barely slept, but with the sunrise he had gone out quickly from the headquarters, a fresh biscuit stuffed into his pocket as an afterthought. The cavalry guard traveled with him, Captain Osband and a small group of horsemen out to the front, leading the way. Osband knew their objective, but Grant understood there was danger still, that somewhere along the rebel position, the response to any talk of surrender could be heralded with violence, some of the rebels certainly believing Pemberton had somehow betrayed their cause. For days now, Grant had known of the grumblings toward Pemberton. Most of that had of course come from the deserters, whose claims of any kind were subject to question. But there was too much of that kind of hostility, too many men referring to Pemberton as a Confederate in uniform only, that Vicksburg was a prize to be handed Grant as part of some grand plan of deception, Pemberton, the Ultimate Spy. He recalled Pemberton's new uniform, all the posturing. He is a man who faces the worst crisis of his life now, a crisis of respect, of disgrace. For an officer, a West Pointer, what is worse than that? Surely, **surely,** he will not deny the only outcome there can be.

Grant realized he was as nervous as he had been the day before, a hard grip on the horse's reins, his breathing short, hard. Osband led him down a steep hill, along a path made wide by the wheels of wagons and artillery, the grass in the narrow fields trampled flat by his men. He passed Logan's headquarters tent, saw the Stars and Stripes. Staff officers saluted him, pointed westward, toward the front, their commander already with his men, and Grant acknowledged their salutes, thought, He is searching for it . . . as I am. We must know.

They crested a steep hill, and Osband held up a hand, the horsemen halting, Grant moving up beside him.

Osband pointed and said, "Sir, General Logan."

Grant saw him now, sitting on horseback, a color bearer and his staff gathered behind him. Out to both sides, blue-coated infantry stood up from their trenches in a wide, uneven line. They were no more than fifty yards from the rebel works, and across the bare field, the massive earthen walls were bristling with activity. Grant pushed the horse forward, moved slowly toward Logan, the man turning to him, a salute, and then a tip of the hat. Grant could see now that Logan had tears on his face.

Grant was still uncertain, his hands twisting in nervousness, and he felt his own stab of emotion, held it tightly, made a sharp nod to Logan, stared out with him to the rebels who stood up high on their own defenses. For a long moment, there was no sound, Logan's men silent, the rebels staring back at them, no taunts, no curses, no playfulness, and no musket fire.

"General Grant," Logan said, "it is a most pleasant morning, sir."

A breeze rose now, soft and warm, and between
the ragged line of rebel soldiers, Grant saw what
Logan had already seen. Along the crest of the defensive works, scattered between the men, there
was a fluttering of white flags.

CHAPTER FORTY-FIVE

SPENCE

SATURDAY, JULY 4, 1863

The silence was unbearable. She crept from the cave at first light, waiting for the shelling to start, but the only sounds that rolled across the hillside came from the people who lived there. She focused on that, a heated argument somewhere down toward Mr. Atkins's cave, could see a cluster of men, hands raised, shouting, violent fury. Cordray broke from the group, moving in long strides up the hill, staring down, one arm in motion, an angry conversation with himself. Isabel Cordray emerged from the cave behind Lucy, drawn by the commotion. She was weaker still, though Lucy was relieved Isabel had finally allowed herself to eat the horrifying fare, goaded on by her own children, who had no qualm at all about what actually went into "squirrel stew." She held Lucy's arm for support.

"What is happening? I know that look. Someone has angered him. Now we shall hear more about it than either of us would like."

Cordray seemed to energize at his wife's appearance, quickened his strides up toward them, and Lucy could see his agitation, the anger still. He softened as he drew closer, eyes on his wife.

"How are you feeling? Are you any stronger?"

"Somewhat. Tell me what has happened."

Cordray lowered his head.

"The rumors of last evening have proven true. Pemberton has surrendered the city. There is great anger, dangerous talk. I must return to our home, make a stand to protect what is still ours. The Yankees are said to be marching into town at ten. There could be great destruction, great peril to any of us. Our officers are, as we speak, laying down their swords in front of our defenses." He stopped, the words choked away by red-faced emotion. "It is the very end of the world."

Lucy walked away, couldn't absorb any more of the man's furious talk, was far more curious about the amazing silence.

"Where are you going, child? You must take care! There is no accounting for what the Yankees will do to us now!"

She glanced back, saw the deep worry from both of them, and shook her head.

"I will take care. I must go to the hospital. The patients there must be looked after."

It was an excuse, the thought of blood and wounds too repellent to draw her anywhere. She climbed the hill to the narrow dusty lane, could feel the heat rising already, another oppressing day, oppressing now for other reasons as well. She tripped slightly, her foot snagging on a ragged piece of metal. She stepped carefully past, reached the road, realized now the ground along the crest of the hill was littered with metal, fragments of shells spread through a pockmarked landscape. She stared at what she knew to be shrapnel, metal torn like paper, jagged edges, twisted, curled, some of it half buried in the ground. The road itself was spread with wreckage, and she knew it had been that way for a while now, something she had grown too used to, had forgotten to see. But in the silence, with no shells streaking the sky, no whistle and roar, no distant impacts and thunderous quakes beneath her feet, it all seemed to rise up toward her, seeking her attention, calling out to remind her what had happened here.

She stood in the road, saw a shattered wagon up the way, wheels tilted inward, the wagon itself a mass of splinters. From beyond the hill, there were men, rough, emaciated, shreds for clothes. She watched them struggling to walk, one man leaning on the shoulder of another, a wound on the man's leg. She knew now: soldiers. But there were no weapons, and she thought of Cordray's words, the swords of the officers. And I suppose, she thought . . . everything else, too.

They continued the climb, saw her now, and she was too tired to feel the fear, all of Cordray's caution. They moved up toward her, one man calling out, "Miss . . . have you anything to eat?"

"I'm sorry. No. I have not eaten at all today."

They moved on toward the road, none of them doubting her, and she called out, "Where are you going?"

They didn't stop, as though momentum was all they had left, one man responding, "Town. The river. Yankees'll be there directly. Might be rations."

She glanced down the hill, saw the caves emptying, Cordray's neighbors spilling out into the rising sunlight, more talk, but many more of them just standing, staring out in every direction with a weary silence, exhausted disbelief. Beyond the hill, more soldiers appeared, wounds again, and she thought of the hospital tents, the men still to recover from all the horrifying things the doctors had to do. I should go there, she thought. They will still require assistance. The Yankees . . . they will not hurt them. They cannot, surely. There is pain . . . damage enough.

Cordray was moving up the hill, a rattle of hot words.

"Now! We must go now! It will not be long, and we could lose everything! There is talk that the Yankees will burn the town, all of it! There is no decency in them. None!"

"Who is saying such things?"

Cordray didn't expect the question, just stopped and waved her away.

"Men who know of such things."

"Officers?"

"I have no time for this, child. I must get to our home. You would do well to seek shelter. There will be Yankee soldiers marching on this road, you can depend on that. This is a day of shame for us all. A day of shame! Pemberton has sold us to the Yankees!"

She watched him go, the long strides again along the rutted road. Out toward the defenses, more soldiers were coming toward her, some on the road, others spread out along the hills, all of them plodding slowly toward Vicksburg. She felt none of Cordray's fury, but began to walk, mindless steps back to her ruins of a house, nothing there to protect. She knew nothing of generals, nothing of Yankees. But there had been blood and brains and limbs and she knew that, over there, there surely had been doctors and nurses, doing exactly what she had done, caring and crying and enduring the worst horrors any of them would ever see. And they will not want more of this. Surely . . . they will not punish us because we chose to defend our homes.

She kept walking, slow steps, the road curving down through a wide gulley, more caves there, the people out in the open, more opinions, more sorrow. Up ahead, a soldier sat beside the road, still wore his small, crumpled hat, some kind of insignia that meant nothing to her. He sat on a log, slumped over, as though this was as far as he could go. She felt a stab of concern, thought, You are still a nurse, after all. Help him.

She moved closer to him, saw a glimpse of awareness on his face, and she knelt low.

"Are you wounded? Can you stand? I'm a nurse."

The man tilted his head, and she saw age, gray hair spreading over his ears, soft blue eyes framed by creases in weathered skin.

"I been wounded, miss. But not for a while now. You're mighty young for nursin'. You been out thataways?"

He pointed toward the defensive lines, and she nodded.

"Near the 3rd Louisiana. We had tents back in the low ground."

"Yep. Took my friend there. Lost a leg, he did."

She stood straight.

"Do you need some help? Are you going to the town?"

He shook his head slowly.

"Not goin' anywhere right now. Yanks'll be through here directly. They'll look after me, I'm guessin'. Captain Seal says we oughta expect some rations. I figure I can wait for 'em. Been waitin' plenty already."

There was nothing angry in his words, none of the spouting off she had heard from Cordray, so many of the others. But she was curious about that, saw a kind of sadness she had seen in so many who had been through the hospitals, the wounded, and the men who carried them.

"You do any fighting out there?"

"Reckon I did. Can't say I kilt no one. Mebbe. They tried mighty hard to stick one in me. Spent days sittin' in a dang hole. Watched some of the others, the ones who thought fightin' was fun . . . watched one boy lose a whole head, 'nother cut slam in two. Yanks know how to use artill'ry, I tell you that."

She was torn now, whether or not to leave the man behind. She looked out across the hillside, saw a scattering of people, nearly all of them moving toward Vicksburg. Many were civilians, and she saw entire families, children urged to keep pace, urgency and panic from their parents.

"I will stay and help you, if you need."

"I don't need, miss. You go on back home. The fightin' is done passed. Even the Yanks done give all they had. No stomach for it, not anymore."

She started to move away, saw a young couple climbing the nearby hill, the woman cradling a filthy blanket. She knew them, saw recognition.

"Mr. Green! I heard. . . ."

They moved toward her, exhausted smiles, and the woman seemed to struggle. They reached the crest and Green said, "I heard you had been nursing the soldiers. Mighty difficult work, Miss Spence. You are to be commended."

"I only wanted to help. Didn't seem right the soldiers should have to suffer, while we . . . well, there was suffering aplenty."

She looked at the bundle in the woman's arms and heard a soft cry.

"How is he, Mrs. Green?"

The woman was pale, her worn dress hanging on her loosely, her husband taking the bundle from her arms.

"Miss Spence, we have been truly blessed. Would you mind terribly examining the boy . . . just for a look? We don't know anything about doctoring."

The bundle was put into her hands, and Lucy saw the pink, teary face staring up at her, a hard, angry twist, the faint coughing cry.

"Oh, my . . . Mr. Green, I don't really know much—"

His wife added her voice.

"Please, Miss Spence. Just a look. Is he going to be all right?"

Lucy pulled the blanket back, exposed the baby's chest, saw nothing to alarm her, the baby no longer crying.

"He's beautiful, Mrs. Green. I think he'll be just fine."

"Oh, thank you. Thank you for that. We just didn't know . . . coming like he did. No place to bring a life into this world."

Lucy held the baby a moment longer, the eyes finding her, soft stare, a tiny hand reaching out from the blanket, fingers smaller than any she had seen.

"I don't agree, ma'am. He was born out here in a cave . . . in the midst of the worst any of us will ever know. He is a gift. There is no doubt about that. He will always know what his parents went through, and I suppose, that is the best experience of all. That no one forget what we suffered here."

She handed the bundle to the baby's father, and Green made a bow.

"You know," he said, "we named him just so. He is William Siege Green. It is a name that will inspire questions all his life."

They moved away slowly, Mrs. Green offering a final thank-you, and Lucy felt drained, the hunger and the weariness pulling her down. She realized the old soldier was still there, had forgotten about him, and she saw him looking up at the Greens, watching them as they walked away.

"They had a child . . . right out here?"

"Yes. I heard about it . . . a few weeks ago. Very kind people. He's a merchant in the town. I didn't know what to tell them. My nursing is very limited. I know wounds, chloroform, things I hope never to see again."

"Then you won't be doin' more nursin'? Shame, that is. This army's not done fightin'. There'll be a call for more like you. Always will be."

She didn't want to think of that, that there would be more to this war, more of . . . this. She stared out to the Greens, saw the woman curl her arm through her husband's, both of them staring at the bundle in his arms. The soldier coughed, then said, "Ah, then, so that's what it'll be."

Lucy felt like sitting, fought against it, the log supporting the soldier too short for propriety.

"I don't know what you mean, sir."

He laughed now, a high cackle.

"Well, you take a lesson from those two. If'n you think you're gonna lose the gumption for fixing up the wounded . . . then you oughta put your care to raising a young'un."

She nodded, didn't know how to respond.

"I must go to the town. You sure you'll be all right?"

"Go on. Tend to your business." She started to move away, and he called after her.

"Miss, for all the trouble you've seen here . . . I wish for you . . . that you'll see happier days."

She saw the warmth in his eyes, couldn't respond. She made a slight curtsy, moved away with slow, soft steps. The people were still filling the road, and there was less of the bickering arguments, less talk of betrayal and anger. The people seemed to strengthen the closer they drew to the town, a calm resolve flowing through them as it flowed through her, that no matter all she had seen, no matter the sickening and the terrifying, the suffering and the torment, she knew that the old soldier had planted in her the gift of hope.

CHAPTER FORTY-SIX

BAUER

VICKSBURG
SATURDAY, JULY 4, 1863

The honor of being the first to march into the town had been given to General John Logan, commanding one of McPherson's divisions. But the ceremony of that had been accomplished quickly, and what followed required far more time and effort. The labor of issuing the paroles, the paperwork that would end the siege had to be completed by both sides, to Grant's satisfaction.

With Logan's division in the town, out along the nine miles of rebel earthworks, the Confederate forces began the process agreed to by Pemberton's surrender. Along the entire front, arms and colors were stacked, the rebel soldiers moved back into the rolling open ground to the rear of their earthworks. Makeshift holding areas were established, and though guards were stationed along the perimeters, the areas bore little resemblance to a stockade. For nearly all of the rebel troops, the first priority was to be fed, and with the promise of rations, they weren't inclined to go anywhere else. The Federal commissary, supplied by a vast fleet of supply boats on the river, immediately complied with Grant's promise to help ease the starvation that had spread through Pemberton's army, and for the first time in weeks, many of the rebels were issued corn, sugar, bacon, and other staples that had long disappeared from their own stores.

In some parts of the line, the rebels did not go quietly, many, including most of the 3rd Louisiana, reacting to the surrender with an outpouring of hostility, nearly all aimed toward their own command. Rather than stacking muskets, complying with the surrender order, some of the furious troops chose instead to smash their muskets against tree trunks, staging what amounted to small-scale riots in their own camps. But that was the exception. Once most of the Confederates had been paraded into their temporary holding areas, the Federal troops were granted permission to fraternize, and both sides found outstretched hands, calls of greeting that belied the reality that these men had done all they could to kill the men they faced now.

Though discipline still prevailed, the Federal provosts and senior officers made little effort to prevent their men from engaging in whatever kind of trade or barter they chose. The soldiers learned quickly how little the rebels had to offer, and so, most of the bargaining went forward with more charity than good business sense. The conversations were mostly cordial, the blue-clad soldiers recognizing that the men they faced now knew full well which side had prevailed. In response to an early outburst of artillery salutes, Grant issued a hasty order that silenced Federal artillery completely across the line, the message to his army clear. There would be no grand celebration at the expense of the captured rebels. Logan's men had marched into Vicksburg to the strains of their own martial music, but even that had been subdued by the sights that awaited them. The destruction in the town kept many of the residents in the street, joined there by straggling soldiers, all of them desperate for food.

For a short while, boisterous recognition of the Federal victory came from the river, several of the navy's ironclads unleashing their whistles and then erupting with artillery blasts that shattered the subdued calm in the town, sending many of the frightened civilians back toward their shelters. Grant had no real authority over Admiral Porter, couldn't order a halt to that cannonade, but Porter himself soon recognized that with Federal troops now looking down on him from the heights within Vicksburg, there was no cause for disrupting what might be a fragile peace.

Bauer had moved through the rebel works, looking for one particular man. He spread out from the men of his own company, searched the faces, ragged beards on sunken cheeks, every rebel soldier seeming too thin for what remained of the clothes he wore. The officers were no different, that what passed still for a gray uniform was more often fragments, tatters that showed the officers had made the same sacrifices as their men. Near Bauer, the other Wisconsin men were doing the same, some of them hesitant, uncertain that these rebels would be open to any kind of cordiality. But that passed quickly, many of the rebels showing a surprising amount of good cheer, as though desperately grateful the fighting was past. Bauer still searched the faces, hoped he would recognize the man, if not by his face, at least by the man's Southern drawl. But that was hardly unique, most of the rebels, particularly the Mississippi troops nearby, speaking with a syrupy slowness that many of the Irishmen in particular seemed to find fascinating. That fascination went both ways, of course, the heavier Irish brogues drawing plenty of attention, good-natured teasing in both directions.

He walked past animated conversations, gatherings where the rebels seemed subdued, probably from fatigue or outright hunger. To one side he saw Willis speaking to an officer, no smiles between them, as though the men in their uniforms knew that there was still a war, that no matter what had happened at Vicksburg, in many other places, soldiers were still shooting at each other. Bauer stopped, watched Willis for a long moment, wanted to approach, but kept away, wouldn't interrupt them. They were, after all, officers.

Bauer couldn't help thinking again of Shiloh, the aftermath so different. There, after a brutal Federal triumph, the rebels had retreated, were gone completely, leaving the horrifying job of burying the dead to the men in blue. Bauer had thought his life as a soldier might end right there, his duty done, that anyone surviving such a bloodbath could never be expected to do it all again. But Willis's grim pessimism had swept away Bauer's fantasy that it was over. He entertained none of that foolishness now, had accepted what he had volunteered to do. His enlistment was for three years, and no matter how many times he had fired his musket, how much of **this** he had experienced, he would continue to go wherever the army sent him.

Another rebel officer approached Willis, and Bauer could see feigned politeness from both men, a cordiality Bauer knew was counterfeit. The man seemed familiar, a lieutenant, his head wrapped in a dirty white bandage. Bauer realized it was the officer whom Willis had spoken to on that awful day in May, the short-lived truce to allow the bodies to be buried. Bauer kept back, could see Willis's formality, contrasting with the rebel's polite gentility, something a **gentleman** did as a matter of course. It had been that way in May, all those good manners, the men in Willis's platoon knowing that once the truce ended, no gentility would prevent the killing.

Another man approached Willis, spoke with his hat in his hand, not an officer. Willis turned, searched the crowd a moment, then saw Bauer, pointed toward him. Bauer was surprised, watched the soldier slip past a crowd of other men, closing toward him. He was a skeleton of a man, shuffling with a pronounced limp, had a short, uneven beard that seemed to have been chopped by a dull knife.

"You! Dutchman! Yep! That's you, ain't it? I 'member how ugly you was!"

The voice came to him now, and Bauer knew.

"You're Zep."

"That I am. And now here we are, standin' out here like one big country picnic. Guess I have to say, we been whipped good."

Bauer struggled to say something.

"I suppose we got the better of it here. I never felt we were better than you. . . ."

"I ain't talking about you, Yank! There ain't a man in this army who don't blame Ole Pem for tossing us into the pit. I got no reason to stick my fist in your face, not one. But if it came to that, I wouldn't back down from you, or any other bluebelly!"

Bauer felt a hint of alarm, tried to measure Zep's anger, not sure what the man might do.

"I don't know about any of that. I don't hate you, or wanna see you dead. I'm kinda glad actually . . . you're not."

Zep looked at him for a long moment.

"I'm no fool, Dutchman. You'd a kilt me just like I'd a kilt you. We just didn't get the chance. Now, all them muskets are in **your** hands, and we're just settin' here waitin' for what's next."

Bauer suddenly realized he had no idea what would happen next.

"Are they . . . are we putting you in a prison camp?"

"You mean, up north? I s'pose, for some. There's a few here says they ain't signin' no parole. My captain says that any man who don't agree to terms will be sent upriver somewheres. There's a few who'd rather go sit in some hole and wait out the war. I suppose there's something to that. This has gotta end someday. Me . . . I done signed the paper. They says we'll be marchin' outa here in a few days, once all the papers are hauled together. We're supposed to gather up at Jackson, or somewheres. That lieutenant over there says Ole Pem expects us to follow him on down the road. This same kinda road, I suppose. Some will."

"You?"

"Nope. Don't mind tellin' you, Dutchman. They let us march out of here, and it's the last this army or this war will ever know about Zep Luvan." He paused, seemed to weigh the wisdom of revealing anything more. "Such men like Ole Pem . . . they treat us like we got no sense of our own. That we'll stand up and die everywhere they tell us to, just 'cause they tell us to. I seen too many die right here. Kin, close friends. Used to think this was worth doin', just 'cause men smarter than me said so. I'm twenty-four years old, and I got a wife, and she's back home wonderin' if maybe I'm a hero, or maybe I'm in a hole in the ground. The best kind of hero is one who comes home and raises a family. Young'uns. My daddy was my hero. That's what I intend to do. Just like him. You bluebellies want to go off and beat your chests about how dang tough you are, fine by me. Long as you keep off my farm . . . and don't mess with my young'uns, I got no beef with you."

Bauer saw resignation on the man's face, but wasn't sure he believed him.

Behind Bauer, a small wagon train rolled closer, blue-coated officers leading the way. Guards were there as well, men with bayonets, which seemed vaguely ridiculous to Bauer. The men around him were more like Zep, weak and hungry, far more interested now in their own welfare than some wild-eyed escape.

"Fall into line out this way! Three lines! We've got bread and molasses. Water, too, if you've got a canteen or a cup. Line up!"

The rebels responded with as much energy as they could muster, their own officers taking charge, and immediately the commissary troops began handing out the rations. Zep moved that way, then stopped, looked back toward Bauer.

"Cain't say it was a pleasure meetin' you, Dutchman. You ain't kilt, so I'm grateful for that."

"Maybe we'll meet again."

"Nope. We won't. 'Cept maybe in hell."

MONDAY, JULY 6, 1863

He walked beside Willis, back toward their own camp. Bauer had tried to find Zep again, curious about the man's dedication, that no matter what his army told him to do, his war was over.

"That's what he said, Sammie. He was just going home."

"Maybe he will. Maybe some officer with a handful of guards will round him up before he gets the chance. These rebel officers aren't quitting this fight. Means too much to 'em."

"They sure don't have much good to say about Pemberton."

"Not one."

They walked along a wide hardpan road, and Bauer looked to the side, saw the great mound of dirt, so familiar now, the same dirt he had watched for weeks. The stovepipes were still there, and Bauer climbed up, a wooden parapet still intact, peered through, was staring straight toward the old tree stump, his own perch.

Willis watched him and said, "Pretty smart of these boys, huh? You did good work on these things. I'm guessing you took down quite a few, maybe right on that spot. You've gotten better at all of this. Didn't think you'd still be here."

Bauer looked at him, felt a stab of hurt.

"Why? You thought I'd run off? That I'd end up a coward?"

Willis held his stare, shook his head.

"Not one bit. I thought they'd get you. You're not a soldier, you're a man in a blue uniform, who's learned how to shoot a musket. Better than most, no doubt. But this isn't for you. A boy dies next to you, and you let it get to you. You can't feel it that way, not and keep your head about you. That's why a man runs away."

Bauer moved back down toward the road, saluted a cavalry officer who rode slowly past, the man returning it.

"Not so. Not at all. You don't tell me why I ran away. That was a long damn time ago. I was scared out of my head, like demons chasing me. You . . . what's wrong with **you**? You're not scared, never. You stand up there like those damn Minié balls are gonna bounce off. I'm gonna watch one get you, I just know it. And when that happens, I'm gonna be mad at you forever. You got no right to be so damn stupid."

Willis looked at him, and Bauer was surprised to see a smile.

"Watch your mouth, Private."

"Well, hell a-mighty, Lieutenant. How can you do that? You got a wife and a new baby back home. I never hear you talk about 'em, never. I'd give anything to have a son, get to teach him all those things a boy needs to know."

Willis stared away.

"Maybe," he said. "This war's gotta end first. Could take a long damn time. Years maybe. You hear about Pennsylvania?"

"The state?"

Willis looked down and shook his head.

"Yeah. The state. I was gonna gather up the platoon, give them the report. Not sure what it means, but Colonel McMahon got the word from General McArthur himself. Said General Grant got a wire straight from President Lincoln. Hell of a fight there, maybe bigger than this one."

"We win?"

"All I know is what the general passed on. It was Lee himself, took on a bunch of boys at some small town . . . forget the name. But yeah, we won, I guess."

"Well, see there? How many more times we gonna win before all those rebels give up? They can't keep losing fights and losing ground. Like that Zep fellow. Blames General Pemberton, says he's not going to fight for him anymore. Look at these rebs around here. They gave us all they had, and we still whipped 'em. Every one of 'em is mad as a hornet at Pemberton. That's gotta be how this ends."

Willis looked at him for a long, silent moment.

"They make fence posts outa better stuff than is in your head. These damn secesh have plenty of generals, and some of 'em are as good as what we've got back there in those big tents. Look how long it took us to grab one stinking little town. Colonel says we got the Stars and Stripes flying up on their courthouse, like that's the most important damn thing in the world. You really think your friend Zep is gonna go home, and if he does, is he gonna stay there? Look how close this whole damn reb army came to starving, right out here in front of us. They're over there filling their bellies full of, hell, I don't know . . . dirt maybe. But if you'd have stuck your head up far enough, one of those boys would have taken it off. Like that damn redhead, O'Daniel. This won't end until all those generals decide to make it end. You and me, Zep, that damn polite lieutenant, we're just out here to do the nasty part."

The words came out of Willis with a rising flow of excitement, and Bauer knew what that meant, had seen it too many times before.

"I wish you didn't like it so much, Sammie. Really

don't." He paused, stared up at the vacant earthworks. "So, what are we supposed to do next? You
get any orders?"

"Not yet. Wish they'd hurry up, though. Had
enough of this place."

"I agree with you there, Lieutenant. Guess there'll
be some other place soon enough."

There were hoofbeats, and Bauer looked that
way, saw a squad of cavalrymen moving up quickly,
riding past now, swallowing both men in a cloud
of dust.

AFTERWORD

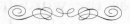

The best Fourth of July since 1776.
—WILLIAM T. SHERMAN

I thought of how many months we had nobly held the place against all the efforts of the Yankee nation, and bore privations and hardships of all kinds. Tears rose in my eyes and my very heart swelled with emotion. Being a prisoner did not in the least affect me, but the loss of the place . . . a great downfall to the Confederacy . . . caused me much pain.
—HUGH A. MOSS,
CONFEDERATE ARTILLERYMAN

The Father of Waters again goes unvexed to the sea.
—ABRAHAM LINCOLN

As we stepped aboard the boat which was to bear us on toward the unknown experiences that awaited us during the death struggles of the Confederacy . . . we became, without realizing all the hardships and bitterness the word implied, refugees adrift upon the hopeless current of a Losing Cause.

—WILLIE LORD, SON OF
REV. W. W. LORD, VICKSBURG

Upon the final surrender of Vicksburg, William T. Sherman, who commands more than thirty thousand of Grant's troops out east of the town, is ordered by Grant to begin the push once again toward Jackson, to eliminate once and for all any threat from the forces commanded by Joseph Johnston. Johnston, who has maintained his position several miles east of the Big Black River, retreats quickly to Jackson rather than engage Sherman in the field. On July 11, Sherman reaches the capital city, and aided by additional troops from both the Thirteenth Corps (Ord) and the Ninth Corps (Parke), Sherman begins a bombardment and general envelopment of the city. Johnston, recognizing the overwhelming superiority of the enemy he faces, withdraws once more. Within a week, Sherman marches again into the state capital with minimal opposition. At first Sherman attempts to pursue Johnston, who has, from all indications, mastered the art of escape. A frustrated Sherman concedes that the blistering heat of the Mississippi summer will do more damage to his army than can be achieved by such a pursuit, and reluctantly, he calls off the chase.

Ordered by Grant to return to his base near the Big Black River, Sherman first lays waste to Jackson once more, including the railroad lines that spread for dozens of miles in all directions. He then returns his forces to their original camps along the Big Black, protecting Vicksburg from any Confederate assault from the east, which never comes.

On July 11, 1863, the Confederate prisoners of war are allowed to begin their march out of Vicksburg. Pemberton holds his hopes high that his army will reassemble itself, though with so much dissension in the ranks, and so much hostility directed toward him, Pemberton sees the value in offering his men a furlough. He grants his army thirty days for whatever personal needs they might have, predicting, as does Jefferson Davis, that those men will once again see the virtue in their sacrifice and return to fight another day. To Pemberton's enormous dismay, an overwhelming majority of the men who surrender at Vicksburg simply disappear from the rolls of the army.

The senior officers under Pemberton's command face more formal rules regarding their paroles. Those men are eventually exchanged against the Federal officers who have been captured by Robert E. Lee two months prior, at Chancellorsville, Virginia. To further aid in bringing the disgruntled troops back into the fold, and avoid violating the terms of the surrender, Pemberton's staff claims that the actual roster of prisoners becomes lost. Thus no official record can be found that would disqualify any man from returning to service. How many of those men actually return is a source of considerable speculation.

As the siege of Vicksburg enters its final days, the events there are overshadowed significantly by events taking place in Pennsylvania. The astonishing loss of life during the Battle of Gettysburg captures the attention of most newspapers and the citizenry in both North and South. But one comparison tells at least part of the story. In the aftermath of Gettysburg, a total of sixty-three Union soldiers are awarded the Medal of Honor. At Vicksburg, ninety-eight such medals are awarded. Nonetheless, little public attention is paid when the final phase of the Vicksburg campaign concludes July 9, with the capture of Port Hudson, south of Vicksburg, the last remaining Confederate garrison on the Mississippi River. For the remainder of the war, the Confederacy is without any control over the most vital artery for supply and transport in North America.

In sheer numbers of men and equipment, the loss of the garrison at Vicksburg is unmatched by any other campaign of the war. While casualty counts pale in comparison to those of Shiloh, Antietam, or

Gettysburg, Vicksburg's loss is a monumental blow to the Confederacy, for reasons that go beyond loss of life. The numbers tell the story. Ulysses Grant succeeds in capturing an entire army, totaling some 29,500 officers and men, in addition to the seven thousand casualties inflicted on Pemberton's army during Grant's overland campaign. In total, Pemberton's army surrenders more than two hundred fifty artillery pieces, more than twenty-five tons of black powder, some fifty thousand muskets, and six hundred thousand rounds of ammunition. In addition, two ironworks inside of Vicksburg itself are lost, which damages even further the Confederacy's ability to replace their lost ordnance.

Though Grant's star rises considerably, it is not until spring of 1864 that Grant will be rewarded with the ultimate prize, command of the entire Federal army. In the meantime, he bases his headquarters again at Memphis. As part of his ongoing operations to strangle Confederate efforts west of the Appalachian Mountains, Grant expends enormous energy reopening the key rail link eastward, the Memphis & Charleston Railroad. Prior to Grant's Tennessee campaign in 1862, the rail line had been a primary east–west artery for the Confederacy. Now it will become just as useful for Grant's Federal army, which will embark on the renewed effort to crush Confederate forces in eastern Tennessee, a campaign that will eventually push into the Confederate strongholds near Chattanooga.

That campaign will continue a drive to devastate Confederate fortunes even further, eventually slicing completely through to Atlanta, across Georgia, and into the Carolinas.

The 1986 edition of the United States Army's Field Manual on Operations describes Grant's campaign thus: "His operations south of Vicksburg fought in the spring of 1863 has been called the most brilliant campaign ever fought on American soil. It exemplifies the qualities of a well-conceived, violently executed offensive plan. The same speed, surprise, maneuver and decisive action will be required in the campaigns of the future."

THOSE WHO WORE GRAY

LIEUTENANT GENERAL JOHN C. PEMBERTON

With his army abruptly scattered, Pemberton is a general without a command. Officially a Federal prisoner, he is immediately exchanged and released by Grant, and by late July 1863, two weeks after his army marches out of Vicksburg, he is reunited with his wife and children at Demopolis, Alabama, where he awaits instructions from Jefferson Davis. But Joseph Johnston files a report that quickly becomes public, laying complete blame for the loss of Vicksburg on Pemberton's actions, including his blatant disobedience of Johnston's orders. Though furious at Johnston's lack of discretion, Davis is overwhelmed by the outpouring of Southern sentiment against Pemberton and hopes to rescue his friend's reputation by convening a court of inquiry. But Davis and the Confederate War Department must deal with the realities of a war that has turned against them, and the inquiry is never scheduled.

In October 1863, Pemberton is summoned to Richmond and is considered by Davis for a new command in Tennessee, under Braxton Bragg, again subordinate to Johnston. But sentiment in the army is strongly against him, and the animosity between Johnston and Pemberton eliminate any chance that the command will ever be realized.

Returning to Virginia, Pemberton awaits some possibility that he will receive another command, offering his services to Davis "in any capacity in which you think I may be useful." Though Davis still regards Pemberton as a close friend, even Davis understands that few in the army would welcome Pemberton as a superior. Accepting his fate, Pemberton resigns his commission as lieutenant general in April 1864, and hopes to make Davis's decision easier by reducing himself to a possible command in his original post, that of a colonel of artillery. Davis accepts the request, and Pemberton assumes command of the Richmond Defense Battalion, and thus serves in support of Robert E. Lee in the campaigns of 1864, which eventually results in Grant's siege of Petersburg.

In early 1865, as the collapse of the Confederacy becomes increasingly inevitable, Pemberton is assigned to a vague post as inspector of ordnance, but by April 1865, he serves once again under Joe Johnston in North Carolina, only as a commander of artillery. With Lee having surrendered at Appomattox, and Johnston doing the same in North Carolina, Pemberton escapes capture and flees to Newton, North Carolina, where he reunites with his family.

Pemberton continues his feud with Joseph Johnston, both men penning memoirs that soundly condemn the actions of the other, including widely differing accounts of the campaign itself, with broad accusations leveled by each man for the other's failures. But Johnston's account, published in 1874, is widely read and thus mostly accepted as fact. Pemberton's memoir takes a far stranger journey. The manuscript is never published in his lifetime, and for all intents and purposes is lost to history. However, in 1995, the manuscript surfaces at an Ohio flea market, mingled with an original manuscript of works by another Confederate general, Marcus Wright. The work is purchased by Civil War enthusiast Alan Hoeweler, who recognizes its astonishing historical value, and the work is finally put into print in 1999.

One recurring condemnation of Pemberton revolves around his presumed choice of July 4 as the surrender date, which many take as a clear indication of his treachery, as though Vicksburg is a "gift" paid to the nation where his true loyalties always lay. Pemberton's explanation is a weak justification of the date, claiming that he had hoped to gain far more lenient terms from Ulysses Grant by surrendering on Independence Day. Though there is no evidence whatsoever to suggest Pemberton was not thoroughly loyal to the Confederate cause, he had every opportunity to accept Grant's terms on July 3 and execute the surrender on that day, thus deflecting, at least in part, the obvious controversy. Since the machinery of the surrender was already rolling forward, his explanation makes little sense. Regardless of the exact date when Pemberton's army lays down its arms, Grant's terms had remained virtually the same.

However, coincidence or not, the city of Vicksburg reacts strongly to the date of the capitulation. Independence Day is not officially celebrated again in the city until 1945.

After the war, Pemberton settles near Warrenton, Virginia, attempting to provide for his family as a gentleman farmer. But life on the land is no better for him than was life as a commander, and embittered by one more failure, he returns to his native Pennsylvania and lives an inconspicuous existence until his death in 1881. His death barely inspires mention in the newspapers across the South. His greatest postwar recognition comes from the efforts of historians, who in 1917 succeed in a campaign to erect a statue of Pemberton at the Vicksburg National Military Park.

> **The weathered bronze statue of Pemberton is virtually all that reminds us of the Pennsylvanian in gray who followed his heart and offered his sword in defense of the woman he loved.**
> —HISTORIAN TERRENCE WINSCHEL

LUCY SPENCE

Though her neighbors, particularly Horace Atkins and John Cordray, offer to assist her in rebuilding her home, Lucy has no desire to remain in Vicksburg. She embarks on a search for her preacher father, which proves fruitless, and she never learns of his fate. Her travels take her to Mobile, where in August 1864 she witnesses the great naval battle there, and in March 1865 she is a resident of the city when the Federal campaign erupts that will eventually conquer it. As the hospitals again require capable nurses, she offers her services and finds herself once more engulfed in the sickening horrors of a wartime hospital, this time caring for men from both armies. But she cannot endure life as a nurse, and vows never to witness combat again.

In Mobile, she marries George Lowery, a railroad manager, and in 1867 gives birth to a boy she names Victor. It is a subtle nod to her home, and a tribute to the sacrifice she has witnessed and suffered there. But her husband does not accept the confines of married life, and once again Lucy finds herself fending for herself, this time with a small child in tow. She seeks work as a private caretaker and serves, among many others, Confederate veterans who still suffer from their wounds. In 1884, her son applies to the Virginia Military Institute, a decision Lucy cannot take lightly. But Victor is a product of his mother's stubborn independence, and she reluctantly consents, under the condition that he never volunteer for service in combat.

Lucy remains in Mobile caring for the ill and injured until her death in 1914, at age sixty-nine. She does not live to see her son, now a captain in the United States Army, as he embarks for France with the American Expeditionary Force. Victor Lowery is killed in action in World War I on the Western Front, at age fifty.

MAJOR GENERAL JOHN BOWEN

Arguably John Pemberton's most capable field commander during the Vicksburg campaign, Bowen is also in command of more action out beyond the defenses of the city against Grant's foray through Mississippi. Bowen succumbs not only to the despair that engulfs his army with their surrender, but also the disease that permeates the entire force. The weakness Grant observes in his former neighbor manifests in a severe case of dysentery. Grant learns of Bowen's illness and offers the services of Federal doctors, a gesture that comes too late. With his wife at his side, Bowen dies on July 13, 1863, nine days after the surrender. He is buried first at Raymond, then moved to the Cedar Hill Cemetery in Vicksburg.

MAJOR SAMUEL LOCKETT

Lockett is easily considered the engineer most responsible for the design and construction of the earthworks that so effectively prevent Grant's army from seizing Vicksburg by brute force. After his exchange and parole, Lockett is promoted to colonel and serves as the chief engineer for the Confederate Army of Tennessee, under Braxton Bragg. As the war ends, Lockett takes his engineering skills into the classroom, and eventually becomes a professor at the University of Tennessee. His reputation brings him a three-year invitation to serve as a consulting engineer for the Egyptian army, which he accepts, traveling to Egypt in 1875.

He returns home to serve as one of the principal assistants for the construction of the pedestal that supports the Statue of Liberty in New York Harbor. Always in demand, he embarks on engineering duties for the governments of Chile and Colombia. He dies in Bogotá in 1891, at age fifty-four.

MAJOR GENERAL
WILLIAM W. LORING

Supported by his superior, Joseph Johnston, Loring manages to avoid condemnation for what can only be described as his abandonment of Pemberton's army after the Battle of Champion Hill. Loring joins his forces to that of Johnston, and eventually serves under John Bell Hood in the ill-fated battles for Atlanta. He accompanies Hood into Tennessee and participates in Hood's disastrous swan song in the battles of Franklin and Nashville. But Loring maintains a solid reputation in the field and returns to action under Johnston in the final conflicts of the war, against Sherman in North Carolina.

Like Samuel Lockett, he is rewarded for his reputation by the government of Egypt, where he serves as brigadier general, his reputation for battlefield command growing far beyond what he had earned in the Confederacy. In 1879, after considerable success in the Abyssinian Campaign, he is awarded the title of Pasha by the khedive of Egypt. He returns home to life as a dignified old soldier, and dies in 1886 in New York City, at age sixty-seven.

JOHN CORDRAY

With the surrender of Vicksburg, Cordray and his family return home to rebuild. He reopens his mercantile business, where he earns a modest living, providing for both of his children, who reach adulthood. But the strains of cave life prove far more damaging to his wife. Isabel dies in September 1863 from pneumonia, at age twenty-six. Cordray remains in Vicksburg, and like so many, he maintains a vigorous animosity toward the Union. The very definition of an unreconstructed Confederate, he dies in 1897, at age sixty-four.

THOSE WHO WORE BLUE

MAJOR GENERAL JOHN MCCLERNAND

Unyielding in his criticism of Ulysses Grant, in early 1864, McClernand's political contacts bring him another command in the field, this time far from Grant. McClernand leads his corps during the Red River Campaign, where he earns no particular distinction, but his ambitions take a severe blow by the elevation of Ulysses Grant to overall command of the army. Ill health and his unfortunate talent for self-promotion result in his resignation from the army in late 1864.

Though McClernand maintains ambitions for command, he is a politician first. In 1873, after serving a four-year stint as a judge, he returns to politics and is active there until the end of his life. He dies in Springfield, Illinois, in 1900, at age eighty-eight.

ASSISTANT SECRETARY OF WAR
CHARLES DANA

Despite the expectations of his superiors that his "observance" of Ulysses Grant will prove detrimental to Grant's career, Dana is surprised and gratified to learn otherwise. What some (including Grant himself) suspect as being a spy mission becomes instead a pipeline of positive and laudatory reports concerning Grant's behavior against the enemy, and with his own subordinates, which helps considerably to secure Grant's command.

After the war, Dana pursues his first love, journalism, and founds and operates what becomes one of New York City's most influential newspapers, the New York **Sun**. He pens a biography of Grant in 1868, and his own memoir, published posthumously. He edits his beloved **Sun** until his death in 1897, at age seventy-eight.

SYLVANUS CADWALLADER

The reporter is the man most singularly responsible for perpetrating Grant's reputation for consistent drunkenness. Cadwallader accompanies Grant's staff through the end of the war, and after Grant's death in 1885, and the publication of Grant's own memoirs, Cadwallader, who believes Grant has downplayed the role of his friend John Rawlins, begins work on his own memoir. He labors for several years, completes the work in 1896, when he is seventy years old, and he dies soon after. The work is not published until 1955, and of course, the claims of Grant's drunkenness are explosive, with no one alive who can dispute them.

In 1864, with the threat of the draft hanging over Cadwallader's head, he takes advantage of the prevailing privilege allowed men of means and purchases a substitute, an African American, to take his place in the army. Revealing this to Grant, Grant responds, "Perhaps the army profited by the exchange."

In the mid-1870s, Cadwallader serves as assistant secretary of state for Wisconsin, and a decade later moves to Springfield, Missouri. Considered a civilian expert, he is consulted frequently by historians throughout the late nineteenth century, and provides valuable insight into the inner workings of Grant's command.

Opinions are considerably divided about the veracity of Cadwallader's anecdotal stories of Grant's bingeing. Southern historians, such as Shelby Foote, tend to accept the reporter's version with more gravity than others, such as Bruce Catton, who describes the memoir as "one more in the dreary Grant-was-drunk garland of myths." Yet it is the writings of the men who were there at the time that seem to deflate the substance of Cadwallader's claims. Chief among those is Rawlins himself, as well as Charles Dana, Horace Porter, and William T. Sherman.

CAPTAIN ANDREW HICKENLOOPER

Considered a rising star among the Federal army's engineers, Hickenlooper is rewarded for his exceptional service at Vicksburg by a gold medal from the command board of McPherson's Seventeenth Corps.

He rises to the position of judge advocate under Grant, and assistant inspector general for Seventeenth Corps. At the war's end, he is awarded a brevet rank of brigadier general.

Returning to his home state of Ohio, Hickenlooper serves as president of the Cincinnati Gas Light Company, becoming a noted expert in the field of public utilities. He enters politics, and in 1879 serves as that state's lieutenant governor. He dies in 1900, at age sixty-three.

ADMIRAL DAVID DIXON PORTER

Foster brother to renowned admiral David Farragut, Porter serves the United States Navy to high honors through the end of the war, notably as commander of the North Atlantic Blockading Squadron. In late 1864, his contribution to the fall of the Confederacy's last major seaside bastion, Fort Fisher, brings him an official letter of thanks from Congress, his fourth such accolade.

After the war, he serves a five-year stint as superintendent of the U.S. Naval Academy, at Annapolis, Maryland. He is promoted to full admiral shortly thereafter, the title made retroactive for his service throughout much of the war.

Penning his memoirs, and numerous other publications, he is regarded as one of this nation's finest naval officers. He dies in 1891, at age seventy-eight, and is buried at Arlington National Cemetery.

AND FROM THESE PAGES

William T. Sherman, Ulysses Grant, Joseph Johnston, Fritz Bauer, Samuel Willis, James McPherson, among many others, have hopes for a rapid end to this war, but those will only be realized when the last great campaigns are waged across lands that have yet to feel the torment and destruction of a human disaster that goes far beyond what any soldier, politician, or civilian could have predicted.

ABOUT THE AUTHOR

JEFF SHAARA is the **New York Times** best-selling author of **A Blaze of Glory, The Final Storm, No Less Than Victory, The Steel Wave, The Rising Tide, To the Last Man, The Glorious Cause, Rise to Rebellion,** and **Gone for Soldiers,** as well as **Gods and Generals** and **The Last Full Measure**—two novels that complete the Civil War trilogy that began with his father's Pulitzer Prize–winning classic, **The Killer Angels**. Jeff was born into a family of Italian immigrants in New Brunswick, New Jersey. He grew up in Tallahassee, Florida, and graduated from Florida State University. He lives in Tallahassee.

JeffShaara.com

Jeff Shaara is available for select readings and lectures. To inquire about a possible appearance, please contact the Random House Speakers Bureau at 212-572-2013 or rhspeakers@randomhouse.com.

LIKE WHAT YOU'VE READ?

If you enjoyed this large print edition of
A CHAIN OF THUNDER,
here are a few of Jeff Shaara's latest
bestsellers also available in large print.

A BLAZE OF GLORY
(paperback)
978-0-307-99064-8
($28.00/$34.00C)

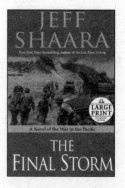

THE FINAL STORM
(paperback)
978-0-7393-7820-5
($28.00/$33.00C)

NO LESS THAN VICTORY
(paperback)
978-0-7393-2862-0
($28.00/$35.00C)

THE STEEL WAVE
(paperback)
978-0-7393-2784-5
($29.95/$34.00C)

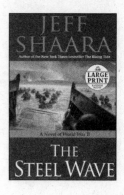

Large print books are available wherever books
are sold and at many local libraries.

All prices are subject to change. Check with your
local retailer for current pricing and availability.
For more information on these and other large print titles,
visit <u>www.randomhouse.com/largeprint</u>.